A Song Called Youth:
Eclipse
Eclipse Penumbra
Eclipse Corona

A Song Called Youth:
Eclipse
Eclipse Penumbra
Eclipse Corona

John Shirley

PRIME BOOKS

A Song Called Youth:
Eclipse, Eclipse Penumbra, Eclipse Corona

Cover art by Paul Morley.
Cover design by Telegraphy Harness.

For more information, contact Prime Books:
prime@prime-books.com

ISBN: 978-1-60701-330-3

• A Song Called Youth •

• An Introduction •
Richard Kadrey

There's an old saw that SF is really about dissecting the present and not about looking at the future, and that's true as far as it goes. Sometimes though, SF can't help but lift the future's skirts for a peek underneath. Look at *1984* and its description of a Total Surveillance society. *Brave New World*'s look at genetic engineering. *Star Trek* practically engineered modern smart phones. Hell, both H.G. Wells' "The World Set Free" and *Superman* described atomic bombs. John Shirley's A Song Called Youth trilogy—the novels *Eclipse*, *Eclipse Penumbra*, and *Eclipse Corona*—is another piece of SF that spray-painted a glimpse of the future on the cave wall without knowing it.

We're living at a strange moment in history. "Interesting times," as the Chinese call it in their famously charming curse. We want power to make our TVs glow and medicine to save our decaying asses but we hate smart people. We whine about Arab oil but go NIMBY when it comes to large-scale alternative energy projects. We want the government to stay the hell out of our lives but we want it to ban gay marriage and porn and to keep that witch-loving Harry Potter from dragging our kids to the devil through the school library. We want reassurance and safety at all cost and we'll suck down snake oil from any carny with a good pitch.

John Shirley saw over the horizon to the post-9/11 fear and loathing idiotscape where the Constitution, the Geneva Convention, and government itself have become mere formalities. Where for-rent mercenaries guard us as long as the money flows and where our desperate need for a strong leader makes the shit sandwich of fascism look a little tastier every day.

And he did it twenty years ago.

The A Song Called Youth trilogy is the story of the world we're knee deep in. And like the best rock and roll it kicks down the walls and busts up the furniture when the action starts and makes you think when you slow down long enough to listen to the words. Living in stupid times doesn't mean you have to be stupid. And maybe with some cunning, crazy-ass energy and balls maybe you can turn things around and make the world a little less stupid. A little less dangerous. A little less suicidal. Hell, that's pretty much what life is and it's what A Song Called Youth is about.

—November 2011

• Biographical Note on John Shirley •
Bruce Sterling

"I first met him in 1977 when he was into spiked dog collars. No one else was ready for his insane novels . . . there just wasn't anything else like that being written then—no hook or label like cyberpunk, no opening—so they were totally ignored. If those books were published now, people would be saying: 'Wow, look at this stuff! It's beyond cyberpunk!'"

—William Gibson

I knew this guy John Shirley when he was the first and only punk science fiction writer in the world.

Back in those days, William Gibson was a hobbyist teaching-assistant who was whiling away his youth, in his ivied meditative fashion, in Canadian junk shops. I was an engineer's kid from a smoggy refinery town who had had my head utterly twisted by three years in India and was hanging out with cowboy-hatted interstellar longhairs deep in the heart of Texas. Rudy Rucker was futilely trying to pass as a normal math professor somewhere in upstate New York. Lewis Shiner was enamored of hardboiled detective fiction and living in Dallas.

But John Shirley loomed on the horizon like some prescient comet. The rest of us paid a lot of attention to him. We were right to do this.

Most of the science fiction writers who later got called "cyberpunks" are and were, at heart, really nice middle-class white guys. They have some pretty strange ideas, but in their private lives they dress and act like industrial design professors. John Shirley was a total bottle-of-dirt screaming dogcollar yahoo.

There were still a few New Wave people around at the time earnestly writing stories with hippie protagonists. The people in John Shirley's stories weren't hippies. They weren't progressive. They didn't mean well. People in John Shirley stories were canaille. They had no brakes. They didn't know what brakes were.

Other people wrote experimental stories with numbered paragraphs, but John Shirley wrote "stories" that were so profoundly fucked-up narratively that you could feel the guy's fingertips trembling spastically on the keyboard. Some of the more daring SF writers of the period were testing the limits of genre. For John Shirley the limits of genre were vague apparitions somewhere in his rearview mirror.

Science fiction is a genre by and for bright people who feel a tad ill at ease in a bourgeois society, a tad under-socialized, but also a tad inventive. . . . Nice people, really. You get used to them. They have a lot to offer, these insect-eating Mensa-freak people who like making puns about neutrinos while sipping ginger ale in the con suite. John Shirley was never like that. John Shirley in his early days was visibly orthogonal to the human species.

I share certain deep and lasting commonalities with John Shirley. We're very near the same age and we've shared some crucial generational experiences. Harlan Ellison was a guru of mine and was kind enough to commission and publish my first novel. Harlan Ellison was utterly enraged with John Shirley and once publicly challenged him to a duel. I once angrily walked out on a bad panel at a science fiction convention. John Shirley liked to topple over tables at science fiction conventions and wallow howling in the crushed ice where the fans had hidden the beer. I listened to a lot of punk music. John Shirley wrote, recorded, and performed punk music.

I think that drugs are an intriguing social and technomedical phenomenon. John Shirley had serious drug habits. I got married and had a kid. John Shirley has been married four or five times and has three kids by two different women. I've written over a dozen books. John Shirley has written more books than I can count, a lot of them under pseudonyms. I once wrote a book with William Gibson. John Shirley is the guy who convinced William Gibson that writing science fiction was a good idea.

I'm kind of interested in military stuff. John Shirley joined the Coast Guard. I took some martial arts classes. John Shirley had a beer bottle broken over his head in a bar brawl. I've moved house a few times in the last thirty years. John Shirley's moved a couple of dozen times during the same period, including a sojourn in France.

The typical Bruce Sterling fan is a computer-science major in some Midwestern technical university. "Stelarc" is a John Shirey fan. Stelarc is an Austalian performance artist who has an artificial third hand, sometimes bounces lasers off his eyeballs, and used to suspend his naked body in midair by piercing his flesh with meathooks.

It may be that it all boils down to this; I am a professional science fiction writer who happened to get called a "cyberpunk." John Shirley is a uniquely authentic avatar of the weltanschauung.

—Adapted from "Foreword" by Bruce Sterling
in *The Exploded Heart* by John Shirley

A Song Called Youth
Book One:
ECLIPSE

John Shirley

*For my sons, Byron and Perry and Julian,
in the hope that I'm wrong about the world
they will grow up in.*

• • •

AN IMPORTANT NOTE FROM THE AUTHOR
This is not a post-holocaust novel.
Nor is this a novel about nuclear war.
It may well be that this is a pre-holocaust novel.

• Prologue •

There was a small bird made out of titanium and glass. It had mechanical wings, electronic guts, and its head was a camera. But it was shaped much like a thrush and was about the same size. Its wings whiffed like a hummingbird's as it flew through the damp, battered city . . . The city was Amsterdam.

In the winter of the year 2039, Amsterdam was occupied by the NATO forces which had, for the moment, succeeded in driving out the armies of Greater Russia, the shock troops of the neo-Com dictator, Koziski . . .

Global warming. Climate change. It had radically reduced the output of Russian agriculture—of the availability of fresh-grown food, and stock feed, in many places—and that meant food had become hard to get. The Russians were on the edge of starvation—some of them over the edge—when Koziski had decided that Russian armies would swarm into Eastern Europe, and keep on going, in order to corral food resources . . .

So far, it was a world war that hadn't gone nuclear.

On the belly of the bird were serial numbers. The bird was a surveillance device, registered with the United Nations Intelligence Regulation Agency. Anyone punching the right serial numbers into a computer modem'd to UNIRA, along with the proper clearance codes, would be informed that the bird was licensed to British Naval Intelligence, under the auspices of the North Atlantic Treaty Organization.

The battery-powered bird had been activated on a British aircraft carrier twenty miles off the crumbling coast of Holland, at the request of the officer in charge of Civilian Law Enforcement. CLE was working out of an apartment building in one of the drier suburbs of half-sunken Amsterdam. The deserted building had been occupied by NATO Forces' Dutch Command Unit as a temporary headquarters.

The CLE officer was an American from Buffalo, New York. His name was Yates. Captain Yates had a memo on his desk from the Second Alliance International Security Corporation (the SAISC, or SA for short) asserting that the SA's supply lines had been "repeatedly disrupted" by the "civilian gang calling itself the *New Resistance*." The SA memo pointed out that it had been authorized by the Hague—those members of the States-General whom NATO had been able to contact—and by the UN Security Council, to police Amsterdam and the surrounding areas. The Second Alliance would see to it that the civilian population remained orderly, as well as safe from looters and other lawbreakers. To do that (the SA response memo went on peevishly), the SA had to move into Amsterdam, and it could not move the rest of its men in unless there were supplies in Amsterdam to sustain them. "I hardly need point out," the memo continued, "that while the SAISC is a civilian private-police force, it must nevertheless work in close cooperation with the NATO military forces, and cooperation is a two-edged sword." Yates frowned, reading that part. Cooperation as a sword? "The terrorist gang known as the New Resistance," the memo shrilled, "is a danger to the NATO armies as much as the SA inasmuch as it commonly steals supplies from NATO forces and disseminates antimilitary tracts which irrationally lump NATO and the Russian forces together as if both were the aggressors in the area."

Yates had shrugged and sent the communiqué to the nearest NATO ship with surveillance equipment, the *Lady Di.*

And the bird had been set free.

But not free to fly about at random. It flew in a widening spiral pattern through the civilian areas, looking and listening for gatherings of "four or more civilians." There weren't many people left in Amsterdam, so the job wasn't as time-consuming as it might seem. When the bird found gatherings of four or more civilians (not very often) it attached itself to the outer wall of the building in which the gathering was taking place, and it laid an egg. The "egg" was actually a tiny hemisphere of nanomaterials that clung to brick or concrete or glass or plasteel and sent out minute sensors. The sensors picked up the heartbeats of people, and if there were enough heartbeats close together, it transmitted a signal. Under martial law it was illegal for more than three persons to gather together without supervision, except in designated areas. The designated areas were under even closer surveillance.

The commander of The Netherlands unit made the gathering-size rule as there had been some trouble with what he described as "low-grade terrorist conspiracies."

Yates, having dispatched the birds to watch for illegal meetings, dispatched another communiqué to the SAISC, telling them what he'd done. Soothing them.

The SA, receiving the message, communicated with their contacts in the USAF Jumpjet Reconnaisance Unit. SA sympathizers in Jumpjet Recon were given the frequency specifics of the transmitting "eggs," and were urgently requested "in the spirit of cooperation," to "triangulate these terrorist cabals and do what is necessary to put them out of business."

The bird flew from one block to another, mile after mile, occasionally attaching eggs. After the third time, it flew past a certain high-rise, where it startled a real bird, a crow, which had been restlessly circling the building.

The crow was shaken by this close encounter with a "UFO" and took itself to the nearest terrace railing to recuperate. It settled onto the railing, looked around, and saw with relief that the bird with the metal wings and a glass head had flown away.

But someone else was there, at the other end of the terrace.

Part One:
SMOKE

• 01 •

"This city is dead." He said it out loud, to a crow. The big black crow was perched on the concrete railing that ran mostly intact around the rubbled terrace. They were thirty stories above the flooded street, where dusk darkened the floodwater to indigo.

The crow heard, tilted a glare at him. Smoke went on, "This city is dead, and I'm someone. I'm still someone. Being here hasn't helped." He spoke to the crow and to the clammy, acidic breeze—it smelled like a ruptured car battery—that lifted the edges of the rain-caked stack of printouts some looter had tossed onto the terrace. "I'm still Smoke, Jack Brendan Smoke, or Brendan Jack Smoke or Smoke Jack Brendan. Mix it up the way you want, it's still there. I thought it would leach off here, crow. Like . . . " He paused, not sure if he was speaking aloud or thinking it now, and wondering which it was. He shrugged and went on, "Like you have a pan of water, nothing else, just dead flat calm water, and you pour, say, a little ink into it, and the ink spreads out, gets all diluted, in a few days, you can't see it anymore. But it didn't work. The ink is still there. I'm still Smoke . . . I could leave Amsterdam, crow. I might not be Jack Smoke where there's enough people. Lost in a crowd. I could go to Paris. There're still a lot of people in Paris."

The crow's claws made a skittering sound as it shifted on its perch. Shifted a little closer to him.

It occurred to Smoke that the crow might not be real; might be a cybernetic fake. But he was past caring.

Smoke put his hands on the railing, felt the concrete's cold bite his palms. He looked at his hands. They seemed creatures apart from him: clawlike gray things, with horny, overgrown yellow nails. He looked that way, all of him: clawlike, gaunt, dark with grime, his layers of scavenged shirts and jackets and pants gone all raggedy edged and uniformly dirt-colored, so he looked like a crow himself, in molting. He had long, matted black hair and beard, and a bird's bright black eyes and an eagle-beak nose. He chuckled softly, thinking that perhaps the crow had mistaken him for one of its own . . .

"It'd be better to be a crow," Smoke said. He looked away from his hands, out over the railing at the city—the necropolis.

This section of Amsterdam was relatively intact, as if mummified, and that amplified the absence of human movement; as if someone had thrown a switch that simply turned off the people the way you'd switch off a hologram: click . . . zip, they're gone.

Smoke tried to visualize Amsterdam the way it had been just five years ago: The streets feverish with cars and buses, most of them self-driving and electric; traffic pulsing on the bridges of the "city of one thousand and one bridges"; flat barges gliding on the Amstel and on sedate, tree-shaded canals flowing slow and thick as green candle wax. It was a city built in rings of streets and canals, most of the architecture remaining as it had been, gabled and red-bricked, when it was built in the seventeenth century. The city had permitted only a few high-rises, in certain zones, like the shell Smoke and the crow perched in now. Now, and all was the same as five minutes ago except it was just a dilute ink-wash darker. There was no going back in time. There was only going forward, one second at a time, as things fell apart.

The clammy wind soughed like an ache through the concrete corridors; the flood made a hollow *whush* like the sea heard in a seashell.

The overcast sky was a lowering ceiling of smudged charcoal black on charcoal gray; the upper reaches of the high-rise faded into cloud, as if the building became less real as it went up and was entirely imaginary at its peak.

Smoke leaned over the balcony and looked down. The floodwaters filling the avenue were sinuous with current, moving, tugging the yellow blob of Smoke's rubber raft tied up at the second-story window ledge. The water was rising. Perhaps the Zaider Zee would return, to reclaim Holland.

"Oh, you could *say* the city was still alive," Smoke said to the crow. It must have been aloud, because the crow fluttered its wings in response. "Because there are still people in it, on the higher ground, squatting here and there. Maybe a few thousand, maybe a few hundred. That's life, but it's the life in a corpse—micro-organisms that live on after the host has died. Hair that grows though the skull is empty. And the SA will be here soon. So the corpse'll be maggoty. And, you could say, 'Maggots are alive.'"

The crow looked interested. "But still, Amsterdam is dead . . . New York is alive, Tokyo and Cairo are alive, very much alive. But this city . . . "

The crow made a caw that somehow sounded reproachful.

"What is it?" Smoke asked. "Is it that I talk to myself? Because talking to a bird, or anything that can't talk back, is really talking to myself? Is that it? I remember being twenty-five and feeling sorry for people who talked to themselves on the street. They were crazy. Or senile. And now I do it—I don't say anything that would compromise Steinfeld, though. So I guess I'm not so far gone. Well I did just say his name. So maybe I'm losing it. And I'm only thirty-five now. I look older, crow, but I'm not. At least, I *think* I'm thirty-five. And something."

The crow cawed again, and Smoke thought it sounded sympathetic.

"I talk to myself compulsively," Smoke said; "I think I once wrote a paper about the phenomenon . . . I tried to make myself stop, for the sake of dignity. But dignity"—he gestured toward the flooded streets—"is underwater, with Rembrandt's house. The water reaches into houses and floats the corpses out . . . "

Color caught his eye. A fantail of sunset red creeping across one of the southeast windows of the building across from him. Windows on the southeast side were often intact, because most of the tactical warheads had detonated in the northeastern part of the city. And the red glaze reminded him to check his radbadge. He fumbled in the folds of his shirts, the four shirts he wore one atop the next, and found the radiation indicator like a convention badge pinned to his rotting jogger's sweatshirt. Only a faint corner of the badge had gone red, which was all right.

"It's all right," he told the crow. "Voortoven says he wishes they'd dropped a Big One on Amsterdam. Instead of torturing us with this slow war. Reneging on their promise to get the third one over in a few minutes. You ever feel that way? Like you wish they'd just *gone for it*? You want some bread? I think it's safe. I stuck a radbadge—I got a sack of them from Steinfeld—I stuck a badge, in the—here it is—" Rummaging in a greasy knapsack. "Left it in overnight, not a smidge of red. So the bread's okay . . . Here." He found the stale bread in its plastic bag, carefully unwrapped it, cursed when a few crumbs dropped. He licked a finger, touched the crumbs, sucked them into his mouth, watching the crow. The crow observed him fixedly, hopping nearer on the concrete rail.

He broke off a corner of the bread and held it out to the crow.

The crow's utter lack of caution surprised him: it hopped up and plucked the bread from his fingers like a man accepting a stick of chewing gum. Casual, familiar.

Smoke watched, fascinated, as the crow placed the crust on the ledge, then held it down with a claw to keep the breeze from stealing it, and meticulously chipped the bread apart, throwing its head back to down the crusty stuff, till only crumbs were left, and the wind got them.

"I'm supposed to be recruiting," Smoke confided to the crow. "Steinfeld says there are likelies here. In one of the rises. Not in this one, though."

He looked out over the city, saw it bruised in sunset. There was another high-rise a block north. It looked as lifeless as this one. He felt an alien touch on the index finger of his right hand and thought, *A bombspider,* and twitched his hand away, revolted—

The crow flapped on his finger, clinging despite his sharp motion, looking at him crossly as it adjusted.

He gaped for a moment and then laughed. "You're trained! You belonged to someone!"

The crow twitched its wings in a way that was eerily like shrugging.

Experimentally, he put his hand to his right shoulder, and the crow fluttered onto a new perch there, settled down, perfectly at home, and all of a sudden Smoke felt just a little bit different. About everything.

• 02 •

Smoke walked into their trap, waited till they'd closed the trap around him, and all the time politely pretended not to know it was happening. He pretended to be watching the L-5 Colony.

The artificial star glittered in the night sky like a fine timepiece, forty degrees from the horizon. He saw it for ten seconds through a break in the clouds, and then it was erased by mist. He wondered if the War had reached out to the Space Colony—halfway to the moon—and, if it had, if anyone was still alive there.

And then the crow tensed and made a rasping sound Smoke was to learn meant *Watch your ass!* . . . and the three men closed in on him from three directions. The crow fluttered; he whispered to it, and it quieted down, pleasing him with its responsiveness.

He was standing at a window, looking out at the gray stalagmite outline of the high-rise where he'd met the crow. "I was over in that 'rise," he told the men, "and I looked at this one and couldn't see a fire or anything moving."

He heard one of them cock a gun.

And then again, Smoke was not so different, even after feeling that things had shifted: he still found himself hoping that the man would use the gun.

But behind Smoke, a man with a leader's voice said, "Turn around."

Smoke turned slowly around and saw a compact young man in his early thirties—but, no. Wrong. Subtract the etchings of wartime stress and fatigue and hunger, and the man was perhaps mid-twenties. He was gaunt from hunger; his chin was just a shade too prominent, like the old drawings of the man-in-the-moon at quarter-phase, and his forehead was high; he had a straight nose; a wry, red-lipped mouth; and small, dark-lashed green eyes rimmed with sleeplessness. His hair was thatchy, oily because it was something he ignored. When it was clean, it was probably blond. He was not more than five-seven, and lean in a weathered brown flight jacket that looked like it had done its flying in bad weather; ancient, faded Levi's; motorcycle boots held together with duct tape.

He was carrying a . . . Smoke stared. "Where'd you get the old Weatherby?" he asked, interested. The boy was carrying a Weatherby Mark V hunting rifle. Gun must be thirty, forty years old, Smoke thought. Bolt action, .460 Magnum. Long, long rifle. Developed for big-game hunting. Anomalous thing to find here, Smoke thought.

The man with the green eyes chuckled and shook his head. His eyes didn't change expression when he laughed. They remained flat, hard, candid. "You're supposed to be scared," he said, "not asking where I got my gun."

"So he knows all about guns," one of the other men said. Moved to Smoke's right. He was a big-framed man who had the look of someone who'd been overweight, starved down to sagging folds. He wore a long black coat, open at the front. And to Smoke's left there was a twitch-eyed vulture of a man breathing noisily through his open mouth. He wore a raincoat and beneath that something so ragged it was unidentifiable. The starved bear carried a .22 rifle, and the vulture carried a sort of mace made from nails soldered to a long pipe. "If he knows about guns," the bear went on, "he ain't some wanderin' tramp."

"That logic is questionable," Smoke said. "A wandering tramp is someone who used to be someone *else*—and when he was the someone else he might have made guns his hobby. I am, in fact, a wandering tramp. That doesn't mean I don't have business. I have business. But I'm not an eye for the Armies. And I'm here unarmed."

"What's your 'business'?" the green-eyed one asked, jeering the word *business*.

Smoke was thinking that the starved bear should have the big Weatherby, and the green-eyed one should have the .22, because he was smaller, and because he was the leader, so he should have known better. But maybe the gun was the totem of power here. And the king should carry the scepter.

"Here's where I take a chance," Smoke said. "I'm going to refuse to tell you my business. Except to say it's no threat to you."

The starved bear took a step toward him, and Smoke closed his eyes and said, "I hope they don't hurt my crow."

Not sure if he'd said it out loud.

"Jenkins," the green-eyed one said, not very sharply. But that's all it took. The big guy stopped, and Smoke, even with his eyes shut, knew the starved bear was looking at the green-eyed one for his cue.

"Lez go through his stuff," the vulture said. "Might be food."

"Animals," Smoke said, opening his eyes. "One's a starved bear and one's a vulture, and you make me think of a coyote or a wolf." He looked at the leader. Again the guy made the smile that didn't travel to his eyes.

"You're just a roost for a crow," he said. "You got a name?"

"Smoke."

"I heard about you, something. Like you barter, black market or . . . " He shrugged. "What's to be so mysterious about?" Smoke didn't answer, so the guy went on, "What's your crow's name?"

"I haven't decided. We're of recent acquaintance. I'm wavering between naming him Edgar Allan Crow or Richard Pryor."

The green-eyed one lowered his rifle, maybe only because it was heavy. "Edgar Allan Crow is corny. What's 'Richard Pryor' mean?"

"He was my father's favorite comedian, and he was black. That's all I know about him."

"We could eat that bird," the vulture suggested. He looked at the green-eyed leader. "Let's eat the bird, Hard-Eyes. Fuck it, huh?"

Hard-Eyes. Quite a monicker.

Hard-Eyes said, "No. Crows are good luck where I come from."

• • •

The clouds had congealed into rain and the rain had wormed and nosed and nudged its way into the high-rise's ten thousand hairline cracks, and it was seeping out of the cracks in the ceiling and dripping with a smell of dissolved minerals into a large bathtub—which someone had dragged from its original mooring just to catch the rain—and into a wooden box which itself was beginning to discolor and leak.

The crow was asleep on Smoke's shoulder.

"I wisht we could have a goddamn fire," Pelter was saying. Pelter was the vulture.

They were sitting on red plastic crates around a dead TV set. The TV screen had been painted with a symbol:

. . . in red paint. They weren't looking at the screen. But it was a kind of chilled hearth for them. They'd eaten a tin of sardines and a pound of cheese Steinfeld had given Smoke "to soften them up." Smoke had brought it out as soon as they'd arrived at the squat. "This's our squat," Hard-Eyes had said, just as if he'd wanted to displace the word *bivouac* in Smoke's mind, in case Smoke was working for the Armies after all.

There was a jumble of old furniture in the room, mysterious geometries in the half-darkness. They'd blacked out the window with three thicknesses of taped-on black plastic; the plastic's wrinkles made glowworms of the anemic yellow light from the two chemlanterns. Smoke said, "You're gonna need a new lump for your lanterns. That solid fuel seems like it's going to last forever, then all of a sudden you're in the dark."

"I don't like the way this guy talks," Pelter said. "He's gonna bring us bad luck."

Hard-Eyes ignored Pelter. He looked across the cone of lampglow at Smoke and said, "You're not talking just about lamp fuel."

Smoke shrugged. "It's all in the lanterns. Energy and attrition and entropy."

Hard-Eyes blinked, looking skeptical. Then his face cleared and he nodded. "And glass going black."

Jenkins and Pelter looked at one another, then at Hard-Eyes and Smoke and then at the floor.

"What's the TV fetish-sign about?" Smoke asked.

He nodded toward the red symbol on the screen. He'd seen it the first time in Martinique, ten years before. He'd seen it on pendants and on screensavers. No one had explained it, except to say, "It's good luck." Later, in Harlem, seeing dead TVs turned into household iconography, he'd figured it was big-city cargo cultism, in a way, and something more: an invocatory variation on the Gridfriend sign.

"You believe in Gridfriend?" Smoke asked.

Gridfriend, god of the global electronic Grid. The Grid gives TV, and news—and credit, which translates into food and shelter. Pray to Gridfriend and maybe the power company's computers lose your bill, and you go an extra month before they turn off your lights; pray to Gridfriend and maybe Interbank makes an error in your favor, computes you five hundred dollars you shouldn't have. And then forgets about it. Pray to Gridfriend and the police computer loses your records. Or so you hope.

"That's not the Gridfriend totem," Hard-Eyes said. "It's Jenkins' thing. It's Jenkins' invocation to the Big Organizer, the god who manufactures patterns—and luck. Jenkins used to do a lot of meth."

"Big Organizer? Just another Gridfriend. You a believer in luck?"

"I make my own."

Smoke smiled at the movie-melodrama sound of "I make my own." It went with the monicker.

"That's why you're here, Hard-Eyes? In this fucking icebox?"

Jenkins snapped Smoke a look. "Hey, you got nothing better goin', Rags. You ain't even got lanterns. You shouldn't be talkin' about our lanterns, man."

The crow stirred on Smoke's shoulder, disturbed by Jenkins' tone. Smoke crooned to it. It tucked its head back under its wing.

He smiled. "Look at that. That's completion . . . This crow and I met today and we're fast friends already. Just like that. Makes me almost believe in reincarnation."

"We should eat 'im," Pelter said, wiping a trail of snot from his bony nose with a crusted sleeve. His eyes were red, swollen, and he coughed sometimes, and now and then his head dipped as if he might fall asleep sitting up. Smoke thought Pelter was sick and would die soon.

"The bird will more likely be pecking your dead eyes out," Smoke said, and then regretted it. He hadn't intended to say it aloud. But Pelter didn't hear. His head had drooped and he was breathing with a bubbling sound.

Jenkins was scowling. "You hear that, Hard-Eyes? His bird pecking Pelter's eyes?"

Hard-Eyes shrugged. "Smoke resents people talking about roasting his designer squab. Makes a man say bitter things."

Smoke laughed. Hard-Eyes made the short, snorting sound that passed for machismo laughter. But his eyes stayed hard.

As the rain made hollow *plips* in the tub of water.

• • •

Jenkins and Pelter were asleep, stretched out on pallets of cardboard. Jenkins slept with his face in his curled arm—like the crow with its beak under a wing—his hands now and then clutching, closing on something he dreamt about; Pelter slept with his mouth open, his breath coming raggedly.

There was only one lantern still lit. As if Smoke had spoken an omen, the other one had used up its fuel and gone out, just like that.

"Not going to make it," Smoke muttered.

"The other lantern?" Hard-Eyes asked.

"Pelter. Maybe the lantern too."

"Pelter's been sick," Hard-Eyes said, nodding.

"Been with you long?"

Hard-Eyes shook his head. "Six, seven weeks. Jenkins has been with me longer. Jenkins, he's not dumb. Just a different focus. He's handy with chip-splicing, accessing, like that."

"Not much use for computer skills in Amsterdam just now." They both smiled wearily at that; it had been too obvious a thing to say and they both knew it.

"You still worried about me?" Smoke asked.

Hard-Eyes shook his head. He smiled flickeringly. "The crow vouched for you."

"I'm a little worried about *you.* You could almost be one of their background men. Looking for the underground. Or for anybody that smells like they wish the Armies would snuff each other and fuck off."

Hard-Eyes shrugged. "You want the story?"

Smoke nodded.

So Hard-Eyes told his story.

• • •

I was in London, (Hard-Eyes said), and I was at a club called The Retro G. They were into cultural retrogressing. That month they had a ska motif, ska music. Two months before they'd had thrash. And before that it was hard core and before that worldbeat and before that angst rock, and before that it was dub and before that it was core-dub and before that, melt-pop, which is what was hot when the club opened. If the club were still there I guess they'd have worked back through the nineteen-nineties, eighties, seventies, sixties, back to rockabilly and bebop and blues. But it's not there now because that part of the town is rubble. Me, I'm from San Francisco, California. I was in Britain for a seminar on Social Democracy. Watered-down socialism. I was a grad student. Yeah, a student with a fucking satchel for carrying his books. Political science major. And deep into applying structuralism to problems of diplomacy. Jesus. And then politics got real for me. The truth behind politics. Aggression and acquisition . . . We were at the Retro G, dancing, and the DJ sliced in that meltpop tune, "Dancing with the Russian Brothers," not part of the ongoing retro motif, so it made you wonder, and then the DJ said it was dedicated to the Russian Brothers who'd just driven their tanks across the frontier into Poland. It shouldn't have been all that surprising; the Ukraine, Belarus, Kazakhstan—it'd all been reunited into Greater Russia not that long before, and did we really think they were going to quit there? But still, we thought he was kidding, until we heard someone else talking about a radio broadcast and we went outside to Dody's car. Dody—man, what an airhead. But she was worried about her business because she marketed designs from some Polish designer. And on Dody's car radio they said the Greater Russian army appeared out of nowhere, no one could understand how they got so many troops to the border without alerting NATO. It was a long time before word filtered back about the maxishuttle drops out of orbit. NATO saw the drops, but the Russians told them it was emergency medical supplies because of some outbreak, and then the fucking troops were in place . . . Okay, that's the version I heard. You hear different versions . . . Anyway, they took Warsaw, moved the Greater Russian Liberation Army's western front HQ in. And this girl Dody, all she could think about was her business going down the drain. I wanted to stuff her up the exhaust pipe of her Jaguar Gasless.

But after that, I was no better. All I could think about was covering my own ass, getting back to the States. Only, you couldn't get a flight out of London, they were all restricted for government use or booked solid. Everyone wanted the fuck out of Europe. You ever read about the Vietnam war? Right, well, you know how when the NVA moved in at the end, there was this rabid scramble to get out of Saigon on anything that moved, people running to cling to the runners of choppers . . . It was like that for a whole continent, in the big cities . . . I went to the airport and some guy was scalping the airline tickets, wanted twenty-five thousand quid each. People climbing over people to buy from the motherfucker . . . People clamoring at the embassy demanding help and getting thrown out and finally breaking windows, getting shot at . . . At the airport somebody once an hour tried to pull off a hijacking . . . it was worse at the docks. But I found a dude with a boat was on his way to Amsterdam, said he knew somebody had a private jet there, could get us both on, and for some reason I bought the story. I was panicked. Yeah, you laugh *now*. He got me to Amsterdam and took my money to "make the connection" for us, and then he never came back, of course. The money wasn't worth much, anyway. But I found him, eight months ago, and he had this Weatherby, he'd looted it from somebody's house. Never gave him a chance to use it on me. I used the twenty-two on him first . . . But wait, I left out a lot. Only, you were probably here for what I left out. NATO forces declare martial law in Holland, Russians move in, Russians get driven back. The riots. The public executions and the riots because of the public executions and then more executions. Me, I watched it all from up here. Tried to stay out of it.

But I'll tell you something funny. It was almost a relief to me. The whole thing. Even the war. It was like—before the war, nothing was real. I mean . . . people talked about things that happened in download movies and VR and online RPG, like they were anecdotes about people they actually knew and . . . It was like our lives before the war were just long, detailed movie lives or TV lives or VR lives . . . I can't explain. But I had this feeling that nothing was real and nothing mattered until the war.

Anyway, I was living with a Dutch girl, Luka. How I met her, she went out one day to try to buy some food, and there was a food riot and she was attacked because she had a bag of food—I'd been in line with her, and when the riot started I helped her get away from it and she was grateful, so she gave me a place to stay—well, okay, maybe it wasn't just gratitude, she was lonely—and it was pretty much an instant thing, like we'd always been shacked up; there were no further questions. She had hair that looked like . . . you ever see cornsilk? She was a big girl, but handsome, Amazon handsome. Always neating things up. Maternal, like your aunt, except in bed. She was . . . And then of course after the Russians blockaded the port and the siege started, the food riots spread from the market to the high-rises. The masses, you know, usually have the wrong idea about who's pulling what strings, and they thought the people in the 'rises were hoarding food, which was bullshit; Luka and I had to stand in the same ration lines as everyone else, but there's no reasoning with hungry people. And they came in and tore the place apart and . . .

. . . and they threw her out a fucking window.

Out a window, and she fell forty stories down, and I opened up on them with my rifle. I was firing at a monster, this mass of arms and legs and screaming heads; it backed out and left some of its parts behind with my bullet-holes in them, and I looked with binoculars and saw they were just ordinary people. I had shot two old women, a fifteen-year-old boy, and a guy who looked a lot like my brother Barry except he had a mustache.

It was a shock. I'd, y'know, shot *individual people*. And everything was changed. The mob came back and some of them had guns now, so I went to the roof and hid in the little house for the elevator motor, and they didn't find me. And they left the place pretty much the way you see it. Then two weeks later the lines broke and the Russians moved in. Occupied the town. And it was just another army. A lot of people thought the Russians would be better than the NATO armies. But there was no food and more people starved . . . You must have been here—No? How long have you been here? Oh, you were in a Camp then . . . And then the Allies tried to retake Amsterdam with the tactical nukes and we couldn't believe it. Small warheads, short-term radiation. No big problem, right? Only kill a fourth of the town's population—you make an omelet you gotta break some eggs. At least a fourth of the town died. In a week. And then the earthworks were sabotaged, and some of the Dutch actually immolated themselves in the squares. The work of centuries to take Holland from the sea reduced to nothing in days, and they couldn't handle it. Some days I understand why they did it and some days I don't. People saw the old men set fire to themselves and most people took no notice. The gangs liked it, though, because it broke the monotony; they made a big production, big joke, of toasting ration bread on sticks over the coals of the guys who . . .

I tried to get out of the city again and stole a boat, but NATO spotters caught me. Convinced I was on a mission for the Russians. They had Jenkins prisoner, too. That's where we met. But he had the brig's lock program dazzled, so he and I escaped, and there was no place to go but here, back here . . . We've done okay. We got a way into the spotter camps, steal supplies now and then. We had to shoot some scavengers one day, but mostly we stay out of trouble, out of anything that looks like it might remotely be considered subversive, and they don't come looking for us. The Armies . . . we don't even talk them down. Either side. Because none of them give a fuck. NATO, the Russians, Americans, Brits, Czechs. Everybody calls them The Armies. Nobody cares *which* army. If you're army, you're The Man in the Helmet . . .

● ● ●

Smoke didn't say anything for a long time. Not even to himself. He was too tired. He knew there was a lot more, but it was more he didn't have to ask about.

A little later Hard-Eyes mentioned family in the States. Mostly he tried not to think about them, because the scramble screen blocked transmissions—all the civvy frequencies anyway and lots of others—so there was no way to get news. Social networking was blocked. Fones blocked. Why torture yourself wondering . . . wondering what it was like in the States now.

● ● ●

From an end-of-term report by thirteen-year-old Gary Krueger, of Cincinnati, Ohio, entitled "The Cause of the War." Gary's report grade was B+.

Different people have different ideas about why the Third World War started. I asked my C-driver Seeker to look in the Internet to see if there was a list of reasons. It found thirty-three reasons which don't agree with each other, and they come from seventeen different groups of people.

The most commonly given reason is the one given by registered members of the Republican Party. They say that Greater Russia has been building up its strength in secret for years. They were making it look like less than it was, with underground training places. Then they saw that the North Atlantic Treaty Organization was not maintaining its strength in Europe and was letting the United States carry the burden, so they saw they had a chance to take advantage of this weakness. Also they say that there were crop failures and industrial problems and all that corruption and mobster activity and other problems in Russia and the Warsaw Pact countries were rebelling and wanted to be independent. So Koziski of Greater Russia, after the coup in 2031, he thought that a war would distract people from these problems and bring the old Warsaw Pact countries back together because they would unite against an enemy. Also the Russians were running out of power supplies and wanted to capture coal and oil and atomic energy plants and microwave receiving stations that get orbital power. They also wanted to embarrass the Americans like they did after the "Bay of Pigs fight," [sic] which was something that happened to the USA in the twentieth century that made the USA let the Soviet Union get concessions, even though this Greater Russian government is a different government than the USSR government.

The Democratic Party people mostly say that the US government pushed the Russian government into starting a war by installing the Milstar 7 and Milstar 8 military satellite systems in orbit. The Russians' satellites weren't as good and they were paranoid that we could use our system to shoot down their missiles and so we could invade them or attack them and they wouldn't be able to defend themselves. So they wanted to take new territory over in Europe to capture Europe ground-based missiles and to create a "buffer zone" to stop invasion, and also, the Democrats agree on this part, they wanted to unite their people against an enemy and make them forget their problems.

The third group of people say that it is because of an "international conspiracy of Jews and Muslims to destroy the United States" that made the Russians do it. I think this a dumb idea because Jews and Muslims don't work together and how could the Jewish people control the Russians when the Russians are persecuting them all the time?

I think the war was caused by all the reasons said by the first two groups.

• • •

A note to Gary Krueger from the teacher: *This is a good report, but I think you use too much Internet material, too much online searching. Too many students do that! That's letting the computer do your work for you. If you do it that way, you won't remember what you learn. Also, be careful when you make sentences not to run them together with so many and's. You are making run-on sentences.*

• • •

The following is a poem written by a student in Gary Krueger's World Affairs class, Barbara Wycowski, twelve years old:

ON A DAY PRETTY SOON

Joe Smith didn't finish eating his apple
Jane Jones didn't finish reading her book
Bob Farmer didn't finish playing his video game
Ann Franklin didn't finish posting on Facebook

Jim Banks didn't finish wrapping his present
Mary didn't finish writing her letter
Dan didn't finish singing his song
Barbara didn't finish writing her poem
Because the hydrogen bombs exploded and
everyone died and the whole world was finished and it
was the end of everything completely and absolutely.

• • •

The following is from a report from Barbara Wycowski for her World Affairs class entitled "Why There Hasn't Been Nuclear War So Far":

. . . In 2030 the USA and Greater Russia signed a treaty called the Conventional War Limitations Treaty in which they agreed that if they had an armed conflict they would limit the use of nuclear weapons to small tactical warheads. The use of those kind would be controlled by an upper limit of how many can be used. A lot of people said that agreeing to make a war in any way was immoral, but this agreement so far has prevented the world war from being a nuclear holocaust. But I think it is only a matter of time and pretty soon it will escalate into a world war, and then we'll all get killed, so I don't know why I'm writing this, except so I can stay in school to make my Mom happy until we're dead . . .

• • •

A photocopy of Barbara's poem and essay was sent by her teacher to her school guidance counselor. On it the teacher wrote, "*I am very worried about Barbara and a lot of other students who seem to have despaired of ever growing up. There is also another group of students who seem to be reacting to the danger of a wide nuclear war by sliding into a jingoism which I also find disturbing . . .*"

• • •

They were lying in the dark, each wrapped in his black-market US Army blanket. The cardboard pallet under Smoke's blanket was cold, slightly moist, enough to give him chills.

Smoke said, softly, "Hard-Eyes."

"Yeah."

Sure, the guy was awake. No way he trusted Smoke yet. Lying there with his old-before-their-time eyes wide open and smoldering in the darkness.

"Hard-Eyes, there are some who are worse than others. Some Armies."

"That right?"

"Yeah, The Second Alliance."

"You call that an army? More like multinational MPs."

"Uh-uh. SA's run by the Second Circle. You know what that is?"

"I saw the NR leaflets. Say they're fascists. Maybe, but no one takes them seriously. Just another gang."

"That's what a fascist army is, a big *gang*. The SA's the Second Circle's army. NATO's using them, but they're using NATO . . . You heard about the new war front?"

"No." The cardboard rasped on the concrete floor—the looters had torn up the carpet—as he got up on an elbow. Hard-Eyes asked, "You been outside?" An edge of accusation. A traveler from outside the city was expected to share news, and rumors—which were indistinguishable. Survival protocol.

"Haven't been outside Amsterdam except once this year," Smoke said. "I've been mostly over by where the port used to be. Last time I was outside I got indentured into the NATO logistics line. Supposed to've been a 'civilian freight porter' with a salary."

Hard-Eyes snorted.

"But you know," Smoke said, "we ate once a day. Guaranteed."

"That's all right. Not bad. And you were behind the fighting."

"Except some of the camp got a dose of forty-four."

"Neurotoxin forty-four? I think that's what's wrong with Pelter. Got a dose of forty-four. He was raving, on and off, when we first found him. It shot his immune system to hell."

"You took in a sick guy? You don't seem like Red Cross volunteers . . . "

Two-second hesitation. Then Hard-Eyes said, "Jenkins knew him. Jenkins is a little limp-dicked in some ways. And it was like taking in a sick cat, nurse the cat to health and in gratitude the little fucker gives you ringworm or something . . . You said 'we' a while ago. About coming into town with someone."

"I came in with . . . " He almost said the name. "A guy who still has connections with the Allies. But they don't run him."

"As far as you know."

"As far as I know," Smoke agreed.

They were quiet for a couple of minutes, because of a spasm of coughing from Pelter. He wheezed for a while and then it subsided. His lungs rattled when he inhaled.

Smoke shivered and pulled his grimy army blanket more closely around his shoulders.

"So how's the front moving?" came Hard-Eyes, suddenly, a sharp question out of the darkness.

"It's moving completely out of Western Europe."

Silence, except for the dull patter of raindrops in the tub.

"Did you hear me?" Smoke asked.

"I heard some horseshit."

"The guy I mentioned, he got it straight from the Allied commander's radio code officer. NATO's leaving a skeleton force in Amsterdam, Paris, Dresden...They've pushed the Russians back, and the story is the Russians are regrouping to hold the line along their traditional borders and around what used to be Warsaw Pact countries. Concentrating on a naval push. The Russians are losing the land battle and winning the sea battle, so who knows how it'll equalize . . . "

"The Russian naval push. Finally. Those outdated nuclear subs. With the nasty missiles . . . " Sounding almost convinced. "Could be rumor number ten thousand five hundred and two." In wartime Europe, contradictory rumors came and went like autumn leaves in a hurricane.

"You know it's not. It feels right."

"And you think the SA will step into the vacuum left by the Russians and NATO."

"You really believe NATO can police the back-territory? That much land? Who's left to do it? Who'd do it here? Paris is hanging together on a smaller police force than New York's got in Central Park. They can hang together because of the military presence. The military moves out and the place is down the drain. And they're moving out, mostly. So the Second Alliance is hired to move in to police things. The UN Security Council sponsored the SA in this."

"The SA . . . " Hard-Eyes was quiet for a moment, then, all in a rush: "NATO couldn't be that . . . I mean, just to turn it over to them. NATO'd try to set up provisional governments modeled on the ones that fell."

"That's what they're calling it: transitional period to get them into the provisional government stage. 'Until autonomy is practical.' In the meantime the SA is providing the men to keep order, supposedly . . . "

"No, dude. Everybody knows about the SA. NATO wouldn't give it *them* . . . "

"Are you serious? Are you that naïve?"

Silence. Then, "I guess mostly it's people in the underGrid that know . . . but NATO couldn't be that stupid."

"NATO is mostly shot to hell except for Scandinavia, Spain, what's left of Britain, the States. And who pulls the strings in the States? SA sympathizers."

After a moment Hard-Eyes said, "No, come on. Okay, maybe it's true. Then what? Is the blockade still up?"

"No, but the SA will be empowered to 'enact migratory containment.' "

"Where'd you get that phrase?"

"Steinfeld has a printout—" Let him think it's a slip. Oh, no, I said the name.

"Steinfeld. You're with Steinfeld."

The rasp of cardboard as Hard-Eyes sat up.

Smoke said, "I'm just a recruiter." Too hasty. "I'm not initiated NR."

"Shit: I've got a New Resistance operative in my squat. The NATO MPs will be dropping in, and we'll all go to the work camps."

"Nobody's made me as NR. I'm freelance. I've known Steinfeld for a while, we were indentured together. He used Mossad connections, got us out. Some others. But I didn't follow him like a puppy, just for that. I'm freelance, Hard-Eyes, for real. I wasn't supposed to bring you along at this stage. But what the hell, come on, come with me. At first light, I'll take you to meet Steinfeld. The man can do one thing for you, in exchange for a little work: he can get you out of Amsterdam. To Paris."

"One crater to another. Foxhole to foxhole. Big deal."

"Now *that* is real, bona fide horseshit, the certified stuff. You know it's better there. Maybe it won't be better for long. But you won't have to stay there long."

Hard-Eyes didn't reply to that. His silence said, *That's hype, and it's all been hype.*

The crow was nestled on the back of Smoke's neck now. It made a small, warm place there with its body. A circle of warmth and mindless friendship three inches across. Thinking contentedly, *They might just kill me in my sleep. It's fifty/fifty.* Thinking that, Smoke focused on the three-inch circle and fell into it, and it was a gateway.

• • •

Smoke sat up and looked through the half-light at Pelter, and knew instantly that he was dead. The crow was gone. Something went cold in Smoke then.

You pathetic asshole, he told himself. You're like a man in prison making a pet of a cockroach.

Jenkins and Hard-Eyes were gone, and Smoke didn't care. Except, he thought, *Those pricks have eaten the bird.*

But he heard a rustling behind him and turned to see Richard Pryor's tailfeathers emerging from his canvas pouch. It had its head in a bag of bread.

Smoke tried not to feel too happy about it, but it was useless. He felt good.

A little dull-blue light shafted glumly from a hole in the ceiling. Probably from a window in the room above. Smoke looked around and saw that Hard-Eyes and Jenkins had taken all their stuff. Were definitely and completely gone. Truth was, he didn't care much. Except he'd liked Hard-Eyes, and he knew Hard-Eyes had the necessary restlessness that Steinfeld looked for.

But fuck it. At least the crow had signed up. "Richard!" Smoke shouted.

The crow fluttered again and backed comically out of the pouch, looked at him with not a trace of remorse. The look said, *Stop yelling, asshole.*

Smoke reached past the crow, into the pouch. The crow hopped onto his wrist.

"Who trained you, huh?"

The crow made a door-creaking sound in its throat.

Smoke fed it the last of his cheese and said, "Looks like I blew the recruiting. They're gone. Their gear is gone, so they aren't coming back. Let's go back to Steinfeld and ask if we can go with him to Paris."

• • •

But in the raft, when he let the currents whirl him through the echoing, swishing canyons of brick and concrete, under cover of the morning fog, he glimpsed another boat behind, and the silvery jut of the Weatherby, and knew then that Hard-Eyes was following him. Simply checking him out. And maybe Smoke would have his recruiting fee after all.

• 03 •

It was utterly artificial, and it was the most natural thing in the world. And the world wasn't a planet anymore.

The world, now, for the Colonists, was an inter-relationship. The world was the inter-relationship between the Colony proper and its tethered satellites; between the Colony and the tethered satellites and the free-orbiting satellites, the moonbase, and various control stations on the planet Earth. Relating by lasered messages, microwaved data input, radio waves, fusion-powered ships. Each unit of information and material relation struggling to assert itself, driven by the will of the builders, despite the flux and surge of solar radiation, cosmic rays. And in fantastic defiance of the flotsam of space: meteors and asteroids.

Their world was a web of data and materialized information, and at the center of the web: FirStep. Or just, *The Colony.* An artificial world, turned outside-in. Artificial, but in his dedication speech, five years before at the official opening of the still-uncompleted Colony, Dr. Benjamin Brian Rimpler asserted that something created of human artifice is more fully natural than a biologically conventional living organism; the Colony, Rimpler said, was a compounding of nature; a splendid elaboration of nature, as an anthill, together with its ants, is a natural growth demonstrating even more principles of nature than a leaf of grass.

Claire was trying to get the general idea—human artifice as a product of nature—across to her first-grade class, and some of them understood, and others were indifferent, and still others rejected the idea out of some undefined resentment against comparing human colonies to insect colonies.

Claire stood on a grassy knoll sculpted to look as if it had come there by geological chance, and around her sat twelve children. Six boys and six girls, as per demographic control.

From the outside, the six-mile-long Colony looked like a cylinder that had swallowed something big and was digesting it boa-style. The bulge at its middle was a Bernal sphere, itself a mile and a half in diameter. The concave interior of the sphere was to have been the main inhabitable area of the Colony. It was Pellucidar. It was Mu, sunken Atlantis, the Hollow Earth. The landscape stretched away to an inside-out horizon, curving up when it should have curved down. The lengthwise axis of the Colony was pointed toward the sun, and sunlight, filtered and reflecting from enormous mirrors, glowed from circular windows at the sunward end of the oblate spheroid and was reflected by other mirrors at the farther end. It was given an auroral tint, at times, by the envelope of heavy gases artificially maintained around the Colony by the Lode-Ice Station. Almost before they'd begun to build the Colony, UNIC—the United Nations Industrial Council—had sent a series of teams into the asteroid belt where high-orbit satellite-mounted telescopes had found huge lumps of frozen gases; the "lodes" looked like great agates, but were in fact more like interstellar icebergs. A series of mining teams in UNIC-owned spacecraft had used channeled-force nuclear blasts to drive a Wagnerian procession of ten-mile-thick lumps of frozen gas back to a synchronous orbit with the slowly growing shell of the Colony. Then they built plants on the frozen asteroids, airtight factories dug into the crystalline surface, which broke the ice down into gas and, after seeding it for heightened energy absorption, routed it via electromagnetic fields into a protective envelope around the Colony: its sole purpose was filtering—it filtered the solar wind and cut back on cosmic rays, making it possible for people to live on the Colony without resorting to strangling thicknesses of heavy insulating materials. From space a comet's tail of gases slowly burning off from the Lode-Ice Station streamed in a spectacular iridescence around the space station, making it look like some celestial tropical fish about to flicker into the deeps.

The Colony rotated once every five minutes, creating a subtle centrifugal artificial gravity. Here on the hill the gravity was slightly less than on the shore of the lake, thirty yards below them.

Overhead, filigreed clouds blurred the land . . . the land that was also overhead.

Toward the sunny end, the arbitrary south, the difference in atmospheric drag between the inner and outer layers of contained air created a hurricane's-eye effect; cloud spirals formed and pulled apart there. You could get dizzy looking into it; you could imagine you were falling—falling up. Look "east' or "west' and you saw the curving vista of brown-and-green landscaping, like a tidal wave of land curling back on itself, a wave never breaking; the landscape was checkered at asymmetrical intervals by the Colony's central housing developments.

Claire and her class sat in a cleared area just above the cactus garden, between the eccentric shapes of gray-green euphorbias and lime-green succulents. The children wore their school jumpsuits, but in the tradition of the Technics Section, the outfits were patched and pinned with ribbons and their parents' work-section badges and viddyprogram logos. The logo patch fad came across like gang colors, a resemblance which made Claire nervous. The most popular patch advertised Grommet the Gremlin. Grommet was a cartoon monster, a *cute* monster, for God's sake, who giggled moronically as he pulled out the wires sustaining your life-support systems if you didn't feed him access credit for sweet-rations. He was a feral, free-floating giga-pet. His bug-eyed face leered idiotically from patches on the shoulders of eleven of the twelve children.

Claire Rimpler wore a white technicki jumpsuit, a kind of bluff social camouflage. But she was Admin, was teaching the technicki children as a volunteer—really as part of her father's program to better relations between Admin and technicki—and had been doing it for two weeks, and for all fourteen days she'd regretted it.

Claire was twenty-one, but looked sixteen when she was smiling. She was small, with a rose-tipped pallor, soft-looking auburn hair clipped short like an EVA worker's; her lips were a shade too large for her doll-like face. Her expressive eyes were brown-black. Her eyebrows were a trifle too thick to be feminine. But the whole, as an ensemble, was far more attractive than she knew . . . Her petiteness and girlish features deceived people into expecting docility. "The truth is, Claire's pure Admin," her brother Terry had said of her. "Gives orders as naturally as a technicki gives back-talk." Her father had lectured Terry about making "classist" remarks about technickis.

No, she'd never been docile. But there were times she'd been passive, introspective, before her brother's death—before Terry had been snuffed into a statistic, in the Third EVA Disaster. Her brother had been supervising a technicki hull-team in the construction of section D, the Earth-end of the cylinder, two years before. An EVA pod had come too close to a tethered satellite. One of the pod's landing struts had snapped the comsat's tether, so the satellite tumbled into the extra-vehicular team on D-sec, striking two, who spun to hit two more, a weightless domino effect that in turn spun thirty-one men off into space, most of them with ruptured suits. Only one of them was recovered alive. Six bodies were never recovered at all. In the wake of the disaster—and with the ongoing problem of the Colony's costs outweighing its financial benefits—public pressure on UNIC had almost cut off funding. Claire's father tried to resign as Colony Committee Chairman and Design Supervisor. New funding had come from select UNIC members, certain big corporate investors, like the Second Alliance. The SA . . . Rimpler had been persuaded to return to work . . .

But her dad was never the same. He wouldn't look out the ports, into space. Maybe he was afraid he'd see Terry floating out there. Floating up to the glass. Staring accusingly.

And Claire was different after that. The occasional moods of passivity vanished forever. She blamed Admin laxity for Terry's death. Which meant she had to become Admin, to set things right. And she was Admin now. Almost completely.

● ● ●

Claire had explained to the children why the land overhead wasn't going to fall on them, and how if they walked in a straight line to arbitrary east they'd eventually come back to the spot they'd left, arriving from the west, all in the same day if one walked fast enough. The children were patient through all this, except, of course, for Anthony, who ostentatiously smoked a syntharette through it all, expecting her to rebuke him for inhaling nicotine vapor, frustrated when she pointedly would not play that game.

They ate a lunch of pressed fruit, from produce grown in the Colony's agripods, and soybutter 'n' jelly sandwiches. And when they'd finished, Claire said, "We're going to have to go back soon. So if anybody has any more questions . . . ?"

Chloe raised one of her small black hands and asked, "Whunna finzuhruzat?" She pointed to the arbitrary north, the inner part of the sphere away from the sun. The land here, between the meager areas of finished developments, looked calico, brown and yellow in patches, with outcroppings of raw blue metal.

"First of all," Claire reminded her, "ask the question in Standard English. Technickinglish isn't what you're here to learn."

Chloe sighed and said, laboriously, "When . . . they are—"

"When are they."

The little girl made a moue of frustration and went on, "When *are they* going to . . . finish the . . . rest . . . of zuh—no—*of that*?"

"Good! To answer your question, the Colony is about two-thirds finished. Maybe five years more and it'll be done."

"But who's going to live in the new part when it's finished?" Anthony asked abruptly, showing off his command of Standard English.

She'd been expecting the question. And she could feel their attention had shifted, suddenly, from whispered jokes, giggling, teasing, complaining—shifted to her. Now, now they were listening.

Maybe we shouldn't bring them on these excursions till we can move them out of the dorms, she thought. Maybe it only makes them feel frustrated.

"Everyone will be able to live there," Claire said. "Everyone! Not all at once. There will be lots drawn to see who's first."

"Who's going to program the lottery computer?" Anthony asked, and she wondered if he was really that precocious or if someone had coached him.

"The computer will be an Admin unit," she admitted, "but it will be fair. Everyone will have a chance."

"But—"

"Now," she interrupted, blithely as she could, standing, "let's go to the arcade!"

"I don't wanna go there," Anthony said, crossing his legs.

Claire jammed a thumbnail in her mouth, began to chew—then remembered the children were watching and quickly pulled it away, using another finger of that hand to point at Anthony. "Tony, don't play that game with me. You love the arcade. You spend hours there. You complained when you had to come out here; you said it gave you headaches. Don't give me that evac about not wanting to—"

"I like it here, and I want to stay."

"Anthony, has someone been—" And then she broke off, seeing the men from TechniWave coming, and she understood it all.

There were three of them. One with the cam-transmitter. Beside him was a guy with his look so burnished he must be the anchorman. And a third guy, an X-factor, might be the one who'd planned this.

The cameraman wore a backpack-fed shouldercam/directional mike and a headset; the cam was mounted on his shoulder like a second, robotic head.

She recognized the reporter, now—Asheem Spengle. He wore the fashionable triple-Mohawk in the technicki colors—white, silver, and gold—and also a white I'm-just-one-of-the-people jumpsuit. He was regular-featured, glib, a human cipher. The third man wore a flatsuit: a suit in which the jacket and vest and tie were false, just lapels and a tie-knot and vest-front sewn onto a one-piece outfit. He was sharp-eyed, coning his lips to seem perpetually thoughtful.

Anthony jumped up excitedly, seeing them. "Misser Barkin!" he began. "I—"

The man in the flatsuit shook his head at Anthony but smiled, showing an overbite.

Anthony caught the cue and shut up. The reporter and the cameraman stopped just a few yards from Claire and the class; the reporter stepped in front of the camera, facing it, his back to Claire, and nodded. The cameraman was already focused, waiting. He hit a switch on his belt. A green light flashed on at the side of the little camera, and Spengle said, *"Routen Admin Park talkwid Adminteach Claire Rimplerner stoods—"* And went on.

Stunned, mentally treading water, Claire listened, translating for herself. *We're out in Admin Park talking with administrative teacher Claire Rimpler and her students and trying to get her reaction on a disturbance that was reported to be taking place here—*

Claire thought, Should I just walk away from it? That might make us look pretty bad. And I'm responsible for the kids. And then they'd just quote Anthony. Or whoever'd coached him.

But then Spengle turned to her and asked her a question.

The camera was on her. His question had been recorded, Claire's reply would be recorded, a recording to be edited for a TechniWave transmission to the whole technicki pop of the Colony.

Translated from technicki:

CLAIRE: If you want to talk to me, I have to know if this is live or recorded.

SPENGLE: We're recording, Ms. Rimpler.

CLAIRE: I had two years of communications, and I know that machine: it can transmit. If you'll do this live so I can say my piece without editing, I'll submit to an interview. Otherwise I can't be sure of getting a fair opportunity to reply.

SPENGLE: I can't guarantee—

CLAIRE: Then I can't answer questions. It's not fair.

Spengle conferred with the flatsuiter.

Claire used the delay to call Admin on her fone. She explained the situation to Judy Avickian in Central Telecast. "Just watch the broadcast, Judy. Ring me if it's not coming through live."

"You got it."

Claire replaced the fone in her pack and turned to Spengle.

Spengle said, "Ms. Rimpler, we'll have link-up in a minute or two. In the meantime—"

He looked at the gawking assemblage of children. "I heard someone up here has refused to go back to the dorms."

"Anthony!" they chorused. "Z'Anthony!"

Claire said, "That's something you must already know, Spengle, since your people—"

Anthony interrupted her by stepping up to Spengle, half turning so the camera could pick him up clearly. He'd been drilled well.

A finger-sized directional mike on the bottom of the camera swiveled back and forth between Spengle and Anthony as they spoke.

"We've got live," the cameraman said, pressing the earplug of his headset.

Spengle nodded, repeated his earlier spiel, and bent to interview Anthony. From technicki:

"Your name is Anthony Fiorello?"

"That's right."

"You're one of the children refusing to go back to the dorms?"

"There's only one refusing!" Claire broke in. Spengle ignored her. And probably it didn't pick up on the mike.

"Why is that, Anthony?"

"It's crowded there and it smells bad and I'm just as good as Admin people, so how come I can't live in the Central with the parks where it's nice like the Admins?" Just a touch mechanical, hinting at rote.

"Anthony—how many people live in Colony? Do you know?"

"Sure, we learned that. About ten thousand people."

"And how many live in Central in the nice dorms, or in the Open out of all that?"

"One thousand."

"Does anything else bother you about all this, Anthony?"

"Well, I came out here and it looks so empty! There's some houses down there, but they're a long way away! There's room here for technics and maintens!"

Claire was fed up. "You want to interview me, it's got to be now. I'm due back at Admin," she called out. "Come on, kids!" She turned to the others. "Get your things together; we're going to have to go soon." Some of them stirred, others stood unmoving, gaping at the cameraman, mesmerized by the technological totem on his shoulder. The reporters, she realized, had usurped her authority over the children. And that was a bad omen.

"Ms. Rimpler," Spengle said, "has just said she *hasn't got time* to talk with us." Heavy sarcastic emphasis on *hasn't got time*. "So we'll have to go back to you, Ben, at TechniWave Central—"

"It isn't true!" Claire shouted, rushing up to the camera. "That's not what I said!—" And then she stopped talking, just stopped, feeling foolish, realizing the light was out on the camera, that it was no longer transmitting and hadn't been for a while.

And Spengle had turned his back to her, was walking away in close, soft conversation with the flatsuiter . . .

Half an hour later Claire stood alone on the platform of the park railstop, watching the car that had come along the axis rail-line to take the children back to the dorms; watching it recede as it carried the children to the north end of the Colony, the dorms and the uncompleted area, while she waited for the train that would take her to the arbitrary south. Hating the glaring symbolism of the moment, she chewed a thumbnail, thinking that once the camera was gone, Anthony had lost interest in boycotting the dorms. He was first on the train, eager for the arcades.

She'd crossed to the southward station and stood looking toward the huge retina-like windows above Admin central. A ring of verdant green encircled the windows. Within the ring, mist curled in gentle spirals, refracting the light in muted rainbows. It was quiet in the parkland; there was a gentle, manufactured breeze smelling of growing things—and only faintly of air filterant—and for a moment the place looked like the paradise it had been designed to be. But then the vent-breeze shifted and she caught the soiled-socks odor of the dorms' overworked air recycler. And the paradise was gone. Paradise has always been fragile.

• • •

"Japanese tourists," Samson Molt said, "never change. The Japanese keep their traditions. Their tea rituals. Their sushi schools and their chopsticks and that Japanese packaging. And the way they act in foreign places is always the same. Since I was a boy, they never changed. They're faddish in some ways—but really, they never change. Could almost be the same tour group I saw in New York as a lad."

Samson Molt and Joe Bonham were lounging at an "outdoor table" at the south end of the arcade. The six clubs, two digital arcades, a handful of boutiques, and two cafés were "the Strip," which was the closest thing the Colony had to authorized nightlife. Molt and Bonham preferred the unauthorized nightlife. But that didn't start for hours yet, end of the third shift, when the maximum number of B-section workers would be freed up to spend cred.

The tourists were eight nearly identical (to Molt's eyes) Japanese with the faddish forehead-strapped cameras, each camera with its remote focuser that snapped down over the right eye, transforming the socket into something reptilian. They wore onepiece Japanese Action Suits, JAS for short, in tastefully splashy pastels, soft material. They chattered and pointed, winking to make the headband cams take pictures. Each stop along the arcade was an orgy of you-take-my-picture-and-I'll-take-yours, posing in front of everything, so that half of what they were photographing was blocked by their bodies.

Molt wondered which ones were industrial spies. The Japanese were said to be planning their own space colony.

Their guide was a tall, demure black woman making a valiant effort to look interested as she droned, " . . . the Colony took twenty-four years to achieve basic livability for non-astronaut personnel . . . " drone " . . . begun in secret early in this century . . . Richard Branson was an . . . " drone " . . . now owned by UNIC, the United Nations Industrial Council, five major international corporations who pooled their resources for matching funds from the UN . . . " drone " . . . The Colony manufactures goods which can only be made in zero or light gravity, as well as operating the first of a chain of interplanetary solar power stations which soak up solar energy and transform it to microwaves transmitted to receptors in the Gobi and Mojave deserts . . . " drone "Although UNIC is still operating in the red, it expects to break even next year and to begin a profit-making phase in the following year . . . We begin our tour at the arcade because it links Tourist Arrival with Colony Open, the parkland area which as you will see in just a moment verges on the paradisial in its . . . " Drone.

The tourists clicked and snapped and chattered on, and the Strip was itself again, shorn of the kitschy glamor of their enthusiasm. Like most of the Colony corridor areas, the Strip seemed more worn, more used, more frayed and grimy than things on Earth, though it had been built only a few years before. Which surprised visitors. They expected the pristine polish of a top-tech chips clinic. But the Colony was almost a closed system. And replacing anything, repainting anything, was more costly here . . .

And now the Strip was like a third-generation hand-me-down toy in a grubby nursery, its colors faded or smeared with the grease of too much touching; like a seaside amusement park long since gone to seed.

Across from the French-style Café Crème was the white seashell-shaped metal awning of the Captain Halfgee club. Soft, moving lights glowed behind the mermaids painted on its plastex windows; two customers came out, still dripping chlorinated water, towels draped over their shoulders, carrying drinks in plastic cups.

The "street" of white synthetics was nine yards wide, and dingy; the ceiling, three yards overhead—unusually high for a Colony corridor—was blue, fluffy clouds painted on at intervals. The clouds looked as if they ought to be laundered with bleach.

Molt's gaze wandered down the street, where the crowd thickened at the one Admin-sanctioned casino. He considered going up for blackjack. But no one in the casino was permitted to lose more than ten newbux in cred, nor win more than twenty, and there was no way, in Molt's view, you could work up a good gambler's sweat when the stakes were so low.

The other clubs and cafés were articulated in bright, brassy, circus-rococo colors, neon-trimmed and flashing, but it was all Admin operated; and to Molt it looked like a miniature setup for children, like the department store "Santa Claus Lane" of his boyhood.

"See the fucking elves making toys," he muttered. Even the Strip's pornography parlor was watered-down, the porn softcore and revoltingly well photographed. Tasteful. Not much fun at all.

He lit a syntharette, not because he wanted one, but because this was one of the few areas in the Colony where the nico-vapor was permitted. And because there was nothing else to do. Just nothing else to fucking *do*.

Molt was a heavy man with a brickish complexion and sharp blue eyes and a tousle of rusty hair. He leaned both elbows on the plastic table, his cup of three percent beer between his hands. He wore genuine faded Levi's, and a real-wool knit pullover, dull yellow, holes at the elbows and shoulder seams. Bonham—a sad-eyed man with thinning brown hair, a long nose—wore a gray pilot's uniform without insignia, two-piece, the short jacket taut across his wide, flat chest. He wasn't a pilot, which is why the uniform had no insignia. The uniform was supposed to help him pick up women. Like Molt, Bonham was a pilot's second, which officially made both men Technic Union. Both had two years of college and, socially, both looked down on technickis. But both men were Neo-Marxists and in the political abstract regarded the technickis as brethren workers.

Bonham had a way of fading in and out of conversations like a radio with a faulty frequency modulator. He could be dreamy and then diamond-hard analytical, by quick turns. He leaned back in his chair, one hand toying with an empty glass, his mind somewhere else.

"Bonham," Molt said, leaning forward, lowering his voice meaningfully. "Fuck these tourists. You want to go to that club they got in the Open?"

Bonham stared glassily at a smudged cloud on the ceiling.

"Joe, dammit!" Molt said sharply.

Bonham snapped his eyes down from the cloud. "Yeah, I heard you. Japanese tourists. Pain in the ass."

"I asked, You wanna go to the club in the Open?"

"The Tavern on the Green? Out in the Admin's Open? You know what that place costs? Three bux for a cup of tea."

"Yeah? It's just—I never been there. But now that you mention it—I can't feature those prices. Forget it."

"Of course, the cost is one way they keep it exclusive, keep the technics and the maintens out. I say we spend the money and make ourselves seen there. A Statement, man."

"Isn't worth the price."

"It would be for the principle of the thing."

"I can't afford the principles. And I'm on probation. If you get drunk, start making speeches, you'll get us into shit with Security." He shook his head dolefully. "Hey, Joe—those new Security bulls they got are *mean*. Fuck it, let's wait for the Afters. You can get something that'll get you drunk, lose some real money, get yourself sick like a man ought to be able to."

Bonham nodded. "Something in that."

The talk and the place were ordinary, and that felt all right: they were between duty-pulls, they had a week, and they could amble through everything and the week wouldn't have to go as fast as usual, if they were careful.

But everything was going to change in twenty minutes.

"You catch the news about the Admin bimbo?" Bonham asked.

"One bimbo at a time. I'm gonna go see—"

"Kelly? She costs more than she's worth, Molt."

"She digs me."

"Whores pretend, Molt, that's all. They're consummate actresses, for one role and one only. And don't try to tell me you made her cum—"

They went on like that for a while, neither man attending the conversation with his whole mind. And in fifteen minutes everything was going to change.

"So what'd you see onna news?" Molt asked, at last.

"Rimpler's daughter. Cute little thing but super-chilled, I heard. She was taking some kubs out into the Open and one of 'em refused to come back, made a great speech how they were being cheated of their fair share of Open. Spengle made her look like—"

"Yeah. Yeah, I did hear about that. Somebody had a handset on the shuttle and—yeah, the technickis on the shuttle were glued on that one, man."

"Smart move, whoever set that up," Bonham mused. "There's a protest tomorrow. You wanna come along?"

"Maybe. But . . . *you* know, Christ . . . " The two men exchanged commiserating looks and sighed. They'd be surrounded by technics yammering technicki at the demonstration. But they had principles to live up to. Molt shrugged. "Where's it going to be?"

"Corridor D-five."

"Yeah, okay. What the hell." He looked at his watch. "Let's go to Bitchie's, it's probably open for—"

"Is that all you ever think about? Listen, you hear about the SWS readings for the dorm sections?"

"The what? Oh. No. What about it?"

SWS: Solar Wind Shield. The atmospheric envelope generated at the Ice-Lode Station. There were persistent rumors that the Admin crews didn't keep the shield's regularity field in place over the Colony's technicki section; that they were indifferent to cancer risks for technickis.

"The reading was negligible, that's what. About as much field as my mother has testicles."

"The field has to be uniform for the Colony to go on working at all."

They argued Colony politics for the next ten minutes. Molt was the voice of moderation. Social Democrat to Bonham's Post-Trotskyite. At least, that's the way Molt was until he got angry, scented violence. But just now, he was quiet as a bomb before it explodes.

In five minutes everything was going to change.

The waitress, Carla, wandered by the tables, picking up glasses, yawning. She was a horsey bleached blonde with a Reservationist's tattoo half showing through her body stocking. Molt and Bonham exchanged banter with her for four minutes.

In one minute, everything would be different.

Carla went inside to bring out two more weak beers. She came out a minute later, without the beer, her hand clapped over her mouth.

"What's the matter?" Bonham asked. "What's the story, Carla?" Molt asked. Their questions jumbled together.

She looked at them, her bloodshot blue eyes stricken, her face paler than usual. She mumbled something through her hand.

Scared by inference, Molt irritably pulled her hand from her mouth and said, "Dammit, Carla, transmit!"

"The Russians. I heard it on the vid just now."

"The Russians what?" Molt asked, thinking, Oh, shit, maybe they finally launched the big ones.

"They blockaded the Colony. Activated their laser platforms, the battle stations . . . Got ships hanging out there . . . *They won't let our shuttles through. We're cut off.*"

Bonham was scared and looked it. But the fear melted away in Molt, and he realized he'd been waiting for this. He'd been holding something back for a long time. This meant he could let it all out. He could kill a few assholes.

Because everything was different. Now.

• 04 •

The rainstorm had blown onward. The sky had cleared, except for a soft breakage of clouds, light blue against the dark blue twilight.

Smoke was at the window, looking out at the sky, squinting as he tried to see some detail of the Colony; but it was just a pale glimmer, a fragment of Bethlehem's marker, forty degrees above the horizon. "They made that thing up there out of asteroids and pieces of the moon." He spoke to Richard Pryor and the crow tilted its head as if listening, and Smoke was grateful. Talking to yourself didn't look quite so undignified when you had something, someone, to pretend you were talking to.

Dignity. A haggard, grimy, stooped, gaunt, bearded man. His gray-shot black beard matted, his eyes too intense, his hands always faintly shaking and dirty as rat's claws. And we're talking about dignity?

But dignity was everything to Smoke.

Hard-Eyes and Jenkins were behind Smoke, their backs to him, talking to Steinfeld and Voortoven and Willow. Yukio was there, too, but he wasn't talking. Smoke knew Yukio was listening, though.

Smoke listened to bits and pieces as Hard-Eyes and Steinfeld interrogated one another. Smoke tuned in and out.

He kept his eyes on the man-spark hanging in the blue-black sky.

(Just below the window ledge, on the outside, gleaming with rainwater, was the egg, the metal bird had attached the day before. It was sending a signal that meant *They're in the room now . . .*)

Smoke looked at the sky, and, now and then, he listened.

"Let's talk basics," Hard-Eyes was saying. "We're talking no salary, not even after the revolution, supposing that ever happens."

"No salary: correct. But I didn't say anything about a revolution. We're not revolutionaries. We're international partisans. We want to re-establish the republics that existed before the war. Elimination of the jurisdiction of the Second Alliance is obviously a prerequisite."

" 'Elimination,' " Jenkins said. "Has a nice clean sound to it." There was no subtlety to Jenkins' sarcasm, "How big you say the SA weighed in at?"

Steinfeld hesitated. Smoke couldn't see him, but he knew the man and his mannerisms. He could imagine stocky, tired-eyed Steinfeld with his long, iron-gray hair neatly parted in the middle, caught up in the back with a twist of wire. With his black beard, the white streak down the middle so neat-edged it could almost have been dyed there. The short, blunt fingers raised, fanned out just above the top of the scarred desk, the deltas of fine lines at his eyes deepening as he concentrated on his reply. His ineffaceable sense of mission never faltering no matter how much he backed and filled and weaved and bobbed in his dealings. *Whop*—the hands coming down flat on the desk as Steinfeld spoke: "Half-million, it's said. And growing."

"Half-million. They have a half-million men in Europe." Jenkins said it with stagey disbelief.

Steinfeld went on to answer the unasked question hanging in the air. "And all told, if we count splinter groups, factions, the NR could muster four, five thousand. But on this front of the resistance, we're not going after them head-on. We sabotage, we guerrilla their flanks, we chew a lot of little wounds in them till they weaken from bleeding."

"Go back to the part about "this front'," Hard-Eyes said. "What's the other front?"

"Negotiating for help. From the Japanese. And others. We're working on it."

"What about the States?" Jenkins asked.

"You must be bloody joking," Willow said. Willow—in olive-drab fatigues, tennis shoes rotting apart, stolen AK-49 assault rifle across his lap. Broomstick skinny, thatch of colorless hair, a beard that belonged on some aging Chinese emperor, bad teeth; spoke in a monotone, the British mumble. "Fucking Yanks wanking off the fucking Nazis." He pronounced it *Nazzies*. "They like the fascist takeover becorz they figure it's either that or commies. And they got big promises for big business deals from the fascists."

"All this . . . " Steinfeld tilting his head back, making the beard jut at the ceiling. So Smoke pictured it (all the time watching the indistinguishable movement of the Colony). "All this . . . supposition. But I do think they have come to *some* accommodation."

"Mark me," Willow said, "they plan to divide fucking Western Europe up betwixt the blewdy power brokers."

"I'm still thinking about 'no salary,'" Hard-Eyes said flatly.

"What do you believe in?" Voortoven asked. He was a broadchested, muscular man, always clean. Curly brown hair.

"What?" Hard-Eyes was a little startled.

"Do you believe in anything at all? You just want money to bribe your way back to the States? You going to play the drifter who does not get involved? Or you are, maybe, a mercenary?"

"We're not above using mercenaries," Steinfeld said, a fraction hastily. "'Mercenary' is no insult."

Voortoven snorted.

Steinfeld went on, "We can't pay money, but we can pay in goods and, eventually, in transportation."

"I want to know what he believes in," Voortoven said.

Forty-five seconds of silence as they waited for Hard-Eyes to declare himself.

Hard-Eyes said, finally, "When I find it, I'll know it."

"To know what we are takes time," Steinfeld said. Steinfeld was Israeli. Long history of involvement in radical movements, Democratic Socialist, but never stained Marxist. It was assumed he had a family in Israel. He'd never mentioned them, but there were pictures in his wallet no one had seen up close. And it was assumed he was run by the Mossad—which might be a wrong assumption.

Hard-Eyes had heard that one, too. "You might be anyone," he said, looking at Steinfeld. "I could get killed and never know who I'd been working for. Dying for."

A full seventy seconds of silence this time. And then Jenkins said, "You say we could trade some mercenary work for *transportation*. We work for you awhile and then . . . "

Smoke stopped listening. He focused on the Colony and said, "Richard, you know how many tons that thing is, up there? More than the membranes of thinking can carry."

The crow fluttered and dug at its breast for a louse.

"You're not impressed? Crows take bright things into their nests, Richard. The Colony construct is both a nest and a bright thing. You know how many tons that nest is, Richard?"

The crow shook itself.

"I don't either. Hundreds of thousands. Millions. At least it'd weigh that on Earth. They're supposed to be making it bigger and bigger. There are no crows there . . . "

Looking at the Colony, a city tossed into the sky, Smoke felt a sucking vertigo. He looked away from it, down to the Earth. He and the crow gazed out at the wrecked harbor, beyond to the Ijsselmeer, and Smoke had a strange sense of being *in place*, wedged somewhere outside the flow of time.

The harbor's flooding had submerged the docks and boardwalks; it had thrown boathouses up past the sidewalks, half crushed them against the swamped bases of the buildings; it had wedged boats into alleys and had made trucks and cars the new housing development of octopi and sea anemones. There was a whirlpool marked by twisting fluorescent foam where the outflowing currents from the rivered streets met the tidal push of the sea. The harbor's sea vista was hobbled by half-sunk ships, boats, tankers jutting like tombstones. There, and there, well apart, were two dull red throbs, where campfires illuminated stanchions and deck fittings on the upthrusting superstructures of two foundered ships; a couple of squatters there, perhaps three more over there, feeling relatively secure on the wrecks with expanses of cold seawater between them and everything else; more security than in the city, where scavengers roamed the rooftops or sculled the narrow, flooded streets in boats.

Smoke's eyes were drawn by movement; the high movement of electric light. One of the Armies' aircraft. There—over the collapsed roof of the warehouse. A USAF jumpjet. Recon patrol, maybe; hovering, and bobbing up and down the way a jet shouldn't be able to, moving almost like a kite. Casimir force combined with standard thrust, tiltable jets. Now and then it darted a searchbeam into windows.

Ought to close this one before it notices us, Smoke thought.

But then the jumpjet veered off, due east. Gone.

Drone of voices behind him. But he was turned outward, to the mortuary peace of the harbor.

A movement of cold air—too slow to be a breeze, more of an oozing than a blowing, numbing Smoke's nose and cheeks, making his ears sting. It was scented with the brine and the clean rot of the ocean—strange there could be a clean rot but in the absence of men it was so—and a trace of oil, and woodsmoke.

A fog was curling in, sending wraith outriders, and tentatively entwining rusty hulls, the wooden snags of pylons, battleship superstructures, and sailing-yacht yardarms. Under the wrecks, the sea drew all light into itself. And yet there was movement there; Smoke thought he saw the ghostly figures of men and women running in slow motion through streets where flame unfurled . . . and this phantasm passed, replaced by the marching of a great army, an army of men in mirrored helmets, their faces hidden in circles of opacity—

Someone was speaking to him. Had been speaking to him for a while. He knew it, just that suddenly. "Smoke! Open your ears!" It was Steinfeld.

"Maybe 'e' deaf," Willow suggested sincerely, "from the shells. I lost some of me 'earing when they was shellin'."

Smoke turned, and Richard Pryor flapped against the sudden motion. "I was thinking, is all," Smoke said.

"You were daydreaming." Steinfeld said. "Best not to show a light."

Smoke closed the blacked-out windows, locked them in place at the bottom.

"And come over here, Smoke. You can hold on to your independence, if you want to keep up the pretense, but I want you to contribute to this."

Smoke nodded, feeling claustrophobic, cheeks and nose tingling in the warmth of the sun-charged heater glowing cherries of red light to his left. The room was rectangular, high-ceilinged—once someone's bedroom. Now the main furnishings were a blond-wood desk, one leg missing, that corner supported by stacked bricks, a few cracked wooden chairs, and a wooden crate. There were two pools of light, at each end of the room—a reddish pool from the heater and a yellow one from Steinfeld's lantern, on a dented cabinet behind his desk. Hard-Eyes and Jenkins leaned against the wall to the right of the desk. They stood there, Smoke guessed, to be near the door and so no one could get behind them. And for the first time he wondered if he'd made a mistake bringing Hard-Eyes here. Hard-Eyes was almost unreadable. The nickel-plated hunting rifle glinted like a frozen lightning bolt in his hands. Jenkins, rifle in hand, bulked beside him, the thundercloud.

Maybe, Smoke thought, these men want to kill us all, and turn us in for bounty. Or maybe they're planning to locate Steinfeld's black-market stuff. Kill us in our sleep, take the stuff.

Smoke wondered, but all he said was, "I saw a jumpjet. USAF, I think. Headed off east."

Steinfeld frowned. Then he shrugged. "Can't go running off every time the fox comes sniffing around, or it'll catch us out of the henhouse . . . " He smiled. "I heard that one from an American soldier from Oklahoma."

Smoke moved to stand against the wall, across from Hard-Eyes.

"You've got an in at both the camps, Smoke," Steinfeld was saying.

"The Russians treat me best," Smoke said, mostly to the crow. The crow made a ratcheting sound. "It was a surprise to me, too."

"You hear a lot about the SA. Let's collate what we've got, for Hard-Eyes and Jenkins. The SAISC was founded by a man named Predinger. An extremely conservative American millionaire. Far right as you can get without being locked up in an asylum. He founded it sometime in 1984, fittingly.

"Initially, the Second Alliance was to be a sort of, um, global security outfit to be used by any international corporation or conglomerate who needed it—something like Xe or Halliburton Security but bigger and with more . . . agenda." Steinfeld shrugged and went on: "It soon became obvious that the SA was in fact an 'antiterrorist' intelligence outfit. Privately owned, to be sure. This was, of course, at a time when terrorists were beginning to make concerted bombing strikes and kidnappings against big business, especially if it was rooted in the United States or in the allied nations . . . " Steinfeld paused to sip from a cold cup of ersatz coffee. He grimaced and went on. "Not surprisingly, the Alliance concentrated on leftist underground political groups, and ignored the rightist variety. It placed a great many people under surveillance, anyone it suspected might have connections with Marxists and hard-core Jewish-rights activists. The SA ignored the anti-Israeli terrorists unless they were clearly anti-American Communists. After a period of surveillance they would take the 'suspects' in for 'questioning'—something they'd do quite without legal authorization, but sometimes with sanction from the local authorities. About two-thirds of the 'suspects' were people with left-leaning tendencies but no actual connection with terrorists. Their inquisitors were always masked. Sometimes the suspects came out of it alive and only bruised, sometimes they disappeared entirely. But—the governments of the countries where the SA operated covered for them. The SA would claim it had fired some people who were 'overzealous.' The furor would die down and the SA would go back to its old activities . . . Radical activism continued to escalate, and in response the SA took to assassinating radical leaders it believed were aligned with activists. Most of the time it was assassinating the moderates who kept the extremists in check. It may have done this knowingly—knowing that when extremists filled the void, the frightened world would tend to tolerate—would *welcome*—the SA's activities. It would grow in respectability and therefore in contacts; with contacts came power and influence. And, of course, all of this was augmented by Predinger's judicious use of cold cash. Campaign contributions, soft money party donations, and some outright payoffs. Bribery was part of the SA's ordinary, day-to-day operation. Once they almost went too far, even for their allies. Their Buenos Aires chief learned that two identified men on their kill list were in attendance at a leftist political rally in a Buenos Aires union hall. The SA simply blew up the hall. Two hundred people were killed. It was never proved against Predinger's people. There is some evidence that the CIA and Argentina's own secret police may have been of covert assistance—"

Hard-Eyes broke in, "This sounds like a lot of propaganda. Left-wing conspiracy-theory stuff. The SA is right-wing, sure—too far right to be running things. But you make it sound like . . . " He shook his head. "You say there is some evidence, and then you don't cite it. Same kinda talk from the Lyndon Larouche Memorial Society. Only, they talk the same way about leftist people."

"In fact, the Larouche Society is one of the SA's cover organizations—"

Hard-Eyes shook his head, chuckling. "Sure. Just like they claim the world is controlled by a secret conspiracy of the British Secret Service in league with Jewish bankers, right?"

Steinfeld smiled. "Coming from the States as you do, I can see how all this would seem like just so much more fringe political background noise . . . But the SA is what I say it is, and here in Amsterdam you will shortly be able to see the SA in operation . . . They're moving in, setting up here. Wait, and you'll see it confirmed. And remember: I'm not a leftist. Here we're in favor of restoring only what existed before the war. Yes, the bad with the good. We are not revolutionaries. We are resistance—to what is shaping up to be a neo-fascist takeover. Spearheaded by the SAISC."

"Why you going to so much trouble to convince us?" Jenkins asked.

"I need . . . " Steinfeld hesitated, looking for the right words. "There are men who are like seeding crystals. You drop them into the solution, and other crystals form around them. I need such men. To form the . . . the core of a much stronger resistance cell. And Smoke here"—Steinfeld gestured helplessly—"he has an uncanny sense for finding such people. He found Voortoven, and Yukio. And he has recommended you." Steinfeld shrugged.

"I'm not sure I should be flattered," Hard-Eyes said.

Steinfeld said, "Do you want to hear the rest of the . . . propaganda?"

"Go ahead."

• • •

When a man tells another man a story, much of the story is untold. That is, it's not told out loud. The unspoken part is the freight of secondary meanings and resonances attached to the spoken thrust of the story. It's a part of the story already understood by the two men. Part of their mutual context.

What follows is what Steinfeld told Hard-Eyes. And here we speak aloud what wasn't spoken at all.

Smiling Rick Crandall. He was one of the youngest Fundamentalist ministers in the country. By the time he was twenty he had his own internationally syndicated program. He was exporting Christian Coalition beliefs and values to the rest of the world, and he was succeeding because he, and his associates, kept tying it in with wealth. Decline or not, America still had the rep for being the wealthiest country. And Crandall kept saying it was his religion and his way of life that made it that way. Predinger bought the station that ran Crandall's show, tripled the man's salary, and gave him a new assignment. He was to be a sort of SAISC goodwill ambassador to the governments of foreign nations, and to other groups who were not government but were sympathetic to the Second Alliance's aims. That was Crandall's job, ostensibly.

But the truth is, Crandall was a recruiter. He used his international fame, or simple bribery, to gain access to people high in governments, people on the fringe of governments, people in opposition to governments. And he recruited them into a new branch of the Alliance. This was called the AntiTerrorist Lobby. And it was a cover. It might have been more appropriately named SAISC Army Recruiting. Crandall was a recruiter for a new, multinational military and political machine. The men inducted into the machine used their influence to legislate a fund that would make their nation an official SA member. They would pay the SA to help them control their domestic terrorism—sometimes real terrorism, just as often it was mere dissent—and they agreed to contribute resources and manpower for the control of *international terrorism . . .*

Each "member nation" provided men—reassigned from the military— for indoctrination in the SA's Worldview Camps. The first and imperative goal of the operators of the Worldview Camps was to instill an absolute and undying loyalty to the SA in all "processees." The processees were taught—brainwashed—to regard the SA as their true father and mother, their sovereign nation, and, most importantly, their link to God Himself. There was to be no possibility of sending men out for Alliance "actions" who were not genuinely loyal to Alliance aims. The Second Alliance had a public credo and a private credo. The private credo was the core of its real identity. It comes in onion-layers. Those who were first-layer processees in the Second Alliance heard a kind of standard Christian Born Again rhetoric. But in the second layer, the Initiates hear a kind of Identity Church theology preached. It is, in fact, a more refined version of the Christian revisionism taught by the Kingdom Message organizers who declared themselves to the public about 1983. That's about when they began to rob banks and armored cars to finance their acquisition of automatic weapons and the other toys of right-wing "survivalists." They called themselves "the Church of Jesus Christ Christian" or "The Covenant, the Sword, and the Arm of the Lord" or "the Aryan Nations" and they held that Jesus Christ was not a Jew, was in fact of Aryan descent; that Great Britain and the United States were the true promised land, the true Israel referred to in the Bible; that blacks and other minorities were mongrel peoples who had no souls and were of no greater spiritual worth than animals. And they maintained that Hitler has been unfairly vilified by the Jews; that the Holocaust never happened. In 1985 there were about 2,500 people in such organizations in the United States—chiefly in Washington, Idaho, Oregon, and California. Many of them were recruited out of prisons, always hotbeds of racism . . . Supposedly there were "several hundred-thousand" sympathizers scattered across the country. Some of the more enterprising members of the Identity Church realized that they looked like country yokels, which kept people who were otherwise sympathetic from taking them more seriously. So they formed a secret society, called the Secret Aryan Fraternity. They linked up with more public groups, like the Georgia-based Council of Conservative Citizens. Groups like these were paranoiacally cautious about publicity, and security.

And, very carefully, the SAF and friends began to integrate their people into urban and suburban middle-class society; into colleges and country clubs and lodges and offices. They began to support political candidates, or mount their own candidacies—without ever honestly declaring their actual political stand. They played moderate or simple conservative—when in reality they were beyond merely "conservative." They were social time-release capsules, moles, of sheer racial hatred. Predinger is believed by some to have been one of the SAF. It's never been proven. It may be just coincidence that the SAF and the SAISC share the same first two initials. But it *has* been determined that Crandall's father was a member of The Covenant, the Sword, and the Arm of the Lord . . . Summary: The SA's general theological creed, its public creed, is ordinary Christian fundamentalism, with no overt racist tinge. Its Initiates are privy to the Identity Church's Jesus-as-Aryan hardcore-racist variation. Initiates administer the general membership. The Initiates in turn are governed by the Second Circle.

The Second Circle, the inner ruling council of the SA, is reported to have a more intellectualized racist vision that doesn't insist on a belief in Jesus' Aryan heritage. Jesus, for the Second Circle, is simply an arbitrary symbol chosen to represent genetic purity. The DNA molecule itself, twisted into a circle, is the Lord's halo . . .

Politically, the SA's private credo was, simply and bluntly: fascism.

And we are not talking fascist here as a left-wing dilettante calls a war-hawk "a fascist," as an insulting term, a mere pejorative. We are talking about definitive fascism. Predinger and Crandall were both, privately, admirers of classic fascist and racist demagogues, including Mussolini and Hitler himself. They were anti-Semitic and anti-black . . .

• • •

"Anti-black?" Hard-Eyes interrupted. "You said they recruited partly from third-world countries."

Dreamily, almost offhandedly, Smoke said, "Actually, they deceived certain black African military dictatorships into providing money and other forms of support. But they kept them in the dark about the real SA political goals. And they didn't recruit soldiers from black countries."

Jenkins looked at Smoke in amazement, hearing Smoke's pedantic side emerge. A scholar hidden in rags and grime.

"The third-world recruits—" Steinfeld began. Then he broke off, listening. Looking at the ceiling.

They all heard it. The rumble and drone of a jumpjet nearby. The Armies—searching for the NR, maybe . . .

Smoke felt a thrill of fear and thought, I'm scared of dying. How long has it been since I felt that way? What's happening to me?

The sound of the jumpjet, the rumble, the drone . . . died away.

Steinfeld looked at his hands. He took a deep breath, and went on. "The third world recruits were obtained mostly from right-wing dictators in Central and South America. And then certain factions of Indians, anti-Semitic Pakistanis, Eastern Europeans—there are a good many Nazi Serbs around . . . But the real core of the SA, its initiate administration, were American right-wing extremists—including sympathizers in the CIA—British, Dutch, and a great many Afrikaners. There are thousands of them . . . They're a separate division of the Alliance, elite troops. The division has a German name which translates as 'Men Chosen to Die First.' The SA's administration is uniformly white. Bravado, you see. Fanaticism. White South Africans from the elite are in charge of the lesser divisions. And the lesser divisions are made up of Spaniards, Italians, Guatemalans, anti-Communist Cuban nationalists . . . "

"Perhaps this is the wedge," Yukio said. Said it succinctly and at just the right moment, a fine and definitive brushstroke. So like him, Smoke thought.

Voortoven nodded and said, "We have men within the—"

Steinfeld cut him off with a glare—Hard-Eyes and Jenkins weren't yet trusted.

Hard-Eyes and Jenkins glanced at one another.

Suddenly everyone in the room knew that if Steinfeld decided he could not trust Hard-Eyes and Jenkins, he would have them killed. And this would not have been the case before Voortoven had said, in that particular context, *We have men within . . .*

Men in place, moles in the Second Alliance, who hope to drive a wedge between the "colored" divisions and their white administrators. It wasn't necessary to say it aloud now.

Steinfeld looked at Hard-Eyes a touch apologetically.

Smoke could see Hard-Eyes' knuckles whitening on the big rifle.

Jenkins had picked up on the tension. He watched Hard-Eyes for a cue.

Voortoven and Willow and Yukio looked to Steinfeld.

Smoke prepared to throw himself aside. His preparation showed only in his reaching, almost languidly, to lay a hand on the crow, so it wouldn't fly away if he had to throw himself down when the shooting started.

Steinfeld opted to go on as if nothing had happened. Continuing the lecture was a way to reassure them. A way to say, *Wait and see.*

"Predinger is said to have died recently, though there are conflicting rumors about that. At any rate, Crandall and his sister have been elevated to supreme command of the SA—"

"*His sister?*" Hard-Eyes' surprise drew tension out of the air. There was soft laughter from Voortoven and Willow.

"His sister," Smoke confirmed. "Ellen Mae Crandall. Apparently she's been a driving organizational force. She did all the dickering when he was first syndicated."

Steinfeld nodded. "They come from a strict Southern Baptist family. Crandall's the spiritual leader of the SA, but for the most part he no longer makes public appearances as a minister—outside the SA. Crandall is the SA's Commander in Chief, though his main military strategist is a man named Watson. A former colonel who worked for the neo-racist underground trying to undermine post-Mandela South Africa . . . The SAISC had its first field-military testing in rural parts of South Africa. They didn't prove out, there, but they learned from it. They've proven themselves militarily putting down insurrections in Pakistan, Ethiopia, Guatemala . . . "

Hard-Eyes showed a touch of impatience, interrupting, "And NATO plans to turn most of Western Europe over to these people? This . . . this cover organization for neo-Nazis? Just like that?"

"They're calling the SA a 'non-Allied security force.' They're maintaining that—and some of them believe it—they're simply hiring a large international security corporation to keep the peace until full political order is restored. They're desperate for order . . . which is roughly why the National Socialists were able to come to power in Germany in the 1930s. People were desperate for stability. Hitler promised everyone economic growth. He promised an end to the political chaos of the Weimar Republic. He promised to reunite Germany."

"Oh, you can't really believe it's . . . like that."

"Not entirely. It's a little cleverer than that. The men in European and American government—especially the Americans and the British—who support 'the SA arrangement,' are part of the new crop of anti-Semites and racists. It's been a growing resurgence for decades. Apologists for fascism like the French New Right, the British National Front. In America, the Council of Conservative Citizens and the US Labor Party . . . the Unification Church . . . others. The SA has been using its media contacts—bought with Predinger's money—for eight years to create an impression of a Jewish conspiracy on which to blame the world's misfortunes . . . And they blame domestic crime on immigrants . . . "

Hard-Eyes nodded slowly. "I saw some of that on American TV . . . None of it real obvious stuff, but . . . almost subliminal sometimes."

Willow said, "Bloody SA's 'police force' is in Italy, Germany, Britain, Belgium, Spain. France soon enough. And 'ere, mate. 'Ere."

"And you think," Hard-Eyes said, looking at Steinfeld closely, "that they and the NATO people who put them in place are setting up some kind of coup?"

Steinfeld nodded. "A military coup for the whole of Western Europe."

There was silence, except for the creak of bodies shifting on chairs. Then, Jenkins asked, "Just how closely in Hitler's footsteps you think these people are gonna follow?"

Steinfeld took a deep breath. "Where they are in place, they have already isolated Jews and blacks and Muslims into barricaded sections of the towns. Crandall is said to hate Muslims even more than Jews . . . "

Hard-Eyes snorted and shook his head. "If it's true . . . what do you think you're going to do about it?"

Steinfeld shrugged. "You know already. A guerrilla war. You want to know more about our strategy?"

Hard-Eyes nodded.

Steinfeld shook his head. "No."

And once again, the men in the room looked to their respective masters for their cues.

That's when a man Smoke didn't know came in. He was a slender black man who wore horn-rim glasses on his nose and field glasses around his neck. There was a submachine gun on a strap over his shoulder. He turned to Steinfeld and then realized that what he had to announce should be said to everyone. He looked around at them and then said carefully, "Jorge got it on the radio. The Russians have blockaded the Colony. The space Colony. Orbital battle stations have gone on full alert."

And once more, every man thought the same thing, so that no one actually said it: *Maybe it's finally coming.*

There was always a feeling that any plans you made, any hopes you drummed up, were empty. Hollow. Like plucking fruit and cutting it open to find it dried out inside. Because it was assumed that, sooner or later, the conventional war would heat up into a nuclear war. And maybe that wouldn't be the end of the world. But it would be close enough.

Steinfeld was the first to shake off the paralysis of despair. "Another escalation." He shrugged. "But it's just taking the conventional war to a new battlefield."

Jenkins shook his head. "What's the point? What's the point of fighting for what's going to be radioactive ashes in a few months?"

Hard-Eyes said, "Maybe it's—"

He broke off, staring at the window. They all heard it. A jumpjet. Close this time. *Close.* The Armies.

Shouts from down the hall, and the roof. Steinfeld's sentries shouting warnings. The jumpjet had come suddenly. That was the jumpjet specialty:

One moment the sky was clear; the next a jet was ten feet overhead, hovering on vertical retros.

The room shivered with the jumpjet's whine and grumble. Hard-Eyes moved toward the door.

The black sentry panicked, went to the window, put his hand on the latch—

Steinfeld stood, turning to shout at him, "No!" But it was lost in the roar of the jumpjet . . .

As the sentry flung the windows open.

The room's lamplight caught the pilot's eye.

Reflexively, Smoke—and Hard-Eyes—paused at the door looked past the sentry and out the window. Everyone in the room was frozen with looking.

The Harrier jumpjet was a swept-wing fighter jet designed in the early 1980s, this particularly adroit model mass-produced only in the early twenty-first century. The two oversized jets on the underside of its wings, computer-controlled for precision, were swiveled to point down, forward, backward, to the sides, so the jet could go virtually any direction; refined computer control and Casimir force generators added extra maneuverability and lift.

It hovered like a helicopter, thirty feet beyond the window, tilted back a little so you could just make out the USAF insignia on the underwings. They could feel the monstrous *engineering* of it, the precisely machined *bulk* of it, its engine heat reaching them, the chemical smell of its burning fuel choking the room.

But looking at it, in that compressed moment, Hard-Eyes thought of it as a plasteel dragon. In Smoke's mind, an insect. Dragonfly, to combine the two, a dragonfly from a Japanese horror movie. Sixty feet long, hovering, trembling as if with metallic rage, tilted up a little as if about to strike. Limned in starlight, glowing nacreously from the cockpit glass, the driver's head was an insignificant arc of darkness within the lozenge of the crystal. Perhaps this was one of those computer-reflexed planes that brought the pilot along mostly for the ride, and just in case. And perhaps the plane made the decision and not the pilot.

The decision to fire. The 60-mm cannon emerged from the socket on the underside of the plane, swiveling to point squarely through the window—the plane pulling back so as not to get caught in the backblast.

In the room, the paralysis passed. Steinfeld scooped up the papers from the desk, and with the expertise of long practice swept them into a vinyl briefcase, vaulted over the desk, and was out the door. Willow and Voortoven were close behind, Jenkins crowding after. Hard-Eyes hesitated, shouting something to Smoke, and Smoke turned, seeing Hard-Eyes raise the Weatherby—

Smoke thinking, the madman's going to shoot at that thing!

The Weatherby boomed. No ordinary rifle. Big motherfucker of a rifle. The so-called bulletproof glass on the jumpjet's cockpit starring, the arc of helmet jerking.

The plane wobbling. Steadying, the 60-mm guns returning to their target. All of this, from Steinfeld's grabbing papers to the gunshot, taking five seconds.

The crow flapped up, cawing, from Smoke's shoulder. He grabbed at it, lost sight of it. Saw instead the sentry still in the open window staring in horror at the plane. The plane pilotless but operating itself cybernetically now. Hard-Eyes trying to pull Smoke back out through the door.

Smoke thinking, We're not going to make it.

He never actually heard the blast.

As the 60-mm cannon fired. It was as if the noise was too profound for his auditory nerves, registering as a squeal like guitar feedback and an ugly metallic ringing. Then heat from a sheet of fire expanded to fill the room; a spatter of warm wetness: blood from the sentry as he was blown apart. All this just the background sensation. The primary sensation was the hardening of the air itself around the blast center. The soft damp air had become a slab of chilled steel that slammed him back into the wall. It *SLAMMED!* him. He could feel his body imprinting its shape in the plaster; feel things straining inside him, buckling—and then giving under the strain, bones creaking and then cracking, all time sadistically slowed so he could savor the hideously lucid sensation of his right arm popping from its socket and his pelvis cracking . . . breastbone cracking . . . cracking . . .

A white-hot freight train of pain roaring down on him.

And—

• • •

He woke, thinking, *Where's my crow?*

He tried to say it, and a steel hammer struck a gong in him and he reverberated with pain. He tried to see, but his eyes were covered by a swarm of black bees.

"Give him more morphine," said a dream-voice. Steinfeld's voice.

Smoke never felt the needle. But its load drew a blanket of translucent numbness over the breakage in him; the pain still glowed, beneath, but muted like coals in a fog.

He opened his eyes: it was like lifting a window that had been painted shut; like it strained his back to open his eyes.

Saw through a feverish mist—a corner of a basement room; part of Yukio walking past; heard Hard-Eyes' voice.

" . . . we want a guarantee of passage out of France whenever we choose to take it."

"If you'll take my word as a guarantee. That's all I've got to offer." Steinfeld's voice. "But you're not fooling anybody. You could have split off from us when we ran, and we wouldn't have stopped you. You shot at the jumpjet to give Smoke time to get out. Who're you kidding? You'd have been safer away from us and you knew it! But you stuck with us."

Hard-Eyes is NR now, Smoke thought. I'm probably internally hemorrhaged, probably die, no doctors, no surgeons. The black bees swarmed over his head again. Stinging. The last thing he thought was, Where's my bird?

• 05 •

Benjamin Brian Rimpler, Ph.D., the sixty-two-year-old Chairman of the FirStep Project, L-5 Colony One, was on his knees, on the white real wool rug in the bedroom of his plush quarters, worshiping a black rubber goddess.

Her name was Hermione, Herm to her friends, Mistress Hermione to Rimpler, when they were role playing. He paid her two hundred newbux an hour to give him relief.

She was well-padded, a tanned Amazon with dyed-coppery hair and white lipstick, white eye-shadow, which contrasted with the head-to-toe skin-tight black-rubber mistress's costume, breast tips and crotch of the outfit cut away to expose opulent rouged nipples—one of them flawed with a curling black hair—and her labia, also rouged.

Her breasts, each separately encased in its own form-fitting sheath of rubber, quivered with her slightest motion, and fairly rollicked with the stroke of the car-radio antenna—fitted with a black plastic handle—that she gripped in her studded right hand. The studs on the back of her hand were implanted into the skin in a connect-the-dots skull. Rimpler loved those little cartoon touches. Hermione was a better actress than the other girls from Bitchie's. But her Queens accent somehow undercut the required imperiousness when she gave him orders.

But when she hit him, Queens reediness didn't matter. The flash of pain sizzled away the illusion's seams. She hit him again, hard. Rimpler made an inarticulate whimper this time, and, feeling nausea building behind the flash, he muttered, "Wait." She was a pro, and she held off. Because there was no question about who was in charge here, really.

Rimpler. Smallish, pallid, blue-veined, bald—shaved bald—just a shade paunchy, his eyes squeezed shut now.

Unlike most of the Colony quarters, Rimpler's Admin Central flat had more than two rooms. It had three, counting the bathroom. He had, too, the condo in the Open. But he didn't use it anymore.

Here he'd dialed the bedroom walls to lozenge-shape. He'd switched off the images of Big Sur which usually glowed from the walls, and he'd dialed the light low, adding a sensuous dollop of red tinge. Penderecki's *The Passion According to Saint Luke* moaned from hidden speakers. "Okay, go ahead . . . "

Hermione looked at her watch and grimaced. When was the old bugger going to get it over with? He was mewling at her crotch, nosing at it like a pathetic blind puppy as she swacked his knobbed back, spat on his egg-head, told him he was cockroach dung—and he was still only half-tumescent!

"You haven't got your mind on your work, you little SHIT!" she hissed, raising welts between his shoulder blades.

Rimpler muttered apologies. Hermione was right. His mind wasn't on the game.

His mind was free-associating wildly, and parts of it seemed to break off from the main mass of his thinking and form venomous TV-eyed organs of pure self-consciousness; treacherous mental excrescencies that watched him, reported on him to some other sneering, sardonic part of his mind.

And the flashes of pain, instead of blinding his mind as they should have, instead of taking him out of himself, this time acted as eidetic drive-in movie screens, looming swatches of luminous white on which the derisive part of his mind projected images . . .

And he saw the thing he had built. He saw it on the screen of flash-pain. He saw the Colony. FirStep, ponderously rotating, a sort of technological totem-pole shape; in silhouette from just the right angle it was an Easter Island figure against the backdrop of space—space, the black and infinitely empty. Space, the brilliantly lit and overflowing with energy. Space, where the spectrum is unleashed.

And he seemed to see the thousands of tons of FirStep in blueprint, its world-class road map of wiring, its clusters of millions of computer chips, a thousand brains for its thousand segments, the people aswarm in it like *E. coli* in the belly of some enormous organism, independent of the organism but interrelated. And he saw its life-support systems, air and water filtration, the dozens of failsafes for airtight integrity against the ever-present gnawing of the vacuum of space, the reaches of insulation and the envelope of the atmospheric filter against the solar wind.

He visualized it in an infrared scan, with its areas of red and yellow for heat energy, its bluer areas where it radiated less heat, its solar-power panels shining with absorbed energy . . .

And he saw the thing in its skeletal stage, slowly coming together, something that had taken twenty years, now forming before his eyes in fast action, growing module by module like a coral reef, the construction pods darting fishlike around it. Growing from section A, a lonely outcropping in an endless sea, to an atoll to an island . . . A, B, C, D, and now E. Years of work materializing in technological crystallization.

And he had designed it, had overseen its construction, had made it grow around him.

Around him! He knew in that terribly clear, terribly ugly instant that it was only a hermit crab's shell. Something he had pulled over himself, taken refuge in to hide his nakedness. The Colony was simply armor for Benjamin Brian Rimpler.

Oh yes: he'd been fascinated with satellites as a boy; with the sky's ponderous celestial majesty; had nurtured a megalomaniacal adolescent fantasy of hoisting his own personal star into the sky. And later, horrified by the planet's swarming malaise, its feverish self-gouging environmental suicide, he'd wanted to create an alternative world, a self-contained, intelligently controlled ecosystem where man—and nature—would be given a second chance. An answer to the population explosion, because it would be the first of many such alternative worlds . . .

Anyway, that's what he told himself. And that's what he told the media. The Colony would employ and house the poor. And in fact the bulk of its settlers were low-income technicki workers. So it looked good. It looked unselfish.

But he saw it, now. The Colony was a monumental act of selfishness. And his obsessive drive to get it built had killed his son.

Here, in the 2/3-grav section, in the exclusive optimum-lifestyle quarters, he had wrapped its vast tonnage about himself in layers of elaboration that seemed, now, only the intricacy of neurosis. Each life-support system, each failsafe and airlock seemed a form of his pathetic anality.

He sat back on his haunches, looked at Hermione, and perceived that he'd allowed a sort of parasite to crawl into his shell with him.

"Get out," he said.

"What? Why, you little worm—"

"No, I mean it. I'm not trying to intensify the game. Get out."

"Hey, don't blame me because you can't get it up. A man gets old and not even the best pro can help. If you'd take some—"

"Get out."

She stepped back, lowering her whip, yawing between two poles, the overawed employee and the professional dominatrix.

"What? The price is still—"

"I paid you in advance. Get out."

Hermione perceived that her license was revoked. She backed away, then turned, without so much as muttering, went to the bed to get her jumpsuit. She'd picked up on his urgency. There wasn't even time to change out of the rubber. The little prick! (And she did mean little!) But he was the most powerful-man on the Colony, except for maybe Praeger. Rimpler could have her jettisoned if he wanted. She went quietly, thinking, I'm in Admin section; I could stop at a credfone and call Praeger. He's into submissives; but what the hell, I can switch . . .

Rimpler watched her go, and one of the fragment outriders of his personality, the autoerotic, infantile part, looked after her with regret and whined to the rest of him. Mentally he slapped it and told it to shut up.

There was to be no more oblivion for him from that direction. It wasn't working anymore. Maybe drugs. Booze. Maybe—

He saw himself in an evac chute. *The gates open, the air sucks out, he's ejected naked into void—*

He recoiled, actually curled up and clutched at himself at the thought.

Terry was—

Recoiled again from that one, too, and tried to think instead about a stiff drink, something to eat . . .

He sat on his haunches, naked, parts of him smeared with Vaseline, his face still damp with her pheromone perfume, his back throbbing with welts, and fought an urge to run to the nearest airlock and jet himself naked into space—

That'd be real freedom, for a moment.

"Dad?"

His gut constricted. A muscle in his back jumped. Fear washed through him, acrid and cold. *Claire.* Claire's voice. He was more afraid of Claire, at this moment, than he'd been of his own ice-queen mother. He was afraid of his own daughter.

If she should see Hermione . . .

But her voice came from the grid in the front door. Hermione was going out by the service corridor. Claire wouldn't see her.

He shouted, "Claire—I'll be right out! I'm in the shower." Then he pressed the door button and said, "seven-three," into the grid. The door analyzed his voiceprint, confirmed it, and opened the front door for her. But left the door to his bedroom locked.

"I'll be right out," he shouted through the door to the living room. He went to the bathroom, let the ultrasound shower cleanse him, shivered with the tingling of it, felt a vague pleasure knowing that a composition by Stravinsky was worked into the sound waves; he couldn't hear the composition at that frequency, but he could feel it.

Still, he wished he could have water. The technickis would get word of it, though, if he had a water system installed. One of them would have to install it, after all. Their commentators would editorialize about wasteful luxuries among Admin elitists. *Admin washunmunener filzerbush*, they'd say. Admin washes in money and our air filter's broken.

Praeger, damn him, had had a water shower installed. The technickis had heard about it, every last one of them, an hour later.

Praeger. president of UNIC's on-Colony board. The sick feeling in Rimpler's gut returned when he thought of Praeger.

He stepped out of the shower, and it sank back into the tiled wall. He went to the mirror, punched 8 on the numbered row of buttons beneath the glass; the mirror reversed itself, showing him its shelved backside. He found the anesthetic spray and coated the welts on his back with it. Again with some regret. Then he dressed in Japanese house pajamas, airy blue silk, and found Claire in the living room. His stomach tightened as she said, "Hi, Dad," with a friendly enough smile, nothing censorious in her eyes.

"How you doing, babe?" he said, bending to kiss her on the forehead. He hadn't seen her for almost two weeks.

"Dad—I'm okay, but—"

He sat down across from her, thinking, *She seems coiled up.*

She wore a light, soft gray suit with a triple-flap skirt; her lips were pursed, her cheeks hollowed.

"You're going to give me more details about the wonderful viddy interview you did—" He laughed breezily. "Forget it! It was a put-up job and by now everyone's realized it."

"Dad . . . "

And then he saw the tension in her posture and the knuckles white on her knees. He thought, Shit, it's Praeger again.

"Dad, when you asked for a four-day in-house vacation—"

"You think it was bad timing? Right after your screw-up with the little technicki kid? I told you—"

"Dad! . . . No. But—I only just found out that you had a no-calls up. I mean, no one could figure out why you weren't making a statement . . . "

"Well—sure. How could I have a vacation, a retreat, if everyone's calling me with the Colony's problems? There's a dozen people happy to—"

"Dad . . . "

This time her voice actually broke. He stared. He hadn't seen her show her humanity like that in years; not since Terry died.

"For God's sake, Claire, out with it."

"Dad, when you sealed the place off, you left it open for LSSE. Right?" There was accusation wrapped in the sarcastic twist she gave to "Right?"

He laughed nervously. "Well, of course!"

LSSE: Life-Support Emergency. There *hadn't* been an LSSE. Impossible.

"Dad—there *was* an LSSE. I mean—this is the sort of thing that keeps happening with you." She was in her bitchily maternal mode now. "Things are flying to hell around you and—Dad, there was a Bright Red. Full alert. *And Praeger gave orders that you were not to be told.* I mean, I don't *know* that for sure but . . . he must have."

He felt himself sinking. "What was it?" His voice a crust.

"Dad—"

"Will you stop saying that and just *tell me*!" His fear of her vanished. He was standing now, arms straight at his sides.

"The Russians have blockaded us. *We're in the war.* The last supply ship was boarded. Captured! There hasn't been another. No ships outgoing. They're even jamming communications. We get through now and then—"

"Why didn't you come to me before? I mean—how long has it been?"

"Three days. Dad, I couldn't get through to see you till today. And you had your screen down. The riots—we couldn't get through because of the riots."

"Riots."

"A man named Bonham has been asking for a general strike. There are four of these organizers really pushing it—a man named Joseph Bonham, a man named Samson Molt—"

"Oh, don't tell me their names, tell Security, I'm not the local thought police. Shit." He found he was staring at his decanters on the table. Wanting a drink and not having the courage even to reach across the table. Afraid the Colony was so fragile it would shiver apart if he moved. His shell, his armor. His insulation from Earth.

"These people are saying that now we're cut off from Earth the techni-class has got to demand rights or they'll be completely powerless when it comes to martial law."

"There's something to that." He laughed bitterly. Now his hands moved of their own violation—squirting gin into a glass. He swallowed it and shuddered. "Praeger'll want—martial law, want to completely subjugate the technickis because of the state of emergency.""

"You *agree* with these people?" More reproach than surprise.

He shrugged, took another drink. Laughed. "Riots!" Shaking his head in wonder. "I designed this thing . . . " He gestured vaguely at the walls, meaning the Colony itself. "And still it's three days before I know we're blockaded. And having riots."

"Dad—Praeger didn't want you to know."

They looked at one another, and the implication hung in the air between them. She gave it verbal shape. "I think there's going to be a coup. I think UNIC wants to take the colony over completely."

• 06 •

FirStep floated in the sea of space, a city afloat in the void.

And Freezone floated in the Atlantic Ocean, a city afloat in the wash of international cultural confluence.

Freezone was anchored about a hundred miles north of Sidi Ifni, a drowsy city on the coast of Morocco in a warm, gentle current, and in a sector of the sea only rarely troubled by large storms. What storms arose here spent their fury on the maze of concrete wave-baffles Freezone Admin had spent years building up around the artificial island.

Originally, Freezone had been just another offshore drilling project. The massive oil deposit a quarter-mile below the artificial island was still less than a quarter tapped out. The drilling platform was owned in common by the Moroccan government and a Texas-based petroleum and electronics products company. TexMo. The company that bought Disneyland and Disneyworld and Disneyworld II—all three of which had closed in the wake of the CSD: the Computer Storage Depression. Also called the Dissolve Depression.

A group of Arab terrorists—at least, the US State Department claimed that's who did it—had arranged a well-placed electromagnetic pulse from a hydrogen bomb hidden aboard a routine orbital shuttle. The shuttle was vaporized in the blast, as well as two satellites, one of them manned; but when the CSD hit, no one took time to mourn the dead.

The orbital bomb had almost triggered Armageddon: three Cruise missiles had to be aborted, and fortunately two more were shot down by the Russians before the terrorist cell took credit for the upper atmospheric blast. Most of the bomb's blast had been directed upward; what came downward, though, was the side effect of its blast: the EMP. An electromagnetic pulse that—just as had been predicted since the 1970s—traveled through thousands of miles of wires and circuitry on the continent below the H-blast. The Defense Department was shielded; the banking system, for the most part, was not. The pulse wiped out ninety-three percent of the newly formed American Banking Credit Adjustment Bureau. ABCAB had handled seventy-six percent of the nation's buying and credit transferal. Most of what was bought, was bought through ABCAB or ABCAB related companies . . . until the EMP wiped out ABCAB's memory storage, the pulse overburdening the circuits, melting them, and literally frying the data storage chips. And thereby kicking the crutches out from under the American economy. Millions of bank accounts were "suspended" until records could be restored—causing a run on remaining banks. The insurance companies and the Federal guarantee programs were overwhelmed. They just couldn't cover the loss.

The States had already been in trouble. The nation had lost its economic initiative in the early twenty-first century: its undereducated, badly trained workers, the outsourcing of jobs and manufacturing made US industry unable to compete with the Chinese and South American manufacturing booms. The EMP credit dissolve kicked the nation over the rim of recession and into the pit of depression—and made the rest of the world laugh. The Arab terrorist cell responsible—hard-core Islamic Fundamentalists—had been composed of seven men. Seven men who crippled a nation.

But America still had its enormous military spread, its electronics and medical innovators. And the war economy kept it humming, like a man with cancer taking amphetamines for a last burst of strength, while the endless malls and housing projects—built cheaply and in need of constant upkeep—got shabbier, uglier, trashier by the day. And more dangerous.

The States just weren't safe enough for the rich anymore. The resorts, the amusement parks, the exclusive affluent neighborhoods, places like Central Park West—all crumbled under the attrition of perennial strikes and persistent terrorist attacks. The swelling mass of the poor resented the recreations of the rich.

While the middle-class buffer was shrinking to insignificance there were still enclaves in the States where you could get lost in the media churn, hypnotized by the flashcards of desire into an iPad-trance fantasy of the American Dream as ten thousand companies vied for your attention, nagging you to buy and keep buying. Places that were walled city-states of middle-class illusions—like the place Hard-Eyes had come from.

But the affluent could feel the crumbling of their kingdom. They didn't feel safe in the States. They needed someplace outside, somewhere controlled. Europe was out now; Central and South America, too risky. The Pacific theater was another war zone.

So that's where Freezone came in.

A Texas entrepreneur—who hadn't had his money in ABCAB—saw the possibilities in the community that had grown up around the enormous complex of offshore drilling platforms. A paste-jewel necklace of brothels and arcades and cabarets had crystallized on derelict ships permanently anchored around the platforms. Hundreds of hookers and casino dealers worked the international melange of men who worked the oil rigs.

The entrepreneur made a deal with the Moroccan government, bought the rusting hulks and shanty nightclubs. And then he fired everyone.

The Texan owned a plastics company . . . the company had developed light, super-tough plastic that the entrepreneur used in the rafts on which the new floating city was built. The community was now seventeen square miles of urban raft protected with one of the meanest security forces in the world. Freezone dealt in pleasant distractions for the rich in the exclusive section and—in the second-string places around the edge—for technickis from the drill rigs. And the second-string places sheltered a few thousand semi-illicit hangers-on, and a few hundred performers.

Like Rickenharp.

• • •

Rick Rickenharp stood against the south wall of the Semiconductor, letting the club's glare and blare wash over him, and mentally writing a song. The song went something like, "Glaring blare, lightning stare/ Nostalgia for the electric chair."

Then he thought, Fucking drivel.

All the while he was doing his best to look cool but vulnerable, hoping one of the girls flashing through the crowd would remember having seen him in the band the night before, would try to chat him up, play groupie. But they were mostly into wifi dancers.

And *no fucking way* Rickenharp was going to wire into minimono.

Rickenharp was a rock classicist; he was retro. He wore a black leather motorcycle jacket that was some seventy-some years old, said to have been worn by John Cale when he was still in the Velvet Underground. The seams were beginning to pop for the third time; three studs were missing from the chrome trimming. The elbows and collar edges were worn through the black dye to the brown animal the leather had come from. But the leather was second skin to Rickenharp. He wore nothing under it. His bony, hairless chest showed translucent-bluewhite between the broken zippers. He wore blue jeans that were only ten years old but looked older than the coat; he wore genuine Harley Davidson boots. Earrings clustered up and down his long, slightly too prominent ears, and his rusty brown hair looked like a cannon-shell explosion.

And he wore dark glasses.

And he did all this because it was gratingly unfashionable.

His band hassled him about it. They wanted their lead-git and frontman minimono.

"If we're gonna go minimono, we oughta just sell the fucking guitars and go wires," Rickenharp had told them.

And the drummer had been stupid and tactless enough to say, "Well, fuck, man, maybe we *should* go to wires."

Rickenharp had said, "Maybe we should get a fucking drum machine, too, you fucking Neanderthal!" and kicked the drum seat over, sending Murch into the cymbals with a fine crashing, so that Rickenharp added, "you should get that good a sound outta those cymbals on stage. Now we know how to do it."

Murch had started to throw his sticks at him, but then he'd remembered how you had to have them lathed up special because they didn't make them anymore, so he'd said, "Suck my ass, big shot"and got up and walked out, not the first time. But that was the first time it meant anything, and only some heavy ambassadorial action on the part of Ponce had kept Murch from leaving the band.

The call from their agent had set the whole thing off. That's what it really was. Agency was streamlining its clientele. The band was out. The last two download albums hadn't sold, and in fact the engineers claimed that live drums didn't digitize well onto the miniaturized soundcaps that passed for CDs now. Rickenharp's holovid and the videos weren't getting much airplay.

Anyway, Vid-Co was probably going out of business. Another business sucked into the black hole of the depression. "So it ain't our fault the stuffs not selling," Rickenharp said. "We got fans but we can't get the distribution to reach 'em."

Mose had said, "Bullshit, we're out of the Grid, and you know it. All that was carrying us was the nostalgia wave anyway. You can't get more'n two bits out of a revival, man."

Julio the bassist had said something in technicki which Rickenharp hadn't bothered to translate because it was probably stupid and when Rickenharp had ignored him he'd gotten pissed and it was his turn to walk out. Fucking touchy technickis anyway.

And now the band was in abeyance. Their train was stopped between the stations. They had one gig, just one: opening for a wifi act. And Rickenharp didn't want to do it. But they had a contract and there were a lot of rock nostalgia freaks on Freezone, so maybe that was their audience anyway and he owed it to them. Blow the goddamn wires off the stage.

He looked around the Semiconductor and wished the Retro-Club was still open. There'd been a strong retro presence at the RC, even some rockabillies, and some of the rockabillies actually knew what rockabilly sounded like. The Semiconductor was a minimono scene.

The minimono crowd wore their hair long, fanned out between the shoulders and narrowing to a point at the crown of the head, and straight, absolutely straight, stiff, so from the back each head had a black or gray or red or white teepee-shape. Those, in monochrome, were the only acceptable colors. Flat tones and no streaks. Their clothes were stylistic extensions of their hairstyles. Minimono was a reaction to Flare—and to the chaos of the war, and the war economy, and the amorphous shifting of the Grid. The Flare style was going, dying.

Rickenharp had always been contemptuous of the trendy Flares, but he preferred them to minimono. Flare had energy, anyway.

A flare was expected to wear his hair up, as far over the top of his head as possible, and that promontory was supposed to *express*. The more colors the better. In that scene, you weren't an individual unless you had an expressive flare. Screwshapes, hooks, aureola shapes, layered multicolor snarls. Fortunes were made in flare hair-shaping shops, and lost when it began to go out of fashion. But it had lasted longer than most fashions; it had endless variation and the appeal of its energy to sustain it. A lot of people copped out of the necessity of inventing individual expression by adopting a politically standard flare. Shape your hair like the insignia for your favorite downtrodden third world country (back when they were downtrodden, before the new marketing axis). Flares were so much trouble most people took to having flare wigs. And their drugs were styled to fit the fashion. Excitative neurotransmitters; drugs that made you seem to glow. The wealthier flares had nimbus belts, creating artificial auroras. The hipper flares considered this to be tastelessly narcissistic, which was a joke to nonflares, since all flares were floridly vain.

Rickenharp had never colored or shaped his hair, except to encourage its punk spikiness.

But Rickenharp wasn't a punkrocker. He identified with prepunk, late 1950s, mid-1960s, early 1970s. Rickenharp was a proud anachronism. He was simply a hard-core rocker, as out of place in the Semiconductor as bebop would have been in the 1980s dance clubs.

Rickenharp looked around at the flat-back, flat-gray, monochrome tunics and jumpsuits, the black wristfones, the cookie-cutter sameness of JAS's; at the uniform tans and ubiquitous FirStep Colony-shaped earrings (only one, always in the left ear). The high-tech-fetishist minimonos were said to aspire toward a place in the Colony the way Rastas had dreamed of a return to Ethiopia. Rickenharp thought it was funny that the

Russians had blockaded the Colony. Funny to see the normally dronelike, antiflamboyant minimonos quietly simmering on ampheticool, standing in tense groups, hissing about the Russian blockade of FirStep, in why-doesn't-someone-do-something outrage.

The stultifying regularity of their canned music banged from the walls and pulsed from the floor. Lean against the wall and you felt a drill-bit vibration of it in your spine.

There were a few hardy, defiant flares here, and flares were Rickenharp's best hope for getting laid. They tended to respect old rock.

The music ceased; a voice boomed, "Joel NewHope!" and spots hit the stage. The first wifi act had come on. Rickenharp glanced at his watch. It was ten. He was due to open for the headline act at 11:30. Rickenharp pictured the club emptying as he hit the stage. He wasn't long for this club.

NewHope hit the stage. He was anorexic and surgically sexless: radical minimono. A fact advertised by his nudity: he wore only gray and black spray-on sheathing, his dick in a drag queen's tuck. How did the guy piss? Rickenharp, wondered. Maybe it was out of that faint crease at his crotch. A dancing mannequin. His sexuality was clipped to the back of his head: a single chrome electrode that activated the pleasure center of the brain during the weekly legally controlled catharsis. But he was so skinny—hey, who knows, maybe he went to a black-market cerebrostim to interface with the pulser. Though minimonos were supposed to be into stringent law and order.

The neural transmitters jacked into NewHope's arms and legs and torso transmitted to pickups on the stage floor. The long, funereal wails pealing from hidden speakers were triggered by the muscular contractions of his arms and legs and torso. He wasn't bad, for a minimono, Rickenharp thought. You can make out the melody, the tune shaped by his dancing, and it had a shade more complexity than the M'n'Ms usually had . . . The M'n'M crowd moved into their geometrical dance configurations, somewhere between disco dancing and square dance, Busby Berkley kaleidoscopings worked out according to formulas you were simply expected to know, if you had the nerve to participate. Try to dance freestyle in their interlocking choreography, and sheer social rejection, on the wings of body language, would hit you like an arctic wind.

Sometimes Rickenharp did an acid dance in the midst of the minimono configuration, just for the hell of it, just to revel in their rejection. But his band had made him stop that. Don't alienate the audience at our only gig, man. Probably our *last* fucking gig . . .

The wiredancer rippled out bagpipelike riffs over the digitalized rhythm section. The walls came alive.

A good rock club—in 1965 or 1975 or 1985 or 1995 or 2012 or 2039 should be narrow, dark, close, claustrophobic. The walls should be either starkly monochrome—all black or mirrored, say—or deliberately garish. Camp, layered with whatever was the contemporary avant-garde or gaudy graffiti.

The Semiconductor showed both sides. It started out butch, its walls glassy black; during the concert it went in gaudy drag as the sound-sensitive walls reacted to the music with color streaking, wavelengthing in oscilloscope patterns, shades of blue-white for high end, red and purple for bass and percussion, reacting vividly, hypnotically to each note. The minimonos disliked reactive walls. They called it kitschy.

The dance spazzed the stage, and Rickenharp grudgingly watched, trying to be fair to it. Thinking, It's another kind of rock 'n' roll, is all. Like a Christian watching a Buddhist ceremony, telling himself, "Oh, well, it's all manifestations of the One God in the end." Rickenharp thinking: But real rock is better. *Real rock is coming back,* he'd tell almost anyone who'd listen. Almost no one would.

A chaotichick came in, and he watched her, feeling less alone. Chaotics were much closer to real rockers. She was a skinhead, with the sides of her head painted. The Gridfriend insignia was tattooed on her right shoulder. She wore a skirt made of at least two hundred rags of synthetic material sewn to her leather belt—a sort of grass skirt of bright rags. The nipples of her bare breasts were pierced with thin screws. The minimonos looked at her in disgust; they were prudish, and calling attention to one's breasts was decidedly gauche with the M'n'Ms. She smiled sunnily back at them. Her handsome Semitic features were slashed randomly with paint. Her makeup looked like a spinpainting. Her teeth were filed.

Rickenharp swallowed hard, looking at her. Damn. She was *his type.*

Only . . . she wore a blue-mesc sniffer. The sniffer's inverted question mark ran from its hook at her right ear to just under her right nostril. Now and then she tilted her head to it, and sniffed a little blue powder.

Rickenharp had to look away. Silently cursing.

He'd just written a song called "Stay Clean."

Blue mesc. Or syncoke. Or heroin. Or amphetamorphine. Or XTZ. But mostly he went for blue mesc. And blue mesc was addictive.

Blue mesc, also called boss blue. It offered some of the effects of mescaline and cocaine together, framed in the gelatinous sweetness of methaqualone. Only . . . stop taking it after a period of steady use and the world drained of meaning for you. There was no actual withdrawal sickness. There was only a deeply resonant depression, a sense of worthlessness that seemed to settle like dust and maggot dung into each individual cell of the user's body.

Some people called blue mesc "the suicide ticket." It could make you feel like a coal miner when the mineshaft caved in, only you were buried in yourself.

Rickenharp had squandered the money from his only major microdisc hit on boss blue and synthmorph. He'd just barely made it clean. And lately, at least before the band squabbles, he'd begun feeling like life was worth living again.

Watching the girl with the sniffer walk past, watching her use, Rickenharp felt stricken, lost, as if he'd seen something to remind him of a lost lover. An ex-user's syndrome. Pain from guilt of having jilted your drug.

And he could imagine the sweet burn of the stuff in his nostrils, the backward-sweet pharmaceutical taste of it in the back of his palate; the rush; the autoerotic feedback loop of blue mesc. Imagining it, he had a shadow of the sensation, a tantalizing ghost of the rush. In memory he could taste it, smell it, feel it . . . Seeing her *use* brought back a hundred iridescent memories and with them came an almost irrepressible longing. (While some small voice in the back of his head tried to get his attention, tried to warn him, *Hey, remember the shit makes you want to kill yourself when you run out; remember it makes you stupidly overconfident and boorish; remember it eats your internal organs* . . . a small, dwindling voice . . .)

The girl was looking at him. There was a flicker of invitation in her eyes.

He wavered.

The small voice got louder.

Rickenharp, if you go to her, go with her, you'll end up using.

He turned away with an anguished internal wrenching. Stumbled through the wash of sounds and lights and monochrome people to the dressing room; to guitar and earphones and the safer sonic world.

• • •

"You gave him to me," Steinfeld said, leaning close to Purchase so he could be heard over the noise of the bar. "And I give him back. And I think we'll both keep him."

Purchase smiled and nodded. "Stisky's a find. A piece of luck."

Purchase was a big, sloppy-bodied man, his hair thin and his face wide. You could hear him breathe, even when he was at rest. But he laughed easily, and he didn't miss much. The two men liked one another, though they were NR for different reasons. Steinfeld had shaped the NR in the image of his own idealism. It was an extension of his convictions—some would say, his almost perverse obsession. Purchase worked for Witcher,

Steinfeld's chief source of funding. But no, Steinfeld reflected, as they slid into a booth in the Freezone cocktail bar, Purchase worked for himself. That should have made him suspect. Only, it didn't. Steinfeld trusted him more than he trusted some of the NR's political zealots.

"Any problem with the blockades?" Purchase asked, toying with his gold choker.

Steinfeld's brow furrowed. "Yes and no. I got through—but it was close this time. No one actually fired on us. But they would have if they'd picked up on us sooner. Sometimes I feel like asking Witcher's pilots not to tell me if we're tracked. I'd rather not know if I'm about to be shot out of the air . . . "

"You bring anyone else through?"

"A few people. We can't get more than a handful out at any one time . . . and it's a risk with just the handful. I won't be taking many more of these trips . . . " He grimaced and changed the subject. "That's a silk suit, isn't it? It's a little hard to tell in these lights, but I think it's *blue*?"

"It is. Dark blue silk." Purchase signaled for a drink. When the puffy-eyed waitress arrived, yawning, rubbing her temples, he said, "I want something big and glittery in an enormous glass. You choose. Something sweet. Sweet as whoever it was kept you up so late last night."

She almost smiled. "Something with a plastic mermaid? A little paper umbrella?"

"Both the umbrella and the mermaid are absolute necessities."

"I'll have a scotch, please," Steinfeld said. "On the rocks." They watched her walk away. She was wearing a gown that picked up wifi signals at random as the signals passed through the room and reproduced Web imagery down the svelte length of her. Collaged faces, mostly fashion models and breakfast-cereal-kids, rippled across her ass and the back of her thighs.

The bar was at the edge of a disco. Minimono droned and thudded on the dance floor. Lights whirled like UFOs landing in an old movie Steinfeld had seen as a boy.

They had to lean over the transparent plastic table to talk, but they'd picked the booth to discourage bugging.

The lights tinted Purchase's face, changing his color as if some expressionist painter were experimenting with his portrait. He was pinkish red dappled with blue when he asked, "How'd Stisky take to training?"

"A fish to water. The more rigorous the better. Well, he was a priest, once, after all . . . Does he have a name yet?"

"John Swenson. The cover had a good foundation: there was a John Swenson born the same year as Stisky. Died five years later. Looked a lot like Stisky did as a kid. His death went unregistered in his hometown—died in a boating accident with his parents on vacation, they all drowned. Death registered in Florida but never entered in computer records. We've put all the rest together. Worked up a set of false memories for mem-plantation . . . I think we've got some likelies, to take the implants . . . "

The expression on Steinfeld's face made Purchase say, "You've got qualms about mem-plants?"

"This business of toying with people's memories—I don't care which side it is doing it—no, I don't like it. It's—" He shook his head.

"Too close to interfering with the soul?"

Steinfeld said, "I am not sure I believe in the soul. But yes, it's too close—to interfering with the soul."

"We're up against it. Outnumbered. We've got to use all the tools at hand. If it's any comfort, we don't implant our own people. We should, but we don't. Just the enemy."

Steinfeld shrugged. "So be it. How high can you place him?"

Purchase fidgeted, looking unsure of himself. The waitress came back with their drinks. Purchase's was some sort of phantasmagorical daiquiri. A cartoon character flew across the waitress's stomach (What was his name? Something the Gremlin) to be replaced instantly by a hydrogen-cell vehicle crashing head-on into another, both bursting into flames. "Cars are crashing in your stomach," Purchase told her.

"That explains my heartburn," she said, snicking Purchase's Worldtalk expense account credit card through the credunit on her hip. She gave the card back and walked away, Marilyn Monroe waving at them from the small of her back. Monroe's breasts superimposed for one delectable instant on the waitress's buttocks.

"People are *wearing* the Grid now," Steinfeld said.

"Just pray to Gridfriend they don't make wallpaper like that. Come to think of it, they probably are making it . . . "

Steinfeld smiled; the smile was barely visible through his beard. He wore a cheap black-and-white flatsuit, a bit tacky here, but passable.

Purchase said, "I think . . . *think*, mind you . . . I can place Stisky—or Swenson, now, if you like—I think I can place Swenson in the Second Circle itself, after a short, ah, probationary period. Within a few weeks."

Steinfeld looked sharply at Purchase. "It took us three years to get Devereaux into the Second Circle. And that was fast advancement. He was in the lower echelons, as you call it, two years and then—"

"I know all that. But . . . " Purchase leaned nearer. "But I've gotten to know Crandall's sister. We modeled her transactional script patterns. She has an affair every two years—almost to the day! Usually something torrid.

Then Rick gets rid of them or she loses interest. We believe that her next one will be somewhat more serious. And it's due in a week—and that's when I'll introduce her to Swenson. She has a growing need for long-term emotional security. We studied her preference profile: Swenson would be her archetype, which is why we picked him. She meets Swenson, Swenson romances her—and we both agree he's got the talent for that—and she will bring him with her. And of course he's done very well in their lower echelons."

"You're very certain of that."

"I'd swear to it: bet a cool million on it."

Steinfeld nodded. "A million. Well—you've just invoked the deity that means the most to you. I'm impressed. All right. If it gets that far . . . Devereaux might . . . "

Purchase shook his head. "You don't really think Devereaux is going to come through, do you? Do you know who's the new SA Security chief? Old Sackville-West. Devereaux's the nervous type. Old Sacks will smell that."

"Then he may smell our Swenson."

"I think not. Swenson has the talent. And he'll have Ellen Mae's support. Trust me."

They took a moment to work on their drinks. Steinfeld looked down, through the table, and through the floor. The floor was transparent; the disco jutted from the side of a highmall rising two hundred stories over the main Freezone helicopter port; far below—and *directly* below—radio-controlled copters rose and landed, dragonfly bright in the ocean-burnished sunlight.

Steinfeld shivered with vertigo. He shifted his gaze to the expanse of cobalt sea. "Funny how from up here, the waves look regular, perfect and orderly. Down close they're all chaotic."

Purchase looked up from his drink. Without quite taking the straw from his mouth he said, "That supposed to be a parable of some kind?"

"No. But I guess it could be: from up here we're taking too much for granted." The waitress walked by, her dress flashing with forty TV channels at once. It made Steinfeld's skin crawl. "How much of that programming"—he nodded toward the televisioned dress—"is Worldtalk's doing?"

"Not a great deal in slices of time. But lots of it in small, regular pulses . . . Worldtalk'll be active on the SA account this week. Naturally Crandall wants me to shepherd it. And I'll have to do a good job of it. You know that."

"For a while. But try not to promote them *brilliantly*. Okay?"

Worldtalk. The globe-straddling agency for public relations and advertising. Purchase was a Chinese-boxes man, working from the inside box out: his own man and yet Witcher's man; Witcher's man and yet Steinfeld's; Steinfeld's and yet the SA's. The SA's and yet Worldtalk's. Steinfeld believed the sequence moved in that order of importance. He had to believe it, because he needed Purchase. There were too few like him.

There was Devereaux, of course. Who just might be a waste.

"You can pick up . . . Swenson, in an hour, at . . . " He took a plastic-tagged hotel keycard from his pocket and gave it to Purchase, who pocketed the key casually but quickly. "He'll be there. Report on placing him to Ben-Simon at the Israeli Embassy. He's still with me. And to Witcher. Let us know if he gets close to them . . . to her."

"You sound as if you doubt Devereaux's going to come through, yourself." (The light shifting, Purchase's face green, then blue.)

"Just thinking in contingencies."

"If Devereaux doesn't come through, we'll have to roll up his backup team, fast."

"They'll have to cope with it themselves. I'm leaving in a few hours. They'll do fine. They're . . . basic. But good."

He looked out over the sea, thinking, *If Devereaux doesn't come through . . .*

• • •

There were eight people in the room, and, each in their own way, they were all killers. No: seven were killers. One was a man who had come here hoping to *become* a killer; to kill one of the other seven people within the hour, in this undersea conference room beneath Freezone.

Freezone's enormous octagonal raft was pocketed with air and layers of flotation synthetics. Most of the buildings in the exclusive Freezone Central complex—walled off from the rest of Freezone to guarantee safety for its inhabitants and visitors—extended like enormous undersea stalactites beneath the "flotation support structure" for greater stability and less vulnerability to winds.

In one of those buildings, the inverted wedge of the Fuji Hilton, Richard Crandall and Ellen Mae Crandall presided over the meeting . . .

The room was dimmed for the briefing screen. Five men and the woman sat at the table. There were two Security men standing behind Crandall at the head of the table. All were bathed in the sickly electronic-blue light from the screen that filled the upper half of the wall to the right of the door.

On three sides, it was a standard convention meeting room, a forty-by-fifty-foot "planning center." The walls were the usual imitation woodgrain, the table matching. The chairs were confoam swivels; soft track lighting overhead was muted now. A bank of remote controls for the screen and room service was inset at one end of the oblong table.

Behind Crandall, the fourth wall was a window of thick plate glass, looking out on the underside of the floating city. The dull blue vista was lit brokenly by flat white rectangles of light staggered along the down-juts of other buildings; the buildings looked like reflections in a pond, upside down. But look closer and you could see men in them: right-side-up men in upside-down buildings. Now and then some glossy, striped, gape-mouthed thing would swim up near the windows, attracted by the lights; jellyfish billowed up, pumping like disembodied heart valves.

Devereaux sat at the table, looking out into the undersea, carefully keeping up his mask of absentmindedness, carefully thinking only about jellyfish. Not permitting himself to think about the act he was about to perform. It was not yet time to think about it.

Best not to think about it at all. Best to let it happen the way an alarm clock goes off.

A voice droned through the air-conditioned room from the bluewhite screen, accompanying the charts and figures appearing and disappearing there. "Alliance registration in Brussels," the voice said, "rose forty-three percent in the last sixty days. Alliance coordinator for Brussels credits this abrupt rise to the anti-Russian/anti-American information campaign. Antipathy to the 'foreign war-makers' has drawn increasing numbers of Belgians into the Alliance, their registration always hinging on the Alliance's guarantee of eventual ejection of all foreigners. Coordinator Casterman expects very little abreaction from Belgian inductees during the Final Phase, anticipating that thorough Camp indoctrination will obviate any significant resentment when, in the words of the resistance leader Chartres, 'the country is taken over by foreigners who promised to protect us from foreigners.'"

Crandall stabbed a button. The narrative froze. He dialed the lights up and turned to Sackville-West, head of Internal Security, asking sharply, "Who wrote that report?" Crandall's faint Southern accent was almost undetectable. He was slender, almost gaunt, his black eyes a little sunken. His wide, flexible mouth could flare into a smile like a dove flushed from cover; could just as easily clamp down into a frown firm enough to use as a metal-shop vise. His hair was receding, and he compensated with long sideburns. A strong nose, craggy cheekbones—a face almost like a beardless Lincoln. He wore a suit and tie, brown leather and cream-colored silk. His sister, to his left, looked unpleasantly like him, to Devereaux's eye. Even without sideburns. Her face was a little softer, her lips redder—but like him. Maybe it was the expression.

"That report . . . " Sackville-West muttered, clearing his throat several times as he looked through his pocket filer. "Ah, that report was written by . . . ah . . . " Sackville-West was a pinkfaced Britisher with three chins and a comma of hair on his forehead. He was always sweating, even in an air-conditioned room. "Swenson wrote the report," Sackville-West said at last, looking up from his console.

Casually, Devereaux raised a hand to his cheek and pressed the stud under the skin, just below his right cheekbone. His Mossad-issue right eye increased its impressions-per-second ratio by five hundred percent. He rubbed at his left eye, as if it were tired, closing it so only the right took impressions. Details normally lost to the human eye showed up in his prosthetic perception: a flicker of fear in Sackville-West, the expression flashing through the face so rapidly Devereaux would have been unable to see it without the implant.

All it told Devereaux was that Sackville-West was physically intimidated by Crandall. Nothing new there.

Sackville-West was repeating, "John Swenson. SA Number 34428, inducted February of—"

"I don't like him quoting Chartres," Crandall interrupted.

"I can see that, Rick." Sackville-West responded, nodding effusively. Calling him Rick but in a tone that meant *Yes, sir.* "But—I think it was just his sense of humor. It says here his sense of irony is strong. I'd evaluate the remark as a kind of smug solidarity with us: mocking the resistance."

"I'm not so sure of that," Crandall said. "Have him observed."

"Quite right, Rick—I've already punched out an order to that effect." He tapped in something more on the pocket filer; its tiny keys were almost too small for his pudgy fingers.

Most of Devereaux's attention went to watching Ellen Mae with his fast-action eye. And something flickered across her face—zip, and it was gone. But Devereaux had seen: anxiety. Concern. For—

For Swenson. So they'd already managed to interest her in Swenson . . .

She glanced at Devereaux, and away. He thought: Mustn't draw attention to myself, rubbing my eye so much.

He opened the left eye and, as if scratching his cheek, switched off the overdrive in the prosthetic one.

Devereaux turned to watch Crandall, who had gone on to comment on the Belgian brief. " . . . I do think, however, that the new disinfo campaign is working very well, and we should continue through the same means—making sure it's as anti-American as anti-Russian. Our friends at NATO"—he smiled, and that was a cue for a companionable chuckle around the table, which dutifully came—"would hardly approve of such indiscrimination, if it came out."

Devereaux smiled and nodded as he was expected to. He glanced at the Security men behind Crandall, essentially mere bodyguards . . . and wondered if they *were* bodyguards. The damn eye-blanking helmets made them maddeningly inscrutable. He thought he felt them watching him.

Don't get nervous, he told himself. Don't think about the job at all. You'll do it when the time comes.

But Crandall was eminently paranoid; his Security knew it, and knew they were expected to be suspicious of everyone. Even now they stood behind him, between him and the window, because Crandall had instantly mistrusted the window when he'd come into the room.

"I just don't like it, my friends," he'd say. "Anybody could frogman right up to the window, fire a subaqueous rocket through it . . . "

But they were behind schedule, and he'd grudgingly agreed to the room with the glass wall.

Crandall switched the report back on. It droned out troop movement figures, confirming the Russian pullback, reporting the taking of crucial sectors. When it began on Paris, Devereaux felt the pressure rising in him again.

He wondered if the detection-shielding on the gun in his briefcase had been adequate. But they'd have arrested him by now if it hadn't been. He wondered, too, if he could shoot the Security men before Crandall, and still be assured of getting Crandall himself. No. He'd have to get Crandall first. Which meant Security would get him. And Devereaux would die.

He remembered a few lines from Rimbaud.

Mon âme eternelle,
Observe ton voeu,
Malgré la nuit seule . . .

My eternal soul,
Redeem your promise,
In spite of the night alone . . .

It was a silent prayer of Devereaux's own, as Crandall stood to offer a prayer for the meeting.

The olive-drab simuleather briefcase was on the tabletop beside Devereaux's notetaker. Devereaux laid his hand on the table beside the briefcase.

It was almost time.

Crandall's prayers took about three minutes. Every head in the room was lowered for the prayer, even the guards. Even Devereaux's. But his finger closed on the latch at the corner of the briefcase. The latch that would release the gun into his hand.

Another thirty seconds, he told himself, as Crandall intoned in polished rhythms, "We're asking your help, Lord, in this your battle, in this struggle to free the earth from the bonds of inbred social sin; from the sickness of miscegeny . . . "

Devereaux had twenty seconds. In those twenty seconds he found himself wondering, remembering—

Stop thinking about it, he told himself. Steinfeld told you, again and again, *When the moment comes, act, don't think. Act, don't think.*

But he saw himself at the New Right meeting, in Nice, raising objections, eliciting odd looks from the other members, realizing that he didn't belong there anymore. Saw himself approached afterward by one of Steinfeld's men. Bashung. Bashung had heard him voice a few cautious misgivings about the proposal to demand that the government oust all recent immigrants from France. Bashung had watched Devereaux through a perceptual prosthetic, identical to the one he now carried in place of his right eye. Had seen the flash of confusion and worry and sorrow and anger the others had missed.

It hadn't taken long to recruit him. They revealed a great many things about Crandall that were usually kept suppressed. They took Devereaux along when they went to record statements by two widows whose husbands had been assassinated by the SA. Bashung and Steinfeld had played video of Crandall's early meetings with his coordinators, at which he made a series of insane statements in tones so calm and measured as to make the hair stand up on the back of Devereaux's neck. Devereaux had entered the New Right chiefly out of his hatred for the Russians. But when you grasped what Crandall's full intentions were . . .

Crandall made the Russians look like playful imps.

Crandall was the one long awaited, long feared. The one they'd all known would come again.

And Devereaux had been recruited and trained to throw himself deeply into bogus support for the SA, to join the SA's ranks, to ascend to this very room, where he was adviser on the French SA takeover.

Devereaux seemed to hear the words of the boy poet again, the debaucher Rimbaud. *Mon âme eternelle* . . . My eternal soul . . .

"And we thank you, Lord," Crandall was saying, "for advancing our struggle. We ask that you take charge now of our eternal souls . . . "

Redeem your promise . . .

"In the name of Jesus the Redeemer . . . "

In spite of the night alone . . .

" . . . we stand against the armies of darkness. Praise God, and Amen."

What was the last line of the stanza? There was another line Devereaux had forgotten. It was . . .

Ah, yes. He remembered, now, as he pressed the switch that ejected the cool grip of the gun into his palm, as the others intoned *Amen*.

He spoke the last two lines aloud as he stood and turned and raised the gun to fire at Crandall. "*Malgré la nuit seule, et le jour en Feu.*"

In spite of the night alone, and the day on fire.

He fired the gun, the Teflon-coated slugs ripping through Crandall's bulletproof vest, but the Security men were already firing back. They *had* been watching him. He tried to track the gun muzzle to Ellen Mae, but the automatic pistols in the hands of the big men had punched holes in him, and he felt a terrible hollowness beneath his feet, as if someone had pulled out the center of the Earth, left it without a core, and it cracked open and he fell into the emptiness and died with a sickening pang of knowing that he hadn't hit Crandall squarely, the bastard would live, the bastard would live . . .

• 07 •

Rickenharp was listening to a collector's item Velvet Underground tape, from 1968. It was capped into his Earmite. The song was "White Light/ White Heat." The guitarists were doing things that would make Baron Frankenstein say, "There are some things man was not meant to know." He screwed the Earmite a little deeper so that the vibrations would shiver the bone around his ear, give him chills, chills that lapped through him in harmony with the guitar chords. He'd picked a visorclip to go with the music: a muted documentary on expressionist painters. Listening to the Velvets and looking at Edvard Munch. Man!

And then Julio dug a finger into his shoulder.

"Happiness is fleeting," Rickenharp muttered, as he flipped the visorclip back. Some visors came with camera eye and fieldstim. The fieldstim you wore snugged to the skin, as if it were a sheer corset. The camera picked up an image of the street you were walking down and routed it to the fieldstim, which tickled your back in the pattern of whatever the camera saw. Some part of your mind assembled a rough image of the street out of that. Developed for blind people in the 1980s. Now used by viddy addicts who walked or drove the streets wearing visors, watching TV, reflexively navigating by using the fieldstim, their eyes blocked off by the screen but never quite bumping into anyone. But Rickenharp didn't use a fieldstim.

So he had to look at Julio with his own eyes. "What do YOU want?"

"N'ten," Julio said. Julio the technicki bassist. They went on in ten minutes.

Mose, Ponce, Julio, Murch. Rhythm guitar backup vocals. Keyboards. Bass. Drums.

Rickenharp nodded and reached up to flip the visor back in place, but Ponce flicked the switch on the visor's headset. The visor image shrank like a landscape vanishing down a tunnel behind a train, and Rickenharp felt like his stomach was shrinking inside him at the same rate. He knew what was coming down. "Okay," he said, turning to look at them. "*What?*"

They were in the dressing room. The walls were black with graffiti. All rock club dressing rooms will always be black with graffiti; flayed with it, scourged with it. Like the flat declaration THE PARASITES RULE, the cheerful petulance of symbiosis THE SCREAMIN' GEEZERS GOT FUCKING BORED HERE, the oblique existentialism of THE ALKOLOID BROTHERS LOVE YOU ALL BUT THINK YOU WOULD BE BETTER OFF DEAD, and the enigmatic ones like SYNC 66 CLICKS NOW. It looked like the patterning of badly wrinkled wallpaper. It was in layers; it was a palimpsest. Hallucinatory stylization as if tracing the electron firings of the visual cortex.

The walls, in the few places they were visible under the graffiti, were a gray-painted pressboard. There was just enough room for Rickenharp's band, sitting around on broken-backed kitchen chairs and one desk chair with three legs. Crowded between the chairs were instruments in their cases. The edges of the cases were false leather peeling away. Half the snaps broken.

Rickenharp looked at the band, looked clockwise one face to the next, taking a poll from their expressions: Mose on his left, a bruised look to his eyes; his hair a triple-Mohawk, the center spine red, the outer two white and blue; a smoky crystal ring on his left index finger that matched—he knew it matched—his smoky crystal amber eyes. Rickenharp and Mose had been close. Each looked at the other a little accusingly. There was a lover's sulkiness between them, though they'd never been lovers. Mose was hurt because Rickenharp didn't want to make the transition: Rickenharp was putting his own taste in music before the survival of the band. Rickenharp was hurt because Mose wanted to go minimono wifi act, a betrayal of the spiritual ethos of the band; and because Mose was willing to sacrifice Rickenharp. Replace him with a wire dancer. They both knew it, though it had never been said. Most of what passed between them was semiotically transmitted with the studied indirection of the terminally cool.

Tonight, Mose looked like serious bad news. His head was tilted as if his neck were broken, his eyes lusterless.

Ponce had gone minimono, at least in his look, and they'd had a ferocious fight over that. Ponce was slender—like everyone in the band—and fox-faced, and now he was sprayed battleship gray from head to toe, including hair and skin. In the smoky atmosphere of the clubs he sometimes vanished completely.

He wore silver contact lenses. Flat-out glum, he stared at a ten-slivered funhouse reflection in his mirrored fingernails.

Julio, yeah, he liked to give Rickenharp shit, and he wanted the change-up. Sure, he was loyal to Rickenharp, up to a point. But he was also a conformist. He'd argue for Rickenharp maybe, but he'd go with the consensus. Julio had lush curly black Puerto Rican hair piled prowlike over his head. He had a woman's profile and a woman's long-lashed eyes. He had a silver-stud earring, and wore classic retro-rock black leather like Rickenharp. He twisted the skull-ring on his thumb, returning a scowl for its grin, staring at it as if deeply worried that one of its ruby-red glass eyes was about to come out.

Murch was a thick slug of a guy with a glass crew cut. He was a mediocre drummer, but he was a drummer, with a trap set and everything, a species of musician almost extinct. "Murch's rare as a dodo," Rickenharp said once, "and that's not all he's got in common with a dodo." Murch wore horn-rimmed dark glasses, and he was holding a bottle of Jack Daniels on his knee. The Jack Daniels was a part of his outfit. It went with his cowboy boots, or so he thought.

Murch was looking at Rickenharp in open contempt. He didn't have the brains to dissemble.

"Fuck you, Murch," Rickenharp said.

"Whuh? I didn't say nothing."

"You don't have to. I can smell your thoughts. Enough to gag a faggot maggot." Rickenharp stood and looked at the others. "I know what's on your mind. Give me this: one last good gig. After that you can have it how you want."

Tension lifted its wings and flew away.

Another bird settled over the room. Rickenharp saw it in his mind's eye: a thunderbird. Half made of an Indian teepee painting of a thunderbird, and half of chrome T-Bird car parts. When it spread its wings the pinfeathers glistened like polished bumpers. There were two headlights on its chest, and when the band picked up their instruments to go out to the stage, the headlights switched on.

Rickenharp carried his Stratocaster in its black case. The case was bandaged with duct tape and peeling with faded stickers. But the Strat was spotless. It was transparent. Its lines curved hot like a sports car.

They walked down a white plastibrick corridor toward the stage. The corridor narrowed after the first turn, so they had to walk sideways, holding the instruments out in front of them. Space was precious on Freezone.

The stagehand saw Murch go out first, and he signaled the DJ, who cut the canned music and announced the band through the PA. Old-fashioned, like Rickenharp requested: "Please welcome . . . *Rickenharp.*"

There was no answering roar from the crowd. There were a few catcalls and a smattering of applause.

Good, you bitch, fight me, Rickenharp thought, waiting for the band to take up their positions. He'd go on stage last, after they'd set up the spot for him. Always.

Rickenharp squinted from the wings to see past the glare of lights into the dark snakepit of the audience. Only about half minimono now. That was good, that gave him a chance to put this one over.

The band took its place, pressed their automatic tuners, fiddled with dials.

Rickenharp was pleasantly surprised to see that the stage was lit with soft red floods, which is what he'd requested. Maybe the lighting director was one of his fans. Maybe the band wouldn't fuck this one up. Maybe everything would fall into place. Maybe the lock on the cage door would tumble into the right combination, the cage door would open, the T-Bird would fly.

He could hear some of the audience whispering about Murch. Most of them had never seen a live drummer before, except for salsa. Rickenharp caught a scrap of technicki: *"Whuzziemackzut?"* What's he making with that, meaning: What are those things he's adjusting? The drums.

Rickenharp took the Strat out of its case and strapped it on. He adjusted the strap, pressed the tuner. When he walked onto the stage, the amp's reception field would trigger, transmit the Strat's signals to the stack of Marshalls behind the drummer. A shame, in a way, about miniaturization of electronics: the amps were small, though just as loud as twentieth century amps and speakers. But they looked less imposing. The audience was muttering about the Marshalls, too. Most of them hadn't seen old-fashioned amps. "What's those for?" Murch looked at Rickenharp. Rickenharp nodded.

Murch thudded 4/4, alone for a moment. Then the bass took it up, laid down a sonic strata that was kind of off-center strutting. And the keyboards laid down sheets of infinity.

Now he could walk on stage. It was like there'd been an abyss between Rickenharp and the stage, and the bass and drum and keyboards working together made a bridge to cross the abyss. He walked over the bridge and into the warmth of the floods. He could feel the heat of the lights on his skin. It was like stepping from an air-conditioned room into the tropics. The music suffered deliciously in a tropical lushness. The pure white spotlight caught and held him, focusing on his guitar, as per his directions, and he thought, Good, the lighting guy really is with me.

He felt as if he could feel what the guitar felt. The guitar ached to be touched.

•••

Claire sat on the couch in her apartment, half the size of her father's, and waited, with quiet dread, for the InterColony news show to come on.

The main room of her apartment was now dialed to living room; the furniture changed shape for bedroom when she told it to. The walls around the screen were translucent, impregnated with a rain forest's greens and scarlets. The image shifted to a rain squall, and the enormous tropical leaves bounced in the rainwater, ran with crystal beads. A hidden aerator issued the scents of a jungle in the rain. She could almost feel the rainwater.

The all-media screen—a glaring anomaly in the projection of the jungle—showed a documentary about the European Congress of the New Right. The sound was turned off, but there were subtitles as the French *Front National* leader made a series of—she thought—wildly inflammatory statements with the calm of a TV chef explaining a recipe. The intense, pallid little man was saying " . . . the inevitability of conflict between cultures with fundamentally different roots can no longer be glossed over. The good intentions of those trying to reconcile Islamic Fundamentalists with Europeans only serve to prolong the pain of social redress. For, I assure you, social redress is necessary. Immigrants from cultures foreign to our own have muddied our cultural waters. It is foolish to assume we will ever occupy the same territory harmoniously. It is naive, unrealistic. This naivete costs us time, money, yes, human lives. The truth must be faced: some races will always be unable to reconcile! The answer is simple: expulsion. It is out of our hands as to whether we are forced to resort to violence in the execution of our solution to the immigrant problem. Cultural vitality and racial purity are synonymous—"

She turned away, sickened. She sensed some obscure connection between the European situation and the Colony.

She made herself a cocktail spiked with an antidepressant neurohormonal transmitter and sipped it, quickly feeling better—artificially—as she waited for the news.

There it was. She dialed up the sound.

" . . . Technicki radical leaders Molt and Bonham agreed today in principle to a meeting with Director Rimpler but said they could not schedule the meeting without a close look at security precautions for both sides."

She shook her head sadly, muttering, "They think we're going to arrest them at a meeting. The depth of mistrust . . . " She took another sip of the medicinal-tasting cocktail, thinking, Everything's worse than I thought it was . . .

The news ran highlights from the last talk between Technicki Union leaders and Admin. There was the flatsuiter, Barkin, speaking in his nasal tone about " . . . a conflict of interest in the Colony's housing directors . . . Admin is being puppeted by UNIC to run things according to UNIC's priorities, and its priority is profit, always. Admin maintains that the technicki housing project for the Open would be much costlier than was originally believed, and that's why it was put off—but they haven't put off developing Admin housing. We have completely lost sight of the fact that the UN's matching-funds program for the Colony was offered because Professor Rimpler promised a home to Earth's disadvantaged—the disadvantaged get here and find themselves in overcrowded, badly filtrated dorms—a drearier home than the one they left behind . . . "

Claire nodded, ever so slightly. There was something to it.

And since then the Russians had blockaded the Colony, cutting off shipments of food and other necessities from Earth. They weren't starving yet, but the warehoused supplies were running low. The technickis were reacting to the increased rationing. Admin was rationed, too, but the technickis were skeptical—and maybe they were right, Claire thought. Were Praeger and the UNIC people really eating less?

InterColony was showing a clip of the Colony riots now. One of the Radics, a guy named Molt, with a pipe wrench in his hand leading a charge down Corridor D. Forty technicki men and women followed behind him—including preteen boys carrying what looked like Molotov cocktails. The faces in the crowd looked almost delirious with release. The image was shot from above and to the side; she guessed it was one of the surveillance cameras. Molt was shouting something through bared teeth. He saw the camera, mounted near the ceiling, and turned toward it, ran at the viewer, threw the wrench. The wrench struck the camera lens—

The image went black.

• • •

Without consciously knowing it, Rickenharp was moving to the music. Not too much. Not in the pushy, look-at-me way that some performers had. The way they had of trying to *force* enthusiasm from the audience, every move looking artificial.

No, Rickenharp was a natural. The music flowed through him physically, unimpeded by anxieties or ego knots. His ego was there: it was the fuel for his personal Olympics torch. But it was also as immaculate as a pontiff's robes.

The band sensed it: Rickenharp was in rare form tonight. Maybe it was because he was freed. The tensions were gone because he knew this was the end of the line: the band had received its death sentence: Now, Rickenharp was as unafraid as a true suicide. He had the courage of despair.

The band sensed it and let it happen. The chemistry was there, this time, when Ponce and Mose came into the verse section. Mose with a sinuous riffing picked low, almost on the chrome-plate that clamped the strings; Ponce with a magnificently redundant theme washed through the brass mode of the synthesizer. The whole band felt the chemistry like a pleasing electric shock, the pleasurable shock of individual egos becoming a group ego.

The audience was listening, but they were also resisting. They didn't want to like it. Still, the place was crowded—because of the club's rep, not because of Rickenharp—and all those packed-in bodies make a kind of sensitive atmospheric exo-skeleton, and he knew that made them vulnerable. He knew what to touch.

Feeling the Good Thing begin to happen, Rickenharp looked confident but not quite arrogant—he was too arrogant to show arrogance.

The audience looked at Rickenharp as a man will look at a smug adversary just before a hand-to-hand fight and wonder, "Why's he so smug, what does he know?"

He knew about timing. And he knew there were feelings even the most aloof among them couldn't control, once those feelings were released: and he knew how to release them.

Rickenharp hit a chord. He let it shimmer through the room and he looked out at them. He made eye contact.

He liked seeing the defiant stares, because that was going to make his victory more complete.

Because he *knew*. He'd played five gigs with the band in the last two weeks, and for all five gigs the atmosphere had been strained, the electricity hadn't been there; like a Jacob's ladder where the two poles aren't properly lined up for the sparks to jump.

And like sexual energy, it had built up in them, dammed behind their private resentments; and now it was pouring through the dam, and the band shook with the release of it as Rickenharp thundered into his progression and began to sing . . .

Strumming over the vocals, he sang,

You want easy overnight action
want it casually
A neat little chain reaction
and a little sympathy
You say it's just consolation
In the end it's a compensation
for insecurity
That way there's no surprises
That way no one gets hurt
No moral question tries us
No blood on satin shirts

But for me, yeah for me
PAIN IS EVERYTHING!
Pain is all there is
Babe take some of mine
or lick some of his
PAIN IS EVERYTHING!
Pain is all there is
Babe take some of mine . . .

• • •

From "An Interview With Rickenharp: The Boy Methuselah," in *Guitar Player Magazine*, May 2037:

GPM: You keep talking about group dynamics, but I have a feeling you don't mean dynamics in the usual musical sense.
RICKENHARP: The right way to create a band is for the members to simply find one another, the way lovers do. In bars or wherever. The members of the band are like five chemicals that come together with a specific chemical reaction. If the chemistry is right the audience becomes involved in this, this kind of—well, a social chemical reaction.
GPM: Could it be that all this is just your psychology? I mean, your emotional need for a really organically whole group?
RICKENHARP (after a long pause): It's true I need something like that. I need to belong. I mean—okay, I'm a "nonconformist," but still, on some level I got a need to belong. Maybe rock bands are a surrogate family—the family unit is shot to hell, so . . . the band

is family for people. I'd do anything to keep it together. I need these guys. I'd be like a kid whose mom and dad and brothers and sisters were killed if I lost this band.

• • •

And he sang,

> *PAIN IS EVERYTHING!*
> *Pain is all there is*
> *Babe take some of mine*
> *Suck some of his*
> *Yeah, said PAIN IS EVERYTHING—*

Singing it insolently, half shouting, half warbling at the end of each note, with that fuck-you tone, performing that magic act: shouting a melody. He could see doors opening in their faces, even the minimonos, even the neutrals, all the flares, the rebs, the chaotics, the preps, the retros. Forgetting their subcultural classifications in the unification of the music. He was basted in sweat under the lights, he was squeezing sounds with his fingers and it was as if he could feel the sounds taking shape in his hands the way a sculptor feels clay under his fingers, and it was like there was no gap between his hearing the sound in his head and its coming out of the speakers. His brain, his body, his fingers had closed the gap, was one supercooled circuit breaker fused shut.

Some part of him was looking through the crowd for the chaotichick he'd spotted earlier. He was faintly disappointed when he didn't see her. He told himself, *You ought to be happy, you had a narrow escape, she would've got you back into boss blue.*

But when he saw her press to the front and nod at him ever so slightly in that smug insider's way, he was simply glad, and he wondered what his subconscious was planning for him . . . All those thoughts were flickers. Most of the time his conscious mind was completely focused on the sound, and the business of acting out the sound for the audience. He was playing out of sorrow, the sorrow of loss. His family was going to die, and he played tunes that touched the chord of loss, in everyone . . .

And the band was supernaturally tight. The gestalt was there, uniting them, and he thought: The band feels good, but it's not going to help when the gig's over.

It was like a divorced couple having a good time in bed but knowing that wouldn't make the marriage right again; the good time was a function of having given up.

But in the meantime there were fireworks.

By the last tune in the set the electricity was so thick in the club that—as Mose had said once, with a rocker's melodrama—"If you could cut it, it would bleed." The dope and smashweed and tobacco smoke moiling the air seemed to conspire with the stage lights to create an atmosphere of magical apartness. With each song-keyed shift in the light, red to blue to white to sulfurous yellow, a corresponding emotional wavelength rippled through the room. The energy built, and Rickenharp discharged it, his Strat the lightning rod.

And then the set ended.

Rickenharp bashed out the last five notes alone, nailing a climax onto the air. Then he walked offstage, hardly hearing the roar from the crowd. He found himself half running down the white, grimy plastibrick corridor, and then he was in the dressing room and didn't remember coming there. The graffiti seemed to writhe on the walls as if he'd taken a psychedelic. Everything felt more real than usual. His ears were ringing like Quasimodo's belfry.

He heard footsteps and turned, working up what he was going to say to the band. But it was the chaotichick and someone else, and then a third dude coming in after the someone else.

The someone else was a skinny guy with brown hair that was naturally messy, not messy as part of one of the cultural subcurrents. His mouth hung a little ajar, and one of his incisors was decayed black. His nose was windburned and the back of his bony hands were gnarled with veins. The third dude was Japanese; small, brown-eyed, nondescript, his expression was mild, just a shade more friendly than neutral. The skinny Caucasian guy wore an army jacket sans insignia, shiny jeans, and rotting tennis shoes. His hands were nervous, like there was something he was used to holding in them that wasn't there now. An instrument? Maybe.

The Japanese guy wore a Japanese Action Suit—surprise, surprise—sky-blue and neat as a pin. There was a lump on his hip—something he could reach by putting his right arm across his body and through the open zipper down the front of the suit—and Rickenharp was pretty sure it was a gun.

There was one thing all three of them had in common: they looked half-starved.

Rickenharp shivered—his gloss of sweat cooling on him, but he forced himself to say, "Whusappnin'?" It was wooden in his mouth. He was looking past them, waiting for the band.

"Band's in the wings," the chaotichick said. "The bass player said to tell you . . . well it was *Telm zassouter.*"

Rickenharp had to smile at her mock of Julio's technicki. Tell him, get his ass out here.

Then some of the druggy feeling washed away and he heard the shouts from the audience and he realized they wanted an encore.

"Jeez, an encore," he said without thinking. "Been so fucking long."

"'Ey mate," the skinny guy said, pronouncing mate like *mite*. Brit or Aussie. "I saw you at Stone'enge five years ago when you 'ad yer second 'it."

Rickenharp winced a little when the guy said *your second hit*, inadvertently underlining the fact that Rickenharp had had only two, and everyone knew he wasn't likely to have any more.

"I'm Carmen," the chaotichick said. "This is Willow and Yukio." Yukio was standing sideways from the others, and something about the way he did it told Rickenharp he was watching down the corridor without seeming to.

Carmen saw Rickenharp looking at Yukio and said, "Cops are coming down."

"Why?" Rickenharp asked. "The club's licensed."

"Not for you or the club. For us."

He looked at her and said, "Hey, I don't need to get busted . . . " He picked up his guitar and went into the hall. "I got to do my encore before they lose interest."

She followed along, into the hall and the echo of the encore stomps, and asked, "Can we hang out in the dressing room for a while?"

"Yeah, but it ain't sacrosanct. You come back here, the cops can, too." They were in the wings now. Rickenharp signaled to Murch and the band started playing.

Standing beside him, she said, "These aren't exactly cops. They probably don't know these kind of places, they'd look for us in the crowd, not the dressing room."

"You're an optimist. I'll tell the bouncer to stand here, and if he sees anyone else start to come back, he'll tell 'em it's empty back here 'cause he just checked. Might work, might not."

"Thanks." She went back to the dressing room. He spoke to the bouncer and went on stage. Feeling drained, the guitar heavy on him. But he picked up on the energy level in the room and it carried him through two encores. He left them wanting more—and, sticky with sweat, walked back to his dressing room.

They were still there. Carmen, Yukio, Willow.

"Is there a stage door?" Yukio asked. "Into alley?"

Rickenharp nodded. "Wait in the hall; I'll come out and show you in a minute."

Yukio nodded, and they went into the hall. The band came in, filed past Carmen and Yukio and the Brit without much noticing them, assuming they were backstage hangout flotsam, except Murch stared at Carmen's tits and swaggered a bit, twirling his drumsticks.

The band sat around laughing in the dressing room, slapping palms, lighting several kinds of smokes. They didn't offer Rickenharp any; they knew he didn't use it.

Rickenharp was packing his guitar away, when Mose said, "You blew good."

"You mean he gave you a good head?" Murch said, and Julio snickered.

"Yeah," Ponce said, "the guy gives a good head, good collarbone, good kidneys—"

"Good kidneys? Rick sucks on your kidneys? I think I'm gonna puke."

And the usual puerile band banter because they were still high from a good set and putting off what they knew had to come, till Rickenharp said, "What you want to talk about, Mose?"

Mose looked at him, and the others shut up.

"I know there's something on your mind," Rickenharp said softly. "Something you haven't come out with yet."

Mose said, "Well, it's like—there's an agent Ponce knows, and this guy could take us on. He's a technicki agent and we'd be taking on a technicki circuit, but we'd work our way back from there, that's a good base. But this guy says we have to get a wire act in."

"You guys been busy," Rickenharp said, shutting the guitar case.

Mose shrugged, "Hey, we ain't been doing it behind your back; we didn't hear from the guy till yesterday night. We didn't have a real chance to talk to you till now, so, uh, we have the same personnel but we change costumes, change the band's name, write new tunes."

"We'd lose it," Rickenharp said. Feeling caved-in. "We'd lose the thing we got, doing that shit, because it's all superimposed."

"Rickenharp—rock 'n' roll is not a fucking religion," Mose said.

"No, it's not a religion, it's a way of life. Now, here's *my* proposal: we write new songs in the same style as always. We did good tonight. It could be the beginning of a turnaround for us. We stay here, build on the base audience we established tonight."

It was like throwing coins into the Grand Canyon. You couldn't even hear them hit bottom.

The band just looked back at him.

"Okay," Rickenharp said. "Okay. We've been through this ten fucking times. Okay. That's all." He'd had an exit speech worked out for this moment, but it caught in his throat. He turned to Murch and said, "You think they're going to keep you on, they tell you that? Bullshit! They'll be doing it without a drummer, man. You better learn to program computers, fast." Then he looked at Mose. "Fuck you, Mose." He said it quietly.

He turned to Julio, who was looking at the far wall as if to decipher some particularly cryptic piece of graffiti. "Julio, you can have my amp, I'll be traveling light."

He turned and, carrying his guitar, walked out, leaving silence behind him.

He nodded at Yukio and his friends and they followed him to the stage door. At the door, Carmen said, "Any chance you could help us find a little cover?"

Rickenharp needed company, bad. He nodded and said, "Yeah, if you'll gimme a hit of that blue boss."

She said, "Sure." And they went into the alley.

• • •

FirStep. The Colony.

They all had to sit on the floor in Bitchie's because there weren't enough chairs. And Molt didn't want some of them on chairs and some on the floor. He wanted them all on the same level, where he could make easy eye contact.

There were twenty-two of them, eighteen men and four women, sitting in a circle on the mattress-covered floor. They were technickis just off the shift, or waiting to go on shift. The little room was fuggy with their smell; the air cycler in this part of the space colony was overtaxed. Had been wafting them green air lately anyway.

Wilson was going on, and on, his technickese slurring the sentences together so the monologue sounded like one big sentence, even translated: " . . . so the thing to do is to push for confrontation and then stop short of the actual confrontation and hold the confrontation out as a threat to make them deal with us because if we really push it and get down to fighting with them we're going to lose but even though they know they're going to win they still don't want the confrontation because it's going to endanger the Colony's air-tigh integ and it'll cost them a few men and it'll be expensive to repair everything that gets busted so I think we oughta . . . "

On and on. Molt had had enough. Wilson was short, thick-bodied, his blond hair had been flared into a corona-shape, was losing its shape like a dying dandelion; he had small, squinty blue eyes and a bulbous nose, little red mouth always going, probably got an in with the pharmacy techs for uppers. Wearing his greasy air-systems mechanic's overalls. Wilson wanted badly to be a radic leader. Molt and Bonham and Barkin were the acknowledged leaders, and Wilson muttered about it because Molt and Bonham weren't real technickis, spoke it with the accent of someone raised in Standard English. Molt's opinion was: Wilson was a grasping scheming runt. Molt had tried to keep Wilson out of this meeting, but the little prick had wormed in, nudged his friends about till they got Barkin to invite him. Little prick'd sell out his granny, Molt thought.

Molt broke in on him with, "You had it a minute ago, Wilson, when you said they're scared of confrontation even though they'd win it. But you didn't carry it far enough." Though of course Molt said it in technicki. "They're scared enough of it, what we got to do is, hit 'em harder, go for it—we got more power than they want to admit because they're scared we'll—"

Bonham broke in, "There's something else we could do."

Molt glared at Bonham. He didn't like being interrupted. And he was beginning to mistrust Bonham, too. All their chumminess had evaporated when they got to be rivals in the new party. Bonham, sitting beside Wilson, shifted, wincing, to keep his long legs from going to sleep, ran his fingers through his hair with that goddamn Che Guevara took on his face, going on, "We could put up a barricade. Several. Take control of the heart of technickitown. That's a confrontation, but then again it isn't. I mean, a *big* barricade, maybe block off Corridor D completely."

"They'd be on us before we got it half done," Barkin said. No flatsuit today, Molt noticed. The fucking hypocrite wearing mech's overalls, like he ever ventured into the repair hangars. He was squatting in a way that kept him from coming into direct contact with the greasy mattress, except for the bottom of his feet. Doesn't want to get dried cum and sweat from Bitchie's customers on his legs. Nice clean mech overalls, probably bought 'em at a costume shop. Christ.

Bonham shook his head. "We stage a diversion, smoke bombs, whatever, up at the main crossover. We have forklifts, everything else we need, get most of it in place in no time."

"You defend a barricade in Corridor D," Molt said, "you got to use guns and you got to shoot to kill. Because they won't stand for a barricade, they'll rush it right off."

Wilson shook his head like a terrier with earmites. "No, hey, I think Bonham's right we'd just fire warning shots, capture some territory, they wouldn't want to move in right away because it'd force confrontation and they don't want that, leastways not yet . . . "

"I'm not so sure they don't want that," Barkin said, but no one was listening, except Molt. They were all jabbering at once now, hot on the idea of a barricade. And then a whistle came through the intercom, signal that the admin bulls were coming down the corridor, were going to raid Bitchie's, so the radics started moving out according to the drill, going out into the little service hallway and through the kitchen; the bulls would find the place empty . . .

But how did they know about the meeting?

• 08 •

It hurt with every breath. But after a while that particular pain was part of the rhythm of being alive, was almost reassuring, and Smoke ceased to take much notice of it. The monotony, and the bedlam noises and smells of the place—that's what was hard to take. He tried to keep himself amused by guessing where he was, what was going on. But the body cast (and damn its itching!) kept him from looking around much. And there was no one who spoke English near him, at first. After a couple of days, he worked out that he was in Belgium, southeast of Brussels, in some kind of military hospital.

After they'd put on the body cast he'd spoken to the doctor only once. "You are lucky," the doctor said, in a heavy Belge accent. "We find no brain damage. Zare ess some internal bleeding and we stop it. You have fracture breastbone, fracture arm, fracture collarbone. Slight concussion. Burns—second degree, not zo bad. You are lucky alzo zince we have . . . " And then he said something in Belgian.

"What's that?" Smoke asked.

"A machine puts a current in zuh broken places of the bone, helps to heal faster. Good-bye." There was finality in that good-bye, and Smoke never saw him again except out of the corner of his eye as he ghosted around the beds of other patients in the big hospital dorm room.

"He is a bastard of a Belge," said the man next to him. A Frenchman. That was all Smoke could tell about him, because his casts made it impossible to turn and look that far to the side. "The Belge are imbeciles, all Belge," the Frenchman said. "And this electricity cure, this will kill you *bientôt.*"

It hurt Smoke too much to talk, at that point, so he didn't reply, and that was their entire conversation. Two days later the Frenchman died.

Sometimes Smoke played with the pain. It came in waves, and when the waves were in a peak, the pain was something palpable. He had always had what he thought of as his inner hand. It was the area low in his chest where he felt the center of his sensations. The place that glows for gratifications and aches for emotional hurt. Sometimes he felt he could shape the locus of sensation there into a kind of ectoplasmic hand—he knew it wasn't ectoplasm, but he pictured it that way—and he could imagine reaching with that hand into other parts of his body, to test them. Reach into the left leg and it will tingle with sensitivity. If it was in pain, he could reach in and touch the pain. Now when the waves of pain came strongest, he reached out his inside hand and caught the waves of pain in the hand and parted them, split them up, or squeezed them like something gelatinous between fingers of internal self-sensation; and this "contact" produced, in his mind's eye, a kind of rainbow-on-oil shimmer he watched with childlike fascination. In this way the pain became objectified into visual terms, and was rendered neutral, defused. The pain became almost painless.

But sometimes the misery of the ward overwhelmed him. The sick were in cots and their cots were everywhere; there were, lately, men laid out on the floor. The place stank, of course, and sometimes the smell was given the extra pungency of humiliation when much of the stink came from himself—the overworked nurses were slow about his bedpans. And the noise of the place diminished at night, but it never ceased. There was moaning and, always, bitching in four or five languages. There were men babbling obscenities, an unceasing bubbling over of mental ugliness, and that was perhaps the worst. He was perversely grateful for the occasional *CRUMP* and quaking of the shellings—or were they bombs?—in the countryside around the hospital. They made it possible to visualize a world outside the infinitely monotonous grind of life in the hospital.

For a time some of the patients were refugees, adding the sirening of wailing children to the dissonant symphony of complaints bouncing from the ceiling. But there was a rule about the hospital being used only for NATO soldiers—Smoke heard a British Red Cross nurse complain about it—and the refugees were moved out to a camp where, it was said, death was certain for the very ill. There wasn't enough food to go around in the refugee camps. In keeping with triage, critically ill refugees simply were not fed.

Smoke had seen the Dutch refugee camps. Had heard the stories . . . Stories of a hundred thousand, two hundred thousand—an ever-swelling multitude of the displaced and homeless tramping the roads outside the European cities. At first they'd fled the war in cars—but the highways had become impassable with rubble and craters, and anyway fuel was hard to get. Now they walked, or pulled carts—often whole families pulling a cart made of a small stripped-down fiberglass car, propane or electric engines removed. Legions of people yoked to automotive shapes, as if enslaved to serve cars . . . Part of a dust cloud in summer, slogging through icy mud in the winter; learning about trenchfoot and scurvy, cholera and hepatitis, gangrene and lice. Some formed tribes for self-protection. The tribes were usually ethnocentric, which festered racial awareness. People who, before the war, had been indifferent to their neighbor's race, were reviling the "scheming Jews hoarding food" or the "thieving Arabs, steal your last crust if you're not watching with a gun in your hand!" By some unspoken consensus, the roads were usually a neutral place, where the tribes merged into one mass of tramping, weeping, cursing, death-eyed misery. Thousands more took to sea in improvised boats and those who didn't founder and drown sometimes found refuge in the Middle East, in Israel and Egypt; a few thousand were admitted to Scotland; thousands more to Canada and the USA. But the anti-immigrant feeling was strong in North America, now, with the global warming crisis and the propaganda, and the quota was quickly filled. The flow of refugees to America became a trickle and then stopped with the near-cessation of civilian air and sea traffic over the Atlantic.

Most of the refugees were trapped in Europe. And most had been cosmopolitan urbanites, whose major baseline concerns before the war had been the acquisition of new technology, or car repair, or money for the August holidays. And now their worries were food, water, weapons, shelter, warmth, medicine. The refugee camps provided enough food to prolong the suffering, but not enough to generate the energy to find a way out of the suffering. The camps were called "the shitpits" by the English speakers. Camp shelters were made from waterproofed cardboard, which turned out to be waterproof for only three or four rainfalls. At first the refugee camps were clean, and run like military bases, dreary but livable. But as the war dragged on the volunteers fell sick, or lost heart; the military could no longer spare men to help out; the Russians blockaded emergency-civilian supplies, believing they might also be supply ships for NATO. The Second Alliance was involved in shipping relief supplies, and Steinfeld claimed they diverted much of it for their own use. The camps swelled and rotted, teeming with people the way cysts teem with bacteria. Riots against the camp administration flared—and quickly died out. They accomplished nothing. But inter-tribal melees followed by guerrilla warfare became a fact of life, as one refugee racial group attacked another for food and medical supplies. And here and there were the advance agents of the Second Alliance, quietly distributing small amounts of food, and great bags of promises. Recruiting those the SA saw as having "special potential." These would disappear from the refugee camps, would turn up later in the Second Alliance, unswervingly loyal to the organization that had brought them out of starvation and squalor and hopelessness, shown them purpose and order and a reinforcement of their most cherished prejudices . . .

Smoke wondered for a while if he would be taken to one of the refugee camps, since he was no NATO soldier. But an orderly wheeling him for the bone-healing treatment, referred to him as "the American soldier." Perhaps he would be taken from the hospital when they discovered the mistake. Or perhaps Steinfeld had arranged this "mistake." Why? It must have cost him several favors. Why had Steinfeld done so much for him? Steinfeld was not an altruist by reflex. Steinfeld was a man obsessed.

Working on the fringes of the New Resistance operation, Smoke had picked up pieces of Steinfeld's history, had fitted them together. Smoke was sometimes privy to intelligence about the NR which didn't reach its rank and file. He had learned that Steinfeld had once been a field operative for the Mossad: Israeli intelligence.

Steinfeld had operated a listening post and then had been promoted to field officer, running agents. As Mossad field officer Steinfeld had run-ins with agents of the Second Alliance as they went about their recruiting. He became interested in them and gathered evidence that their ranks were riddled with active anti-Semites, including men who, decades before, had sheltered the doddering, wheelchair-bound Nazi war criminals from war crimes investigators. Steinfeld became a bit shrill in trumpeting the dangers of the Second Alliance to the Mossad. He was believed to have lost his objectivity. This, combined with his known sympathy for the Palestinians, cost him his post. He was pressured into resigning. He set up his own network, "going indie," at first cadging funds here and there from sympathizers— some said even from Palestinians. Now, an American businessman named Quincy Witcher paid Steinfeld's bills. And no one was quite sure why.

Steinfeld had his sympathizers in the Mossad; occasionally one of these gave him intelligence, or a little extra credit-grease, or food, or weapons. The Mossad brass pretended not to know about this, because Steinfeld was still useful to them. But he was also on their yellow list: the list of those who would be assassinated, should the correct juxtaposition of circumstances arise; should Steinfeld be viewed as dangerous. There were those who would have relegated Steinfeld to the red list: assassinate ASAP. *Suppose he was captured?* they argued. *He has seen us on the inside; there is much he knows.* Still, over tea in commissaries and wine in the better restaurants in Tel Aviv, it was decided that Steinfeld would not be shot or blown up or poisoned, at least not right away. Not by the Mossad. After all, he was doing work that was useful to the Mossad, but which they could truly disavow.

Lying rigid in his plaster carapace like a paralyzed lobster, staring at the same grime spots on the yellowing ceiling week after week, Smoke thought about Steinfeld a great deal. So it was somehow not a great surprise when Steinfeld came to see him. It was as if Smoke had conjured him.

Steinfeld was wearing a blue nylon windbreaker. It rode up a little on his big belly. The New Resistance was based in Paris now, which was relatively comfortable compared to Amsterdam.

"Looks like there's more to eat in Paris," Smoke rasped when Steinfeld sat carefully on an unsoiled corner of Smoke's bed.

Steinfeld smiled and nodded. He looked at the IV stand, then at the lesions on Smoke's forearm. "You don't look so bad," he said. "Except for this arm. What's this?"

"It became infected," Smoke said. "The IV needle. They put it in the wrong place a few times, missed the vein. What's worse is when they forget to change the bottle. The damn thing empties and turns vampire, sucks blood out of me. The blood runs up the tube. Hurts like the devil."

Steinfeld said, "They have too much to do."

"I know. I don't complain—anyway, they ignore complaints."

"But once," Steinfeld said, looking at him, "you tried to tell them you are not a soldier, that you should not be here. So I heard."

"They don't listen no matter what you say."

"If they had, you'd probably be dead by now. Do you still have a death wish, Smoke?" Steinfeld asked.

Smoke said nothing.

"I think you do. That's the only problem with it."

"With what?"

Steinfeld said, "With the fact that you owe me now, Smoke."

Smoke said, with a faint smile, "I see."

Steinfeld nodded.

"You have plans for me," Smoke said.

Now it was Steinfeld's turn to say nothing.

"It itches in this cast," Smoke said. It was good to have someone to complain to.

"Yes. And the food here is . . . ?"

"Execrable," Smoke said.

"Go on," Steinfeld said.

"They rarely change the sheets," Smoke said with alacrity, "and they rarely turn me. I get bedsores, which they sometimes allow to become infected. Then they give me a general antibiotic, and the sores ease, and then they forget to turn me and the sores come back. And so forth. The crying of the others is an assault on sanity."

"I would say that it is better to be in such a place than dead in a shell of a building in Amsterdam—given that you won't be here forever. But we come again to the problem of your death wish."

"Are the others alive? Hard-Eyes and the others?"

"So far as I know. I've been away from Paris for a while."

There was something more that Smoke wanted to ask, but he felt foolish. And in this place there was little dignity; what one could scrape up, one hoarded.

He didn't have to ask it, as it happened: Steinfeld guessed what was in

Smoke's mind. "The crow lived, and came along to the boat. I have it in my flat, in Paris. Someone's taking care of it."

Smoke felt an absurdly profound relief.

Steinfeld stood up. He took a chocolate bar and a vitaminpak from his pocket and put them in Smoke's usable hand.

"They're giving me a treatment with electric currents to heal the bones," Smoke said to keep Steinfeld there just a little longer. "A Frenchman told me it would hurt me, but I think it's helping. The pain is much less, It's just a few weeks since they started doing it."

Steinfeld nodded. "It works. We'll come to get you when they decide the casts can come off."

He turned to go. Smoke said quickly, desperately, "Tell me something. Anything. I need something to think about. You have plans for me. Tell me about it. Something."

"There isn't much I can say here."

"Then only what you *can* say."

Steinfeld nodded at the IV bottle. "I'll see to it they refill that thing."

"Tell them to take it away. I don't need it. Tell me something, Steinfeld."

Steinfeld took a deep breath, tugged at his beard, blew the breath out again. He looked at Smoke. "I know who you are. I found out the day before the jumpjet hit us. For a while I too thought Smoke was a nickname."

"Wait—" Smoke felt he was going to choke.

But Steinfeld bulled grimly on. "You don't want me to talk about it. You've become expert in not thinking about it, and you don't want me to undermine that expertise. Tough. You wanted something to think about. So think about this: you're Jack Brendan Smoke. You're American. You were in Amsterdam when the war broke out, to see a psychiatrist at the Leydon clinic. Before that, you won the United Nations Literary Committee prize for your *Search for a Contemporary Reality*. You were the spokesman for all the people who felt lost in the accelerated rate of change. You wrote a second series of essays in which you said, generally, that there were people manipulating the Grid for political ends, and you named Worldtalk. You predicted a return of fascism and you quoted something you'd heard about the Second Circle, the secret inner circle of the Second Alliance. The ones who make the SA's long-term goals . . . That essay was never published. Evidently someone at your publishing company was SA. Some men came to the clinic in ski masks. You were taken in the night and they—"

"Please . . . " A great weight on his chest made it hard to breathe. "Steinfeld . . . "

"They tortured you. They gave you a drug that made you feel that you were choking . . . "

He stopped, seeing Smoke was gagging. He waited. After a minute the spasm passed.

Smoke lay staring at the ceiling, breathing shallowly.

"I'm going to go on, Smoke," Steinfeld said.

Smoke just lay there.

Steinfeld said, "They wanted to know who you got the information from. About the Second Circle. You didn't tell them. They tortured you in many ways. In many imaginative ways. And then the choking drug, again. They tried to move you to another place, where they had access to extraction. You escaped, en route, and went back to the hospital, where you broke down completely. You were sent in secret to another clinic. The men would have found the clinic anyway, eventually, would have come for you again—if not for the war. That was the day the Russian tanks crossed into Germany. And a little while later the Russians were moving in on Amsterdam, and they shelled the city. Your clinic was shelled. Almost everyone killed . . . "

"I was in my safe, locked room," Smoke said, taking it up in a small voice. "But then the wall was blown in. I went to get someone to put the wall back. They were all dead. Except Dr. Van Henk. I saw him—his face was bloody. The sight of him bloody like that frightened me. I don't know why it affected me so strongly—I ran from him, we lost sight of each other in all the burning. Was it Van Henk who—?"

"Yes. I had this from Van Henk. He's still alive. So far as I know."

"I was the only patient not killed. Wherever I went there were only the dead. I wandered out of there. Sometimes the choking, from the drug—it would start again. It seemed to come back, maliciously, after me. The choking and the dead everywhere . . . For a long time I couldn't remember who I was. When I could remember—I wanted to forget again. Wanted to be someone else . . . " His voice was cracked glass.

Steinfeld said, "Sometimes your face looked familiar to me. But under all that grime . . . and the way a man gets wasted . . . " He shrugged. "So you wanted me to tell you something. There's this: you were a great writer. A great speaker, great humanist. The torture didn't break you—but then again it did. Even so, Smoke: you could help us. In the States the only ones who believe that the fascists are coming again are the ones trying to help them. As for the others—" He shook his head sadly. "Worldtalk pushes their buttons. But if people keep speaking up in the underGrid . . . You *could* help us! People remember you."

Smoke said, "I *can't*."

"Sometimes I see a man who's broken, or bent by torture, and I know he'll never change. Never heal. When I saw you with that crow," he smiled ruefully, "I knew you would heal. That meant the other possibilities I saw in you could become real. Now you have something to think about."

Steinfeld nodded, once, to say good-bye and went away. Leaving Smoke to just lie there, staring at the ceiling.

• • •

Hard-Eyes and Jenkins were walking through the Parc Monceau. It was the flaccid end of late afternoon; the trees stood leafless and stark as nude crones. The forest looked dead, and misty wet, all grays and blue shadows and browns leached of life. But the smell of moldering leaves was good. Hard-Eyes inhaled it in hungry breaths and the cold air bit at his sore nostrils; pins and needles danced in his cheeks.

The HK-21 assault rifle in his hands was cold as a stone crucifix and felt nearly as heavy. He was tired; he was hungry. One meal a day was not enough.

"Steinfeld promised us more to eat," Jenkins complained.

Hard-Eyes had been thinking the same thing, but he said, "We're lucky to get what they give us. You get a look at that refugee camp outside town?"

Jenkins grunted. "You got a point." His hands were red from cold on the blue steel and plastic stock of his assault rifle. They'd traded in the Weatherby and the .22 for more practical weapons.

Hard-Eyes glanced over his shoulder, wondering why the instructors were hanging back so far. And then he stopped.

He couldn't see them at all now.

"They're fucking with us, Jenkins," Hard-Eyes said.

Jenkins stopped and they watched the trail behind them, expecting to see their guerrilla-warfare instructors strolling around the bend, through the attenuated bristle of bluish underbrush. Nothing.

There were no bird sounds. There had been, a few minutes before.

Hard-Eyes swallowed.

"Those guys don't like us," Jenkins said, his voice hushed. "What'd they say about 'robber packs'?"

"Said we hadda be careful because the noise of the gunfire might attract robber packs. Guys that live on the other side of the park, in the shack slum over there."

"Shit!—you think they set us up?"

"Steinfeld wouldn't risk men like that."

"But I'm telling you *these guys don't like us*. They've decided that Americans suck. They think we're CIA or some shit. And Steinfeld ain't around."

"They don't like us but they wouldn't—" He broke off, staring through the mist. There were men coming out of the woods.

The trees to the right of the trail were not thickly dispersed. The well-spaced trunks came together in the compression of distance, becoming a corrugated wall of gray about fifty yards away. From here it looked liked a solid wall of trees. So when the men came out of that solid-seeming wall it looked as if they were squeezed out, like man-shaped drops of liquid. They looked as gray as the tree trunks, except there were smears of orange-pink for faces and pencil-thin strokes of blue-black and brown in their hands. Rifles.

Hard-Eyes counted eight and after that stopped counting. And looked for a place to run to. To his left was a broad, cracked parking lot. The French government scarcely existed now, and the skeleton of it that remained had no resources for park maintenance, so the parking lot was choked with blown branches and leaves; here and there were the rusty humps of stripped and abandoned cars. But the cars were too far away to be used for cover. He and Jenkins would be shot in the back if they ran across the parking lot.

The trail up ahead looked safer, but the instructors had told them, "When pressed, ask yourself if this is a situation when we must disperse—or regroup? The answer depends on the nature of the enemy and their position with relation to your own unit's command."

If Hard-Eyes ran ahead, the enemy would become a wedge between Hard-Eyes' unit and the unit's command, the instructors. The command would be threatened, hemmed in by the enemy and when possible he was to regroup to protect command.

So Hard-Eyes said, "Back down the trail."

Jenkins said, "Shit, man—"

"Come on!"

The pack was close enough so that Hard-Eyes could make out the features in the orange-pink smudges. He turned and ran.

Hard-Eyes thought, This isn't the enemy, this is a bunch of half-starved Parisians hoping we'll be carrying something valuable or edible.

And he thought, The instructors have set us up so the robber pack becomes "the enemy." Like this is a war game where the other side doesn't know it's playing a game.

And then he thought, The fucking instructors are hoping we'll get our asses blown away. Or maybe we'll burn down a few of these problem thugs for them.

. . . As he heard the first popping sounds, and the echoes like a sheet of aluminum shaken to simulate thunder. A piece of turf threw itself in the air near his feet. Irrationally, he leapt back, as if the bit of jumping ground itself were the threat.

Hard-Eyes ran on, Jenkins a little behind and falling farther behind. The trees danced crazily past; the sky made a jerky windshield wiper movement. He ran past a tree and it spat bark at him; a piece of yellow wood-flesh showed where the bullet had scored away bark.

He heard Jenkins returning fire behind him, a thudding rattle, probably no hope of hitting anyone, trying to suppress them.

Thirty feet ahead the trail sank into thickets of blue bushes. There was not much cover at the opening of the trail between the bushes. If the pack got directly behind them, they would simply stop and shoot down the line of the trail, and cut them down.

If they reached that first bend, cutting left into the bushes, they might make it.

But just then Jenkins stumbled and gave a strangely high-pitched cry as he went down, skidding over the iron-hard, iron-cold earth, his rifle clattering. Hard-Eyes wanted to run on, part of his mind already making up excuses.

But he stopped. Huffing and cursing, he turned, going upstream against his own impulse to *get the fuck out*, fighting the current in himself. He heard a scornful humming, and he knew that a bullet had missed his head by an inch or two. Jenkins was getting to his knees, puffing. How could they miss him? He was such a big target! Hard-Eyes bent and tried to help him up, but Jenkins shook his arm off—both of them annoyed—and said, "Just cover me," as he reached for his rifle.

Hard-Eyes turned and opened up without aiming, the automatic rifle jumping in his hand; he felt like a fool when he saw that he'd shot six holes in the bole of a tree between him and the pack. Then he saw one of them coming at him from the right. The man paused about forty feet away and raised the rifle to his shoulder, aiming, like a man shooting at rabbits. He had a big nose, weak chin, gaunt cheeks. He wore a tagged brown cap. He fired. The bullet cut the air overhead. The man struggled to reload his rifle . . .

Hard-Eyes swiveled the HK-21 and fired another burst from the hip. He had ludicrous mental images of himself as a boy taking turns with his big brother cutting the lawn because when you started the lawn-mower it made a noise like the assault rifle. He saw himself spraying a water hose at his brother—shooting an automatic weapon sometimes felt like shooting a high-pressure water hose at someone; when you were close enough to the enemy with no time to aim, you pointed the hose, raking back and forth, and hoped for the best. The man in the brown cap spun half around and staggered, dropped his rifle, but didn't fall. He looked confused, then he turned and ran, holding his side. Wounded. Others were coming on through the trees, spread out. Hard-Eyes emptied the magazine at them, firing in little bursts. They dodged behind trees for cover—and then Hard-Eyes realized that Jenkins was up and running for the brush.

Hard-Eyes ran after him. Someone on his left shot at him. He felt a tightening sensation at the left side of his head: entirely psychosomatic; that was the place he imagined the bullets would hit him. Anticipating the sickening crack of a bullet impacting. Jenkins was about ten feet ahead, running with a wallowing motion, with poor coordination, looking as if he'd like to throw the encumbering rifle away.

And then the brush was sweeping past and Hard-Eyes felt a surge of relief as he turned the bend in the trail. For the moment he was out of their line of sight. Up ahead the trail stretched straight for a ways. That would be a good place to get shot in the back.

"Jenkins!" he hissed. "Hey—go find the instructors, I'm gonna be here in the brush on the left side, left side going this way, don't shoot in it when you come back even if you hear gunfire in it 'cause that'll be me!" He couldn't be sure Jenkins heard, but Hard-Eyes thought he saw him bob his head in response.

Hard-Eyes angled left, then pressed close to the brush, turned to move back up, parallel to the trail. The brush here hooked in a question-mark shape, roughly, and he was moving up the stem of the question mark toward the inside of its hook. The pack was on the other side of the hook. He was breathing hard as much from fear as exertion, his breath smoking out white in front of him, and he thought, What if they see my breath steam above the brush; they'll know my position . . .

He heard a babble of voices in French. He pressed into the wall of brush at the hook of the question mark, biting his lip to keep from yelling when a twig stung his right eye, other tiny jags raking his cheek and neck and hands.

He turned sideways to elbow deeper into the brush, thinking, Maybe this is stupid, maybe the brush will just hold me in place and I won't be able to run, and they'll see me in here and shoot into it till they get me.

He scrunched down, so that the thicker part of the brush was over him, and he felt better about it, because he could move here, the branches making arches over him. He heard voices and footsteps. He began to worm between the thick, horny stems of the bushes toward the bottleneck in the trail, dragging the rifle in his right hand, trying to keep dirt out of it. Pulling himself along on his elbows. The cold ground sent an ache up through his elbow bone. His cheek itched fiercely where the twigs had lashed him. His eye burned where it'd been scratched. It hurt when he blinked.

He could see the trail through the screen of brush now. He brought the rifle up and wedged it into firing position against his shoulder, about thirty degrees out of alignment with his body, his elbows planted, the breech propped in his hands, and sighted at the trail. And then he heard the French voices again and knew they were arguing. Some wanted to go down the trail into the brush. Others thought it might be too dangerous. Then three of them trotted down the trail, in a formation neat as bowling pins. He angled the rifle up a little more and then thought, Shit, I didn't put another clip in it! Idiot!

He laid the gun down, quietly, carefully, as they drew abreast of him. The front man was just fourteen feet away, ten feet beyond the screen of brush. Hard-Eyes reached behind him, fished in his pack. The angle was awkward. He ground his teeth in frustration. The man was walking past. Still fishing in the pack, Hard-Eyes felt something metallic cold under his fingers. He drew it out and looked at it. A full clip. He ejected the other clip and slapped the full one in—and heard a shot. Someone was bending to look in the brush. A rifle barked and a piece of twig lopped neatly in two, fell delicately across his rifle barrel.

Hard-Eyes sighted on the guy crouching in the trail. He took a deep breath, let it out, and when it had gone out of him and his body was still before the next breath, he squeezed the trigger—and at the same time the other man fired. Something sizzled past Hard-Eyes' right cheek. The man who'd shot at him did a little dance of frustration, dancing backward—no, that's not what he was doing, he was staggering back as Hard-Eyes' assault rifle stitched three rounds into his chest. Hard-Eyes expected to see bloodied holes but the places the bullets struck looked like black dots. The guy fell. Hard-Eyes kept firing, raking, centering the sights on the silhouettes of two other running men . . .

The rifle kicking his shoulder, acrid blue smoke clinging to the arching brush just overhead. A twig smoldering from muzzle flash. His ears aching with the detonations, the vibrations.

The men had stopped running. Were all, like him, on the ground; but they were on their backs. One of them making a mewling sound and a pedaling motion with his feet. Another turning to vomit blood. Hand clawing the ground. Twitching. Then not moving at all.

Hard-Eyes waited, but no one else came down the trail. After a while, when his hands were going stiff with cold, his elbows aching, his cheek throbbing, he heard Jenkins shout something. And then French voices behind him, and he knew one as the petulant voice of one of his instructors.

There was another sound: *wham wham wham wham wham wham*. After a moment he realized it was the sound of his heart pounding. He was amazed that he could hear it so clearly.

He wormed up, thrust head and shoulders out of the brush just enough to look down the trail both ways. He saw no one either way, except the dead. The three men he'd shot were all dead now. They weren't silhouettes anymore. But he couldn't help noticing that one of them was just a boy. Maybe fifteen. A boy with a rifle gripped in his white hands.

He stood up and brushed thorns and dried leaves off himself, feeling dizzy but energized.

Thinking, with more wonder than regret: They were just hungry. That's really all it was.

His instructors came around the bend in the trail, their rifles raised.

"Hold your fire!" Hard-Eyes yelled. Or tried to. The words came out mush because his mouth was numb from cold. His right ear felt cold too. Funny: just the right one.

They slowed, looking at him. They were frowning. He knew they'd have some complaint about how he'd done it. Jenkins was right: They didn't like Americans. But Hard-Eyes knew he'd mostly done it right.

Jenkins came lumbering along. He stared at Hard-Eyes open-mouthed.

"Your ear," he said. "You lost an ear."

• • •

Molt was walking down the corridor, thinking he'd got off at the wrong level. It felt like Level 02. He felt heavier here than he should.

The corridor was deserted, which he thought was strange, too. It should be work time in this section. Wilson had said they'd meet on Level 00. He was sure of that. He was sure he'd pressed 00. But he saw a coordination indicator, Level 03, Corridor C13—no indicator for function.

He was in a part of the Colony he'd never been in before. The walls were the same kind of utilitarian studded gray metal you found down in Recycling or around a power station.

I pressed 00, he thought. I'm sure I did.

He turned to go back to the elevator. A section of the ceiling four inches wide slid down to become a wall, in front of him, ceiling down to floor. *Zi-ip*: that fast. It was a transparent wall, plastic but thick, and he knew he'd never be able to break it. He stared, feeling a panic of the sort he hadn't felt since having his first really bad childhood nightmares. He touched the wall to be sure it was real.

He looked around, gut clenching with a growing suspicion.

He'd pressed 00, but the elevator had taken him to 03. The bastards could control the elevators independently. Of course. They had brought him here.

He looked down the hall. There were other sections of the ceiling that looked as if they could slide down. He was sure he hadn't seen a ceiling like that at launch level or at the dorms. But he had seen them somewhere. Around Admin—when you went to Admin to get your pay chit stamped you saw ceilings with those sections in them, and you wondered what they were . . .

He backed away from the transparent wall, turned, and ran. He got forty feet. Ten feet ahead of him another section of wall slid down. He was boxed in.

He slowed, the run becoming a trot and then a walk. He walked up to the wall and pressed his forehead against it, looking down the stretch of empty corridor on the other side. He was breathing hard, clouding the transparent plastic. He slammed his fist against the wall—three times, almost fracturing the bones of his hand. He knew he couldn't break the wall. He hit it to let them know how he felt. Because he knew they were watching him.

He looked at the metal corridor walls between the transparent barriers, wondering . . . what next? Poison gas maybe? Or maybe he'd be ejected into space. No. The liberal wimps in Admin—at least on the Rimpler side of the board—didn't have the honesty to do it that way.

There was a door in one of the walls. It was opening.

Slowly, sliding back into the wall. It whirred faintly.

Molt thought, I'm expected to walk through there. Fuck that.

He moved to where he could look through the door without standing too near it. Through the doorway he saw an almost bare room. There was a rectangular panel in the wall that would be the cot, when it was pulled out. There was a toilet, a sink, a shower stall. Air-conditioning vents—not big enough to crawl through. That was all. A detention cell.

He sat down with his back to the wall across from the door. He wasn't going to give them the satisfaction of seeing him walk in here. Not right away.

He wondered, idly, why they'd done it this way. If they'd tracked him, why hadn't they sent the bulls in to arrest him?

Because the sneaky bastards knew if they'd sent the bulls in, it would have been a political act. It would have martyred him. They had to do it so no one would see. This way they could spread rumors he'd deserted to the other side or gone into hiding. Make him look like a coward.

Wilson. That skeevy runt must have sold him out.

He looked around, wondering where the cameras were. He looked at the ceiling and nodded to himself. Somewhere in the ceiling, one of those panels is two-way.

He stood up and dropped his pants . . .

• • •

In the Admin conference room, they sat around a table shaped like a backward S and watched Molt on the screen. Molt dropped his pants, took hold of his dick, waved it at them, pointed at it with his other hand, and mouthed, clearly, *Suck this, you motherfuckers.*

Claire winced and looked away.

The curves of the S-table were softly contoured. Praeger sat inside the curve across and to the left from Claire. Her father sat in the form-fitting chair across from her. Ganzio, the Brazilian UNIC rep, sat to her immediate left, scowling. He'd been here for an inspection visit—and had been stranded when the Russians had blockaded the Colony. He wanted to go home.

Judith Van Kips, the Afrikaner rep, sat to Gaazio's left. To Van Kips' left sat Messer-Krellman, officially the union rep appointed by UNIC— puppeted by UNIC. Across from Messer Krellman was Scanlon, the Colony Security chief.

The room was lit with soft, shadowless indirection. On Claire's far right, at one end of the cornerless, roughly rectangular room was the screen, and on the screen was Molt. On Claire's left, opposite the screen, was a bronze sculpture of a flock of birds taking flight from a pond.

Claire glanced at Molt, saw he was doing something even more obscene now, and fastened her eyes on the sculpture—with almost equal distaste. The sculpture seemed as false, as abstract and convenient, as UNIC's protestations of classless fairness. Everyone will have a chance here, Admin had been saying over InterColony channel. Everyone will have an opportunity to move into the Open when the time comes. When the blockade is lifted, we'll discuss pay raises and greater recreational credits. But in the meantime . . .

In the meantime they discussed security measures.

"Isolating this man isn't going to isolate the rebellion," Claire said. "The rebellion is widely supported. And it'll continue to be supported in the Colony—as long as we're hypocritical. We complain of not having money to improve their housing, but we sink four million newbux into expanding the security system—well before the rebellion began. And two million more into Admin housing improvements—"

Scanlon said, "Looks like we improved security not a moment too soon. The riots . . . "

"The riots don't *have to be*," Claire said wearily. "There would be no riots if the technickis were given what they were promised in the Articles. The technickis are convinced we've betrayed their trust."

"Are they really convinced?" Praeger asked. "I think not." Praeger was half-bald, and his pinkish head always made Claire think of a pencil eraser rounded by use. His eyes were weak, and he had some kind of phobia of implantation eye operations, so he wore thick, rimless glasses. His lips were bloodless, the same color as the skin of his face. He was thick-bodied, an athletic man—something you wouldn't think he'd be, looking at his head—and muscular under the gray three-piece suit. "They're reacting to stimuli, according to their social programming. They could just as easily react another way—with other stimuli. And if we're wise, we'll provide that."

"And let them know only what we want them to know," Rimpler said suddenly, startling them with his humorous tone. "And if they find out about the rest—tell them it's a communications problem." The "communications problem" was a reference to Praeger's failing to inform Rimpler of the emergency while he was on vacation. Praeger had claimed he'd given the order to a subordinate, who'd failed to implement it by simple oversight. In due course Praeger had produced a subordinate who claimed to be responsible for the error. The man had been put on pay suspension, and probably been well paid off. "Just a little commun-i-ca-shuns prob-lemmmm," Rimpler said, dreamily singsong. Making Claire think of the dormouse at the mad tea party. And making her think, What's happening to him?

Van Kips sighed. "I really think there's no point in dragging that one over the coals again, Doctor." Pursing her lips—the severest expression she allowed herself. Or, perhaps, that Praeger allowed her. Supposedly, she worshiped Praeger. She was an implausibly beautiful woman. Shaped to some artist's conception. Metal-flake blue eyes; a model's narrow, doe-elegant face. Her long, perfectly straight flaxen hair was parted in the middle, to fall over her shoulders with impossible artfulness. She wore a dove-gray suit and white silk blouse; the suit clung to her tall, willowy body when she moved. But now she sat rigidly upright, her hands folded in her lap. Moving only her eyes when she looked at someone.

"At this point," Praeger said, "it's meaningless to try to pin down the cause of the riots. First, we must quell the riots, the vandalism, the strikes. If we come out now and say, Yes, you're right, we've been remiss—well, that would encourage them in the idea that violence is the way to get through to us. The violence must cease before we concede anything."

"I sure have to agree with that, Bill," Scanlon said, in his faint Southern accent. He was a big, boyish-looking man, with tired eyes and a lot of seams in his wide, friendly face. Friendly face, and he'll have a jolly twinkle in his eye, Claire thought, when he gets around to ordering my arrest. "If we give in now we'll have to give in every time they threaten us. Things'll just get worse—for them and for us, too." He shifted in his seat and waited for a response, smiling like an angel. Claire remembered having heard he was some kind of born-again Christian.

"For them and for us, too?" Claire said. "That 'them and us' mentality is one of our problems. I move we release the prisoners Security took during the riots, on their own recognizance. Just to ease the tension a bit. Then we try to set up another meeting with the Radics—and we allow them to send a technicki representative to the meetings. Those aren't such great concessions."

"Jack here," Praeger said, nodding toward Messer-Krellman, "represents them. He's the union rep, is he not?" Messer Krellman was a ferret-faced man with a bored expression and a habit of sighing after each statement.

"Yes, I seem to recall that's my function," he said sarcastically and sighed, looking with mild reproach at Claire.

Claire shook her head. "It should be a *technicki* rep! Born and bred a technicki! Someone who speaks technicki because he was raised in it. Jack has simply lost their confidence. It wouldn't be a concession to—"

"It would," Praeger said. "Because it's on their list of demands. Along with the release of so-called political prisoners. His demands." Nodding now at the screen. At Molt.

"Look at him," Judith Van Kips muttered, shaking her head. "This is one of the technicki leaders. You'd want someone like this at our meetings? *Here?*"

"He's not a technicki, actually," Claire said. "Not precisely . . . We'd pick someone more, um—"

"Look at him," Van Kips repeated, hissing it.

On the screen, Molt was pivoting in a circle, wagging his dick at each point of the compass.

Judith Van Kips made a noise of revulsion. "The man is evidently on drugs."

Rimpler shook his head. "I think not." He chuckled. "Molt knows we're watching, but he doesn't know where we are, so he's saying fuck you in every direction, just to make sure we get the message."

"You seem to approve, Doctor," Ganzio, commented. He was a slim, dark man with a mustache so neat-edged it looked stenciled, and small, forever-shifting black eyes. He wore a gold-colored suit, which everyone privately thought vulgar.

"Oh, no, no," Rimpler said airily. "But one has to admire his nerve."

Molt was making an even ruder gesture now, and Praeger stabbed a finger at the tabletop's terminal. The image on the screen reticulated, folded into itself, was replaced with a view of the Strip. There was a crowd around the café, listening to someone standing on a table speak. Praeger punched for a close-up on the speaker. The image zoomed in. It was Bonham. They didn't have the audio on, but the crowd looked mesmerized by the speech. "Now, there's a fellow with talent," Praeger said. "Suppose he was speaking for *our* benefit. And suppose we controlled the technicki TV channel. If we provided the right stimuli, the technickis would drop their inane, self-indulgent rebellion of their own initiative. Willingly."

Claire felt a chill. She looked to her father, wishing he'd take some active part in supporting their side of things. He was looking wistfully at the refreshment panels in the wall across from him, probably wanting to dial up a cocktail.

Maybe it had been a mistake to insist he come to the meeting at all, Claire thought. He had changed, in the last few years. In the beginning, her father had considered the Colony an extension of himself, and, if anything, he'd been a micromanager, too fervently responsible for its development and maintenance. And then Mother had left him, refusing to make the move to the Colony. He'd considered it a personal betrayal. Claire had been almost relieved by the divorce, really—she'd never felt close to her mother. The woman was cold, self-involved . . . As if to compensate for his wife's betrayal of his dream—she had called the Colony "a vanity unprecedented in the history of mankind" and "a monument to the misbegotten"—Rimpler was more control-compulsive than ever.

But with Terry's death, he began to change. At first he became, by turns, defensive, sullen, inward. That stage had also been marked by feverish overwork.

And then he'd collapsed, in Admin Central Command, after spending twenty straight hours overseeing the installation of the new computer system—and dealing with all the problems that arose while the old system was down. Then came another stage, a sort of manic-depressive period. Claire suspected he was using his pass to the pharmaceuticals storerooms too liberally. He'd begun using intermediaries to hire girls out of Bitchie's and the other technicki Afters. And he became increasingly abstracted at work—as if he was thinking only of getting home, to another sexual psychodrama . . .

Still—he'd done what was expected of him, as an administrator—until the riots, and the news that he'd debauched right through a Colony life-support emergency. He reacted as if the Colony itself had rejected him. And he buckled under the psychological disorientation brought on by the sudden loss of control. Became childlike, prone to tantrums. Now, too often, she found herself forced into the role of chiding mother. He seemed to enjoy seeing her in that role—and at the same time he was afraid of her. More than once she'd found herself sick inside with self-disgust when she'd realized he'd drawn her into some almost incestuous dominatrix-style role-playing. She'd refused to play along—and he withdrew even more into drugs, drink, the search for oblivion—and when the real world intruded on his quest for oblivion, he responded by jeering at the thing he'd devoted most of his life to building . . .

What was it Praeger had said?

. . . provided the right stimuli the technickis would drop their inane, self-indulgent rebellion of their own initiative. Willingly.

Claire took a deep breath and turned to Praeger. "You feel they can be swayed with a broader media campaign. It won't work. Not with the blockade building up the pressure, making everyone a little more afraid every day . . . "

Praeger said, "Media campaign?" He seemed abstracted. He smiled faintly. "Not precisely. Nothing so transparent . . . I think we've lost sight of the problem at this meeting. The problem is sabotage! The problem is a life-support risk! *This is a life-threatening emergency,* Claire! For their sakes as well as—well, for everyone's sakes, we have to take the reins in our hands. All of the reins."

Claire looked at the screen. "They're not so stupid as to damage the life supports. They don't want to eat vacuum any more than we do."

"When people get excited," Praeger said calmly, "they tend to forget common-sense considerations. The thing could get out of control—farther out of control than any one of them would like. An individual technicki is logical—a mob of technickis is not."

"And you propose to defuse them by taking control of their media? That'll only infuriate them!"

"You misunderstand me. I mean—we'll control it indirectly. They won't know we're doing it, if we do it right."

"But that's . . . " She was at a loss for words. She looked again to her father. But he was standing up.

"Well, it's been delightful," Rimpler said. Smiling vacantly. He walked to the door, without saying anything more; without even looking around. Leaving her alone with them.

Claire grated, "Dad! Dammit—take some responsibility!"

He paused at the door, turned to her the look of a bad little boy caught doing what he shouldn't.

She looked away. Scornfully: "Oh, forget it. Go on."

He shrugged, turned, and opened the door. She thought, Maybe he manipulated me. Knew I couldn't handle that little-kid shit. Knew that'd force me to let him go . . .

Scanlon was looking thoughtfully after Rimpler. Something icy-cold about the expression on Scanlon's face frightened Claire.

Rimpler closed the door behind him—effectively closing the door on his leadership in Colony Admin.

Praeger was gazing at the screen. "This man Bonham could be very useful to us," he said.

Messer-Krellman said, "I believe Claire made a motion a little while ago. Does anyone second it? Should we vote on it?" He liked the formalities. And he knew how the vote would turn out.

"Don't bother," Claire said. "I suggest we table any further action till 0900 tomorrow. We all need to think about this. Just keep in mind: the situation is explosive, with the blockade of the Colony. They know the Colony is blockaded, they know resources will run low. They're going to be more insistent than ever—you won't be able to manipulate them." She got up and followed her Father out the door.

She paused for a moment before going out, and looked over her shoulder.

Van Kips and Praeger were looking at the screen. Praeger said something to Van Kips. She nodded.

Feeling helpless, Claire left the room.

• 09 •

Rickenharp put on his dark glasses, because of the way the Walk tugged at him.

The Walk wound through the interlinked Freezone outfloats for a half-mile, looping up and back, a hairpin canyon of arcades crusted with neon and glowflake, holos and screens. It was involuted, intensified by layering and a blaze of colored light.

Stoned, very stoned: Rickenharp and Carmen walked together through the sticky-warm night, almost in step. Yukio walked behind, Willow ahead, and Rickenharp felt like part of a jungle patrol formation. And he had another feeling: that they were being followed, or watched. Maybe it was suggestion, from seeing Yukio and Willow glance over their shoulders now and then . . .

Rickenharp felt a ripple of kinetic force under his feet, an arc of wallow moving in languid whiplash through the flexible streetstuff, telling him that the breakers were up today, the baffles around the artificial island feeling the strain.

The arcades ran three levels above the narrow street; each level had its own sidewalk balcony; people stood at the railing to look down at the segmented snake of street traffic. The stack of arcades funneled a rich wash of scents to Rickenharp: the french-fry toastiness of the fast food; the sweet harshness of smashweed smoke, gyno-smoke, tobacco smoke—the cloy of perfumes; the mixed odors of fish-ka-bob stands, urine, rancid beer, popcorn, sea air; and the faint ozone smell of the small, eerily quiet electric cars jockeying on the street. His first time here, Rickenharp had thought the place smelled wrong for a red light cluster. "It's wimpy," he'd said. Then he'd realized he was missing the bass-bottom of carbon monoxides. There were no combustion cars on Freezone. Some parts of America still permitted pollutive, resource-greedy gasoline cars, and Rickenharp, being a retro, had preferred those places.

The sounds splashed over Rickenharp in a warm wave of cultural fecundity; pop tunes from thudders and wrist-boxes swelled in volume as they passed, the guys exuding the music insignificant in comparison to the noise they carried, the skanky tripping of protosalsa or the calculatedly redundant pulse of minimono.

Rickenharp and Carmen walked beneath a fiberglass arch—so covered with graffiti its original commemorative meaning was lost—and ambled down the milky walkway under the second-story arcade boardwalk. The multinational crowd thickened as they approached the heart of the Walk. The soft lights glowing upward from beneath the polystyrene walkway gave the crowd a 1940s-horror-movie look; even through the dark glasses the place tugged at Rickenharp with a thousand subliminal come-hithers.

Rickenharp was still riding the blue mesc surf, but the wave was beginning to break; he could feel it crumbling under him. He looked at Carmen. She glanced back at him, and they understood one another. She looked around, then nodded toward the darkened doorway of a defunct movie theater, a trash-cluttered recess twenty feet off the street. They went into the doorway; Yukio and Willow stood with their backs to the door, blocking the view from the street, so that Rickenharp and Carmen could each do a double hit of blue mesc. There was a kind of little-kid pleasure in stepping into seclusion to do drugs, a rush of outlaw in-crowd romance to it. On the second sniff the graffiti on the pad-locked, fiberglass doors seemed to writhe with significance. "I'm running low," Carmen said, checking her mesc bottle.

"Running low on drugs? Whoever heard of *that* happening?" Rickenharp said and they both burst in peals of laughter. His mind was racing now, and he felt himself click into the boss blue verbal mode. "You see that graffiti? *You're gonna die young because the ITE took the second half of your life.* You know what that is? I didn't know what ITE was till yesterday, I used to see those things and wonder and then somebody said—"

"Immortality something or other," she said, licking blue mesc off her sniffer.

"Immortality Treatment Elite. Supposedly some people keeping an immortality treatment to themselves because the government doesn't want the public to live too long and overpopulate the place. Another bullshit conspiracy theory."

"You don't believe in conspiracies?"

"I don't know—some. Nothing that far-fetched. But—I think people are being manipulated all the time. Even here . . . this place tugs at you, you know. Like—"

Willow said, "Right, we'll 'ave our sociology class later children, you gotter? Where's this place with the bloke can get us off the fooking island?"

"Yeah, okay, come on," Rickenharp said, leading them back into the flow of the crowd—but seamlessly picking up his blue mesc rap. "I mean, this place is a Times Square, right? You ever read the old novels about that place? That was the archetype. Or some places in Bangkok. I mean, these places are carefully arranged. Maybe subconsciously. But arranged as carefully as Japanese florals, only with the inverse esthetic. Sure, every whining, self-righteous tightassed evangelist who ever preached the diabolic seductiveness of places like this was right—in a way—was fully justified 'cause, yeah, the places titillate and they seduce and they vampirize people. Yeah, they're Venus's-flytraps. Architectural Svengalis. Yes to all the clichés about the bad part of town. All the reverend preachers—Reverend who, Reverend—what's his name?—Rick Crandall . . . "

She looked sharply at him. He wondered why but the mesc swept him on.

"All the preachers are right, but the reason they're right is why they're wrong, too. Everything here is trying to sell you something. Lots of lights and whirligig suction to seduce you into throwing your energy into it—in the form of money. People mostly come here to buy or to be titillated up to the verge of buying. The tension between wanting to buy and the resistance to buying can give you a charge. That's what I get into: I let it tickle my glands, but I hold back from paying into it. You know? Just constant titillation but no orgasm, because you waste your money or you get a social disease or mugged or sold bad drugs or something . . . I mean, anything sold here is pointless bullshit. But it's harder for me to resist tonight . . . "

Because I'm stoned. "Makes you susceptible. Receptive to subliminals worked into the design of the signs, that gaudy kinetics, those fucking on/off bulbs—makes you flash on the old computer-thinking models, binomial thinking, on-off, on-off, blink blink—all those neon tubes, pulling you like the hypnotist's spiral pendant in the old movies . . . And the kinds of colors they use, the energy of the signs, the rate of pulse, the rate of on/offing in the bulbs, all of it's engineered according to principles of psychology the people who make them don't even know they're using, colors that hint about, you know, glandular discharges and tingly chemical flows to the pleasure center . . . like obscenities you pay for in the painted mouth of a whore . . . like video games . . . I mean—"

"I know what you mean," she said, in desperation buying a waxpaper cup of beer. "You must be thirsty after that monologue. Here." She shoved the foaming cup under his nose.

"Talking too much. Sorry." He drank off half the beer in three gulps, took a breath, finished it, and it was paradise for a moment. A wave of quietude soothed him—and then evaporated mesc burned through again. Yeah, he was wired.

"I don't mind listening to you talk," she said, "except you might say too much, and I'm not sure if we're being scanned."

Rickenharp nodded sheepishly, and they walked on. He crushed the cup in his hand, began methodically to shred it as they went.

Rickenharp luxuriated in the colors of the place, colors that mixed and washed over the crowd, making the stream of hats and heads into a living swatch of iridescent gingham; shining the cars into multicolored lumps of mobile ice.

You take the word *lurid*, Rickenharp thought, and you put it raw in a vat filled with the juice of the word *appeal*. You leave it and let the acids of appeal leach the colors out of *lurid*, so that you get a kind of gasoline rainbow on the surface of the vat. You extract the petro-rainbow on the surface of the vat with cheesecloth and strain it into a glass tube, dilute heavily with oil of cartoon innocence and extract of pure subjectivity. Now run a current through the glass tube and all the other tubes of the neon signs interlacing Freezone's Walk.

The Walk, stretching ahead of them, was itself almost a tube of colored lights, converging in a kaleidoscope; the concave fronts of the buildings to either side were flashing with a dozen varieties of signs. The sensual flow of neon data in primary colors was broken at cunningly irregular intervals by stark trademark signs: Synthlife Systems and Microsoft-Apple and Nike and Coca-Cola and Warner Amex and NASA Chemco and Brazilian Exports Intl and Exxon Electrics and Nessio. In all of that only one hint of the war: two unlit signs, FABRIZZIO and ALLINNE—an Italian and a French company, killed by the Russian blockades. The signs were unlit, dead.

They passed a TV-shirt shop; tourists walked out with their shirts flashing video imagery, fiberoptics woven into the shirtfront playing the moving sequence of your choice.

Sidewalk hawkers of every race sold beta candy spiked with endorphins; sold shellfish from Freezone's own beds, tempura'd and skewered; sold holocube pornography key rings; sold instapix of you and your wife, oh that's your boyfriend . . . Despite the nearness of Africa, black Africans were few here: Freezone Admin considered them a security risk and few on the contiguous coast could afford the trip. The tourists were mostly Japanese, Canadian, Brazilians—riding the crest of the Brazilian boom—South Koreans, Chinese, Arabs, Israelis, and a smattering of Americans; damned few Americans anymore, with the depression. Screens scanned them, one of them caught Rickenharp with a facial recognition program and on it a sexy animated Asian woman cooed, *"Rick Rickenharp—try Wilcox Subsensors and walk in a glow of excitement . . . "*

As they got deeper into the Walk the atmosphere became even more hot-house. It was a multicolored steam bath. The air was sultry, the various smokes of the place warping the neon glow, filtering and smearing the colors of signs and TV shirts and DayGlo jewelry. High up, between the not-quite-fitted jigsaw parts of signs and lights, were blue-black slices of night sky. At street level the jumble was given shape and borders by the doors opening on either side: by people using the doors to check out malls and stimsmoke parlors and memento shops and cubey theaters and, especially, tingler galleries. Dealers drifted up like reef fish, nibbling and moving on, pausing to offer, "DH, gotcher good Dee Ech": Direct Hookup, illegal cerebral pleasure center stimulation. And drugs: synth-cocaine and smokeable herbs; stims, and downs. About half of the dealers were burn artists, selling baking soda or pseudostims. The dealers tended to hang on to Rickenharp and Carmen because they looked like users, and Carmen was wearing a sniffer. Blue mesc and sniffers were illegal, but so were lots of things the Freezone cops ignored. You could wear a sniffer, carry the stuff, but the understanding was, you don't use it openly, you step into someplace discreet.

And whores of both sexes cruised the street, flagrantly soliciting. Freezone Admin was supposed to regulate all prostitution, but black-market pros were tolerated as long as somebody paid off the beat security and as long as they didn't get too numerous.

The crowd streaming past was a perpetually unfolding revelation of human variety. It unfolded again and a specialty pimp appeared, pushing a man and woman ahead of him; they had to hobble because they were straitjacket-packaged in black-rubber bondage gear. Their faces were ciphers in blank black-rubber masks; aluminum racks held their mouths wide-open, intended to be inviting, but to Rickenharp whispered to Carmen, "Victims of a mad orthodontist!" and she laughed.

Studded down the streets were Freezone security guards in bullet-proofed uniforms that made Rickenharp think of baseball umpires, faces caged in helmets. Their guns were locked by combination into their holsters; they were trained to open the four-digit combination in one second.

Mostly they stood around, gossiped on their helmet radios. Now two of them hassled a sidewalk three-card-monte artist—a withered little black guy who couldn't afford the baksheesh—pushing him back and forth between them, bantering one another through helmet amplifiers, their voices booming over the discothud from the speakers on the download shops:

"WHAT THE FUCK YOU DOING ON MY BEAT SCUMBAG. HEY BILL YOU KNOW WHAT THIS GUY'S DOING ON MY BEAT."

"FUCK NO I DUNNO WHAT'S HE DOING ON YOUR BEAT."

"HE'S MAKING ME SICK WITH THIS RIP-OFF MONTE BULLSHIT IS WHAT HE'S DOING."

One of them hit the guy too hard with the waldo-enhanced arm of his riot suit and the monte dealer spun to the ground like a top running out of momentum, out cold.

"LOITERING ON THE ZONE'S WALKS, YOU SEE THAT BILL."

"I SEE AND IT MAKES ME SICK JIM."

The bulls dragged the little guy by the ankle to a lozenge-shaped kiosk in the street and pushed him into a man-capsule. They sealed the capsule, scribbled out a report, pasted it onto the capsule's hard plastic hull. Then they shoved the man-capsule into the kiosk's chute. The capsule was sucked by mail-tube principle to Freezone Lockup.

"Looks like they're using some kind of garbage disposal to get rid of people here," Carmen said when they were past the cops.

Rickenharp looked at her. "You weren't nervous walking by the cops. So it's not them we're avoiding, huh?"

"Nope."

"You wanna tell me who it is we're supposed to be avoiding?"

"Uh-uh, I do not."

"How do you know these out-of-town cops you're worried about haven't gone to the locals and recruited some help?"

"Yukio says they won't, they don't want anybody to scan what they're doing here because the Freezone admin don't like 'em."

Rickenharp guessed: the *who* they were avoiding was the Second Alliance. Freezone's chairman was Jewish. The Second Alliance could *meet* in Freezone—the idea was, the place was open to anyone for meetings, or recreation; anyone, even people the Freezone boss would like to see gassed—but the SA couldn't *operate* here, except covertly.

The fucking SA bulls! Shit! . . . The blue mesc worked with his paranoia. Adrenaline spurted, making his heart bang. He began to feel claustrophobic in the crowd; began to see patterns in the movement around him, patterns charged with meaning superimposed by his own fear-galvanized mind. Patterns that taunted him with, *The SA's close behind.* He felt a stomach-churning combination of horror and elation.

All night he'd worked hard at suppressing thoughts of the band. And of his failure to make the band work. *He'd lost the band.* And it was almost impossible to make anyone understand why that was, to him, like a man losing his wife and children. And there was the career. All those years of pushing for that band, struggling to program a place for it in the Grid. Shot to hell now, his identity along with it. He knew, somehow, that it would be futile to try to put together another band. The Grid just didn't want him; and he didn't want the fucking Grid. And the elation was this: that ugly pit of displacement inside him closed up, was just gone, when he thought about the SA bulls. The bulls threatened his life, and the threat caught him up in something that made it possible to forget about the band. *He'd found a way out.*

But the horror was there, too. If he got caught up in this . . . if the SA bulls got hold of him . . .

Fuck it. What else did he have?

He grinned at Carmen, and she looked blankly back at him, wondering what the grin meant.

So now what? he asked himself. *Get to the OmeGaity. Find Frankie.* Frankie was the doorway.

But it was taking so long to get there. Thinking. The drug's fucking with your sense of duration. Heightened perception makes it seem to take longer.

The crowd seemed to get thicker, the air hotter, the music louder, the lights brighter. It was getting to Rickenharp. He began to lose the ability to make the distinction between things in his mind and things around him. He began to see himself as an enzyme molecule floating in some macrocosmic bloodstream—the sort of things that always OD'd him when he did an energizing drug in a sensory-overflow environment.

What am I?

Sizzling orange-neon arrows on the marquee overhead seemed to crawl off the marquee, slither down the wall, down into the sidewalk, snaking to twine around his ankles, to try to tug him into a tingler emporium. He stopped and stared. The emporium's display holos writhed with fleshy intertwinings; breasts and buttocks jutted out at him, and he responded against his will, like all the clichés, getting hard in his pants: visual stimuli; monkey see, monkey respond. He thought: *Bell rings and dog salivates.*

He looked over his shoulder. Who was that guy with the sunglasses back there? Why was he wearing sunglasses at night? Maybe he's SA—

Noooo, man. *I'm* wearing sunglasses at night. Means nothing.

He tried to shrug off the paranoia, but somehow it was twined into the undercurrent of sexual excitement. Every time he saw a whore or a pornographic video sign, the paranoia hooked into him as a kind of scorpion stinger on the tail of his adolescent surge of arousal. And he could feel his nerve ends begin to extrude from his skin. After having been clean so long, his-blue mesc tolerance was low.

Who am I? Am I the crowd?

He saw Carmen look at something in the street, then whisper urgently to Yukio.

"What's the matter?" Rickenharp asked.

She whispered, "You see that silver thing? Kind of a silvery fluttering? There—over the cab . . . Just look, I don't wanna point."

He looked into the street. A cab was pulling up at the curb. Its electric motor whined as it nosed through a heap of refuse. Its windows were dialed to mercuric opacity. Above and a little behind it a chrome bird hovered, its wings a hummingbird blur. It was about thrush-sized, and it had a camera-lens instead of a head. "I see it. Hard to say whose it is."

"I think it's run from inside that cab. That's like them. They'll send it after us from there. Come on." She ducked into a tingler gallery; Willow and Yukio and Rickenharp followed her. They had to buy a swipe card to get in. A bald, jowly old dude it the counter took the cards, swiped them without looking, his eyes locked on a wrist-TV screen. On his wrist a miniature newscaster was saying in a small tinny voice, " . . . attempted assassination of SA director Crandall today . . . " Something mumbled, distorted. " . . . Crandall is in serious condition and heavily guarded at Freezone Medicenter . . . "

The turnstile spun for them and they went into the gallery. Rickenharp heard Willow mutter to Yukio, "The bastard's still alive."

Rickenharp put two and two together.

The tingler gallery was predominantly fleshtone, every available vertical surface taken up by emulsified nude humanity. As you passed from one photo or holo to the next, you saw the people in them were inverted or splayed or toyed with, turned in a thousand variations on coupling, as if a child had been playing with unclothed dolls and left them scattered. A sodden red light hummed in each booth: the light snagged you, a wavelength calculated to produce sexual curiosity. In each "privacy booth" was a screen and a tingler. An oxygen mask that dropped from a ceiling trap pumped out a combination of amyl nitrite and pheromones. The tingler looked like a twentieth-century vacuum cleaner hose with an oversized salt-shaker top on one end: You watched the pictures, listened to the sounds, and ran the tingler over your erogenous zones; the tingler stimulated the appropriate nerve ends with a subcutaneously penetrative electric field, very precisely attenuated. You could pick out the guys in the health-club showers who'd used a tingler too long: use it more than the "recommended thirty-five-minute limit" and it made your skin look sunburned. One time Rickenharp's drummer had asked him if he had any lotion: "I got 'tingler dick,' man."

"To phrase it in the classic manner," Yukio said abruptly, "is there another way out of here?"

Rickenharp nodded. "Yeah . . . Uh—somewhere."

Willow was staring at a teaser blurb under a still-image of two men, a woman and a goat. He took a step closer, squinting at the goat.

"You looking for a family resemblance, Willow?" Rickenharp said.

"Shut your 'ole, ya retro greaser."

The booth sensed his nearness: the images on the sample placard began to move, bending, licking, penetrating, reshaping themselves with a weirdly formalized awkwardness; the booth's light increased its red glow, puffed out a tease of pheromone and amyl nitrite, trying to seduce him.

"Well, where *is* the other door?" Carmen hissed.

"Huh?" Rickenharp looked at her. "Oh! I'm sorry, I'm so—uh I'm not sure." He glanced over his shoulder, lowered his voice. "The bird didn't follow us in."

Yukio murmured, "The electric fields on the tinglers confuse the bird's guidance system. But we must keep a step ahead."

Rickenharp looked around—but he was still stoned: the maze of black booths and fleshtones seemed to twist back on itself, to turn ponderously, as if going down some cubistic drain . . .

"I will find the other door," Yukio said. Rickenharp followed him gratefully. He wanted out.

They hurried through the narrow hall between tingler booths. The customers moved pensively—or strolled with excessive nonchalance—from one booth to another, reading the blurbs, scanning the imagery, sorting through fetishistic indexings for their personal libido codes, not looking at one another except peripherally, carefully avoiding the margins of personal-space.

Chuffing, sighing music played from somewhere; the red lights were like the glow of blood in a hand held over a bright light. But the place was rigorously Calvinistic in its obstacle course of tacit regulations. And here and there, at the turns in the hot, narrow passageways between rows of booths, bored security guards rocked on their heels and told the browsers, *No loitering please, you can purchase more time at the front desk.*

Rickenharp flashed that the place wanted to drain his sexuality, as if the vacuum-cleaner hoses in the booths were going to vacuum his orgone energy, leave him chilled as a gelding.

Get the fuck out of here.

Then he saw EXIT, and they rushed for it, through it.

They were in an alley. They looked up, around, half expecting to see the metal bird. No bird. Only the gray intersection of styroconcrete planes, stunningly monochrome after the hungry chromatics of the tingler gallery.

They walked out to the end of the alley, stood for a moment watching the crowd. It was like standing on the bank of a torrent. Then they stepped into it, Rickenharp, blue mesc'd, fantasizing that he was getting wet with the liquefied flesh of the rush of humanity as he steered by sheer instinct to his original objective: the OmeGaity.

They pushed through the peeling black chessboard doors into the dark mustiness of the OmeGaity's entrance hall, and Rickenharp gave Carmen his coat to hide her bare breasts. "Men only, in here," he said, "but if you don't shove your femaleness into their line of sight, they might let us slide."

Carmen pulled the jacket on, zipped it up—very carefully—and Rickenharp gave her his dark glasses.

Rickenharp banged on the window of the screening kiosk beside the locked door that led into the cruising rooms. Beyond the glass, someone looked up from a fat-screen TV. "Hey, Carter," Rickenharp said.

"Hey." Carter grinned at him. Carter was, by his own admission, "a trendy faggot." He was flexicoated battleship gray with white trim, a minimono style. But the real M'n'Ms would have spurned him for wearing a luminous earring—it blinked through a series of words in tiny green letters—*Fuck... you... if... you... don't... like... it... Fuck... you... if*—and they'd have considered that unforgivably "Griddy." And anyway Carter's wide, froggish face didn't fit the svelte minimono look. He looked at Carmen. "No girls, Harpie."

"Drag queen," Rickenharp said. He slipped a folded twenty newbux note through the slot in the window. "Okay?"

"Okay, but she takes her chances in there," Carter said, shrugging. He tucked the twenty in his charcoal bikini briefs.

"Sure."

"You hear about Geary?"

"Nope."

"Snuffed hisself with China White 'cause he got green pissed."

"Oh, shit." Rickenharp's skin crawled. His paranoia flared up again, and to soothe it he said, "Well, I'm not gonna be licking anybody's anything. I'm looking for Frankie."

"That asshole. He's there, holding court or something. But you still got to pay admission, honey."

"Sure," Rickenharp said.

He took another twenty newbux out of his pocket, but Carmen put a hand on his arm and said, "We'll cover this one." She slapped a twenty down.

Carter took it, chuckling. "Man, that queen got some real nice larynx work." Knowing damn well she was a girl. "Hey, Rick, you still playing at the—"

"I blew the gig off," Rickenharp cut in, trying to head off the pain. The boss blue had peaked and left him feeling like he was made out of cardboard inside, like any pressure might make him buckle. His muscles twitched now and then, fretful as restive children scuffing feet. He was crashing. He needed another hit. When you were up, he thought, things showed you their frontsides, their upsides; when you peaked, things showed you their hideous insides. When you were down, things showed you their backsides, their downsides. File it away for lyrics.

Carter pressed the buzzer that unlocked the door. It razzed them as they walked through.

Inside it was dim, hot, humid.

"I think your blue was cut with coke or meth or something," Rickenharp told Carmen as they walked past the dented lockers. "Cause I'm crashing harder than I should be."

"Yeah, probably . . . What'd he mean 'he got green pissed'?"

"Positive test for AIDS-three. The HIV that kills you in three weeks. You drop this testing pill in your urine and if the urine turns green you got AIDS. There's no cure for the new HIV yet, won't be in three weeks, so the guy . . . " He shrugged.

"What the 'ell is this place?" Willow asked.

In a low voice Rickenharp told him, "It's a kind of bathless gay baths, man. Cruising places for 'mos. But about a lotta the people are straights who ran out of bux at the casinos, use it for a cheap place to sleep, you know?"

"Yeah? And 'ow come you know all about it, 'ey?"

Rickenharp smirked. "You saying I'm gay? The horror, the horror."

Someone in a darkened alcove to one side laughed at that.

Willow was arguing with Yukio in an undertone. "Oi don't like it, that's all, fucking faggots got a million fucking diseases. Some side o' beef with a tan going to wank on me leg."

"We just walk through, we don't touch," Yukio said. "Rickenharp knows what to do."

Rickenharp thought, *Hope so.*

Maybe Frankie could get them safely off Freezone, maybe not.

The walls were black pressboard. It was a maze like a tingler gallery but in the negative. There was a more ordinary red light; there was the peculiar scent that lots of skin on skin generates and the accretion of various smokes, aftershaves, cheap soap, and an ingrained stink of sweat and semen gone rancid. The walls stopped at ten feet up and the shadows gathered the ceiling into themselves, far overhead. It was a converted warehouse space, with a strange vibe of stratification: claustrophobia layered under agoraphobia. They passed mossy dark cruising warrens. Faces blurred by anonymity turned to monitor them as they passed, expressions cool as video cameras.

They strolled through the game room with its stained pool tables and stammering holo-games, its prized-open vending machines. Peeling from the walls between the machines were posters of men—caricatures with oversized genitals and muscles that seemed themselves a kind of sexual organ, faces like California surfers. Carmen bit her finger to keep from laughing at them, marveling at the idiosyncratic narcissism of the place.

They passed through a cruising room designed to look like a barn. Two men ministered to one another on a wooden bench inside a "horse stall" with wet fleshy noises. Willow and Yukio looked away. Carmen stared at the gay sex in fascination. Rickenharp walked past without reacting, led the way through other midnight nests of pawing men; past men sleeping on benches and couches, sleepily slapping unwanted hands away.

And found Frankie in the TV lounge.

The TV lounge was bright, well-lit, the walls cheerful yellow. The OmeGaity was cheap—there were no holo cubes. There were motel-standard living-room lamps on end tables; a couch; a regular color screen showing a rock video channel; and a bank of monitors on the wall. It was like emerging from the underworld. Frankie was sitting on the couch, waiting for customers.

Frankie dealt on a porta-terminal he'd plugged into a Grid-socket. The buyer gave him an account number or credit card; Frankie checked the account, transferred the funds into his own (registered as consultancy fees), and handed over the packets.

The walls of the lounge were inset with video monitors; one showed the orgy room, another a porn vid, another ran a Grid network satellite channel. On that one a newscaster was yammering about the attempted assassination, this time in technicki, and Rickenharp hoped Frankie wouldn't notice it and make the connection. Frankie the Mirror was into taking profit from whatever came along, and the SA paid for information.

Frankie sat on the torn blue vinyl couch, hunched over the pocket-sized terminal on the coffee table. Frankie's customer was a disco 'mo with a blue sharkfin flare, steroid muscles, and a white karate robe; the guy was standing to one side, staring at the little black canvas bag of blue packets on the coffee table as Frankie completed the transaction.

Frankie was black. His bald scalp had been painted with reflective chrome; his head was a mirror, reflecting the TV screens in fish-eye miniature. He wore a pinstriped three-piece gray suit. A real one, but rumpled and stained like he'd slept in it, maybe fucked in it. He was smoking a Nat Sherman cigarette, down to the gold filter. His synthcoke eyes were demonically red. He flashed a yellow grin at Rickenharp. He looked at Willow, Yukio, and Carmen, made a mocking scowl. "Fucking narcs—get more fancy with their setups every day. Now they got four agents in here, one of 'em looks like my man Rickenharp, other three took like refugees and a computer designer. But that Jap hasn't got a camera. Gives him away."

"What's this 'ere about—" Willow began.

Rickenharp made a dismissive gesture that said, *He isn't serious, dumbshit.* "I got two purchases to make," he announced and looked at Frankie's buyer. The buyer took his packet and melted back into the warrens.

"First off," Rickenharp said, taking his card from his wallet, "I need some blue blow, three grams."

"You got it, homeboy." Frankie ran a lightpen over the card, then punched a request for data on that account. The terminal asked for the private code number. Frankie handed the terminal to Rickenharp, who punched in his code, then erased it from visual. Then he punched to transfer funds to Frankie's account. Frankie took the terminal and double-checked the transfer. The terminal showed Rickenharp's adjusted balance and Frankie's gain.

"That's gonna eat up half your account, Harpie," Frankie said.

"I got some prospects."

"I heard you and Mose parted company."

"How'd you get that so fast?"

"Ponce was here buying."

"Yeah, well—now I've dumped the dead weight, my prospects are even better." But as he said it he felt dead weight in his gut.

"'S your bux, man." Frankie reached into the canvas carry-on, took out three pre-weighed bags of blue powder. He looked faintly amused. Rickenharp didn't like the look. It seemed to say, *I knew you'd come back, you sorry little wimp.*

"Fuck off, Frankie," Rickenharp said, taking the packets.

"What's this sudden squall of discontent, my child?"

"None of your business, you smug bastard."

Frankie's smugness tripled. He glanced speculatively at Carmen and Yukio and Willow. "There's something more, right?"

"Yeah. We got a problem. My friends here—they're getting off the raft. They need to slip out the back way so Tom and Huck don't see 'em."

"Mmm. What kind of net's out for them?"

"It's a private outfit. They'll be watching the copter port, everything legit . . ."

"We had another way off," Carmen said suddenly. "But it was blown—"

Yukio silenced her with a look. She shrugged.

"Verr-rry mysterious," Frankie said. "But there are safety limits to curiosity. Okay. Three grand gets you three berths on my next boat out. My boss's sending a team to pick up a shipment. I can probably get 'em on there. That's going *east*, though. You know? Not west or south or north. One direction and one only."

"That's what we need," Yukio said, nodding, smiling. Like he was talking to a travel agent. "East. Someplace Mediterranean."

"Malta," Frankie said. "Island of Malta. Best I can do." Yukio nodded. Willow shrugged. Carmen assented by her silence.

Rickenharp was sampling the goods. In the nose, to the brain, and right to work. Frankie watched him placidly. Frankie was a connoisseur of the changes drugs made in people. He watched the change of expression on Rickenharp's face. He watched Rickenharp's visible shift into ego drive.

"We're gonna need four berths, Frankie," Rickenharp said.

Frankie raised an eyebrow. "You better decide after that shit wears off."

"I decided before I took it," Rickenharp said, not sure if it was true.

Carmen was staring at him. He took her by the arm and said, "Talk to you a minute?" He led her out of the lounge, into the dark hallway. The skin of her arm was electrically sweet under his fingers. He wanted more. But he dropped his hand from her and said, "Can you get the bux?"

She nodded. "I got a fake card, dips into—well, it'll get it for us. I mean, for me and Yukio and Willow. I'd have to get authorization to bring you. And I can't do that."

"Know what? I won't help you get out otherwise."

"You don't know—"

"Yeah, I do. I'm ready to go. I just go back and get my guitar."

"The guitar'll be a burden where we're going. We're going into occupied territory, to get where we want to be. You'd have to leave the guitar."

He almost wavered at that. "I'll check it into a locker. Pick it up someday. Thing is—if they watched us with that bird, they saw me with you. They'll assume I'm part of it. Look, I know what you're doing. The SA's looking for you. Right? So that means you're—"

"Okay, hold it, shit; keep your voice down. Look—I can see where maybe they marked you, so you got to get off the raft, too. Okay, you go with us to Malta. But then you—"

"I got to stay with you. The SA's everywhere. They marked me."

She took a deep breath and let it out in a soft whistle through her teeth. She stared at the floor. "You can't do it." She looked at him. "You're not the type. You're a fucking *artist.*"

He laughed. "You say that like it's the lowest insult you can come up with. Look—I can do it. I'm going to do it. The band is dead. I need to . . . " He shrugged helplessly. Then he reached up and took her sunglasses off, looked at her shadowed eyes. "And when I get you alone I'm going to batter your cervix into jelly."

She punched him hard in the shoulder. It hurt. But she was smiling. "You think that kind of talk turns me on? Well, it does. But it's not going to get you into my pants. And as for going with us—What you think this is? You've seen too many movies."

"The SA's marked me, remember? What else can I do?"

"That's not a good enough reason to . . . to become part of this thing. You got to really believe in it, because *it's hard.* This is not a celebrity game show."

"Jesus. Give me a break. I know what I'm doing."

That was bullshit. He was trashed. He was blown. *My computer's experiencing a power surge. Motherboard fried. Hell, then burn out the rest.*

He was living a fantasy. But he wasn't going to admit it. He repeated, "I know what I'm doing."

She snorted. She stared at him. "Okay," she said.

And after that everything was different.

Part Two:
KESSLER

• 10 •

His name was James Kessler, and he was walking east on Fourteenth Street, looking for something. He wasn't sure what he was looking for. He was walking through a misty November rain. The street was almost deserted. He was looking for something, something, the brutally colorless word *something* hung heavily in his mind like an empty frame.

What he thought he wanted was to get in, out of the weather. Walking in rain made him feel naked, somehow. And acid rain, he thought, could make you naked, if you wore the kind of syn-threads that reacted with the acids.

Up ahead the eternal neon butterfly of a Budweiser sign glowed sultry orange-red and blue; the same design since sometime in the twentieth century. He angled across the sidewalk, pitted concrete the color of dead skin, hurrying toward the sign, toward the haven of a bar. The rain was already beginning to sting. He closed his eyes against it, afraid it would burn his corneas.

He pushed through the smudge-bruised door into the bar. The bartender glanced up, nodded to himself, and reached under the counter for a towel; he passed the towel across to Kessler. The towel was treated with acid-absorbents; it helped immediately.

"Get any in your eyes?" the bartender asked with no real concern.

"No, I don't think so." He handed the towel back. "Thanks." The tired-faced men drinking at the bar hardly glanced at Kessler. He was unremarkable: round-faced, with short black hair streaked blue-white to denote his work in video editing; large friendly brown eyes, soft red mouth pinched now with worry; a standard printout grey-blue suit.

The bartender said something else, but it didn't register. Kessler was staring at the glowing green lozenge of a credit transferal kiosk in the back of the dim, old-fashioned bar. He crossed to it and stepped in; the door hissed shut behind him. The small screen on the front of the fone lit up, and its electronic letters asked him: Do you want Call or Entry?

What did he want? Why had he come to the kiosk? He wasn't sure. But it felt right. A wave of reassurance had come over him ... *Ask it what your balance is*, a soundless voice whispered to him. Again he felt a wave of reassurance. But he thought: Something's out of place ...

He knew his mind as a man knows his cluttered desk; he knows when someone has moved something on his desk—or in his mind. And someone had.

He punched ENTRY and it asked him his account number and entry pin. He punched the digits in, then told it he wanted to see his bank balance. It told him to wait. Numbers appeared on the screen.

$NB 760,000.

He stared at it. He punched for error check and confirmation.

The bank's computer insisted that he had 760,000 newbux in his bank account.

There should be only 4,000.

Something was missing from his memory; something had been added to his bank account.

They tampered with me, he thought, and then they paid me for it.

He requested the name of the depositor. The screen told him: UNRECORDED.

Julie. Talk to Julie. There was just no one else he discussed his projects with till they were patented and on-line. No one. His wife had to know.

Julie. He could taste her name in his mouth. Her name tasted like bile.

Julie had been home only a few minutes, Kessler decided, as he closed the door behind him. Her coat was draped over the back of the couch, off-white on off-white. She liked things off-white or gray or powder blue, and that's how the place was decorated. Kessler liked rich, earthy colors, but she considered them vulgar, so that was that.

She was bent down to the minifridge behind the breakfast bar. She stood up, a frosted bottle of Stolichnaya in her hand. "Hi, Jimmy."

She almost never called him Jimmy.

Julie came out with a vodka straight-up and a twist of lime for each of them. He'd learned to like vodka. She padded across the powder-blue rug in bare feet, small feet sexy in sheer hose; she was tall and slender and long-necked. Her hair was the yellow of split pine, cut short as a small boy's, and parted on the side. She was English and looked it; her eyes were immaculate blue crystals. She wore her silk-lined, coarse-fiber, off-white dress suit. She looked more natural in her suits than in anything else. She had "casuals" to wear at home, but somehow she never wore them. Maybe because that would be a concession to home life, would almost be a betrayal of the corporation family she belonged to. Like having children. What was it she said about having children? *If you don't mind, I'll continue to resist the programming of my biological computer. When DNA talks, I don't listen. I don't like being pushed into something by a molecule.*

He took off his coat, hung it up, and sat down beside her on the couch.

The vodka, chilled with no ice, waited for him on the glass coffee table. He took a drink and said, "There's seven hundred and sixty thousand newbux in my bank account." He looked at her. "What did they take?"

Her eyes went a little glassy. "Seven hundred and sixty thousand? Computer error."

"You know it's not." He took another sip. The Stoli was syrupy thick from being kept in the freezer. "What did you tell Worldtalk?"

"Are you accusing me of something?" She said it with her icy Oxbridge incredulousness then, like, I can't believe anyone could be so painfully unsophisticated.

"I'm accusing Worldtalk. And . . . you're *theirs*. They do as they like with you, Julie. If Worldtalk says it's not *team-playing* to have kids, you don't have kids. If Worldtalk says listen for anything that might be useful, you listen. Even at home. You know, you wouldn't have had to quit your job—I can understand you wanting to have a career. We could have had the kid with a surrogate or an artificial womb. Gotten a nanny. They don't want employees, at Worldtalk, they want to *own you . . .* "

"It's childish to go over and over this. Worldtalk has nothing to do with my decision not to have children. I worked *eight years—*"

"I know it by rote: you worked eight years to be assistant second vice prez in the country's biggest PR and advertising outfit. You tell me *having children* is demeaning! Eight years licking Grimwald's boots—that's demeaning! Going to Worldtalk's Family Sessions for hours at a time—"

She stood up, arms rigid at her sides. "Well, why not! Corporation families *last*."

"A 'corporate family' isn't a real family. They're using you. Look what they got you to do! To *me!*"

"You got some seven hundred thousand newbux. That's more than you would ever have made on any of your harebrained schemes. If you worked for one of the big companies you'd be making decent money in the first place. You insist on being freelance, so you're left out in the cold, and you should be grateful for what they—" She snipped the sentence in two with a brisk sibilance and turned away.

"So we've dropped the pretenses now. You're saying I should be grateful for the money Worldtalk gave me. Julie—*what did they take from my memory?*"

"I don't *know!* You didn't tell me what you were working on and—anyway I don't believe they took anything. I—goddammit." She went to the bathroom to pointedly take her Restem, making a lot of noise opening the prescription bottle so he'd hear and know it was his fault she had to take a tranquilizer.

• • •

Kessler was in a bar with his attorney, Bascomb. Herman Bascomb was drunk, and drugged. The disorder of his mind seemed splashed onto the room around him: the dancers, the lights, the holograms that made it look, in the smoky dimness, as if someone was there dancing beside you who wasn't. A touristy couple on the dance floor stopped and stared at another couple: horned, half-human, half-reptile, she with her tongue darting from between rouged lips; he with baroque fillips of fire flicking from his flattened nostrils. The touristy couple laughed off their embarrassment when the DJ turned off the holo and the demon couple vanished.

Bascomb chuckled and sucked some of his cocaine fizz through a straw that lit up with miniature advertisements when it was used, lettering flickering luminous green up and down its length. Bascomb was young, tanned, and preppie; he wore an iridescent Japanese Action Suit.

Sitting beside him, Kessler squirmed on his barstool and ordered another scotch. He wasn't comfortable with Bascomb like this. Kessler was used to seeing Bascomb in his office, a neat component of Featherstone, Pestlestein, and Bascomb, Attorneys at Law, friendly but not too friendly, intense but controlled.

My own fault, Kessler told himself; chase the guy down when he's off work, hassle his wife till she tells me where he hangs out, find out things I don't want to know. Like the fact that he's bisexual and flirting with the waiter.

The bar was circular, rotating slowly through the club, leaving the dance floor behind now to arrive at the cruising rooms. As they talked it turned slowly past flesh-pink holographic porn squirmings and edged into the soft music lounge. Each room had its own idiosyncratic darkness, shot through with the abstracted glamour of the candy-apple-red and hot-pink and electric-blue neon running up the corners to zigzag the ceiling like a time-lapse photo of nighttime traffic. The kitschy design was another annoyance for Kessler.

Bascomb turned on his stool to look at the porn and the live copulation; his mouth was open in a lax smile. Kessler looked over his shoulder. Again in the dimness the holos were nearly indistinguishable from the real article; a drunken swinger tried to fondle a woman with four breasts, only to walk through her, discovering her unreal. "Do we have to talk here?" Kessler asked, turning back to the bar.

Bascomb ignored the question and returned to an earlier one. "The bottom line, Jim, is that you are a nobody. Now, if you were, say, a Nobel-Prize-winning professor at Stanford, we might be able to get you your day in court, we might get a grand jury to investigate the people at Worldtalk . . . " Bascomb was talking without looking away from the intermingling porn and people. "But as it is you're a mildly successful video editor who makes a hobby of working up a lot of rather ingenuous media theories. Every day some crank or someone looking for attention announces a Great Idea has been stolen from their brains, and ninety-nine percent of the time they turn out to be paranoids or liars or both. I'm not saying you're a paranoid or a liar. *I* believe you. I'm just saying I'm probably the only one who will."

"But I have the seven hundred sixty thousand NB . . . that shouldn't be there. That ought to be proof of something."

"Did you request the name of the depositor?"

"Unrecorded."

"Then how are you going to prove a connection?"

"I don't know. But I know an idea was stolen from me. I want it back, Bascomb. And I can't work it up again on my own from scratch—they took all my notes, files, recent research, everything that could lead me back to it."

"Sucks." Bascomb said sympathetically. They had rotated into the lounge; people on couches watched videos and conversed softly. Sometimes they were talking to holos; you knew when you were talking to a holo because they said outrageous things. They were programmed that way to ease the choking boredom of lounge-bar conversation. "I want it back, Bascomb." Kessler repeated, his knuckles white on the rim of the bar.

Bascomb shrugged and said, "You haven't been in this country long; maybe you don't know how it works. First off, you have to understand that . . . " He paused to sip from his cocaine fizz; he became more animated almost instantly, chattering on: "You have to understand that you can't get it back the way it was taken. Whoever it was probably came in while you were asleep. Which adds credence to your theory that Julie was involved. She waits up or pretends to sleep, lets them in, they gas you to keep you out, shoot you up with the receptivity drug. They've got microsurgicals in the big box they've brought with them, right? They look at the screen they've set up that translates your impulses into a code they can understand. They get some dream free-association maybe. But that tells them they're 'on-line' in your brain. Then they put a request to the brain, fed into it in the form of neurohormonal transmitter molecules they manufacture in their box—"

"How do you know so much about this?" Kessler asked, unable to keep the edge of suspicion out of his voice.

"We get a case like yours once or twice a year. I did a lot of research on it. The ACLU has a small library on the subject. It really gets their goat.

We didn't win those cases, by the way; they're tough to prove . . . " He paused to sip his fizz, his eyes sparkling and dilated. Kessler was annoyed by Bascomb's treating his case like a conversation piece.

"Let's get back to what happened to me."

"Okay, uh—so they made a request to the biological computer we call a brain, right? They asked it what it knew about whatever it was they wanted to take from you, and your brain automatically begins to think about it and sends signals to the cortex of the temporal lobes or to the hippocampus; they 'ride' the electrochemical signals back to the place where the information is stored. They use tracer molecules that attach themselves to the chemical signals. When they reach the hippocampus or the temporal lobes, the tracer molecules act as enzymes to command the brain to simply unravel that particular chemical code. They break it down on the molecular level. They extract some things connected to it, and the chain of ideas that led to it, but they don't take so much they make you an idiot because they probably want your wife to cooperate and to stay with Worldtalk. You might not be close but she's doesn't need the guilt. Anyway, the brain chemistry is such that you can ask the brain a question with neurohumoral transmitter molecules, but you can't imprint on the memory, in an orderly way. You can feed in experiences, things which seem to be happening now—you can even implant them ready-made so they crop up at a given stimulus—but you can't feed in *ready-made memories*. Probably that's 'cause memories are holographic, involving complexes of cell groups. Like you can pull a thread to unravel a coat fairly easily but you can't ravel it back up so easily . . . Look at that exquisite creature over there, she's lovely, isn't she? Like to do some imprinting on her. I wonder if she's real. Uh, anyway . . . You can't put it back in. They take out, selectively, any memory of anything that might make you suspect they tampered with you, but lots of people begin to suspect anyway, because when they free associate over familiar pathways of the brain and then come to a gap—well, it's jarring. But they can't prove anything."

"Okay, so maybe it can't be put back by direct feed-in to the memory. But it could be relearned through ordinary induction. Reading."

"Yeah. I guess it would be better than nothing. But you still have to find out who took it. Even if it turns up as someone else's project—proves nothing. They could have come up with it the same way you did. And you should ask yourself this: Why did they take it? Was it simply for profit or was it for another reason? The bigger corporations have a network of agents. Their sole job is to search out people with development ideas that could be dangerous to the status quo. They try to extract the ideas from the guys before they are copyrighted or patented or published in papers or discussed in public. They take the idea from you, maybe plant some mental inhibitors to keep you from working your way back to it again. If you came up with an idea that was *really* dangerous to the status quo, Jimmy, they might go farther than a simple erasing next time. Because they play hardball. If you keep pushing to get it back, they just might arrange for you to turn up dead. Accidents happen."

• • •

But riding the elevator up to his apartment, trying to come to terms with it, Kessler realized it wasn't death that scared him. What chilled him was thinking about his wife.

Julie had waited till he'd slept. Had, perhaps, watched the clock on the bedside table. Had gotten out of bed at the appointed hour and padded to the door and ever-so-quietly opened it for the man carrying the black box . . .

And she had done it simply because Worldtalk had asked her to. Worldtalk was her husband, her children, her parents. Perhaps most of all her dreadful parents.

And maybe in the long run what had happened to him, Kessler thought—as the elevator reached his floor—was that the Dissolve Depression had done its work on him. For decades the social structures that created nuclear families, that kept families whole and together, had eroded, had finally broken down completely. Broken homes made broken homes made broken homes. The big corporations, meanwhile, consumed the little ones, and, becoming then unmanageably big, looked for ways to stabilize themselves. They chose the proven success of the Japanese system: the corporation as an extension of the family. You inculcate your workers with a fanatic sense of loyalty and belonging. You personalize everything. And they go along with that—or lose their jobs. So maybe it started with the Dissolve Depression. Jobs were more precious than ever. Jobs were life. So you embraced the new corporation as home and family system. The breakdown of the traditional family structures reinforced the process. And you put your employer above your true family. You let its agents in to destroy your husband's new career . . .

And here we are, he thought, as he walked into the apartment.

There she is, making us both a drink, so we can once more become cordial strangers sharing a convenient apartment and a convenient sex life.

• • •

"Aren't you coming to bed?" she called from the bedroom.

He sat on the couch, holding his glass up beside his ear, shaking it just enough so he could listen to the tinkle of the ice cubes. The sound made him feel good and he wondered why. It made him visualize wind chimes of frosted glass . . . his mother's wind chimes. *His mother standing on the front porch, smiling absently, watching him play, and now and then she would reach up and tinkle the wind chimes with her finger . . .* He swallowed another tot of vodka to smear over the chalky scratch of loneliness.

"You really ought to get some sleep, Jimmy." There was just a faint note of strain in her voice.

He was scared to go in there.

This is stupid, he thought. I don't know for sure it was her. She hadn't *exactly* admitted it. "That was just a hypothetical," she'd said later.

He forced himself to put the glass down, to stand, to walk to the bedroom, to do it all as if he weren't forcing himself through the membranes of his mistrust.

He stood in the doorway and looked at her for a moment. She was wearing her silk lingerie. She was lying with her back to him. He could see her face reflected in the window across from her. Her eyes were open wide. In them he saw determination and self-disgust, and then he knew she had contacted them, told them that he knew. And the strangers were going to do it to him again. They would come and take out more this time—his conversation with her about the money, his talk with Bascomb, his misgivings. They would take away the hush money they had paid him since he had shown he was unwilling to accept it without pushing to get back what he had lost . . .

Go along with it, he told himself.

That would be the intelligent solution. Let them do it. Sweet nepenthe. The pain and the fear and the anger would go with the memories. And he would have his relationship with his wife back. Such as it was.

He thought about it for a moment. She turned to look at him.

"No," he said finally. "No, we don't have enough between us to make it worthwhile. No. Tell them I said next they'll have to try and kill me."

She stared at him. Then she lay back and looked at the ceiling.

He closed the bedroom door softly behind him and went to the closet for his coat.

• • •

They hadn't taken the money yet. It was still there in his account. He had gone to an all-night credit kiosk, sealed himself in, and now he looked at the figure, $NB 760,000, and felt a kind of glow. He punched his fone and called Charlie Chesterton.

The screen asked him, "You want visual?"

"No." he told it, "not yet."

"Sap?" came Charlie's voice. "Huzatun wushant?"

Wake Charlie out of a sound sleep, and he'd talk technicki. *What's happenin'? Who's that and what do you want?*

"Talk standard with me, Charlie. It's—"

"Hey, my neggo! Kessler, what's happening, man! Hey, how come no visual?"

"I didn't know what you were doing. I'm ever discreet." He punched for visual and a small TV image of Charlie appeared below the fone's keyboard. Charlie wore a triple-Mohawk, each fin a different color, each color significant; red in the middle for Technicki Radical Unionist; blue on the right for his profession, video tech; green on the left of his neighborhood, New Brooklyn—an artificial island. He grinned, showing front teeth imprinted with his initials in gold, another tacky technicki fad. And Charlie wore a picture T-shirt that showed a movie: Fritz Lang's *Metropolis*, now moving through the flood scene.

"You went to sleep wearing your movie T-shirt, you oughta turn it off, wear out the batteries."

"Recharges from sunlight," Charlie said. "You call me to talk about my sleeping habits?"

"Need your help. Right now, I need the contact numbers for the Shanghai bank that takes transferals under anonymity . . . "

"I told you, man, that's like, the border of legality, and maybe over it. You understand that first, right?"

Kessler nodded.

"Okay, neggo. Fuck it. Set your screen to record . . . But for the record this is on you, *I* ain't doing any such transferral . . . "

• • •

Bascomb's office was too warm; Bascomb had a problem with his circulation. The walls were a milky yellow that seemed to quicken the heat somehow. Bascomb sat behind the blond-wood desk, wearing a stenciled-on three-piece suit, smiling a smile of polite bafflement. Kessler sat across from him, feeling he was on some kind of treadmill, because Bascomb just kept saying, "I really am quite sure no such meeting took place between you and me, Kessler." He chuckled. "I know the club very well, and I'm sure I'd remember if I'd been there that night. Haven't been there for a month."

"You weren't enthusiastic about it, but you told me you'd take the case." But the words were ashes in Kessler's mouth. He knew what had happened, because there was not even the faintest trace of duplicity or nervousness on Bascomb's face. Bascomb really didn't remember. "So you won't represent me on this?" Kessler went on.

"We really have no experience with brain tampering—"

"That's funny, your saying that. Considering you obviously just had firsthand experience, pal."

Naturally, Bascomb gave him that oh-no-don't-tell-me-you're-into-that-conspiracy-shit look.

Kessler went on: "And I could get the files that prove you have dealt with the issue in court. But they'd only . . . " He shook his head. Despair was something he could smell and taste and feel, like acid rain. "They'd tamper with you again. Just to make their point."

He walked out of the office, hurrying, thinking, *They'll have the place under surveillance. But no one stopped him outside.*

• • •

Charlie was off on one of his amateur analyses, and there was nothing Kessler could do, he had to listen, because Charlie was covering for him.

" . . . I mean," Charlie was saying, "now your average technicki speaks Standard English like an infant, am I right, and can't read except command codes, and learned it all from vidteaching, and he's trained to do this and that and to fix this and that, but he's like, socially inhibited from rising in the ranks because the economic elite speaks standard real good and reads standard alphabet—"

"If they really want to, they can learn what they need to, like you did," Kessler said irritably. He was standing at the window, looking out at the empty, glossy ceramic streets. The artificial island was a boro-annex of Brooklyn anchored in the harbor. It looked almost deserted at this hour. Everyone had either gone into the city, or home to TV, or to a tavern. The floating boros were notoriously dull. The compact flo-boro housing, squat and rounded off at the corners like a row of molars, stood in silence, a few windows glowing like computer monitors against the night.

But they could be watching me, Kessler thought. *A hundred ways they could be watching me and I'd see nothing.*

He turned, stepped away from the window. Charlie was pacing, arms clasped behind him, head bent, playing the part of the young, boldly theorizing radical. "I mean, I've got some contacts on the space Colony, up on FirStep, and they're getting into some radical shit there—and what is FirStep, man, it's a microcosm of society's class issues . . . "

The apartment was crowded with irregular shelves of books and boxes of ancient compact disks; Charlie had hung a forest of silk scarves in the Three Colors, obscuring the details like multi-color smoke. "And in Europe—that shit's getting *serious*—"

"Yeah, wars are serious, Charlie."

"I don't mean the fucking war, neggo. I mean the side effect. *Chegdou,* you know what's happening in Europe, man? The SA is taking over! And it's all being manufactured over here. Fascism, a fait accompli."

Kessler groaned. "Fascism! Don't give me that leftist catch-all cliché. It's bullshit."

"How can you say that after what's happened to you?"

"What's happened to me is business as usual. It's not really political."

"Business as usual is the very definition of politics in a world where corporate identity is more global every second. And anyway—you didn't used to be so negative about this shit. Maybe they cut some of your political ideas, neggo. I mean: How do you know? You don't remember—" He grinned. "Remember?"

Kessler shrugged. He felt like throwing in the towel, giving Worldtalk the fight. Maybe Julie was right.

"If you'd just talk to this guy I want you to talk to, man."

"I don't need any lectures from any more knee-jerk leftist theorists who'd probably give their right eye to be the rich and corrupt men they whine about."

"You're doing a devil's-advocate thing now, Jimmy. You trying to talk yourself into giving up?"

Kessler shrugged.

Charlie looked at him, then went back to pacing, talking, pacing. "This guy I want you to meet—he's not like that. He's only in town a week. He's not an armchair theorist. He's not really a . . . what . . . I don't think he's a *leftist* exactly. I mean, he came here to get some financial support for the European resistance, and he had to run the blockade to do it, almost got his ass blown out of the water. His name's Steinfeld, or that's what he goes by, he used to be—what's the matter?"

A warning chill; and Kessler had turned, abruptly looked out the window. Three stories down she was a powder-blue keyhole-shape against the faint petroleum filminess of the street. She paused, looking at the numbers.

She might have guessed where he was, he told himself. She had met Charlie; heard him talk about Charlie. She might have looked Charlie's address up. She went to the front door. The apartment's bell chimed and he went to the screen. "It's your wife." he said. "You want me to tell her you went overseas? Japan?"

"Let her in."

"Are you kidding, man? You *are*, right? She was the one who—"

"Just let her in." There was a poisoned cocktail of emotions fizzing in him: a relief at seeing her, shaken in with something that buzzed like a smoke alarm, and it wasn't till she was at the door that he realized the sensation was terror. And then she was standing in the doorway, against the light of the hallway. She looked beautiful. The light behind her abruptly cut—sensing that no one was now in the hall—and suddenly she stood framed in darkness. The buzzing fizzed up and overwhelmed the relief. His mouth was dry.

Looking disgustedly at Kessler, Charlie shut the door.

Kessler stared at her. Her eyes flickered, her mouth opened, and shut, and she shook her head. She looked drained.

And Kessler knew.

"They sent you. They told you where to find me," he said.

"They—want the money back," she said. "They want you to come with me."

He shook his head. "I put the money where they can't get it—only because it's part of my proof. Don't you get sick of being puppeted?"

She looked out the window. Her face was blank. "You don't understand."

"Do you know why they do it, why they train you with that Americanized Japanese job-conditioning? To save themselves money. For one thing, it eliminates unions. You don't insist on much in the way of benefits. Stuff like that."

"They have their reasons, sure. Mostly efficiency."

"What's the slogan? *Efficiency is friendship.*"

She looked embarrassed. "That's not—" She shrugged. "A corporate family is just as valid as any other. It's something you couldn't understand. I—I'll lose my job, Jimmy. If you don't come." She said *lose my job* the way Kessler would have said *lose my life.*

Kessler said, "I'll think about going with you if you tell me what it was . . . what it was they took."

"They—took it from me, too."

"I don't believe that. I never believed it. I think they left it intact in you, so you could watch to see if I stumbled on it again. I think you really loved them trusting you. Worldtalk is Mommy and Daddy, and Mommy and Daddy trusted you . . . "

Her mouth twisted with resentment. "You prick." She shook her head. "I can't tell you . . . "

"Yeah, you *can.* You *have to.* Otherwise Charlie and me are going out the back way and we're going to cause endless trouble for Worldtalk. And I know you, Julie. I'd know if you were making it up. So tell me what it was—what it really was."

She sighed. "I only know what you told me. You pointed out that PR companies manipulate the media for their clients without the public knowing it most of the time. They use their connections and channels to plant information or disinformation in news-sheet articles, on newsvid, in movies, in political speeches. So . . . " She paused and took a shaky breath, then went on wearily. "So they're manipulating people, and the public gets a distorted view of what's going on because of the special interests. You worked up a computer video-editing system that sensed probable examples of, uh, I think the phrases you used were, like, 'implanted information' or 'special-interest distortions.' So they could be weeded out. You called it the Media Alarm System." She let out a long breath. "I didn't know they'd go so far—I thought they'd buy out your system. In a way they did. I *had* to mention it at Worldtalk. If I didn't I would've been . . . disloyal." She said *disloyal* wincing, knowing what he would think.

But it was Charlie who said it: "What about loyalty to Jim Kessler?"

Her hand fluttered a dismissal. "It doesn't matter at this point whether it was wrong or right. It's too late. They *know* . . . Jimmy, are you coming with me?"

Kessler was thinking about the Media Alarm System. It didn't sound familiar—but it sounded *right*. He said, slowly, "No. You can help me. If you testify, we can beat them."

"Jimmy, if I thought they—No, no. I—" She broke off, staring at his waist. "Don't be stupid. That's not—" She took a step back and put her hand in her purse.

Kessler and Charlie looked at each other, traded puzzlement. When Kessler looked back at Julie, she had a gun in her hand. It was a small blue-metal pistol, its barrel tiny as a pencil, and that tiny barrel meant it fired explosive bullets. *They* had given it to her.

"Do you know what that gun will do, girl?" Charlie was saying. "Those little explosive bullets will splash him all over the wall." His voice shook. He took a step toward her.

She pressed back against the door and said, "Charlie, if you come any closer to me, I'll shoot him." Charlie stopped. The room seemed to keen ultrasonically with imminence. She went on, the words coming out in a rush: "Why don't you ask him what that thing in his hand would do to me, Charlie. Shall we? Ask him that. Jimmy has the same kind of gun. With the same goddamn bullets." Her voice was too high; she was breathing fast, her knuckles white on the gun.

Kessler looked down at himself. His arms were hanging at his sides, his hands empty.

"Lower the gun, Julie, and we can talk." Charlie said gently.

"I'll lower mine when he lowers his," she said hoarsely.

"He isn't holding a gun." Charlie said, blinking.

She was staring at a space about three feet in front of Kessler's chest. She was seeing the gun there. He wanted to say, *Julie, they tampered with you.* He could only croak, "Julie . . . "

She shouted, "Don't!" and raised the gun. And then everything was moving: Kessler threw himself down. Charlie jumped at her, and the wall behind Kessler jumped outward toward the street.

Two hot metal hands clapped Kessler's head between them, and he shouted with pain and thought he was dead. But it was only a noise, the noise of the wall exploding outward. Chips of wall pattered down; smoke sucked out through the four-foot hole in the wall into the winter night.

Kessler got up, shaky, his ears ringing. He looked around and saw Charlie straddling Julie. He had the gun in his hand and she was face-down, sobbing.

"*Gogido*," Charlie said, lapsing into technicki, his face white.

"Get off her." Kessler said. Charlie moved off her, stood up beside her. "Julie, look at me." Kessler said softly. She tilted her head back, an expression of dignified defiance trembling precariously on her face. Then her eyes widened, and she looked at his hips. She was seeing him holding a gun there. "I don't have a gun, Julie. They put that into you. Now I'm going to *get* a gun . . . Give me the gun, Charlie;" Without taking his eyes off her, he put his hand out. Charlie hesitated, then laid the gun in Kessler's open palm. She blinked, then narrowed her eyes.

"So now you've got two guns." She shrugged.

He shook his head. "Get up." Mechanically, she stood up. "Now go over there to Charlie's bed. He's got black bed sheets. You see them? Take one off. Just pull it off and bring it over here." She started to say something, anger lines punctuating her mouth, and he said quickly, "Don't talk yet. Do it!" She went to the bed, pulled the black satin sheet off, jerking it petulantly, and dragged it over to him. Charlie gaped and muttered about cops, but Kessler had a kind of furious calm on him then, and he knew what he was going to do; and if it didn't work, then he'd let the acid rain bleach his bones white as a warning to other travelers come to this poisoned well—this woman. He said, "Now tear up the bedsheet—sorry, man, I'll replace it—and make a blindfold. Good. Right. Now tie it over my eyes. Use the tape on the table to make the blindfold light-proof."

Moving in slow motion, she blindfolded him. Darkness whispered down around him: She taped it thoroughly in place. "Now am I still pointing two guns at you?"

"Yes." But there was uncertainty in her voice.

"Now take a step to one side. No, take several steps, very softly, move around a lot." The soft sounds of her movement. Her gasp. "Is the gun following you around the room?"

"Yes. Yes. One of them."

"But how is that possible? *I can't see you!* And why is only the one gun moving—the one you saw first? And why did I let you blindfold me if I'm ready and willing to shoot you?"

"You look weird like that," Charlie said. "Ridiculous and scary."

"Shut up, Charlie, will you? Answer me, Julie! I can't see you! How can I follow you with two guns?"

"I don't know!"

"Take the guns from my hands! Shoot me! Do it!" She made a short hissing sound and took the gun from his hand, and he braced to die. But she pulled the blindfold from him and looked at him.

Looked into his eyes.

She let the gun drop to the floor. Kessler said, softly, "You see now? *They* did it to you. You, one of the 'family.' The corporate 'family' means just exactly nothing to them."

She looked at his hands. "No gun." Dreamily. "Gun's gone. Everything's different."

Siren warblings. Coming closer.

She sank to her knees. "Just exactly nothing to them," she said. "Just exactly nothing." Her face crumpled. She looked as if she'd fallen into herself; as if some inner scaffolding had been kicked out of place.

Sirens and lights whirled together outside. A chrome fluttering in the smoky gap where the wall had been blown outward: a police surveillance bird. It looked like a bird, hovering in place with its oversized aluminum hummingbird's wings; but instead of a head it had a small camera lens. A transmitted voice droned from the grid on its silvery belly: "*This is the police. You are now being observed and recorded. Do not attempt to leave. The front door has been breached. Police officers will arrive in seconds to take your statements. Repeat—*"

"Oh, I heard you," Julie said in a hollow voice. "I'll make a statement all right. I've got a lot to tell you. Oh, yeah." She laughed sadly. "I'll make a statement."

Kessler bent down and touched her arm. "Hey . . . I . . . "

She drew back from him. "Don't touch me. Just don't! You love to be right! I'm going to tell them what you want me to. Just don't touch me."

But he stayed with her. He and Charlie stood looking at the blue smoke drifting out of the ragged hole in the wall, at the mechanical, camera-eyed bird looking back at them.

He stayed with her, as he always would, and they listened for the footsteps outside the door.

•••

"Why should we leave when we don't know who it was who bailed us out?" Julie asked.

She sat hunched over, hollow-eyed. She seemed to be holding on, in some way.

Kessler nodded. "It could be Worldtalk's people, Charlie."

Charlie shook his head. "I saw the guy in the outer office. He's one of ours."

"Yours, Charlie," Kessler said. "Not mine."

They were in Detective Bixby's office, sitting wearily in the plastic chairs across from Bixby's gray metal desk. The overhead light buzzed, maybe holding a conversation with the console screen on the right of the desk, which hummed faintly to itself. The screen was turned to face away from them. On the walls, shelves were piled high with software, cassettes, sheaves of printouts, photos. The walls were the grimed, dull green such places usually are. Bixby had left them to confer with the detectives in the new Cerebro-kidnapping Department—the department that handled illegal extractions. The door was locked, and they were alone.

"At least here we're protected," Julie said, digging her nails into her palms.

Charlie shook his head again. "I called Seventeen, he said Worldtalk could still get at us in here."

"Who the hell is Seventeen?" Kessler snapped. He was tired and irritable.

"My NR contact—"

He broke off, staring at the desk. The console was rotating on a turntable built into the desk top, its screen turning to face them. Bixby's round, florid face nearly filled the screen.

"'S'okay," Bixby said. "CK's taking your case. Your video statements are filed, and your bail is paid. That'll be refunded soon as we get the owner of the building to drop the charges on the blown-out wall. Should be no problem. If you want protective custody—maybe not a bad idea—talk to the desk sergeant. Door's unlocked." As he said it they heard a click, and the door swung inward a few inches. They were free to go. "Good luck," Bixby said. His face vanished from the screen.

"Come on." Charlie said. "Let's do this fast before the fucking *door* changes its mind."

•••

The basement room was dim and damp, and old, cracking apart. A man was waiting for them there. The man was sitting on a cracked, three-legged wooden chair, just under the single light bulb; he sat with the chair reversed, resting his arms on the back, one leg extended to compensate for the missing chair leg. He smiled and nodded at them.

Kessler looked at Charlie, and Charlie shook his head.

"Is he from Worldtalk?" Kessler asked.

Julie's voice was hollow. "I don't know him. I don't know. Maybe they hired him."

The man said, "I work with Worldtalk. I work with the SA. And I work with Steinfeld," he said. "Not in that order." He was a big, soft bodied man, and he was too smug. He had an executive's neutral blue-gray hair tint, with just a streak of white, indicating he'd "risen in the ranks." Maybe he'd started as an accountant, or a typing-pool supervisor; he was entitled to wash the tint out, but some executives kept their early rank marks as a kind of warning: *I fought my way up, and I'm still willing to fight, so don't fuck with me . . .* He wore a dove gray suit, a real one, and the choker that had replaced ties in the upper classes.

"Man, you took out of place here," Charlie said.

The man in the gray suit chuckled.

The basement was empty on one end, the other dominated by a pile of detritus, accumulated junk from the old tenement above, including a lot of torn up carpeting gone mildewy gray, looking like The Thing That Lived in the Cellar.

"I'm Purchase," the man in the gold choker said.

He extended his hand and they shook all around. But no one else gave a name. Purchase's hand was warm and moist.

Charlie shrugged. "This must be the guy."

Purchase looked at his watch. "You were expecting a guy who looked like John Reed, maybe?"

Kessler looked at Charlie. "Isn't there a password or code phrase or something?"

Purchase answered for him. "The meeting place is the password. Who else would be down here?"

Kessler stared at Purchase. "I don't like anything ambiguous. You say Worldtalk, you say SA, you say Steinfeld. I mean, for all I know, I'm not really seeing you. Maybe they came in last night, maybe they treated me and Charlie and Julie so we share the same hallucination. Maybe they're trying to propagandize—that revolutionaries are really a lot of fat cats. Like the IRA and PLO chiefs who used to make fortunes off the black market. Maybe you're not here and I'm talking to an empty chair."

Purchase nodded. "That's not *impossible*, but it's pretty unlikely. You stood watches, last night, I presume. Anyway—I'm not a revolutionary.

Never said I was. I'm an employee. I work for Steinfeld, while pretending to work for the SA, while pretending to work for Worldtalk. SA thinks I'm their man in Worldtalk; but I'm Steinfeld's man in the SA. Only, I'm not a radical. Not unless it's radical to want the United States to stay the United States. I'm a patriot—and I'm a mole, planted in Worldtalk. And I'm placed to keep an eye on the people who want to make the United States the Fascist States of America. Is that explicitly enough? Two days ago I got the Worldtalk memo about Mr. Kessler's program. I happen to know that Steinfeld is working up something similar. He wants you with us. By *God* this is stupid. It's cold in this dump. Do we have to go into this here? There's a van upstairs, big and comfortable, right across the street. We'll talk on the way."

Kessler hesitated. Maybe he should still go to the ACLU.

But Charlie and Julie had insisted they had to go into hiding. "This Steinfeld will help me get my work back? My life?"

"He'll help you. If you help him."

Kessler took a deep breath, and nodded.

They went upstairs.

Part Three:
SWENSON

• 11 •

Ellen Mae Crandall stood at the head of the table, in Conference Room B, seventieth floor of the Worldtalk Building. It was an oblong table in an oblong room, a room with the usual imitation-wood-paneled walls and thick umber rug. There was just a trace of the shabbiness—a smutching of the transparent table, a fade in the color of walls and carpet—that such new places acquire after a remarkably short usage.

Sitting to her right, watching her without staring at her, John Swenson was thinking that Ellen Mae Crandall resembled her brother to an unfortunate degree. What were pleasingly masculine features on her brother were coarse on Ellen Mae. She had the heavy eyebrows; the deep, intense brown-black eyes; the wide, flashing grin showing a piano-keyboard spread of teeth, perfect and spotless, all the black keys missing . . .

Swenson smiled at the thought. There were no black keys in the Second Alliance. But some of the piano's hammers were black. They used whoever they had to use.

Ellen Mae wore a black shirt-suit with a lacy white collar. She looked pale, and her eyes were sunken even deeper than usual.

Swenson, conscious of his youth and good looks and trying to de-emphasize them—the last thing he needed to contend with was envy-seeded suspicion—sat across from Colonel Watson.

The Colonel was one of those ageless outdoorsmen who might be as young as forty-five and as old as seventy—he was closer to the latter. His florid face, weathered by the tropical sun during a hundred campaigns to suppress black independence, was British resolute, and British classic. His smoky-blue eyes flickered up and down the table, filing reactions, attitudes, levels of competence. Swenson considered him the number two power in the SA.

Sitting beside Watson was corpulent, nervous Sackville-West, head of Internal Security, breathing noisily through his mouth, scribbling notes which he screened with one cupped, doughy hand, like a priggish schoolboy who suspected his neighbor of cheating on exams.

The rest of the table was taken up by Spengle, Gluckman, and Katzikis and their secretaries—since the transcribing computer built into the table provided copies of all that was said, none of the secretaries were needed; they were there for reasons of pomp and Swenson ignored them. His mind was on Ellen Mae.

But Swenson was going to move carefully, softly, delicately. He had been investigated once, after the attempted assassination, and he had weathered it, had in fact come out of it in a position of strength. But two investigations would be one too many.

And Sackville-West trusted no one except for Crandall.

Ellen Mae called the meeting to order. She smiled and said, "The first order of business is to tell you that Rick is off the critical list, and his condition is now listed as serious. But Dr. Wellington informs me that Rick is pulling through with flying colors and is expected to be on his feet in two weeks—"

There was the expected murmur of relieved pleasantries around the table, Swenson carefully adding his own sigh of happiness.

"Now normally—" Just a touch of mischief in her voice, a mama with a Christmas surprise. "—I'd lead the opening prayer myself. But today, Rick is going to do it."

Heads snapped up. A few of the lower-echelon people muttered concern. Swenson waited, expressionless, guessing what was up.

Ellen Mae tapped out a brief order on the keyboard built into the table in front of her. A wafer-thin video screen hummed down from a slot in the ceiling behind her. She stood to one side. The room darkened; the screen lit up.

Rick Crandall faded in, in slightly drained colors; the picture was a little fuzzy around the edges. Crandall looked pale, but better than Swenson had expected. Makeup? Probably. Crandall was propped up a little in a hospital bed. An IV tube led from a wall panel to his arm.

Crandall smiled.

There was a stirring around the room in response. That smile was short of a grin, but it was strong, and certain, and it sent a thrill of reassurance through every one of them.

"G'mornin, friends," Crandall said in his soft Southern accent—so soft it was almost missing. "I want to thank you all for standing by me in this time, and for holdin' the fort for me. I have a report here . . . " He gestured toward something off-camera. " . . . that informs me you have been faithfully manning the watchtowers. I'm feeling a whole heckuva lot better and looking forward to being back at Our Work in two or three weeks—that is, unless the doctor's maybe a Democrat or a Jew! And I guess if he's one, he's the other."

A ripple of laughter around the room. That Rick.

"Now if I could . . . "

Swenson said it in his mind along with Crandall, he'd heard it so often, *Now if I could just have your attention for the most important business in the world, we'll say a prayer.*

" . . . business in the world," Crandall was saying, "we'll say a prayer."

He closed his eyes and tilted his head down a little. Everyone in the conference room did the same thing.

" . . . Lord, we beseech you to let us learn from our mistakes; to care for one another so deeply we will not allow our brethren to stray for a moment from Our Work, which is *Your* Work; to give us the strength to persevere in this moment of vulnerability; to know the Devil when he stands among us. Lord, you sent the Devil among us, to teach us a strong lesson. You struck the stigmata of the Christian Warrior into me, to humble me and to illuminate the gravity of Our Work; Lord, we beseech you . . . "

The prayer came rhythmically, in something near a monotone, but it never droned. It conveyed urgency, but it was never hysterical.

Crandall was wounded, and sick, and this was probably taking a lot out of him, but you had to hand it to the guy, Swenson thought, he had the art down and he could lay it out from a hospital bed and still make you shiver way down in your bones.

He explained things in the prayer, simply and with finality: the would-be assassin had been the Devil's man, just that simple. In order to prevent such a thing from happening again, to prevent another diabolic incursion, we must search ourselves, and those around us: we must increase security and we must watch one another like hawks, in God's name. There are traitors afoot.

And Crandall had rung in stigmata. Without saying it directly—that would be sacrilegious—he had managed to imply that in being shot he was martyred, that in some sense he was a stand-in for Christ Himself.

And they would buy it, Swenson knew. The word *stigmata* would start a train of associations in their minds, as Crandall knew it would, and sooner or later they would proclaim him Messiah.

And Swenson thought, *Oh shit, Devereaux.*

Devereaux's mission was totally misbegotten. *I told them, use a bomb. The mission had to be a suicide. I told them a bomb.*

But then, a bomb hadn't worked when they'd tried to kill Hitler.

As the prayer ended and the lights came up, Swenson caught Sackville-West looking hard at him. The old man seemed an incompetent dodderer and more than once Swenson had wondered if he deliberately played that up to make his enemies underestimate him. And just now he was watching Swenson.

Making Swenson think: *I let myself slip out of character.*

And you can't even do that in your thoughts. Steinfeld had warned him. *You're an idealist, John, and you're too well motivated for deep penetration; they'll sense you, they'll smell you out, because you can't bury it deep enough.*

But Swenson had been the one, because Ellen Mae wanted him close to her, so there was nothing else for it.

Swenson forced himself into the role. He put a hand to his eyes and thought about Crandall and saw him as his Uncle Harry, whom he'd loved; Uncle Harry, who'd died of cancer; the method acting pushed his buttons, and the tears came. Reverential tears.

He cut it off quickly. Don't overdo it.

Ellen Mae smiled down at him. She stood close beside him, her bony hip pressed against his arm; she reached down and squeezed his shoulder reassuringly. Her own eyes glistened with tears.

"He'll be back. He'll be back soon," she said softly.

"I know," Swenson said, smiling bravely.

• • •

In one of the notebooks in which Rickenharp wrote ideas and lyrics, the last thing he'd written was: *Synchronicity laughs when we see it and laughs when we don't.*

At the precise instant Swenson was replying to Ellen, a long way away, Rickenharp was saying, "Yeah, I know." Because Carmen had just said, "What did you expect? It's not easy and it's not fun and it's not romantic."

"I *mean*," she went on, "did you expect there would be a kind of TV fadeout on our shaking hands, agreeing to take you with us, and then maybe a quick cut to the action, some street fight in which you blow away the enemy, and then cut to the scene where you get your medals?"

"*No*, I didn't fucking expect that," Rickenharp growled. "But this is fucking ridiculous. I didn't know heaps like this still existed anywhere."

Yukio shrugged. "It's a typical Maltese fishing trawler."

Yukio, Willow, Rickenharp, and Carmen were huddled miserably in the hold of a fishing boat. A lantern swung pendulously with the wallowing of the creaking boat. An engine rattled and coughed somewhere behind them. The hold stank of rotting fish blood, and Rickenharp kept waiting to get used to it and he never did. Every breath was a fight with gagging. He was cold. The hold was clammy. The inner bulkhead behind drank heat from him. But if he sat anywhere else, or in the middle, he got seasick. He'd already thrown up twice, in the far corner, and he didn't want the dry heaves. The swinging lantern made him sick, but he didn't want the darkness either.

He'd sat hunched like this for hours. Somewhere between five and twelve hours—probably closer to five—and it seemed like days. He coughed, and he felt faintly feverish.

I'm getting a fucking cold, he thought.

But he'd complained once, and he wasn't going to let himself complain anymore, because Carmen's tone told him she was one step from contempt for him.

And the worst of it, the deep muddy trench of it was, *the drugs were gone.*

Here he was, slogging along in a boat Frankie's source used for smuggling drugs, among other things, but the hold was empty now, and they'd gone through Carmen's supply and Rickenharp's three grams—one gram ruined by a slopover wave when they'd boarded from the rowboat . . . They'd done them all, and now he felt burnt and enervated, and he was on a tightrope over the pits of the various pits of his personal hells, pits he knew like a man six months in solitary knows his tiny cell.

How much longer? he wanted to ask.

Is it much farther to Denver, Mom?

Your father's fed up with hearing that. You kids play with your holo-boy or something . . .

The fever rose, and warmed him, and he slipped into a pleasant delirium; driving with his parents across the country, he could almost feel the vinyl of the car's seats against his cheek . . .

We'll never get there, the little boy whined, in the delirium.

"We'll get there." Carmen's voice, from somewhere. "Or we'll drown and it won't matter."

•••

"Nationalism is the key to any nation." Watson was saying. He smiled urbanely. "Seems obvious, doesn't it? The very impulse that normally serves to exclude foreign control can insure the *success* of foreign control—if the key is turned from within the target country."

Watson was standing at the mini-terminal where Ellen Mae had stood; across from him Swenson took notes at his mini-terminal.

"We have NATO's leave," Watson went on, glancing at his notes, "to establish behind-combat policing bodies in Belgium, France, Norway, Spain, Greece, Italy, and, very soon, Holland. England for the foreseeable future will continue to be administered by the National Front, but—" he smiled "—the distinction is superfluous." Chuckles around the table. "They're all doing Our Work . . . "

Swenson smiled companionably. *Doing Our Work.*

"Our Work" meant full control over the countries in which the SA was established. It meant a takeover. It meant the Eclipse project.

" . . . establishing Our Work in these countries is simply a matter of utilizing each target nation's nationalist sentiment, a sentiment that is, everywhere, stronger than ever. The scenario is as follows, and I give it to you in a brief, general way with the understanding that the details that will come later are most important:

"Each target country is already in desperate need of order. Like Lebanon in the last century, the targets are unable to police themselves and have requested outside assistance. The SAISC being the only 'independent' security force large enough, being multinational, and being essentially a business without political loyalties—"

Here he paused to smile and they were allowed to chuckle again.

"—was awarded the policing contract for the target countries without significant dissent from the United Nations. The majority of our troops were in place as of last Friday midnight. Paris remains an exception; the war has severely damaged logistic channels into France. The troops will be airlifted in as soon as the neutrality agreement is finalized with Moscow. Once we're in place, the Russians will find out just exactly how 'neutral' we are . . . " Watson paused for another round of polite chuckling. With Crandall there was never a need for the polite response; the group responded to him naturally, liturgically, sincerely. But, of course, Watson was a typical high-military British bore. " . . . Each target nation has assigned a native liaison to coordinate policing efforts between the SA and the target's government or provisional government. In every single case, I'm proud to announce, our liaison was placed by the SA's Advance Services Bureau. The liaison is one of us. In each case it is a man with a public reputation for nationalistic sentiments. The man in France is Le Pen, great grandson of the last century's famous Front National organizer. The popular sentiment for nationalism has grown in France as in the other nations as a result of the incursion of immigrants, who take jobs away from nationals, and who transform their neighborhoods into something alien; and the Third World War itself, which, of course, has not made the common people pleased with foreigners. Steeped in this sentiment, young Le Pen is one step from the presidency.

"Our procedure in France will be roughly as follows: First, our troops will arrive and restore order. The food rioters, the looters, the bands of thieves, and the various terrorist and radical factions will be arrested, shot, and generally discouraged. Second, we will arrange it so that Le Pen will take credit for the restoration of order. Third, an information campaign will convince the public that Le Pen is in complete control of the SA troops, and that the presence of the troops is equivalent to the triumph of French nationalism. The problem, of course, is that most of the SA troops will be foreigners—the contradiction will be ironed out by inducting increasing numbers of sympathetic French nationalists into SA forces, and by creating the illusion that the SA is the tool of the French people, and completely in their control. Fourth, French troops thoroughly indoctrinated into the SA way of thinking will by degrees completely replace the rank-and-file of street-visible SA troops. But their superiors will ultimately be SA proper. Now . . . " He paused dramatically, looked up and down the table, and made eye contact. "Now, if we follow this simple formula, and follow through on its one thousand and one necessary details, we will, in less than five years, control every West European country of any significance. To put it bluntly, Europe will be ours. And we will begin to clean it up. The Zionist/neo-Stalinist conspiracy that controls half of the continent, and the Muslim conspiracy that controls the rest, will be eliminated, and eliminated with finality. *The solution is at hand.*"

• • •

Hard-Eyes and Jenkins sat side by side in twentieth-century steel-and-wood classroom desks. Jenkins looked fairly miserable. He was too big for the desk. Hard-Eyes felt all right. He was full; they'd just come from lunch. They ate well here, as Steinfeld had promised, and the room was warm, heated by an oil furnace in the basement of the old Paris school, an *école supérieure*; the vents gave out slow-rolling waves of warm air and a faint petroleum scent, a kind of industrial perfume which Hard-Eyes somehow found comforting. He was warm and well-fed. On an age-darkened bulletin board to one side were posters from twenty years before, extolling in French the virtues of democracy for some Parisian civics class. But listening to Steinfeld drone about guerrilla cell organization, Hard-Eyes was alternately mangling his own favorite victim of persecution, his right-hand thumbnail, and with his other hand nervously tracing the scorings of initials carved into the blond wood of the desk top. He felt himself careening, tottering on the edge of the abyss that was his future.

Steinfeld was saying, "Internal cadres organize into cells of three persons, only one of the three interfacing with command or other cells. A cell of three persons is the standard cell formation used in a classic guerrilla movement." As he spoke he drew a diagram on the blackboard.

And Hard-Eyes kept up an internal dialog with himself.

They are liars, he thought. All intelligence services employ liars, or, make liars of their employees; they have to, it's a necessary job skill. So Steinfeld might be working for anyone, including the fucking Russians. Who am I really working for?

What difference does it make? You know why you're doing it. For food and shelter and in the hopes you'll make contacts that'll get you back to the States.

Sure, okay, but the Second Alliance could be funding and directing this whole thing, could be behind the resistance to the Second Alliance! Some kind of disinformation system, say; or maybe creating a semblance of a resistance in some way gives them authority to use greater force, which would consolidate their power in the region.

Wha-at? Bullshit! Paranoia! I mean, come on.

Yeah? You can't *be* too paranoid anymore.

Yes, you can. Paranoia is a skill, neggo.

And then he forced himself to listen to Steinfeld, who was talking about propaganda teams, armed and unarmed. Winning hearts and minds . . .

• • •

A week after that, and they were on a roof, looking down through a sheer, misting rain, at Place Clichy. There were no cars in the *place* that late afternoon. Preparing for the demonstration, the police had rerouted the automotive traffic around the square; the traffic didn't amount to much anyway, with the gas shortage, and because a quarter of the city's streets were impassable with rubble from the Russian shellings.

But the square was filled, was overflowing with people. Every age, every profession—but mostly people who had been middle class, and lower middle class, Steinfeld said. All of them white.

Steinfeld was there beside Hard-Eyes and Jenkins and little Jean-Pierre and Hassan . . . Hassan the faintly smiling, who had come from Damascus to join the New Resistance. Sometimes Hassan said that the Muslim Holy Alliance would send troops to help Steinfeld, because the SA had already begun registering Parisian Muslims, and because the Front National wanted to expel all Muslims from France . . . But the Islamic troops never came. Hard-Eyes supposed that they could not bring themselves to take orders from a Jew.

They were crouching in a small space between an ornamental balcony railing—wrought iron, the paint flaked off it, rust burning through—and a dormer window, looking down past the slick, runneling tiles at the demonstration forming up in Place Clichy. There was a statue in the middle of the square, but it was hidden behind bunting and placards and banners and French flags. Hundreds of people in the crowd waved smaller flags; the surface of the crowd had a plumage in the colors of France, as if the collective entity that was the demonstration was a kind of bird showing its tail feathers to declare itself to others of its kind.

In the foreground was a temporary wooden stage, about ten yards wide and two high, erected that morning. The NR operatives were seeing it from behind. Over it was a white awning and it was backed in a sheet of the same white material, so that they couldn't see the speaker on the stage. But they could hear him; his turgid intonations boomed from the stage PA and echoed off the buildings around the square. And they could see his shadow. Stage lights threw his shadow on the white stage backdrop, outlining him as if for a Japanese shadow play. And the shadow he cast was larger than life, a shadow Goliath waving his arms and gesticulating, pointing a trembling finger at the sky. It was the gigantic shadow of Le Pen, the Front National candidate, great-grandson of Le Pen, who had also been the Front National candidate. When the war situation shifted sufficiently to permit an election, this Le Pen would stand a good chance of being elected. So Steinfeld told them . . .

Steinfeld translated the speech for Hard-Eyes and Jenkins as it went into its dramatic climax. "He's saying, 'And now the diadem of Europe has been crushed; the gem of France lies in its wreckage. Who is to be blamed? Clearly, the Russians are responsible. They began the war, they invaded Allied territory, and they have tried to take Paris! But who is it who has sabotaged the metros, blown up the power stations, burned the Civil Defense headquarters? Those who are the servants of the Russians, the slaves of the new KGB! Where do they come from? The third world, and the Middle East, where the Russians wield control! The foreigners who we welcomed into our nation, and who repaid us with their cultural pollution, with espionage, and sabotage! All *to prepare the ground for the Russian Union's destruction of our city!* The Muslims, the Jews, the Algerian Communists, the Portuguese Communists—*the poison! The Poison!*' "

The crowd's response was thunderous.

"They really believe that?" Jenkins asked incredulously. "Things break down, so they blame immigrants?"

"You have penetrated the heart of their argument," Steinfeld said dryly.

For a moment Hard-Eyes wondered if Steinfeld was translating accurately. Maybe he was distorting . . .

But Hard-Eyes could see genuine rage in the crowd's fist-shaking, in the excessively energetic way the flags were waved, in their voices, and most of all in the posturing of that enormous shadow . . . That strangely familiar silhouette with its rhythmically gesturing arms . . .

And he could see the advance SAISC men around the edges of the crowd, and behind the stage, arms crossed over their uniformed chests . . .

And he knew the truth again, when he saw the Second Alliance reaction to the counter-demonstration arriving from the side street. The counter-demonstration consisted of half a hundred spectacled students and dark-faced Algerians chanting, *"Fascisme? Non! Fascisme? Non!"*

"Brave and stupid." Steinfeld muttered.

. . . as the SA ran to intercept the counter-demonstration, the security bulls wielding nightsticks, drawing guns. Twenty SA bulls in wedge formation rammed into the counter-demonstration, sticks swinging. The Front National crowd turned to follow them. The candidate shouted something inaudible in the roar of the crowd . . . The regular police, briefed for this, were holding their positions at the street corners . . .

"If you looked sharply," Steinfeld said, "you might have seen two members of the counter-demonstration backing out through their own demonstration just before the SA moved in. Provocateurs, setting up the real counter-demonstrators. They're either SA or Le Pen's agents. Or both . . . " He went on with the cool objectivity of a TV commentator talking about the decline and fall of Rome. *And on that same day the barbarians massed outside the gates of Rome* . . . "What you are seeing is part of the 'strategy of tension.'"

"That was a strategy the old school terrorists used," Jenkins muttered. He had turned away from the riot in the street below and lit a cigarette. Hard-Eyes continued to watch the riot, fascinated.

"The extremist right-wing propagandists coined the term to speak about the left, yes. But it is the right who most efficiently use terror. Terror and disruption of services creates an atmosphere of tension which sets the stage for a rightist takeover. Provides a rationale for liquidating a leftist threat. *Agents provocateurs* infiltrate the leftists, media for terrorists, bombings, plant evidence, incriminate detainees with their 'confessions' . . . There were other, earlier European extremist right-wing terrorist groups. One of them, founded by Stefano Delle Chiaie in the last century, has grown very large, and simply merged itself with the Second Alliance. It wasn't very well organized in the twentieth century. It didn't have a centrally coordinated body or even a headquarters. It was loosely structured, a circle of friends, really, neofascists and old-guard Nazis. Sometimes it was assisted by the CIA, because it was so fervently anticommunist. American intelligence recruited and sheltered Nazis after World War Two, you know. Those who were valuable to it. Those Nazis survived and went on to become part of the loose rightist organization. It factionalized, and that kept it from being efficient—until Crandall came along. He has a talent for finding some kind of ideological common denominator. He brought them all together under his umbrella. And now they're here. Their work is as you see it. Here before you . . . "

Staring down at the riot, the flags and the bloodied clubs upraised, hearing the dull thud of gunshots now, Hard-Eyes had a revelation; personal, internal revelation. It had been percolating in his mind for days. He'd been asking himself why he did it, why he stayed with Steinfeld. There were rumors of a route to Freezone, and from Freezone it was possible to work your way back to the States. It was risky, but not as risky as staying in Paris. So why did he stay?

Because he had spent his youth fighting a sense of unreality; a feeling of insignificance and transience. Partly it was the Grid, the outgrowth of the Internet, the spawn of the mating of television and the Web. It shaped the prevailing iconography, the backdrop Hard-Eyes had grown up in, middle-class urban America. As it shaped London, Paris before the war, Tokyo, New Delhi, Capetown, Rio de Janeiro, Hong Kong . . . As it had been tincturing Russia, yes, even the People's Republic of China for decades. Steinfeld thought that the Grid was, perhaps on some collective unconscious level, the real reason the Neo-Communists in Russia had begun their post-Glasnost aggression. After the fall of capitalist post-Putin Russia, and the shambles of the new global recession, Russia had descended into near anarchy, giving the new authoritarian state the mandate to re-establish Communism. The new Soviet needed to pirate resources by conquest to stabilize its power. But it feared the Grid: The satellite transmissions blanketing the Earth with every frequency of the Grid. They tried to impose a Soviet-like censorship but Russia was pervaded with illegal satsend receivers; the black market in them boomed uncontrollably.

Hard-Eyes understood their fear of the Grid very well.

The minimono star Callais becomes hot. Overnight his image is everywhere. Endorsing in videos, holos; dancing, singing with charming minimono lugubriousness on animated T-shirts, and in playback glasses and on holo-posters and on screens in cars and buses and trains and planes and singing out of the radio . . . Or someone pushes a new style of clothing computer-designed for a computer-evaluated subtype: Westerclothes for the Distinctively Rough-Edged Man. *He's a Westerclothes Man!* . . . Political candidates packaged like a candy bar, like a line of clothing or a cigarette, while the politician's actual political reality almost entirely undefinable . . .

Worldtalk with its glassine fingers in the news broadcasts, the printouts. Shaping, shading the data: Illusionists in the pay of special interests. There was, once, an American Underground—but one was never sure who the real enemy was. Who, finally, was responsible for the Dissolve Depression and the rooftop shacktowns it created; the increasing blasé acceptance of the USA as a nation under siege from within, manning the barricades with the growing legions of hired cops, gypsy cops, rent-a-cops, uniformed thugs insulating the rich from the poor?

The Grid shaded it all beyond clear seeing. War-support propaganda. Styles of talking popularized by characters from TV shows. Catchy expressions deliberately created by TV-show packagers. Media-propagated intellectual fads, health fads, and art fads. Fads on fads within fads— gushed out from the great cornucopia of the Grid. The latest celebrity scandal—and sometimes the celebrity didn't exist as a physical person. Some were, all along, purely digital creations.

All of it transient, the day-by-day changing shape of the national self-image. Each man reduced to the status of a single pixel in a wifi transmission.

And now, in that split-instant, in a flash insight into his personal mental cosmos, Hard-Eyes knew why he was going to stay and why he would fight beside Steinfeld.

Because this . . .

. . . the SA cops in their beetle-wing helmets using their clubs, the confrontation with the true predator; with a clearly distinguishable evil.

. . . this was *real*.

•••

Bonham was standing in line, staring at the plastic-sheathed metal wall. The pilots called the Colony's walls "bulkheads," and the irritated Colonists had called the pilots "bulkhead blockheads"; now with the blockade they were "blockade bulkhead blockheads." To Bonham, it was a wall, and when he'd worked on the spaceships' shuttles the ship's "bulkheads" were walls, to him. He didn't like NASA jargon, he didn't like working for NASA, and he made up his mind he wasn't going to work out-Colony anymore. They didn't pay him for those kinds of risks. The Russians might take the next step, go from blockading to shooting ships out of space, and no way Bonham was going to put his ass on the line for a handful of newbux once a month.

One part of Bonham's mind was tracking angry free association; the next level down was watching the line of people waiting to get into the main shop and thinking, *There'll be nothing but crap left by the time I get in there. There has to be a way to get in sooner.*

He looked over his shoulder, spotted Caradine and Kalafi in the line down the hall behind him. He made the hand sign that said, *I'm going to initiate a resistance action, are you with me?*

Caradine and Kalafi signaled support. They were acknowledging his leadership and that felt good.

So Bonham took a deep breath, stepped out of line, and walked to the turnstile, ignoring the frowning clerk. He turned and looked down the line and shouted, "You want to know the truth about what's going on here, people? They're using the blockade as an excuse to hoard supplies! Admin gets all the supplies they need! The only way we're going to get what we need is *to take what we want!*"

They looked back at him with fear and uncertainty. But the cooling system was only intermittently functioning again and they'd been waiting there an hour and a half and the line was moving like a dying centipede and all they wanted was goddamn toilet paper and their protein-base ration and their rabbit meat ration and maybe some frozen orange juice . . .

So when Kalafi and Caradine joined him—and the three of them broke the line, pushed past the clerk at the turnstile, began the looting—the whole damn line followed their example. Bonham felt a surge of adrenaline-fueled pleasure in being at the cutting edge of the riot.

The rioters were whooping and cackling and feverishly scooping and grabbing, sweeping armfuls of groceries into their carts and bags, running out past the checker when they had all they could carry, kicking tables of cans over just for the hell of seeing them fly and clatter, terrifying the regular security guard—an old man in a uniform.

But some part of Bonham's mind wondered where Molt was, and listened for the amplified voices of Security bulls.

So he left the shop as soon as his cart was full, just as the good stuff was beginning to run out and the crowd was losing its mischievous-kid holiday mood and beginning to get genuinely surly. Bonham shoved the choicest of his groceries in a box, picked it up, and ran for it, not thirty seconds before Security got there. The cameras swiveled to watch him go.

• • •

"It's sad that you never knew Paris," Besson was saying.

They were sitting beside the window in a café in the Eighteenth Arrondissement, Hard-Eyes and Jenkins and Besson. Besson made Hard-Eyes think of Baudelaire; he had the bulbous head, that forgotten hairline; the hurt, accusing eyes; the bitter mouth; and the threadbare dandyism. He wore an old-fashioned vested sharkskin suit and a bow tie; a gold-plated watch chain looped over his thin middle. Besson had sold the watch itself, a year before, when the Russians had the city sealed off and the first famines came. His shoes were taped three times, all the way round, and he'd put blacking on the tape to try and make it took like part of the shoe. His vest was missing three buttons, and he was unshaven. His nails showed negative quarter-moons of black. But he was elegant; still, he was elegant.

He smoked the wretched C-rations cigarette down till it burned his yellowed fingers. He sighed, crimped it carefully out, and put the eighth-inch butt in a Prince Albert tin he kept in a jacket pocket. "The bastard Yankee soldiers gave me one cigarette. Not even a chocolate bar. I'm not pretty enough, eh?" He gave a mirthless laugh. As if on cue, a truckful of American soldiers trundled noisily down the street. The truck ran on compressed hydrate crystals; the septic smell of methane trailed the truck as it swung, grinding as it changed gears, around the corner.

"Most of the Americans will be gone tomorrow," Besson said, and there was no regret in his voice.

Jenkins and Hard-Eyes looked at one another. Hard-Eyes shrugged.

Jenkins had tried to talk Hard-Eyes into surrendering to the American soldiers, pretending they were just lost American expatriates. More than once they'd thought about it, in Amsterdam. But the Americans didn't send you home, word had it. They press-ganged you into civilian work crews. Or, worse, the COs had the power to draft you on the spot.

"You have never seen Paris," Besson said mournfully. He gestured contemptuously at the tired, wounded city around him. The café faced a narrow, brick-paved street below the Sacré Coeur. The onion dome of the ancient cathedral was just visible above the red tile rooftops; the overcast sky was breaking up in the late-afternoon breeze. Propaganda leaflets whipped down the gutter. The tall, stately buildings, narrow houses crowded together in gray stone and red tile, windows shattered out of them, were gap-eyed, lifeless. Most of the chimneys were mute, spoke no smoke; the sidewalks were scabbed with trash, a neglect unknown to Paris before the war. The café itself was almost empty. There were no supplies—it sold no beer, no liquor, only weak tea and a few exorbitant bad wines. The big copper espresso pumps were empty; Parisians were complaining as much from the loss of their daily caffeine as from the famine. The café owner kept the establishment open mostly out of habit. There were two old digital pinball machines against the wall, dead, cold as tombstones; there was no power. But the newly arrived SA technicians had gotten the natural-gas pumps working. There was gas, to heat the tea Hard-Eyes and Jenkins and Besson sipped beside their fly-specked window.

"This café, now, at this hour, should be overflowing with people," Besson said. "In the next room, they would fill their salad plates and eat, and the waitress would come to tell them the daily carte . . . They would have wine, and café after, a fine black café. Les Halles! I lived in Les Halles, I had a bookstore. I knew your Steinfeld very well in those days. He would come in, and we would argue . . . " There was a flash of genuine pleasure in Besson's eyes for a moment. "How I loved to argue with him! Wonderful arguments! We both enjoyed! And Les Halles—the tourists were the life of the place, and there were musicians and jugglers to take money from the tourists. The French musicians would try to sing American songs, the Americans stranded in Paris would try to sing French Songs. Or Paris on a rainy night—you walk on the streets almost empty, and then you are filled with the romance of your misery. Just when you are cursing the rain, you see the glow of a *brasserie*, the light laughing out of it. There was a bread seller, Prochaine. He was said to make a wonderful bread, and the reputation of this bread was such that people would stand in line two hours to buy it, to buy one loaf, sold only in his shop. It was a heavy bread, not dark and not light, a little sour but also sweet, and it was moist . . . crystalline. *Comprends?* A very simple bread, and profound, *mes amis*. You could taste one bite for an hour. This *pain-Prochaine*, it was Paris. Just five years ago, my friends . . . Prochaine is dead now, and his son is dead, and when the Russians held the city, the Allies bombed a big gun in Les Halles, antiaircraft gun, and now the neighborhood is . . . " He shrugged and sipped his tea.

"And now the SA is here," Jenkins said.

Across the street, a man was putting up a poster. He peeled the backing-paper off and pressed it onto the big gray stone wall, beside the wide stone stairs terracing up to the cathedral.

The posterer was a knobby teenage boy in a ratty sweatshirt. His hair was twisted up into a flare topknot over his head, in imitation of last year's American fashions; but the tint was six months overdue for renewal; and he'd had to hold the shape with rubber bands.

Besson sighed. "Why do you Americans send us your stupid hairstyles?"

Hard-Eyes was laboriously translating the poster. It came out as something like:

THE *FRONT NATIONAL* HAS COME TO THE RESCUE OF THE FRENCH PEOPLE!! WATCH FOR THE SOLDIERS OF THE *STRATEGIE ACTUEL* AND STRUGGLE BESIDE THEM TO REBUILD PARIS!! THE *STRATEGIE ACTUEL* HAS RESTORED THE GAS!! FIGHT THE CONSPIRACY OF FOREIGNERS!!!!!!!!!!!!!

The boy continued down the block, peeling the backing off the posters, sticking them up, leaving the slick brown backing to curl like oversized pencil shavings on the cracked sidewalk. He put up three more posters, each one different, and yet each one the same as the last.

The second said: "WHY HAVE WE ALLOWED THE ZIONISTS TO RAPE PARIS?"—and nothing more.

The third said: "PARIS IS A JAIL AND THE FOREIGNERS ARE THE JAILERS . . . BUT FRANCE HOLDS THE KEY!!

A fourth said: "FOOD AND FREEDOM IS ON THE WAY! DON'T LET MUSLIMS, JEWS, OR LIARS TAKE IT FROM YOU!

Each poster was printed on a different color paper, with different styles of lettering. They were not of uniform size. They might almost have been put up by different organizations.

"When the electricity comes on, they'll start the radio propaganda," Jenkins said.

Besson snorted. "How? The Russians blew up the power plants."

Jenkins said, "Saw something out at Rond Point Victor Hugo. They had a receiver on a truck. A microwave power receiver. Maybe SA owns one of the power gathering satellites. Maybe they'll beam it down here. Not enough for a whole city—but enough for, say, a fifth of the town, two days a week. The people'll be glad for what they get. They'll know who to thank . . . "

"And the SA can cut it off when they want. When it suits their purposes," Hard-Eyes said.

"This talk disgust me!" Besson declared, flapping his hand dismissively. "You disappoint me. You are talking politics. I thought you were men of refinement. Do you think it was politics that made our situation? No, my friends. It was aggression. Politics is only the snorting of the bull before the charge. But—I can see that Steinfeld has chosen you well."

Hard-Eyes looked sharply at him.

Besson laughed. "I said the right thing, no? This bastard Steinfeld, he chooses men he knows will catch the disease of politics! The secret idealist, eh? Someone—Jean François—said to me, 'Why should I work with Steinfeld? He is a foreigner pretending to fight for France. There are Yanks and Brits in his troops. Maybe they are CIA, maybe British secret service . . . Why should they fight for us?' But I told him to remember the German resistance to the Nazis in World War Two. Not so much resistance, but it was there! The resistance against the Nazis was every kind of man, in Germany. There were Communists and conservatives and everything between. There were foreigners and there were fanatic German nationalists who simply hated Hitler."

"But why not you, Besson?" Jenkins asked. "Is the SA really much better than Hitler?"

"Why not me, because I am not one to march in parades—even clandestine parades! I watch them from my window. When my wife . . . died . . . she . . . " He stared out the window, tried to swallow the sorrow. "That part of Paris is poisoned now. We will not use the big bombs, they agreed, eh? So they use the *leetle* nuclear bombs. What do they call them?"

"Tactical." Hard-Eyes said.

"Yes. They only burn up a square kilometer, eh? Three square kilometers on the edge of Paris, one inside. Poisoned with radiation! So—it is okay to poison us only a *petite* amount, bit by bit? That is like choosing to torture a man to death instead of killing him cleanly . . . " He stood up abruptly, upsetting his chair, and walked stiffly out into the misting rain, without so much as an *au revoir.*

Hard-Eyes hugged himself, feeling cold.

"It's crazy, staying in this town," Jenkins said. But he said it musingly. There was no implication in it.

Hard-Eyes nodded, wondering, Why *are* we doing it? And the answer came: So that the world means something.

The boy came into the café and asked the shopkeeper if he could put a poster in the window. The shopkeeper shook his head, once, and hooked a thumb at the door. The boy made a great show of writing down the address of the shop.

Hard-Eyes thought, Surely it hasn't come to that, surely not so soon . . .

But when they came to the café the next day, hoping to find Besson there, the café keeper was sorrowfully boarding up the windows. Someone had smashed out the glass, and on the wall beside the broken café window was spray-painted, in French, HE COLLABORATES WITH THE ENEMIES OF FRANCE!

So they walked back to the hostel Steinfeld's people had put them in and said nothing on the way. They passed a supermarket, gutted and burned out in the lootings, and the posters were everywhere.

• 12 •

In Manhattan, and in the "A" building of the Second Alliance International Security Corporation, across the street from the Worldtalk Building, John Swenson typed up a coded communication to a man named Purchase. He told his terminal to send the communication to Purchase's terminal, across the street and up forty floors. The communication was a message within a message within a message. To a man who was an agent within an agent, within an agency. Message *one* told Worldtalk that SAISC's security preplanning for the Eighth International Congress of Orbital Manufacturers was complete. Message *two*, hidden within the signals for the first, was from the SA's Second Circle, the ruling committee, to Purchase the SA agent. So far as the SAISC knew, Purchase was one of eighteen Worldtalk executives with greater and lesser degrees of loyalty to the Second Alliance. Message *three*, secreted within the second, was from Swenson the NR agent to Purchase the NR agent. Warning him that SAISC was making plans to implement a full corporate takeover of Worldtalk—the world's biggest public relations firm and potentially the most powerful tool for propaganda known to modern man . . .

Swenson sighed and wondered if he had done well to send it through an SAISC terminal. How closely was Sackville-West monitoring everything that went out? There was no such thing as an unbreakable code. He looked at his watch. Ellen Mae ought to be alone in her office about now. He picked up a sheet of computer printouts and walked down the hall. Her door was open. He knocked on the frame and went in.

"What have we got here?" Ellen Mae Crandall asked, in her most musical voice, as Swenson laid the printout on her desk. "You could have *sent* it," she added, nodding toward her desk terminal. She smiled. She'd said it to give him his opening.

Swenson said smiling softly, "Maybe it's because any excuse to see you personally . . . " He shrugged. Ellen Mae blushed, really blushed, by God, and he wondered if he'd gone too far.

She looked hastily at the report. "Oh, the FirStep Colony. Is this from Praeger?" She frowned. "Why didn't he send it to me directly?"

"He sent it to Colony Intelligence Director—which as of this morning is yours truly."

"Oh, I forgot! There's so much, without Rick, to keep track of . . . " She sighed. Playing helpless female now.

He put his hand on her arm, telling himself to ignore the arm's slight excess of black hairs, and said, "He's going to be back with us soon."

She swallowed, flustered, but gave no sign she wanted him to take his hand away.

Purchase was right about her, Swenson thought.

She glanced over the report. "What's, um, the gist of this?"

He straightened, and put his hands in his jacket pocket. "There isn't a lot to it. They can't get anything but short transmissions out, and fewer of those lately, with the Russians sending out their scrambling signal. Rimpler is possibly cracking under pressure. He's unstable anyway. He's got a lot of popular support but among the technickis there are two other men Praeger thinks he can put in to replace Rimpler. On the technicki level, of course. Rimpler's daughter is a problem . . . "

She wasn't listening, she was staring straight ahead with a patently artificial look of having remembered something important. "Oh, my gosh."

Oh, my gosh? Swenson thought. Aloud he said, "Something wrong?"

"I've just realized I've got to get a full report on this to Rick, tomorrow. I've told him he shouldn't work, but he—well, you know how he is. You can't keep him away from it. If he were in a hospital maybe we could, you know, encourage him to take it easy, the doctors have some kind of authority there. But he's out at Cloudy Peak Farm, and he's just like Daddy was—once he gets on the farm, he's the Farmer and no one can say a word to him!"

Swenson chuckled, and thought, maybe the polite chuckling all the time is the hardest part of all.

She went on, "I promised him I'd get this to him—you know, my own analysis. But I don't think I can do it alone, and with everything else . . . " She turned to him as if she'd just thought of it. "John, do you think you could come out to the farm tonight? We could work late, so I could have it in the morning . . . "

"I'd be honored." he said, and in a way it was true.

And this time he was careful not to put his hand on her arm. It was all still a question of timing.

"Security will pick us up at six, at the front door." she said briskly, turning all studiedly businesslike.

"I'll be there with bells on," he said, knowing she liked old-fashioned expressions. He smiled at her and went back to his office. And couldn't suppress a stab of pity for her . . .

• • •

As the helicopter settled down over Cloudy Peak Farm, Swenson hung on to the straps and closed his eyes. He didn't mind flying—it was coming down or going up to begin the flying that scared him. It wasn't the sky, it was the ground. The ground could be hostile to flying things. It smashed them, if they weren't careful.

And he'd already seen the Crandall's farm on the helicopter's first circling approach . . . A river cut a purple trail through the moonlit trees. The moonlight showed a great swatch of lawn, the glistening snail tracks of two steel fences, and the cluster of trees around the main house. Smaller servants' houses huddled to one side. Behind the house a barn, according to rumor, sheltered a few cows, a couple of sheep, horses—but it wasn't really an actual farm anymore. It was "a combination of pastoral religious retreat and Second Alliance planning center," to use Purchase's phrase.

He felt a sudden queasy hollowness in the pit of his stomach that told him the helicopter was dipping, spiraling down. In his mind's eye he saw it crash; saw himself burning alive in the wreckage.

He felt a cold sweat break out on his forehead and told himself fervently, "This is stupid," and then realized he'd said it aloud. But the thudding chop of the blades had blotted it out.

If they asked me now, he thought, right now, right this second, who I am, what my business is, I might blurt the the truth. *My real name is John Stisky and I'm working undercover for the NR, the New Resistance, an organization that wants to destroy you, all of you . . . Now, what do you think of that? Because the fear made him mad, made him want to blurt everything. Tell them more than they asked. Tell them and tell them—*

Thud. A disappointed whine as the engine cut. He opened his eyes—and drew back, startled by a man with eyes like a falcon, a beak of a nose, and a slash for a mouth, looking right at him, staring. Swenson almost said, *My real name is John Stisky and—*

And then falcon-face said, "You all right, sir?"

Swenson looked at the man's flat-black Security uniform, and panic passed. Just an SA Security guard. "I'm fine. I'm not so good at flying. A little dizzy for a moment—problem with the balance in the inner ear. Only happens when the altitude drops too quickly. No problem."

He brushed the man's hands away from his safety belt, unbuckled it himself, and stood. His knees wobbled and then found their strength. He took a deep breath and stepped out and down, needlessly ducking his head under the slowly spinning blades. He stood in wet ankle-deep grass and felt the relief rush over him, and once more he was John Swenson, deep in character, when Ellen Mae put her hand on his arm and led him to the house. "Are you all right, John?"

"Sure." He smiled sheepishly. "I'm not much for chopper flights."

"Maybe a glass of wine and some dinner. We can work after dinner."

"Now you're talking."

She squeezed his arm, pleased at his familiarity, and he thought, I'm doing it right.

• • •

Memo from Frank Purchase to Quincy Witcher—High Encryption Protocol.

Subject: John Stisky

. . . was a priest of the Holy Roman Church assigned to the Diocese of Managua, Nicaragua. Within three weeks of arriving in Managua he came into conflict with his immediate superior, Father Gostello (see attached transcript of recorded fone interviews), when he requested leave to participate in a demonstration at the American Embassy protesting the occupying American army's refusal to consider a timetable for electing a new Nicaraguan governing body; Stisky defied Gostello and attended the demonstration. He was arrested in the course of a riot, and in jail met Father Encendez. Fr. Encendez had been four times censured by the Church for unauthorized political activity in the wake of Pope Peter's encyclicals denouncing Church involvement in progressive political causes. Encendez was later dismissed from the priesthood (as a move of conciliation to the occupying American Forces), when he published an article in an American news printout alleging that General Lonington, Director of the Nicaraguan Occupation, was "connected with anti-Semitic and anti-Catholic organizations and had in his boyhood several times attended meetings of the Ku Klux Klan-related Council of Conservative Citizens . . . may have been instrumental, as a young lieutenant, in helping Nazi war criminals escape an Interpol investigating team." Encendez continued his organizing after leaving the priesthood and in April was found shot to death in a muddy ditch ten miles south of Managua. Stisky pressed for an investigation and charged that Lonington had business connections with the Second Alliance Corporation. Crandall's church had already begun recruiting in Managua, and was the only American church organization allowed free rein there; Stisky pointed out that Lonington was a member of that church, and he demanded Lonington's removal. Stisky was subsequently defrocked . . . No conclusive evidence indicating a homosexual relationship between Stisky and Encendez, but Stisky's college records show that for several months he was a member of the New York University League of Bisexuals . . . He left the university to enter the seminary in 1994 . . . Stisky's father was Jewish, his mother half-Jewish, but both his parents were atheists, and conceptual artists. His swing toward the Church might be considered an intellectual rebellion against both his parents' philosophy and their chaotic lifestyle . . . His relationships with women typically are abbreviated and stormy . . . He received psychiatric treatment for a nervous breakdown in July, spending two months in Fairweather Rehabilitation Center . . . his instability is a double-edge sword. It is connected with his extreme motivation—his hostile feelings for the SA are as heartfelt as any I've encountered—and his tendency to slip into quasi-pathological sub-characters. The latter tendency, when trained, is clearly useful in an undercover operative but adds to his unpredictability. Stisky is essentially a gifted amateur. Nevertheless, in the course of his chance meeting with Ellen Mae Crandall, last August sixth, she showed a marked interest in him . . .

• • •

"I think we could break it down in three steps." Claire told her father. They were sitting in the living room of Professor Rimpler's apartment. Rimpler sat across from her, slumped over the dialed-up hump of the floor he used as a coffee table. There was a tray of liquors in crystal decanters on the table hump; the walls were dialed to light green, the light was adjusted to resemble the indirect shafting of sun through forest boughs. Claire sat on a confoam chair, her hands clasping her knees, watching her father with growing distress, thinking, *He's coming apart.* "The first step," she went on, trying desperately to engage his attention, "is to talk to this man Molt. He was one of their chief organizers. We can convince him that we're on his side. Second, we release him and he goes to the technickis and speaks for us. Third, to show our good will, we make some concessions. We release the looters from detention, we do double-checks on the field strength around technicki quarters to make sure they aren't getting extra radiation—I mean, why not? The whole thing'll defuse."

"What makes you think we're on their side?" her father asked, casually.

She looked at him in shock. "What?"

"You heard me. Yes, the technickis are in fact being discriminated against, to some degree. I'll tell you something else, Claire my dear— Praeger and his people have seen to it that blacks, Jews, and Muslims are no longer being advanced in Admin! Oh, yes! I know for a fact that he plans to weed them out under one pretense or another, when the blockade is lifted. There's discrimination for you. But we don't *dare* point it out—if Praeger falls, we fall. Things are at that kind of boiling point." His voice dropped from brisk to weary, cynical, marking his shift in mood. He poured himself a tequila, mixed in lime juice and grenadine, then drank off half of it and stared dully into space. "The Ozymandias principle," he said, mostly to himself. "The bigger the enterprise, the more ridiculous you look when you see it was all for nothing, when entropy makes a joke of it."

Claire stood, and moved to sit beside her father; but he only hunched even more. He wore white shorts beginning to yellow; a button-up shirt opened to show the steel-wool hair of his chest; on his feet were decaying thongs. He smelled sour. His eyes focused only on his drink. He held the glass up to the light; the beaded crystal was transfixed by a beam of emerald.

She put an arm over his shoulders; they felt thin and bony. He shrank from her touch, and she dropped her arm. She spoke in a parody of a teacher's recitation: "Dad—if a small meteor impacts the Colony's outer skin, the break is sealed up with the Rimpler alloy. All through the hull is a layer of Rimper Alloy. If the alloy is kept at ninety-two degrees, it's liquid; if the cold of space breaks in, it freezes instantly, fills the hole, restores airtight integrity . . . I make that little speech to the kids when I take them out to the hull observation station. Professor Rimpler made that alloy, I tell them, and he designed this home in space, and he's always trying to make it better for them. There's no alloy that reseals things if we break up in a civil war, Dad. We have to seal the civil breach. And it's you people expect to do it. You have to go on viddy and talk to them. You have to patch up the holes for them."

He pressed the cold glass to his forehead. Tonelessly he said, "If you can get Molt to help us, then maybe. But don't count on any help from him. They went down to interrogate him an hour ago . . . "

Claire stood and backed away from him. She looked at him hard, trying to recognize him. "Dad—how do you know these things? Praeger's 'racial weeding' . . . their plans for Molt . . . ?"

He gestured vaguely toward his console. "When I designed the comm system I . . . built a few safeguards into it. I can monitor Praeger's instructions. I get them all routed to me automatically; I have his code, too." He shrugged. "If you get Molt, I'll talk to the technickis. But just for you. Not because I care about them. They're a lot of *E. coli* in the belly of the beast."

She stared at him. And thought: *Let it go.* If that was his attitude about them, it was something that she couldn't change. Not now.

Claire turned and spoke to the door panel; it slid aside and she walked down the hall to her apartment, where she changed into her Admin Governing Committee jumpsuit, thinking: *E. Coli in the belly of the beast?* There was something pathological about putting it that way.

She pinned her Security pass to her collar, needing the semblance of authority. She took her father's private lift three levels toward Admin. Security level was the entire floor below Admin—like a moat around a castle. As the lift stopped, a panel over the door lit up red with the words SECURITY—PASSES ONLY.

Her palms were damp. She wiped them on her hips and told herself, "You are in charge."

The door opened and Claire stepped into the hallway. A camera looked at her. She held up her pass for the camera to see. Nothing stopped her as she walked down the hall.

She hesitated at the glass doors. Someone had stenciled *Happy Holidays* and a cluster of holly leaves on the glass, and she remembered that it was near Christmas. They would put the big artificial tree up in the Open soon. But no, not with all the vandalism that had been happening. The technicki vandals would make a wreck of it.

She went through the door. A young man smiled up at her from behind the glassy desk. Four small TV monitors to his right showed all four access corridors to Security. There was no need for him to watch them, really; the computers did it quite efficiently alone. But where possible her father had arranged for a human being to oversee cybernetic functions; the other engineers had hinted that the human backup arrangement was irrational, even eccentric.

The young man in the flat-black SAISC uniform kept smiling as he said, "How can I help you, Ms. Rimpler?" His face was pretty, almost angelic, but his hand lay on the desk within reach of the summons button. She and her father had been in Denver for a UNIC meeting when Praeger had revamped Security. They'd come back and found Second Alliance International Security Corporation men setting up new surveillance gear and sentry teams strategically throughout the Colony; the grim, gray-black uniforms could be glimpsed wherever the corridors made a nexus . . .

The SAISC struck her as altogether too secretive an outfit, almost cultish. There was, after all, its connection to Crandall, who was close to being a cult leader.

"I need four men to escort a prisoner from lockup," she said, trying to sound assertive. "Samson Molt."

The receptionist's smile froze right where it was.

"Let me see what I can do—" He turned to the terminal, tapped a fone number; a face appeared on the screen. She couldn't see it clearly from this angle, but she thought it was Scanlon's. The receptionist was going to the top, which seemed out of sequence. "Ms. Rimpler is here, asking permission to see a prisoner, Samson Molt . . . "

"To escort him out of there," Claire broke in. "I want to take responsibility for him. He is to be remanded to my custody. I need a few men to help me—"

Scanlon's voice, like his digitally compressed face, was too flat, too oblique.

"The situation is dangerously unstable, Claire. Molt's release would contradict the public information we've already given out; we've had to say repeatedly that we don't know where he is."

"No one believes that anyway."

"I'm sorry, Claire, but if you'd like to put in a formal request for his transfer, we will process it and try to give you an answer within two or three weeks."

"This is ridiculous, Scanlon. I want to talk to you face to face." But the screen went blank. "I'm sorry," the receptionist said blandly, the smile now completely gone. "He's out doing fieldwork. If you'd like to make an . . . "

Claire turned and walked out; it was as if she were swept along by something, washed into the elevators, and not until she'd gone down to Central Telecast and found Judy in the commissary did she really take note of her surroundings.

Claire looked around the commissary, blinking, and then sighed and sank into the cracked blue plastic seat across from Judy Avickian. Judy was small, eyes nearly black, waist-length curly black hair braided for work, looped over one shoulder to dangle in front of her white and gold skin-suit. Judy liked things white and gold; her earrings were ivory on gold wires. There was a suggestion of a mustache just above the corners of her pale lips, but it wasn't much more than a shadow, and she was an attractive woman; attractive and strong. She and Claire had had a brief fling, and then Claire had shrugged and said, "I guess I'm just heterosexual." Now they were friends, but when certain subjects floated by on the conversational stream, Judy's tone became acrid.

The room was too well lit, as cafeterias have always been; the vending machines built into the walls hummed, but behind the glass, the shrink-wrapped, vitamin-injected food in the little slots looked, in that harsh light, like wax imitations.

"You look pissed off," Judy observed.

"You know it." Claire told her what had happened at Security Central. "Two years ago it would've been unheard of. Those people worked for my father—for the Colony. Now they've . . . "

Judy nodded slowly, her eyes gazing at something inward. "The SAISC are invited in where there's a power vacuum. Where somebody in collaboration with them plans to fill the vacuum." She looked at Claire. "I was talking to a woman, the mother of a kid they arrested. She hasn't seen the kid in a month. They won't grant her visitor's privileges. She thinks something's wrong, She thinks they hurt him. Maybe he's dead. They hit him three times with an RR stick. He was thirteen years old."

"What's an RR stick?"

"Recoil reversal. The recoil you'd normally feel when you hit something, the kinetic energy, is rerouted back into the point of impact a split-second later—it's like the stick hits you twice when they hit you with it only once. The guy using it can't judge how much force he's used . . . "

"Jesus. When did you see her?"

"Two days ago. We've been gathering material for a story on it, but I'm not sure they'll give us permission—" She shrugged. "The bottom line, Claire, is that UNIC is taking it all away from your father."

Claire blinked and said, "I don't think it's quite that, uh . . . "

Judy shrugged and shook her head at the same time. "You want to get in to see Molt?"

Claire nodded.

"And you want my help?"

Claire nodded again, watching Judy. The bitterness was there. Judy's tone said, *I tried to warn you about this before. You should have trusted me, listened to me. Stayed with me.*

Judy stood up. "Then let's go get my class."

• • •

There were four of them, Judy, Angie, Belle, and Kris. Belle and Kris were sisters, both of them tall and black. Angie was Swedish, blond and blue-eyed, her expression always fierce; she was a bulky, high-breasted, big-boned woman, and she wouldn't have looked out of place in one of the last century's National Socialist paintings of Aryan peasants. But Angie, Judy's instructor, was fervently Neo-Marxist.

They were Admin, and educated in standard English. But they were strongly sympathetic to the technicki cause.

They wore black exercise leotards, fencing masks, corrugated chest protectors. They looked like umpires for a woman's baseball team, Claire thought. Only, Angie and Judy carried nunchuks.

Angie had always looked at Claire with a kind of your-time-will-come disdain; she took off her mask just to let Claire see that expression now as Claire took charge.

"I'm going in first," Claire said. "I'll leave the door unlocked. When you hear me shout, come running."

Judy shook her head vehemently. "I think we'd better go in with you now."

"I don't want to provoke them. It'll be better if I can get Molt on sheer authority. If I can't, you'll hear from me." She tapped the comm button on her collar.

Feeling a little dizzy, she turned to the door.

This is rarefied air for me, she thought. Goddammit, Dad, if you were here . . .

She took the code key from her pocket, looked at the coordination indicator: Level 03, Corridor C13. She was near the outer shell. She could feel it—the gravity was faintly greater near the outside of the Colony.

The codekey looked like a small handgun with a crystal muzzle; she turned the two dials at the back of the key to read 03 and C13; then she pressed the codekey to the lock panel and the door opened.

She expected to see a guard on the other side, but there was no one. A sheet of transparent plastic wall blocked her way, forty feet farther on. But she knew what it was, one of her father's security precautions, and she'd come prepared.

She dialed the codekey, and pressed it to the bulkhead. A small red arrow lit up on the bottom dial, pointing upward. She kept the key pressed to the wall, and moved the key upward; it chimed. The codekey communicated with the regulator on the other side of the bulkhead, and the plastic wall slid up.

She walked on, heart pounding, feeling like a burglar.

A door was open on the right. From inside it came a single drawn-out note, and after a moment she recognized it as sound made by a human throat: a high, fluting note, curling from fear to despair—and abruptly cutting off.

And then a voice, someone else's voice: "The simple thing would have been to get a neurohumoral extractor up here, take it all right out."

"Scanlon had a requisition in for one, Doc." Another voice.

"But you can't get anything through the blockade, and they're hard to get anyway. Illegal as hell. Problem with customs."

"Is it illegal now? I've been up here too long—I didn't know."

Claire made herself walk up to the open door and look in.

There were three of them who were *like that.* Faceless in helmets. And the horror of their faceless heads was tripled: one would have unsettled her, but three splintered her will. The helmets they wore, blanking out their faces with opaque blue-green visors, looked like things made of beetle wings. They were NA "security bulls." And she thought, security *bulls* is wrong: they're like insects, insects big as men.

They were bent over the man strapped to the bed. *Molt.* She saw what they'd done to him. She bit her lip. To one side, a white haired, white-coated doctor looked faintly querulous as he glanced up at her from his instruments. Like something startled from feeding.

Claire stepped back, turned, pressed herself against the corridor wall, beside the door, and stopped thinking. She shouted into her comm button. She heard footsteps inside the cell, and a helmet-muted voice saying, "I don't know but we're sure as hell gonna find out who she is."

Claire was remembering a time as a little girl when she'd walked in on her parents and her dad had been all tied up in thin white ropes and her mother was standing over him with a whip and Daddy's face was all welted and, not understanding the sexual game, she'd thought, *If Mommy could do that to Daddy, she could hurt me, too.* It had turned her world view upside down. And she felt the same way now.

The Colony was something maternal to her, and now, beyond all reason, the Colony was hurting its children.

A sudden, cruel pain in Claire's right shoulder and she looked around to see the blank beetle-wing face distorting her reflection. The pain was his hand clamped on her. She pictured an insect claw clamping her shoulder, and she bit off a scream; and then the helmeted head tilted up to look past her, and magically, the carapace cracked down the middle.

Angie had come.

Angie followed up with a karate kick. The man staggered back, letting go of Claire's arm. The other women closed in as the second and third of the helmeted guards stepped out the door, electric stun batons swinging.

Judy pushed Claire out of the way; Claire fell back, and as she fell she saw something strange: Judy and Kris slapping the back of the beetle helmets. It seemed strangely like the sort of helpless-female gesture they abhorred, that slapping motion—and then Claire fell onto the floor. She lay still for a moment, trying to get her breath, then sat up and stared: the bulls were slapping at themselves, were screaming, writhing on their hands and knees, trying to claw their helmets off. Judy and Kris had—with what resembled ladylike slaps—attached high-frequency warblers to the helmets. Pain-inducing sound waves reverberated inside the helmets.

Then Judy and Angie and Kris stood around the fallen men and worked them over with nunchuks, whipping the chained clubs to strike in the unprotected places between the armored segments built into their flat-black uniforms. In their fencing masks and chest protectors, pounding mechanically with the nunchuks, the women looked as inhuman as the Security bulls . . .

Claire yelled, "Stop it stop it stop it!"

Then Angie was looking down at her, through the fly's-eye grid of the fencing mask. "What was it you said about using your 'sheer authority'?" she said.

Judy said, "Shut up, Angie." She helped Claire to her feet, and Claire made herself go in to help them take Molt off the bed. She didn't look at the unconscious men on the floor.

When they stepped into the room, Molt saw them and screamed, clawing at his straps, trying to get away from them.

• 13 •

It would be a real mistake to underestimate Ellen Mae Crandall, Swenson told himself, as he watched her talking to the Los Angeles SA recruiting staff on satvid. She likes to play shrinking violet, take-me-in-your-strong-hands, but for her it just might be a game, almost as vicarious as reading a romance novel. Or maybe that's wrong. Maybe when she changes, when she gets soft and pliable, she means it.

Maybe she's both people.

"Just make absolutely completely sure there's a clear division of intel awareness between the first two levels and the third. Need-to-know is the axis of the organization," she told the man on the screen.

Swenson, sitting hunched over the report spread out on the long wooden table, looked up again at the stainless-steel cross on the antique cabinet across the room. His eyes were drawn to it, again and again, and he knew that was dangerous.

It'll suck me right out of character, he thought. I could become Father Stisky.

He'd half expected to find swastikas on the walls at Cloudy Peak Farm. Portraits of Hitler. Something. But there was only the small German "iron cross" insignia, hardly noticeable, engraved into the intersection of the three-foot Christian Cross on its maplewood stand.

The long, narrow, book-lined room was log-cabin styled; halflogs on the inside and outside concealed the wall's electrical and electronic guts. There were tinted-glass Tiffany lampshades over the imitation gaslamps curving from the walls. An enormous flagstone fireplace hulked at one end. Swenson had looked twice to be sure the logs burning in the fireplace were real. In the acid-rain states it was illegal to cut trees for firewood. There just weren't enough trees left for that luxury.

The house wore its wood the way status-conscious socialites had once worn their minks. It had been "made out of the wood of the trees they found growing right here on the land, the way my brother wanted it," Ellen Mae had told him. "He likes things natural and simple, the way God likes them. God gave us dominion over all things of this world."

That's his problem, Swenson thought. He confuses what he likes with what God likes, all the way down the line.

And then he chided himself for falling out of character. *Don't even think things like that.*

She was standing over him now, and he looked up into her face—a face that looked craggier than ever in the uneven light, and he felt a purl of despair. *I not only have to make love to this woman, I have to do it well. I have to make her want more.*

"How's it look?" she said.

He stammered a moment, then realized she meant the report. "Um—I think it's just about ready."

Ellen Mae placed a hand on the table close to his left elbow and bent over him to look at the report, her arm around him like a schoolteacher looking at the work of a favorite child; his skin crackled with the slight furriness of her cheek. He felt a wave of revulsion—followed quickly by arousal, and he wondered where *that* was coming from.

"It looks fine," she said, scanning, flipping through it. Probably not really looking at all. Her breath smelled like iron.

She straightened and put her hands on his shoulders. "Let's visit Rick and we can give him this."

Oh, shit, he thought.

But aloud he said: "Great!" Sprightly as he could make it. He shuffled the papers together, put them in a folder, and added, "But maybe he'll want to see this as a readout. I could put the corrections on a datastick—"

"He wants it tonight if he can get it," she said. She sighed. "He shouldn't be working at night—he shouldn't be working at all—but just try to keep him from it."

Ellen Mae said it reverently.

• • •

It was like finding a secret passage that led from a home into a hospital.

They turned a corner, and the wooden hallways ended. Abruptly, they were in a long white hall: white tile floors, white walls; shiny pieces of medical apparatus on steel tables equipped with rollers, looking malevolently arcane, waited to be wheeled in to Crandall's room if the doctors needed it. There were three doctors here, specialists who were staying on at Cloudy Peak while Crandall was convalescing.

Were the doctors in the SA? Swenson wondered. They must be, for security reasons. Swenson reflected on the surprising number of educated men in the SA. Even intellectuals. But then, the driving force of the neofascist French New Right were its intellectuals. It was an old paradox: a powerful mind was no proof against stupidity. Ideas rooted in brutality had an emotional origin. Emotion could make any notion seem reasonable. *Stay in character, even in your mind.*

There was an SAISC guard standing in the doorway, his face hidden in a dark green-blue helmet. He stood with his legs braced apart, one gloved hand clasped over his wrist. He was like a living gun.

But he stepped aside, seeing Ellen Mae. She didn't even glance at him; it was as if he were a wall fixture.

And then Swenson followed her through, and there was Crandall, in bed, smiling up at them.

Swenson smiled back. But he couldn't look Crandall in the eye. So he looked around the room. On the tables beside the bed were framed pictures, some of Ellen Mae alone, one of Ellen Mae and their parents, who were said to be living on a ranch somewhere in New Mexico. In the picture Ellen Mae and her parents were sitting together on the bench of a picnic table. Ellen Mae looked like her father.

And she looked like Crandall. And Crandall had a lean, wolfish face that might have belonged to a backwoods imbecile—except for the personality shining through it, transforming it in some subtle way. The personality, the benevolence on a foundation of sheer self-certainty, made that inbred country face something magnetic.

Crandall had never been married. He said he was married to his mission. But in total there were four pictures of Ellen Mae, and Swenson wondered if there was some kind of repressed undercurrent of incest between Ellen Mae and Smiling Rick Crandall.

A bank of instruments clicked and peeped on the wall behind Crandall. From one of them a tube had extruded to sink its single silvery fang into a vein in Crandall's left forearm.

The room was decorated in soft white; the cabinets across from the bed were topped by pots holding a small forest of cream colored flowers. Swenson pictured the SA bomb detection team going through each vase and afterward meticulously putting the flowers back the way they'd been, and he almost laughed aloud.

He became aware of the tension knotting his chest then; he could see his own impending hysteria like the foreshortened horizon of a cliff's edge in the distance.

He fought it by sinking roots into the character, into Swenson.

Here's the trick, Purchase had told him. You have to be like a perfectly camouflaged bug in a fone. If it's made right, the antibugging team could take the fone apart and not find the bug. You've got to operate like a fone, buzz like a fone, do everything that a fone does, just exactly, and not transmit until it's time to transmit and then do it without breaching the illusion you're just a fone. You've got to think you're an ordinary "fone" until that moment.

But still, he thought, I could grab the guard's gun, I could kill them both right here. Sacrifice myself. Get it over with.

Only that wouldn't stop the SA. There was still Watson, and the others.

So he looked at Crandall and told himself, *This man's a hero. This man's a martyr. This man is here on a Holy Mission for God. This man is here to purify the world.*

And looking at Crandall, you could believe it. Even when he sat up, and they could see the bandages swathing his bony chest, and he muttered as he fumbled with the TV control unit to make the thin, filmy screen unreel from the ceiling.

"Something coming on TV, I want ya'll to see it," he said.

The viddy membrane dominated its part of the room. It held a perfect 3D image of a submarine surfacing, the water parting for the vessel like lace-edged stage-curtains.

" . . . As the art of making the ocean 'transparent' has improved," the commentator said, "techniques for making Russian submarines quieter improved almost simultaneously. This Russian 'bottom-crawler,' when in its cruising mode and not using its treads to crawl on the bottom, is outfitted with a new sound-damping device which absorbs the noise of its nuclear reactor's noisy cooling equipment, making it virtually impossible to detect with the sound surveillance system of hydrophones the Navy has planted along North America's continental shelf. Russian teams of saboteurs comb the shelves in bottomcrawlers, destroying fiberoptic sensor cables where they find them, further reducing our ability to detect enemy subs. The NSA has reported that the Russian ability to detect our submarines is enhanced by a new system of ocean-bed-implanted computers which monitor seabed vibrations and search for turbulence-vibrations typical of submarines. These developments threaten the delicate balance of deterrence that prevents the use of strategic nuclear weapons in the Russian-NATO war. If the Russians can detect American submarines carrying nuclear weapons, they could eliminate them, making a Russian first strike more practical."

Crandall switched off the sound. Images of deep-sea military juggernauts hunched silently across the screen. "Now, of course," Crandall drawled, "Mrs. Anna Bester might just be angling for more military funding, releasing this stuff. I had my misgivings about a woman president, but by gosh, the woman is no weak bleeding heart . . . But if this new threat to American subs is on the level, the SAISC might just have what they used to call a 'window of opportunity.' Our clandestine surveillance department has come up with something new we just might be able to trade to the Department of Defense for a little unbending on Our Work in Europe. If they gave us better logistical support, we'd have the European situation sewn up."

My God, Swenson thought. It hit Swenson like a blow to the stomach. *They're moving into everything.*

"The DoD has shown some interest in the new thing from Armaments," Ellen Mae said. "They'd like to see the Jægernaut field-tested . . . "

Crandall glanced at Swenson—and Swenson felt a chill.

"I think it's best we hold off on talking about that, Ellen Mae honey." Crandall said.

Because I haven't got a top-level SA Security clearance, Swenson thought.

Or is it more? Do they suspect me?

Purchase's people had gone to elaborate lengths to build up an identity for John Swenson: Birth certificate and baby pictures planted in a small Midwestern town; elaborate schemes to obtain letters of recommendation from SA members and supporters who were led to believe they knew Swenson when they didn't: Purchase had access to Worldtalk's memory-tampering systems. He fed false experiences into the men who were to give the recommendations; they seemed to remember Swenson's assistance, Swenson's right-wing politics, Swenson's sacrifices and invaluable advice.

Sackville-West had six hours of video interviews with SA sympathizers who "remembered" Swenson. And all the documentation was there.

But maybe Crandall smelled a ringer.

There'd been just the faintest flare of suspicion in Crandall's eyes, somehow not at all incongruous with the smile, when he'd shaken Swenson's hand.

Was it suspicion . . . Or jealousy? Swenson wondered. Crandall would know that Swenson and Ellen Mae were on the verge of becoming an item.

Suddenly Swenson was uncomfortably aware of the armed guard standing behind them, quiet as a piece of furniture, lethal as a bullet.

Crandall changed the subject, and Swenson forced himself to listen to Crandall's diatribe on a threatened liberalization of the ironically-named Antiviolence Laws of 2025.

" . . . The principle is very simple, as I see it, John," Crandall was saying. "And since it was voted into law, violent crime has been reduced in the country. I don't know the precise statistics . . . " He looked at Swenson.

Swenson knew he was being tested. The John Swenson created by Purchase was supposed to be an expert on the Antiviolence Laws. They'd steeped him in them. He knew the statistics, all right.

Swenson nodded and said, "Violent crime was reduced by twenty percent in the first five years, then by thirty-eight percent in the second five years, and now we're down forty-one percent. As I understand it, the program as it stands calls for the death penalty for the second homicidal violent crime—the first in cases involving sadism or torture—and for the third occasion of non-homicidal but nevertheless violent crime. Constitutional rights to appeal are suspended after the second conviction. The convict is to be executed within twenty-four hours of conviction, as inexpensively as possible. Senator Chung and Senator Judy Sanchez are leading the fight calling for the law's repeal . . . " Swenson paused, wondering if he was reciting *too* well. But Ellen Mae was beaming, nodding encouragingly, so he went on. "They are, I believe, uh, pointing up statistics showing that more people are executed who are later shown to have been innocent . . . But, of course—" He shrugged expansively, as if he couldn't understand how they could so stupidly miss seeing the obvious. "—the program's architects knew perfectly well that more innocent people would be convicted, by accident, because of the hastening of the judicial process . . . But because the program reduces violent crime by creating a stronger deterrent, and by taking killer-types not only off the street but out of the world, there are also fewer *victims* of violent crime. Which compensates for the rise in the number of innocent convictees. Victims of crimes are innocent, too."

Swenson cleared his throat apologetically, as if to say, Sorry about running off at the mouth that way. He looked modestly at Crandall and waited for the verdict.

Crandall grinned and said, "My Good *Lord* but he's got the gift, don't he!" He turned to Ellen Mae. "I wonder if Mr. John Swenson here could be convinced to do a little testifying for the CSO when they give their testimony in *support* of the Antiviolence Laws next month . . . ?"

"Well, don't look at me!" she said, laughing. "Why don't you ask him? He's standing right there."

Crandall lowered his voice to a stage whisper. He pretended to talk to her behind his hand. "You think ah dare tuh?" His accent deepening for the sake of humor.

Ellen Mae giggled.

Swenson thought, The CSO: Commission for Social Order. Controlled by the SA. Funded by the SA's friends. Advocates of a more "broad-minded" interpretation of the Constitution . . . Advocates of the imposition of martial law in high-crime areas. Most of the country's military manpower, including the majority of the Reserves and the National Guard, were either fighting the Russians overseas or massed along the USA's coasts. The implementation of martial law would require that some paramilitary, mercenary, or private police force be hired to supplement the urban police. And the biggest such organization was the SAISC.

Swenson marveled at the scale of Crandall's ambitions. But was it Crandall—or was it Watson? Or was there someone else, someone less public?

"Well, now, John boy, I was just wonderin' . . . " Crandall began, drawling it out slowly to give him his cue.

Swenson chuckled and said, "By some chance I happened to overhear. I'd be honored to testify for the CSO."

And he'd do it with conviction. He'd been a Jesuit for a few years—and he'd never believed in God. He could be an intellectualized fascist, too. He was good at playing parts, at being anyone but a man named Stisky.

•••

Ellen Mae Crandall came to him just five minutes after midnight, wearing an oversized, remarkably non-erotic bathrobe.

She was playing the lost, weak woman now. Her eyes were large and shiny in the dialed-down light of the hallway. She was carrying what he thought was a glass of warm milk, and her voice was slightly slurred. He smelled brandy on her.

"Hi . . . Could I talk to you about something? I'm sorry if you were asleep. I just—"

"I couldn't sleep, in fact," he said, moving back from the door to invite her in.

Swenson was wearing a bathrobe over pajamas. He felt strange in pajamas—he never wore them normally, but they seemed appropriate in this house. There wasn't even a computer console in his room.

Ellen Mae looked to see that the hall was empty. Then she padded into the room. He closed the door behind her. There was a moment of awkward silence. She held the glass up between them. "You—you really have to try this. It's my mother's recipe . . . " He smiled and took it gratefully, glad he wouldn't have to do the job without having a drink in him. He sipped and almost spat it out in his surprise. It was eggnog, with brandy in it. Thick, creamy, almost without sweetening. He thought of semen. He said, "Whoa. It's good."

"A little libation lengthens the life, my grandmother used to say."

Quoting her goddamned grandmother, he thought. And then he warned himself: *Get into the role!*

She rubbed her eyes. "My eyes are so tired. Looking at a screen all day . . . "

Swenson knew what that meant. He turned and dialed the light lower. "How's that?"

"Better."

"Come and sit down, and tell me about it."

In the dimness, he almost liked the way she looked. Or maybe it was the brandy.

She sat down beside him; the bed didn't creak—they never did anymore.

He took one of her hands between his, smiled, and said, "Tell me about it."

It was all in his voice. He felt her squirm a little with pleasure.

"Well, you know, I love Rick. I really believe in my heart he's been chosen by God for a special mission. I'd never say this in front of him because he won't have anyone putting on airs for him, but I truly believe he's the most important man in the world today. Not because of what he is—but because of what he'll be. But . . . I have to have some life of my own, outside of Rick. You know—a little more life than Our Work." She made a soft sound of guilt and indecision. "I don't know—maybe I'm wrong to want it—"

Again, he knew his cue. "Not at all."

"But—Gramma always said, 'Follow your heart.'"

He listened to her in wonder. She could talk blithely and with expertise—about demographic surveys, clandestine cellular organization, and security enforcement techniques. And out of the same mouth she spouted this incredible *corn*.

"Does—does Rick disapprove when you have a private life?"

"Well—he disapproves of, you know, anything *intimate* that happens outside of marriage. And I have to be very careful about getting married because it's a media event."

"Of course. But if you are discreet . . . "

He could almost feel her blush. "Yes, but . . . it's a sin."

Uh-huh, he thought.

He didn't believe for a moment that she or Crandall gave a damn, as it were, about sin. Except for the cameras. Not in any real way.

"I understand," he said gently, pressing her hand. "But—surely God understands your special predicament. And in any event, Jesus said even the worst sinners are forgiven if they genuinely ask. You'll be forgiven."

"Oh . . . " Just melting now. He'd said it right.

She bent and rested her head on his shoulder, tilted up just enough.

He let go of her hand, slid his right arm around her waist, and bent to press her wiry lips with a kiss.

He had been afraid he'd be unable to get it up for her. But his imagination performed the miracle for him. In fact, her angular body was not so different from that copper-skinned boy's, the boy later found in a ditch with so many holes punched into him, like Saint Sebastian transfixed by arrows . . . It was the image of Saint Sebastian writhing in martyrdom, the arrows so stiff and masculine in his wounds, that made Swenson stiff and masculine, made it possible to transfix her, to pretend, to pretend within the pretense.

How our special pathologies do serve us, he thought, as he pressed her back onto the bed.

• • •

When Rickenharp came out of it he sat up—and almost fell over with the weakness.

"Too soon." Carmen said, pressing him back. He lay back and felt better. He was still weak, but the gnawing soul-horror was gone. All he felt now, besides weak, was hungry.

The world shook around him, like it was laughing, a growling sort of laugh, and then he put it together. He was in the back of a truck. They were on the flatbed. The light came from the space between the tailgate and the canvas cover over the rusty slats.

It was bluish light, and he thought it might be dawn. The air on his face was cold, but warmth seeped up from the engine, and a faint scent of methane.

"I'm hungry as a bastard," he said. His throat was dry, he realized as he tried to talk. It came out a rasp.

But she understood. "We haven't got any food. Maybe next stop, if we're lucky. Anyway, your fever seems to be gone."

"Where are we?"

"Northern Italy. North of Naples. You've been out for days. Willow . . . " She paused and he saw the flash of her teeth. "Willow wanted to dump you, more than once. I was inclined to agree with him. Keeping you isn't practical. But Yukio says you're some kind of samurai. He wants you along." She shrugged.

Italy? Fucking crazy. He closed his eyes and visualized sausage tied up in strings and platters of steaming pasta.

He could smell the sea in the breeze now, as they took a curve, and a fresh wind hit them.

What was it she'd said?

Willow wanted to dump you. I was inclined to agree with him.

They'd almost thrown him overboard into the Mediterranean. No doubt for the "greater good."

"My fans," he muttered.

"What?"

But be didn't have anything to say to her.

To hell with her.

• • •

Ellen Mae was gone when Swenson woke. There was a silk rose lying on the pillow beside him. The brandy-eggnog glass was gone. He had, literally, a bad taste in his mouth.

Swenson sat up and his head throbbed. Wan sunlight filtered through the yellow-curtained windows to either side of the bed.

A discreet tap came from the other side of the door. He groaned inwardly, thinking, *Not her again so soon!*

But he put on his robe and said, "Come in."

It was a uniformed houseboy, an old man with age-blurred eyes, silent except for his labored breathing as he wheeled in the breakfast tray and poured the coffee. Somehow, Swenson was surprised that the old man wasn't black. But he thought, Of course not, they wouldn't trust black servants, they could be infiltrators.

The old man shuffled out and Swenson lifted the old silver cover off the plate. Bacon and eggs and biscuits. None of it looked synthetic. It would be interesting to see what they tasted like.

But he almost gagged on the bacon. You could really taste *the animal* in it.

There was a note in an envelope on the tray.

He assumed it was from her, but it wasn't.

Welcome, John! Meet me out at the front gate at 0900.

—Watson

So Watson was here. Swenson glanced at his watch. Almost eight.

He got up and dressed, muttering, "Oh-eight-hundred. Shit." But he almost ran to get there on time.

Outside, he found a sky the color of granite, the sun a blur of brass behind the overcast. And the massive posts of the original front gate were granite, old granite torn three centuries before from the ancient New England hills, much of it painted bright yellow and red by lichen. The old stone fence to either side of the gates had fallen down in places. But it didn't matter; a few feet in from the stone fence the steel-mesh barricades loomed, two of them, crested with concertina wire.

A pair of German shepherds paced restlessly between the steel fences—seeing Swenson they threw themselves against the links, making the fence ring like chain mail as he approached the first checkpoint. He expected the dogs to bark, but they didn't. They snarled, furrowing their muzzles, fixing their yellow glares on him. He remembered the strong taste of the bacon, and his stomach lurched.

His shoes crunched in the agate cinders of the drive. A helmetless SAISC guard looked at him with a dilution of the same look the dogs gave him. The guard stepped out of a small wooden shack on the other side of the hurricane-fence gate and said, "Name, please?"

Stisky.

He almost said it. And what frightened him was this: it hadn't been an accident. He badly wanted to say it.

The guard was blond and blue-eyed. The blue eyes were narrowed now. Because Swenson had hesitated.

"John Swenson."

The guard nodded, his eyes still narrowed. "The colonel's gone on already. Said you could catch up with him at the chapel."

The flat blue eyes regarded him steadily, the glare gone, only unflinching appraisal now. The eyes were lined with white-blond lashes, long and soft as a small boy's.

"Where's the chapel?"

The guard pointed. It was off to the northeast, half-hidden in the oak trees that fringed the grounds. Looking at it, Swenson felt a spike of ice through his belly.

The chapel was beautiful. And he was afraid of it. Moving like a wooden soldier, he began to walk toward it.

It was a simple chapel of white wood, with stained-glass windows. He couldn't make out from here what the figures in the stained glass represented.

The chapel stood almost demurely in a stand of oak trees shaggy with moss and mistletoe. Swenson crossed a lawn to reach it, his shoes getting soaked by the dew in the fragrant grass. He shivered. It was a chill, clammy morning. There were wraiths of fog, yet, under the oak trees. Fallen leaves whispered beneath his feet as he walked up to the chapel's front steps. The chapel was bigger than he'd thought. Room for two hundred.

The oaks creaked faintly in a puff of breeze.

Oaks, he thought. *Druidic.*

He opened the green-painted chapel door.

There were two Nazis, in full uniform, kneeling before the altar, pig-shaven heads bowed in prayer.

To one side stood Colonel Watson, in a neat gray suit and trenchcoat, his face florid with the chill. On the other was Sackville-West, sitting in a pew, head bowed, hat in hands.

Over the altar was a twelve-by-eight-foot oil-painting, professionally but cornily rendered, showing Jesus sitting on his throne, his face uncharacteristically creased in a scowl of judgment. On his head was a circlet of oak-leaves. Sitting at his feet were Rick and Ellen Crandall, painted with just a little flattery, both in white robes. There was a steel cross on a blond-wood stand under the painting, and imprinted at the intersection of its bars, no bigger than a silver dollar, was an "iron cross." To either side of the dais area were furled flags—an Old Glory, a Confederate flag, and one he didn't recognize, its insignia folded away. White tulips stood in a silver vase on the altar, a floral benediction.

The room blushed with rosy light from the stained glass. He looked at the stained-glass figures and didn't recognize them.

There were paintings along the walls to either side of the pews. He couldn't make them out from here, except that they were neurotically intricate and allegorical, with figures suspended in the heavens in hallucinogenic clusters.

Swenson couldn't move. He was transfixed there at the entrance. He told himself, *Don't be stupid. Don't be a child.*

But he stayed where he was until Watson looked over and beckoned.

He walked down the aisle past the empty pews toward the black-coated backs of two Nazis in full, mid-twentieth century SS uniforms, kneeling at the altar in silent prayer.

Watson stepped out of the chancel, and with the exaggerated quiet of a man wary of a sacred moment, walked down the outside aisle, then gestured for Swenson to join him three pews back.

The two men sat down side by side on the hard wooden pews.

"Sackville-West wants you along," Watson said, more a mutter than a whisper.

"Along on what?"

Watson snorted and nodded toward the two Nazis, figures from a propaganda painting. "We're going to 'initiate' those two nitwits . . . " He shrugged, and the briskness of the motion told Swenson that the colonel was irritated; irritated just short of fury. "A man named Strawling from Idaho—he attended one of our conventions out in Orange County. By some administrative mistake, this man Strawling was allowed into the SA-Initiates meetings, attended Special Services, the whole bit. Got himself all excited. Turns out he belongs to the National Socialist White People's Party! We'd had no idea, of course. We don't need unsubtle dunderheads among the Initiates . . . But somehow he slipped through the screenings . . . He told his pal, the one kneeling there beside him, and they came out here . . . Just drove up to the goddamn gate at dawn, told the guards they wanted to see Rick Crandall. They heard about the assassination attempt—wanted to be his bodyguards!" His voice dripped with contempt. "They were all got up like that! At the gates of Cloudy Peak Farm, dressed like *that*! Like old school twentieth century Nazis! Christ, if some reporter was hanging around . . . " He shook his head. "Naturally we didn't let them in to see Rick. The guards rang Sackville-West and old Sacks rang me out of a sound sleep and we went to see Rick. He said they should make their peace with God, so here they are. I don't know why Sacks wanted you along—" Swenson felt Watson look at him. "But I think it's a kind of initiation for you, too. Not the kind those two are getting, of course . . . "

Swenson nodded. He sat like something carved into the wood of the pew, remembering the Second Circle, and the Services, the pageantry of it, and how he'd almost lost himself . . .

• • •

Excerpt from a memo
From: Frank Purchase to Quincy Witcher

Thought you would be interested in the following letter from Stisky to Encendez. Father Encendez was in prison at the time of the letter's composition. The letter was never mailed. We found it when we went through Stisky's effects.

. . . the truth is, I never believed. When I entered the Church, I "suspended my disbelief" like you do when you're reading a novel. You believe in the novel's subjective world while you're reading it, but of course you know it's all made up. But you prefer to believe, while you're reading, because you love the intricacy, the marvel of it, the sublime distraction of it. I feel the same way about The Church. The Church is a she, and I once fell in love with a woman, and knew that, despite all she said, she didn't love me back, not really. The love I fantasized was unreal, and I knew it, but I made myself believe in it because it was a delicious reassurance. The Church has a thousand volumes of love letters it has written to itself, in the form of the Apologias and so forth, in all their manifestations. The Church is a beautiful lie. I saw no harm in the necessary casuistry. And it gave me a base to work from, to help the poor. I wanted to get in among the people who needed me, and it put me there. I wonder about my own underlying motives, though. The pageantry of the Church, the patina of glamour on the rituals; the pleasantly musty homeliness of a Jesuitical library; the asceticism so weighty with our self-congratulation. But most of all the pageantry, like the tarted-up garishness of a Parisian whore, the rituals, the accoutrements, all of it seduces me . . .

As you can see, our "Swenson" has a profound psychological need for ritual. The more dramatic the ritual, the better. Again, his predilections are a double-edged sword. I worry that when he undergoes the SA's Second Circle training program, and sees the neofascist splendor of their Services, he may fall under their spell. He denied his faith, in private, and he was rebellious, but ultimately his actions bespoke a strong loyalty to the Church, until he was defrocked. If he develops the same neurotic attachments to the rituals of the SA's inner circle, we may lose his loyalty entirely . . .

• • •

They were walking through the slowly dissipating mists, under the oak trees. An SAISC guard in full mask walked ahead, carrying a rifle, like a platoon patrol's point man; then came Swenson with Watson and the two Nazis walking to Watson's left. Behind them were two more faceless SA guardsmen.

They strolled along a trail, under a tracework of damp black twigs having the look of old electrical cords. Winter-withered ferns arced dripping to either side; there was a smell of rotting wood and mushrooms. A single blackbird trilled and warbled and trilled yet again. Swenson was cold. He zipped up his jacket and balled his hands in his pockets.

He thought he could feel the guards looking at his back.

The Nazis were wearing their shiny billed caps now. There was a young one with beetling brows and a weak chin, and an older one with a face like a knot of old tree wood. They both had Western accents; they'd come from northern Idaho. "The panhandle," they said. They both owned businesses out that way, but they'd decided coming here was more important. A man had to choose between profit and duty sometimes, the young one had said. No matter what they said, Watson acted as if he saw the perfect rightness of it. He nodded and said, "Mm-hmm, oh, I agree," now and then. Their dress uniforms were knife-creased, neat as a pin, complete with swastika armbands; their boots spit-polished. Swenson saw Watson wince when he looked at the armbands.

The two men didn't seem to understand what was happening. Except that, now and then, the older one glanced nervously over his shoulder at the guards.

They came to another steel-mesh fence; the sentry let the German Shepherds tug him along between the inner and outer fences.

The trail veered left, hooking back toward the chapel, and they turned to follow it. They walked along silently for another hundred feet and stopped when they came to a small clearing. The brush had grown up thickly around the clearing. To one side was a wooden bench cut from a log. Watson smiled wearily at the Nazis and said, "Sit down, boys." They looked dubiously at the log; the dampness would stain their uniforms. But they sat.

Suddenly the older one, licking his lips, looked up and said, "Maybe we shouldn'ta come here like this. Guess we shoulda called. But we got the runaround when I tried to write. I figured I had to go right to Reverend Crandall. But if you say we leave, well, I guess we'll sure leave."

"Nobody said anything about your having to leave," Watson said neutrally. He took a neatly folded handkerchief from his coat pocket and blew his nose on it. "You see," he went on, "we have us a problem." His shift into rustic speech mannerisms was more friendly than mocking. "Now, it's like this. You had access to things you weren't supposed to have access to. Just a mix-up. Ours really. But people at your level of activity aren't supposed to be seen in association with Reverend Crandall. It's not good public relations. You're not even supposed to know how to find him. I just hope and pray no one was watching when you folks drove up dressed like that: Now, we can't take the chance that you'll leave here and tell some more of your people where to find Rick. And then again, you represent a security risk in other ways. We don't want people running around who might feel rejected, and become disgruntled with the Reverend. Especially not people with a bombing record." He looked at the young man, who went pale. "You see, young man, we know all about you already. We know where your friends and family are . . . How many others did you tell?"

"Nobody else!" the older Nazi said indignantly. "I knowed it was top secret."

Watson smiled. He glanced at Sackville-West. The old man shrugged.

"I believe you." Watson said. "But . . . we'll have to look into that."

It had taken the younger one a while to get the upshot, but he burst out, "You saying we oughta be ashamed to come here dressed like this? This uniform symbolizes our martyrdom to the Aryan cause! We're pariahs and we know it and we do it 'cause it's right! All over the world people are interbreedin' with animals! White women and men having congress with black animals and stinking up their blood with the blood of monkeys!"

"Very colorful way to put it." Watson said, dabbing daintily at his nose with the handkerchief. "You know, in a way I almost agree with you."

"Almost!" The young Nazi looked at the impassive faces around him, at the faceless helmets, and let his exasperation carry his voice into shrillness. "Hey now, I got to get this straight. Do you folks believe in the Triumph of the White Race or *not*?"

Watson looked musingly into his handkerchief. "I suppose you deserve an answer at least . . . My boy, the answer is yes and no. I believe in it, but not the way you believe in it. You see, I happen to believe that Negroes are in fact an inferior race, in a certain sense. For example, some claim they don't pan out on the genetic scale for intelligence quotients. But you know that conclusion could be disputed, and I'd be willing to listen to evidence that maybe they're as intelligent as we are, after all. Maybe they are. Maybe they're not a *bit* inferior. I don't know. Rick Crandall doesn't know. And what's more, we don't care. We happen to think, first of all, that miscegenation—interbreeding—is a bad thing, leading to genetic impurity, but not because the other races are low but because it creates too many uncontrollable variables in the genetic process."

"Genetic process! You people believe in *evolution*?" the younger one sputtered.

The older one had put his elbows on his knees and his head in his hands. He groaned and shook his head. "Best not get us in any deeper, Elwood."

"Well now, we believe that genetics is God's Tool," Watson said. He chuckled at some private joke and went on, "Now, in the beginning, could be that God created the world in seven days. Like it says in the Book. But after that, after he sent Adam and Eve out of Eden, he used genetics to do some of his work here . . . " He cleared his throat, and Swenson, watching him, felt sure that Watson didn't actually believe in Creationism of any sort. Swenson felt light-headed. He almost laughed aloud.

"We in fact believe," Watson went on, warming to his subject, "that racism, as it's called, ought to be an instrument of administrative policy in the coming world government. And we know precisely how to use the social phenomenon that historians call 'fascism' to further that ambition. But you gentlemen have made the fatal error of mistaking the means for the end. And the . . . *trappings* you've chosen are no longer appropriate. They are socially poisoned by the awkward people who wore them before."

"Awkward?" the young man was shocked. "You talking about *Adolf Hitler*?"

His outrage was palpable.

The older Nazi groaned, "Dammit, Elwood, shut up. Shut the hell up."

"Hitler?" Watson shrugged. "Hitler was a madman. Worse, he was unsubtle and inefficient—Well, you could argue that he very efficiently got rid of the six million Jews, and, of course, he did us all a favor—those people are too smart for their own good, or ours. But otherwise—"

The young man sprang up with tears in his eyes. "I ain't gonna listen to any more of this!"

"You won't have to," Watson said gently. He stepped back.

Sackville-West stepped back, well out of the way. Swenson mechanically followed suit.

Not you, Swenson, you're going where they're going.

Swenson froze.

And then he realized he'd heard it in his mind. No one had spoken to him. The voice was a product of his suppressed terror, the twisting fear that he had been brought out here to be executed—

The two Nazis jumped to their feet and turned to run. The guards pointed their guns and opened up, and the terrible thing was, there was almost no sound.

The automatic weapons were fitted with suppressors. They made only soft, stammering hisses as the two Nazis exploded with blood under the impact of scores of rounds, as if magic made them open up with little faucets of red, made them dance and spin . . . in the quiet morning . . .

Then they'd fallen, slumped over the log side by side.

Swenson thought, *I should be happy.* Two more Nazis dead. Killed by their own kind. Steinfeld didn't even have to waste bullets on them.

But he felt only a kind of gnawing numbness.

He seemed to see the body of a beautiful, copper-skinned young man dead in a ditch, riddled with bullets.

And then he visualized the painting of Saint Sebastian, skewered with arrows . . .

Oh, no, he thought. *Oh, God, no. I've got an erection.*

And the sickness passed.

A fourth guard strolled up, carrying two body bags. "Where will he take them?" Swenson heard himself ask dazedly.

"We have a crackerjack incinerator here," Watson said. "Just the best."

"Waste of time, all that speechmaking." Sackville-West said. He was notorious for his taciturnity.

Watson smiled and said, "Where's your feelings, Sacks? They had their hearts in the right place, after all. Anyway, I thought our friend Mr. Swenson here could use some clarity on where we stand."

No one spoke for a few moments. Swenson peered up through the interlacing branches, trying to see the sun. The sky beyond the naked twigs was uniformly steel gray. The woods were silent, except for the strikingly unnatural sound of the body bags being zipped up.

• 14 •

"Hey—how about leaving me a gun?" Rickenharp said. "What the hell. I mean, if I have to stay in this fucking truck alone—this fucking truck I've been in all fucking day long. Not to complain or anything."

Carmen paused, straddling the truck's closed tail-gate, and looked back at him. She'd just said, *Stay here, don't move, if anybody speaks to you play dumb. We're going to see if the pass is open.*

Now she was a silhouette, spiky black against the deep indigo of the late evening sky. Even her cold-plumed breath showed in silhouette.

And Rickenharp was sitting with his back to the cold steel, his muscles cramping with the chill of it.

Carmen made a hissing sound of impatience and swung back into the rear of the truck. She crouched by her pack, and he heard the crisp sound of nylon rustling. She took a wedge of darkness from the pack and, moving crabwise, came to hunch beside him.

He felt something cold and heavy pressed into his hands. She was a figure of darkness giving him the means to kill. "It's a machine pistol," she said.

Her hands were still on the pistol, and the pistol was in his hands. It was an assassin's benediction. She was touching him via the pistol.

There was a faint, neat-edged click in the darkness.

The gun glowed in his hands; it shone from within.

The pistol was transparent and electrically lit up. It was framed with stainless steel; the inner sections of the gun were made of glass-clear hyper-compressed plastic. He could see into the magazine, could see the bullets in the clip like a row of robot larvae. A tiny light in the pistol's butt and another under the breech gave the gun an eerie blue glow.

She ticked a black-painted fingernail against a stud just above the trigger guard. "That's the safety. *Up* is safety off. After that all you have to do is aim and squeeze the trigger. Those are .22 rounds. Not big, but very precise. The small rounds give you a clip of forty . . . "

Willow hissed from the tailgate. "Put out that bloody light in there! And come *on*!"

She showed Rickenharp the light switch on the back of the butt and flicked it off. "Light shows up your position—it's only in case you have to check the gun when you're under cover. Don't shoot unless you're sure someone's shooting at you, or about to. You might shoot a friend by accident. These plastic guns look like children's toys. They're not." She moved away and slipped out of the truck.

He wanted to ask her, *What made you so sure I didn't know anything about guns?* But he realized it was a stupid question.

Carefully, holding the gun up so he could see it against the screen of night sky above the tailgate, he took the grip in his hand and slipped his finger into the trigger guard.

He looked at it for a moment; in the darkness it was like an outgrowth of his arm. And a door opened inside him, and something slithered out of the door, leaving a trail of thrill behind it.

Rickenharp drew the gun close to his chest, between both hands, and looked out into the night.

Now and then he had to shrug down farther into his coat, to shake the shivering off. He took deep breaths, trying to stoke oxygen fires in himself, and thought, *Christ! Maybe I'm drugged-out delirious. Maybe I'm still back in Freezone, hallucinating in my shit-hole hotel room. Or maybe I really am somewhere in the Alps with a machine pistol in my hands.*

He thought of Ponce and the band. That scene ain't real, you Gridnipplers. THIS is real! Gridfriend help me, this is real.

He wiped his nose on his sleeve and listened.

No sound, except the the snap-sound of the wind whipping the canvas. The minutes passed—or maybe they didn't. He wasn't sure how long it was before he heard the voices.

Guttural voices. Foreign language.

He thought, *Russians.*

Willow had talked about it, blasé as a trucker talking about the highway patrol. "Some of the Alps are Russian and some parts aren't, and the bloody borders keep shifting. NATO territory today is Russian tomorrow and vice versa, like," he'd said.

. . . Crunch of footsteps . . .

I'd have heard gunfire if it was the Russians, he told himself.

But not necessarily. Yukio, Willow, and Carmen might have walked right into a trap—been forced to surrender without firing a shot. Maybe a mile down the road they're tied up, lying gagged in the back of another truck. Russian truck. Or SAISC—worse. And the SA could be anywhere.

The talking had stopped. *Crunch.* Footsteps again. Closer.

He brought the gun around and rested his elbow on his right knee. He trained the gun on the rear of the truck.

And the Russians torture everybody for intelligence nowadays, Willow had said. Even sheep farmers.

He reached across the top of the gun and flicked off the safety.

The guttural voice again. He tried to be sure of the language. Couldn't hear it clearly enough.

A creak as someone stepped onto the rear bumper, two shapes blurred together in the rear, the guttural voice again, and then the rear of the truck lit up—

It lit up with strobe flashes, four of them, going off like flashbulbs, making the scene at the rear of the truck into a choppy motion-picture sequence: Carmen, hand lifted over her eyes, mouth opened to shout, a strange man beside her in a watch cap, his eyes wide; Carmen with two red holes in her chest; Carmen with arm flung up; Carmen falling back.

The back of the truck echoed, a metallic lisp for each gunshot.

And Rickenharp realized he'd squeezed the trigger.

He thought, Willow said something yesterday about meeting some Swiss friends.

And then: I shot Carmen.

• • •

"The truth is," Molt was saying, "there are two factions in administration. One faction is basically in favor of martial law in the Colony. Their attitude is something like, the danger to the station's life-support system is too great if they let things go on."

Bonham sat in the After, listening to Molt talk on an old twelve-inch TV sunk flush with the wall, thinking, *Molt sounds tired, mechanical. Barely maintaining.*

And the TV in Prego's After was tired itself, barely maintaining, the talking-head image of Molt warping into the outline of a peanut shell, making Molt look even more tired.

Bonham nestled back in the easy chair. The chair took up half the room. Like everything else in the small room, the chair was frayed, ripping out at the seams, and grimy. The walls were papered with fading printout porn; marker graffiti overlapped unreadably on the walls between the printout girls. There was a mattress behind the easy chair stained with a revolting potpourri of effluvia. This end of the Colony had some kind of heat-convection problem and Prego had been issued a space heater to compensate; the heat rose and its waves lifted the papery girls by the corners of their pages; the heat had activated the decay factor built into the paper, so that the underprinting was showing through: TIME TO RECYCLE ME. There was a heap of Prego's laundry beside the TV set; its sourness dominated the room.

There were three rooms in Prego's After; the other two malodorous, trashed-up rooms were bigger, crowded with people drinking Prego's foul home brew; *fermented garbage,* Molt called it. Bonham had the door closed and the TV turned up as loud as it would go, to beat the sounds coming from the other rooms: laughter, minimono blaring; he had to strain to hear as Molt, on TV, went on, " . . . The other faction is . . . I believe . . . sincerely interested in negotiating a compromise with strikers. The blockade state of emergency is a time when we should all be working together to survive . . . " He paused to glance at his notes. Bonham saw that Molt's hands were shaking and he blinked too often.

Molt was replaced by Asheem Spengle; the technicki commentator's triple-Mohawk was comically warped by the distortion in the upper half of the screen so that he looked like a tropical bird. He said something in technicki, which was translated at the bottom of the screen in subtitles. " . . . And that was our excerpt from Radleader Molt's media conference, which he gave yesterday after his release from Colony Detention . . . We noticed that more than once Radleader Molt referred to a written text in giving his statement. We cannot help but wonder who wrote that text. Was it indeed Radleader Molt? Or was it written for him by Colony Admin? Molt's statement was followed by an endorsement from the Colony's own founder, Professor Rimpler, and his daughter Claire . . . Clearly Molt's involvement with these two high administration figures sheds doubt on the sincerity of his—"

Bonham changed the channel, muttering, "Bullshit."

Another news show, this one in Standard English delicately articulated by an anchorwoman who looked like she was from the Middle East: " . . . have renewed their demands on a document teletyped to Admin officials today; the council of radleaders demanded a timetable for technicki integration into Admin housing projects in the Open, technicki representation in all

Admin governing committees, guarantees of improved living conditions, and removal of SAISC 'conflict prevention guards' from technicki gathering places and hallways . . . " Bonham leaned forward, seeing himself on the screen, a slightly wobbly image, a burst of static fuzzing the anchorwoman's words. He caught, " . . . Bonham, chairman of the Radleader council, speaking today . . . "

Then he heard his own voice and hated the sound of it over TV. It sounded bloodless, too high-pitched. And Prego's damn screen was warping his image, making his head quiver like a soap bubble. He heard himself say, " . . . amazed they think we can be manipulated with double-talk out of George Orwell like 'conflict prevention guards.' Storm troopers are storm troopers."

Bonham shrugged. It was okay. Sometimes they used a slice that made you sound a fool. But that one went right to the point.

The anchorwoman was going on to something not directly related to Bonham, and Bonham began to lose interest. " . . . Full power was restored to the top four sublevels today by Admin technicians, despite technicki striker efforts to sabotage the conduits to—"

" 'Con-dew-its,' " Bonham said. "Nobody uses that word anymore. But I like the shape your lips make when you use it."

He kicked the switch with the toe of his rubber cowboy boot and sadly watched the lovely brown-eyed face compact and vanish into itself.

He looked at his watch, and thought, *I'm late, just about the right amount.*

Bonham got up, stretched, and picked his way through the room, through the door to the next, larger room crowded with partiers, thudding with minimono; he moved deftly through the tangle of legs, avoiding the ones who deliberately tried to trip him; he blinked against the thick smoke, thinking the smoke seemed to be moving to the music (but that couldn't be possible, could it?), and found the door.

The After was illegal, and Admin was beginning to crack down on places like it, correctly figuring them to be hotbeds of radical fermentation. So he paused at the monitor screens, checked the hall for bulls, swiveling Prego's camouflaged TV camera both ways. All clear.

Bonham opened the door, stepped through, closed it quickly behind him. Rubbing his eyes, he hurried down the corridor to the nearest crossover.

He passed a gaggle of technickids graffiting the corridor wall; they froze when he turned the corner, looking over their shoulders at him. He smiled and shrugged, and they grinned, relaxing. There were four of them, all about eleven years old, and they were in four colors: Hispanic derivation, black, Caucasian, and one that was maybe southeast Asian. Their jumpsuits were tricked out with buttons and patches—their parents' tech rating patches, next to minimono wiredancers looking dolefully out from glossy buttons, as unreal as the buttons showing cartoon characters.

The corridor here was riotous with graffiti, almost black with it in places; the sloganeering that had begun it was clotted over with obscenities and identities and gang symbols. There was more gang graffiti lately, and he wondered if it was time to take the techni-kid gangs seriously as a threat.

The door into the crossover for the Open had been vandalized off its hinges. Halfway down the crossover, an SAISC guard blocked the way. Maybe the guard was that far back from the door because the ones who stood right in the doorways were just begging for a lob. Bonham had once lobbed a Molotov himself, and then thought, *Am I crazy? If this place burns down there's nowhere to run to.*

Could the Colony burn? Some said yes, some said no, some said portions of it could, and there might be flammable insulation in the walls, and if flammable wire burned back to that flammable insulation, the place could fill with smoke, and even though there were theoretically enough gas masks and shelter-suits to go around, word was about a third of them had been vandalized or decayed past use . . . Bonham occupied his mind that way, trying to throw off the jitters and only making it worse as he walked up to the armoured guard.

He couldn't look up into that blue-green curved-mirror face, he just couldn't make that, so he looked at the middle of the gray-black chest and said, "Bonham, security pass 4555." The bull tapped his wrist console. "Repeat."

Bonham repeated it for the voice analyzer; the analyzer transmitted to Security Central's computer, which compared the registered sound waves with Bonham's own, checked the code number, and flashed a picture of Bonham to the tiny screen on the inside right of the guard's mask.

"Go ahead, sir, and have a nice walk," the bull said, stepping aside.

Bonham walked past, and looked at his watch. He picked up his pace . . .

. . . She was where she said she'd be, and she had only one bodyguard with her.

Judith Van Kips stood in the very center of the construction site. The fiberplas frame of the unfinished condo rose around her like a cage. It was a gilded cage, because the Open's light had been filtered and tinted red-gold to make a sunset; in another hour it would be dark. The corridors, too, would dim, normally, in order to produce regular circadian rhythms. But they were well-lit full-time since the strikes, the riots . . .

The light from the sunward glass made black bars of shadow across the red-dirt site, across Judith Van Kips' long, straight flaxen hair and the black uniform of the masked guard behind her.

Heart pounding, Bonham stepped through the frame of the door, thinking, If I change my mind and back out now, the bull's going to grab me, and they won't let anybody bust me out like Molt.

"That's close enough," she said.

Bonham stopped ten feet from her. "I don't like the bull listening."

"He's my Personal. We can trust him. Hold still now."

He waited it out, rigid and sweating, as the SAISC guard ran a weapon detector over him, then patted him down.

The bull put the instrument back in his belt pack and drew his gun. Judith Van Kips smiled when she saw the fear on Bonham's face.

"It's just in case," she said.

Bonham shrugged, just as if he hadn't been a fraction of a reflex away from rushing that gun. "You and Praeger bought that bozo Spengle."

She didn't say anything to that.

He went on, "I'm going to cost more than Spengle." He smiled. "Some journalists are more expensive than others."

She waited.

The breeze, the carefully engineered breeze, played with the precisely cut ends of her flaxen hair, drifting them across her carefully engineered face, a face too perfect to be natural.

"I want the money, and I want out. Home. Earth. Maybe—" He shrugged. "Trinidad might be nice. Or Freezone."

"The blockade." Her voice was almost inflectionless.

"Don't bullshit me. I know about the treaty. They're going to allow limited shipping to go through. For food, basic supplies. Bare minimum, no import, no export, freeze on all transport. But ships coming in will have to go back. Some of your people will be going back on them. I want to go, too."

"Where did you hear about the treaty?"

"One of my boys—maybe I'll call him my *Personal*—he, uh—he has got the touch, and Gridfriend's always at his elbow. He sucked your commlines. He and I are the only ones who know. Unless—" He shrugged. "Unless he blows it. But I don't think he will."

"His name."

Bonham shook his head.

She looked at the bull, as if thinking of having the name squeezed out of Bonham. But she thought better of it. Praeger had plans for Bonham.

Finally, she shrugged. "Keep an eye on your friend. And be careful no one learns about the treaty. We've gone to great lengths to keep it out of the media."

"Is it you, jamming transmissions from Earth?"

"Some frequencies yes, some frequencies no. As for moving you to Earth, it might be possible. I'll speak to Praeger. If he authorizes it, you'll be told by coded comm, same code as previously."

"I want the money in a sealed credit-cassette. A tamper-proof credette. Twenty-five thousand newbux."

"That's five thousand more than we agreed on."

"I'm doing more than risking my life. I'm betraying my people. And I got to live with that. In a way I'm throwing away a lifetime."

"You're not betraying anything you really believed in, or you wouldn't be capable of doing it at all. I personally will authorize the additional five thousand. But there will be no more."

"Okay. So what do you want me to do—precisely?"

"First, reinforce Spengle's intimation that Molt might be under someone else's control. Second, and most important, militate against any compromising with Admin. Insist it must be all or nothing."

Bonham's stomach flip-flopped with sheer disgust. Disgust with them—and disgust with himself, because he knew he'd go through with it. If he pushed the technicki radleaders into an 'all or nothing' posture, Admin would be "forced" into complete martial law, multiple arrests, sweeps of technicki quarters.

And executions.

Legally, Admin had the power to declare martial law. Once martial law was declared, Admin was authorized to execute anyone it regarded as threatening to the airtight integrity and general life-support-profile of the Colony. The accused had the right to *one* hearing. After the hearing, execution could take place, at the council's discretion.

It was spelled out in the fine print of every Colony resident's contract. And it was there because, despite all the engineering and fail-safing, the Colony was fragile. It wouldn't survive a full-scale uprising. Some of the technickis knew that—others considered it Admin propaganda designed to keep the proletariat down.

"All right," Bonham said at last. "But I want you to know why I'm going to do it."

She snorted softly. "You do? Then you're a weak man. But go ahead."

You're a weak man. He wanted to tell her to fuck herself. But he had to go on with his rationalization. The urge was overpowering. He knew it was pathetic, but he couldn't keep it from coming out.

"I'm going to do it because the Colony is a dead loss. Because the Colony is not going to make it. Within a year, it will be a dead shell. Everyone in it will be dead. So it doesn't matter."

She looked at him steadily. "You know something we don't? Has someone built a large bomb, for example?"

He shook his head. "Nothing like that. I think the risk you're taking is going to get out of hand. I think you underestimate how angry these people are, how irrational they are, and how far they're willing to go. They have to be stopped—or everyone will die."

"You underestimate Praeger." Something discreetly worshipful in her voice when she said *Praeger*. "He's planned for all of that. I have been authorized to inform you that Praeger thinks highly of your ability to manipulate crowds. You have talent. On Earth or in the Colony, we will have other uses for you. You can take that as a guarantee that you will be paid as promised."

She turned and walked away.

The security bull stayed where he was, between Bonham and Van Kips. Watching. Ready.

Bonham turned away and walked on leaden legs out of the site, through the long grass, and into the gathering shadows of the Open's parkland. An SA Security patrol trundled by in a small vehicle like a golf cart, shining hand-spots into the dark places.

Shine them into my gut, Bonham thought.

The patrol flashed a light over him and drove on, probably already informed of his authorization. They all knew just where he was.

They were going to have other uses for him, she'd said. *Oh, shit. Oh, God.*

He walked through the gate into the crossover, and down the transparent-plastic corridor leading to the Technicki Quarters level.

There was the guard, halfway across . . .

No. He was closer to the door now, bent forward a little. Listening.

A shout echoed down the corridor, from the far door beyond the guard. The guard started toward the door. Bonham fought an urge to warn him.

The guard reached the door, drew his club, looked out.

A flutter of red light trailing through the air . . .

A lob, Bonham thought, as a Molotov cocktail exploded in the center of the guard's chest; a second burst on his helmet.

His scream was amplified by his helmet mike.

The armored guard staggered backward, flailing, already a human torch, a man of fire like something from the vision of an Apostle. He clawed at the extinguisher on his belt, but the second lob had dripped its gel over his faceplate and he couldn't see to use it. The guard suits were supposed to be fireproof, but the underground's technicians had worked up a new burning agent that ate right through the nonflammable' synthetics making up the guards' armor. The fire reached the burst-charges of the teargas grenades in the guard's pouch, and they blew and sent shrapnel into him . . .

The guard fell, flailing, and a third lob hit him. Bonham backed away, feeling the heat on his face, smelling petroleum base, burning plastics. The sound of sizzling plastic was overlaid by screams.

A bit tardily, the Colony's bulkhead sensors detected the fire and activated sirens, mechanical screams augmenting the burning man's own cries. The sprinkler system came on—but only sporadically, here and there down the hall. It had been vandalized. The fire-suppressive liquids didn't reach the burning guard. The guard's mask was melting onto his face.

Bonham thought, Someone's been cutting corners on their armor. It's not supposed to burn *that* easily.

Portions of the helmet were burned away; part of the face was exposed. Bonham thought, Did my people do it? Or was it Praeger's agents, setting the stage for martial law? Did this guy's armor burn so easily because he was issued a suit intended to burn?

And as Bonham turned to run, he thought, When it burns, you can see it: there's a man inside that suit. A man.

Behind him, the man stopped his thrashing. SAISC guards arrived in patrol jitneys. The smoke rose black as anger.

                          • 15 •

The lovemaking happened in stages. In the first stage Swenson was going through the motions, playing images in his head so he could maintain tumescence, feeling as if he were in a gym, working out on a press bench; in the second stage he found pleasing familiarity in her angles and planes, and he descended into the mindless enjoyment of yeasty genital communion; in the third stage he began to hallucinate.

He saw things, as he did things to her—to her and to the copper-skinned young priest he was unable to disentangle from Ellen Mae.

He saw—

She was a hard-bodied woman, tensile and angular, and Swenson saw himself rearing above her—and then he saw a hammer pounding a nail into a board.

And now a hammer pounding a nail through a man's palm.

Pull back from that riven palm, to show the man's arm on the raw wood of the cross, the sag of his body against the upright piece. Back up, flashback now: he saw the First Sorrowful Mystery. Swenson, as Father Stisky, had taught Nicaraguan children how to say the Rosary. He'd had to explain how the recitation of each "decade" was accompanied by meditation on the fifteen events of the Mysteries. The Joyful Mysteries, the Sorrowful Mysteries, the Glorious Mysteries. Sometimes the children were frightened when he taught the Sorrowful Mysteries. Perhaps frightened by something in the good father's eyes. The Sorrowful Mysteries told of the agony of Jesus . . . The First Sorrowful Mystery was Jesus in the garden of Gethsemane, a copper-skinned, Hispanic Jesus praying for the sins of the world. On to the Second Sorrowful Mystery, in which Jesus is scourged by the guards and the spiteful Jews who condemned him to Crucifixion. On to the Third Sorrowful Mystery, and Swenson saw Jesus carrying the cross up the hill to Calvary. On to the Sorrowful Mystery of the Crucifixion, Jesus nailed to the cross, the nails going into His palms, into the wood, the hammer driving the nails, driving His blood into the flesh of a tree, driving the nails into the wood, driving the nails, pounding in, in, until the blood—

He screamed as he came, a scream of anguish.

He saw the two Nazis, kneeling in the chapel, saw the bullet holes appear in their backs like stigmata. They're dying for their cause, though they know it not, he thought.

And then it faded as Ellen Mae, beneath him, gasping, asked, "Are you all right?"

"Yes. It's taken care of."

"What? What's taken care of?"

"I—I don't know. I'm not thinking straight." He smiled, tried to make out she was making him muddled with desire. "You devastate me."

What *had* he meant by *It's taken care of?* He'd been repeating something.

Something Watson had said. They'd been in the kitchen, coming in through the back door. Ellen Mae was up making bread from scratch. It was something she did in the mornings. She said it was her "meditation time." She hadn't looked at Swenson at all. She was kneading dough, and she glanced up at Watson and said, abstractedly, "Did you take care of those awful men?"

Watson nodded. "It's taken care of."

"Oh, good. I don't like those sort of little backwoods Hitlers around, they upset Rick. Would you like some coffee?"

Listening, Swenson had been sure she hadn't meant, *Did you send them away?* She had meant, *Did you kill them?* Casually as a farmer's wife asking if he'd slaughtered a pig for supper's pork chops.

Why was he bothered by the execution of the NeoNazis? Vile men, after all, by any measure. The world was better off without them . . .

That morning, he and Watson had sat in the kitchen breakfast nook, just the two of them, drinking coffee, eating sweet rolls.

Now, more and more, he felt as if he were watching himself on a screen. Stisky watching Swenson, and Swenson wasn't Stisky anymore, and Stisky wasn't sure he could control Swenson . . .

"I've had my eye on you for a while, John," Watson had said, smiling his most avuncular smile.

Swenson searched Watson's face for double-meaning, saw nothing but the smile.

"We monitored you at the Service. When Rick was preaching on the video, there and, ah . . . well, Old Sacks did it, really. Via wires in your robe. Test your response. Everyone to be admitted to the circle was monitored. Of everyone there—you showed the most positive response. Your pleasure centers were working overtime. Your pulse was up where it was supposed to be and . . . I won't go into all the details. Suffice it to say, we feel you're rated to be a deacon in the Second Circle." He had the look of a father who's just told his teenage son he's getting a new Mercedes for his birthday.

Swenson looked appropriately gratified.

And now, lying beside Ellen Mae, he thought, *They don't know who I am. They think I'm Swenson. I'm Stisky. And yet they know who I am better than Steinfield does. They know me.*

God help me.

Agnus Dei, qui tollis peccata mundi, miserere nobis.

• • •

James and Julie Kessler sat on the sofa together, watching television. This hotel room had a holocube above the screen, for the holo channels, but Kessler had turned the holo function off. He didn't like seeing miniature 3D people caper through deodorant commercials on the other side of the coffee table. With the ordinary TV, you could maintain your distance more easily; when they were three dimensional, they were more intimidating, and you almost felt compelled to buy whatever it was they were selling—or to shout at them to leave you alone. And of course they couldn't hear you.

So they were watching the low-income transmissions. "What time is it?" Julie asked.

Kessler felt a twinge of irritation. "What difference does it make? We're here at least till tomorrow night. Nothing changes. We aren't expecting anyone and we can't go out."

"I just like to know," she said gently, touching his arm.

He put his hand over hers and sighed. "Sitting around and relaxing is making me tense."

"At the risk of annoying you again—*exactly* what did Purchase say last night?"

He shrugged. "Basically, we wait. They'll protect us in the meantime. They'll contact us."

"I don't mean basically."

"Well—he said the hotel is owned by his people. He said Worldtalk's people are looking for us. Worldtalk has been taken over by the SAISC. The SA has its own intelligence service. The New Resistance people are setting up a kind of 'underground railway'—only it'll be by Lear jet—to some island in the Caribbean."

"I understand that much but—*what* island? And what'll it be like there? I mean—it could be a prison for all we know."

"I don't think so. Steinfeld was . . . I just believe him. We'll have a cottage and be protected. I'll work with his people to develop my screening program. Purchase has gotten his hands on some of the program through Worldtalk. They can use it to counteract the SA's propaganda—that's something valuable to him. They wouldn't brutalize us when they need my cooperation. That wouldn't make sense . . . But they won't tell us where the place is precisely, because if the SA finds us before we're moved, then, uh . . . " He shrugged.

She squirmed against the cushions, her hand tightening on his arm. "Maybe we should . . . I don't know . . . go off on our own somewhere. Like Canada. Maybe we're taking risks with these people that—well, what do we know about them?"

"I was impressed with Steinfeld. The feelings we have about people *have* to matter. Anyway, I've known Charlie for years—he's part of it, and he's going with us."

"It couldn't be," Julie said, "that you like the fact Steinfeld is taken with your program? An ego decision?"

He opened his mouth to deny it, and then thought better of it and said, "Maybe that too. So what? What difference does it make where we go? Running is running, hiding is hiding."

She didn't say anything for a while.

He tried to take an interest in television.

Channel 90 was occupied with the televising of a National Spirit Rally. Five hundred grade-school children in red, white, and blue marched across a football field in formation, creating an eagleshape with the flags they carried. A hundred more in the stands above lifted composite cards to make up a picture of the maternally beneficent—kind but firm—face of Mrs. Anna Bester, president of the United States of America. The children sang the hit pop tune "We're Gonna Kick That Russian Butt!" until a large holo of Mrs. Bester appeared on the stage, smiling and waving—

Kessler changed the channel.

Channel 95 showed the young country-pop singer, Billy Twilly, winding up a song with a grave endorsement of "Anna's new program." As his band played softly behind him, he strolled across the stage with his head down, one hand in his pocket, like a humble man a little embarrassed by the great responsibility that has been thrust upon him. He stopped, looked up into the lights and said, "Anna's new program is more than just a new ID system. It's safety—safety from the threat of terrorism for every American. Last year a thousand people were killed by terrorist bombs around the country. The only way we can be sure that the bombing is stopped is by identifying everyone, clearly and without any mistake. Some call it submitting to authority—I call it friendship—and faith. Faith in Anna Bester, and in the United States. Now, I'd like to sing—"

Kessler-changed the channel, muttering, "I'm not sure anyone *needs* my program—some of this stuff is so . . . "

"It's not always so obvious," Julie said.

Channel 98 was a technicki channel . . .

" . . . *Soisezim, whudduhfiugyuhmina* . . . " the comedian said, running a hand nervously along his quadruple-Mohawk. "*Neesud, hey*—"

Kessler changed the channel.

It was a CGI cartoon. Grommet the Gremlin, grinning toothily, his sine-wave eyes sparking, flew in loop-the-loops around a tight formation of Russian skatebombers, nipping in to effortlessly pluck rivets from their wings.

The wings fell off, and the planes hung for a moment in the air, as if unable to decide to crash. The Russian pilots looked in consternation at one another, and one of them said, "I told you, comrades, we should've got planes built in America!" And then the cartoon plane spiraled down and exploded into flames, the pilot's head and arms flying bloodily off to bounce into the air, Grommet the Gremlin using a pilot's severed bloody-stumped arm like a baseball bat to whack a severed head into—

Julie changed the channel.

On Channel 100 a man wearing a headset whispered confidentially, "I never miss *anything* on the Grid! A Gridfriend brand portable satlink puts me in touch with—"

Kessler changed the channel. Commercial. A young woman in a bikini strolled across her sundeck. The man beside her looked nervously around and said, "You sure it's safe to sunbathe? I mean—"

"Sure, silly! We've got Second Alliance Security here! It covers the whole development! There hasn't been a sniper here since the SAISC came around!"

A trustworthy male voice intoned, voiceover, "Second Alliance International Security Corporation—The Only Real Security is Full Security!"

Kessler turned the TV off.

They sat for a moment staring at the blank screen.

"You're depressed," she said.

He shrugged. He squeezed her hand. "Don't worry about it."

"I have to tell you something. The reason I'm worried about where we're going . . . "

He looked at her. He knew. He felt a wave of joy, a wave of sheer dread, a wave of anxiety, a wave of joy . . .

As she said, "I think I'm going to have a baby."

• • •

Hard-Eyes and Jenkins were awash in fog. They were walking across a bridge over the Seine; the morning fog was thickest here, rising from the river to hide most of the city from them. The sun was a hot pearl in the east.

"Trouble with these black-market assholes," Jenkins said, "is you can't find the bastards in the same place twice in a row. Where he is yesterday, he isn't today. But with any luck . . . "

"Can he get coffee?"

"Claims he can," Jenkins said, shrugging. "Claims he can get genetic pharms, too. Morph-trance, epinephrine, norepinephrine, neurotransmitters . . . "

"How's he get this stuff?" Hard-Eyes asked, looking around—not seeing much but billowing fog.

"Certain brigades, American army spikes the food with combos of that stuff to make the men more combat-ready. Lots of adrenocorticotrophic hormone . . . Some of the experimental troops are outfitted with injectors. Little box strapped on near the kidney, shoots 'em up with what they call chemcourage. Some real berserker shit. They're experimenting, trying to get a combination that makes them careful but not paranoid, aggressive but not likely to attack their COs—"

"Sick shit to do to a soldier."

"Yeah. Anyway, this guy works in the Yanks' camp."

"You calling them Yanks, too? You're a fucking Yank yourself, Jenkins, me neggo."

"Yeah. But—you see enough of this shit, you don't wanna be a Yank. I mean—Yank or Russian either. They can *all* kiss my ass." They paused, listening. Distant, hollow thuds. A long shivery metallic shriek. A quick succession of booms. Silence.

"How close does that sound to you?" Jenkins asked nervously.

"A few miles away. Hard to tell in the fog, but it sounded like it was coming from north of the city."

"Fuck. Fighting moving back to the city. Just fucking great."

"Hell with this coffee dealer. Let's see if Steinfeld's back. They said last night he'd be back."

"They said he'd be back every night for a week."

"Let's look in . . . Shit, here comes a patrol truck." They saw the black silhouette of an SA patrol truck, just a squarish bulk in the fog, coming onto the bridge.

Jenkins was over the bridge rail first, Hard-Eyes a half-second later. They hung from the rail, heads below the stone edge, the column of a bridge lamp hiding them, the toes of their boots on a two-inch ledge taking some of their weight.

The truck moaned slowly nearer . . . and nearer. The river susurrated below them. Hard-Eyes could feel its cold breath on his back. The river's splashing seemed amplified by the overarching bridge. A spotlight came on, atop the truck's cab, as it drew close; the truck slowed, and the small spotlight beam slashed like a saber through the fog and flashed over them, and Hard-Eyes thought, *They're going to see us.* There was a second of uncertainty. In that second, he realized two things: first, that he and Jenkins must not be taken. The SA was dragnetting anyone who couldn't be definitely identified as French, US Army, or a soldier of the NATO forces. And even the French were suspect if they were not registered with the Front National, or if they were Jewish, Muslim, or Communist. Those taken vanished into the SA's Center of Preventive Detention. The SA was said to be using an extractor for some, torture for others. There were rumors of exterminations, but there was no proof. And there were no investigative journalists looking into it. Invoking their NATO-granted power of martial law, the SA had simply closed down the local Internet news sites, and the few remaining print publications. The TV transmitters had been destroyed by the Russians. If Hard-Eyes and Jenkins were taken, the SA would soon know whatever they knew about the New Resistance. There was no way of keeping anything back from an extractor.

So, in that second, Hard-Eyes knew that if they were seen, he and Jenkins would have to jump into the river.

His second realization was, they would probably not survive the river. At this time of year it was high and cold. Exposure would kill them or would drag them down till they drowned.

And that's why he was NR.

Because this . . .

. . . the truck passing, slowing, searching for them with its spotlight, the confrontation with the predator, the imminence of a mortal choice . . .

. . . this was real.

The truck came to a stop. The spotlight beam kept moving.

The light passed over the stone railings, swept past Hard-Eyes and Jenkins, lifted to hold for a moment on the black metal statuary, sweating with fog, mounted on columns along the rail. As if these figures from mythology were objects of suspicion.

And then the truck rolled on.

They waited, fingers freezing to the stone balustrade, till the truck's red taillights were completely swallowed by the mist. Then they climbed stiffly over the rail and, thrusting numb fingers into coat pockets, they walked on, side by side, saying nothing.

But inside himself, under the layer of silence, Hard-Eyes had a buzz on.

• • •

By the time Jenkins and Hard-Eyes reached the safe-house, they were both hoping Levassier had gotten some food in. Their meals had been cut to once a day, and the once had not come for the past two days. They found Levassier on the third floor of the safe house, which had become an infirmary.

The old pile had been built in the mid-nineteenth century and hadn't been renovated since the mid-twentieth. You passed through two old cast-iron doors, brass knobs in the center of each, and into a courtyard, conscious you were being watched as you approached, and watched as you entered, though you saw no one watching at all; no cameras, no one at windows. The white-painted wooden shutters on the windows were kept open. The curtains were not drawn. Lights showed, even on the dormer windows of the red tile roofs. Every care was taken to make the house look as if it kept no secrets. The SA used roving cameras, the bird-drones; if a camera should flutter up to the window, hover like an oversized aluminum hummingbird to peer electronically through, it would see kerosene lamps, or the few electric lights if it was during an accredited electricity ration period for the area. The remote-control operator looking through the bird's camera-eye, gazing in rapt boredom into a TV screen back at the SA center, would see a banal, shabby room, containing, perhaps, a wan child listening to the propaganda broadcast on the radio, or two old women commiserating. Levassier, Steinfeld's adjutant, fretted that some alert inspector might notice that the rooms seemed too small for the volume and style of the house. He might realize there were other rooms he wasn't seeing.

Having passed inspection twice, Hard-Eyes and Jenkins stepped through a closet, through a hidden door, and into the infirmary, where Levassier was said to be with his patients.

Levassier was a doctor, and an old-fashioned radical—yes, a *Marxist*—but Steinfeld had said, "I forgive his politics in gratitude for his morality."

The strange truth was, politics were irrelevant in this particular political battle. And this was another reason Hard-Eyes remained in Paris.

The infirmary was a long, windowless room, fuggy with continuous human occupation and bad ventilation. Three walls wore faded lily-patterned wallpaper, water-stained at the upper corners; the fourth wall, built by NR personnel to cut the original room in half, was an ugly thing of cinder blocks and drippy mortar. There was barely room to pass between the end of the second-hand hospital beds and the papered wall. The room was lit by two dim bulbs in the cobwebbed ceiling, at either end of the room. As Hard-Eyes and Jenkins entered Levassier was cursing the lack of adequate light. He was bending over a man wearing a chest cast in the middle of the three occupied beds.

Levassier was an intense, birdlike man, big-nosed and pale, his eyes magnified in thick rimless glasses. He sniffed continuously from a cold he'd had all the time Hard-Eyes had known him. He had the pinched lips of a zealot, and little sense of humor. He wore a white doctor's coat now, probably for its psychological value to the patients.

"*C'est la merde,*" he muttered, "*C'est la merde.*"

Hard-Eyes found a lighter in his pocket. It was nearly empty, there wouldn't be another, so he hoped Levassier appreciated it: he crossed to the middle bed, bent over the patient, and flicked the flame alive, throwing a small pool of yellow light.

Levassier said, "Eh?" and looked up, annoyed at the distraction.

"Light for your work," Hard-Eyes said.

"You will eat soon enough; do not cuzzle up to me." Levassier said.

"That's *cuddle* or *cozen*," Hard-Eyes said, grinning.

"*Arrete!* You frighten zuh bird! It makes droppings when it is afraid! Disgusting to have it here, but he won't let us take it away . . . "

Hard-Eyes saw the bird then, a big black crow perched on the gray tube-steel frame at the foot of the bed. It cocked its head and caught the reflection of his lighter flame in its eyes. It cawed, showing a snippet of pink tongue. Hard-Eyes switched off the small flame and put the lighter away. He looked at the man in the hospital bed more closely now.

"Smoke?"

Smoke nodded, smiling very faintly. "It's good to see you're still with us, Hard-Eyes. I've only been here three days from Brussels. Waiting for Steinfeld. No one's told me a thing."

"You don't look the same," Jenkins said. "I mean, you don't look like you."

"I've put on weight. They cleaned me up. Cut my hair." Hard-Eyes stared at Smoke, thinking he had a striking face, now that the grime and beard was gone. A little pinched, the eyes deep-set, but aristocratic; something illuminated about it. The word *saintly* came into his mind, and in sheer embarrassment Hard-Eyes tried to banish it, but it wouldn't go. Saintly.

Hard-Eyes looked away. "Who else have we got here?"

A girl, asleep or comatose, was lying on her back, her chest bandaged, her mouth open, looking parched. Her hair was spiky.

"That's Carmen." Smoke said. "Accidental gunshot."

The third patient looked over, hearing that. He was gaunt, big-eyed, his face mobile, too elastic. On the verge of madness, Hard-Eyes thought. He was sitting on the edge of a bed. Perhaps he wasn't a patient at all. He was wearing a leather jacket. His hair was short, streaked, but it had lost its shape, whatever it had been. He looked vaguely familiar. From the earring, jacket, the hunched attitude on the edge of a bed, Hard-Eyes judged him to be a retro-rocker of some kind. He had the habitual sullen posture of a rocker missing his stage, and missing the activity of his scene.

"That's Rickenharp," Smoke said. "He hasn't said anything in three days. Since he came in with her. He shot her himself. Accidentally. Apparently he wasn't sure who it was, but he hadn't intended to shoot, and his finger twitched on the trigger." Smoke shrugged with his eyebrows. "Amateur with a gun. He's making a great thing of not forgiving himself. He's tried to maintain a vigil. Tried not to sleep. Gave in last night, poor fellow. He's very . . . dramatic. But then, Rickenharp's a stage person."

Smoke was speaking so that Rickenharp would hear him. Maybe trying to jolt him out of his funk.

"Rickenharp . . . " Hard-Eyes repeated. "The guitar player?"

Rickenharp looked up at him, unable to conceal his gratitude, and a friendship was born.

• • •

"What you have to understand, dear Claire," Rimpler was saying, "is that we are all trapped into what we are by what we thought we were."

"Dad . . . " But she didn't know quite how to say what she needed to say.

They were in her father's apartment, in the Admin quarters of FirStep, the Colony, and they had just finished watching InterColony evening news. A report on the shortage of air filters due to the blockade, causing worsening air quality. Small protest fires set here and there about the Colony were exacerbating the condition. (Claire thought, The *air* here is fine. Admin has a different ventilation system. The best filters go to Admin.) Reports of more rioting. Arrests. Three rioters hospitalized. The man Bonham was everywhere, throwing fuel on the fire, somehow the police never touching him, though they had arrested most of the other leaders.

Rimpler had turned the newscast off halfway through. And he'd made himself a drink. He wore the same shorts, the same grimy bathrobe. He hadn't shaved.

He sat on the rug beside the sofa, making another drink, humming to himself. She watched as he dropped a pill into the drink. It fizzled.

"Dad—what are you putting in your drinks?"

"A little something to give them more punch. Making them into Punchy Punch." He sipped, and shuddered. Then his eyes became languid, the lids drooped, and he began to talk. "When you're a young man, or woman, Claire, you try to build things. Businesses or homes or books or space stations or . . . schools of ideas. You have a wide freedom of choice as a young person. Relatively speaking. As you grow, you build on to what you've built, and on to that, and onto that, and you attach yourself to it, and you create a sort of web of . . . of conceptions and misconceptions of the world. Wrong or right, these ideas solidify around you, and hem you in. And you do things in accordance with the ideas, and, then . . . why then you must justify what you do, if you are to live with yourself. So your choices diminish *until you are no longer making them*, you are simply building a pattern on a pattern. It's like a man who's built a skyscraper with his own two hands—I saw a Popeye thing like this as a boy on TVLand—the skyscraper got to be up in the clouds, and he was up there, atop it, but he hadn't built stairs and there was no way down or off, so he had to keep building, up, up . . . Where he gets the materials I don't know, and there the analogy breaks down . . . "

He's completely maundering, Claire thought. Who's Popeye?

"Dad—we've got to make up our minds where we stand on this thing . . . "

"But that's what I've been trying to tell you. I've built myself into the Admin and I must support Admin. Right or wrong. I've gone as far as I can with you."

"You know there's no 'right or wrong.' The way things are now, Admin is just plain wrong."

"Yes." Dreamily. "I believe we are."

"But you don't care."

"I can't do anything about it."

"Even if you can't take a stand, you can help me in other ways. I'm barred from council sessions now. You're not."

"I'll tell you what I learn . . . if they let me go," he said, nodding.

"How can you accept it all so passively!"

"Please don't shout."

She felt near weeping. "You weren't like this before."

"No. But since then I've seen them. I've seen *into* them. And this man Molt must go. His being here risks the peace of my retreat . . . " He gestured at the room around him with his drink. "My . . . hermitage, my dear, dear child. You fail to understand how serious our Praeger is. Because you don't know *who* he is. Praeger is one of the chiefs of the Second Alliance. They wish to make the Colony their world headquarters—when the blockade is lifted. Crandall wants to come here. He feels safer here. Ironic, as things are now. But if they could perfect their control, they could turn the place into a perfect police state. It would 'hum with harmony,' to use Praeger's charming phrase. It would be safer for Crandall."

"How did you get all this?" Her voice came out a croak. "About the SA's plans for the colony and . . . ?"

"You always seem surprised by my keeping tabs on the thing I built myself. Why, my dear child, I tapped their comms . . . they had run tether satellites out to transmit past the blockade . . . to Crandall's farm. To a man named Swenson. And a certain Watson. Even their names sound alike to me. Swenson and Watson. Praeger and Jaeger. These people are the vectors for the new conformity, and maybe they'll all change their names to sound alike, Watson, Wilson, Winston; Crandall, Kendall, Randall, Rendell—"

"Dad—you're saying that the Security Section is now a political organization?"

"It's run by one. The new fascists, dear girl."

The door opened.

Claire looked up at the door in shock. No one was supposed to be able to open it from the outside with a key, except . . .

Except Security.

Two Security bulls stood in the door, one with a face, the other faceless. But the one with a face might just as well have worn a helmet, for all his expression told them. It was friendly, with a faint regret. He was a Security administrator whose name she couldn't remember. He was here for the sake of decorum. Professor Rimpler was not some technicki bumpkin.

"Professor Rimpler." the administrator said politely. "Claire Rimpler. I have executive orders to bring you with me, for questioning and detention, in connection with a detention-cell breakout and the maiming of three guards."

"May I finish my drink?" Rimpler asked. Casually, just as if he didn't know full well that these men had come to take him to prison; as if he didn't know that it was a prison he would never come away from.

"Certainly, sir," the administrator said, smiling.

"Took them a while to make up their minds they could politically get away with arresting us," Rimpler mused, rattling the ice in his glass. "Or maybe they simply needed time to arrange the appropriate political background."

"As to that, I couldn't say, sir," the administrator said, glancing at his watch.

Claire looked around. The moment, the arrest, made everything look different. *How little we normally notice,* she thought.

Now the whole room seemed to spring into relief. The walls were adjusted to a soft, dimpled texture, making her think of a padded cell. The two men standing in the arch of the doorway were remarkably detailed; she saw every fiber in their armored suits, every stud on their belts, every pouch and fastener and wrinkle. She noted the play of light across the faceplate of the one on her left. She heard a faint squeak and rustle of synthetic material as he shifted his weight. She could hear him breathe, very faintly, through his helmet amplifier, even dialed to low output.

She was listening for something else. *Molt.*

Molt was in the next room, sleeping. He slept whenever they would let him, taking tranks cut with antidream. The administrator hadn't said anything about him; hadn't looked at the bedroom. Maybe they didn't know he was here.

She'd taken pains to make them think Molt was hiding somewhere behind the Corridor D barricades, with the other radicals, technickis and the Admin progressives like Judy and Angie and Belle and Kris who were sympathetic to the tecknickis. She looked at the guard's RR stick, on his belt. His right hand was resting on its pommel. Not threateningly. A little behind the stick was the gun in its locked holster.

Claire listened . . .

Molt sometimes moaned in his sleep.

Professor Rimpler finished his drink, sighing, setting it down with a *clack.*

He stood and said, "Well, shall we go, Claire?" The Security administrator smiled approvingly.

The bedroom door opened. The administrator looked at it, his smile fading. The bull drew his RR.

There was a faint hiss.

A small hole, a centimeter across, appeared in the center of the guard's chest. He shouted some meaningless monosyllable.

The administrator threw himself down.

There was a *whumpf* and the guard's suit expanded like a balloon, in a split-second puffing the chest to four times its normal size. Blood jetted from the tiny hole, squirting out in a neat arc. The bull's arms snapped up and down, once, and he fell over backward. He hit the corridor's floor with a wet sound, blood fountaining in a thin stream from the single hole. His suit began to deflate. Slowly.

Molt stepped through the open bedroom door and pointed the thing in his hands at the administrator on the floor. The man was getting to his feet and now truth showed in his face: it was contorted with naked fear.

Claire shouted, "Don't!"

But the thing in Molt's hands—it looked to her like a little bicycle tire pump she'd had as a girl—hissed again and a hole appeared in the man's back as he turned to run; the suit expanded; blood splashed out from the collar. The man tried to scream, but all that came out was a gurgle. And the blood kept coming.

She thought, *It's so red. There's so much of it and it's all so red.* She looked away. The man scraped at something on the floor, moving spasmodically . . . wet sounds.

Then the room was quiet.

Molt's heavy face was dead. His eyes were lifeless. He slurred as he spoke. "It worksh like you shed, Rimpler. Right through the shuit."

Rimpler nodded, his head tilted to one side. "The only one in the Colony. Far's I know. But maybe not: Praeger requisitioned explosive bullets. Not that all explosive bullets are necessarily fired from—"

"How can you talk that way! Like hunters over deer!" Claire burst out. Her stomach churned. She was shouting to keep from throwing up.

"It's a way of adjusting," Rimpler said, bending to make himself a drink.

A flash of heat went through her. She knocked his hand down, and his glass broke against the table. He stared numbly at the fragments.

"Dad, we have to go! *Now!*"

"Oh, no. You and Molt go. I'll report that this was done by rioters."

"They won't believe that. They'll arrest you. They don't *extract*, Dad. They *torture*."

He sighed. "I suppose . . . they won't leave me alone."

Molt was dragging the bodies inside. "They have a transmitter in the suit," Molt was saying, pronouncing his words more carefully. "If it'sh cut off, it shets up an alarm, and they send someone to inveshtigate."

Claire looked at the leaking suits, the bodies, then at her father. "So let's go *now*, dammit!" She wanted more than anything to get away from there.

As they went down the hall—her father in his absurd shorts and sandals and bathrobe, Molt in a grimy technicki jumpsuit, she in her Admin jumpsuit—Claire knew that she wanted to go farther than simply away from this end of the Colony.

She wanted off, and down. To Earth.

• 16 •

The message encoder worked like this: Swenson sent a e-message from the SAISC administration to Purchase at Worldtalk.

It was a non-classified message re the acquisition of Worldtalk by the SA Corporation. The message was relayed in groups of signals, each group of signals representing a group of letters. The interval between the transmission of a group of letters was supposed to be uniform. But certain groups of letters arrived fractions of a microsecond later than they should have; a half-microsecond late corresponded with a certain word; one-tenth of a microsecond later corresponded with a certain letter; one-eleventh with another letter, and so forth. Purchase—having reception software equipped to listen for the encoded delays—received first the ostensible message; then—after securing his comm line—he told his console to listen for the delays, make the letter and word correspondences, and print out the decoded message. The message from the SA Second Circle to SA-initiate Purchase read:

> Joseph Bonham, political liaison apprentice, arriving on treatied Russian exchange ship from Colony, transfer to SA shuttle orbit, L2, 2-10/0800 EST, arrival New Brooklyn seaport 01100 EST. Meet with double Security, supervise transfer of Bonham to Detention Unit Three for extraction and implantation.

There was a third message hidden within the second. After the second message was decoded, it was transmitted from the computer to the printout mechanism; another decoding unit in the printout mechanism—a unit known only to the NR—heard another set of fractional delays in the transmission of the group of signals, a kind of meaningful computer stuttering, and translated them into the third message, which it printed out after the second.

In the message from Swenson, the SA Second Circle operative to Purchase, the SA Second Circle operative, was a message from Stisky/Swenson, the New Resistance agent, to Purchase, the New Resistance agent.

The message read:

They are prepping me to give Senate testimony against reform of the Antiviolence Laws. Have asked me to stay on at Cloudy Peak. I cannot manage it much longer. Psychological pressure too great. Give me orders or get me out. They are trying to obtain memory extraction experts. They also plan to provide DoD with new submarine silencing techniques in exchange for covert federal backing of SA projects. Tell me what to do, let me do it, and get me out, repeat, get me out. They are going to hold a Service soon.

Purchase read the printout twice. On the outside, he looked like a businessman who was annoyed by a sudden burden of extra work. Inside Purchase, bridges were buckling, guy wires snapping, ceilings falling in.

He glanced abstractedly at his office door, as if simply letting his eyes wander. But looking to see if anyone was in the hall.

No one.

He got up and closed the door. He transferred the message to a high-priority garbled transmission unit, rerouted it through a coded modem—which he had to take from its hiding place in his closet and interface with his system—and relayed the message to Steinfeld, via Joseph Bensimon, the NR contact at the Israeli Embassy. Bensimon would relay the message to the Israeli Secret Service, the Mossad, who, if they could get through the various static blocks, would send it via satellite to Steinfeld.

There was another *if*: if Steinfeld was still in the Mossad's good graces. The Israelis had had a generation of peace, after the Arab Spring and the Cairo 13 Treaty; Jordan, Kuwait, Egypt, Lebanon, the Saudis, Iran. and the State of Palestine signed the treaty, after Israel signed a pledge to accept a Palestinian state and after it ceased building new settlements. (Iran had come into the fold when the regime of the Ayatollahs had fallen to reformists.) Israel was neutral in the US/Russian confrontation, even when the war moved into the Middle East, as the Russians tried to capture oil fields in the few Arab nations aligned with the West. So far, the Russians had left Israel out of it. Israel's frontiers were massively defended. The Knesset had gone from pugnacity to moderation, and Steinfeld was regarded by some Israelis as a firebrand, a fanatic who saw Nazis under every bed.

But Purchase sent the message, after which he detached the special external modem unit and packed it into a Styrofoam-and-cardboard container in his closet, so it looked like an ordinary extra kept in case of a breakdown.

Then he sat at his desk, drinking cold coffee from a plastic cup. There was a hairline crack in the cup; coffee leaked through in beads to run down onto his hand. He stared at it, thinking, *By the time we get advice from Steinfeld it'll be too late.*

He sighed. Stisky had been his project. His enthusiasm. Witcher had said, "The guy's almost too good to be true." And Witcher had been right. Stisky/Swenson had sat in on the last planning session with Steinfeld, before they'd placed him in the SA's Second Circle. That had been a mistake.

Stisky knew some things. He knew too many names.

And they had a memory extraction man now. They would do a routine extraction on everyone, and if they asked Stisky/Swenson's memory center the right questions, they'd know about Purchase, and they'd know where Steinfeld was.

Swenson was your idea, he thought. *Take responsibility.*

He turned to the console and told the computer he wanted to send a message to Cloudy Peak Farm.

• • •

Rickenharp was trying to understand. Some of the talk at the conference table was in French, some in English, some in Dutch. He'd made out that the French resented meetings carried on in English, but Jenkins had pointed out that at least half the "active" members of the Paris NR—active meaning those prepared to take up arms at any time—were English speaking, and they translated everything. Then the French guy—actually an Algerian immigrant—had complained that this Steinfeld was recruiting all the wrong people and perhaps they should replace Steinfeld with a Frenchman.

But when Steinfeld came in, sitting in the empty chair at the head of the table, the French guy shut up, just like that.

Everyone shut up. They were like children fighting till the teacher came back into the room.

And it was a schoolroom, the teacher's conference room of the old *école*, with its cracked plaster walls and the oily warmth from its furnace. The school was receiving its electricity ration today and they had electric light, for now; old, humming, tubular fluorescent lights. The room—half its original size—was without windows; the windows had been covered by a false wall, to deceive the spy birds. Two guards stood at the two doors at either end of the room. Each with an old Uzi slung over his shoulder. The actives at the table were armed only with whatever they could carry without showing it. It was considered cloddish to display your guns, except in an actual firefight. But the bigger guns were nearby, under the coatrack, in a case, and loaded.

There were fourteen people around the long, gray-painted metal table, sitting in rickety plastic chairs, daydreaming about coffee. Four women, ten men.

So this is the Paris resistance. Kind of pitiful, really. Does that make it more heroic?

Song lyric in there somewhere . . .

Smoke sat on Steinfeld's right, Yukio on his left. Hard-Eyes sat beside Rickenharp, Jenkins on the far side, both of them silent and bored. Yukio and Willow sat across the table from Rickenharp.

Carmen was there, sitting beside the doctor at the corner. She had insisted. Rickenharp stole glances at her. Her complexion was gray, but there was no droop in her posture. She'd changed her look, Rickenharp thought. And then he realized that what she was wearing wasn't a "look." She was wearing fatigues and a flak jacket because she meant to fight, and she wanted everyone to know it. She hadn't said anything to Rickenharp since she'd regained consciousness. He'd tried to apologize, of course. (Thinking: How do you *apologize* to someone for putting bullet holes in their chest?) She'd acted as if she hadn't heard. There was no angry chill about it. It was as if she'd made up her mind that he didn't exist.

I'm an embarrassment to her, Rickenharp thought.

Somewhere in Italy—somewhere inside him—he'd made up his mind to get the hell back to the States or Freezone at the first opportunity. He'd played at being one of the guerrillas, almost believed it, especially when he'd pictured telling the band about it. But he'd had no real intention of going *through* with it. Not after that ride in the boat.

And then the gun. The feeling it was an instrument he wanted to learn to play. And then—

He squeezed his eyes shut, but the image came. Carmen falling back, those little neat round holes punched into her . . .

But now it was different. Now he *wanted* to be NR. It was as if he'd been slapped awake. Sitting there with his eyes shut, he thought: *Until I shot her, I was asleep, sleepwalking through ego games.*

The rest of the world had been unreal, except in the way it reacted to him; the way women reacted, or an audience. But now it was as if he'd been slapped—

"And who's this? Is he asleep?" Steinfeld's voice, and suddenly Rickenharp knew Steinfeld was talking about him.

Rickenharp opened his eyes and looked down the table. Everyone was looking back at him, except Carmen.

"I'm not asleep," Rickenharp said.

"This building is no longer a school, in the traditional sense. So don't sleep in it," Steinfeld said. His voice was mordant. Some of them laughed, and Rickenharp realized it was a joke.

Steinfeld, though, was not laughing. He was waiting.

"I'm Richard Rickenharp," he said. It felt clumsy in his mouth.

"I'm sponsoring him," Hard-Eyes said.

Carmen looked at Hard-Eyes, annoyed, and Rickenharp had to smile.

"Me too," Jenkins said. "I'm, uh, sponsoring him too."

Steinfeld tugged at his own beard, hard, as if wondering if it was a fake. "But isn't this the young man who—?" He looked at Carmen.

Oh, God, Rickenharp thought.

But Rickenharp cleared his throat (Thinking, *For God's sake, don't let your voice quaver!*) and said, "I'm the guy who shot her. I take responsibility. I shouldn't have insisted on having a gun when I didn't know how to use it . . . "

"I'm not at all sure it's your responsibility," Steinfeld said, surprising only Rickenharp.

Carmen was looking at her hands folded on the table. She nodded. "It was my fault. I should never have given it to him. I knew he didn't know how to use it. And it wasn't an emergency."

Steinfeld nodded. "Still—if he's to be an active . . . " He shrugged.

"We've put in ten days target practice in the catacombs," Hard-Eyes said. "Rickenharp's working hard. He won't make the same mistake."

The catacombs. Rickenharp seemed almost to hear the echoes of the gunshots ringing off the curved stone walls. *Smelling the wet mineral smell of the place, the underscent of sewage, then the smell of gunpowder. Seeing the cold gray stone reach of the subterranean target-practice room, with its woebegone, ravaged wooden silhouettes. Feeling the gun cold in his stiff hands, then feeling it grow warm with its compressed internal explosions. Hearing the hail-clatter of spent shells hitting the floor. Visualizing a guitar but holding the machine gun and fighting the urge to—*

"He's learned fast. He can take the weapons apart and put them back together. He's accurate. He's careful. We work on hand-to-hand; Jenkins teaches him field communications. He works hard."

—the urge to laugh.

"Mr. Rickenharp is a . . . performer, right?" Steinfeld said. "And we are not performing here."

"I know that." Rickenharp began. "I—"

"Are you trying to make up for shooting Carmen by working hard to be one of us?"

Rickenharp sensed that Steinfeld considered that kind of motivation insufficient. But he also sensed Steinfeld would know it if he lied. "Partly.

But—" He reached for words and couldn't find them, but plunged into trying to explain anyway. "It's *more*. Everything's different when you—well . . . it's like you're . . . like that Poe story where the guy is tied to a table and there are rats all around him. But in my version, it's like the guy was asleep, and there was someone there trying to untie him and save him from the rats, and a rat bites the guy who's tied up, so . . . uh, when he wakes from the pain, he strikes out and accidentally hurts the guy trying to untie him and then he realizes what he's done so he wants to kill the rats but it's also because it made him realize, you know, something he never realized before: *the rats are all around him*—"

"Oh, for God's sake, stop babbling!" Carmen said, very definitely looking at him now—looking two round neat bullet holes into him.

But Steinfeld was shaking, silently shaking, and after a confused moment Rickenharp realized he was laughing.

"Well—" Steinfeld tried to speak but the laughter made it impossible. He had to wheeze for a moment. Then he tugged on his beard and, with an effort, stopped laughing, and shook his head, his face red. "Well, that's a wonderfully, uh, baroque explanation, my friend; and the frightening thing is I know just what you mean!"

Some of the others were laughing now, the English-speaking ones. The French speakers looked confused.

Carmen permitted a smile to lift a corner of her mouth, for just a moment.

Rickenharp saw her as she'd been at the club, bare-breasted and spike-crowned. He wanted her, and he knew that, now, he'd never make the move. Having made a small *faux pas*. Having *shot* her.

Steinfeld raised a hand, and the laughter died down.

Rickenharp felt a strange combination of mortification and deep relief.

"Does anyone else sponsor our young singing poet here?" Steinfeld asked.

"Yes. I do," Yukio said.

"Yeah," Carmen said, with a sigh. "What the hell. Me too. I mean, if Yukio does." Shrugging.

Rickenharp was limp with relief at that.

"The sponsors will be responsible for this man's further indoctrination, briefing, and training," Steinfeld said, all business now. "Just see to it he isn't prone to being a dilettante, or being a, what's the word, a grandstander. In fact—I wonder if he's aware . . . " He looked at Rickenharp. "That if he tried to go to the States and tell the media all about his heroic 'journey' with the resistance, and write songs about it, and draw attention to us. We'd kill him."

Rickenharp looked back at Steinfeld, and swallowed. The guy was not kidding.

Steinfeld kept looking at him, eyebrows raised. "Well?"

"I do understand that," Rickenharp said. "I wouldn't do that anyway. I understand why you think I would."

The NR leader looked at Rickenharp for another long, assessing moment, then nodded. Steinfeld took out a handkerchief and mopped his brow. "It's hot in here. Now, first the good news—I did bring a little coffee and a few other items back for the actives."

There was a general murmur of pleasure at that.

Steinfeld gestured to the doctor, who translated for those whose English was shaky. "*Il fait chaud ici . . .* " Levassier began.

"Just the important stuff, Claude." Steinfeld said.

The doctor nodded curtly and translated the part about the coffee. More murmurs of pleasure. He waited, as Steinfeld went on.

"But as for our steady supplies . . . "

Steinfeld told them that the food ration would be reduced by one-third, but it would be twice a day. They were running out of furnace oil. There would be measures taken to conserve all supplies . . .

And he told them that the Russian/NATO front was holding steady forty miles north of Paris. Both sides were showing great restraint in the use of tactical nuclear weapons, which meant that fallout dangers were minimal just now.

The seat of France's right-of-center government had been moved to Orleans, about one hundred fifteen miles south of Paris. The government currently had very little influence on affairs in France outside Orleans and the provinces of Guyenne and Provence. Of the other provinces, those not controlled by the Russians had fallen under the authority of local petty demagogues whose power was in actuality reliant on their working relationship with the Second Alliance. The badly decimated, desertion-plagued French military was chiefly occupied in maintaining logistics for the NATO forces at the Front, or in protecting the government at Orleans. The few French soldiers remaining in Paris were attachés to the police department and were effectively absorbed into the Second Alliance, since the SA had been given authority over the police. As a sop to the hard-line nationalists, Le Pen had been appointed Minister of the Interior, his principal responsibility now the administration of the police.

The police and SAISC troops were largely occupied in rounding up anyone the SA's intelligence branch designated as a "criminal or disruptive element," i.e.: Communists, dark-skinned immigrants (for whom suitable crimes were invented), left-of-center Jews, and dissidents of any kind. And, as an afterthought, looters and conventional outlaws.

Steinfeld went on, "The line will hold steady in France for a while, I should think, unless the Russians manage to take out Milstar 2."

Milstar 2, the USA's orbital military warning/communications/ observation system, was protected by a series of orbital battle stations and watched over by a "fence" of tethered satellites. The Russian disadvantage in space technology had so far kept Milstar 2 safely insulated.

"Our source in the Pentagon informs us," Steinfeld said, "that the Russians are about to launch new anti-sat weapons, specifically to take out Milstar. If they're successful, NATO will find it more difficult to watch its back: and as we found out at the beginning of the war, its back is space. The Russians could shuttle troops in behind NATO lines . . . " He paused for the translator. Then: "The city would once more become a battleground. More accurately, it would quickly become rubble. If that happens, the SA will dig in behind NATO lines. We will follow the SA, wherever they go, to disrupt them in any way we can. In the meantime, we—"

"C'est suffit!" the Algerian said. "I am need to know this: What have we been waiting for? We do nothing but print posters . . . C'est merde. Why do we not fight? We do not use the explosives, the guns, we keep them like a greedy child hiding his toys! Only a little, we use, here and there. Nothing. Why are we wait? Eh? Why we wait for big push?"

"It's very simple." Steinfeld said with a wintry smile. "You've been waiting for me. The waiting is over. I'm here. And now, we go on the offensive."

• • •

Corridor D was choked with debris, with bad smells and the atmospheric tension of relentless jeopardy. Belle had told Claire, "We call it Alphabet Town. After a neighborhood in old New York, where the avenues were named A, B, C, D . . . "

Claire sat with her back to the wall, behind the barricade, supposedly on duty. There were four others on duty. Two technicki men, up above on ladders, looked through the notches atop the barricades. Angie and Kris below, in the truck cabs, were looking down the empty corridor in front of the barricades. And Claire knew Angie was quietly, urgently hoping to see someone coming. Someone to shoot at.

Claire was supposed to act as a messenger and gofer for the barricade guards. Mostly, she brought coffee. The corridor here was a litter of trash, trampled beyond recognition; the news sheets were still soaked from the riot hoses the SA bulls had used before the barricade had gone up; empty emergency ration canisters clattered underfoot whenever she went back to the corridor rest station to try and find a toilet that wasn't stopped up.

And the air filtration was working at one-quarter efficiency. It smelled like a maggot's belch.

At the back of her throat, the odor was met by the smoke from the empty, rusting lubricant drums fulminating under the vent behind the barricade. Technicki rebel bravos stood around the barrel warming their hands, spitting into the flame to watch it hiss, laughing and bullshitting. The air vent sucked at the black smoke but much of it slithered away and coiled near the ceiling, increasing her sense of choking submergence . . .

"Wonderful," Claire said, now, tasting her own bitterness as she stood up, looked through a crack between boxes, down the corridor at the sacked shopping mall: the shop doors slack-jawed on their hinges, department store mannequins with heads twisted to look over their backs tangled in torn-down, charred drapes. Shards of plate-glass windows on the floor were a fallen, frozen mockery of the stars outside. She muttered, "The only thing they haven't done is take shit from their diapers to draw pictures on the walls."

Goddammit, she'd grown up in the Colony. True, she wanted to leave it—she realized now she'd always wanted to leave it—but in some way it was part of her. It had been her home for years. It was a frontier outpost for mankind. It shouldn't be treated like this.

D was one of the main corridors. It was twenty-five feet from the floor to the glowing strip along the ceiling's center, and fifty feet wide. Before the barricade, D had been busy with jitney traffic or small electric trucks towing a train of supplies; with bicycles and tribikes, and electric mopeds. There were two trucks here now, nose-to-nose across the corridor, part of the front-side barricade. The barricade was reinforced by ore crates filled with crushed asteroid rock hijacked from the storage bins at the south end's smelting works, moved into place with forklifts and stacked to within a foot of the ceiling. The truck cabs doubled as lookout stations. The armed lookout would open the driver's side door and climb in, lean on the window frame of the passenger's side door, to watch the corridor through the door window. A rear barricade blocked off access from the corridor's end, sixty yards behind them.

There had been a Security station by the mall. The 9th Precinct, Belle called it. It was burned out and abandoned after the first riots, and a panicky Security bull had deserted his post without clearing out the station's small armory. The rebels had found four 30.06 rifles—semiautomatic, gas operated with computerized sighting scopes—and a crate of shells; they'd found one .22 pistol with a magazine of thirty explosive bullets. They'd found a launcher for teargas canisters and four guns that fired only rubber bullets.

"Most of the Colony bulls don't like to use their guns because of the danger of ricochet damage to the ship's life support," Bonham had said at the bonfire meeting at the edge of the Open. "But the walls are heavily reinforced. The bulls are too careful. We don't have to be. Most areas there's no real danger to life-support systems from bullets, or even explosives. The station was built to weather a variety of internal disruptions."

Thinking about that statement now, Claire wondered if she should try to convince them that the Colony was more fragile than they knew. But she was Admin; she was barely tolerated. She and her father were constantly watched, and Claire didn't feel safe unless Angie was with her. So Claire thought, *I wish you luck.* And she said nothing.

She buttoned up the collar of her coat and thrust her hands quickly back into its pockets.

The cold that seeped in from space, when colony maintenance decayed, had a whole different quality from cold on earth. It gave you a sensation in the bones that seemed to resonate with thoughts of death, absolute death, final death.

The fucking bulls, she thought, sitting down on the crate. The fucking SA bulls had shut down the general heat conduits. There were local heat generators drawing on sunlight collector stations. But it wasn't enough. It was supposed to be for emergencies.

Now and then a friendly lady-voice, an Admin Voice, asked them in technicki to remove the barricades and come back to work, so that Admin could turn full heat back on and begin work restoring air quality . . .

And what was her father doing? Chuckling. Rimpler strolled up to Claire, hands shoved in his coat pockets, collar turned up. Looking around and chuckling. "It's all been an experiment," he explained. He spoke mostly in non sequiturs now. "It's a great experimental organism, the Colony. When it goes wrong you learn something from its death, and you say, 'Aha. Why didn't I see this before?' This—" He pointed at the barricade. "This is arteriosclerosis. You want to know why I'm not angry about what they're doing to the thing I made—because *we* did it, *we* grew it, *we* crossed the orange tree with the parasitic vine . . . I've *been* angry. Praeger used to make me angry. Remember?" Chuckling. "Sometimes I still feel it. But it's not just anyone's anger. If I'm anything, I'm a refined man." She saw he'd put on his greasy bathrobe over the overalls they'd given him. His hair was matted, his chin a cactus, his teeth yellow and going green. "There is something exquisite in the delicious, intricate rage of a refined man. The rage that soars! The rage that writes Damn All Children on every balloon released from the Venusian Palace in Disney City! Maybe I should have made this place into a sort of big amusement park, my dear . . . Yes, the next one shall be a . . . " And he wandered off, as if his feet were following the train of his free association.

Claire stared after him. She wanted to find a place to cry, just to get it out. *My father's gone insane, and I don't think he's ever getting better.*

Someone was striding over to her.

She looked up. It was Bonham.

She looked down.

"We've got the microwave working in the cafeteria," Bonham said. "There's hot food. You can go if you want. Your father's there."

"Thanks," she said woodenly, then stood and turned to go.

He held her with his tone when he said, "You look pretty unhappy. Things could be worse. The technickis wanted to ransom you."

"Admin wouldn't give up a toothpick for us."

"That's what Molt told them."

Claire glanced at Molt, who was sitting on a torn mattress near the fire, holding the pistol he'd used on the guards. He was looking at the wall graffiti like an archaeologist trying to puzzle out an obscure hieroglyph.

She snorted. "I'm surprised he spoke up."

"We had to ask him what he thought. He's changed. He used to be . . . boisterous. I heard him speak twice since coming here. *Twice.* Both times to answer questions." Bonham shook his head. "It shows what torture does."

She said nothing. She waited for him to let her go. He was in charge here.

"You want out," he said suddenly. Sudden and soft, a whisper.

She looked at him.

He answered her unspoken question. "Yeah, out of the Colony. Off. Down. *Earth.*"

She kept looking at him, waiting. He leaned toward her. He was too lean, too hungry, and his breath smelled of canned stew.

"Claire—I can get you out. I'm going myself." He started to glance over his shoulder, then realized it looked craven, and stopped the motion.

"The blockade," she said.

"There's a way past. It's arranged. If I take someone—it'd be dangerous, but I have a pass to get to the docking bays. There's a way."

"Why? Why risk it to take me?"

"I watched you for a long time." He hesitated, looking for a way out of the awkwardness of his desire. There was no way out, so he said it bluntly, "I wanted you. I want you now."

Her heart was thudding. Her stomach coiled and uncoiled and coiled.

Out. Off. *Down!*

That was the thudding.

But with him. That was the coiling sensation. Revulsion.

He'd sold them out. She knew that and had nearly told the others. Now she was glad she hadn't. Because she wanted out.

Out.

"I can't go the way they want me to." Bonham was saying. "I had a warning from someone on their side—The SA's going to take me if I go back their way, for brainwashing. Hardcore extraction and conditioning. If we go back my way, we can use the NR for an escape route."

"What's the NR?"

"New Resistance. Antifascists."

She snorted. "Do they know who you sold out to?"

His face went blotchy red. "I—it was because the place is doomed. It's going to die. You and I know it. So I do what I have to, to get off."

Off.

"Is there . . . a bargain we have to make?"

"An understanding."

"Okay," she said, hating herself for the first time in her life. Down.

After a moment she added, softly, "I do want to go."

To Earth.

• 17 •

The message was for Watson, but Ellen Mae was the only one in the room when it came in at Cloudy Peak Farm. The main console was in the living room, its screens looking alien in their glossiness against all that wood under the deer antlers and the badger pelt. She was walking through on her way to the kitchen to make the bread, her mind sorting details for the upcoming Service, and the console lit up just as if her passing by had wakened it.

She glanced over the message, saw it was coded. No one else here so she used the password. The console scanned her retina, then gave her the message. It was for Watson, and she almost lost interest and then her eye caught a name—*Swenson*.

She read it all carefully then.

It was from Purchase. Requesting the presence of John Swenson at the Worldtalk Building in New York. Some executive there had met Swenson, had taken a liking to him, wanted to make him permanent liaison between the SAISC and Worldtalk, this meeting very important to facilitate smooth acquisition of Worldtalk, urgent that Swenson come to New York immediately . . .

Nonsense, she thought. Worldtalk was already as good as acquired.

Purchase was kowtowing to his Worldtalk boss, that was all. Forgetting who he answered to, really answered to.

Ellen Mae deleted the message. The hair rose on the back of her neck as she did it. This was against procedure. Rick wouldn't approve. Watson wouldn't approve. Sackville-West would positively glower.

But she didn't hesitate. She sent Purchase a message: *John Swenson has more important work to do, right here. Don't contact us again unless it's really urgent.*

And she signed it *Crandall*.

Well after all, she was a Crandall, wasn't she?

Feeling deliciously mischievous, she went to make bread dough, smiling as she thought, *I did that just like the lady spies in the old movies.*

•••

Swenson was sitting alone in the chapel. Outside, the snow fell in bleached-white flurries. The snowfall rippled the light, making the stained-glass figures seem to quiver as if they were about to move.

It was chilly in there; he had his hands tucked in his armpits. He was looking at the figures in stained glass. After looking a long time, he'd decided that one of them was definitely Charles Darwin. Another was Gregor Johann Mendel. How did Crandall square this with Christian Fundamentalism? With creationism? He didn't try. The "Christianity" Crandall showed the public was not the strange faith he practiced in private.

The pseudo-Christianity of the Second Circle was almost crypto-druidic. Its imagery was pastoral. Its interpretation of genetics was almost fertility worship. Its intellectual content owed something to the Sociobiologists, even more to Nietzsche and Bergson and Heisenberg. It had its own mythology. Its own vision of the future.

The Second Circle's vision of the future came into the chapel, with Watson.

It was a boy.

Watson was wearing a heavy wool overcoat. There were snowflakes melting on his shoulders. The boy wore a gray-black SA uniform, charmingly miniaturized, down to the overcoat and the black gloves. A black watch cap was half tucked into Watson's coat pocket. The boy held his own black-billed cap in his hands. They stood at the beginning of the aisle, between the first set of pews, a few yards to Swenson's right. They looked around, Watson looking at the chapel as if he'd never seen it before. He stood behind the boy, one weather-reddened hand on the boy's shoulder.

In college, John Stisky had written a paper on Fascist Ideology. Looking at the boy with Watson now, he remembered a line from the English fascist

James Barnes: *The present* Weltanschauung *of fascism may be summed up in one word—youth.*

He was a little surprised to see the boy had brown hair. He'd expected blond. But then, Crandall's vision of the earth-born purity of American fascism was rooted in the American countryside, especially the West. Crandall collected Frederic Remington originals. Cowboys were most often depicted as having brown hair.

But blue eyes, oh, yes, and his features were from another of Crandall's collections: His Norman Rockwells. The painting of a bright, tolerant, curious young WASP boy scout.

"That's Darwin, isn't it?" the boy asked, looking at the stained glass.

Watson smiled. "Very good."

But Watson's smile was replaced with a mild frown of concern as he turned to look at Swenson.

"You're not feeling well this morning, John?"

"I'm all right, thanks. Just thoughtful. Distracted. There's . . . so much to do."

"I know how you feel," said Watson and went on, perfectly serious: "It staggers the mind, the job we have ahead of us. The shaping of a world!"

Swenson realized that Watson was talking portentously for the boy's sake. "I assume our friend here is . . . ?"

"This is the lad," Watson said proudly. "Jebediah Andrew Jackson Smith."

The boy looked humbly down.

"Our new junior deacon!" Swenson said, kindly. "Welcome."

And as he said it he thought, *Maybe this is the one I should kill.*

Jebediah Smith was Crandall's great experiment. "The proof of the pudding," Crandall had said. "And the cream of the crop."

Jebediah was one of a group of ten-year-old boys and girls raised in Colton City, the SAISC's "ideal town." Swenson had never been there. He'd only recently acquired the security clearance that made it possible. He'd seen pictures. It looked like the Hometown USA section of Disney City. Except, in the background, you could see the guard towers. Colton City was in a "low-fallout probability" area, in northwestern California. It was highly protected, insular, and permitted no tourist traffic. Its town motto was "Colton City: Beautiful, Comfortable, Safe, and Christian." Jeb and twelve others had been raised in the town's Christian Fellowship Center. Jebediah was supposed to be "deeply and resolutely imbued with our principles."

"I feel a Power in this place," the boy said, with complete assurance. He walked up the aisle, alone, unafraid, and stepped up to stand beside the altar. He put a hand on the altar and looked around. "I feel a Power here," he repeated. "I feel this place is chosen as the place for a new beginning. A new creation."

Holy shit, Swenson, the former priest, thought to himself.

Because there was nothing like a false note in the kid's voice, nothing histrionic or rehearsed. The boy was speaking out of his depths.

God help him, Swenson thought. What had they done to him?

Watson said, "You just look around to your heart's content, son." There was a touch of awe in Watson's voice now. He looked shaken.

He sat down beside Swenson, said softly, "The boy still amazes me."

Swenson nodded.

Watson looked at him. "Want to tell me about it, John? I mean—what's troubling you?"

Swenson wanted to. He wanted to tell him what was really bothering him: Sackville-West was going to put some of them under extractors, and John Swenson would be one of those extracted, and they would ask him about himself, and find out his history was false, and ask him about his real one, and they'd hear all about the NR, and Steinfeld, and Purchase. And there would be a bloodbath along with his own execution. *And so you see, Watson*, Swenson would say, *I was just sitting here wondering if I should try to borrow a car, maybe make up a reason to drive into town, get past the gates, run and hide. Only, Watson, I have a feeling they won't let me leave till after the information extraction.*

But that was not the worst of it. Not for Swenson. The worse part was, he was beginning to feel like he belonged here, in this chapel. Like he *should* tell them everything.

He watched the boy Jebediah, who was staring up at the oil painting of Crandall sitting with Jesus, the boy maybe wondering where he would fit into the painting. A boy with a sense of destiny . . .

"You don't want to talk about it, John?" Watson went on. There was no suspicion in his voice.

But Swenson knew he had to respond, and quickly. Watson sensed he was gnawed at by something. They all knew about him and Ellen Mae, of course. All the more reason he must be monitored very closely. He had to give Watson something . . .

Swenson sighed. "Perhaps I *do* need to talk to someone about it . . . I guess I worry that we might be betraying young Jebediah here, and all the other young ones. We might be moving into this thing too fast. Biting off more than we can chew. It's *the war* that worries me. We're deploying thousands of troops in a war zone and the risk that the war trend will change, that the front will move back to include, for example, Paris. That our outposts will be overrun by the Russians . . . " He shook his head. "It seems like an awful risk. A gamble. We're biting off too much too soon and we're risking the overall Program . . . "

Watson nodded appreciatively. "You're a wise young man. We are risking a great deal—but not everything. Unless the Russians win the war, we will prevail, John. At the moment, they're losing. You see, the war works in our favor simply by being there. It acts as a kind of . . . a kind of *eclipse* that blocks out basic values, conventional morality, leaves people open to extremes they wouldn't consider any other time. Take World War One, for example. After the Treaty of Versailles, Europe was at a loss. It was a junkyard. Everyone was looking for someone to blame for their plight. In Germany, national pride was nearly shattered. People were desperate for direction, identity. National Socialism offered them someone to blame. They could blame the Jews and their friends the bankers. It offered them pride: in national identity. It offered them a way out of the Depression and want: the Nation would take responsibility for rebuilding, for providing work and food. But for that, they told the people, we'll need control. Socialist control. 'Only, don't get the idea we're Marxists! We're *National* Socialists . . . '" Watson shrugged. "The same situation exists now. There are millions of homeless since the advent of the war. The refugee camps are swelling—our recruiters are finding them very fertile ground indeed. Do you know what a refugee camp is? It's a microcosm. The camps automatically divide up by race. That's instinct. The wogs on one side, the Africans over there, and the European natives over here. But the Red Cross and the other people who run the camps give out the food evenly. And there isn't really enough. So the hungry native Europeans see the immigrants, the various shades of darkies, getting a good deal of the food. And they resent it . . . and they listen to us when we talk." Watson was becoming excited now, relishing his old pseudo-intellectual fashioned racism. He ground the palms of his hands together like a man trying to crack a walnut.

Jebediah had come to listen, standing by gravely, nodding as if he understood as an adult would. And who knew how much they'd tinkered with the boy's brain? Perhaps they'd robbed him of his childhood, Swenson thought. Perhaps he did understand Watson's twisted logic.

Watson was saying, "I'll tell you what these people in the camps are—they're base clay! They're malleable!'

"What shape will we make them into?" the boy asked, surprising them both again.

"The shape of salvation!" Watson said. "Salvation for the very clay we're shaping. We're teaching them strength and a taste for purity! Our people—

yes, white people, Western civilization's people—will better survive and prosper if they expel foreign impurities. Impurities of blood, religion, culture, and economic philosophy: the decadence we've all been living in is like the . . . the excretion, the bodily pollution of those foreign influences . . . "

Swenson nodded and patted Watson on the shoulder, just admiringly enough so it was believable. "You could be a preacher yourself. A good one."

Watson chuckled and said, "Oh, Rick's preacher enough. But of course I do write . . . uh, *help* him write his sermons."

Watson mused silently for a moment. Swenson shifted on the hard pew, aware his legs were going to sleep, his feet numb from the cold. He wanted to go back to the house, but this seemed a holy moment for Watson, and he sensed he'd best let it round itself out.

"The ironic thing," Watson said, "is that it doesn't matter if we're better than they are, or *not*. It was what I was telling the two bumpkins from Idaho. It doesn't matter if we're better than the Jews or wogs. We're *different*, and . . . " He gestured toward the stained-glass figure of Darwin. "And we must struggle with them, win out over them. We must show who is the fittest! Not superior, fittest."

Swenson said, "Yes, I think I . . . "

Watson turned sharply to him. "*Do* you see? Really? The Russians may overrun some of our positions—but in the meantime our men are planting the seeds of the new shape among the common people, the common clay. We make contacts, we develop relationships. We attach strings. And when the new shape arises . . . Ironic, again, to think of the Jewish legend of the golem, the man-thing made from clay . . . When our golem arises, it will answer only to us."

Jebediah's eyes shone with an understanding that should have been beyond a ten-year-old boy.

If Steinfeld saw this boy, Swenson thought, he would be afraid. He would want to kill him.

But Swenson knew he couldn't do it.

Watson was looking at the boy with a kind of quiet wonder. And perhaps a trace of fear. He had forgotten about Swenson's misgivings. He stood, and stretched, and said expansively, "Well! Let's go back to the house where it's nice and warm and have some cocoa, shall we?" He turned to Swenson. "Coming, John? A little hot cocoa, eh?"

Swenson smiled, falling back into character, letting the character drive for a while. "Just what the doctor ordered."

He stood and stamped some feeling into his feet, then followed them out the door, hearing Watson say, "You see, Jeb? We're all family here."

• • •

Swenson had seen them arriving at Crandall's compound all day. By sunset, there were forty of them. Twelve of them were children, grave and soft-voiced and much doted on.

At a few minutes after eight that evening, they all set out for the chapel again, this time as part of a candle-light procession. Swenson, like the others, wore the gray-black hooded robe, and held a red candle in a black wooden holder. The night was almost windless; the flames guttered only slightly as they trudged across the snowy meadow between the house and the chapel.

Swenson walked along, looking at the ground as if afraid of stumbling. And he was: afraid he'd fall if he looked up at the chapel. But Ellen Mae moved up beside him, whispered in that Hallmark Card tone of hers, "Look at the chapel! Isn't it beautiful!"

So he had to look. It glowed against the backdrop of the woods. Light from the windows made a broken, mixed rainbow across the virgin expanse of snow—and the snow was iridescent, crystalline, immaculate.

"The snow around the chapel looks like a clean soul," she said, and it should have made him recoil inside with contempt. That saccharine drippiness. The show window of a religious souvenirs store.

But it was a measure of his mood, his susceptibility, that he looked at the snow and thought, *Yes, like a clean soul.* "We walk our footprints across it like sins," he said, saying things himself that would have made him chuckle back in the seminary. "And by morning the Lord wills another snowfall to cover it all. His redemption falls from heaven."

She reached out and briefly squeezed his arm. He felt a surge of emotion. Real emotion, real feeling for her; for the chapel, the procession. At the same time thinking, *Someone get me out of this.*

The chapel's light glowed out the door and windows. A floodlight illuminated the steel cross up top. *A thing of steel*, he thought. In his mind's eye he saw Jesus—no, it was Rick Crandall—waist deep in hordes of unclean Muslims and Jews, dwarfish things only coming up to his waist, clawing at him, and Crandall had the steel cross in his hands, was using it like a battle-axe to sweep them from his path, smashing with it, blood flying . . .

He shook himself, to make the image go. A little hot wax dripped on his hand from the candle he carried, and he cherished its burning reproach.

The snow squeaking under his feet. The chant beginning when they were halfway to the chapel. Crandall and Watson, at the head of the procession, leading the litany.

THE INVOCATION: Who is our Lord?
THE RESPONSE: Jesus is our Lord.
What is His will?
His will is purity.
What does He purify?
The world He purifies.
What is His sword?
Our Nation is His sword.
Who is our Lord?
Jesus is our Lord.

And on. Crandall and Watson chanting the invocation, all the others responding, Swenson too—feeling emotion tremble in his voice, and thinking he heard distant thunder. No, he had heard a single snowflake fall in the forest. Thus the Lord hears all.

Someone get me out.

The children chanting the response: *Our Nation is His sword.*

And then Swenson saw the copper boy.

Swenson stared and stopped walking for a moment, so that someone behind him made a tsk of irritation, and Ellen Mae took his arm, whispered, "Are you all right?"

Swenson moved on mechanically but stared at the copper boy, who moved to keep pace with the procession but didn't walk; his feet didn't quite touch the snow. Didn't change his pose. The boy was standing nude, arms down at his side, giving Swenson a puzzled smile. The smile seemed to ask, *Why are you with them?*

Ellen Mae looked in the direction Swenson was looking. "What is it?"

She doesn't see him, he thought.

He shook his head and kept trudging, staring at the boy, waiting for the mirage to vanish.

It wasn't really a boy—the youth was on the cusp between boy and man. He'd been precocious, graduating from a high school in Managua at sixteen, going right into the Jesuit college . . . Found in a ditch, the mud mingling with his blood, plants to grow in his decayed flesh . . .

. . . Swenson/Stisky . . . saw Saint Sebastian lying in the snow, near the procession, the saint breathing hard in a kind of ecstasy of mortification, and with every breath the arrows would sink themselves into him more deeply . . .

But it wasn't Saint Sebastian, it was the copper boy, bleeding with the red arrows, the arrows whose fletches were candle flame, the boy saying,

"John, you wrote me a letter once, about the Church . . . you said, It's the rituals that matter. Nothing else matters. The historical vindication of Jesus doesn't matter. The Christian philosophy doesn't matter. Faith doesn't matter. For me, the rituals, the compression of symbols, the march of our apotheosized yearning for security . . . the sense of family, of belonging . . . and the glamour of the Church's sweetly absurd artifacts . . . This is what matters to me, what holds me. It's a kind of fetishism, you said, John, remember? A terrible compulsion that works on me quite apart from my political considerations . . . I hate the Church the way a junkie can hate his dealer. Get away before it's too late . . . Remember?"

"A ritual is a ritual," Swenson said.

"What?" Ellen Mae whispered.

He shook his head. He looked at the chapel. They were almost there. He felt the chapel door pulling him. He visualized a fish in a stream reaching a dam, sucked into the spillway. Plunge through into a shining lake where all is enclosed by bank and you never have to wander again . . .

"No," the copper boy said. *"Fight the pull! It's your sickness."* Swenson looked and now the boy was dressed as a priest at mass. The black, the gold. *"Don't go in there, or you will lose me,"* the boy said. But now his face changed, becoming more mature—now he was Father Encendez. *"These people murdered me, John."*

What does He purify?

The world He purifies.

Through the open door he could see the holographic projection floating above the altar: a shining molecule of deoxyribonucleic acid, DNA, the double-helix model, turning, shining like a sort of Christmas tree bauble, the images of Jesus and Rick Crandall behind it.

He thought, *If I go in, I'm lost.*

But the current was ineluctable: it came from inside him, and a man cannot bite his own teeth. The current swept him along.

The procession took him into the chapel, and the ritual began.

• • •

The occupation army had blocked off the roads leading out of the immigrant ghettos in the Twentieth Arrondissement: Algerian ghettos, Congolese, Pakistani, the others. There were SA observation posts in the corner apartments of the buildings overlooking the intersection. Inside the ghetto, the SA proceeded with its registration of all foreign-born residents, or those whose parents were foreign-born. Immigrants were allowed outside the ghettos only if they had SA work permits and photo ID. Once a week, police examiners entered the ghetto bearing lists provided by collaborators; "proved and potential" insurgents were rounded up and taken in two trucks out past the roadblocks, past the checkpoints and the observation stations, into moonlit streets under the cold glitter of the winter sky.

On such a night, at 8:30 p.m. the gray-and-olive four-ton SA trucks with their load of prisoners drove down rue Hermel to rue Ordener, turning at the church across from the *mairie* of the Eighteenth Arrondissement; the ancient mayorage had once housed a police station, now it was a bombed-out shell. Most of the neighborhood, the streets below the hill of the Montmartre, had become architectural crusts, the outlines of the stone row-houses filled with rubble. In the faces of the deserted buildings their windows shadowed deep blue, their cornices and figured-stone ledges picked out all sickly in the chilled aluminum moonlight. One lane of rue Ordener had been cleared of rubble. The trucks turned past the former metro station . . .

And Steinfeld, in the ruins of the *mairie*, threw a switch. The street blew up ten feet in front of the lead truck, the driver suddenly faced with a fountain of burning asphalt. The truck fishtailed to a stop at the edge of the crater, flame licking up at its grille. It tried to back up, but the second truck, just coming to a stop, was still in the way.

Hard-Eyes was the first out of the eastern exit, Yukio out of the western, followed by Jean-Pierre, Rickenharp.

Behind Hard-Eyes came Jenkins and Willow and Hassan and Shimon.

Hard-Eyes was laughing to himself, all the bottled-up sense of urgency boiling out, a rifle fitted with an M-83 grenade launcher in his hands as he angled left. He stationed himself behind the street-lamp that stood in the rubble choking the sidewalk like the single tree surviving a forest fire. The armored windows of the stymied truck were opening for the driver's gun muzzle as Hard-Eyes propped the M-83 on a metal collar around the post and aimed.

He heard a crackle in his headset, then Steinfeld's voice telling the others, *Hold your fire unless you see them outside the truck, until Hard-Eyes—*

Hard-Eyes squeezed the trigger, and the rifle's muzzle jumped, the launcher hissed, there was a splendid Fourth-of-July BOOM, and the truck's right front tire flew into rubbery flinders, was replaced by a ball of flame; the truck chassis lifted up like a clumsy steer rearing back to stamp a hoof; the blast flame lit up a piece of street and the truck's underside for a full second—then the truck fell back down onto the flame, splashing it out, huffing a ring of smoke. He could see the axle was bent, the engine twisted unnaturally out of its case, forcing the torn hood back; the oil-spattered engine looked like some primeval hatchling half out of its metal egg. Then smoke twisted up around the engine, small fires licking after it.

Hard-Eyes felt a bubble of elation expand and pop in him. He laughed again, and all his senses hummed; the cold night air crackled on his hands and face. The smell of burning, of cordite and nitro and blood, made his heart pound . . .

He was chambering another round, a grenade no bigger than two fingers together, when Yukio opened up on the SA in the second cab—or maybe the enemy fired first, it was hard to tell, the flame seemed to leap out simultaneously. Hard-Eyes was aiming, firing, without thinking, without having to, and the second truck's right front end blew out.

Just over his head, sparks flew from the old iron post. It took him a moment . . .

And then he knew they had made him, were firing at him, and his cover was scanty. His scalp contracted with fear. He heard Steinfeld shout, "Give Hard-Eyes covering fire!" He glimpsed Rickenharp up and running toward the truck, firing the Uzi-3, a double-barreled submachine gun, letting go from both its barrels, shouting something; the truck door swung open, a man flopped out . . . Hard-Eyes thought, *That guitarist's got balls.* He ducked back, hunkered behind a big fallen cornice on a pile of debris, almost immediately bullets skittered across rubble just by his head. Not a better spot, maybe worse. Raised his head a fraction to see a man getting out of the truck on the other side, firing through the smoke and flame rising from the twisted hood, returning Rickenharp's fire. Rickenharp running toward the back of the truck . . . 9-mm rounds kicking chips out of the street at Rickenharp's heels.

Steinfeld's voice in his headset shouted, *"Hard-Eyes, if you're clear, run back of the station, come round to the rear of the truck, supervise the liberation—"*

He wasn't clear but Hard-Eyes ran, thinking, *Any second now I'll know what it feels like to get a rifle slug in the side of the head.* Maybe it wouldn't feel like anything, if he was hit by an explosive round. His nervous system would be exploded with the rest of him before it could transit the information. *Sure, keep telling yourself that.*

Then he was at the back of the truck and Yukio was there ahead of him, had cut the chains looping through the steel rings (Where was Rickenharp? He heard the maniac rattling of the Uzi-3, realized the rocker had circled behind the truck's driver, was taking him out . . . heard Willow shout from the back of the second truck, yelling at the prisoners to get out, but where were the guys who'd guarded them? Watch it, watch your ass, those guys must be . . .) The prisoners—dark faces, leaping out, looking around, eyes wide—

Suddenly a man without a face, SA bull in full armor was there, tracking the pistol to Jean-Pierre. Little Jean-Pierre in his black cap, face blacked out, funny little guy, would scream like the devil if you beat him at checkers and beg you to play again. Standing between Hard-Eyes and the bull. Jean-Pierre's back to the bull. Yukio turning, trying to shoot past Jean-Pierre. The armored SA soldier pointing something, it was hard to see in the shadow of the truck—Hard-Eyes was trying to get a firing angle—the dark killing thing in the bull's hand spraying white fire. Jean-Pierre's head erupted, bits of it flying out to carry the cap off—

Yukio fired and the bull staggered. But he was armored, was still on his feet, tracking the gun toward Yukio. Hard-Eyes thought, *If I hit him at this range with a grenade, it'll kill Yukio, too.*

Then Rickenharp was running up behind the bull, shoving his gun against the back of the guy's neck, under the helmet—at that range no armor's going to help—

The helmeted head lit up with the fire behind it and tilted from the neck at a strange angle . . . the bull staggered and fell . . .

The prisoners were running helter-skelter for the subway station, Jenkins and Willow herding them. Sporadic fire racketing as the others exchanged rounds with two SA bulls crouching in the rubble across the street.

Hard-Eyes fixed on them, crouching behind an overturned stone bench, firing at someone he couldn't see. He raised the M-83, set up a grenade round and tracked till he felt that little interior bell ringing: *You're sighted in.*

He fired and the bench flew backwards, maybe five hundred pounds of stone leaping back and smashing the men. *Damn, it makes you feel bigger than human. And then sick.*

Steinfeld was shouting, *"Retreat, trucks coming!"*

Hard-Eyes ran through the veils of smoke, saw someone kneeling, trying to get up, blurred through the smoke but—*It's one of ours.* Hard-Eyes bent to help him up—*oh, it's Hassan*—bullet through his leg, looked like it had taken out the man's knee; he was going to need a brace . . . The two of them running like men in the three-legged race . . .

Down they went into the wrecked Metro station, flashlight beams whipping, all wavery with the running of those who carried them . . .

Someone else, Rickenharp, was helping him with Hassan, who in his pain was shouting for Allah. Then they'd reached the station, were onto the tracks, the pool of light around the lanterns. Sympathizers who'd waited there took Hassan onto a stretcher, the Arab trying not to weep with the pain and then giving in, and they hurried down the tunnel to the camouflaged entrance that led into the sewers, and the escape route, Hard-Eyes thinking, *My mouth is so dry. Lips chapped. Wish I had a beer.*

• • •

In the Cloudy Peak farmhouse. Walking down the hall. The copper boy was gone. But some small, still voice tried to tell Swenson, Now's your chance, go and get into a car, smash through the gates, Stisky, *run* . . .

The guard was walking ahead of him, down the hall. Escorting him to the extraction. "Just a routine CC extraction, sir." Cerebro-Chemical extraction.

Just draw out a little of your brain juice, sir, through a straw, sir, won't hurt a bit, sir, won't damage you, won't erase anything, it'll just tell us exactly what you've been up to and that you're not who you're pretending to be and who all your associates are. Sir.

They'd tried to do them all before the Service. But Swenson had been last on the list, and they'd been running late, because one of the servants, it turned out, had been a member of the Communist Party, and had to be dealt with, though in all probability his membership had been a caprice of years ago, and chances were he was utterly loyal to Crandall . . .

It was nearly midnight. The guard had hidden a yawn behind his hand. Had shrugged apologetically when Swenson had asked, "Can't it wait till tomorrow?" The guard wasn't wearing his helmet, a sign that this was more or less a formality. He had his gun, the kind that fired explosive pellets, strapped to his thigh. Unlocked. He had his back to Stisky. Most of the house was asleep. Stisky . . . Swenson . . . could grab the gun, put the man down, run for the garage, get a car, and with a little luck get away.

So why didn't he do it?

It was as if he were still in the procession. He was floating along, still seeing the Service, the DNA icon slowly rotating there; what a marvelous thing when the boy Jebediah came to stand before the altar and the holo image of the molecule descended to enclose him, began to spin, and the chanting reached a climax, and the wooden bowl was passed, in it the oak leaf, and a little blood from each was taken so that the oak leaf was floating in blood when it reached Swenson . . . Stisky . . . Swenson . . .

"An end to wars," Rick Crandall told them, "when all bloods are of the same blood, when only one race remains. Will that race be divided against itself? It will not."

Run, Stisky.

The beauty of the children's voices lifted in hymn, singing, *Our Nation is the Sword.*

And they were all united in their unthinking, unquestioning belief in Rick Crandall. I was the fly in the ointment, Swenson/ Stisky thought. I was the muddying track in the white snow. A man divided against himself.

Run.

The guard was opening the door for him, and he stepped through, carried through by the current, and it was too late to stop. He didn't look at the technicians. He saw Ellen Mae at the foot of the bed, whispering urgently to Sackville-West, the old man scowling as he listened, shaking his head now.

She doesn't want him to do it to me, Swenson realized. *Because she's afraid they'll extract the details of my relationship with her, she's afraid they'll hear about all the things we did . . .*

Poor Ellen Mae.

Thinking of the boy dead in the ditch, Swenson took off his shirt and lay down on the bed. They opened their bags and black boxes, and they put a plastic breathing mask over his face, and he smelled what sleep smelled like.

. . . He couldn't remember a transition. The mask had come down, and he'd gone out and they'd done the extraction. Now he felt as if his head were a balloon half filled with air, flaccid, beginning to fill up, and as it filled, a sensation grew taut in his head. Pain. Another sensation in his chest.

Iron filings. That was the taste in his mouth as he woke, looking at the room through a layer of gelatin. Hearing a technician say, "He's coming out of it sooner than the others . . . " But they had it. He could see it in Ellen Mae's face, looking at him in horror, shaking her head, telling Sackville-West it must be a mistake.

He heard himself talking. "I betrayed you as much as I betrayed Steinfeld when I let them do it, do the extraction . . . And I *did* let them. Understand that. Tell Rick. I could have found a way out. I could have run! But it was my confessional." Aware of the guard standing close beside the bed, taking handcuffs from his belt. The man was left-handed. His gun was on his left hip.

"I cared about you, Ellen Mae," he heard himself say. "Come and say good-bye to me. I only did what I was trained to do. So come and say good-bye."

Sackville-West shrugged.

Ellen Mae moved around to the left side of the bed. The guard on Swenson's right opening the handcuffs. The blurriness was going from his eyes.

My arms don't work very well, he thought, as he lifted them to embrace Ellen Mae, felt her wet cheek against his. But they'd work well enough. They'd taught him about those guns. Purchase had sent him for weapons training. Poor Purchase, they'll get him now.

Sackville-West coming around to the left side of the bed to tug at Ellen Mae.

The sensation in his chest was a keening, a violin playing high C. The violin player stopped playing but the string continued to resonate as the player tightened it with the peg, tightened the string, made it tighter, the string about to break, so tight it's going to break, stretching . . . to . . .

He reached up and took the gun from the guard's holster and heard someone shout a warning as he pressed the gun between himself and Ellen Mae and pulled the trigger twice.

. . . stretching up to break. Snap.

As the pellets exploded he thought, *I should have shot Sackville—*

Didn't even have time to complete the thought before the thunder consumed him. The thunder of a single snowflake hitting the ground.

• 18 •

Had she slept? Claire wasn't sure. Yes, she must have, because her father was gone from his sleeping bag, and if she'd been awake she'd have noticed his going.

Claire sat up and looked around at the stainless-steel and fiberplas panels of the cafeteria kitchen area. They'd policed the trash yesterday so the room was mostly clean, but the air was fuggier than ever. The lights were dialed low for sleeping. Angie and Judy were bedded down under the counter, sleeping in the same bag. So they were lovers now. So what.

Then she had a sinking sensation, followed by a rasp of annoyance, as she realized she had her period. She could feel it, sticky, a little wet. Great. There'd be blood spots in the sleeping bag, blood on her underwear, she didn't have another pair. And, goddamn it, she didn't have any tampons. There just weren't any left. She reached down to the bottom of her sleeping bag, where she'd stashed a roll of toilet paper. She used a swatch of it to clean blood from the inside of her thighs, then rolled some of the soft synthetic paper around two fingers, making a makeshift sanitary napkin, and positioned it. She sighed, and unrolled her jumpsuit which she'd used as a pillow—and climbed into it, then went to see if they'd turned off the water, so she could rinse out her underwear.

"Oh, thank you, Gridfriend," she muttered, when she saw the toilet was unstopped. Some technicki plumber had finally earned his rating. She used the toilet, then tried the suction flush. Working! The water in the tiny bathroom's tiny sink's tiny tap was running, too. But not much longer, she thought as she rinsed out her panties. The hot-air hand-dryer was running, so she used that to dry them. Mostly; they were still damp when she had to put them on because someone was banging on the door. She climbed into the jumpsuit, difficult in the constricted space, and went out. It was Angie. "Everything's working today."

"They turn off the water tomorrow, your father says." Angie pushed hurriedly past her into the bathroom.

"Does he know that for sure?" Claire asked through the closed door.

"You tell me. We woke him up, asked him to come to tell us what he thinks Admin will do, or how we get to supplies. But he's not much use. Talks crazy half the time. Everybody's getting mad at him, they think he's faking."

"They're stupid." Claire said.

What now? Find her father? But he made her mad, too . . .

She started to walk away and heard Angie shout, "You bastards!"

And then the Pleasant Lady spoke from the wall speakers. "Corridor D, your water has just been shut off. Your electric power will follow and finally airflow. The air you have is bad, but it's not as bad as having no air at all. It's time to come home now. Those of you who are sports fans might be interested to know that tomorrow is the playoff for the opening of the technicki teams Jai Alai champ series. Those who come out today will receive a full pardon and free passes to the games. Those who do not come out will be arrested, tried, and sentenced." Maternal regret in her voice; *hurts me more than it hurts you.* She repeated the message in technicki.

"Pricks," Claire muttered.

There was a banging behind her, and Angie burst out of the bathroom, her face red, her eyes blinking too often, the way they did when she was trying to hold her anger in check. "Your father is lying to us on purpose!" she shouted. "He said we would have water today."

"You said yourself he was only guessing."

Angie shouldered Claire aside, and Claire stared after her in the shock of sudden realization: *It won't be safe for me among these people much longer.*

When Claire returned to the place below the microwavers where her sleeping bags had been, she saw Bonham and her father coming down the aisle together. Were they drunk? The way they walked . . .

No, her father was hurt, and Bonham was helping him walk.

Not such a bad guy, Bonham, she thought. And then she wondered if she was only trying to prepare herself for having to be his whore.

Professor Rimpler was grinning at her, and that made his smashed lip, his swollen eye look worse. His feet were bare, and one of them looked swollen.

"Dad . . . " Feeling her voice cracking. "What did you do this time?"

She and Bonham helped the old man onto his sleeping bag. He immediately turned onto his side, away from her, sighing.

Bonham took her arm and led her a little ways away, looked around. They were alone. "I think he provoked them on purpose. They were already hostile but . . . he told them they were going to die, that the bulls hold all the cards . . . " He shrugged. "Then he started to babble. Something about a hermit crab, we're all hermit crabs fighting for a shell, we should give up and crawl away . . . Molt hit him. I tried to stop them but it was all too fast: someone hit him in the foot with a gun butt. Then your father started laughing, hysterical laughter. They moved away from him. You know what I mean? I think your father is exaggerating his . . . his mental problem. Was maybe having a nervous breakdown, but now he's playing it, real cagey about it. So they don't expect much of him."

She stared at him, thinking about it. Then, slowly: "Maybe you're right . . . Was Angie there when they hit him?"

"No. Why?"

"She used to be my friend. Judy and Angie. Lately . . . " She shrugged. "What now?"

He glanced around again, crossed his arms over his chest, leaned a little nearer. "We leave when the lights go out. They'll turn out the lights in a day or two. I'll have a flashlight. We'll go back to rear launch."

"It's closed down, guarded."

"The guards'll be expecting us. It's part of the deal."

Her stomach twisted. But she said, "Okay. They expect three of us?" Looking at him meaningfully, waiting to see if he'd say, *Your father can't go.*

"They expect only me. But they'll let us through if I insist. I have a priority pass and that means anyone I authorize." He hesitated.

"Yes? What else?"

"Molt. I'm worried about Molt. I think he suspects." He shrugged. "Nothing I can do about it . . . "

He broke off suddenly, stepped back from her. Angie was coming toward them.

Claire thought, *When the lights go out . . .*

•••

"You know what's funny?" Rickenharp said. "That you can get used to being shelled. Bombs exploding around and after a while it's like being used to traffic noises."

"I am no bloody *way* getting use to it," Willow muttered.

They were in the basement of the safe-house, tiny dirt-floored rooms once part of *les caves*, the wine cellars, when the building had been someone's house.

Rickenharp said, "I mean, anyway, its just like I imagined it. Something hits, and the place shakes, a little dust comes down from the ceiling. You feel a vibration go through you. Only it sounds different than I thought it would. Sometimes. There's a kind of whining sound after the blast. I think it's metal breaking—"

"Rickenharp," Hard-Eyes said suddenly, "you proved yourself on three raids now. You did great. Everyone thinks so. You got balls. But Rickenharp, shut the fuck up."

Rickenharp shrugged and shut up.

Hard-Eyes was far from used to the shelling. It scared him more than a firefight, though he was probably less likely to get killed here. It scared him because he was helpless. The whole shebang could come down on his head, and it was no use trying to shoot back at it. There was no strategy except run to a hole and hide in it. You just sat and waited to see if your number was up. It sucked.

The Front had moved back. The US Army had been backed into Paris, and now the Russians were shelling it. Rubbling all that history.

The town was down to a fourth of its population, maybe less; more streaming south every day, running from the shelling. Thousands were clogging refugee camps, trading one kind of suffering for another. But maybe it was better than being stuck in the ghettos, hammered helplessly by shells.

He looked at the others in the light from the lantern, trying to get his mind off it. Rickenharp, Willow, Yukio, the doctor, Jenkins, Carmen. The others in other cellars. Everyone here looking sullen, or looking as if they were trying to keep from looking scared, except goddamn Rickenharp, that brain-damaged asshole, expression on his face like a kid watching fireworks. *Ceiling falls in and we'll see if you're having fun, pal.*

There was a little room left near the door. He was surprised Smoke wasn't there. Smoke usually hung out with Yukio.

"Where's Smoke and the—" He broke off as they heard the thud, felt the vibration pass through the room, chattering teeth as it rippled through them. Dirt sifted down from the ceiling.

"Smoke's gone to the States," Carmen said. "You were out on a hit, you weren't in on that. Steinfeld set up—"

Another thud, another nasty vibration, feeling closer now.

She went on, her voice straining for normalcy. Rickenharp was looking at her, not smiling now. Thinking what Hard-Eyes was thinking: Carmen's scared, wants someone to hold her, but her pride won't allow it.

She said, "Steinfeld set up a route, everything. Smoke's going to do some kind of lobbying in the States to get backing for us."

Jenkins said, "That old burn-out?"

Carmen said, "Steinfeld says Smoke's not a burn-out. He used to be some kind of traveling reformist. Philosopher, writer. Then something bad happened and I guess he gave up, lost touch . . . He's like, changing, Steinfeld says. Says he used to talk to himself all the time. Now he talks to the crow or to people and that's all. He writes stuff in notebooks . . . Steinfeld says he's got some kind of special talent . . . "

Hard-Eyes thought of the scarecrow Smoke had been when they'd met. He nodded. "Yeah, he changed."

They were silent for a while. So were the cannon.

The Algerian came to the door, a lantern in his hand. *"Okay ici? Bon. Steinfeld dis, C'est fini."*

"What's 'e fooking know about it?" Willow said irritably.

Yukio said, "His listening station in the north. He picked up their radio commands. We have the code."

Hard-Eyes felt something unwind in him. He was going to live another day.

He found himself looking at Carmen. Thinking, Funny how, after you almost get snuffed, you want to fuck.

But she was looking at Willow.

Hard-Eyes shrugged. No accounting for taste.

• • •

Kessler's first impression of the island was of a strange, almost featureless flatness, and a blaze of light.

Julie put down her hand-luggage, and fished in her purse for her sunglasses. "This light's *great* for my headache," she muttered, slipping the dark glasses on.

"It was a long flight," Kessler said. "You'll feel better after you get some rest."

"I just can't sleep on airplanes. I'm afraid they'll crash while I'm asleep."

"That's the best time for it if—oh, there they are." Charlie was coming toward the Lear jet in a three-wheeled jitney; the jitney's driver was an islander, skin so dark he was almost purple. The pilot and the steward came down the metal steps behind Kessler. The pilot pointed a plastic matchbox at the plane and pressed a button; the steps retracted, whining, and the door sealed itself.

The jitney pulled up, Charlie jumped out, grinning under his mirrorshades, and pumped Kessler's hand. "'Sap, man!"

"Hi, Charlie . . . This is all our luggage, just carry-on."

"Shit, I came here with less than that. Come on."

They rode the jitney across sticky black asphalt smelling of hot tar, through the heat-shimmer to the little glass-fronted airport building. There was no customs at all. "This island is *ours*, Jimmy," Charlie said. "No one comes here but NR. If they do, they're arrested, and put under an extractor . . . "

Kessler grimaced. Charlie said, "Yeah, I know. I don't like the fucking things either. This one's the only one we got. Anyway, anybody comes to the island by accident, they take 'em into custody—but they let 'em go later if they extract out legit."

"This island got a name?"

"Merino. No government except a little police force, and Witcher acts as a kind of local judiciary, when he's here. He's here a lot now. He's getting paranoid. Officially, Merino's a territory belonging to—um, I'm not supposed to tell anybody what it belongs to, because if you got extracted they'd know what area to search through . . . I found out by asking the locals. And then got a big lecture about it. When it comes to extractor proofing, ignorance is safety. Anyway, Witcher's got a deal with the country that the island belongs to. He owns it—shit, it's only about thirty-five square miles."

Kessler shrugged. He was enervated and logy as they got into a limo. It felt cold after the heat outside.

"Oh, God, air conditioning," Julie said gratefully. They rode along a white crushed-shell road, between rows of palm trees, parallel to a glittering white-sand beach. The sea was a vast blue gem.

They drove through two checkpoints, past electric fences crested with barbed wire; under the unwavering gaze of CCTV cameras that rotated smoothly to watch them. Past guards with rifles.

Julie looked at him, and he squeezed her hand. He knew what she was thinking. That this might turn out to be a kind of prison for them.

Kessler said, "Charlie—they let us come and go from the compound as we please?"

"Absolutely. But they give you a list of things you can talk to the locals about. They speak a dialect sort of half Spanish, half English. They understand you, though."

They were driving through landscaped estate grounds now, cacti and exotic plants he'd never seen, flowering on both sides. A fountain. A tennis court. But at intervals: concrete bunkers, showing the snouts of heavy machine guns and small cannon.

They passed through a gate, and into a kind of small village. Cottages, two cafés, two bars. They pulled up in front of a whitewashed cottage with red shutters and solar panels on the roof.

"This is your place," Charlie said proudly. "Bigger'n your apartment in New York. Witcher really set it up nice for us here."

They went into the cottage. Inside it was shady, cool, comfortable. Wicker furniture, an old-fashioned wooden four-poster bed. Julie lay back on the bed, took off her sunglasses, and threw an arm over her eyes. But Kessler knew she was listening as he and Charlie talked.

"Witcher's okay," Charlie was saying. "A little straight. A capitalist—but then so are you. He's . . . You know—gets his money from a private cop company, in competition with the SA, and from patents on surveillance devices. His people developed camera birds. So sure, he's straight. But he's a good guy."

"Why's he do it? Why's he fund the NR?"

"Not even Steinfeld's sure. Witcher says he hates racists and anyway the SA's his biggest business competition. But I don't know. Thing is, you can trust him. You can feel it."

"Steinfeld here?"

"No. He's stuck in Europe. Maybe in deep shit . . . You'll get the whole briefing later. There's a guy coming, Jack Brendan Smoke."

"Yeah. I read him. He was way ahead of everyone else—"

"He's going to be working with you, to counter Worldtalk's subliminals and the PR for . . . You'll get it all after dinner."

"Okay. But—" Kessler hesitated, not sure what it was he wanted to say. What was bothering him was, he supposed, simple disorientation. And worry. Could he really trust these people?

"Hey, Jim—" Charlie put his hands on Kessler's shoulders. "You won't have to stay in this place forever, but you got to understand: *this is home!* These people have been through it all—with Worldtalk or the SA or the fucking CIA. There's a woman here who was extracted by Worldtalk—you can talk to her. I'm tellin' you. The fences are to keep the enemy out, not to keep us in. You're home, man. You're home . . . "

• • •

Purchase was sitting in one of Worldtalk's video conference rooms, thinking he needed to go to the enzymologist and have his stomach acid turned down again, when Fremont on Screen One said, "Look, let's boil the problem down to its basics. We have journalists, congressmen, you-name-it—not too many, but then, any amount is too many—accusing the SAISC of anti-Semitism, of creating racial pogroms in the war zone, of misusing NATO funding, of—hell, everything."

Chancelrik, on Screen Three, said, "Basically they're hinting the SA chiefs are actual *fascists*, for Christ's sake. Well in fact—I don't know if you fellas saw this report—that there's a group that calls itself the New

Resistance responsible for—" He paused to read off a printout. "—thirty-five military attacks on SAISC stations and personnel in six European capitals, and according to this source they're spreading propaganda calling the SA 'Nazis' outright."

"Okay," Fremont said, "that's the upshot. But you note that ninety percent of the accusations have to do with things happening in the war zone. We can point up that things in the war zone come to us garbled because of the difficulty of getting clear information through the Russian blockade, all the antisat scrambling, you-name-it. Any thoughts on that, Purchase, my boy? Heard scarcely a peep from you."

"Uh-huh. What I think is . . . " Purchase contemplated the faces on the screen—Fremont transmitted from LA, Chancelrik from Chicago, Barley from Miami. " . . . I think you're on the right track, Sammy, and uh—" He thought desperately, managed, "I think we should suggest through our news-sheet editorializing channels that there's a kind of prejudicial attitude here, behind these accusations, because, uh, our lady prez has come out as a supporter of the warzone policing program so, uh, basically what we have is the Democrats seizing on an issue, spouting a lot of hearsay and, uh . . . "

Something about the way Barley was clearing his throat a little too loudly into his headset made Purchase realize he was blowing it. Barley said, "I think—correct me if I'm wrong—I already brought up that point, remarkably close wording—"

In his humorous drawl, kidding him about it.

Purchase said, "Of course, sorry—I'm out of it today, little personal problem. Uh, in fact I've got to make a call about that, do you guys think—"

"Hey, you take as long as you want, Purchase, my boy!" Fremont said.

"Sure! Go ahead!" the other two chimed in.

"Thanks." But he knew as soon as he was out of the room they'd say: *Isn't it a shame about Purchase, guy isn't keeping it together anymore.*

He stood up and put his screen on hold, then went down the hall to his office, thinking that maybe it was stupid to wait it out.

He'd been waiting for word from Swenson—or about Stisky. Confirmation that Stisky's cover was blown. But maybe it was a mistake to wait. Maybe he should run—*now.*

He'd told himself he had work to do here. It was a crucial time. If he could find a way to sabotage the SA's Worldtalk propaganda campaign . . .

No. He made up his mind. The risk was too great. He'd leave here, join the others in Merino. He was holding back out of sheer inertia, really. Habit. He'd come to the office every weekday barring holidays for eight years, and old habits—

The thought broke apart and spiraled into irony: *Die hard.*

Because when he stepped into the office he saw the two SA bulls in full armor standing to either side of the door. He saw them reflected in the window beyond his desk.

"Mr. Purchase," one of them said. Wearing the helmet they wear when they come to take people away.

"Okay," Purchase said. "I understand."

Thinking, *Try to call the cops?* These guys had no real legal authority to do more than detain him, as long as he didn't resist. But they'd never let him call the cops. They planned to take him somewhere quiet, and interrogate him, and eventually kill him.

He turned to face them, smiled, and said, "Let's go." He started to go out the door between them—then stopped and snapped his fingers as if just remembering something. "Uh—you mind if I get my wife's picture from my desk?"

One of the guards turned his opaque faceplate toward the desk. "There's no picture on the desk, sir."

"It's in the drawer," he said, turning to the desk casually as he could manage, his heart pounding, sweat starting out on his forehead. "I don't like to have her on the desk there staring at me accusingly all day, so I keep her in the drawer—" Little chummy laugh there. "But I'd like to have the picture"—opening the desk drawer—"to look at now and then." Reaching in.

"Mr. Purchase, I'm getting a rising heartbeat rate and a respiration signal on you that's a little worrisome. I think you'd better hold it right there—"

As Purchase turned with the gun in his hand.

But the one on the right had taken a step closer and had his RR stick out. The stick was already whistling down at his head, and Purchase didn't even get the pistol's safety off. He felt the crunch and the explosion of pain, and nothing else.

The bull had hit him a little too hard—maybe because of the gun—and Purchase was still comatose in an SA-owned hospital six months later when, after the fourth extraction try proved futile, the euthanasia judge signed the papers and Worldtalk pulled the plug.

And then Purchase finished dying.

• • •

The Radic technickis controlled only a relatively small part of the Colony. The back section of Corridor D and, for a while, about half the technicki dorms. On the twenty-seventh day of the occupation, a little over two months after the Russians had blockaded the Colony, Security stormed the barricaded dorms and retook them. About twenty percent of the Radics were taken prisoner. And Security found the body of Guy Wilson, ripe from decay, in Wilson's sealed dorm room. Wilson had been beaten to death, "probably with the butt of a rifle." The Admin—not citing its evidence—officially charged Samson Molt with Wilson's murder, *in absentia*. It warned the technickis, over InterColony and intercom, that Molt was "still at large."

In fact, Molt and the Radics' hard-core had been driven back, into Corridor D. They sealed off the corridor behind them and now occupied the burnt-out corridor mall, the cafeteria and its kitchens, and the corridor's main passageway. But they were in touch, via hastily rigged wifi transmitters, with technicki sympathizers on the outside of the barricaded area. And it was this source that got word to Bonham and Molt that the bulls were coming in force now from every main access, were massing around the bend in the corridor and in the transverse passage that led into the corridor area from the dorms. They were carrying flashlights and rifles.

Minutes after this report came through, the lights went out in Corridor D.

Immediately there were panicky shouts insisting that no one panic, no one panic, and flashlight beams stabbed at the ceiling, the walls, as if trying to see through them, to see the unseen enemy . . .

Bonham had known the exact time the power cut would come. He and Claire had rendezvoused at the intersection of Corridor D and Transverse 67. Forty yards back from the front barricade. The front barricade, on the Admin side, was the most heavily guarded.

The rear barricade had only three men on it, because the sympathizers on the outside had not reported significant Security activity in the end of the corridor. The Radics' sabotage had wrecked transverse access to the rear barricade area. The bulls couldn't get through that way without clearing away great mounds of debris.

The only other way they could come from behind would be from the rear launch levels. The Security bulls could, conceivably, take pods or repair shuttles from the Admin area through space to the rear launch and get at the back barricade that way. But the rear launch levels were far smaller than the Admin launch levels. They could accommodate only two small vehicles at once . . . And only about five men could come through the small airlock at any one time. The process of bringing in men that way would be time-consuming and could be monitored by the Radics' crudely rigged TV surveillance system. But the power cut had turned off the Radics' surveillance gear as well as the lights. The rear was blinded. The three men on the back barricade argued about what to do—the Radic-occupied territory was clearly being attacked from the front, one of them argued, so they should go and help support the front barricades. The others argued for staying where they were.

• • •

Bonham and Claire waited in a dark doorway to one side, listening to the argument.

Claire whispered, "What if they stay on the barricades?"

"They'll let me through. They're used to seeing me as a leader." But there was no certainty in his voice.

The pitch-black corridor area was shot through with lances of light. Pools of illumination danced over walls and ceiling, quivering with an urgency that corresponded with the shouted directions, and arguments, and more cries of "Don't panic!" And thirty feet to Claire's left, the senior of the three guards was shouting, "All right, fuck it, we'll stay, but if Molt . . . " The rest was garbled by interruptions from the others.

Claire huddled against the cold metal wall, chewing a knuckle, searching through the fragmented darkness for a glimpse of her father in the patches of light. "Goddammit, where's Dad? . . . Damn him! I told him, I wrote it down for him where we'd be—"

"You should have brought him with you."

"Molt had me on barricade duty. It wasn't safe for Dad to be out there with me where everyone could see him, he'd start ranting and they'd—you know—"

She shrugged. He didn't see her shrug in the dark, but he understood her.

• • •

The old man was crouched under the big mixing table in the cafeteria kitchen, smiling absently in the darkness. The darkness was almost complete. Now and then a light splashed the wall across from him as someone carrying a flashlight ran past. His world was dark but splashed with light; it was cold, and yet he felt feverish, and that was like space itself: black but shattered with light, cold but charged with radioactive heat. Maybe, he thought, this is an old-fashioned omen. A taste of what's to come—when the Colony's turned inside out and we're all dissipated into the void.

Rimpler's back ached. Without thinking, he shifted his position to ease the ache. That turned him enough so he could see the luminous dial of the pocket watch Claire had scrounged for him. Automatically, he registered the hour, and saw it was past time for him to meet Claire.

The time demanded a decision. And a decision came, one that had been struggling to get out of him for days. He'd sat there in the darkness for an hour, not thinking about any one thing in particular—but all the time some part of his mind had been thinking, and by degrees coming to one starkly unavoidable conclusion. He'd had a towering responsibility, had willfully taken it on himself. And just as willfully had thrown it aside.

Jettisoned it. And now he was going to have to try to find it again. And never mind that it was impossible, and that it was too late. He was going to have to try and take it back.

He wondered if he should try to explain to her, make her understand what he had to do. How would he put it? *Claire—I made it possible for thousands of people to move into another world, to start over, and they turned against me and I handled it badly. And I lost the world I made . . .* He could imagine her response.

"You telling me that Jehovah has been disenfranchised?" She had more of her mother in her than she liked to admit.

I've been asleep, Claire. I put part of myself to sleep because of what happened to Terry—and because the thing I spent my life building fell apart around me. Now I'm going to take charge again, and make it right.

What would she say to that? She'd say it was a childish fantasy. That it wouldn't work. And he knew it probably wouldn't work.

He remembered telling Claire about the tower a man built himself into over the years, the tower of convictions and habits and ineradicable decisions. He visualized his own personal tower of Babel, and in the vision he saw it tottering, beginning to shiver apart . . .

And the trouble was—he wasn't in that tower alone. He had every man, woman, and child in the Colony up there with him.

Feeling his way along the wall, he crept out of the kitchen and into the cafeteria, straightening up to look around. Ahead was the door into Corridor D. The lights and shouting danced together there. He walked into them.

And out into the chillier open spaces of the corridor.

Someone loomed over him: a big, angry man with a gun in one hand and a flashlight in the other. Molt himself.

"Where are they going to come from, Rimpler? Where will the bulls come from? From the dorm crossovers? From the rear? The front?"

"Probably from the front," Rimpler replied distractedly. "I intend to meet them, to tell them that I'm taking over again, so there's no need to worry about it. We'll negotiate a settlement with you people. It will include an amnesty."

Molt stared at him, open-mouthed. Rimpler had forgotten that he was a beaten-up old man, grimy, hair matted, chin stubbled. That he'd been behaving half-cracked for days. It was as if a Bowery bum wandered into the mayor's office and announced he was taking over. "You pathetic old has-been!" Molt burst out. "You've really lost it this time."

Rimpler snorted. "So I'm crazy? You're locked in here, surrounded by hostile professional warriors far better armed. You have almost no light and you'll soon have no air. You're wanted for murder! And *I'm* irrational?

You got yourself into this, Molt. You're a glory-hounding leech who's dragged a lot of discouraged people into the shitpit which is your natural home. Now go and tell them that I'm—"

But Molt had stopped listening. He was looking around, his face—lit from beneath by the flashlight in his hand—was grim with suspicion. "Where's Bonham?" He demanded suddenly. He grabbed Rimpler by the neck and shook him, threw him to the floor. "Where the hell's Bonham? The lights are out, the bulls are coming—and Bonham disappears!"

Rimpler sat there on the floor, stunned. Molt reached down and pulled him to his feet, shook him again. Rimpler felt as if everything that had gone wrong, all the forces that had gone wild around him, were incarnate in Molt; were wrenching Rimpler's shoulder, shaking him, screaming at him. "*Where's Bonham?*" Molt shouted.

"He's gone!" The reply coming from deep inside him somewhere. "Gone! He and Claire went out the back way—by now they're gone! You can forget him!"

"*What?* You old *pig!* Why didn't you—?" He couldn't articulate his outrage, after that. Molt shouted in wordless fury, and brought the flashlight down, overhand, hard onto Rimpler's head.

Rimpler saw it coming, and time seemed to slow so he could appreciate the sight . . .

The shining electric comet arcing down to him, a light roaring to hit him right between the eyes. Rimpler shouted: "Terry!" He heard a crunch, and then a crash resounding like the fall of the Tower of Babel.

•••

Claire saw the luminous dial of Bonham's watch as he raised it to check the time.

"Right about now," he said.

Five breathless seconds passed. And then they heard the rattle of semi-auto rifle fire from the front barricade. The rifle fire was instantly followed by the big, sloppy *HUH-UMP* of an explosion as the bulls fired a concussion shell into one of the barricade's trucks; a rumble as part of the barricade collapsed. More rattling gunfire, flicker of flames growing from the front of the corridor. A rackety mechanical noise followed by a *SCREEEE* as Security used a bulldozer of some kind to push the ore crates out of the way. More gunfire, strobe flashes, another explosion she could feel vibrating in the metal of the wall. Her nails dug into her palms, her eyes hurt from the strain as she tried to see her father in the confusion of running men, flashing lights, fencing flashlight beams. Instinctively she started toward the front, calling, "Dad!"

Someone grabbed her arms, pulled her back. After a moment she knew it was Bonham, whispering urgently in her car. "You can't do it! You'll get shot if you go up there! Look—they're gone from the rear!"

The eruption at the front had drawn the guards off the rear barricade. He dragged her to one of the jitneys used as barricade support.

She stopped resisting Bonham when she saw looked over her shoulder and saw Molt jogging clumsily after them.

Molt shouting, "Bonham! You ain't goin' nowhere, man!" Still twenty yards away, Molt stopped and raised the rifle . . .

The light was all patchwork around Molt. For a moment he stood there with his back to the conflagration at the barrier, like a man in a cave standing silhouetted against a campfire. He was outlined in flickering light, his face in darkness.

Then the muzzle flash lit his face as he fired at Bonham—three rounds, all three missing, pocking bullet dimples into the metal of the jitney's cab. Bonham let go of her and turned, climbed into the jitney, and through it to the other side of the barrier.

Claire stood snake-fascinated, staring at Molt, who was moving toward her again, centering the rifle on her chest . . .

Screams echoed from the front barricade. The bulls had broken through. Claire saw seven, maybe eight Security bulls in full armor, opaque faces catching the uneven light, as they ran up behind Molt, shouting with amplification, "SAMSON MOLT, DROP YOUR WEAPON, YOU ARE UNDER ARREST—"

Molt spun, pointed his rifle at the nearest bull, and fired. The man staggered but kept coming, raising his own weapon and a flashlight. Molt threw the rifle aside and drew a pistol.

She heard Bonham shout, behind her, "*Claire!* Come on! They're waiting for us out here!"

Molt fired the pistol, a pistol using explosive armor penetrating ammo—a guard fell, his armor ballooning. His amplified scream echoed with ear-ripping shrillness off the steel walls . . .

Molt ran shouting at the guards . . . flashlight beams whipping around him . . .

Claire squinted, trying to see her father . . .

Bonham shouted at her from behind . . .

And then Molt stopped as one of the guards shot him. Molt seemed surprised that the bullet hadn't hurt him much. Then he laughed and moved toward them again.

And, running at them with his gun upraised, howling with laughter—he exploded. The small explosive bullet buried in him detonated and the red of the explosion's flash was complemented by the red of blood-splash.

We forget we're made mostly of red liquid, Claire thought. But now she could see it was so—as Molt became a fountain of red liquid. She felt a few hot red drops spatter her forehead.

She saw the bulls move toward her, booming. "CLAIRE RIMPLER, YOU'RE UNDER ARREST—"

Dad's gone, she thought. It's hopeless.

She turned and climbed frantically through the jitney built into the barricade, trying to worm out the window on the other side, all the time expecting to feel an armored hand clamping her ankle to pull her back. But Bonham's hands, instead, pulled her through the jitney's window and past the barricade. She was in semidarkness, on her knees. Amplified shouts from behind her: "CLAIRE RIMPLER—"

"Why are they trying to arrest me?" she gasped at Bonham. "You said you arranged it."

"The arrangement had to be secret. Only a few of them know. Come on!" Bonham helped her up, and they ran around a corner, down a transverse passage, up a ringing metal stairway, following the blob of Bonham's flashlight jiggling on the wall—coming out on the access to the launch deck.

It was lit up, here, and there were uniformed men standing around, looking bored, waiting for them.

Claire screamed with frustration.

Bonham said, "It's all right—they work for Van Kips. It's part of the deal."

One of the men demanded, "You got the transport authorization?"

"Yeah, yeah . . . uh . . . here it is . . . " Bonham handed the man a paper.

"Okay. Come on."

And Claire burst into tears.

Her father was gone. She had abandoned him.

• • •

URGENT: Witcher to Steinfeld

Decoded:

They extracted Stisky. He is reported dead. Ellen Mae Crandall reported dead. They have Purchase. You are compromised: they know your location. Repeat, they have made Paris as the location of NR field leadership; you in particular. Message intercepted relaying orders from Watson, Paris to be sealed off, the city to be "taken apart if necessary." New weapons deployed. Leave Paris, repeat, leave Paris . . .

• • •

URGENT: Bensimon, Israeli Embassy, to Witcher

Decoded:

Your message transmitted on to Steinfeld. However, Russian damage to allied sats and other factors make Steinfeld copying message unlikely. Computer report: probability only seven percent that Steinfeld received message. Strategic good news: high-level decision in Tel Aviv resulting from new intelligence confirms extreme anti-Semitic activity SA prompting Mossad to take active part against SA. Will do what we can to get Steinfeld and cadre out.

Part Four:
HARD-EYES AND HARPIE

Hard-Eyes and Rickenharp were picking their way through the ruins of Paris, en route to checking out the landing pod Steinfeld claimed was coming down a kilometer northeast, when they saw Besson frying the last two fingers of his left hand.

They could see Besson—his image distorted but recognizable—through the fire-warped bubble of the burnt-out McDonald's plastic window. He was cooking something they couldn't see, at that point, using the grill's abandoned bottle of propane. True to form, Besson had camped out just two blocks from the Arc de Triomphe, on the Champs-Élysées. What was left of the Champs-Élysées . . . Besson was never far from the arch; his wife had been buried alive after a direct hit on their apartment building a few hundred yards from the monument.

And Besson returned to the shell of the building at night, to talk to his wife.

Rickenharp claimed he'd seen her himself; translucent and luminous, she drifted over the rubble, smiling enigmatically. So he said.

Maybe he *did* see her. Because two days after the front moved on north again, leaving Paris in the hands of the SA, the *Strategie Actuel*, and a few beleaguered cops, Rickenharp had made a deal with a black marketeer, traded an antique Chinese jade-and-silver bracelet ("First thing I bought when I got the royalties on my first hit. Everybody else bought a car.") for half an ounce of blue mesc.

You do enough blue mesc, you see anything you want.

It was a damp, chill evening; gloomy but suffused with the pearly gray afterglow. There were shreds of fog gathering, knitting together in the blue shadows of the ruined walls.

They stood outside the wrecked MacDonald's, the steel of the Belgian assault rifle growing cold in Hard-Eyes' hands as the dusk wore into night. There was a .45 holstered on Hard-Eyes' right hip. Rickenharp carried something he'd scavenged from an SA ordnance dump: a Heckler and Koche Close Assault Weapon System (CAWS) automatic shotgun, model three. Gas operated with recoil assist, bullpup layout, internal operation floating system; 12-gauge. It was a thirty-four-inch gun, with the flash-hider, squarish, made of lightweight permaplast, carbon-fiber and plastic, stronger than steel. Twenty-round box. Rickenharp carried a pouch of seven ready-loaded boxes, and he'd practiced slapping them into the magazine till he could do it faster than the eye could follow. The CAWS was lethal out to 150 yards.

Rickenharp said, "What you think, neggo? Let's go see how old Besson's getting on. We're, like, the only civilians left in Paris unless you want to count the cannibals in Pigalle."

Hard-Eyes shrugged. "Steinfeld won't like it. We gotta get to the thing before the fashes do, Harpie."

"Probably not a landing pod the spotters saw, man. How likely is that? Orbit drop pod? Sure. More likely helicopter. Talk about fashes, it was probably them." The fashes: the Fascists.

"Yukio saw the sensor profile and he knows spacegear. But fuck it, let's look in on Besson." He stepped into the MacDonald's as he spoke, "Five minutes tops and—oh, shit." That's when he saw what Besson was cooking. His fingers . . .

They'd gone into the refugee camp, recruiting, more than once, and they'd seen things there, that—well, this shouldn't have bothered Hard-Eyes as much as it did.

His gut contracted as he watched Besson stab a fork into his fingers and bring them to his mouth, start chewing, his eyes blank. He had a submachine gun, a Russian model cadged off some corpse, slung on a strap over his right shoulder.

"Hey, Besson, man, uh—" Rickenharp said softly. "Put down the gun and—everything. You come with us, we'll find you some rations, man. We didn't know you was so hard up." Stupid thing to say: everybody was hard up. Rickenharp's pale face had gone grim; his Adam's apple bobbed on his long neck as he swallowed to keep from gagging.

Besson looked at them—and growled.

Looking into Besson's small red eyes, at the sores on his emaciated face, his scalp and hair missing in patches, Hard-Eyes knew he was burnt. Gone, blown. He'd gone into the neurotoxin-dusted sectors, maybe without knowing it, scratching in the rubble for food, and the stuff was killing him slowly, making him mad first, as it was designed to do . . .

And now he was pointing the machine gun at them, holding it against his hip with his good hand. One of his charred fingers still clenched in his teeth. He growled again—a warning, like a dog with a bone.

He'd probably shoot at them if they moved, even if they backed away. A man got that way if he was yellow-dusted.

So Rickenharp pretended to faint.

He fell into a swoon, sighing, falling flat out on the shard-strewn floor. Besson gaped, confused. The charred finger fell from his mouth. Finally, his burnt brain decided: something moved, and even if it was only to fall, better shoot it.

So he lowered the gun to point it at Rickenharp on the floor.

Hard-Eyes drew his sidearm and did Besson a favor.

Besson fell with a neat round hole through the forehead, and Rickenharp, lying on the floor, started to sob.

Hard-Eyes felt empty. He reached down and pulled Rickenharp to his feet. "What you gonna do if we run into Carmen's patrol, she sees you like that," Hard-Eyes said, a catch in his voice. "Cut it the fuck out."

Rickenharp staggered out the door and took deep draughts of the cold night air. Hard-Eyes came to stand by him. "Later on," Rickenharp said, "we take his body to his old house, bury him with his wife."

"Okay . . . He's better off, Harpie."

"Yeah. I guess." He took an old, ornate snuff box from his pocket, opened it, scooped a strong hit of blue mesc with a thumbnail grown extra long for just that purpose. He snorted it up, and, still sniffing it back into his sinuses, said, "Yeah—" Sniff. "Probably better off now—" Sniff. "Than he has been for years." Sniff.

Hard-Eyes watched dolefully. "Hodey, I shouldn't be trusting you with a gun anywhere near me when you're on that shit. I'll be glad when you run out."

"Hey, it just makes me a better shot."

"Sure, if you're shooting at gray aliens and fairies."

"Hey, I'm the head producer, the programmer of my hallucinations, neggo."

"Just fucking come on." Hard-Eyes led the way off through a narrow side street, the buildings on the other side mostly intact, heading northeast again.

"You believe in life after death, Hard-Eyes?"

"I don't know." He didn't believe in it at all, but he didn't want to say that to Rickenharp just now.

"I do." Sniff.

"What a surprise."

"I mean, something's up with this life. It's weird we're alive. So it'd be weird if we're . . . " Sniff. " . . . just alive for this little blip of time, man." Sniff.

"Will you stop sniffing that crap? Dammit, you're gonna make some mistake . . . Seriously, you oughta give that mesc crap up."

"Tell it, Hard-Eyes: it's brain rot. Stay real, stay real, neggo! Brain *dam*-aaaage!" He grinned. His features were lean and smudged and hollowed and wiry, and when he grinned, it pulled his face into something that would have given chills to a horror-flick makeup artist.

But when Hard-Eyes didn't respond to the grin, it faded, and Rickenharp shrugged and said, "Yeah, well—I gave up the stuff twice before; last time it was for a long time. But here I figure it doesn't matter if I fuck up my health, because how long am I gonna have my health here? We're likely to get popped before we get outta here, I don't know if anybody clued you in on that classified secret."

"Hey, you know something? Steinfeld says we don't talk unless necessary when we're out, because the fashes got listening posts everywhere, and not just radio, they use boom mikes, too. Okay? If you think you can shut up on that crap you're packing in your sinuses."

"You pissed off at me?"

"No."

"I mean, we never follow that rule—"

"Rickenharp—"

"I know. Shut the fuck up. Right?"

Hard-Eyes smiled. They pushed on, passing through a region of flattened buildings, seeing the cat-sized gray rats ooze through the broken ends and endless jumble, and Hard-Eyes couldn't keep from thinking that Besson's death was a bad omen. That the ax was falling, and he'd just heard the whistle of its coming.

They turned a corner, and there was the blackened wasteland of the Parc des Buttes Chaumont. "There's the park," he whispered. He pressed himself to the corner of a building and peered across the Avenue Simon Bolivar at the park. A layer of black smoke hung over the pitted earth. The street was cluttered with cars, some burnt-out, some overturned, all covered with a layer of ash. Nothing moved. As they looked, the darkness seemed to settle in, running the shadows together.

"Okay," Rickenharp said. They moved across the sidewalk, picking their way through rubble from a looted storefront, brick chips and glass crunching under their feet (too loud, dammit!). They felt vulnerable out in the avenue as they hurried on, crouching between the cars, jogging for the park.

Hard-Eyes thinking, *We're moving like the fucking rats. Becoming like them.*

Then they were in the park, trudging between the craters, through the rubble, smelling the char. Seeing a group of disjointed skeletons, gray-white in a blackened, wheel-less US Army jeep.

"Shit," Rickenharp said, "there's no goddamn landing pod."

But there was. They found it at the far end of the park, beyond a copse of trees burnt like used wooden matches, shriveled and black; beyond hummocks thrown up by shell blasts; beyond hulks of exploded armor and a bone-dry pit once a duck pond. In the one relatively level field remaining in the park, a squat, six-legged landing pod, like some myth-sized mechanical spider, sat steaming in a crater rim kicked up by its own retros. A little ways away, deflated, was an anomalous swatch of woven silvery fabric; the shriveled bag of the parachute-balloon that had slowed the pod's descent. The pod was just a silhouette against the skull-colored ruins at the edge of the park; its slatted ports giving out downslanting beams of red light near the thick, charred heat shield.

They could smell its fuel, its hot metal—and they saw shadowy figures moving near its jointed legs.

The shadow-people moved out from under the pod. Three people, walking toward them on what was left of the asphalt path.

Hard-Eyes moved off the path; Rickenharp moved where Hard-Eyes moved, following his lead. It had been that way as long as they'd known one another.

They squatted behind a hump of crater edge, watching the strangers and looking around. Why hadn't the SA Fashes come to check out the pod? Maybe they were busy. The Parisian NR's ranks had grown; about half of every group of prisoners they liberated joined them. The city looked dead, but a great deal went on in it. Steinfeld gave the Fashes a lot to do.

The three strangers walked nearer. The one in the lead carried a flashlight, its beam of blue-white swiveling over the scarred earth like a blind man's cane. Hard-Eyes checked his rifle, switched it to auto, raised it, at the same time squinting through the dark, trying to see what uniforms the strangers wore.

Rickenharp whispered, "Yo, Hard-Eyes, what if there's Jægernauts out at the edge of the city like Steinfeld said? If they're active, they'll pick up the heat register from the landing pod. They'll come."

"Ease your ass, hodey. You're all paranoid. It's the blue . . . *Shh.*"

The strangers on the path had come parallel, were walking past.

Hard-Eyes stood, raised the assault rifle, and barked, "Freeze! Drop your weapons!"

The strangers froze. Two sidearms fell to the gravel.

Hard-Eyes moved in closer and around in front of them, keeping the rifle leveled at a woman and two men. He saw in the glow of the flashlight the young woman had short-clipped, soft-looking auburn hair; a pixyish face; strangely doll-like lips; and big, intelligent-looking, dark eyes. She was short and slender, wearing a gray Colony staff one-piece jumpsuit. She looked familiar, too.

"We're neutral," said the thick man beside her. He had a thick nose, small eyes, and an ash-colored crew cut. He wore a pilot's jumpsuit, and a heavy pack on his back. "Refugees from FirStep. The Colony."

"Who, uh, are you with?" the second man asked. Thin guy, brown-haired, sad eyes.

Rickenharp for once was struck dumb. He was staring at the girl.

"Train that light at the ground," Hard-Eyes said.

She tilted the light downward. He moved in to retrieve their guns. Two small pistols. One of them for explosive pellets.

"Let's have the pellets, too," Hard-Eyes said.

The skinny one glanced at the others, then handed over a canvas packet the size of a deck of cards. Hard-Eyes stowed the weapons in his belt. The skinny guy took a step toward him—

Rickenharp popped the CAWS butt into the hollow of his shoulder, took a bead on the lanky one's chest, and rasped, "Don't you move that neutral ass again, friend."

The man became a statue. But a talking statue. "Ah, right. I'm Frank Bonham. This is Brett Kurland—our pilot. And this is Claire Rimpler. She's the daughter of Dr. Benjamin Rimpler."

Hard-Eyes clicked. "I thought I'd . . . Yeah, okay." He lowered his rifle. "'S'okay, Harpie," he told Rickenharp.

Rickenharp kept his gun level. "Say what?"

"Said put away your piece. I recognize her." He was embarrassed to say it. "I did a paper on the Colony-administration system for a sociology class. I watched an interview with Rimpler and his daughter. That's her. She was a kid then. They're Colony. Neutral."

"Neutral is bullshit." But Rickenharp lowered the shotgun. He went on, "Neutrality doesn't mean shit if they meet the SA. The fashes don't care if you're Russian or American or Australian or a dog. In Paris, anyway, if you're not fash, you're the fashes' enemy."

"Fashes?" the girl asked.

"Tell you all about it on the way," Hard-Eyes said, looking at the sky. He'd heard something . . .

"On the way where?" Bonham asked.

"Our bunker." Hard-Eyes was scanning the rooftops.

"Hey," Rickenharp said, sounding like a kid at his aunt's picnic basket, "you got any goodies in that pod? Like coffee? Freeze-drieds? Fresh water?"

"It's all here in my pack," Kurland said brightly. Trying to sound helpful.

"Put out the light." Hard-Eyes said suddenly.

Claire switched the flashlight off. They looked to see what he was staring at.

Lights were approaching over the ravaged skyline. "Jumpjet." Rickenharp said. "The trucks'll be right behind." He turned to Hard-Eyes. "Let's make for the metro —"

Hard-Eyes hissed, "Run! The bastard's moving in!"

The wedge shape of the jumpjet was approaching with jerky movements; like a dragonfly, darting ahead, pausing, darting ahead. Now and then it stopped in midair to shine its spots on the ground, moving on slowly now, tacking the light along the path—stopping to hover over the pod.

Hard-Eyes and Rickenharp, Claire and Bonham and Kurland ran through the shadows. They ran down a six-foot-deep erosion ravine toward the rue Botzaris. Across Botzaris, hot with exertion now, they made their way gasping through a maze of abandoned, rotting furniture spilled from the back of a deserted, wheel-less furniture truck, then down the rue de la Villette toward the metro station. Hard-Eyes heard Claire cursing between gasps. This was probably not what she expected to find on Earth.

When they got to the metro entrance, Claire switched on the flashlight, and they ran down the steps. They paused in the rubble at the bottom to catch their breath. It was an eerie, oppressive place in the glow of the flashlight. "We'll have to crawl to get past the rubble here," Rickenharp said. "But after a few feet it opens up, we can walk . . . "

Claire dropped the flashlight, and sobbed out of the darkness. Bonham picked up the light, and touched her face to comfort her. Hard-Eyes felt strange, seeing that. He didn't like Bonham touching her.

Neither did she. She slapped his hand away. Her voice was cracked as she said, "I'm . . . it's stupid to cry now."

"Good a time as any," Hard-Eyes said. "We can sit down for a few minutes, we're under cover now." He tugged her wrist, and she hunkered down to sit on a slab of broken concrete, atop the rubble heap.

The flashlight was pointed downward; he could just make out her shoulders shaking as she sobbed. "I don't know . . . " she muttered. "But God . . . I wanted to come back so bad . . . But it's so strange here, it's like . . . it's heavy and cold and exposed . . . and it's worse than the Colony . . . "

"Not worse," Rickenharp said. "We got a sky here. And there's parts of the planet—big parts—the war hasn't touched. You hang in there, you can go see 'em."

Hard-Eyes said nothing. Let her believe it. But the chances were, none of them would get out of Paris alive. After a while, she said, "Okay. Let's go." Her voice was steady now. Hard-Eyes took the flashlight, and they went on.

•••

Walking down the tunnel. Flashlight beam flaring the red eyes of rats, spotlighting fist-sized mutant roaches.

Rickenharp sighed, world-weary, when Claire fell in beside Hard-Eyes.

"What's at your . . . headquarters?" Claire asked.

Hard-Eyes snorted. "Headquarters consists of a hundred raggedy guys and a few women sitting in the basement of a bombed-out apartment building. Cleaning guns, arguing politics, reading. Playing cards with a deck that's wearing see-through. Guys from every nationality . . . Most of them speak English. It's not cozy there, but we got some chemheaters, ersatz coffee, small store of canned food. Now and then we find somebody's hoard in the ruins . . . We got to turn down this tunnel, we can't go on that way 'cause the tunnel's collapsed . . . "

"Your friend said something about the SA."

"Fashes. Neofascists."

"The Second Alliance."

He looked at her. "That's right."

She laughed bitterly. "We have that particular species of cockroach on the Colony, too. They took over. A coup, really. They're calling it an emergency police action. When we left they'd overrun everything. They're in complete control there now. Martial law. Praeger's little dictatorship. My father . . . "

"I was going to ask you if he was still . . . how he was."

"I think he's dead. He . . . " She shook her head, her eyes closed. After a moment she opened her eyes and said, "Bonham had a pass on to an outgoing ship, but we had to hijack the pod when we got to Station One. They had us scheduled to go down in the States, and I'm pretty sure the SA would have arrested me there. And Bonham thinks they wanted to brainwash him. So we had to steal an unscheduled pod, and we happened to be over Europe, and Bonham heard the NR was in Paris . . . " She shook her head. Her voice was dry, so dry it cracked. "We didn't know it was like this."

"It wasn't this bad till they sealed off the town. No one goes in or out, unless they crawl the whole way maybe. Lot of people are starving. They got wind that Steinfeld is here . . . "

Rickenharp said sharply, "You're talking a lot, man. If they got extracted . . . " He licked his lips, twitching from blue mesc.

"Fuck off," Hard-Eyes growled. "SA already knows everything I've said."

"Steinfeld is your leader?"

Hard-Eyes nodded. "They're flattening the city looking for him. Methodically trying to dig him out . . . There's no fuel left in that pod?"

She shook her head.

He shrugged. The fashes had it now anyway.

She said, "I can't believe what they've done to Paris."

"Most of it was done by the Russians and the Americans. Rickenharp there, and me, we were Americans. We fucking swore it off."

"What kind of people are in the Second Alliance army? Around here I mean."

"They're a mix. A lot of them are Hispanic and Italian, but none of the Latins rise far in the ranks. Around here, mostly British, Afrikaner whites, Lebanese Phalangists."

"So—what are you people going to do?"

He shook his head grimly. "You picked a bad LZ. You put your foot in a bear trap. We're just hanging on, hoping some of our allies get through. They tried to run a chopper in for Steinfeld once—it was shot down. They'll try again. Well, there's something else . . . "

Rickenharp looked at him. "Hard-Eyes, man, she could be captured."

Hard-Eyes nodded. "But I'm going to tell her anyway. Coming down in this shit, the woman's got a right to know. We get captured, you think we could keep anything back, the equipment they got? They'd get it from us, too, Harpie."

"Go on, blow it then. Shit," Rickenharp muttered.

Hard-Eyes hesitated. Maybe Rickenharp was right. But he was tired. And it seemed important that she know. He glanced at Claire—and found it impossible not to trust her. "Our people are moving in from the other capitals, planning to drive through to get to Steinfeld. If it weren't for the rest of us trapped in here, I think Steinfeld would tell 'em to forget it, write him off. Because it probably won't work. The SA lines around the city are tight and well entrenched. And they got the Jægernauts."

"What's that?"

"A—killing machine. *Big.* Hard to describe. Anyway, we've changed our base op three times in three weeks. They're crowding us in. Maybe we'll just take our stand around the arch and let 'em know we're there. Get it over with, take a few of them out with us. Free the rest of the NR to go on. We'd be martyrs. Good political strategy—if anyone ever hears of it."

"You mean—take a stand and let them kill you?"

"Uh-huh."

"Like the three hundred Spartans. Romantic."

Rickenharp cawed at that. His voice trembled a bit, his eyes blinking too much, as he chortled, "Romantic. Yeah. Mostly it sucks."

"Why—why take your stand around the arch? You mean the Arc de Triomphe, right?"

"Uh-huh." He shrugged. "Maybe it's foolish. Corny political symbolism. Trying to rally the French behind us. The arch is one of the few places of old Paris left standing mostly intact. So it's the symbol of the NR. It's on the NR flag. We had a prisoner tell us the fashes are planning to use Jægernauts level the arch. 'To try to crush what can't be crushed,' Steinfeld says. Meaning our spirit, I guess. Sometimes he talks that way. Makes speeches about dying meaningfully and . . . all that. We make fun of the way he talks but—" He broke off, embarrassed.

He never had to explain Jægernauts to her. Except to say, later, "They were built by a Second Alliance armor subsidiary, a German firm run by a guy named Jæger." He didn't have to explain because when they came up out of the metro station at Clichy, they heard the world-filling roar of a Jægernaut. Saw it a few minutes later when they were jogging along the sidewalk, a few blocks from the new safe-house.

Rickenharp and Hard-Eyes looked at one another. And started to run.

But it seemed to Claire that they ran the wrong way:

They ran into the cloud of dust that surrounded the Jægernaut, Hard-Eyes shouting for her and her companions to wait where they were.

• • •

The ground shook and the air itself shook, with the noise of the killing machine, the THUNK-rumble-THUNK-rumble. The crashes, the squeal of snapping metal, crystallized steel grinding stones into dust . . . They saw it up ahead, lit up along its axis; yellow and red lights that made the dust cloud glow . . .

The Jægernaut loomed above them, a five-story double swastika of plasteel, wearing the dust cloud like its cloak of power.

Hard-Eyes squinted up at it, his eyes burning, lungs wracked with the smoke billowing from the rubbled gap where the building had been: the building that had housed their headquarters.

The Jægernaut finished it work. It hadn't spotted Hard-Eyes and his companions. Plowing through massive buildings as a tank would plow through a fiberboard house, it crashed away from them; bricks rained to either side of it like spray at the prow of a boat. It used tight microwave beams to soften up the stone and iron as it shouldered through . . .

The whole machine was a giant wheel without a rim. Like two rimless wagon wheels with eight-jointed spokes on each side. Hydroplas "muscles" kept it churning, digging, gouging, plowing through, looking to some like a Rototiller—but fifty yards high. At the axis, between the two sets of gouging spokes, was the nuclear power source, and you'd be sorry if you blew that part up. Each spoke was four yards thick. The power source remained stationary; the axis turned around it. The Jægernaut was terrifying to behold, even before it began to move. It was the ideal instrument of state terrorism. A half-dozen could level a city in under a month. And they were a bitch to bring down.

Rickenharp and Hard-Eyes forced themselves to clamber over the remaining crust of wall, coughing through the smoke and dust. They felt the thrum of the departing Jægernaut, heard its monumental clanking, the shudderings so heavy in the air it was like moving through another medium, a kind of shock-wave liquid . . .

Then they climbed down into the smoking socket where the New Resistance HQ had been.

A small fire burned in someone's leather jacket, where a chemheater had been smashed. The fire-flutter was the only motion—the smoke rising in wisps like the departing wraiths of the dead. Here and there were hanks of skin, hair, shredded fatigues. A bloodied yet bloodless hand thrust like a claw from one of the mounds of rubble. Bloodied black bandannas now mingled indistinguishably with the flesh and brains of the wearer.

The Jægernaut had gone over the place more than once.

Hard-Eyes felt a jolt as he found what was left of Jenkins. His heart turned to slag inside him.

"They're all dead," Rickenharp said shakily, sounding like a lost child.

Hard-Eyes shook his head. "No—they . . . maybe some got away . . . " It was a dream. He tried to imagine how it had been real. "The sentries . . . the fashes send commandos to kill the sentries. Then they bring the Jægernaut in on quiet trucks. Auto-assemble the parts maybe a block away. Activate it, it unfolds itself—it's pretty compact when it's folded up . . . And it comes down on them before they know what's happening . . . "

Rickenharp said, in a voice kept carefully flat, "It makes a lot of noise coming. Even if it was close—must have been some of them got out of the building. *Must* have been."

They looked around a little more. Found nothing alive; found pieces of their friends.

The sound of the Jægernaut was receding now. It was like an iron foundry walking away.

Another sound came. A humming, grinding of gears. Jeeps. Trucks.

"Fashes coming to check it out, man, Harpie," Hard-Eyes said.

Rickenharp just stared around him, mouth slack, eyes smoldering with growing rage—a hair-trigger rage. Very carefully, Hard-Eyes laid a hand on Rickenharp's arm. Rickenharp whirled and pointed the shotgun at him, squeezed the trigger, snarling.

The safety was on. Hard-Eyes swallowed to force his heart down out of his throat and said, "It's me, Harpie. Jesus fuck."

"Sorry. I . . . "

"You *gotta* get off that blue mesc shit."

"It's not that . . . " Rickenharp's eyes overflowed. Tears streaked the grime on his cheeks. "They're . . . "

"I know. I'm telling you man, *had* to be some of 'em got away. Hey, the fashes are coming. We can kill some of 'em if we—if we get to high ground. Okay?" Rickenharp let Hard-Eyes take his arm and steer him out of the ruins. The noise of trucks got louder. Hard-Eyes saw a light stab through the smoke, seeking. "Shit, where's—"

Then Claire and Bonham and Kurland ran up, coughing in the smoke. "There's soldiers," Bonham said, gasping. "Are they—"

"They're SA," Hard-Eyes said. "Come on." He led them down the street, away from the sound of the approaching men. Out of the thick of the cloud, down one of the twisting, twenty-foot-wide side streets.

They paused here to catch their breath. "Shit, I'm exhausted." Claire said.

Hard-Eyes looked down the alley, saw a man silhouetted at the other end. Carrying a gun. Hard-Eyes raised his assault rifle. But the man waved and spread his arms, gun out to the side, offering his chest as a target. Surrendering. Walking nearer.

Then Rickenharp said, "All *ri-ight!*"

It was Yukio, in khakis and black bandanna. Over his shoulder was a rifle fitted with an M83.

He walked up, his face blank, lowering his arms. Hard-Eyes put a hand on Yukio's shoulder. The Japanese was rigid with grief. "There are two others who made it," he said hoarsely. "But the rest in the HQ are dead. This is the second family I've lost to them."

"Who made it?" Rickenharp asked.

"Willow and Carmen. They went out to find . . . privacy. We were having a party. This is why—we drank too much. Or we would have heard it coming. Steinfeld gave us the last case of wine." He smiled weakly. "You missed the party."

"Party?" Rickenharp's tone was pure incredulity. "What the fuck?"

"For Steinfeld. Ten minutes after you go out, a call comes through: the Israelis captured an SA jumpjet. Room for two passengers. They sent it through for Steinfeld and Dr. Levassier. Steinfeld goes to direct the assault to get us out. It will fail." He shrugged. "Steinfeld is out, though. He is safe, for now. He can go on. It hurt him to go. I saw it. But he knows where his work is. He went."

"Steinfeld is out!" Rickenharp said. His mood did another wild swing. He danced around, pretending to play the shotgun like it was a guitar. "*Fuck* these fascist pricks!"

"Keep your voice down, Harpie," Hard-Eyes said.

Yukio was staring at the newcomers. "From the pod? Colony people?"

Hard-Eyes nodded. "Let's move out."

"Where to?" Claire asked, slumping against a wall.

"Shelter, for now," Hard-Eyes said. "Till we can regroup with another cell."

"Gimme shelter, the man says." Rickenharp chuckled. "Gimme, gimme, gimme. I know a place. Wait'll you see, Hard-Eyes. Come on. One block."

• • •

Hard-Eyes sat with his back to a wall, his assault rifle across his knees. It was an old gun, from late in the last century, repaired twice in the NR machine shop. They were camped out in the wreckage of what had once been a music-supplies store. Yukio, Hard-Eyes, and the refugees from the Colony, hunkered behind the sales counter. There was a smashed-open cred-scanner lying on its side like the skull of a beheaded robot, and there were sheets of music printout scattered yellowing on the floor and nothing else except the faint glow of a Coleman and the flicker of the chemheater in the back of the hall.

Turned out Rickenharp had stashed the lamp and the heater here. This is where he'd come, those times he'd disappeared.

Down the hall, the Rimpler girl was lying on a bed of sheet music, near the chem-heater, snoring softly. Bonham and Kurland sat near her, whispering. Across from Hard-Eyes, Yukio sat with his head on his arms, arms propped on knees, knees tucked against his chest, muttering Japanese in his sleep.

Hard-Eyes whispered, "Rickenharp?"

Rickenharp's voice from the other side of the counter. "I'm still on, man. Still wired. Get some sleep. I'm watching."

Hard-Eyes put his head on his arms, imitating Yukio, and drifted into a fitful sleep, waking now and then at little sounds. He heard Rickenharp sniffing something up—probably synmorph this time, to take the edge off the blue, and to keep from thinking too much about the friends who'd been butchered, pulped, during their only celebration in six months. Drifting . . .

Next thing he heard was Bonham and Kurland arguing; hearing Kurland's accent more clearly now. "But we can't know that these 'fash' people are, ah, you know, the way they are advertised to be by their—" Kurland lowered his voice. "—by their *opposition*. I mean, the opposition always describes the other side as bad news and bloody tyrants . . . Now, if we explain to these Second Alliance people we're not subversives, we're neutral, surely they—well, I think we should go to them, and—"

Bonham said, "Oh, don't be stupid. They'd ID me; they know I skipped out on them. They'd ship me to one of their rehab camps. You they'd read as a possible accomplice—you took a bribe from us, so you'd worked in someone else's employ against them. Claire worked against them, so they want her in their clutches. Forget it."

"But, I say—"

"I said *forget it.*" A lot of authority in the weedy little guy's tone when he wanted it.

So Bonham had collaborated. Hard-Eyes filed it away, and went back to sleep.

• • •

"Dammit, Hard-Eyes, wake up!"

Hard-Eyes sat up straight, wincing. His back ached from the cold concrete wall. "Whuh you want, man. I go on watch?"

"No, Yukio's standing sentry . . . C'mere."

Hard-Eyes stood, stretched, and, carrying the assault rifle, followed Rickenharp down the hall, past the Colony refugees sleeping around the metal shell of the chem-heater. Hard-Eyes glanced at Claire. Her face in sleep like something from a Pre-Raphaelite painting. He felt a pleasant tug, looking at her. He smiled, seeing she was sleeping with the machine pistol Yukio had given her; it was clutched to her chest the way a little girl sleeps with a doll . . . They walked past, down to the left. Down the stairs into a musty basement storeroom. Rickenharp switched on a flashlight.

"I was poking around here once . . . I saw these boards looked recently nailed on, like somebody was hiding something back here . . . " He laid the flashlight on the top of a stack of cardboard boxes, so the beam faced the wall, spotlighting a door. The door was boarded over. He pulled at the planks and they came away easily. He'd pried them away before and then put them back; loosely reinserted the nails.

He tossed the boards aside with a crash that made Hard-Eyes flinch, shined the flashlight through the low doorway.

"Check it out!'

Hard-Eyes bent and went in, Rickenharp following with the flashlight.

It was a small room, twenty by five feet, just a long closet, filled with musical instruments. Mostly guitars, amplifiers, speakers, microphones, and PA equipment.

Hard-Eyes shuddered with intuition and a sense of displacement, staring at the hoard. To Rickenharp, it was the Treasure of Tutankhamen.

"Eyes, my man, this is Kismet." His voice thick with conviction. "Destiny. I was intended to find this stuff. I feel like Ali Baba . . . I guess these were like demonstration models the music store hid down here when the Russians started shelling. There's even a tuba over there. Can you believe it? I tried twenty music stores, man, before I couldn't find anything that wasn't busted. But I knew it was there waiting for me in one of 'em . . . "

"Too bad you can't use it. Got no power. And the fashes would hear."

A grin lit up his corner of the room like an electrical arc. "Oh, yeah? Look-a-that!" He stuck out his hand. A chromium cube glittered in his palm. "You know what that is? That's a Firestormer, made by Marshall Amps. Intense battery power for the biggest amp concentrated in that little thing. Costly sucker. Good for five days of top-volume playing. And scan this: Earphones. Two sets. They plug into the amp. Built-in volume controls. I can play and the fashes won't hear a note. You wanna hear something? I already got the guitar tuned . . . "

Feeling like he was denying food to a starving man, Hard-Eyes said, "Uh, not just now, man. I'm pretty tired, got a headache."

"Headache? Great. Just put the headphones on. I'll clear your headache up. There won't be room for an ache in your head! I got me an old Telecaster here, 'bout fifty years old, works fine . . . I crank this sucker like so, jack in here, insert the battery here . . . " The amplifier's lights winked hot red in the semidarkness. Rickenharp had left the flashlight on the floor. He bent near it to snort a long line of blue mesc from the back of his hand. A bluish light bled up from the flashlight to accent his face eerily, as if he were glowing from the drug.

Hard-Eyes sighed, put on the earphones, and turned the volume low, prepared to listen to a twenty-minute self-indulgence, electric ego-swell tedium, maybe some interminable variation of one of Rickenharp's favorite twentieth-century tunes.

Rickenharp strapped on the guitar, put on the earphones so he could hear himself . . .

A hummm in the earphones . . .

The first chord rang like a church bell. Long and slow and full. The second quivered bluesy like a woman wailing at a New Orleans funeral in the churchyard where the bell rang. Rickenharp was playing a funeral dirge for their friends, dead under the crystallized-steel jackboot . . . And then he played a theme that resonated anger, vengeance, renewal of purpose; picking up the tempo, doublepicking for a rhythm section, and he was off and running, rocking for real. The notes pealed and tripped, dashed into speed-rapper's digressions, dashed on, paused like a comedian timing an irony, and then seemed to carry on a monologue that had a rhythm to it like Rickenharp's style of talking. They segued back into the thematic riff and—okay, Hard-Eyes was impressed.

Finally, Rickenbarp was finished. Hard-Eyes took off the earphones. His ears rang.

"Rickenharp, man, I had no idea."

"This is my instrument. Could have been custom-made for me."

"You want a hit of this blue, Eyes?"

"No, hodey, come on, you know me better than that. But play another tune. I'm not quite deaf yet." He put the earphones back on.

• • •

Rickenharp and Hard-Eyes were smiling when they came out of the back room.

There was no one in the hall. Hard-Eyes frowned and flicked the HK's safety off. He led the way up the hall, thinking, *All that noise in the earphones, anything could've happened out here, we'd never know it.*

They went up to the counter. Heard a rustle, an urgent whisper, couldn't make out what was said. Hunched over, they moved around the counter, looked out into the main room . . . Room strewn with fiberplas crates, the guts of a smashed piano, broken glass. A little light bleeding across the room from the busted-in windows on the left. Movement to the right, behind the crates. Rickenharp turned that way, stepping out from the cover of the counter.

Then Hard-Eyes saw the men in the doorway to the left. "Harp—" he began.

But Rickenharp stepped into the open, and the darkness was splintered by muzzle flashes; the walls echoed with thudding automatic weapons. Rickenharp went spinning, falling. Two stray rounds slammed into the broken piano, making plaintive, discordant notes . . .

Hard-Eyes bellowed and jumped out to fire at the door with the HK; it leaped in his hand, funneling his anger; the room lit up with strobe flashes from the muzzle. One of the men yelled hoarsely and fell. Hard-Eyes instinctively moved back to the cover of the counter.

In the strobe from the gun he'd seen Bonham and Kurland lying facedown on the floor, hands behind their heads. The men had come in, seen them in the main room maybe. They'd surrendered . . . Where was Claire?

"Rickenharp? Yo, Harpie!" Hard-Eyes hissed.

"I'm . . . okay, man."

"Don't move."

Hard-Eyes peered over the top of the counter at the door. Saw no one.

He bent and moved on into the middle of the room, groped till he found Rickenharp. "Where you hit?"

"Leg. Hip."

"I gotcha." He slung the assault rifle over his back, bent to help Rickenharp.

But before he could pick Rickenharp up, light stabbed from the doorway. A man barked, "Hold it, drop your weapons!"

Hard-Eyes looked, blinking in the light. Above the glare he made out three men coming in, weapons raised. SA Regulars. No heavy body armor on them. But they had the drop on him.

"Harpie . . ."

"I say fuck 'em," Rickenharp said.

Rickenharp had his CAWS across his chest. Grimacing with pain, he sat up, fired across his body at the men in the door. The autoshotgun roared like a small cannon, booming and leaping in his hands, and the man in the lead was torn apart by four 12-gauge rounds at a range of thirty feet, his left arm separating from his shoulder; his body, seeming to liquefy, splashed back on the others. Then the booming stopped and Rickenharp hissed, "Fucker's jammed!'

Hard-Eyes was trying to bring his HK into firing position, but it was too late, the other SAs were firing; Rickenharp grunted and fell back; 9-mm rounds were whistling so close by Hard-Eyes' head he could feel the friction, and any split-second now one would—

Claire popped up from behind a crate like a jack-in-the-box, the machine pistol blazing, rattling in her hands. She sprayed wildly at the door—both men went down.

The flashlight was lying in the doorway, still shining, making a reflecting pool of puddling blood.

Hard-Eyes was shaking, his heart hammering in his chest.

He told himself, *Get calm, get calm.* Rickenharp was alive, his head bleeding, trying to get up. "Lay still, ya damn fool," Hard-Eyes told him. He walked on wobbly legs to the door, picked up the flashlight, wiped warm slick wetness from it on a SA uniform. He straightened—and the flashlight beam fell over Yukio. He seemed to be embracing someone.

He was lying facedown atop an SA regular, his right hand still on a knife stuck in the dead man's throat. His side was bloody. His left arm was shot through, a welter of blood and protruding bone splinters. But he was breathing.

Claire walked up from behind. She said, "Kurland went to look out the window. Yukio told him to go back inside. They argued, and then the SA men came. Yukio shot one of them. Another one shot Yukio, and Yukio dropped his gun and fell down. But when the guy came to check him, Yukio jumped up, stabbed him, and they fell down together . . . And then

some more SA came and Kurland surrendered . . . And then you came . . . "
She shrugged.

Her voice was dead; her face was expressionless.

Hard-Eyes looked at Rickenharp. Kurland was there, spraying a
dressing on Rickenharp's wounds from the first-aid kit in his backpack.
Claire took another medikit from a belt pouch and bent down to see what
she could do for Yukio.

Hard-Eyes went to the door, looked down the streets. "They were
probably just a patrol. Maybe we're okay here."

He went back inside. Kurland and Bonham were carrying Rickenharp
into the back room. They laid him down by the chemheater. He was
unconscious, bleeding from the right temple.

"Lad took a ricochet, maybe just a fragment, from the size of the entry
wound," Kurland said. "That second salvo, after he shot at them . . . maybe
not too bad, though . . . Might be just badly stunned."

Hard-Eyes and Claire—she was stone-faced, efficient—dragged the dead
SA patrol to the back of the main room, hid them behind the flattened piano.

They laid Yukio beside Rickenharp. Yukio stared at the ceiling, ground
teeth against the pain but making no other sound. Hard-Eyes injected
him with synthmorph from the medical kit, and he gave out a long, soft
sigh, and went almost immediately to sleep. Hard-Eyes used a field cast-kit
to set Yukio's broken arm in a temporary plaster brace. The wound in
Yukio's side was superficial.

• • •

It was about four a.m. when Rickenharp woke and asked Hard-Eyes to
shine the flashlight in his eyes. His voice was raspy. Hard-Eyes shrugged,
got up, and shone the light in Rickenharp's eyes.

"Do it, Hard-Eyes. Shine the light on me . . . "

"I'm doin' it already, man."

And then they knew he'd gone blind.

"Bone splinter probably," Rickenharp said, trying to sound clinical.
"Severed the ol' optical nerve. Or maybe a blood clot."

"Shit, man, we'll get you out; they'll operate . . . "

Rickenharp said, "Blind." Tasting the word. More amazed than horrified
at first. "Blind. What a scene, man. An Anti-scene, really. *Blind.*"

The bullets Rickenharp had taken in the leg had made flesh wounds,
and missed the arteries. But he was weakened and lay on his back near
the chem-heater, head pillowed on Hard-Eyes' rolled-up jacket, playing
the Telecaster, listening to himself on the earphones. A little behind him
stood the small amp, its red light glowing like a supernatural eye, as if
Rickenharp's demon crouched protectively near.

After a while, he stopped playing but, smiling faintly, seemed still to be listening to something. "Hey, Hard-Eyes," he rasped.

Hard-Eyes went to crouch near him. "Yeah?"

"Take the earphones off me. Put 'em on. Listen." Hard-Eyes took the earphones and listened. He heard static and, very faintly, a voice.

Hard-Eyes burst out, "It's Willow! Willow's voice! . . . This thing picks up one of our frequencies!"

"Yeah, they do that sometimes. You hear what he said?"

"Yeah, he's repeating it over and over. All units meet at rendezvous twenty, oh-nine-hundred. Damn—What was R-twenty?"

"You're supposed to have it memorized, expert! It's the southbound platform at Metro Franklin Roosevelt. That's on the Champs-Élysées—not far from the arch. Oh-nine-hundred. Tomorrow morning. You know, things happen real symmetrically, Hard-Eyes. We get a little good luck, a little bad luck, a little good luck. Latest good luck, we snag this regroup message. Latest bad luck, we're on the wrong side of the fucking arch. Nazi shit-heads're camped all around it. We could get *to* the arch but not past it. On one side is the yellow-dust zone, on the other side they got their headquarters. The streets are blocked off unless we go right under the arch . . . So how do we get through to regroup at Frankie Roosevelt?"

"We'll figure something."

"Hey—that was a rhetorical question. 'Cause I got something figured, man. I want you to promise you won't fuck me up on this. Give this to me. My last gig, Hard-Eyes. Listen . . . "

• • •

"This is bloody stupid." Kurland muttered.

It was an hour before dawn. They were trudging through the gouged streets, through blue-black shadows and silver-limned patches of fog, through rubble and char and the cold smell of ashes. And they were carrying sound equipment on their backs.

Hard-Eyes could hardly believe it himself. But when Kurland kept complaining, Hard-Eyes said, "There's no talking him out of it. We're gonna do it. So shut the fuck up."

Rickenharp, leaning on Claire, grinned at that. "Good to hear you say that to somebody else, Hard-Eyes."

"You shut the fuck up, too."

Claire was carrying a guitar and medical kit. Kurland had the PA horns. Yukio carried weapons—and a rhythm box. Bonham had cords and mikes, miscellaneous hardware, and Rickenharp's shotguns. Hard-Eyes had two portable amps strapped to his back and the assault rifle in his arms, the M-83 over one shoulder. They carried their gear through the twisted stub of a skyscraper, between fantastic shapes of melted glass and plastic; through the ribbed remains of a cathedral; through a field of ravaged mannequins where a department store had stood. All the time sweat was running icy under their clothes.

"Fucking absurd, I'm telling you," Kurland growled, as he shifted the weight of an amplifier.

Claire said, "The war is absurd. Racism is absurd. This—" She gestured at the wreckage of Paris. She didn't have to finish the sentence.

"I just hope I don't get rained out," Rickenharp said.

They hid from passing patrols twice, and then crept on, concealed by mist and the night and the megalomaniac overconfidence of the fashes.

• • •

And then they'd reached the Étoile. The Star. The arch stood at the center of the twelve-pointed star where the avenues met. It had been decreed by Napoleon in 1808, begun by Chalgrin the same year, not completed until 1836. Made of massive stone blocks, the Arc de Triomphe was fifty yards high, forty-four across the front, twenty-two on the side. Its facades were intricately carved, its arch sheltering the flame of the unknown soldier. Long since gone out, overwhelmed by the wind of a thousand thousand unknown soldiers passing on . . .

On the face of the arc facing the Champs-Élysées was the high-relief group, a carving representing the departure of the war volunteers. The central figure was the Marseillaise with her wings spread, her out-thrust sword pointing the way, her mouth opened in an eternal shout, a shout carved in stone.

The Arc de Triomphe was bullet-scarred but still standing.

Nearly dawn. The night sky relented a little, admitting some blue. Most of the fashes were encamped on the far side of the arch. To rendezvous with the NR, Hard-Eyes had to get past them.

There were a few sentries on this side of the arch—but between Hard-Eyes and the sentries was the cover of overturned trucks, crashed hovercars, gouted tanks, rubble, and long shadows.

Aching under their burdens, they crossed the Étoile; crouching, darting through the twisted wreckage, Kurland and Bonham with their thoughts written on their faces: *This is irrational, this is insane.*

Just inside the door that led to the stairwell, in one of the arch's massive legs, two neofashes squatted by a sickly-yellow chem-fire.

Hunched down behind a truck, Hard-Eyes screwed the sound suppressor onto his assault rifle. He crept around the circular curbing surrounding the arch till he was out of the line of sight of the sentries, and then dashed back to the arch's support, pressed himself flat against the stone. He listened, heard soft, unconcerned voices from inside. A trapezoid of sulfur-colored light projected onto the concrete from the door to his left.

Don't let 'em get off a shot, he told himself. Quiet, got to be fast and quiet. He edged up to the door.

"The bloody resistance is a bloody fucking joke," said someone inside. "Waste of time to be sitting out here for a bunch of ticked off frogs and wogs."

Hard-Eyes smiled. He pivoted, turning to step through the door, tracking to center his sights as the men looked up, gaping. The rifle's suppressor hushed the report of the bullets, as one man fell over backward, his chest opening up with faucets of blood, while the second was training a submachine gun at the intruder, at Hard-Eyes, who was thinking, *Right through the brain so he doesn't get a shot when he goes down*. Letting his trained fingers do the work, the HK spitting flame, hissing, licking away the top of the guy's head; the man spun, blood spiraling from his shattered skull, the gun clattering to the floor. That was the only sound the gun made.

And they had taken the Arc de Triomphe.

• • •

They carried the equipment up piece by piece. Up the stairwell inside the arch; up to the observation deck at the crown. Claire and Hard-Eyes helped Rickenharp climb the stairs. They set up the equipment, jacked in Rickenharp's guitar. Rickenharp sat on the amp, to everyone's amazement meticulously tuning up the guitar in the earphones, the chill, damp wind whipping his hair. Charcoal-edged, silver-hearted clouds flowed behind him. Rickenharp smiled crookedly, as he tinkered with the guitar settings, looking weaker, paler than ever. Yukio sat beside him setting up the grenade launcher, the automatics.

Hard-Eyes made them up two shots apiece with the syringes from the medikit; each shot contained a solution of one part blue mesc, one part synthmorph, one part energizing vitamins. Just to see them through. He made it in a tin mess cup belonging to the dead sentries.

Kurland stared but said nothing.

"It's funny, the arch being the symbol of the NR," Rickenharp whispered. "I mean—seems like I remember it was all about Napoleon. A fucking tyrant."

"Became a symbol of the French Republic," Yukio said, finishing setting up the weapons. He sat back, resting, his voice distant, eyes closed. "Democracy. Anyway, we appropriated it. Gave it our own meaning. Fascism is anti-traditional. What's good in tradition is what makes people want to fight Nazis . . . Arc celebrates culture, tradition, for us. Not tyranny . . . for us it's not about tyranny . . . "

"Rickenharp," Hard-Eyes said, as he pulled back on the syringe plungers to suck the solution through the needle, "an operation might restore your eyesight. Or a transplant or a prosthetic."

"Come off it, man. That whole side of my body's going numb. I still got strength in my arms, my fingers. But it won't last long. Something's busted in my brain, Hard-Eyes. Always was—" He grinned. "But now it's fucked up for good. You guys won't get through unless Yukio and me create a diversion. And Yukio and me—we're screwed anyway. He ain't gonna leave his arch. Made up his mind when our compadres got flattened. These Japanese motherfuckers are crazy!" Said admiringly. "And Yukio feels bad, man, that he didn't get it, too. With all of his friends. And . . . " He gave a crooked smile.

"It's the band, though, really. Isn't that it, Rickenharp? You got it in your mind your career is dead. And that's your whole identity. So you think you got to die, too. Rickenharp, buddy, it's *dumb* to—"

"No, Hard-Eyes," Rickenharp broke in. "Don't tell me my big moment is dumb. No, you don't see. This *feels* right. It's like I been rehearsing my whole life for this gig . . . "

"Harpie . . . "

"No, I mean it. I ain't hopin' for nobody to talk me out of it. Now scan this, man . . . " His voice got some of its old excitement back in it. "The Jægernauts, they got cameras on 'em, at the stationary part of the axle, right? You can see 'em pop out of the slot when they want a good TV-shot to show the troops for the Triumph-of-the-Will scam. You know? They'll show us getting plowed under and they'll send it back—with sound, man! Back to that neofash hometown in California and show it to the kids and the young ones, and the kids'll see me, they hear the tunes, they might react differently than what the fashes expect, right?"

"Maybe so, Harpie." Not believing it for a moment. But let the guy have his fantasy.

"Anyway, I always wanted a live gig on TV. They made us lip-synch."

He grinned and there was blood on his teeth.

So Hard-Eyes gave the primed syringes to Yukio, embraced Yukio and Rickenharp, and went to the stairs without a word. When he looked back, just before going through the door, he saw Yukio taking a red ribbon from his jacket, winding it around his head, kneeling in preparation for a Shinto ceremony.

• • •

Hard-Eyes and the refugees hid themselves in a tangle of cold, twisted black armor and waited for daylight. They were in the back of what had been an old half-track. Once, Bonham tried to hold Claire's hand. She jerked it away from him and shut her eyes. His expression went hard, but he said nothing. After a while he climbed off the back of the half-track and went around the front, where, in the cover of an overturned truck, he pissed against the half-track's engine.

Hard-Eyes could see only a bluish section of Claire's face, enough to see she was awake. "Suppose we get through," he said. "What will you do? If you could go anywhere, do anything? Dumb question, I guess: You'll try to get back to the States."

"No. Where's this thing headquartered? The Second Alliance I mean."

"The military headquarters? Main one is supposed to be in Sicily."

"So why don't you hit the island?"

"Not enough manpower—or seapower. NATO's guarding it. NATO thinks—or claims it thinks—that the SA is just a privately owned peacekeeping force like it pretends to be. Sort of high-quality mercenaries subcontracted by the UN and NATO. So we got to get past NATO too. And those guys aren't our enemies. But Steinfeld was working on a way to get in, before they found him."

"He'll try it, sooner or later."

"Uh-huh."

"I want Praeger," she said, her voice chillingly flat. "If we can get to the Second Alliance's command, we can bring Praeger to justice."

"Who's Praeger?"

"We get out of Paris alive I'll tell you about it." Daylight wasn't long in coming. Hot-metal blue edged the ragged, truncated skyline when they heard the first amplified note pealing over the square, that bizarre church bell again, declaring a new and electric morning.

They heard, from ten yards away, the captain of a passing neofash patrol burst out, "What the bloody 'ell is *that*?"

Claire almost wept with silent laughter. She whispered, "What kind of music's he going to play?"

"It's mostly retro-rock, twentieth-century stuff . . . but it's more than that," Hard-Eyes murmured.

Rickenharp began with a bash-out of the Blue Öyster Cult's "Cities on Flame with Rock 'n' Roll," slammed on to The Clash's "London's Burning," and then segued into Lou Reed's solo version of "White Light/White Heat." Rickenharp had jacked a mike into one of the amps and he bellowed the lyrics in a voice that made Hard-Eyes sure Yukio had given them the shots. Rickenharp was coming on to his last high. The digital rhythm box started, thudding out a martial backbeat that shivered like controlled thunder from the faces of the wrecked buildings around the Étoile.

It was still dark enough for Hard-Eyes to lead the others through the shadows around the perimeter of the Étoile, in the ruins, and over the dead fountains, toward the Champs Élysées.

Now Rickenharp was segueing from a Sisters of Mercy cut to a Nine Inch Nails tune: "Head Like a Hole." He yowled, *"Head like a hole, black as your soul, I'd rather die than give you control!"* his voice echoing thinly up and down the Champs-Élysées. And then an updated "Street-Fighting Man." Each chord peacock-tailed out into beautiful distortion, echoing around the wide, breezy, broken space of the Étoile.

Hard-Eyes chuckled and hefted his assault rifle, muttered, "Christ. He's pulling it off!" They were crouched behind an overturned troop transport truck. He peered out between a bent-out fender and the grille at the entrance to the street. Dozens of SA entrenched there, staring up at the arch, mouths agape. Maybe Rickenharp had been wrong about how they'd react . . . If they didn't take the bait, Hard-Eyes and Claire were fucked . . .

Rickenharp, banged through some mid-1980s tunes. The Clash, Dead Kennedys, The Fall, New Order, U2, The Call, and Killing Joke's "Requiem." Into the nineties with Panther Modern's "Sometimes It's Better to Die."

He paused, made a chord oscillate drunkenly, and yelled, *"Hey! You pathetic wimps frightened of a guitar?"* Bellowing it so loud his voice fuzzed in the amp. But they understood him. Louder now: "YOU! YOU LIMP-DICK INTESTINAL WORMS! YEAH, YOU, THE BRAIN-WASHED, PECKERWOOD BIGOTS! RIGHT: THE SHIT-EATING DUMB-FUCK RACIST PRODUCTS OF BACKWOODS COUSIN FUCKING! LET ME BE MORE EXPLICIT! I'M TALKING TO THE FAGGOT SA NAZIS SUCKING THEIR THUMBS OVER BY THE METRO SIGN! *YOU PUSSIES SCARED OF A GUITAR?* COME ON! COME ON, YOU COWARDS!"

There was another minute of debate amongst the SA. Then the fash commander gave the order—and the SA charged the arch, spraying its crown with automatics. Dust and chips of stone flew from the top, where Rickenharp howled on at them. "COME ON, YOU PHILISTINE PECKERWOODS, *LET'S GO!"*

Yukio waited till the neofascists were halfway there before opening up on them. He'd set up two grenade launchers, already had them cranked for range.

Three explosions burst before the arch like giant flame-hands flashing open. Fragments of concrete and metal rained. Dust bloomed . . . and cleared.

As Rickenharp played the Stooges' "Search and Destroy" . . .

Twelve of the Second Alliance assault force were sprawled there, broken and unmoving.

Six more kept coming—Yukio stopped them with short, precise machine-gun bursts. Another wave of them came on, took cover in shell-holes, began returning fire. Yukio kept moving, kept low, kept firing. He had a better angle for shooting than they did. And all the time Rickenharp's guitar wailed and roared . . .

Yukio fired an M-83 round across the Étoile; it blew up in the commander's tent, setting it on fire. Another M-83, and another. The SA ran helter-skelter for cover, their lines in confusion.

Beyond the burning tent, forty yards beyond, Hard-Eyes could see the metro entrance he wanted.

"Come on!" he shouted. *"This is it! Run like a bastard!"*

He took Claire's elbow and—Bonham and Kurland close behind—they sprinted across the open side-street. They were almost there before the regrouping sentries spotted them.

"Down!" Hard-Eyes shouted. He and Claire flung themselves down behind an overturned lamppost.

Bonham threw himself flat just behind.

Kurland panicked, gaping around, shouting, "We gotta go back, we gotta . . . "

A burst of machine-gun fire caught him in the mouth, blew his upper teeth up, through his sinuses, through his brains and out the back of his head; and he fell like a puppet with its strings cut.

The machine gun was set up in what had been a magazine kiosk, its muzzle flaming over scraps of posters advertising *Le Opéra*. It was in a spot that would be hard for Yukio to hit.

"HEY, YOU IN THE MAGAZINE STAND!" Rickenharp's voice boomed. He paused to giggle into the mike. An amplified giggle heard through the popping of gunfire. "HEY, YOU WITH THE MACHINE GUN! COME ON! GIVE ME YOUR BEST SHOT, YA NAZI COCKSUCKER!"

Hard-Eyes smiled.

The machine gun fell silent for a moment. The muzzle swiveled to the arch. Some officer shouted, "Ignore that arsehole, you bloody fool! Cover the—"

But the officer was too late—Hard-Eyes gestured for Claire to stay where she was, then he jumped up, zigzagging, running, thinking, *Maybe this time I'll find out what it feels like to get it in the head. Maybe it's the biggest goddamn rush you can imagine.*

As 72-mm rounds whined up, ricocheting from the street near his ankles . . .

But he reached the kiosk, circled it, found a hole in the side, shoved the muzzle of his assault rifle through, and squeezed out his clip, raking back and forth over the kiosk. The muzzle of the machine gun tilted back, leaking a little smoke. He signaled Claire. She and Bonham jumped up, sprinted to him. Hard-Eyes slapped another clip into the assault rifle. Yukio was firing to give them cover as they ran for the metro entrance. Blurred glimpses of SA soldiers . . . the whine of rounds sizzling the air around them . . .

And then they were down the steps, under cover.

"Oh, shit," Bonham said, gasping. "The entrance's blocked."

"Looks like it but it's not, really," Hard-Eyes said. "We set 'em up that way . . . Dig there. The stone with the paint splash on it. Pull it out, start digging. It's just camouflage." Bonham and Claire began to dig.

Hard-Eyes turned and went back up the stairs, to look out over the metal-strewn battlefield to the arch, trying to see Rickenharp. There—a tiny figure on the crown of the arc, almost unseeable. But hearable. His voice and his guitar, kicked through those mean little Marshalls, were audible even over the gunfire. Some original tune now, Hard-Eyes suspected. He couldn't make out the lyrics, but he knew what it was about. He'd heard a thousand permutations of it, over the years. It was an anthem, and it was about being young. A song called *Youth*.

And then the Jægernauts rolled in from the east and west, two of them converging on the arch. They came on like the neofascist war machine itself; they came on like mortality. Killing machines as big as five-story buildings, they cast shadows that drank up whole blocks . . . From here they looked like five-story spoked wheels, the spokes digging into whatever was in the way. There were clouds of dust, showers of bricks. The neofashes scattered, cheering, pulling back. Yukio kept sniping at the fascists, and more than one fell.

The echoes of his gunshots rolled like bass lines for Rickenharp's electric wailing. Rickenharp had cranked the amps all the way up; he could still be heard over the squealing of the oncoming Jægernauts. The two sounds went well together.

It was monumental, that destruction. The two Jægernauts converged on the Arc d'Triomphe from opposite sides, began to grind gigantically away at it, spinning in place at first like the wheels of a mud-stuck Hummer, then biting into the corners, crunching down as the microwave beams took the fight out of the stone. Yukio's bullets whined off the blue-metal scythes, the Jægernaut's spokes. Metal bit down on stone with a screaming that was another kind of heavy-metal jamming against Rickenharp's final chords: fat blue sparks shot out from the machine's grinding spikes; cracks spread like negative lightning through the huge monument; the hundred-pound head of a Valkyrie snapped from her stone neck and tumbled, bounced from a shelf of stone to fall and shatter on the grave of the unknown soldier; the arch's great crown bent, buckled inward . . . and all the time, *the whole time*, Rickenharp played on, a solo fast as he could play it, keening and ascendant, Rickenharp standing on an up-jutting stone, the last upper corner of the arch; a tiny figure of pure defiance silhouetted against the sky; Rickenharp the performer playing this one for all it was worth . . . the cracks spread farther . . . the microphones picking up the sound of the monument's cracking, crunching, rending . . . a final furious and defiant guitar chord—one last thunderous guitar chord!—and a last burst of gunfire from the arch's top—

And then the arch fell into itself—and was replaced, for a moment, by a great pillar of dust and a monolithic silence. Silence. Silence. Silence. No guitar. Silence.

Hard-Eyes thought, My friends are dead.

On the outside, he showed no flicker of emotion. On the inside, a raincloud was bursting.

The Jægernauts, walked over the rubble, stamping back and forth, grinding the remains of the monument into powder. Powder, and blood.

The Arc de Triomphe, the flag-ensign of the New Resistance, the symbol of the struggle against the neofascists—was crushed into gravel; was flattened. The Arch of Triumph was gone.

But Hard-Eyes knew who was triumphant. As he turned to go into the tunnel, he seemed to hear Rickenharp's final chord echoing on, and on.

• Epilogue •

The frightening thing about racism is that it can be made to sound rational.

—Jack Brendan Smoke,
Essays for the Year 2040, "Too Long Anno Domini" (Witcher Press)

"I've got good news for you, Smoke," Witcher said.

Witcher's private jet had been circling Manhattan for half an hour as it awaited landing clearance for JFK International, in Queens. The interior of the jet was clean, and brightly lit, and new-smelling. The only passengers, aside from the staff, were Witcher, Witcher's secretary—who was asleep in the bed compartment—and Jack Brendan Smoke. And Smoke's crow.

Smoke was wearing a light cotton suit the color of ashes. They had picked it out for him at Freezone. Complete with fashionable notched turtleneck—an alternative to the gold choker.

Smoke was still gaunt. But they'd had him on a rehab diet, and his eyes were bright. They'd even cleaned his teeth, implanted new ones to fill out the gaps. He would be able to walk the streets of New York and pass as an affluent citizen. But he felt displaced. Lost. It seemed he identified with the wreckage he'd left behind.

There was a lounge, with a wide observation window, and Smoke sat at the bar, looking out the window at the island of Manhattan gleaming austerely in the ascetic sunshine of a cloudless winter day.

Witcher was in his late sixties, but he had a good glandularist, good enzymists, good telemerase virologists—and he looked about forty. He'd allowed a little silver to streak his shoulder-length, neatly clipped brown hair and his short, equally neat beard. He wore a brown suit with leather shoulder insets. He'd kept his wide mouth and flattish nose and deep-set brown eyes. He could have afforded something glamorous.

"What's the good news?" Smoke asked, without looking away from the city.

"Have a look." Witcher slid a glossy printout across the brass bar to Smoke. He'd just brought it back from his office, in the rear of the jet. Smoke picked up the printout.

The plane tilted a little, and Smoke's glass of club soda slid away from him. He let it go. The bartender caught the glass before it fell.

Witcher glanced at the bartender, then said, "Go ahead on up to the bed compartment and have a rest, Jerry, if you would." When he was gone, Witcher said, "The hell of it is, Jerry's been with me twenty-two years. Loyal as they come. We should be able to say anything in front of him—but with extractors . . . " He made a dismissive gesture. "Loyalty means nothing."

Reading the printout, Smoke took a deep breath and let it slowly out. Then he smiled. "Steinfeld, Hard-Eyes, Carmen, Willow, Levassier, Hernandez . . . Who are these others?"

"Refugees from FirStep, apparently. The girl claims to be Professor Rimpler's daughter, Claire Rimpler. She's joined the NR. She says her father was murdered on the Colony. We've had no confirmation of that from Colony Admin. The other guy—this Bonham—has some kind of deal he's trying to make with us. I'm not sure what it is, yet . . . There's a story behind this Colony refugee thing. We can use it at the news conference."

Smoke turned to the crow in its cage on the floor. "You hear that? Steinfeld, Hard-Eyes, some of the others—they got through!" The crow tilted its head and seemed to shrug as it ruffled its feathers.

Smoke turned to Witcher. "How'd they do it?"

"What Steinfeld calls "pincer Coordination." The units trapped behind the lines hit the SA roadblocks at the same time Steinfeld's people hit them from the outside. Two-thirds of the NR trapped in Paris got through and got away. They're camped somewhere in the French Alps now. There's a list of the confirmed casualties here."

Smoke nodded, but he didn't look at the list.

"How long will we be in New York?" Smoke asked.

"Four days. We can't stay long—the public exposure is a risk for you. You'll be heavily guarded, of course, but . . . "

Smoke nodded. "I know. Where do we go after New York?"

"The Antilles. A little island where . . . you'll see."

"This man Kessler is there?"

"He is, yes, with his wife. You and he'll be working closely together—at least, that's what Steinfeld's hoping."

"In some ways Steinfeld's very . . . practical. But he's also a wild-eyed idealist like a college kid of twenty. With his fantasy of restructuring the Grid itself. Giving the media back to the people. Raising consciousness in one global flash . . . " Smoke shook his head.

"You think it can't be done?"

"I think any real social restructuring is unlikely short of nuclear holocaust. But . . . " He smiled wanly. "But of course we'll try." He looked out the window, at New York City. "Why do you do it, Witcher? You can't be making a profit on this. You don't strike me as an, um . . . "

"As the humanitarian type? I'm not. I admire brave men, but . . . But mostly, it's business. Three times the SAISC has tried to take over Witcher Airlines, Witcher Computers—three times each. The SAISC is a corporate predator. They started it—I'm just fighting back."

Smoke shook his head. "That's not the reason." Was Witcher the twenty-first century's Oskar Schindler? Or was there something else, something hidden several layers down?

He tried to see what was at the very tip of the Worldtalk Building. The plane was tilted, circling the south end of the island, swinging in toward Queens, and he felt as if there were an invisible string connecting the tip of the building and the plane, the plane spinning on the string like a child's toy.

"Well, now," Witcher said, "you're a sharp man. Steinfeld said you were. You're right: it's not the real reason. Someday I'll tell you the reason, maybe. When it's safe."

A blank TV screen behind the bar flickered and then lit up with a fish-eye image of the cockpit. The copilot turned to look at them. "We have clearance, sir. We're making our final approach."

Witcher nodded at the screen. "It's about time. Double-check to see that our security meets us."

"Yes, sir." The screen went blank again.

Smoke said, "Of course, the good news from Paris is also bad news. Because it means the Second Alliance have Paris to themselves. Just so much more captured territory."

"They had it already—too many of the French were with them . . . " Witcher shrugged. "And the rest of Europe is falling in step."

"There are plenty of French who are not collaborating. And Steinfeld's still in France." Smoke murmured, "And Hard-Eyes. And the others. And they haven't given up."

The plane passed over the city, and Smoke had a glimpse of the traffic sweating through the avenues . . . The urban organism humming with life . . .

"This city is very much alive," Smoke said softly, to the crow. "But then, so was Amsterdam, not so long ago."

THE END OF VOLUME ONE

A Song Called Youth
Book Two:
ECLIPSE PENUMBRA

John Shirley

For Stephen P. Brown

• Prologue •

A man and a little girl were strolling down a white beach, in hazy sunshine, in the heart of the twenty-first century. The Caribbean surged lazily beside them, white capping crystalline blue. The man was tall and dark and gaunt. A crow perched on his left shoulder, a blot of blackness on the beach, its head ducked against the sun. The girl, who walked between the man and the lapping lacework fringe of the surf, was about nine or ten—no one was quite sure of her precise age. She was dark brown, her wavy black hair caught up in the bright yellow scarf common to the women of the island of Merino. She had hold of the belt loop on the man's left hip, holding it as if she were holding his hand. It was too warm to hold hands.

The man and the little girl wore sandals made from tire rubber and hemp; he wore khaki shorts and a blue silk shortsleeved shirt; it was an expensive shirt but he'd lost three buttons from it and hadn't bothered to replace them. The girl was wearing a yellow cotton shift.

The man was Jack Brendan Smoke. The little girl was named Alouette.

Smoke had adopted her a few weeks earlier. She was a child of this island. Her parents had died a year before, in a hurricane.

"Do you think I'm a clever girl?" she asked him. Her island accent was strong, but her English was good.

"Yes. You are the cleverest girl your teachers know. But you mustn't hold yourself above the other students."

"I won't. But if you think I'm clever, why don't you tell me things?"

"What things?"

"What your work is. Why you came here. What your people are doing. I know they're doing something special."

He hesitated. Then he decided. "All right. You know about the New-Soviets?"

"Yes. Well . . . I've heard of Soviets, in Russia. I didn't know they were new . . . "

"The *New*-Soviets came into power after Yeltsin and his successors failed to keep Russia thriving—Russia was weak from corruption, in the years after Putin. They couldn't pay the people who kept the country together. They had to find a way to strengthen the country again. Sometimes war stimulates economies. The NATO nations were aggressive, they argued about the oil near the North Pole and . . . all that gave them a good excuse. So, you know what they did?"

"They invaded Eastern Europe because they were afraid of the aggressiveness of the Yankees. The Yankees were very aggressive. The Yankees were stealing their oil."

"That was their excuse. There was arguing about NATO presence in Eastern Europe and the oil in the Arctic Circle—the Russians said it was theirs. Moscow believed—or pretended to believe—that the allies were building up a force to use against them, to seize the oil. The New-Soviets said 'a good offense is the best defense.' Do you know why there wasn't a nuclear war?"

"Because of the Conventional . . . "

"The Conventional Aggression Treaty."

She nodded, as if he were a student giving the right answer. "And because of the warning systems."

"That's right. It just wasn't practical. It would've been what is called Mutual Assured Destruction." He wondered if she'd learned this by rote only, or if she understood it. Then he wondered if anyone really understood it. "Do you know what happened because of the third world war in Europe?"

"The armies destroyed lots of cities and everyone went into refugee camps and there was riots and people stealing everything and . . . and robbers."

"Exactly. The New-Soviets and the United States let their bulls loose in the world's china shops and everyone suffered. Because of that, NATO hired . . . you know what NATO is?"

"Yes." A little annoyed. "Of course!"

"Okay. Well, you're young but you're more educated than a lot of kids from my country. NATO hired the biggest international private police company. They provided security patrols and antiterrorist squadrons and all kinds of mercenary business. They are called the Second Alliance. You see, at the turn of the century NATO bombed Kosovo, and terrible chaos resulted in that area, in the Balkans. The Albanians had an entrenched organized crime outfit that spread out everywhere in Europe, selling heroin and guns and dealing in prostitution and such, and in the aftermath of the war the crime and violence got so terribly awful in Kosovo and the surrounding areas—so NATO was trying to prevent more of that. It's sort of ironic, really, considering what happened. They hired the Second Alliance and they were exactly the wrong people to hire. Did you know all that?"

"No," she admitted.

"The Second Alliance International Security Corporation. We just call them the SA. NATO hired them to police Europe, to keep order behind the lines. They were a big army all by themselves. Bigger than anybody thought. And nobody knew they were waiting for a chance like this. There was a conspiracy . . . Well, anyway, they occupied lots of Europe behind the lines of fighting. They took control of it. And it turned out that the people who ran the SA were Fascists."

"Fascists are Nazis. I saw them in movies. They torture people and kill Jews for being Jews. They want to control everything."

"More or less correct, at least in World War Two. Especially the German Fascists. The SA, now, is controlled by some very, very extremist Fundamentalist Christians who aren't really Christians at all. Christ would have been saddened by them. Unlike most evangelists, the SA and their friends are believers in racial purity. Genetic purity. A man named Rick Crandall in America, and another man named Watson in Europe, those are their top people. Rick Crandall is a preacher of sorts. They have power in the United States now, too. They have friends in the government. Maybe even the president."

"Mrs. Bester?"

"Yes. President Bester. And they control some very big American companies. They're using them to influence the American people through the media. There's a depression in the United States. Because terrorists destroyed the banking system. Some people think President Bester provoked the New-Soviets into aggression so she could have a war that would help the economy and big business. Anyway, the depression and the war make a lot of pressure on people, and that makes them think that Fascism might be all right . . . for a lot of reasons. And the Fascists control the Space Colony now. They took it over."

"The Space Colony! I wanted to go there!"

"You know all about it?"

She nodded eagerly. "It's a building in space—a building bigger than Merino. Floating out there!" She pointed at the sky. "Thousands of people live in it. It has trees and everything, way out in space! It's closed up so the air can't get out, and it recycles everything. But the New-Soviets have . . . stopped people . . . "

"Blockaded it."

"Yes, blockaded it in space, so it's running out of food because it can't raise enough for all its people inside."

"Yes. When we take it back from the Fascists, we can go there for a visit."

He didn't say, "*If* they take it back." Not to her.

"That's what your work is, then? To take it back?"

"Yes. And to help Europe get away from the same people. It's the work of a great many others: to give Europe back to its people. The Second

Alliance used tricks and set up puppet leaders so that the people of Europe think they have their own leaders, but those new leaders really belong to the SA. And the SA is promoting Fascism in the people. They're hungry and angry and they want order, and Fascism promises food and order, so they think they want Fascism. But they don't know it means they won't have any freedom and they'll have to hate their neighbors.

"How are you fighting these people?"

"We have the New Resistance. The NR. We're fighting them with guns and with information."

"With guns?" She looked at him. "You? You might have to fight with guns?"

He put an arm around her shoulders. "No. Not me. I use words and ideas. I'm no good with guns. People like Steinfeld and Hard-Eyes are using guns and strategy and tactics . . . "

"Steen-field. Hard-Eyes."

"They're leading our guerrillas—that's *guerrillas*, not—"

"I know the difference between guerrillas and gorillas." She rolled her eyes at him. "We used to have guerillas fighting here."

He smiled. "Sorry again. Let's head back now and get something to drink. I'm thirsty."

"Yes." They turned and moved away from the water toward the NR compound.

"Hard-Eyes," she said when they were almost to the road, "is a stupid name."

Smoke laughed. "You're right. Hard-Eyes is an American named Dan Torrence. The nickname sort of embarrasses him now."

"I can see why."

"But he's a good man. He doesn't think he's better than anyone else, and he has given himself completely to the Resistance. Because he saw what the Fascists did to some people, and he saw what the future could be like."

"Why do people decide to be Fascists?"

"Almost anyone could be Fascist under the right circumstances. If they get scared enough. It's because, you see, most people live their lives like sleepwalkers. They're not really awake, though they think they are. And sleepwalkers are easily led. That's why we have to fight it so hard. Because it never quite goes away."

SOUTHEASTERN FRANCE. THE ALPS.

Three olive-drab trucks and an icy-blue dawn. The shadows were still black in the craters on the two-lane mountain road angling up through the French Alps. The dark steel of the sky to the east was going blue-white between the snowy peaks but the rough texture of the peaks' western faces was yet etched by the passing night; the dawn light created a kind of ecliptic corona around the silhouetted mountaintops.

In the lead truck, Dan "Hard-Eyes" Torrence was riding shotgun, literally holding a twenty-round CAWS fully automatic shotgun propped up between his legs. Steinfeld was driving. It was a stolen US Army truck, an old Ford diesel built in the twentieth century. It creaked with age and overuse, its mileage indicator long since numerically exhausted. The rusty floor was cracked; engine heat pushed fumes up at them, along with the grunt and clash of the gears as Steinfeld downshifted for the steepening road grade. The headlights flickered when the truck hit a pot-hole, the beams swiveling out over the canyon drop-off to their left as Steinfeld swung the truck around to avoid a crater. On the western side of the road, a craggy cliff face rose two hundred feet above them before sloping back toward the top of the ridge; snow, loosed by the vibrations set up by the truck, skirted down from shelves in the rock to glitter in the headlight beams. There hadn't been a fresh snowfall for three days. Morning melt-off and the passage of other vehicles had cleared the road of most of it. Now and then the rumbling engine roared in frustration as they hit an icy patch and the wheels spun, Steinfeld cursing through his thick black beard as he wrenched the wheel in search of traction.

Dan Torrence was tired. He was gritty tired and aching tired; physically, mentally, emotionally tired. He cranked the side window open a little more, to let the cold air wash over his face, revive him a little. He wouldn't let himself sleep, because Steinfeld was there, and Steinfeld never seemed to sleep, never showed his weariness except a sort of tangible moodiness, a tendency to lapse into scowling silences. There were forty-four of them in three trucks, moving southeast toward northern Italy, as they had been for almost four days. They were supposed to rendezvous with the rest of the French NR in twelve hours.

But most of the French New Resistance probably wouldn't make it. Most of them were probably dead, or swallowed up by the SAs "preventative detention camps." And two hundred of them had died when they'd broken through the blockade around Paris. They died to get Steinfeld safely through. Which, perhaps, was why Steinfeld never seemed to sleep.

Torrence had lost his three closest friends in Paris, at the end. Rickenharp and Yukio and Jensen. Killed by the Fascists; crushed by the Jægernauts like small animals under a jackboot heel.

But he'd found Claire. They'd met in the wartime chaos of Paris.

Now she was curled up in the back of the truck, probably asleep beside Carmen and Willow and Bonham and the others. Claire was a short, frail-looking woman who'd killed seven of the enemy back in Paris, one of them with a knife.

Torrence wanted to climb into the back of the truck and curl himself up around her, try to keep the warmth of her humanity from slipping away into the mountain shadows.

But he remained sitting stiffly in the passenger seat, staring blearily out the mud-spattered windshield. Feeling his eyelids twitch from exhaustion, his back ache from the hours in the truck.

Steinfeld shifted his bearlike bulk in his seat, stretching as much as he could in the cab's confines, wincing.

"Find cover soon, Hard-Eyes," he muttered.

Torrence heard himself say, "Don't call me that, anymore. Call me Torrence. Or Dan."

"Oh?" Steinfeld looked at him but didn't ask why. He shrugged. "Well, Torrence—satellites'll pinpoint us. New-Soviets will think we're NATO; NATO'll know us for Unauthorized in this area; they'll collate it with the Fascists." His voice was gristly with fatigue.

Torrence nodded. "You know a place?"

Steinfeld shook his head. "Don't know this stretch. Just hope I'm where I think I am."

A single short honk from the track behind them.

Torrence felt a chill, then a hot surge of adrenaline wakefulness. They wouldn't be honking unless something was wrong.

He looked in the passenger-side mirror. "They're stopped—looks like they're stuck . . . "

Steinfeld cursed in Hebrew and pulled over, close under the cliff side. He put the truck into park, left it idling as he got out, breath pluming in the chill air, and went back to see what was wrong. There wasn't enough room between the truck and the mountain for Torrence to get out on the right side, so he slid across the seat and climbed out the driver's side door, grateful for an excuse to stretch.

Levassier was the driver of the second truck. He was standing in the headlight beams, arguing in French with the big, bald Algerian, an NR guerrilla Torrence barely knew.

Levassier had driven a little too close to the edge of the road, on the eastern side. The road's shoulder was badly eroded by winter weather and the shock of air-to-ground missiles that, earlier in the year, had torn up parts of the roadbed. The road had crumbled away under the left front tire, and the truck was beginning to tilt toward the ravine. The Algerian—Torrence hadn't found a chance to learn his name—was saying, so far as Torrence could make out, that Levassier should simply back farther up onto the road. Levassier was making grand gestures that seemed to say, "What an imbecile!" as he maintained that there was ice under the rear wheels, so the truck wouldn't make progress backward, but might well slip about, slide into the ravine if they tried.

Steinfeld was crouching, looking at the rear wheels of Levassier's truck.

Torrence lifted the edge of the canvas tarp and looked into the rear of Steinfeld's truck. Claire was sitting up, with her back to the truck cab, staring into the shadows. He looked for Bonham, the other refugee from the Colony, saw him curled up on a sleeping bag, snoring through his beakish nose, wide mouth open. Reassured to see that Bonham wasn't sleeping beside Claire, Torrence looked over at her again. She didn't look up at him. He could just make out her eyes, open in the darkness, staring at the truck bed. Blinking, staring.

Why wasn't she asleep? Why was she sitting there in the dark, staring at nothing?

Steinfeld shouted, "Torrence!"

Torrence walked back toward Steinfeld. Looking at the sky as he went, wondering if they were under surveillance. And wondering if a Second Alliance patrol plane might not happen by. Or the New-Soviets. Or NATO.

Everyone was their enemy.

Steinfeld had appointed Torrence as captain. He had no bars, no insignia to show his rank. He wore blue jeans and a ski jacket and black hiking boots. But Willow and Carmen and the Spaniard, Danco, went instantly into position when he told them, "You three—grab the S.A.G. and the grenade launchers, stand watch for air attack."

Torrence walked on, found Steinfeld and Burch unloading a heavy tow chain from the rear of the third truck. Burch was a stocky, glum black from the People's Republic of Central Africa. He wore a parka and wire-rimmed glasses.

Without looking over, Steinfeld said, "Torrence, detail a crew to hook this up."

Half an hour later they were still trying to safely move the teetering truck. It was packed with ordnance; there wasn't room for the stacks of rifles and ammo boxes in the other trucks, and Steinfeld didn't want to leave it behind, so they continued to struggle with several tons of metal poised on a cliff edge. Torrence had cut his hands on the chain as they added manpower to the rear truck's pull. His hands ached with the cold; the knuckles were swollen. The shadows had shrunk, the growing light was blue-gray; it was a watered-down light, but they no longer needed the headlights. The sun was edging over a mountaintop that looked to Torrence, in his weariness, like a Klan hood slightly cocked to one side. There was just a faint suggestion of sun warmth on the top of his head.

They couldn't back the towing truck very far, or it would have gone over the edge behind it. So they couldn't use its full power to move the one it was pulling.

Steinfeld made up his mind. "Unload the rest of the gear, anything useful; we'll run the truck over the side, make do with two. Hope they'll get us up over the pass."

Torrence gave the orders. All the time looking at the sky, or at the first truck, wondering about Claire. He looked up at the austere mountain-sides; listened to the men talk, their voices sounding tinny and lost in the mountain vastness. Thinking he'd be moved by this place, another time—the scenery, the heady purity of the morning air . . . but now it was just another pain in the ass, something to hump over, trudge through . . .

He heard a distant thudding sound. Soft and repetitive but distinctly man-made in its ominous regularity.

He looked around, frowning, losing the sound in the noise the others made as they unloaded a crate of ammunition . . . there it was again, louder.

He felt his scalp tighten, the hair rising on the back of his neck. He looked around for Carmen, saw her perched on a boulder with a grenade-fitted rifle in her arms. She was looking at the sky, frowning. He started toward her.

Steinfeld shouted, "Where are you going, Torrence?"

Torrence opened his mouth to reply—and the reply caught in his throat when he saw Carmen pointing, and then saw what she was pointing at.

Three aircraft. A jet accompanied by two helicopters. They were side by side, in close formation, coming at them from the east over a serrated shoulder of mountain, a little more than a quarter of a mile off, and closing. It looked like one of the new stealth models of the Harrier jumpjet, shaped like a hunchbacked triangle, flat black; not particularly fast, but lethal in its copterlike maneuverability. And flanking the jet: the autochoppers, American made, equipped with sidewinders and 7.62-mm miniguns.

They could spray a target area with six thousand rounds per minute . . .

He opened his mouth to shout a warning but Carmen was already shouting; the others saw the aircraft now too. Levassier was looking through field glasses. He must've seen the Second Alliance Christian crosses on the undersides of the jumpjet's wings, the black and silver of its trim because he shouted, "SA!"

They could hear the thudding of the chopper blades clearly now and the whine of the jet. Coming in slow for a jet.

Maybe, Torrence thought, *they'll see the Army trucks, take us for NATO.*

No. They'd see we're all out of uniform. They've been looking for us in this area. There are a half dozen other telltales. They'll know.

As he thought this, he was looking around. There was no time to drive the trucks out of the way. They'd have to find cover.

The cliff face to their right, on the western side of the road, rose about a hundred feet. But about forty feet ahead of the lead truck, there was a fissure running back into the cliff. It looked as if it might be wide enough to run into, but narrow enough to give them cover. He couldn't see anything else.

Steinfeld had come to the same conclusion. He was shouting orders. Everyone was running now; some of them with crates of ammo slung between them; some running to the lead truck, shouting at the others to get out, make for the fissure: Levassier arguing that they should get in the trucks and drive like the devil. But the trucks would make excellent targets on the road.

Torrence shouted, "Get what you can carry and run for that opening in the cliff! Go, go, *go!*"

The jumpjet and the copters were almost on them; they occluded the sun, sending their shadows racing like hungry panthers ahead of them. The cannons mounted on the nose of the Jump Jet were tilting downward. The jet and the autochoppers swung off to the north, and for a giddy moment Torrence thought they'd decided not to engage—but then he saw they were coming around for a strafe run, angling to follow the north-south course of the road so they could come in low. The choppers followed the jet in precise flight-path replication: they were Bell *Heeldogs*, unmanned, entirely automated, robot pilots responding to the orders of the human pilot in the jet.

Weariness was forgotten. Mouth dry with fear, Torrence looked around for Claire, saw her climbing out of the back of the truck, carrying a light machine gun, her face white, her lips pressed to a thin line. She was the last out. Steinfeld and the others were mostly up ahead. Someone—Burch, maybe—had gotten into the lead truck, was starting it, and driving ahead to block the gunships from the main body of guerrillas. Drawing fire.

Hot knives clashed in Torrence's lungs as he ran to Claire, shouting, "Leave the fucking gun!" She shook her head angrily, continued to carry it, staggered under its weight. He slung the CAWS over his shoulder and wrenched the machine gun from her, tossed it aside, took her elbow, and dragged her along, knowing that if they survived, she'd lecture him about women carrying their own burdens.

But he didn't care because now the autochoppers had let go four sidewinders. He heard a quadruple thud and the scream of rending metal as the missiles struck the two rear trucks; Torrence felt heat on his back, and the arrogant shove of shockwaves. He stumbled, but Claire steadied him and they ran on, the world dancing jerkily around them—

Something sizzled past them, drawing a line of white exhaust in the air, the line finishing in the back of the lead truck, which still trundled awkwardly up the road, and a second later the truck Torrence had ridden in all night was consumed in an orange-red ball of fire.

Heat and the zing of shrapnel. Reflections of fire shimmering from the patches of snow; a long, thudding echo off the mountainsides.

Burch, one of the best of them, was dead.

Claire shouted, "Here they come!" and tugged Torrence into the poor shelter of a boulder jutting from the cliff as the Harrier and the auto-choppers bore down on them. The rocks around them spat chips and sparks as the steel-jacketed rounds impacted. Something stung Torrence's cheek; something more slashed at his neck. He and Claire tried to press farther into the hollow; their backs were bruised by knobs of cold rock.

Torrence thought, *If they pull up and turn toward us, we're fucked. They'll mince us.*

But the killing machines kept going, chasing the main group of the rebels, who'd just reached the fissure, twenty yards ahead; Bonham paused at the opening to look back, probably looking for Claire—then he ducked inside. Carmen was crouched in the opening with her rifle propped on a small boulder; she fired, and a grenade arced up, only to bounce off the underside of an autochopper before exploding; the chopper rocked in the air but showed no other effect as it whipped by, following the Harrier.

Torrence pulled at Claire's arm, and they were running toward the fissure, wondering if they could get to it before the choppers and the jet circled back. They ran past three bodies sprawled in red splashes. No time to see who they were.

The jet slowed, stopped in midair, and the autochoppers obediently came to heel.

Take out the jet, Torrence thought. Somebody take out the fucking jet.

The jet and its faithful dogs were coming at them, about fifty yards up, angling down, red sunlight gleaming on the cockpit and flashing off the steel curve of the autochoppers' blind front ends.

Running hard, Claire beside him, Torrence saw an autochopper swiveling toward him and Claire, lining them up in its sights. He felt her hand in his, palm moist with sweat, fingers rigid with tension, and there were things he wanted to tell her—

And then she was pulling him into the shadows of the crevice as 7.62-mm minigun rounds screamed off the rock a few feet behind them. Someone returning fire with the ground-to-air missile launcher . . . a satisfying *ka-whump* as the missile struck an autochopper.

Torrence threw himself down into a pebbly alcove between two, low boulders, Claire hunching down beside him, both of them gasping, shaking with fear, but amazed to be alive, feeling a transitory buzz of triumph . . . until he saw that Potter and the Algerian were splashed over the rocks near the entrance to the crevice. They'd been caught coming into it.

Torrence felt despair drag like a heavy lead weight. But he forced himself to get up, look for Steinfeld.

There were four volunteers near the entrance to the fissure, shooting at the aircraft in order to draw fire, to give the others a chance to move back into cover, away from the road. The fissure was about forty feet deep, V-shaped; it was about eighteen feet across at the top, narrowed to a snow and pebble-packed floor, angling upward toward the mountainside; there was a slight overhang on the south side that gave them a little aerial cover. The sun shone almost directly into the crevice; the bluish light was broken up here and there by sharp blades of shadow.

"How . . . how many of us?" Claire asked, arms propped on her knees, face buried in her arms.

He said, "Looks like we're down to about thirty-two." She said something more, but he couldn't hear it because of the bark and chatter and scream of gunfire from the front of the fissure. Steinfeld and Levassier were just turning a corner farther down the crevice, moving up to deeper cover. Cursing as they slipped on patches of snow and uneven rock, other guerrillas carried wounded, and a few crates of weapons, food, guns. They hadn't gotten away with much.

The wounded were giving out short, sharp cries of pain with each jolt as they were moved.

Some mocking inner voice told Torrence: *You wanted to be where the conflict was real. This real enough for you?*

The remaining autochopper opened up with long, blanketing bursts of its miniguns at the four guerrillas drawing fire at the opening of the fissure.

Torrence saw the rough *V* of the fissure's opening blur with dust and rock chips and smoke and spattered blood. He saw the bodies of the four volunteers jerking, slamming against the stone with the impact of the bullets: four people, gone instantaneously. Each one had a life history; parents, family, friends, perhaps children. The ribbon of each one's life history—summarily snipped.

He saw the *Heeldog* hovering fifty feet up, wind from its rotors swirling dust and smoke and snow. Like an opaque-helmeted SA security guard, it had no face. It was computer-driven; it was a machine for hunting, for killing, and nothing more.

The jet was coming in from the opposite direction looking for targets. Claire had gotten her breath. She stood and they followed the others back into the fissure, feeling like small animals running from an exterminator.

They turned the corner in the fissure just as the rock behind them erupted with a cannon shell from the jumpjet. The ground seemed to ripple; the shock thickened and distorted the air, and the ground seemed to leap out from under Torrence . . . till he found himself lying facedown, his ears ringing.

Thinking, *Have I been hit?* Someone was pulling at his arm, shouting over the screaming roar of the jet, the thump of the autochopper blades, "Get up, damn you, Torrence!" Claire's voice. "Come on, Danny!"

Torrence? Danny? He remembered the names, remembered everything that had brought him here. It seemed nonsensical now—even as he forced himself up, got his rubbery legs moving, as he and Claire stumbled back into the crevice: it seemed absurd, a meaningless exchange of chaos. *They throw chaos at us, in flying bullets, shrapnel, explosions; we throw chaos back at them. Waves of chaos heaved back and forth, driving me up a mountain for two days, then on foot into a mountain fissure. Waves of chaos driving us like field mice before a thresher. Small animals under the jackboot again . . . The Jægernaut that had killed Rickenharp as he played his guitar . . .* The ideological origin of the conflict was an excuse. The conflict, the killing, had a life of its own.

And he wanted out of it, just then. In that exhausted, meaning-drained instant he wanted to hide in a hole till the wave of chaos passed him by; till he could crawl back down the mountain, find his way to the sea, to a ship or a plane, back to the USA and the walled-in enclaves of safety his parents lived in . . .

But then he looked at Claire and saw no despair in her. He saw fear and anger, but no tears. He felt her hand in his, and the sensation was somehow the organizational locus for meaning. In that instant all meaning proceeded from her touch. Steinfeld, the New Resistance—all that was distant just now. Now they were running, struggling to survive, together; and that *together*, by itself, had to be meaning enough, paltry though it was. It was like using a small, leafless tree as your only shelter against a raging desert sandstorm.

There were three more volunteers up ahead, where the fissure widened for a short distance. They were setting up a missile launcher, which wasn't much more than a ten-foot tube of olive-drab metal on a tripod. A rifle fitted with a grenade leaned against the stone wall to one side. The jet and copter were converging overhead.

Torrence had a choice, then. He could pick up the rifle, join them in drawing fire away from Steinfeld, and be killed. Or he could tell himself: *I'm a captain, officers are necessary, important to the Resistance, I'd be squandering a resource if I sacrificed myself. And Claire is with me. I brought her into the NR. I feel responsible for her.* Tell himself all of that . . . and use it as an excuse to scramble for safety.

Some irresistible clockwork mechanism of his personality made the choice for him. He pulled away from Claire as they came up to the volunteers, shouted, "Go on, join Steinfeld, I'll be there in a minute!"

"That's bullshit, Torrence! Come *on*!"

But he'd grabbed the grenade rifle, was wedging it in the hollow of his shoulder (wondering if she was going to get killed because she wouldn't leave him here, killed because of his gesture, his gesture of self-lessness ultimately selfish because it sacrificed her too), aiming at the autochopper . . . its blades blew grit in his eyes . . . he saw the jet loom up, its wings vibrating from its hover-retros; he felt it emanating heat, poised over them like a monstrously oversize sword of Damocles . . . he shifted aim and fired . . . the grenade arced toward the jet and—didn't explode. A bum charge. *Fuck!* He was going to die for nothing . . .

The chopper's miniguns opened up, but it was a few yards too far south, and most of the rounds rang off the rock overhang; a ricochet caught one of the volunteers in the eye, a young black woman who clutched at her bloody socket, screamed and crumpled as the other two fired the missile. The launcher belched: white flash and a white rope of smoke behind the missile. It struck the sidewinder tubes on the right side of the autochopper. At the same moment the jet's cannon fired—its aim thrown off by the shockwaves from the exploding autochopper, its shell struck the rock wall over the two surviving volunteers.

Torrence seemed to see an orchid of fire that blossomed gigantically to consume his field of vision, and he felt himself flying backward—

•••

Torrence came to himself sitting with his back to the curved stone, a patch of snow chilling his tailbone. His head seemed to reverberate with a metallic singing. Red and blue smoke swirled. The red smoke wasn't real; it vanished. The blue smoke remained, so he decided it was real.

Claire?

He turned his head, and winced. Saw her sitting beside him, laughing to herself. Her upper left arm was laid open, thickened blood making the cloth of her coat indistinguishable from the torn flesh of her wound. Her hysterical laughter was almost lost to him through the roaring, metallic ringing in his ears. He looked up (flinching with head pain) and saw that the sky was clear over the fissure. Where was the jump jet?

The natural stone wall across from him was painted uniformly red. The paint was still wet. He looked at it for a long time before he knew it was blood.

A man's raggedly severed arm lay nearby in an iridescent patch of snow; the fingers were curled as if the hand were playing the piano. The skin was blue-white.

All the time there was the hissing, roaring, in his ears, an aural motif for the scene.

And then Willow and Carmen were there, bending over him. Their faces seemed fish-eye distorted. Willow was a gaunt, straw-haired Brit, with bad teeth and a perpetual air of quiet suspicion; Carmen was a lanky punk in an Army surplus ski trooper's jacket, waterproofed green canvas with a hood; the hood was thrown back to show her ring-clustered ears, her black hair shaved on the sides and the back of her head, spiked like a paradoxical anarchist crown atop.

"Anything broken, mate?" Willow asked. Each word accentuated by the white puffs of his breath in the cold air.

Torrence thought about it. Decided Willow meant bones. He moved experimentally. The movements brought some aches and a whirligig of nausea. But none of the grating pain accompanying broken bones. "I think I'm all right. Just kinda . . . blurry."

"You'll be okay," Carmen said.

Claire had stopped laughing; she sat rocking with pain, silent. Carmen put a tourniquet on Claire's arm, and then she used a medikit to clean and close the wound. Claire made hissing sounds between clenched teeth.

"It's a nasty-looking cut, but it's shallow," Carmen said. "Artery's intact. Nothing embedded. Looks worse than it is." Torrence didn't want to move. He wanted to lie there. Stay there. Sleep, maybe.

He must've mumbled something aloud about it, because Willow said, "We got a camp, up the crack. Sleeping 'ere's not on for you, mate." Willow helped him up. Torrence groaned.

"The jet . . . " Claire said huskily.

"Gone," Carmen said. "I think it was damaged when the second chopper blew. But it'll be back. *They'll* be back. Trucks are gone. We can't use the road. Steinfeld says we hide up in the mountain . . . "

• • •

THE ISLAND OF MERINO, THE CARIBBEAN.

Jack Smoke tapped the broad, wafer-thin computer screen and said, "They're somewhere in here . . . about ten miles northeast of the Italian border." The big, glossy-black crow perched on his shoulder fluttered a little when Smoke moved.

Witcher, standing beside Smoke, was frowning at the map on the screen. He nodded and tapped the terminal's keyboards for zoom magnification on one small segment of the map. That part swelled to fill the screen. "There's nothing much around there. No villages . . . just the pass . . . "

"And it's a high elevation, not much cover except rocks. They're exposed."

Smoke and Witcher were in the Comm Center, at the place called Home: the heavily fortified New Resistance world headquarters on the island of Merino somewhere between the Antilles and Cuba. It was hot and oppressive between the thick, white-painted concrete walls, the gray concrete floor splashed with paint around the edges where the painter had been sloppy; white plastic, aluminum, and black plastic equipment crowded the room, and in some places you had to turn sideways and press hard to get through between the monitoring gear. Two technicians sat at satellite link monitors at the other end, recording information about SA, NATO, and NSR troop movements, and alert for information pertaining to Steinfeld. The technicians were a man and a woman; the man was black. Both were topless, wearing only shorts, because the room was stifling, turgidly hot. Smoke and Witcher each wore white shorts, sandals. Witcher wore a gold polo shirt, darkened by sweat to clay color under his arms. Smoke wore a flower-print Hawaiian shirt, mostly blue. And in a way he wore the crow.

Smoke was silently cursing Witcher's fear of air conditioners. Mention air conditioners and Witcher'd mutter darkly about "lethal mutations of the American Legionnaire's bacterium." But Smoke had come to accept

Witcher's fits of hypochondria, his mercurial shifts from expansive openness to tight-lipped reserve. Witcher was the angel of the New Resistance, its billionaire backer, and if his eccentricity should shift him from supporting the NR, the resistance might well collapse.

They were too dependent on Witcher, Smoke decided. Perhaps Steinfeld should take steps to reduce their reliance on him.

"Smoke," Witcher said suddenly, "what about the contingent at Malta? We could air-drop some assistance."

Smoke shook his head. "That'd be just another group of NR trapped in the area. We're too badly outnumbered to help Steinfeld that way. If we could get the men in, it'd have to be from a high-altitude drop. The airspace there is monitored by three armies. If we had some helicopters, something that could fly in under radar, but big enough to pick up forty men . . . " He shrugged.

Witcher grimaced. "We tried." He'd dispatched a ship disguised as a tanker, with six copters; hidden in holds designed for oil. One of the NR's American operatives had been captured, interrogated with an extractor. He'd known about the tanker, because he'd supervised the construction of its false walls. The extractor, a device using molecular biology to extract information from a subject's brain, had told the SA about the tanker and its destination. The SA pulled strings, claiming there was a terrorist plot afoot, and NATO simply sank the ship, fifty-five miles west of the Straits of Gibraltar.

"Maybe we could stage a diversion, draw the SA away from him," Witcher said.

"I considered that. But we've intercepted their field transmissions. They've ID'd Steinfeld. They're certain it's him. Getting him will be first priority."

"So what do we do?"

"Hope Steinfeld finds a way out on his own."

"You saying there's nothing we can do for him?"

"It looks that way." Smoke's voice was flat, emotionless. But he reached up and stroked the crow, as if comforting it.

• • •

SOUTHEASTERN FRANCE.

If was late afternoon when Torrence woke, but in the cave it was twilight. It was a shallow cave, only forty or fifty feet deep, with a high, cracked ceiling that effortlessly swallowed their campfire smoke. Torrence sat up and looked around.

He was in the back of the cave, sitting on a sleeping bag. Claire lay on a bag beside him, asleep. He wanted to reach out, stroke her hair, but he didn't want to wake her. And they'd never made love; there was no real physical intimacy between them.

The fire popped and sizzled. It was a skewed pyramid of thin, twisted tree branches gradually collapsing into the wavery column of yellow flame. The wounded lay nearby, seven of them; one groaning, the others too quiet. Two of them looked like they'd died. On the far side of the flame the little Spaniard, Danco, sat with an old AK-47 across his knees, staring into the fire. Danco had a brown, saturnine face; bristling, arching eyebrows; a small, pointed beard; and the devil's own red mouth. He wore fatigues, a watch cap, and a battered brown leather jacket.

Torrence looked at his watch and saw that the crystal had splintered into a coarse star; the digits were frozen.

He stretched, biting his lip at the pain. It felt like he had some cracked ribs, bruises, and a lot of little wounds.

He felt dull, creaky with aches, hungry. But the disorientation, the panic—all that was gone.

Scowling and muttering, Levassier came into the cave carrying a packet of freeze-dried soup mix and a bucket of snow for melting. Torrence tried not to stare at the food. They might not have enough for anyone but the wounded.

But everyone ate. Bonham sitting near Danco on the other side of the fire, eating greedily, staring at Claire and Torrence. Claire woke when she smelled the food cooking. By degrees, as the guerrillas talked over the mess kits of soup and canned stew, Torrence pieced the picture together. They'd found the cave a mile and a half up the mountain from the road. There were twenty-five of them intact enough to fight.

Two SA jets had gone over, probably looking for them. The sentries were fairly sure they hadn't been spotted. There was cloud cover, blocking satellite reconnaissance. Steinfeld had used a pack-radio to try to reach the other SA units, and the Mossad, transmitting coded messages. No reply so far.

The SA was probably triangulating troops in the area by now. They'd be along soon enough.

So what do we do? Torrence wondered. It would be tough to run farther, with the wounded, and with scarce supplies.

Steinfeld looked grim.

After the meal—it would be their only meal that day—Torrence stood a watch outside the cave. The clouds that had drifted in at midmorning had thickened, began to unspool thin streamers of sleet. Torrence trudged from one miserably uncomfortable spot to another in the shallow, open area of broken rock outside the narrow cave mouth, slipping on ice-glazed patches of gray snow. A faint wash of smoke drifted out of the cave entrance but was quickly sucked away by the drizzly wind. The wind burned his nose and ears, and the auto-shotgun was a dead weight on its shoulder strap.

He was dismally grateful when, an hour after sunset, just when it was getting *really* cold, Steinfeld sent out the dour, pallid Frenchman, Sortonne, to relieve him.

Torrence found Claire sitting cross-legged on the sleeping bag, cleaning a rifle, forehead creased with concentration. Danco had taught her how to clean the rifle just the day before.

Now Danco watched, grinning, as Torrence sat down beside her, his hands and fingers tingling in the sudden warmth from the campfire.

They didn't speak for a while. Then Claire said, "The sky clear out there?"

"No. You wondering about the Colony?"

She hesitated, then nodded, frowning over the assault rifle. She'd put it back together perfectly. "No news. When I left, it was on the verge of anarchy. And the New-Soviets were closing in. I'm not even sure if the damn place is still up there. Just to see it . . . "

He asked, "You can see it with the naked eye?"

"If you know how to look. It looks like a star."

"I guess you're not used to being down here yet. Joining the NR is a bad way to readjust to the planet."

She stared at her grime-blackened hands, her broken, dirt encrusted nails. She shrugged and looked around. "Actually . . . " She smiled sadly. "The cave is sort of comforting—the Colony's corridors weren't so different, really . . . God, I just wish I could know if . . . " She broke off, squeezing her eyes shut.

"Wish you could know if he's dead?" Torrence asked.

After almost ten seconds she nodded, very slowly. "If Dad is dead."

They didn't speak again for nearly two hours. The fire burned low; darkness gathered itself around them. Steinfeld, Levassier, and Danco talked softly at another campfire nearer the front. Most of the others were asleep.

Torrence and Claire sat side by side on the sleeping bag, knees drawn up, hugging themselves for warmth. Suddenly she said, in a whisper, "It's getting cold in here. But I . . . it's like I can hardly feel the cold, like the feeling is in someone else. I left the Colony to get away from the fighting, and to get away from the way the place was falling apart—the place I lived all those years—and, shit. Look at me."

"You could get to the States. Steinfeld could probably arrange it."

Mentally adding to himself, *If we get out of this alive.*

She shook her head. "The Second Alliance took the Colony. Enslaved everyone there. It was bad enough I ran away from the cocksuckers once. I couldn't live with twice. I want to stay where the fight is—the fight against the SA. And for Dad's sake, this is my way to fight Praeger." It was difficult to make out her expression in the dimness. "Maybe I should've stayed in the Colony. Fought them there."

"What would have happened if you'd stayed?"

"I'd have been arrested. Interrogated. Probably killed. They'd have made it look like the rebels killed us, I guess."

"So how can you feel guilty about not staying? You couldn't have fought them, you were trapped, cornered."

"Feelings aren't rational. I mean, how many times in a person's life do they feel guilty for something they can't really control?"

He had to concede that. "Know what you mean."

"And today I got so . . . I just *felt fucked*. Those things that weren't even human were hunting us . . . those unmanned flying *machines* . . . " Her voice broke. "I was more scared than I thought a person could be without their heart blowing up."

"Me too."

"Were you?" She sounded surprised.

"Scared shitless." He reached out, tentatively laid his hand on hers. Started to withdraw when he felt her move but she turned her hand palm upward, squeezed his hand, leaned toward him, and pressed her head against his shoulder.

Torrence had an overwhelming urge to embrace her—and he gave in to it. She returned the embrace. He felt her shaking as she sobbed softly.

He held her for a long time, being careful of the wound on her arm, till it was too cold to stay atop the sleeping bag. "Let's get under the covers," he whispered. "And sleep," he added, to let her know he wasn't going to make a move on her.

She nodded. They took off their boots and climbed into the double sleeping bag. Both of them smelled sour. But it had been a long time since that had mattered.

They held one another against the cold, and the fear.

He'd almost gone to sleep when he felt her moving against him, a kind of blind nuzzling of her hips. He felt his cock harden; she felt it, too, and pressed her crotch against it. Both of them ached, and her wound burned on her upper arm—but that made the caressing more piquant, a deeper relief. She unbuttoned her blouse and pressed his rough hands to her breasts.

There was some fumbling with zippers, and pants buttons, but in a few minutes they were joined, with Claire on top, straddling him, sighing softly, almost sobbing; she was very warm, and very wet, inside. And when she came, she pulled his face to her breasts and he was amazed—exquisitely amazed—to experience the sheer, silken luxury of them here, in this place, this animal's den on the cold shore of a battlefield.

• • •

At ten the next morning Steinfeld, Levassier, Danco, and Torrence held a conference. They looked at maps on the glowing blue screen of a hand computer; they collated what data they had about SA, NATO, and New-Soviet troop movements and came to a bitter conclusion. To leave there was probably suicide. To stay there was to await execution.

They decided to go through the mountains. The wounded would have to be abandoned—or put to death. No one said this but everyone knew it. There was real sorrow in Steinfeld's eyes.

They'd never had to do it before. Torrence wondered if they could bring themselves to go through with it.

The question was moot, because before the guerrillas could move out, the enemy came.

They heard the thudding of choppers, and an electronically amplified voice booming outside the cave entrance, its absurd verbosity echoing between the rocks: "*This is the Second Alliance Security Force acting on behalf of the North Atlantic Treaty Organization. Come out of your camp unarmed, with your hands on top of your heads. If you surrender, you will not be harmed. Repeat, if you surrender . . .*"

There was no question of surrender. They would put them under extractors. You can't keep anything back from an extractor. They'd know what Steinfeld knew, and that would mean arrests, hundreds of arrests . . .

Steinfeld looked almost relieved. They wouldn't have to abandon the wounded.

They looked at Steinfeld. Steinfeld said, "Deploy for defense."

• 02 •

Seen from Earth, it was a star. But inside . . .

Dan "Hard-Eyes" Torrence had a sister. He assumed she was safe in the same fortresslike housing project their parents lived in, near New York City.

But Dan Torrence's sister, Kitty, had married while he was in Europe. She'd married a technicki, a black technicki in fact, and she'd emigrated to FirStep, the Space Colony, to be with her husband, Lester, who was a communications technician. That was just before the New-Soviets blockaded the Colony.

She'd married, but her best friend, a feminist, had persuaded Kitty to keep her last name. She was still Kitty Torrence.

Kitty's job on FirStep was simple and ugly. She kept the sludge pipes in the recycling center from clogging. Kitty was a wide-framed woman, her hair brown and coarse, her features blunt, hands and feet a little too big. She'd once overheard someone calling her "horsey." Okay; she was not a pretty woman, and not unusually intelligent. But she was strong and determined, and her eyes were a nice shade of blue, almost violet, and Lester adored her.

The recycling center was an enormous barn-shaped room with aluminum-gray walls and six-foot-thick flat-black pipes. The joints of the pipes were dull silver. Harsh fluorescent light buzzed overhead; steam and rancid smells escaped from loose pipe joints; the atmosphere was faintly cloudy, like a glass of gin left out for a couple of days.

Kitty's legs hurt, and she was thirsty. Parched. Her lips were cracked. There was a steady, dull background heat in the room, and in it swam the human odors wrung from the disposable clothing. The heat, noise, and smell were always there, and after a while it felt strange to go out into the corridor where the air was cooler and cleaner—and so much quieter.

Because the pipes roared all day. They roared and groaned, as discarded one-use garments and other refuse from the previous two days, heated by the same chemical process that liquefied it, bubbled and slopped through the pipes. No one knew why the pipes gave out those pathetically human groaning noises, but the superstitious technickis assumed the ghosts of Samson Molt and Professor Rimpler were trapped in the pipes, because probably Admin had simply fed them into the recyclers. The younger technickis—the younger ones were more superstitious—would hear the groans and mutter, "Cover me, Gridfriend . . . "

The four biggest pipes emerged from the wall to the right, slanted down to the first separation vats; a plethora of smaller pipes sprouted from the vats. A catwalk ran along the pipes and around the enormous vats, and Kitty walked along the catwalk, checking to see that the pipes weren't clogging. The colonists used disposable clothes most of the time because laundering would consume too much volume, too much water on the Colony, and because there were strict weight limits on what could be shipped up from Earth; the weight allowance for clothing was small. Each dorm or living unit had its own garment printer; blocks of the raw garment material, to be fed into the printer like reams into a photocopier, were delivered once a week. Some wore cloth clothing on the Colony; there were even boutiques. But most preferred the economy and flexibility of disposable clothing. Print it out in any style you programmed the printer for that day. Wear it twice and toss it into the chute. The chute took it to the sludge pipes, where it was soaked in Breakdown, which broke it down into sludge with the other recycled trash; its main components were drawn by inertia and the Colony's centrifugal force down to recycling, down to the big pipes where Kitty walked along the catwalk.

Kitty was five months pregnant, but it didn't show a whole lot. She wore a shift to help conceal it. She was afraid they'd lay her off if they knew she was pregnant. But the supervisor was technicki; she knew what conditions were like for technicki, she knew Kitty and her husband needed the work credit.

Every five steps Kitty had to stop and slide open the little window on the top of the pipe; usually a little sludge spat up at her when she did this and she'd snatch her hand away to keep from getting sludge and Breakdown on it. She'd hold on to the rail and peer into the pipe, and if she saw it was gumming up, she'd use the sludge fork clamped inside the window to clear away the blockage. Then she'd close the window and go on to the next joint. And when she got to the vat, she'd cross over to the other side, go back up the next pipe. And when she got to the wall, she'd cross over, go back down the pipes again. On and on like that all day.

She guessed it was better than working down in Fecal Sewage where Mary Beth worked. There weren't enough jobs to go around, because the traffic between Earth and the Colony was so reduced, and the Colony had been damaged in the vandalism, sabotage, the riots of the Technicki Rebellion. Now that the comm transmitters were damaged and they were waiting, endlessly, for comm parts to be sent from Earth, Kitty's husband had to make do with occasional video maintenance work. The Colony wasn't going to let anyone starve, it was said; if you couldn't pony up the work-cred for food, they gave you rations—bad food and not enough of it. These were difficult, transitory times, Admin told them. Have to tighten the belts a few notches. But it would be over soon.

The rebellion was over, after all. The mirror-helmeted Second Alliance security bulls were everywhere. Praeger and the Admin council had complete power. The union assemblies had been suspended. Martial law was in effect.

But somehow the sabotage was still happening. The TV lines had been disrupted by some vandal—wild laughter, static, distorted images. The extra air-purification parts in storage had been damaged by runaway warehouse robots. The food in cold storage was damaged when the refrigeration had turned itself off, refused to go back on for twenty-four hours. And yet there seemed to be no whisper of an active technicki rebellion . . .

What would happen, she wondered, if the New-Soviets won the war on Earth? Would they take over the Colony? Would they blow it out of the sky?

A broad ripple of nausea ran through her; the rancidness from the pipe seemed to deepen, the heat seemed to increase. She had to stop and lean on the railing of the catwalk, turn away from the pipes, and retch for a few moments. God, how she had wanted to get pregnant, have Lester's baby. A beautiful little golden baby, caramel colored like its dad . . . but she regretted it now—now that she had to hide it. If they found out, they'd make her leave her job, go to Colony parenthood monitoring to see if they'd even permit her to have the baby. And since Lester was black, and the Second Alliance was running things, they probably wouldn't issue the permit. They'd find some excuse to disallow it. Unless she could wait long enough, so the baby was a *fait accompli*. But moments like this . . . feeling sick and too heavy and tired all the time . . .

She saw the supervisor, Mrs. Chiswold, standing by the vat, looking up at her with a worried expression; probably worried she'd have to let Kitty go.

Kitty smiled, and stretched as if she'd just been taking a little rest, then stamped back to the pipes, forced herself to stare into the endless subterranean river of sludge. And let her mind wander till she found herself wondering what had become of her brother, in Europe. Danny. Poor Danny. He was probably dead.

• • •

SOUTHEASTERN FRANCE.

Torrence was thinking, *We'll probably be dead by sunset, the latest.*

He and Claire and Danco were hunkered down in a shallow, crater-shaped depression atop a house-size mound of rock, waiting for the SA choppers to make another pass. They squinted against the austere winter sunlight, shivered when the breeze knifed them. Torrence's hands were stiff on the auto-shotgun. Claire, sitting beside the small missile launcher, blew in her hands to keep them warm.

"How they find us?" Danco wondered aloud, his dark eyes darting from side to side as he scanned the cloud-lidded sky. He said something else, but it was lost in the rattle of gunfire as Willow's group met another onrush from SA ground troops, up ahead, with a wall of bullets.

"Probably found us with infrared scans," Torrence said. "This is a good area for it. Not much else up here that's warm to confuse the tracking.

Doesn't matter." He heard the resignation in his own voice and thought, *I
sound dead already.*

"It matters how they did it," Claire said. "They could use the same
technique on the other Resistance outfits . . . "

Torrence nodded. She was right. She was right a lot of the time.

He heard a rattle of pebbles behind him and looked over his shoulder.
Bonham and Sahid—a Palestinian whose shattered right arm quivered in a
rude splint—were dragging the wounded out of the cave on sleeping bags,
and into the shelter of another cluster of rocks. Bonham looked as if he
were thinking of surrendering and he probably was. Sahid was a pinched,
yellowish man whose lips hung slack as, wincing with pain, he tugged the
wounded guerrilla with his left arm.

Nature had anticipated their need for a good defensive setup. The
tumble of rocks, some ancient glacial deposit, was arranged in a kind of
half-moon shape an acre across around the cave opening, with the moon's
curve facing outward from the cave; the maze of rocks was made up of
granite and basalt, gray and dull black, knobbed and craggy, but most of
them roughly squarish or beveled like housetops, ten to twenty feet tall;
between them ran crooked corridors of stone; the floor of each "corridor"
was of smaller rock mortared together with snow.

The guerillas were looking east; the sun was almost overhead, here and
there glancing brightly off the assault rifles of the three other NR teams
placed in the warren of stone; four more were dug in around the approach
to the cave.

Claire and Danco were to operate the launcher. Torrence was there
because that's where Claire was. The three of them were sitting ducks up
here for the choppers—but they had to be on high ground to get a good
shot with the launcher.

The SA had unloaded troops from two transport choppers, long helis with
two sets of copter blades each; they'd let them out down the mountainside a
ways at a safer LZ: Maybe a hundred SA Regulars, without heavy armor or
the visored helmets, but well-armed, fanning out to approach the cave area.
They might well have rained missiles on the NR position from above, but
Torrence's guess was they wanted some intact prisoners for interrogation.

Willow had waited till the SA regulars were almost on top of them
before jumping up and opening fire. The SA, caught by surprise, lost eight
men before getting under cover—they'd expected the Resistance to hole
up closer to the cave. A man sat behind a damaged, unusable machine
gun in the mouth of the cave—a Frenchman Torrence didn't know.
Terminally wounded, the Frenchman had volunteered for decoy duty.
Suicide. Torrence thought he should go and talk to him, let him know it

mattered, let him know he wasn't forgotten. But it was too late; he had to stay in position.

"Here comes another chopper," Claire said.

Bonham was alone now, dragging the last of the wounded from the cave—as Torrence watched, Bonham stopped, startled, dropping his end of the sleeping bag at the sound of an assault-rifle burst somewhere not far behind him. He turned and looked in that direction, seemed to waver on the point of running.

Torrence muttered, "Breached our flanks," as he turned and started down off the rock, half sliding down a snow-and-ice-encrusted incline. Claire would be all right for awhile.

He made the ground and ran through the chill shadows, between the high rocks, toward Bonham. Hissing, "Get 'im undercover, damn you!"

Bonham cursed but bent and dragged the unconscious man off to the right as behind him two SA regulars emerged from a crevice, their guns still smoking from the execution of the NR sentries they'd surprised.

They were Hispanic, maybe Guatemalan, in gray-black uniforms, trousers tucked in at the boots, and SA-insigniaed ski jackets with imitation sheepskin collars. They carried assault rifles, grenades on their khaki belts buckled over the coats. They were fifty feet off.

And they were looking at the mouth of the cave where the Frenchman sat hunched over the machine gun, forty feet to their right. Their attention was focused on the cave. Torrence approached in heavy shadow. They hadn't spotted him. One of them raised a rifle, pointed it at the quiet, hunched figure behind the heavy machine gun. Torrence realized the guy on the MG had already died. The other SA tapped his friend's shoulder and shook his head. Reached for a grenade. The machine gunner seemed to be looking toward Torrence, away from the approaching soldiers.

Torrence heard the thwacking blades of approaching helicopters. He ignored it, moved forward carefully, trying to make as little noise as possible, keeping close to the craggy rock wall on his right, thinking, *Any second they'll realize the machine gunner's dead, they'll look up, see me, open fire. Those assault weapons have better accuracy than the shotgun at this range.*

The soldiers were moving closer to the machine gun. One of them had a grenade out, put his other hand on the pin. The choppers thwacked nearer. Torrence was thirty feet away from the two SA. Twenty-five . . .

His foot dislodged a stone. The SA looked toward him.

Torrence ran at them screaming, hoping to unnerve them into paralysis as he leveled the shotgun, bracing it against his hip, squeezing the trigger.

It was like firing a small cannon. The 12-gauge rounds slapped into the chamber at a rate of three per second. The gun leapt in his hands, viciously wrenching his wrists, kicking bruises into his hip, thundering so the rocks echoed big rolling booms and the shadows vanished in strobing muzzle flash and—

In four seconds he'd sent twelve 12-gauge rounds into the two men, the load spreading just right at this range but compact enough to rip deep, slamming the two soldiers off their feet, and even before they struck the ground, more rounds slashed into them so that their bodies jerked around in the air . . . spinning, blood flying . . .

They fell like things that had never been alive, their rifles clattering. One of the men almost torn in half above the waist.

Torrence saw the grenade, with its pin gone, rolling on the ground nearby.

He leapt for a boulder as the grenade went off, felt a hardened slab of air smack him in the back, send him head over heels so he ended on his back with his head pointed back the way he'd come.

He lay there for a moment breathing hard, feeling that icy pinching in the back of his legs that said he'd been hit by grenade fragments. Hoping the flak hadn't severed tendons. He lay there, trying to sort out the sounds. A harsh rattle of a chopper's minigun (maybe cutting Claire to pieces: *Fuck, Torrence, don't think that*) and a dull thud, a whoosh, an explosion— that would be Claire and Danco's surface-to-air. *WHAM.*

He sat up, glimpsed a ball of fire tipping down into the rocks, vanishing in some fissure, huffing up blue smoke after itself . . . heard a ragged cheer . . .

They'd gotten one of the choppers.

Buoyed by elation, he got to his feet. He was dizzy, and his legs hurt like a bitch, but it didn't feel bad. He'd taken small fragments mostly in the meat of his thigh. It hurt when he walked, but . . .

But he hurried toward the rock Claire was on, heard the brittle *snap-snap* of rifle fire, saw Danco opening up on someone below, then ducking down from return fire. Judging from the down-slant of Danco's rifle a moment before, his target was close to the rock. Torrence circled the rock, heard two voices that sounded Dutch, maybe Boer—Afrikaans. The rock up ahead was shaped like the prow of a ship; the mazelike way between the rocks angled sharp right and left around that prow. He angled left, had to turn sideways to slip through the narrow passage. The rock's dull-knife edges against his tailbone, shoulder blades. And then he emerged into a wider corridor. It was brighter here and he blinked against the sudden sunlight as he turned the corner and saw two, no *three*, SA regulars just under thirty feet down the narrow rock corridor from him, hunched down, one of them fitting a grenade on a launching rifle, the other two slapping fresh clips into their magazines. *Shit*: Torrence realized he'd dazedly forgotten to reload. The magazine on the auto-shotgun now held only four or five rounds. It'd have to be enough—they'd spotted him; one was raising a rifle, shouting, "Hold it right there!" The others snapped their heads around to look, jerky with fright. Torrence and the one who'd spotted him opened up at the same time. But in a place like this, Torrence had the advantage. The assault rifle ricocheted its rounds off the rock just over Torrence's head, rock chips hissing away as Torrence squeezed out the rest of his magazine, the shotgun painfully loud in the enclosure, hurting his arm like a son of a bitch now.

He was too close—too close because he got a good look at their faces. Blue-eyed Dutch faces, rosy-cheeked, all three of them probably teenagers. Racists, yes; Fascists, yes; maybe even brainwashed robots in a sense. But they had faces that registered fear and hope and even a kind of wistfulness. And he had a split-second flash-card image of those faces as boys, three boys playing where they weren't supposed to be . . . caught by the adults and punished . . .

Dan Torrence closed his eyes against what his auto-shotgun did to those boyish, blue-eyed faces. One of them screamed. Kept screaming, one long, screaming tone, like someone continuously pressing down a car horn. Was still alive, screaming as Torrence opened his eyes and stepped over to him . . . the young soldier's red-splashed body, bubbling blood, mingled with the others in the narrow space . . . broken bodies crammed in one atop the other between broken, blood-dripping rock . . . the boy screaming because his face was gone and part of his head and most of the fingers on his left hand . . .

Torrence retched. Then took a deep breath, got control of his lurching stomach, and pulled the knife from his belt, bent, slashed through the boy's windpipe and jugular.

The knife was a little dull; took several seconds. Torrence trying to ignore the spongy feeling transmitted through the knife: flesh resisting, parting raggedly, making him remember cutting through the neck of a chicken on his uncle's farm as a boy.

He heard himself speak, was surprised to hear what he said—surprised by his own words: "I'm sorry, son. Just let go and it'll be all right. Go home to your ancestors!"

Stomach pirouetting, Torrence turned away. He wiped and sheathed the knife, and started to walk away from the dead . . . and stopped, looked at the auto-shotgun in his hand: *His rosy cheek torn from the bone of his jaw.*

Torrence tossed the shotgun aside.

He turned and went through the ordnance that had been dropped by the enemy dead. He selected an M-20 US Army assault rifle, automatic, and a pouch of ammunition. Then he went in search of communication with the living.

• • •

Many miles overhead, a satellite turned its cold eye on the maze of boulders, the stony ridges of the mountain, the patchwork snow and sere granite. Over the mountains to the west, other satellites watched the deserted shore as well as a picket of New-Soviet ships on the ruffled jade of the Atlantic Ocean. Scan the sea, league on league, mile on mile: When the reach of sea seemed infinite, finitude came as a shore, like a slap in the face. American shores, studded at regular intervals with new batteries of antiaircraft weapons, new radar installations, preparations for a New-Soviet invasion. (Moot preparations: if the invasion began, the Americans would launch a preemptive nuclear strike. The New-Soviets knew; so far they hadn't tried it.)

American satellites watched over the new Air Force installations, over receiving stations for the microwave power beamed from solar-collecting stations in orbit. Some of the satellites were controlled from the CIA installation at Langley. Around the installation rose fences, wire, cameras, checkpoints enclosing a series of nondescript government buildings with polarized windows.

Focus on one of those windows. A square of blueblack in synthetic stone. Beyond it sat a man named Stoner, alone but for the camera that watched him. He was hunched over a WorkCenter keyboard. Corte Stoner was both large and small; his upper half was large, with a thick chest, wide shoulders, and a well-padded middle; his legs were shorter than most, his hips seemed almost miniature. He had a pudding-bland face, except for his sharp blue eyes. His short brown hair was combed and brilliantined in strict imitation of an old photo he'd seen of Hank Williams. He wore jeans, a red plaid shirt made of real cloth, and a cream Western-style jacket.

But his mind was focused through his sharp blue eyes on the screen, sifting data. Finding in it events and observations that were like pottery shards to an archaeologist; he could fit them together, come up with a whole more than the sum of the parts. He could see the man hidden in the file.

It was Corte Stoner's job to turn the file and its data back into a man. To do that, he had to reconstitute the man in his own mind.

Just now he was studying the thin file on a man named Daniel Torrence. Called by his guerilla companions "Hard-Eyes."

The file had been provided to the CIA Domestic Branch by the Second Alliance International Security Corporation; the file's approval-of-transfer had been initialed by Sackville-West himself. Evidently the SA held Torrence in high regard as an enemy combatant.

Stoner sat back in his chair, felt a tingle of gratification as it readjusted its contours to his movement. He patted his shirt pocket for his cigarettes, thinking he might slip outside for a smoke break, and then remembered that his wife had taken the cigarettes that morning; had kissed him and taken them from his pocket at the same time. "You're giving them up, remember?" she said.

He smiled and sipped tepid ersatz coffee, to give his hands and mouth something to do. The war had interrupted coffee shipments; the Russkies at the Panama canal.

The file said that Torrence had been a college student at the outset of the war. An American, born in Rye, New York, he had lived most of his life just north of San Francisco, in Marin County. Upstate middle-class family. He'd gone to London to study political science. He seemed to be "doing it to have something to do," according to the dean at the New London School, in England. Some kind of exchange-student thing. He leaned toward Democratic Socialism but with "no particular zeal." When the war began, Gatwick air traffic was tied up, so Torrence tried to get out through Amsterdam, found himself stuck there instead. Became leader of a gang of scavengers ducking the worst of the war as it moved through the Netherlands, trying to survive day-to-day and "presumably waiting for transportation to the States." Recruited into the New Resistance by unknown persons, "probably in return for promises of food and eventual transportation home." Evidently Torrence became ideologically entangled. Became convinced that the NATO forces and the SA were in some kind of racist collusion, judging from the text of pamphlets the NR circulated (File Appendix 12, Sec. C & D).

Stoner shrugged.

So what was the big deal? The agency had given the NR a Focus One rating. That meant that all overseas experts and a significant number of Stateside personnel were to focus on the guerrillas. There were less than two thousand active guerrillas in France. Admittedly they'd significantly inconvenienced the so-called "peacekeeping" private army, the SA. But essentially they had to be some sort of bandit outfit, just another gang of scavengers feeding off the leavings of those two monstrous predators, the New-Soviet and NATO armies.

Why was CIA Domestic so involved in this? There weren't likely many NR agents in the United States. They were not known to sell information to the New-Soviets. They had performed no bombings, no robberies. They *had* been linked to two assassinations—one attempted and one successful. Rick and Ellen Mae Crandall. But the New Resistance had a sort of feud with the Second Alliance people—it wasn't really a matter of National Security. The SA was supposed to be an employee of the USA, and NATO—but not synonymous with its interests. Keep tabs on them, yes—but Focus One?

There was a war on, after all. Common sense dictated, from Stoner's viewpoint, that all available agency personnel focus on counterintelligence; on countering the New-Soviets. Sure, the SA was performing a useful service for NATO by keeping order behind its lines, discouraging saboteurs, helping stabilize logistics. But the CIA, it seemed to Stoner, was allotting too much manpower and too many man-hours to the concerns of the SA. The president herself had signed a Classified Executive Order adjuring them to "give all necessary aid to NATO's peacekeeping force."

And the file on Torrence had been stamped *PrS.—Priority Subject.* Stoner read:

Torrence quickly graduated from a complete outsider to become one of the top five operatives in the European NR. He has been directly involved in every major guerrilla action since his recruiting, and one eyewitness described him as "ruthless and a little crazy when he's leading an attack" (extractor ref. SA872) and "a leader, but also the guy is a dog at Steinfeld's heels" (ibid.). Subject believed to have engineered the capture of the Arc de Triomphe shortly before its Jægernaut demolition in SA Operation Cold Bear and the subsequent evacuation of Steinfeld and NR core from Paris.

This subject experienced a profound motivational shift, with subsequent radicalization, after Paris training. Computer personality analysis and projections foresee extensive militant political involvement and volatile potential for Movement Leadership. Long-term survival of subject Torrence is counter to the best interests of SAISC/CIA projects. Advise subject be terminated with extreme prejudice . . .

"Can't kill what you can't reach," Stoner murmured. He glanced over the text again and his eyes stopped on *the best interests of SAISC/CIA projects.* When had it become SAISC/CIA projects, in that order, with that sense of cohesion? There was an *Extractor Reference* in the file. Some captured NR had been "extracted" by SA operatives. The SA had access to extractors? That was news to him. And Operation Cold Bear—military nomenclature.

There was a Big Military slant to the SA, though they were supposed to be more like a private cop force with army methods. And the guerrillas claimed the Second Alliance was actively racist. It made Stoner nervous, because it made him wonder about Kupperbind.

Emmanual Kupperbind, CIA liaison to the Mossad. Kupperbind had submitted—unsolicited—a report on the "extra-contract activities" of the Second Alliance International Security Corporation in the Netherlands, Belgium, Italy, and France. He'd claimed the Second Alliance International Security Corporation itself was a security risk. He alleged "systematically racist activities" and "the implementation of a European apartheid" that would, among other things, inevitably alienate Israel, at a time when American intelligence was already in danger of losing access to Israeli intelligence—some of the best in the world.

Not only had Kupperbind not been taken seriously at the agency, he'd been recalled and put out to pasture. Retired four years early.

There was a rumor that Kupperbind's dismissal was entirely a function of agency politics: Pendleton, the Director, was said to have gotten his job partly through the influence of the SA's panel of international security "experts"; the panel advised the president, from time to time, on terrorism and saboteurs. Pendleton owed the SAISC favors, it was assumed.

Whatever, all copies of Kupperbind's report were gathered up and shredded.

All except one. Stoner had a copy. He hadn't read it in detail. He'd been busy, and the whole thing had smelled of eccentric alarmism.

But when the clerk had come around asking for the report, Stoner had made excuses. Told them it was locked up in one of his cabinets and it was a hassle to dig it out just now when he had so much work to do. He'd drop it off later that afternoon.

Only he never did drop it off. He wasn't sure why he'd never turned the report over. Ought to get rid of the damn thing.

But, after all, he was under assignment to study the so called New Resistance. The NR existed—so it said—to oppose the Second Alliance and "the conspiracy for which it is a façade." And any information on the Second Alliance could conceivably apply to his investigation of the NR. He could read Kupperbind's report. Skeptically. Perhaps pan a few small nuggets of useful information out of the silt of Kupperbind's paranoia.

He was startled by a buzzing from his console, almost jumped out of his chair.

Words flashed for his attention on the screen: *Incoming call, switch to one mode for receive.*

Stoner punched for One Mode. The file page on the screen compressed to a thin line; the line expanded to become something else entirely. A man's face. Unger.

The TV image of Unger smiled. Squat, almost jolly face, laugh lines around the eyes, always smiling when he first saw you, hail-fellow-well-met. Always wanted something. Stoner had never trusted Unger, but Unger was section chief, so Stoner smiled and said, "What can I do for you?"

"You could switch on visual so I can see if it's you or somebody doin' an impersonation!"

"Sorry." He tapped transmission tie-in with the webcam.

"There you are, by God! How's it hangin', Kimosabe?"

Stoner winced inwardly. Kimosabe. Where'd he get that stuff? Something to do with being playful about Stoner's "rodeo drag."

"Fine. Great."

"Good—well, hey, Kimosabe, we're just trying to get some loose ends tied up here, and we find, going over the checklist for Recalls, that you never turned in that File-178 Report-43 we asked for. Says here you promised to bring it in yourself."

Stoner felt a chill at the synchronicity of it. File-178 Report-43 was the Kupperbind report. Should have just done a scan on it. "Well, I'll look it up, see what I got. I don't know as I have it; they maybe forgot to check it off when I brought it in. I'll see."

Unger's video grin melted into something flat. "Say there, Kimosabe, we got a Focus One on the NR. That file concerns the NR; we need it in here right away. We're just anal about proceedure, when it comes to Focus One."

The file's more about the Second Alliance, Stoner thought. But he said, "If I've got it, you'll sure get it. Right away."

Unger nodded. Stoner hoped Unger was going to break the connection, but after a moment of silent two-dimensional staring, he said, "I wonder if we could take a quick meeting, say in the commissary in about an hour. We need to talk. Things are moving. Changes coming down. We need to know which side of the changes you stand on, Corte."

"Uh . . . I've got a lot of . . . "

"Seriously, Stoner. The commissary. One hour."

"Uh—okay. I'm there."

Unger broke the connection. Stoner thought: We need to talk?

•••

SOUTHEASTERN FRANCE.

Claire almost shot Torrence when he turned the corner. He saw her shudder, the color draining from her face. She lowered her rifle.

Claire and Danco were crouched in the frozen rubble between two sheer rock walls, under the boulder they'd used for surface-to-air launching. A curtain fringe of thin ice hung in little gray spears down the shadowed rock walls beside them. Both Claire and Danco were haggard; Claire was trembly with cold or fear. Torrence wanted to go to her, put his arms around her, but he thought she might resent being comforted in front of Danco, so he held back.

"Your shotgun," Danco said. "Damaged? It works no more?"

"It works too well," Torrence said. He looked up, hearing a fresh spate of gunfire. Unconsciously he'd turned so that his back was to the rock, Claire and Danco on the left, a view down the crooked corridor of chill stone to his right.

Movement down there. Hard to make out clearly in the shadow what it was. But in that direction . . .

"Here they come," he muttered.

Danco's walkie-talkie was nattering at him. He pressed it to his ear, frowning, then nodded. "Okay. *Sí.*" He put the walkie-talkie back on his belt and told them, "We regroup around the cave. The SA, they are pressing. They are coming in to finish us."

• • •

A cold, weary late afternoon. The sunlight streaking pale between the megalithic stones imparted no warmth. About twenty guerrillas were posted at the openings between the rocks, and in the approaches to the cave from the sides. Two more NR—Sahid and the fatalistic Sortonne— crouched in the crater atop the square boulder, a little bit in advance of the main group; Sortonne with a rocket launcher, Fahid beside him to help reload.

It was quiet. The enemy had moved into position, probably deploying seeker missiles, maybe light artillery.

Steinfeld's command group squatted on its haunches, mouths and nostrils trailing steam as they talked, hands tucked in their armpits for warmth.

Steinfeld saying, " . . . the extractor makes it that way. The only course we can take from here. We hit them with everything, we force their hand . . . "

Steinfeld hesitated, his mask of calm slipping. It hurt Torrence to see it. He relied on Steinfeld's courage, his seeming indefatigability. But being cornered one too many times had worn Steinfeld down.

Steinfeld looked at the ground, and when he looked up at them again, his gaze was broken. He couldn't look directly at any of them. He said, "I must insist that you kill me the moment the line breaks. Be sure to shoot

me in the head, several times. A shot to the body won't necessarily . . . "
He cleared his throat.

Levassier turned away, cursing in French.

Torrence felt leaden. Like he'd never get warm again. They'd patched
him up, but he was suffering from blood loss, dizzy when he moved too
quickly. It didn't matter, obviously. He looked up toward the line at the
edge of the amphitheater area around the cave mouth—a woman there, an
NR Guerilla, toppled over backward. They heard the distorted crack of the
gunshot a half second later, echoing *shuh-shuh-shuh* through the twisted
corridors of rock. The woman lay on her back, staring sightlessly, a bullet
hole in her forehead. It was Angeline, someone he scarcely knew. Steinfeld
was bellowing orders, and Torrence automatically went into position with
the others. Claire came up beside him, with the black woman, Lila, and
they crouched behind a block of stone the size and shape of an overturned
credit-transfer booth.

Ahead, the crooked corridors of rock were sunk in shadow; dark,
hunched figures shifted there. Lila said, "We cannot see them. Their
uniforms are colored like the rock." She took a flare gun from a pack lying
on the ground beside her, dropped a shell in it, fired it; the shell arced
up, down, and splashed the gray dimness with sparks and the blue-white
dazzle of burning magnesium. Someone screamed, and even Claire smiled
at that. *Burn, you bastard, because you're going to kill me.*

And then they saw something else in the light of the flare.

Torrence remembered snorkeling once, off the coast of Florida, seeing a
shark nosing slowly toward him among the coral formations. That's what
this thing looked like, from here. The shark in the undersea maze had
swum past, ignoring him. This one wouldn't do that.

It was a seeker missile, moving slowly—not much more than hovering
in place, just drifting forward as it picked out a target—held up by jets
on its underside, its tail rocket dormant, waiting for the missile's micro
computer to make a decision, wavering in and out of the flare light behind
it. The self guided drone was a sleek thing of shiny chrome, a sensing grid
on its nose looking for heat in human-body outline. Nosing this way, that.
Why was it taking so long?

Maybe it was confused by the still flickering flare, reflected from the
cold rocks. Soon it'd pick out the heat from a group of people, though, and
it'd find its way—

One moment the self-guided missile was drifting in and out of shadow,
almost absently; a split second later, rattlesnake flash, it struck, impacting
with the top forward edge of the cratered boulder where Sortonne and
Sahid had been . . . Had been.

Torn outlines of the two men were flung from the fireball; dolls from which some sadistic kid had torn the hands and heads. Warm droplets spattered Torrence's cheek. Chunks of rock flew from the blast, and a small boulder smacked meatily down onto Levassier's shoulder—smashed down himself now, shoulder crushed, upper arm nearly mangled away, hanging by shreds. Steinfeld was running to him, removing his belt for a tourniquet. Torrence felt blood—Sortonne's? Sahid's?—running down his cheek toward his mouth. He smeared it away with the back of his hand so he wouldn't have to taste the blood of other NR. Blood already cold to touch.

Shouts of outrage from his fellows; someone sobbing; spastic volleys of gunfire; two more on the line fell back, one gut-shot, shit from his ruptured intestines adding its ugly tang to the iron taste of blood in the air and the scratchy tang of gun smoke; the writhing as a rift through his neck pumped out his life. There was no helping him without too much risk, they had to ignore his frantic hand signals—*Help me!*

Try not to see him, look down the sights of your gun . . .

"Don't shoot without a clear target!" Steinfeld yelled.

NR firing slowed and stopped. Echoes and then quiet. Torrence looked for the enemy and saw no one . . .

Motion. Gleaming metal motion. Another seeker. The sight freezing his bowels as it nosed into a band of wan sunlight, sniffing for group heat.

Torrence squeezed off a three-shot burst at the seeker, hoping to detonate it while it was still a hundred yards away. Glimpsed sparks as the rounds ricocheted from stone. Anyway, it was well armored, you'd have to hit it precisely, squarely, in the nose, almost impossible at this range. Try again—no, wait!

Claire had taken something from Lila, was up and running ahead of them, toward the missile.

"Claire!" Torrence heard himself shout.

She was bending beside Sortonne's body, lifting it up, her hands under its armpits, her face twisted. What the fuck was she doing? Recovering bodies? *Now?*

The seeker missile was drifting closer, its tail rocket beginning to show flame as it picked out a target. Any second it would lance out, blow two or three or five of them to shreds.

Claire had set up Sortonne's body so it leaned on a boulder. She fired the flare gun into it and turned to run.

The body's chest erupted with the burning flare.

The missile sensed the flare heat, saw the body outline; the heat more than enough for a group. It streaked to the decoy, exploding it along with bits of boulder. Still running, Claire stumbled, caught in the shockwave or by shrapnel, fell flat, skidding. Torrence shouted something and vaulted over the boulder, ran to her, picked her up in his arms . . . she was heavier than she should have been; his legs were wobbly. He felt a stickiness on the back of his legs; he'd started bleeding again. Someone, maybe Steinfeld, was shouting to him to let her lay and get under cover. But he staggered back to the low boulder with her, the others laying down suppressive fire to give him cover.

He laid her on her back behind the stone. Bullets ripped the air overhead. His ears ached from the gunfire noise of the guerrillas, just to his left. Claire's eyes were open, moving. Alive. But registering nothing.

A tympanic roll announced the tons of killing machine suddenly blocking out the sky overhead, a machine giant's voice booming shakily through the thudding. copter blades, *"If you surrender, you will not be killed. If you surrender . . . "* The words were shattered by light machine-gun fire as someone opened up at the copter; it returned fire with its miniguns, and the machinegunner screamed. All the time Torrence was looking at Claire's face. Was she hit? Internal bleeding?

"Claire?"

Danco and Lila were shouting something at him. "More choppers!" someone yelled, and something more in French. He looked up and saw a group of large brown choppers moving in, guns alongside firing. Red stars on the helicopter's doors. New-Soviet choppers. The New-Soviets were involved now. Why? He didn't really care.

His eyes stung from dust in the rotor backwash. "Claire . . . ?"

A shell burst threw bushels of the stony ground into the air somewhere behind him and slapped him down with the hot ripple of its blast, sending a single sharp ringing tone through his head as he fell sprawling across Claire. *Am I hit? Is she hit?*

"Claire?"

After a moment Torrence realized he was lying facedown across her, his body making an X with hers. And he was holding his breath. He let it out, becoming aware of a whirlwind of noise and motion, of people running nearby, fire chattering in their hands. It seemed to him that it was all mixed up now; it wasn't the enemy over there, NR here—the enemy had overrun them, were all around; the NR was there, too, emerging and sinking in smoke. He saw two SA regulars running up the slope toward him. He rolled off Claire to his rifle, rolled into prone sniper's position, popping the gun into the hollow of his shoulder, firing instantly, and one of the SA fell. The other one was still coming, pointing a submachine gun right at Torrence. Any second he'd feel the slugs. But the submachiner seemed to gush fire and he fell, writhing in flame, shrieking . . . somebody'd hit the guy with an incendiary grenade . . . after a moment the soldier lay still, facedown, quietly burning. But the New-Soviet choppers were looming like great golden dragons overhead as they descended, rotors whipping the smoke.

"Dan?" Claire's voice. "Let's get up, let's get under cover." Sounding weak. But she was all right.

But . . . *Fuck, the New-Soviets are going to take us, Torrence thought. Fuck that. They'll torture Claire and then they'll execute us. That's what they do. Wring you for information and kill you for convenience. I got to kill her myself. Save her from torture.*

Rifle in hands, he got to his knees beside her. She was turned on her side, away from him, starting to get up.

He pointed his rifle's muzzle at her head. *So they don't torture her.*

He pulled the trigger.

Nothing.

No ammunition.

He tossed the rifle aside, looked around for another gun.

And then Steinfeld was kneeling beside him, pulling him up.

"Got to kill her before they . . . " Torrence said. Or tried to say, he wasn't sure which. He felt like he was made of soggy cardboard. His lips didn't want to work; his tongue felt thick. He managed, "They'll take her . . . "

The choppers were settling down in an open space just ahead of him. The SA had taken cover, driven back by cannon blasts from the New-Soviets.

Steinfeld said, "They're not Russians. That's cover. Kind of camouflage. That's the Mossad. They got transmission. They've come to get us out."

Torrence must have lost consciousness for a while. But not more than a few minutes. Because when the fuzziness around him resolved, he saw he was inside a helicopter, hearing Steinfeld say, "They've gone into the cave. They sent in ten regulars, it looks like . . . I doubt they send in any more. Go ahead, Danco."

Torrence heard Danco chuckle as he reached for the remote-control detonator.

Torrence found himself wanting to say, *Don't trigger the detonator. Don't kill them. I know what they are. I know they're enemy, I know they killed my friends, I know they're some kind of Nazi and I know what that means, but it's enough, it's too much now, so let them go, just let them go, please let them go, it's all too fucking much . . .*

Torrence was distantly aware that there was a field IV plugged into his arm, a Mossad medic kneeling beside him holding up a plastic bottle of plasma, Claire sitting up across from him, her leg bandaged, staring into space, but she was alive, Lord, she was alive . . .

He heard Danco laughing. "Hey, *pendejos, vaya con Dios!*" as he threw the switch on the detonator. And the cave blew, taking ten SA with it.

Torrence thought: *I'm glad they're dead. I have to be glad of it or nothing means anything and everything I've done and everything that happened—all of it was meaningless. Accept it. They needed to die.*

He felt the acceptance lock into place in him; he turned away from the thought that just a little more of his humanity might've gone when the acceptance came.

Ten more of the enemy were dead. That was all.

He smiled and went back to sleep.

• 03 •

LYONS, FRANCE.

Jean-Michel Karakos stood at the window looking at the prisoners in the detention pens below. On either side of him stood the pale Dr. Cooper and the pink Colonel Watson. Behind Karakos loomed an enormous Second Alliance guard—the man must have been close to seven feet tall. Karakos could feel the man back there, hulking over him.

Karakos's hands were cuffed together, and the cuffs were locked to a chain around his waist.

Karakos, Watson, and Cooper were looking through the polarized window at a nightmare concocted with the simpleminded efficiency of a high-school science fair project.

Cooper was about forty, Karakos guessed, though it was hard to tell with an albino. He was stooped, potbellied; he had one pink eye and one blue eye, hair that looked like mold, and an unsettling waxiness to his skin. It looked as glossy as a balloon. He wore a blue lab smock over a tweed suit.

"It's an interesting experiment," Watson was telling him. "It was Cooper's brainchild." Watson was a tall, thick-bodied Englishman in his early fifties, with a round, weathered face, a brickish complexion, and poker-chip blue eyes. He wore a black-and-silver Second Alliance officer's uniform but stood in a kind of boyish slouch, as if to defuse the harsh punctilio implied by the regalia. He was the Chief of Tactics, a title that encompassed a great many public and private responsibilities. Some said he was the number-two man in the Second Alliance.

"Oh, well," Cooper said with a modesty that was clearly insincere, "the experiment is actually an old sociobiological concept—we're merely bringing it to life."

"You are a sociobiologist, then?" Karakos asked, as if he were a magazine interviewer and not a prisoner.

"A sociobiologist? No, we're beyond that here." They were standing at the second-story polarized window that looked out over detention pens ten, eleven, and twelve. Karakos didn't know where he was; he'd been brought here in the back of a big windowless truck, packed in with seventy others. The trip had taken only half an hour—he was sure only that he was still in France. The building was big, drafty, echoey, built of a dull white alloy that looked like plastic, but was in fact alumitech.

Watson had the air of a proud man of property giving a friend the tour, telling Karakos they'd put the place together from its component parts in two weeks, once the foundations were sunk. There were fifteen "pens," most of them not visible from here; pens ten and eleven were side by side under the window; pen twelve was as big as ten and eleven together and ran alongside them to the right. Each pen was separated from the others by two chain-link fences, and each fence's crown of thorns was concertina wire. Between the two fences was a five-foot concrete path patrolled by helmeted SA guards.

Karakos was deceptively brutish-looking. He was stocky, brown-eyed—his eyes were sunken now, from poor diet. He had thick lips, a wide mouth full of widely spaced teeth from which the gums were beginning to recede; oily, stringy brown hair; and eyebrows that grew together. He wore a detainee's polyplas bright orange overalls—for maximum visibility in case of escape—and a yellowed T-shirt. He had ten days' growth of coarse brown beard, and in the months he had been in detention, he had been so long without a bath that he could no longer smell anything but himself. He was not an elegant figure. But as Watson had written in his Extraction Experiment 5F evaluation for Sackville-West, *"Karakos was one of the NR's most effective propagandists. His scathing attacks on the SA (for the banned newspaper* Égalité*) were noteworthy for their eloquence and sheer panache, and it is said he worked closely with Steinfeld planning the NR's first field campaigns."*

"No," Cooper was saying, "I'm not a sociobiologist. We left that behind years ago." Tight, smug smile. "I'm a social geneticist."

Karakos noted Watson's reaction, an arch look that Cooper interpreted as humorous acknowledgment, but which probably signified Watson's barely contained contempt for the albino. Cooper was, after all, a genetic aberration himself. But he was useful to the SA.

Was there a way to drive a wedge between the two men? Karakos wondered.

You're grasping at straws, he told himself.

But Karakos; had the habit of hope. It was a survival skill, for the "detainees." A monstrously false term, *detainees*. As if it was only temporary. As if they'd ever go free.

"As you can see, Jean-Michel," Watson began, "the detainees in the three pens are divided, roughly, into three skin-color groups." Watson's manner, talking to Karakos, was amiable, respectful, with a touch of the paternal. Just as if he wasn't a prisoner wearing handcuffs and guarded by a giant professional thug in a mirrorglass helmet. Watson went on, "And, in fact, each of the three pens is on a different dietary regimen. The black-skinned group in number ten are fed rather well and given a number of privileges, such as cigarettes, the others don't receive. The brown-skinned group in eleven is on an average diet, with average privileges. The lighter-skinned coloreds—half-breeds, essentially—in pen twelve are being nearly starved. Dr. Cooper's theory holds that interracial mistrust is *instinctive*, but that instinct is often dormant until survival-stress factors are significantly increased. You'll note the subjects are in most cases imprisoned, in this experiment, with their families, in order to tap into their protective instincts. Each penned group has been informed that fighting is to be severely punished—the equivalent of the civilizing social inhibitions that check violence in urban settings—but Dr. Cooper believes that given a sufficient increase in survival-stress factors, all such restraints will be overwhelmed and aggression will take place."

"People who starve get angry, yes," Karakos said. "And they'll strike out against whoever's around. Race has nothing to do with it."

"We have another group, on the other side of Control, in pens thirteen, fourteen, and fifteen," Cooper said, in an oozily patronizing tone. "In those pens the races are mixed: light-skinned side by side with black and so forth—and we find that they do not respond to survival factors nearly so uniformly as those who are incarcerated with their own race."

"Even if it's true," Karakos said, shrugging, "it doesn't prove anything about the superiority or inferiority of races involved."

"We have other experiments . . . " Cooper began a little angrily.

But Watson cut him off with an incisive hand motion. "It's of no real relevance in the long run, which race, if any, is the superior. First you must understand that this experiment is laying the groundwork for experiments on a larger scale in the outside world. We can induce race war with the right social pressures applied . . . "

"*Colonel . . . *" Cooper said warningly.

A flicker of satisfaction showed on Watson's face. *He's using me to bait Cooper,* Karakos thought.

Watson went on blithely. "The question of race superiority is only of academic interest—to me, at any rate. What matters is that races are inherently programmed to be in conflict with one another, under any sort of real stress—and the only true path to world peace is to see to it that the conflict is resolved by carrying it to its logical conclusion; its final solution . . . "

Karakos shook his head in disbelief. "I always assumed that you wanted to, ah . . . "

"To enslave?" Watson smiled. "Or perhaps merely to exploit the other races?" He chuckled. "It's no longer practical. There's too much uncontrolled information polluting their cultural integrity, poisoning them with discontent and ambition. No, in the long run the only real solution is genocide. *Many* genocides. Oh, for now we need the lesser races for economic reasons. But we're already at work breeding a sub-race of workers who'll be quite incapable of challenging us. We call them 'subjugate breeds.' The subjugates won't be human at all, you see. No smarter than dogs or horses, but they'll be idiots savants when it comes to carrying out whatever low work need be done—technicki work, grunt work."

Cooper was fuming. Even the silent SA guard behind Karakos was shifting restlessly. In a carefully flat tone Cooper said, "Colonel, you have a tendency to enjoy the sound of your own discourse to the detriment of security . . . " Watson silenced Cooper with a look. It wasn't a hard look, particularly. Once more, it was incisive. "When I speak to Karakos, I'm speaking to a blackboard."

Karakos knew what he meant. He meant the extractor. He meant he would be *erased*.

They'd already put him under the extractor once, for interrogation purposes. But they hadn't gotten anything useful: The resistance had shifted its headquarters since he'd been imprisoned. All the partisans he'd known about had long since fled France. He had no idea where Steinfeld and the others were now.

But next time the SA would erase him, would take not only his personality, his convictions, but also everything he knew that might be useful to the Resistance. And now he knew something that could make all the difference. If the rest of the world could be told . . .

Karakos felt sick with responsibility. He had to get word out somehow. Because Watson was not insane. He was probably a sociopath, yes, but not truly insane. It seemed impractical: a plan to exterminate every race on Earth but the Caucasian—and the Caucasian's special "subjugate breeds." Wildly impractical.

But maybe not. The Second Alliance's New Life Lab was known to be involved in genetic engineering of microorganisms. And during the Middle Ages a single strain of microorganism, the bubonic plague, wiped out something from one third to one half of the population of the world. Indiscriminately, of course. But suppose someone engineered a discriminatory virus or bacterium? Some had claimed that the CIA, in the twentieth century, had come close to developing a germ that killed only Slavic races . . . like the New-Soviets. But the project had been canceled as impractical because too many Americans had Slavic blood.

But suppose the SA developed genes that were more selective. That killed only the black race, the Jewish race, the Chinese.

"But what would you do about the New-Soviets?" Karakos asked.

"The New-Soviets will lose the war," Watson said. "We'll absorb them. Racially they're close enough to us that . . . "

"Colonel Watson," Cooper interjected, student now, "suppose something were to go wrong—an attack on this building, say—and this man were by chance to go free? He—"

"He'll be taken care of very soon, I assure you, Cooper," Watson said sharply. Losing patience. Dropping Cooper's *doctor* honorific.

Karakos thought, *They're off-balance with conflict now. Try it.* "I understand your multiple genocide is even now being cooked up in the New Life Labs." Deadpan. Trying to sound as if he knew it to be true.

Watson and Cooper were staring at him. Watson had gone almost as white as Cooper. He began, "We extracted you, you had nothing about . . . " But then he snorted and shook his head ruefully. "You are playing a little game with me." His bluegray eyes had seemed watery; the water turned to ice now, as he stared at Karakos. He'd been wheedled into an admission. He'd been manipulated, and it was as if Karakos had spat a wad of phlegm onto Watson's ego. Watson went on. "You shouldn't play at such things, you know. I have you, you see. I *own* you now. I can do as I like with you. And I really don't think you've quite considered the implications of that."

Karakos's stomach lurched.

"I brought you here," Watson said, "to prepare the ground for you in some way. Or to prepare the ground *in* you. The extractor will change you, yes. We will erase you, rebuild you from the ground up—but simply chemically installing a new mind-set in a man doesn't seem adequate to me. I felt you needed to be prepared. I feel that somewhere in you there's a seed of genetic purity that resonates with the beauty of what's happening here—a beauty that emerges from truth."

"You're preparing me . . . mystically?"

"Spiritually, perhaps." Some of the edge had left Watson. "I . . . always felt you were rather wasted on the other side. I suppose I wanted to try to convert you the ordinary way first." He shrugged. "Strange impulses arise in one from time to time." He looked down at the pens. "Ah. The fourth stage. Have a look, Karakos."

Karakos forced himself to look. Till now, afraid of his own anger, he'd tried not to look at the pens too closely. Now, he saw the prisoners squatting in groups, held nearly motionless by the weight of misery. Saw that the privileged detainees had clothing; the others were humiliated by being kept naked and shivering with cold. Saw them huddled for warmth and rocking on their heels, mothers clasping listless infants. Some of the younger men seemed to have gone into the gray blankness of simple despair; others were looking around with a maddening repetitiveness: Look first this way, see the fence, the locked gate, the guards, the wire; look *that* way, see another fence, wire, guards; look another way, see the wall, the opaque window behind which they knew more of their captors watched them; turn, look behind, and see the fence, the guards, the walls. Start over again: see the fence, the locked gate, the guards, the wire . . . No matter how many times you looked, it was still the same.

Even from here, Karakos could see the marks of malnutrition on the unprivileged prisoners; the distended bellies, the sores, the dullness in their faces. But all of them, from time to time, glared sullenly at the other pens.

The gate opened, four SA guards strolled into the non-privileged pens, picked out prisoners at random, and began to beat them. "And, of course," Karakos said, his voice just a croak now, "those in the privileged pens are not usually beaten."

The prisoners were cringing, running, clawing at one another to get out of the way as the guards swung cattle prods and Recoil Reversal sticks.

"You begin to see," Cooper remarked, "how very animalistic the prisoners are. They revert so easily."

"Animalistic?" Karakos could not believe it. He fought himself, feeling the dull throb of hatred inflame and squirt searing bile in him. He wanted to lunge at Cooper.

But he didn't move. It was as if he stood balanced on the tip of a flagpole. He didn't dare to move. He simply stood at the window, trembling, sweat running into his eyes, as Cooper spoke into a microphone, ordering the guards; and as the guards opened the gates between the pens.

As pens eleven and twelve were opened onto number ten.

The guards withdrew from the area. None could be seen from the pens.

Slowly the larger group, made up of the prisoners in eleven and twelve, began to move toward the frightened, huddled blacks in ten.

It began gradually. But in ten minutes the fighting had begun, and in fifteen minutes four, perhaps five, of the blacks had been beaten to death by the prisoners from the other cages.

Karakos was choking, gagging. Not with squeamishness—he was beyond that—but with undirected rage at the way these people had been shorn of their humanity, twisted into new shapes; all the hunched shapes of brutality.

"I think we have room forty-four set up for Jean-Michel, don't we?" Watson said, speaking into a fone he'd taken from his belt. "Good."

I have to make them kill me, Karakos thought. Or they're going to use me and I'll be part of this.

This—the men tearing other men to pieces below. And women. And children.

He could no longer contain himself. He slipped from the flagpole, turned toward the guard, and, forgetting his cuffs, tried to raise his fists against the man and screamed in frustration when the shackles restrained him—and something bit him on the arm. He looked, saw that Cooper had given him an injection. He had time to think, *They're going to use me.* And to feel the horror that followed on that thought, before all thinking was eclipsed and the darkness was complete.

• • •

WASHINGTON, D.C.

"So what did Unger say?" Howie asked.

Stoner shrugged. "Not much—just something ambiguous about how things are 'hopping' and 'we're all gonna have to watch our step, you read me, Kimosabe?'"

Howie laughed.

The two CIA career men were in a bar in Washington, D.C., on Connecticut Avenue. It was not a fashionable bar. It had a twentieth century jukebox, its music the umpteenth reissue of Patsy Cline or George Jones, twentieth-century country music instead of Minimono or chaotics or ska-thud or angst rock. The floor was wood instead of concrete or plastipress, and it sagged in places with age. The bar stools weren't confoam; they were torn, taped-up vinyl. There was a mirror behind the bar instead of a vidflasher.

Howie and Stoner were sitting in a scarred wooden booth drinking Lone Star beer, imported from Texas, and talking shop. They were almost the only people in the bar, except for a barfly on a stool at the far end talking to the bleached blond barmaid, and a snoring fat man four booths away. It was eight p.m., and Stoner was tired from work—but at the same time he was wired on a nagging anxiety that never quite articulated itself.

Howie was a barrel-chested black man of fifty, wearing halfglasses and four gold rings on his left hand. An enormous white cowboy hat was tilted back on his head—he'd worn it as a joke, because Stoner was a country-music fan. Howie's right eye was electronic, an implant; it moved a little differently than the other, but it was fairly realistic. They'd even traced fake veins on the corner of the white. When you looked at the iris closely, you could see the overlapping sections of its shutter closing.

"Unger came into AD this morning," Howie said. Once a field agent, Howie now worked in the CIA Domestic's Accounting and Disbursements office. "Said he had a special project needed funding and the director was unavailable, could he talk to our supervisor? What the hell, he thinks Fench is going to give him money without top-off approval? Man's crazy." There was something more than office-gossipy derision in Howie's voice; something personal, even sullen.

"All he wanted from me—in a material way—was the Kupperbind file," Stoner said, watching Howie's face.

"Was that all." Flat like that. No question mark.

"And he mentioned you."

Howie had been staring at a moth-eaten elk's head over the bar. Now his eyes jerked back to focus on Stoner; the artificial one took a micro-moment longer to line up with the other.

"How's that implanted eye treating you, Howie?"

"Okay. I had some ghost-image problems with it. It picked up some TV station, I was seeing football players running through my office. And one of those AntiViolence executions, some guy getting his head blown open in front of a studio audience . . . I saw that while I was in the fucking cafeteria trying to eat my dinner. Blew away my appetite. Had to get my eye reinsulated. What'd Unger say about me, goddammit?"

"He said he heard you were a good buddy of mine. I said yeah. He said, 'Alignment is everything, Stoner.' I said, 'Huh?' and he said, 'You should be careful who you pick to be your friends, Kimosabe. Pick people who're on their way up.'" Stoner waited for Howie's reaction. Howie just sat there, looking leaden, motionless, staring at his beer bottle. "What is it with you and him, Howie? What the hell was he talking about?"

"He was talking about the new Hiring Assessment Program, man. They make it sound nice with a name like that. Whitewash it." He smiled bitterly at some private joke.

"Go on."

Howie shook his head. "He's an asshole, but he gave you good advice. You don't want to know any more about it."

"Yeah, I do. Come on, man. We known each other for a while. Hell, I married your niece, Howie. Come on."

Howie sighed. "Okay. You asked for it. You're going to think it's paranoid bullshit, though. You ever wonder why I'm in AD now, after eighteen years in the field?"

"Sure, I wondered." With a little embarrassment, because he'd assumed Howie had fucked up in some major way.

"Let me tell you something, I wondered too. I got twelve Special Commendations, I figured that was enough. I applied for desk work, figured something supervisory in Langley. Department Chief. Wanted to settle back with my family. So they transferred me, all right—to the fucking accounting department. Man, I got seniority, experience, training, education, and know-how over every fucking one of my five immediate superiors. You know? I got my masters in psych, I got . . . " He broke off, swiped at an imaginary fly. "They don't care about any of it. They said the Assessment Program evaluated me as being best suited for accounting. So I looked into this Assessment Program. It's supposed to be based on a new 'personnel efficiency study.' Only there never was any such study. It just doesn't exist. The whole thing was cooked up by Unger and the director, and so far it's only been applied to blacks, Hispanics, Orientals, Jews, and anyone who's even politically moderate. Nobody else."

Stoner stared at him and shook his head in disbelief. "You're saying they're using this Assessment Program for racial discrimination? To 'keep the niggers down?' Howie—this is the twenty-first century. Even the CIA has to worry about race-discrimination suits . . . "

"Do they? All that's going to be quietly scotched by Congress, after . . . Well, the HAP program is just for starters. When they can, they fire blacks. Or . . . well, remember Winston Post?"

"Tall guy, used to be a basketball player, worked in personnel?"

"Yeah. It was him who first found out that this 'efficiency study' was bogus. He started complaining, talking lawsuits. Where is he now?"

"Come on—it was a car accident, man, brakes went out, that could happen to anyone."

"Sure happened at a convenient time. And that was a brand new car the brakes went out on. Eight hundred miles on it. His wife tells me she called an ambulance, but it didn't come for almost an hour and a half. She asked them how come they took so long and they said some plainclothes cops pulled them over and hassled them. And Winston bled to death in the wreck."

"Jesus. That sounds like . . . "

"Yeah. But don't say you heard it here. I'm retiring as soon as I can. I'm getting out, man."

"Maybe I ought to get out too."

"What for? If Unger bothered to warn you, means he wants you to change sides. They've decided you're valuable. You got that famous memory of yours, that talent for data search. And you're not exactly a liberal. They know you got a bug up your ass about Communism."

"Christ, the New-Soviets are blockading the Atlantic ports, fighting over the Panama canal, blockading the Space Colony, and they fucking invaded half of Europe, and you're telling me I got *a bug up my ass* about 'em?"

"Anyway, you and Unger are in the same camp that way—he hates the Reds too and anyone they can call 'socialist.' So they want you solidly with them when they purge the Agency. And when they purge the rest of the government, and maybe the whole fucking country . . . "

"Hey—now you're getting paranoid."

"Right. Sure. But you know who's behind this Assessment Program? Our friends in the Second Alliance. The SA. Post saw the memo—it was on their recommendation. Who you know that's more racist than the SA, man, huh? You read that Kupperbind file. And where's Kupperbind now? Let me tell you something, Stoner . . . these bastards have just begun. Before they're through, it's going to be a white, white world, my friend . . . "

• • •

THE ISLAND OF MALTA.

"We can't really be alone," Steinfeld said. "But sometimes it feels as if we are."

Torrence nodded.

They were in a villa on the island of Malta, in the Mediterranean Sea. A little chill was creeping into the evening air, but compared to the Alps, it was almost balmy here. Deep winter in Malta was like early fall in New York.

The villa was a Mossad safe house. It was high and narrow, an anomaly in the landscape. Nothing but trees and scrub and boulders around it for ten acres square. The villa's designers could have sprawled it out comfortably, like many Mediterranean country houses. But they'd chosen the gaunt effusion of an Italian town house. It was three narrow stories, with a balcony on each of the upper stories; the top balcony faced north, the lower faced east. There was a ten-foot brick wall around the property, topped with barbed wire. Cameras and infrared detection devices were snugged discreetly in the trees. It was perfect for the Mossad's purposes: It commanded a view of the fields and olive orchards beyond its grounds; it could be defended from the balconies in two directions, and the wall would help ensure privacy. To the east, beyond an olive orchard, was the sea. To the south, forty yards behind the house, was the barn, actually a hangar, just big enough for a chopper with its switch-back blades secured.

Steinfeld, Torrence, Claire, Danco, and an Englishman named Chiswell were sitting around the old wooden table in the gray stone kitchen. Chiswell was a tall, basset-faced man with wispy brown hair and a melancholy intensity.

Torrence shifted in his seat, wincing, feeling the bandages rasp on his wounds. He sat on pillows, because the Mossad medic had dug some fragments from his buttocks.

They were into their third cup of coffee after dinner. They were cleaned up, in fresh clothing, and well-fed, and in safe, warm surroundings—and they all felt like hell.

The light was fading, the room darkening visibly minute by minute. No one felt like getting up to turn on the light. Their faces were increasingly veiled by deepening shadow.

Steinfeld sat across from Torrence, hunched over the table, an empty pewter coffee cup between his hands. He turned it back and forth in his palms like a potter. "What we've got is this: about four hundred troops coming from France, Italy, Holland, Switzerland. Solely NR. And we're in touch with the alignments: the Communist party of France, the Italian Leninists, a cadre of anarchists . . . all of them have gone underground, so it's hard to say how many they number, and harder still to work steadily with them. But we're in touch. The Communists, especially, are doing some very good organizing." He sounded distant, almost mournful.

Claire sounded even more distant when, her voice almost too faint to hear, she asked, "Isn't it . . . unwise to bring everyone here? We'll all be one target, then." Torrence looked at her, wondering again if she'd been through too much. She was wearing a gray, much zippered pilot's jumpsuit the Israelis had given her. As she spoke, she sat with her hands folded in her lap, looking out the window at the tangerine smear of sunset.

Steinfeld said, "Yes, it's a risk for us all to regroup in one place. But the Fascists have made it impractical for us to work the way we worked before, at least for now. They've got complete military control of France, Belgium, Holland, Germany, Spain, Portugal, Austria, Northern Italy, and Greece. They're consolidating control in six more countries, including England. Legally speaking, their control is supposed to be temporary, and it's supposed to be only in terms of law enforcement, but in most places they've succeeded in placing their puppets in administrative positions. They've got a lot of grass-roots support from the white, native Europeans because the SA does tend to bring order to chaos, wherever they appear, things do become orderly, and where there are still rails intact . . . "

He didn't have to say it: the trains run on time.

Steinfeld went on. "And, of course, the white Christians see them isolating the Algerians and the other blacks and immigrants in assigned ghettos, arresting anyone black or Arab or Jewish who so much as sneezes. And the white Christians who are prejudiced respond favorably when they see that. And even the ones who were formerly liberal . . . " He shrugged. "Jack Smoke once said that social chaos has a way of making conservatives. When there is privation, famine, constant danger, some low instinct seems to make people suspicious of strangers, or of anyone at all different. Open minds will slam shut . . . " He paused to sigh. The darkness thickened in the room. "There are only a few courses open to us. We can run to the States and work there to try to awaken the public to what's going on over here. The SA's American people are manipulating the news, censoring things without seeming to. Here, they don't permit journalists to accompany NATO troops in Europe. People in America don't know what's happening here. But Smoke and Witcher and their team are working on changing that already, and if we leave Europe, the continent's only resistance core will be gone."

• • •

By insisting on keeping all political activity out of the NR—except, of course, for its primary mandate—Steinfeld had made the New Resistance a resource available to Communists, capitalists, anarchists, republicist conservatives, liberals; all flavors of those persuasions, as long as they were opposed to the Second Alliance. New NR recruits sometimes joined on their own; others might be assigned by the Socialist Workers Party, or the Libertarian Party—but all were required to take a mortally serious vow that clearly stated they would put all political disagreements with other Resistance fighters aside, giving first priority to the struggle with the New Fascism. Steinfeld's organization supplied the sundry Communist and anarchist resistance cadres with money, weapons, and sometimes hiding places; in return, the cadres provided intel, safe houses for traveling NR actives, and sometimes military reinforcement. They coordinated their sabotage efforts, and together managed to keep the SA off-balance.

Occasionally there were polite ideological arguments in the NR ranks. Some of the republicists muttered about the danger of giving Communists resources that would help them survive so they'd be around after it was all over.

But Steinfeld had said, "There will always be Communists. I'm against all dictatorships—even dictatorships of the proletariat. But we have to learn to live with Communists."

At such times Levassier, who was a Trotskyite, would complain bitterly of Steinfeld's patronizing tone with respect to the People's Revolution, and he would insist that the dictatorial phase of Communism was only temporary, in order to enforce revolutionary reforms, and he would go on to quote Marcuse's claim that the so-called free world was a dictatorship that used media and conformist conditioning to enforce its dominion. "Zuh Grid," Levassier said: "All zuh television and Internet, all electronic media, banking computer systems, all of zis—this is their gulag . . . "

NR political discussions were always mild and rhetorical, never became real infighting.

They were all too urgently aware of the real fight.

• • •

"If core NR escapes to the USA," Steinfeld said, "we weaken the other resistance groups. But—SA surveillance on the continent is so tight, we're finding it tougher to get away with anything. And people are frightened." He made a gesture that almost seemed to convey despair. It was difficult to tell; his face was lost in shadow. "They're beginning to turn our people in."

"So what does that leave us?" Torrence asked.

And the room grew darker yet.

Steinfeld took a deep, rheumy breath. "The Fascists have two European headquarters—Paris and Palermo. The Sicilian headquarters is also their center of communications, and one of their top air bases. According to our information, Colonel Watson and five other top Second Alliance officials will be in Palermo in early March to evaluate the European situation. They'll be in conference with Crandall by satellite. If they decide the situation is amenable, they'll move into the second phase of their campaign to take control of Europe. They'll announce something called the Self-Policing Organization of European States. SPOES will claim it's the core of a new economic and political unity that will protect it from the ravages of New-Soviet and American interference, and from the war itself. It will be . . . "

" . . . A new Axis," Danco burst out. "Mussolini, Franco, Hitler, and Tojo, in the last century. Now we will have Le Pen, Sinsera, and the other SA puppets."

Steinfeld said simply, "Yes." After a moment he added, "In effect, they will be announcing the birth of a new Fascist state."

No one spoke for a full minute. Then Torrence said, "You want to raid their Palermo HQ? That it?"

Steinfeld grunted in assent. His chair creaked mournfully as he shifted his weight, leaned back.

Torrence looked out the window. The last shreds of saffron light were melting away. A single ray of orange-red flicked on as a cloud shifted at the horizon. And suddenly switched off, as the sun sank farther, as if someone had thrown a switch to turn off a searchlight beam.

Steinfeld said, "I have in mind a large, concerted raid, timed to hit the island when they're having their conference. Ideally we will kill Watson and some other top people, destroy their sat dishes, their transmitters, whatever aircraft are on the ground. It won't stop their push, but it will slow them. The longer they wait to put SPOES into effect, the more chance we will have to warn people about what's coming."

Chiswell said, "Rather awfully breezy, the way you say it, Steinfeld—but that island will be defended like nowhere else in their territory. I don't think we have the manpower or the air power to make it work. Unless the Maltese help us."

Steinfeld said, "They're Socialist, so they oppose the SA. But not actively—not even very vocally. They give us shelter, but no help with materiel or troops or transportation. The Mossad will provide some planes, some choppers, some amphibious vehicles. But it must operate secretively too. There's a severe limit to how much they can help us. Witcher is doing what he can, but he's finding it tough to get anything through the Atlantic Blockade."

"Then we do what we can with what we've got," Torrence said, thinking, as the room grew darker still. *And we'll probably die doing it.*

A young black woman came into the room; Lila, an NR captain from Martinique. She spoke to Steinfeld in rapid-fire French. He nodded, replied in the same language. She left. Steinfeld said, "It seems Levassier is going to live. He will lose an arm, however." Cold silence till he went on. "And one other piece of news: Michael Karakos has escaped from the detention camps. He's on his way to us. He's a good man. He'll be a great help."

And the darkness in the room was almost complete.

• 04 •

There was a can of people, floating in space. It was the Space Colony, FirStep, but to Russell Parker, just then, it was only a very big tin can.

Russ Parker—he thought of himself as Russ—was Chief of Colony Security. He sat at his desk in Central Admin, hating his job, hating his current home (if you could call it a home), hating his boss, and hating himself. And asking God's forgiveness for all that hatred.

It had just hit him as he sat there looking over his schedule of interviews for the day: *He hated.* It had boiled up in him from somewhere hidden and it had come as a complete surprise.

A bit of scripture popped into his head, Romans 12:20. . . . *if your enemies are hungry, feed them* . . .

But, Russ added to himself, try not to feed them your soul.

Russ was six-foot-two, weighed in at two twenty-five. He wore an Admin sky-blue Security jumpsuit—the color of the original security force's uniforms, before the SA—and an old-fashioned wristwatch with a watch face and hands. He was middle-aged but boyish-looking, blue-eyed, tanned, seam-faced, and he usually managed a friendly expression. He sat in a compact office, twenty feet by thirty, with the claustrophobic seven and a half feet between floor and ceiling, typical of the Space Colony's offices; the walls were postered with old *Arizona Highways* photos of the American Southwest's deserts and mesas and sunsets. His desk was real walnut—he'd built it himself, having imported the wood over a six-month period a piece at a time—and centered on it was a white plastic computer console.

He wished to God you could smoke on the Colony. Even after all these years . . .

Russ took a deep breath and closed his eyes for a moment, leaned back in his squeaking swivel chair—he refused to let them oil it, he liked it to squeak—and put his booted feet on the desktop.

He'd just come from his session with Dr. Tate, the Admin chief psychiatrist. Had gone to him about his ulcers, which his physician felt were stress-related. Tate seemed to've had a partial rejuv, had his face and back rebuilt, so he looked thirty years younger than his sixty-five—and Russ himself was fifty but Tate seemed paternal somehow, anyway. He'd expertly gotten Russ to talk about himself. Airing the misgivings he'd been having about the job, and how the job conflicted with his religion.

Prompted by Tate, Russ realized that only part of the hatred was real. The part about hating *himself.* The rest of his feelings about the job, the place, were colored and exaggerated by his self-hatred. Russ Parker was a Christian, and his self-hatred, as Tate had hinted, was rooted in the shame of religious hypocrisy.

That thought came to him while he was looking at the list of names on the computer screen.

Beside the name of each Security Risk he was to interview was a short summary of the interviewee. Ninety percent of them were either black, Jewish, or married to a black or Jewish person. The other ten percent were Marxists or known to be associated in some way with the people who'd fomented the Technicki Rebellion. The list just didn't make sense—there was no particular correlation between the technicki rebels and race. Only thirty percent of them had been members of a racial minority group. And those weren't the ringleaders. The issues giving rise to the Technicki Rebellion just weren't race-related.

The Colony's new chief administrator was a man named Praeger. The list had been made up by Praeger's special committee on post-rebellion security measures. And everyone on the committee was, like Praeger, an SA Initiate.

Russ took a deep breath, turned in his swivel chair, and tapped the button that would buzz Administration for video conference. He glanced at his watch. It was three p.m., Colony Time. Praeger should be back from lunch by now.

Praeger's cybercam image appeared on the upper left-hand screen of the four monitors, two stacked over two, that stood to the left of Russ's work console. Praeger said, "Hello, Russ, what can I do for you?" Wearing his rimless Coke-bottle glasses, running a hand over his eraser-pink bald head, making an inquisitive cone of his prissy red lips.

Russ controlled his surge of revulsion and said, "Well, now, Bill, I was just looking over the list of Risks, and I just can't see why most of them are on there. I feel it's inappropriate to use race as . . . um . . . "

"Everyone on the list is there for a good reason," Praeger said briskly, as if he were impatient with stating the obvious. "The reason doesn't necessarily show up on the stats attached to the list. Sometimes the reason isn't provided. Our agents just give us the names, and there are too many names for them to get specific about each one. We want you to interview them and see what you can find out. Look for connections to rebels of course—but, really, anything problematic at all."

Russ struggled to maintain his mask of serenity. Like nothing rattled him. Objecting mildly, "That doesn't make sense, either. They know I'm Security Chief. I expect they're not likely to open up to me. No, sir. And, hell—I don't know what I'm supposed to be lookin' for. "

"Don't you?" A hint of real annoyance in Praeger's flat voice now. "Saboteurs, for a start. Who sabotaged the food refrigeration? Who's been interfering with InterColony TV transmissions? Who's been freezing up Admin's elevators?"

"Probably just servicing breakdowns, Bill. We haven't got the parts—"

"Some of those systems were newly installed."

"There was no direct evidence that it was sabotage, the way I heard it."

"Electronics informs me that they think it was done with a power surge, which was deliberately introduced into the systems."

"I've got that report. I see it as a lot of wild digging for excuses to cover up the fact that they can't find the real problem."

"They might as well say that the statement you just made is *your* way of covering up *your* inability to find the saboteurs."

There was a tense silence. Then Praeger chuckled, to let Russ know that what he'd just said wasn't serious. But they both knew it hadn't been entirely a joke, either.

Behind that chuckle was the slightly veiled implication that Russ's job might be on the line.

Sure, Russ had come to despise the job. But he was trapped on the Colony till the blockade was lifted. If he resigned, he'd be an object of suspicion. He'd be on the list that was on his computer. He just might be arrested on general principle.

"Maybe you don't know, Russ—there've been reports of unusual activity at Life Support Central," Praeger said.

"I've got that one. Wild changes in power output levels. You think it's connected to the power surges in the other parts of the Colony?"

"I don't know. But I want you to see what you can find out about a kind of technicki cult around Professor Rimpler."

"A what? A *cult*?"

Rimpler? Rimpler was dead. Bludgeoned by Samson Molt during the uprising. Rimpler, who'd founded the Colony, had turned against its Admin Committee, had become a rebel sympathizer.

Praeger shrugged. "For people who work every day with state-of-the-art hardware, the technickis are remarkably superstitious. Evidently some of them believe Rimpler's spirit is haunting the Colony. It could be that this cult around his 'spirit' has found out about his, ah, cerebral/cybernetic interface . . . which is now in place in Life Support Central."

"Run that 'un by me again there, boss, will ya? About that interface?" Drawling it, making light of it. But Russ was stunned.

Praeger sniffed. "It's not so unusual. Been done before. When we found his body, it wasn't quite brain-dead. He was interested in cerebral/cyber interfacing, he had all the equipment here to experiment in it . . . and the life-support computer system was on its last legs. We didn't have time to get in a new life-support computer—we can't get in the equipment fast enough with the blockade. The air was getting bad. It's that simple. We risked a total breakdown in life-support systems without some kind of guidance computer. A brain interface was the quickest way—the only way we had. The principle of cerebral interfacing . . . "

"I understand the principle." Human brains store much more information than a computer in a *much* smaller space, and they respond to some things more quickly; brains could be grown, or surgically removed, from people who've signed their bodies over. Once perfected, using an interfaced human brain as an extension of a computer costs less than an elaborate computer storage system. "But, Bill . . . " He shook his head again, laughed hollowly. "It's all experimental! And, anyway, it'll never be practical for the Colony's *life support!* We discussed this, and the committee voted against it! Brain tissue is too fragile; it deteriorates, ages, has a number of unpredictable qualities . . . and—for God's sake!—you used *Rimpler's* brain? I mean—Rimpler?"

"As for its deteriorating—the wetware link is only a temporary expedient till we get a hardware system. We're keeping the tissues alive with a nutritive fluid. It's fascinating, really, don't you think? Just being able to access all the right parts of the brain to use . . . remarkable. Admittedly, it's an experiment that, ah, *interests* me . . . "

Russ suspected that Praeger took some kind of perverse pleasure in using his old adversary's brain tissue as a convenient spare part. It was like a medieval ruler making the skin of his enemy into a seat covering for his chair, or drinking ale from his skull. It was a celebration of his complete triumph over him.

Praeger, Russ thought, *you're a sick man.*

Praeger went on. "And as for its being *Rimpler's* brain—this isn't a Gothic by Mary Shelley, Parker. Do you suppose we sent Igor out for a good brain and he dropped it, came back with Rimpler's? There's no shred of Rimpler's personality left in it. We have a primitive extractor here . . . not adequate for interrogation, but it *will* erase. Rimpler's memories were erased. A great deal of the brain was cut away; we're only using the tissue that's interfaceable. Dr. Tate used electrochemical amino-acid breakdowns to translate the computer's impulses into neurohumoral transmission units which . . . "

"*Dr. Tate* did this?" Russ broke in, startled.

"Yes." Praeger's expression was as glassy and flat as the TV screen. "Why?"

"Uh—nothing." So Praeger was working closely with Tate. How much had Tate told him about Russ's problems? Did he stick to professional confidentiality? *Was Tate SA?*

"It could be some of our Security Risks know about Rimpler's brain," Praeger said. "There could be a connection."

"Seems pretty farfetched to me. And interrogating people in this arbitrary kinda way . . . To be honest, I don't think excessive security is *good* security. It makes people angry at authority, makes them hard to deal with—we could end up *making* rebels. I just don't see the necessity."

"You don't see the necessity." Praeger's voice was terribly calm. He reached for something offscreen, punched some buttons. An image appeared on the lower right-hand TV monitor . . .

It was a telescopic TV image of a spacecraft; something like a standard space shuttle but knobbier, with heavily bolted plates, and generally cruder: a New-Soviet vessel. Their spacecraft always looked directly descended from the *Monitor* and the *Merrimac*.

"You see that?" Praeger asked.

"I see it."

"They're out there. The New-Soviets. Less than a hundred kilometers from our outer hull. Directly in the way of the approaches to our hangars. They're armed. They have—you see the dishes?—a great variety of communications gear. They could be communicating with someone on the Colony, for all we know. They could even have had accomplices at the air locks."

Russ listened with amazement to the rising tone of hysteria in Praeger's voice. Praeger looked cool, but . . . he'd begun talking rapidly, and his pitch had risen half an octave.

"I see," Russ said slowly. Soothingly. (Thinking, *This man is making life-and-death decisions about people . . . about me . . . he's capable of having me killed.*) "Well, uh, I surely see your point and, ah, that puts a different light on things." Adding humbly, "I'll get right on it, Bill."

"You do that, Russ."

Praeger cut the connection.

Russ stared at the blank screen, thinking that he just hadn't had the courage to bring up his real objection to the brain interfacing. It seemed immoral. Blasphemous somehow.

But Praeger would've laughed at that. Praeger was an atheist.

And now he was expected to take part in systematic racial profiling. And he just couldn't see any way out of it.

Russ turned slowly to his console, to the list of names. Thinking, *God forgive me.*

The first five people on the list were all waiting in the outer office.

He noted the first name on the list and called his assistant on the intercom. "Sandy, send in Kitty Torrence, please."

• • •

THE ISLAND OF MALTA.

She saw men who were also wild dogs. Wolves, jackals, wild dogs. They went on their hands and feet, running in a crouch; unnaturally long arms, unnaturally short legs. Each lean muscle clearly etched in the moonlight; skin mottled pink and mange-gray. Hairless but for a strip of fur down the back. Wagging, semi-tumesced sexual organs. Their hands and feet black with grime, their faces—

Their faces were the worst part. She saw lust for murder and rape in those faces. But—and this was the horror that kept her from looking twice—they were human expressions. Expressions that, till now, she'd glimpsed in men's faces for only a microsecond before the veil of civilizing conditioning was drawn again.

There were two packs. One had made a sort of camp around the mouth of a burrow, a small cave in a bank of dirt, under the dark cypresses dripping with Spanish moss. Smaller dogwomen licked and suckled dogman-infants. Others stalked the edges of the feces-littered camp, snuffling the hot swamp breeze, tick-studded ears listening, sorting through the croc grunts and cricket calls. Listening for . . .

A splashing. Pricked-up ears caught a rustle, a panting. A prescient silence.

And then the second pack lunged from the shadows, attacking the camp.

She saw two of them rending one of the dogwomen; the dogwoman bitch tried to run but was caught with one set of jaws on her rump, the other on her neck, pulling her two different ways, pulling her apart so blood spurted, hotter than the steamy night air. While three more leapt on her husband, rending with toothy jaws and filthy talons.

She saw one of them raping a mother whose breasts swung heavy with milk under her as she tried to claw away from him, as he sodomized her while biting into the back of her neck . . . biting deep. She saw them maim their victims so they could no longer move and then the victors thrust their human faces into the wounds of the still living—

Claire sat bolt upright in bed, choking, trying not to vomit, but a sound between a gurgle and a scrape was all that escaped her throat.

The room yawed, and a dark, tooth-bared man-face thrust itself into her line of sight.

She screamed and clawed away from it. It was barking at her.

"Claire! Hey, Claire!"

The last membrane of the dream dissolved.

It was Torrence. *Danny.* It was Danny. She looked around, found she had backpedaled off the bed, had fallen, was sitting on the cold floor, her back against the cool wallpaper. Sweating. Her tailbone bruised.

"I'm sorry," she said. Her voice sounded funny in her own ears. "I . . . shit, what a nightmare."

"Sounded like it was. You okay?" As he bent over her, nude, he helped her to stand. His touch on her arm making her skin crawl (a flash of the filthy talons ripping pink into red).

She pulled away from him. Wearing only panties, she went out the bedroom door and down the dark hallway. It was three in the morning. The house creaked with her footsteps. It felt fragile and porous around her, after the Colony; you could feel all its boards straining in the night wind to burst free of their nails. (Nails! God, the house had been nailed together! One step from mud huts . . .)

Claire found the bathroom and gratefully turned on the light, looked around at the old ceramic surfaces of the sink, the bathtub—she looked quickly away from the tub. It had brass legs shaped like an animal's, complete with claws . . .

She washed her face and smoothed her hair and tried to calm herself. At last she went back to the bedroom.

She stood for a moment in the door of the bedroom, looking at Torrence in the indirect light from the floor lamp. She felt all right about getting back into bed with him, now. He looked normal, relaxed, friendly. He was lying on his back, hands behind his head, nude under a sheet; she could see the outline of his penis angling to one side like a clock's hand at three o'clock.

She felt a sexual stirring, which played tag with the half-suppressed sense of loathing left over from the dream . . . Paradoxical, going from a loathing of male murderousness to the damp edges of desire—some kind of primeval programming . . . The killers can provide food, shelter . . . She shuddered. But the desire didn't go away . . .

"Want to tell me about the nightmares?" he asked.

"No."

"You sure? Maybe it'd help."

"*No.* Men are arrogant. Think they can analyze everything, cure everything."

She could see a flicker of resentment in his face. He'd been trying to help her.

"Did Steinfeld decide for sure?" she asked.

"About the raid? Yes."

"What, um, are they going to do with Bonham?"

He glanced at her, probably wondering how she felt about Bonham. She'd promised herself to Bonham, and in return he had agreed to get her safely down to Earth. He'd done his part; she'd reneged on hers.

He said, "I don't know. Bonham seems to think we have some kind of obligation to him. He wants money, a passport, transportation to the States. He claims he can give us some useful information about the Colony—he did say one thing that grabbed Steinfeld's interest. That Crandall's planning to use the Colony as his headquarters once the New-Soviet space blockade is lifted. But I don't think Steinfeld trusts Bonham enough to let him go."

"When he's frustrated, he's dangerous."

"We'll watch him." He turned on one elbow, looked at her for a moment, bent and kissed her. Claire responded, but weakly.

Then she turned her head away.

She felt her face contort as she fought tears.

"What's wrong, Claire?" he asked, with as little pressure as possible in the question.

She bubbled it out all at once, her voice pitching on the edge of a whine. "I'm all—all just . . . shit . . . It's weird, I was wondering when this'd . . . see, I've been . . . with you guys, I've been killing people. I never thought I could really kill anyone. It seems so—this is a smug term but—so *unevolved*. And then I got caught up with you guys . . . and I killed those men. And I didn't feel *anything* about it! It was so amazing how I didn't feel disgust or remorse or . . . or anything. But I guess *I did*, because it's all coming out now. Here, where the pressure's less. It comes out in the nightmares and—God, when I saw you kill people with that shotgun . . . I mean, you're all *my friends,* and my friends are tearing bodies apart with these tools *made* for tearing bodies apart, and . . . how could I just *accept it?*"

He absorbed this for a few long moments. Then: "Like you said, you *didn't* accept it. But you coped with it. You think there was anything else we could've done?"

"Yes. We could have let them kill us. Maybe that would be better than having to tear people apart."

He didn't say anything for a few minutes. Finally she looked at him and asked, "You mad at me?"

He shook his head. "No. I do know what you mean. But, Claire—they're planning *another Holocaust.* All the signs point to that. If we don't stop them, more people will be murdered."

"We have to murder a few to keep them from murdering a lot?"

"That's it. If you insist on calling what we do murder."

After a moment she said, in a small voice, "I guess. I guess it makes sense. But—"

"I know how you feel. It's like nothing makes sense when you see it happening. I felt the same way more than once."

"But, Danny . . . you *like* killing people."

He tensed. "What? No! Or . . . the truth is, I do and I don't." He seemed desperate, then, to change the subject. He turned over, sat on the edge of the bed. "I like this old house. I wonder who it belongs to, really. You know, the others are all crammed together in six rooms. Steinfeld was almost sentimental, giving us this room to ourselves. Something about morale—theirs as much as yours and mine. Hey!"

He'd noticed light glinting off something half-hidden behind a rack of thirty-year-old yellowed English paperbacks on a wall shelf. The glint of a bottle. He got up, crossed to it, pulled it out. Accidentally tipping an old collection of Clive Barker stories onto the floor.

"Scotch!" A stubby, triangular bottle, half full of amber liquid. *Pinch*, it was called.

He brought it back to the bed, unscrewed the cap, and sloshed some into the empty water glass on the bedside table. Drank off half. "Damn!"

"Well, don't *hog it.*"

Twenty minutes later they both felt considerably more relaxed. In fact, she felt a little too relaxed. Any more Scotch and she'd get the spins.

Then she was in his arms, felt her body acting almost on its own, undulating against him in that way he liked . . .

They kissed for a long time and then . . .

"No, wait," she said.

He flinched. His erection was so rigid it looked painful.

She smiled apologetically. "I want to, but . . . we can't actually fuck, okay? It's too much like something in my dream. It's too much like stabbing tonight. But maybe . . . "

He relaxed as she ran her still Colony-soft fingers over him, drew sensations from him, began to squeeze and pump.

He was lying sideways, his head tilted over hers so he could kiss her, trace her lips with his own tongue, her right breast nuzzling his chest as he gently parted her labia with the index and middle finger of his right hand, dipped into the wet core of her, gathering a little lubricant onto the tip of his finger, running it up onto her clitoris. She groaned and pressed against him, her hand working at him . . . Some minutes later she gasped, bucked her hips, and he let go the orgasm he'd been holding back . . . holding it back with an exquisite desperation . . . and he came, too, across her heaving belly.

Later still, as he sat up to pour them both a drink, they heard a truck approaching, saw lights prying at the shade from the drive outside.

He looked out the window onto the front of the house.

Two men he remembered from the Mossad were getting out of a van, carrying submachine guns. Now there was a third man walking ahead of them into the house, unarmed but apparently not their prisoner. *One of our people,* he thought, straining to see who it was.

The man seemed to feel Torrence watching. Just before stepping onto the porch, he looked up at the window. Torrence saw his face clearly then.

"Who is it?" Claire asked.

"It's Michael Karakos," Torrence said.

• 05 •

Lyon, France.

Watson was summoned to the Comm Center, in the Lyon SA installation, at three in the morning.

His bedside console had chimed, its screen lit up with three sets of identical numbers: 33-33-33. The code for the SA's final authority. Watson dressed hastily, woke his personal bodyguard, Klaus, who always slept in his clothes, and together the two of them trudged across the frozen mud of the compound, past the guards at the checkpoints, who stepped reluctantly from their heated stations to approve passage. Watson and Klaus continued into the cube-shaped building with its rooftop orchard of antennas and sat-dishes.

Watson was mildly surprised to see that the big, warm, console-crowded viewing room was dark—except for a single green-glowing screen at the far side.

He stood in the doorway for a moment, staring at the screen, pinching the bridge of his nose. He was getting one of those blasted sinus aches from the cold.

Klaus stood behind him, a foot taller than he was, and sixty pounds heavier. Tonight Klaus made him nervous. Not because he was big. Not even because he was wearing that damned opaque helmet. But because Watson had realized that Klaus was not at all stupid. And therefore his loyalty could be an act.

Across the room, that green light glowed, like some kind of grave-yard phosphorescence. A gravestone of green light pulsing alone in the darkness—for him, for Colonel Watson, for no one else.

Get a grip on yourself, man. "Klaus, turn on the blasted heat, eh?" Watson said, fumbling for the light panel. His fingers brushed the panel, and the lights came on, in sequence across the room—flick, flick, flick, flick. He crossed to the screen, footsteps echoing in the room's chill metallic spaces, eyes blinking in the harsh blue light, as Klaus lumbered away to find the thermostat.

Watson activated the console, and the holotank above and behind the screen lit up. He'd grumbled about the expense of having a holotank installed here. TV would have done as well, he'd thought. But now he saw why Crandall had insisted on it.

His gut twisted as Crandall appeared in front of him, lifesize in the holotank, his three dimensional image glimmering as if from some numinous inner fire.

Crandall was sitting in a plain wooden armchair, his head tilted forward a little, his eyes shadowy, that same shadow playing around the faint smile. His craggy face looked gaunter than ever. His short hair, combed back from the angular forehead, had thinned. And there was something curiously inert about the set of his legs.

It occurred to Watson that he hadn't seen Crandall standing for a while, not since the night of the ritual in the Cloudy Peak chapel. The night Johnny Stisky killed himself and Crandall's sister, Ellen Mae.

Crandall had been secretive about the extent of his wounding after the assassination attempt . . . after the NR had tried to kill him . . .

Maybe he was crippled and didn't want them to know because it would reduce his power over them. He was supposed to be a man Protected by God himself. He was almost the Messiah—he allowed some to suggest that he *was* the Messiah. Would God allow his Christ to be a cripple? (What was that old American expression, "Christ on a crutch"?)

"Well, Colonel," the figure in the holotank said in his soft accent, "I've heard some mighty disturbin' reports. I know that you would be unable to sleep well till you cleared up the matter with me. How about you do a little quick explainin'."

Watson shook his head. "Rick, I—"

"Now, I see that I'm-sorry-Rick-I-don't-know-what-you're-talking-about look on your face, so I'll pretend you're not joshin' me, and I'll tell you here 'n' now: You've been telling our enemies all about our most classified project."

Watson did indeed know just what Crandall was talking about. And knowing made him feel like he was coming down with the flu. Weak, feverish, and green around the brisket.

"I deny telling an enemy about anything classified," he said, gazing serenely up at Crandall, hoping his face was as proud and unafraid as he was trying to make it look. The holocameras in a semicircle just above the holotank showed his image to Crandall, transmitted by satellite across the ocean. To Cloudy Peak Farm, where Crandall had remained, with tripled security, since the Stisky affair. Watson had heard Crandall was living behind bulletproof glass now, with only his doctor having physical access to him. And Crandall wasn't even sure he trusted his doctor.

Crandall asked, with soft incredulity, "You deny it? Do you think you're in some headmaster's office, Colonel? Are you a boy denying having stolen the sweet biscuits?"

"I deny that Karakos is an enemy, Rick. At the *time* he was, technically, but . . . ah . . . "

"I'm familiar with your plans for him." The Southern drawl had left his voice, bit by bit, replaced by the bitter cold of crystallized steel. "Suppose something had gone wrong. Suppose he'd escaped. Suppose he'd won his way to the NR. They have media contacts in the States. How long before the headlines read, second alliance plans world genocide?"

"Rick—"

"What is it you're about to say, Colonel? That no one would believe we'd attempt something so impractical? Ah, but everyone is familiar with the 'wonders of neurotech,' Colonel Watson. Don't you think American journalists are capable of putting two and two together?"

The inside of Watson's mouth had turned to cardboard. "Ah, well, Rick—"

"You have lost the privilege of using my first name, Colonel."

Watson felt a deep, deep chill run through him.

"The truth is," Crandall went on, "you're a windbag. You've always been a windbag. You're also a talented man, but that's not enough. We need reliability. And you simply like to talk. To boast, to pontificate. It's in your character. It's a weakness, Colonel."

Crandall was talking quickly. Was himself strangely loquacious today. With that and the gauntness, Watson began to believe the rumors he'd heard were true: Crandall was taking some kind of amphetamine.

Crandall leaned back in his chair, and the chair creaked. Equipment at Cloudy Peak Farm picked up its creaking, transmitted the creak of the wood to a satellite somewhere over the Atlantic, which sent the creak down to the receiver on the roof of the Comm Center: the sound of wood creaking. "We're taking under consideration the possibility that you might be better off if part of your, well, now, your background on all this were extracted . . . "

"No!" Watson burst out. If they extracted his knowledge of Project Total Eclipse, his whole relationship with the SA would be surgically altered. He might be used as a soldier, a strategist, but he'd no longer be an insider. His power would be irreparably undercut.

"You might not like the alternatives, Colonel," Crandall said softly.

Watson swallowed; his tongue sandpapered the roof of his mouth. "See here, Reverend Crandall—I admit I've been a trifle, ah, insubordinate. Truth is, I find it hard to continue working with the albino. He's obviously a genetic inferior. His hubris is insufferable. I suppose what happened was a product of my distaste for him. I realize that's no excuse. I can assure you that from here on in, I'll keep a tight rein, ah, on my tendency to, ah . . . "

"Very well."

Those two words opened a floodgate of relief in Watson. Those two words meant he was not to be killed. He was aware that it might've gone either way. There was a reason that Klaus was standing behind him.

"But you do know, I'm sure, that your restraint will be closely monitored."

"I . . . I would have it no other way, Reverend Crandall."

"All righty, let's get on up the hill a ways. What else've you got to tell me, Colonel?" Crandall's false Southern affability had returned. He leaned his chin on his fist and yawned.

"Very good, sir," Watson said. "We're triangulating in on the People's United Front . . . and ah . . . "

"I don't want to hear about every diddly-squat little Commie outfit. The New Resistance is our priority, Colonel."

"The NR. Yes. We, ah, believe Steinfeld and his planning council to be somewhere in the Mediterranean, possibly on the coast of North Africa. We have, of course, our man in the field, who has every likelihood of linking up with them, and we expect a message from him shortly. In the meantime . . . "

"You *had* them, Colonel. Your people had the resistance cadre trapped. And now you don't even know where they are."

"Reverend Crandall . . . " Watson paused to contain his anger. He took a deep breath. "Reverend Crandall, I was not in charge of that operation; they didn't have time to consult me. I was here, shoring up security around the project installation."

"You want to pass the buck? Fine. But from here on in, Colonel, I want you to leave *basic* security to Sackville-West. You are to go to our installation in Sicily, immediately, and you are to work from there to find Steinfeld and his people. I want them found, and I want them completely *gone* from our hair. They're small, but they're more dangerous than they look. Steinfeld has a knack for uniting factions. I know the knack when I see it: I have it myself. Take him seriously, Colonel."

"Reverend . . . "

But Crandall had cut the transmission. His smiling face rippled as the image faded, the ripple distorting the smile, warping it—or perhaps revealing it for what it was.

And then the holotank was dark.

Watson turned away, stifling a curse. Crandall could still be listening.

A giant's silhouette hulked in the doorway, across the room. Klaus. When had he moved over there?

Watson frowned in irritation. The man had a way of staring at you . . .

Watson shrugged. He crossed the room, muttering, "Let's go."

A minute later, as their feet crunched the pockets of ice in the compound's frozen earth, Klaus said, "Colonel . . . ?"

Watson glanced at him. "Yes?"

Klaus stopped in the middle of the compound and looked up at the stars. The stars were reflected, cold and brightly impassive, in the arc of Klaus's visor.

"Well, what is it, Klaus? It's cold out here."

Klaus looked toward him again. At least, his helmet was tilted down. "I could not help but overhear your exchange with the Reverend Crandall. He's right about security matters, of course . . . "

"Just who do you think you . . . "

"But on the whole I question his competence to continue as our leader."

Watson stared at him, astounded that Klaus would speak treason so bluntly.

Klaus reached up and twisted a series of studs at his neck. The helmet's visor slid upward. Watson could see his craggy Eastern European face, with its hawkish black eyes and short-clipped black beard, the broad, red-lipped mouth. And he saw conspiracy in that face.

"He's going to be looking for mistakes, Colonel. And everyone makes mistakes sometime. You make fewer than most, of course. But eventually . . . and when you slip up, he's going to over-react, as they say in America. Perhaps the time has come to look for a way to . . . well, to remove him from real power. He is a necessary figurehead. But there is no reason he should have to be a *living* one . . . "

Watson glanced around. There was a guard at the fence, but he was well out of earshot. "You're suggesting we . . . but the man's so heavily guarded." *This is insane. Am I actually considering this proposal?*

"Opportunity, Colonel. The opportunity will come. My brother, Rolf, is one of his private guards. The time is not yet here. But it will come."

"And what do you expect to gain?" Watson's teeth were chattering from the cold now, but he stood fascinated, staring up into Klaus's monumental confidence.

"A promotion. Sackville-West's job. At twice his salary."

Watson said, "This is a loyalty test of some kind. You're working for Crandall."

"You control a staff who can operate an extractor. I will submit myself to it, if you wish. Look into my mind. See the truth."

After a moment Watson nodded. "Very well. But we will not move against him until I decide the time is right."

"Of course, sir." Klaus reached up and snapped his visor shut.

They started back to the officer's quarters. Watson thinking, *Have I made the wrong decision? Have I let my anger with Crandall push me into making a fatal mistake?*

Overhead, the constellations turned, swinging slowly, slowly, through the night . . . and one star crossed the path of another.

• • •

Washington, D.C.

Janet Stoner was peering through the slot between two other condos, onto the next street. A boy wearing a transparent anti-acid-rain slicker bicycled by, his tires slicing puddles.

It was Saturday afternoon. The rain had stopped. Everything was soaked in a pearly gray light. Corte Stoner and his wife were on the back terrace of their Georgetown condo, sitting under the rain-scarred plastic bubble. Janet was sitting in the wicker rocking chair, looking pensively out through the plastic pane. She wore a white sweater and cream pants and ticked orange-painted, manicured nails against the wicker chair's armrest.

Stoner was aware his wife had gained weight in the three and a half years since Cindy's birth; there were lines at the corners of her eyes, and she was less energetic than she'd been when she and Stoner had married. Yet Stoner was still in love with her, and they both knew it; the knowledge was held in a quiet confidence between them.

Through the open sliding glass doors Stoner could see Cindy—her skin not the dark black of her Mama's, but more cocoa—sitting raptly in front of the wall console watching a computer generated cartoon in which blond, blue-eyed Danny Angel and his sidekick, Bucky Blast, foiled another plot of the evil New-Soviet scientist, Dr. Darkinsky. Reflected cartoon colors crawled over Cindy's face.

"You go over everything, Corte?" Janet asked dryly. "You check the Bible in my desk drawer? Might be a bug in there, baby." She was sitting with her feet tucked under her for warmth. It was a little chilly on the porch. She was looking at the black satchel sitting beside Stoner's easy chair. It contained detection equipment, Stoner had been at it all morning and into the afternoon. He was fairly sure they weren't being bugged, at least out here. But he knew it couldn't last.

"We're clean so far," he said.

"If you want to talk to me without worrying about surveillance, why don't we go out somewhere noisy?"

"I wanted to know about the house. I just wanted to know."

She said, "You're taking this pretty seriously."

"You afraid I'm going paranoid?"

She shrugged. She smiled. "I go with you, baby. Anywhere, even to paranoid."

He glanced at Cindy. Danny Angel was over, some noon news show had come on. Cindy was spelling words on her I Teach Myself computer, sitting cross-legged and holding the little robin's-egg-blue console in her lap. Smart kid.

Stoner took a deep breath and told Janet about the Hiring Assessment Program weeding the non-Caucasians and moderates out of the CIA's power structure; told her about Howie; told her about the Kupperbind file. Told her, last, as unsensationally as possible, about Winston Post.

She was a strong woman. Just a little catch in her voice when she said, "You really think they . . . " She glanced at Cindy, lowered her voice. " . . . you think they murdered him?"

He nodded.

"And you think they're watching you?"

He nodded again. "It's only a matter of time before they start home surveillance. And they're already reassigning my workload. I was keeping tabs on NR data. The Resistance people in Europe. They've taken me off that."

"How, uh, how far do you think they'll go?"

"I don't know . . . but right now I think Unger figures to use you against me for leverage, keep me in line behind him, so I support him in everything."

"What do you mean, *use me against you?*" She was outraged now. Violated.

"Their rationale is, blacks and other 'coloreds' are prone to sympathy with radical groups, because the radical groups are actively anti-racist. So blacks are Security Risks. So is anyone closely associated with blacks." He shrugged. "They haven't used the Assessment Program to reassign me, because I've got a lot of seniority. Which means clout. I think they'd be more likely to arrange another 'accident.'"

She stared at him. "Jesus, Corte."

"You think I'm . . . going off the deep end over this?"

She shook her head slowly. "You never talked much shop with me, all these years. You were real tight-lipped. It was part of your job to be, I guess. If you're telling me things now, you got to be worried for real, for serious reasons."

He nodded, smiling ruefully. She was too smart to simply assume that he was right. She'd had to reason it out. "I can't play along with them, Janet, even if they weren't going to go after me. I can't handle it. It's . . . I'd be a traitor to my country to play along with them. Because they're traitors. This bullshit is un-American."

"Now I got something to tell you that you maybe didn't know."

He waited. She'd genuinely startled him.

"About my brother. I told you he was working overseas for SOCK-Vuh . . ."

"For what?"

"Shell-Oil-Coca-Cola-Viacom."

"Oh. SOCCV. Pronounce it Sock-Vee. What about it?"

"That was a lie. There's another reason you never met him. Stu's in New York. He's in the Black Freedom Brotherhood. But so far as we know, he hasn't got warrants out on him. I don't condone the Brotherhood, they're terrorists. That's what I told him too. But . . . he's my brother."

"Okay. You think the Company knows about him?"

"We don't know if they do. There's nobody looking for him as far as I'm aware. You people know about all of 'em?"

"Of course not." He shook his head. "Christ, what if Agency finds out . . ."

"I know. Eventually . . . so, I was thinking . . . well, first: What're you going to do about all this?"

"Do? I'm going to see how bad it looks. Try to confirm my suspicions. If it looks bad, I take you and Cindy and we run."

"Uh-huh. Where? Where that's worth going to?"

"What else you want me to do?"

She hesitated.

"Go on," he said.

"Okay, um—well, look, honey . . . if we got to run, it's better if we have something to run to. An umbrella. Some people have already got shelters set up. Now, I don't condone the Brotherhood—and I wouldn't want to join them. But they could help us, put us in touch with these other people . . ."

"What other people?"

"The New Resistance."

His eyes widened. "You want to join the NR?"

She shook her head. "But they could *help* us. Maybe they'd expect something in return. Information, something. Why not?"

"But they're guerrillas. Criminals."

She shrugged. "Supposedly. And supposedly—so is my brother. But if you think the Company is going to kill you . . . what else have we got?"

He tried to think of a reply. He couldn't. He heard the TV talking with newscaster semi-seriousness in the next room, something about another acid-rain alert. Secretary of the Interior warning that acid rain falling in the Midwest could cause wheat and corn shortages, but "*famine* is too strong a word." At this time.

That morning, the president had asked Congress to give her emergency powers of absolute authority on a temporary basis—to keep order as the danger of a New-Soviet first strike increased; citing the New-Soviet destruction of two US orbital antimissile battle stations; citing also increased domestic terrorism from "race extremists on the left"—meaning black and Jewish activists. *Insisting* that the grant of absolute authority was only temporary . . .

They were making it sound as if the threat of all-out nuclear war was nearing the flashpoint. Hearing that, he should have been scared. But all he could think about was: *Criminals. We'll become criminals if we run to those people.*

When Janet asked again, "What else can we do?" he still had nothing to say.

• • •

The Island of Merino, the Caribbean.

"The strange truth is," Smoke was saying as his crow, Richard Pryor, fluttered restlessly on his shoulder, "most people don't see the Grid. That is, they don't know it for what it is when they see it. They aren't able to step back from it. Or they think it's only the Internet or the Web or something—and that's only a quadrant of it. Let's step back from it now and look at it squarely . . . " He turned and switched on the big videoscreen that stretched across the wall like a blackboard behind him. It hummed, flickered with light . . .

It was hot in the briefing room, though it was seven in the evening. The windows were open. Mosquitoes whined and ticked at the screens. Glancing out the window, Charlie saw the searchlight on the guard tower swinging over the sandy ground outside the NR's Coordination Center.

He looked back at Smoke, and shifted on the metal chair, wincing at the pain in his buttocks. His fingers hovered over the keyboard of his lap console.

Charlie Chesterton was one of the people they didn't make metal chairs for; he was too skinny for them. He was tall, bony, a little round-shouldered, a touch weak-chinned. He was twenty-three, and he wore his hair in a young man's fashion: the triple Mohawk; three fins, each a different color and each color significant, the middle one signifying he was a Technicki Radical Unionist; the one on his right was blue for his profession, digitech; the one on the left was green for the neighborhood he'd grown up in the floating boro of New Brooklyn. He was wearing a sleeveless clip T-shirt, this one looping through a Jerome-X video, the same scenes over and over.

There were six other NR trainees in the hot room, in the New Resistance CC, on the tiny island of Merino.

Behind Smoke, the screen, volume muted, flashed through its parade of media baubles, a weirdly inappropriate backdrop for him.

Smoke, in his sleeveless black jumpsuit, was gaunt, hawk-nosed, tired-eyed, dark; his movements were swift, almost abrupt. But sometimes he'd slide seamlessly into a deep calm that seemed so smooth, so untouchable, you felt you were looking into the face of a man who'd spent his life in a monastery.

He had a look on his face like that now as he paused, faintly smiling, looking sedately at them from the front of the briefing room.

And then he came out of it with a sudden slash of his hand, making them rock back in their seats, his crow flapping irritably to a perch on the windowsill, as he said, "It's going to shape you, your family, your friends, unless you—unless we—shape the Grid first! Learning to shape it starts with redefining it. The Grid is a three-leveled system. The first level is Worldtalk-type packaging of products, people, ideas, styles of behavior, socially useful prejudices, and, of course, some 'news,' all mixed into a solution of entertainment or simple distraction. That level is then fed into the second level, which is all the transmissions: all forms of TV and holo transmission; Internet, obviously; standard radio and bone-implant receiver radio; home consoles, schools consoles; smartfone tabloids; daily news-sheets you buy at the printout kiosk; electronic billboards, video billboards; every other kind of long-range communications between computers. Visorclips, earmites, downloads: all filtered through the Grid in some way. Even Charlie's T-shirt there . . . "

Charlie shifted uncomfortably in his seat. Smoke's crow tilted its head to peer at him suspiciously with its glittering eyes.

Charlie wanted badly for Smoke to like him. He'd read all of Smoke's essays, books of them written before Smoke had been caught up in the chaos surrounding the war in Europe. Smoke had been abducted by the Second Alliance, tortured, escaped through one of the war's multitude of wild variables; wandered lost in the deepest circles of a private hell. And had come back, resurrected from what his public had thought was his death and what had been, at least, the death of his sanity. He had emerged not unscathed but unbroken. Jack Brendan Smoke was a legend in the underground.

Smoke went on, "The third level of the Grid are the receivers, the public. The electronically enhanced collective unconscious. The important thing to remember is that while the Grid is made up of three levels, it's *all one system*. And the third level dovetails back to feed into the first . . . It is a baseline, common-denominator system, in service of someone's zero-sum game—except when it is used for something greater. It has the potential—as we have seen in the Internet—for a horrible abuse or a transcendent usage. It can be a sketch of our potential greatness. Let me just drop in this quote . . . " He shuffled through some papers, found the quote. "From Teilhard de Chardin: 'In the perspective of a noogenesis, time and space become truly humanized—or rather super-humanized. Far from being mutually exclusive, the Universal and Personal . . . grow in the same directions and culminate simultaneously in each other.'"

Charlie blinked. "Noogenesis"?

There was only the downside of the Grid, so far as Charlie could see, on the big screen . . .

As if bemusedly sharing Charlie's thought, Smoke paused and looked at the screen, shaking his head, smiling sadly. On the screen, a sex-com sniggered by, then a commercial for a new securicomp that monitored the entry of strangers into a subscribing neighborhood—delivery men, workmen of all kinds, would-be renters, shoppers: all were observed, digitized, analyzed. The camera/computer system looked for type-anomalies, such as racial variations, economic class variations, clothing style variations; a scaling up of type anomalies might mean the neighborhood was in danger, would send a signal for hyperalertness.

The neighborhood security team that used a TADS—Type Anomalies Discrimination System—protects its neighborhood in advance, the commercial suggested soothingly. The slogan: *TADS weeds out weirdos!*

"There you go," Smoke said, tapping the words appearing at the bottom of the screen under the TADS ad: *A Second Alliance International Security Corporation product . . .*

"Jaysiz," Charlie murmured.

"Yes," Smoke said. "They are becoming ubiquitous."

The screen flicked to a newsblip of the successful retaking of Vienna, and President Bester saying, "We're making great strides! With your support we'll win the war—and without recourse to nuclear weapons!"

Then: a ten-minute "Science Special" suggesting "new studies by experts would seem to indicate that interracial marriages create offspring who seem to be unusually vulnerable to disease or birth defect." The study, of course, was a lie. And then came a five-minute evangelical program . . . and then a sitcom—which Smoke fast-forwarded through, using delay-programming, to show a white couple, Dan and Joanie Clifton, are annoyed by Mr. and Mrs. Wog, the Pakistani couple who'd moved in next door; whose overwhelming curry cooking smells and practice of defecating in the hallway give rise to a number of hilarious remarks on the part of Mr. Clifton . . . and then a public-service commercial informing the public that New-Soviet spies are rife in the tech centers, best not to speak to anyone you haven't known for years . . .

"That sitcom is only available in Fundie regions," Smoke remarked, "—parts of the South, Idaho, southern Washington State. It's not syndicated in California, and other places where American minorities and progressives still have some power. But for how long? It's available over the Internet, of course—as so much racist propaganda is . . . "

Smoke thoughtfully scratched the crow under the beak. "In the hands of the Second Alliance the Grid saturates the public with wave after wave of pseudo-information, each wave hitting all the local receiving centers, the cities, more or less simultaneously. There's more, and coming faster, than ever before. Doesn't matter if it's a lie or not, it's all information.

"People receive the information simultaneously, and they soak it up passively. If for example the government claims there's a new strain of AIDS that you get only from talking to antiwar-activists, then fifty-seven percent of the people hooked into the Grid will believe the antiwar-activist-AIDS story implicitly, instantly. Everyone they run into has heard the same thing. They all got it at once. So it seems to confirm itself by its very instantaneous prevalence. Since no real substance exists in this hypothetical broadcast, there's nothing much to stimulate questioning. There's simply the basic bullshit story line, and 'testimony' from a few 'experts' the government keeps on tap for when it needs their tailor-made quotes to give the appearance of credibility. Maybe a visual flash of a chart to give us an impression that some serious study's been done. And bang! everyone believes it. And it becomes 'true' for the public, as a kind of Consensus Reality develops from the instantaneousness and ubiquity of the story. That sort of thing makes the Grid a powerful tool for shaping society.

"And none of this was lost on Crandall and the other planners for the SA. The SA had the foresight to buy the world's biggest PR outfit, Worldtalk.

"They're still reasonably subtle in their use of the Grid, but they're getting bolder. They're blaming the depression on immigrants, non-Christians, the so-called 'Zionist conspiracy'; and they can blame the war on the New-Soviet, of course. Although our intelligence indicates that the New-Soviet has been trying to broker a peace deal, an effort Mrs. Bester has ignored." He looked at the crow—and smiled. The bird seemed to be listening to him raptly. "The public's being programmed to be knee-jerk supportive of the government and, by extension, the SA, which, as a 'private-sector' security and peacekeeping force, is now operating under a government contract. All classes of the Caucasian public are being programmed to blame its ills on outsiders, immigrants, non-Caucasians. It's being set up to give its backing to a race war."

On the screen was a "public-service ad" warning that "visitors from other countries" have "inadvertently introduced" a series of new flu viruses recently, particularly one strain that may be fatal to children. *Until the crisis is past, it might be best if your children played only with native-born Americans.*

US Weather Service acid-rain alert, keep windows closed, don't go out without goggles tonight.

Fallout shelter drills for all public schools announced tomorrow. Public service announcement: "Remember, harboring draft resisters or deserters is giving aid to the New-Soviets." The announcement concludes with a slogan from the US Department of Public Information: "The only way to win the war is to win together! Warning: Illegal TV or radio transmissions will be traced! Perpetrators will be prosecuted! The underGrid is the underworld—don't let criminals whisper in your ears!" Premiere of a new night-time drama, *Ghetto Cop*. Slogan: *"He does what he has to."*

Smoke continued. "And there's only one way to sensibly fight it. We break into the Grid, we reprogram it where we can, we use Jim Kessler's antipropaganda software to force the Grid to reveal itself for what it is. We step up our input into the underGrid. We try to reach concerned journalists in the overGrid—sure, there are some. The Grid is really too vast for the SA or the government to control effectively. It's more porous than they know. We *can* get into it. Jim Kessler's going to be here . . . " He glanced at the wall clock. " . . . in just a few minutes, to train you in doing just that."

A weary hour later, after Charlie's fingers had begun to ache from tapping notes into his console, training was over for the night. Charlie rose to follow the others out of the room.

Smoke was standing near the door, the crow perched on his right hand. He held it near his cheek and murmured to it.

Charlie was feeling logy, thinking of bed. He stretched, rubbed at his numb buttocks once, and started to walk out past Smoke.

"Hold it, young Chesterton," Smoke said, looking at the crow but smiling for Charlie's benefit.

Charlie stopped, waited, wondering if Smoke was going to reproach him for something.

"You'll continue antipropaganda training, Charlie," Smoke said, "but we won't be placing you in a network mole position."

Charlie stared at him. "I can do it. I was a little sleepy tonight, but I followed the whole . . . uh . . . "

Smoke shook his head. The crow cawed raspily, almost like laughter. "No problem with your alertness. We need you elsewhere. You know about video-evidence tampering? The AntiViolence Law programming?"

"Just the first briefing. Not much."

"We've got a special project for you. You'll be part of a team that's going to be working with a US senator."

Charlie stared. "What? A US senator!"

"Oh, yes. If you volunteer."

Charlie shrugged. "You're Smoke. You're Jack Brendan Smoke. Without you, man, I'd still be asleep. You need it, you got it."

• • •

THE SPACE COLONY. MARRIED WORKERS' DORMITORIES.

Lester was home, just stepping into their unit. Kitty Torrence heaved herself off the bunk and couldn't keep from groaning. She ached in a dozen places; when she stood, the dull aches became sharp ones, making her suck air through her teeth. The baby squirmed in her swollen belly.

"*Duhgedda* . . ." Lester began.

"Lester, we said we weren't going to talk technicki because the baby should learn standard, right? We got to get in the habit before . . ."

"All right, okay. Don't get up, I said."

"Got to. Time to fix dinner."

"Kind of thing it is, I can do it just as well. Your belly like that, isn't room for two of us to walk around in here, anyway."

She laughed and lay down; the dozen aching places that had begun to scream quieted to whining.

She watched him fix dinner. On the Space Colony, while they were on rations, "dinner" meant he took two airline-food trays from the storage unit and put them in the microwave.

"Be good when we can afford some real food around here," Lester muttered. He was a small, wiry man; it was as if he'd been bred for the twenty-five-by-thirty-foot studio unit they shared.

There was a queen-size bunk in its own nook, a wafer-thin sofa that folded down from the wall, a "kitchen" area with a "dining bar" about the size of a card table. There was thin foam rubber over the floor; the walls were coated in light blue syntex, which was mottled around the edges with mildew. Once a week she hung fresh drapes of garment material over the bed alcove and above the little sofa. The light was from a soft white ceiling fixture. A small videoscreen was flush with the wall to the right of the door, which covered the screen when the door was open. Just now it was clicked to a soothe-scene. There was a selection of six soothe scenes. It also served as a TV for the techniwave channel and the twice weekly movies Admin was supposed to provide. It was also the monitor for the house Intranet. Mostly they used it for movies—only there'd been more equipment failures, and they hadn't had a movie for a month. Lester frowned over the videoscreen, trying to change channels. "It's fuckin' up. You'd think with my training I could fix it but . . . problem's not in this unit."

"What you trying to get?"

"The mountaintop scene. Where you can see the wind blowin' the snow off the mountain." Lester's favorite. "There it is . . . see if I can get it in better . . . "

"I guess you'd rather play with that thing than give me a kiss. I don't blame you, the way I look now."

He chuckled and came to her, bent to kiss her. "You are the prettiest thing in creation. Of course, I need an eye implant pretty bad."

She pretended to punch him in the shoulder. He acted as if she'd broken his arm, making the arm swing loosely, hamming it up. She smiled up at him. *He may be small but he's a handsome man. And he's smart.*

The microwave went *ding*! and he got their meal. He put pillows behind her so she could sit up, leaning against the wall, holding the tray on her pregnant belly. He sat beside her, scowling as he ate. He resented the airline food. It was an issue with him.

The nausea caught up with her halfway through the meal, and she put the tray aside. "You were later than I thought you'd be. Does that mean, um . . . "

"That they gave me work? Wish it did. Another bullshit day wasted in a waiting room. No fucking work. Another week of subsistence creds. I'm late 'cause I stopped off at Bitchie's to talk to Carl." He hesitated. "And the others. They asked me to . . . just to talk . . . " He sounded almost puzzled.

The others. He'd gone to a meeting, then. *Colony New Resistance.*

The only argument she'd had with Lester in a month happened after they'd gone to an NR meeting together. The New Resistance rep, Carl Zantello, had said some things about Admin and the Second Alliance she thought were crazy. He'd claimed they were part of some enormous racist conspiracy. Crackpot stuff. She'd agreed that Admin was mishandling the Colony, was treating people badly. But saying they were part of a new international Nazi party or something . . . Zantello was watching too many movies, she'd told Lester. And Lester had yelled at her that she'd believe it if she were black, because if she were black, she'd feel the way SA people looked at blacks; she'd notice how they related to the other races, the way they treated them.

A black man could *feel* it all coming down. Maybe some kind of survival skill evolved in American blacks, Lester said. A keen awareness of prejudice in others; a talent for sensing the plans that followed the prejudice.

A tendency to slide into plain old paranoia, she'd said.

Two weeks after the meeting she'd been called to the Security office, to see Russ Parker. Not a bad man, she thought.

But he'd talked to Lester, too, and Lester had come home angry. *"They've been watching me,"* he'd said.

"So—they asked you to make a speech?" she asked now.

"Kind of." He grinned. "I guess it was, yeah. I talked about the prejudicial work-assignments. I swear to God—l never expected to see this on the Colony in the goddamned twenty-first century. It's like all that Civil Rights work never happened—it took so *little* to start them backsliding. They're hiring Caucasians, and a few ass-kissing Spanish and Japanese. And nobody else is getting work assignments. So nobody else is getting anything but subsistence creds. Most of the technickis— even the white ones—are bitching about it. In private. But everybody's afraid to bitch in public because of the 'preventative detention' bullshit." He ticked off the names of the technicki political prisoners on his fingers. "Judy Wessler, Jose Arguello, Abu Nasser, Denny Bix—all of 'em arrested, no one gets to talk to them. Shit, we don't even know if they're still alive." He took a deep breath and then, staring fixedly at the snowy mountaintop scene, said, "So me and Carl decided the time's come for another general strike."

"Lester . . . " She wanted to shout at him. But she knew how he'd react. She needed to change her tactics. She carefully modulated her voice and said, "Lester, you're right. We should all go on strike again. It's called for. But—we got to think about *timing*. While the New-Soviet blockade's on, the SA can do what they want with us. I mean, you said they were some kind of Nazis, right? And they know you're a socialist. Black is bad enough—but socialist! If they're fascists, they don't have any conscience about hurting people—maybe even killing people—that stand up to them. Especially black socialists, Lester."

"That's exactly the reason we ought to stand up to them," he said. "Because it's immoral to give in to people like that. And giving in's even more dangerous, maybe, in the long run, than fighting them now. They're consolidating their power. We've got to take some of that power from them while we can. We got to face the risks."

She repressed the outburst of exasperation she felt at his bravado. Holding back wasn't easy—being pregnant made you cranky. She wanted to yell, to grab him and shake him. But it was especially unwise to argue when you were in the Colony housing units. The claustrophobic compactness of a unit acted like an electrical transformer on the current of anger, pulsing it up to absurd extremes.

"Okay, Lester—yes, we ought to stand up to them. But . . . but don't you think it'd be more, um, more powerful . . . that it'd give us, you know, a better chance, if you wait till the blockade's over? So they don't just use it as an excuse to come down on you? They've got to lift the martial law alert eventually."

He frowned, and shook his head. But after a moment he said, "Maybe. Maybe so."

The videoscreen gave off an uncharacteristic crackle. In the image, electronic snow fell over the mountain snow. They stared at the screen, both wondering the same thing: Are they bugging us? Listening in on this? Is it that far along?

And then a voice spoke from the intercom grid over the door. It was a computer simulation of a woman's soothing but firm voice. *Little Mom*, some of the Colonists called her. Or else they called her *Libish*: Technicki for "lying bitch."

"Please take note. Please take note," the voice said sweetly. "The Boulevard of Lights" . . . that was Corridor C . . . "—has been sealed off due to flooding. Do not attempt to enter the corridor until entry is reauthorized. The corridor flooding is believed to be caused by sabotaged pipes. If you have any information about the vandals, your security report will be treated confidentially. Should your report lead to the apprehension of the vandals, you will be rewarded, also in confidence. Remember, helping Security maintain order is helping *you!* Thank you for helping yourself!" She repeated the message in technicki.

So someone had sabotaged the pipes at Corridor C . . .

Kitty looked at Lester questioningly. He shook his head. "It wasn't us."

The videoscreen gave out another raucous buzzing—and then the image cleared. Kitty and Lester stared at it. They looked at one another; then back at the screen.

It was different. The scene was an endless digital loop, and it should always be the same sequence, wind blowing soft banners of powdery snow from a Himalayan mountaintop; feathery whiteness blown from the stark, dignified peak, trailing into crystal-blue sky. But now there was *a man* in the mountaintop image. He was sitting on the mountain's peak, kicking the snow up with his feet like a little kid, laughing. He was *nude*, for God's sake, on a mountaintop. And he was an old man. Skinny, potbellied, white-haired. And evidently crazy.

"*Yugg'nshid!*" Lester swore in technicki. "*Hooftzit?*"

"I don't know," Kitty murmured. The image of the man was small. It was hard to see his face. "But he looks familiar . . . "

• • •

In another part of the Colony, at exactly that moment, someone else found the image familiar.

"Shoot me for a wetback, but by God I think that's Professor Rimpler!" Russ burst out.

"It is indeed," Praeger said. He was on a separate screen in Russ's office, monitoring the transmission anomaly from his quarters. "This reinforces my opinion: There is a Rimpler cult. And they've broken into our system somehow."

"Maybe you're right. I don't know what else it could be. But if the guy's a hero to them, why they making him look . . . like that? Like he's gonzo-whack. Seems to me—shit!" The mountaintop image had vanished, replaced by a close-up of Rimpler's leering face. The face tried to speak, but the words came out garbled.

The image on the screen flickered, vanished. The snowy mountaintop returned, sans Rimpler.

"What are our chances of tracing the source of the superimposed images?" Praeger asked.

"I don't know. I'll have to ask the techs. But until we know when it's going to happen ahead of time, it's hard to be prepared to trace anything . . . "

"Then have the computer continually monitor all channels for anomaly. At the first anomaly it should trace automatically."

"That'll take time to set up—in fact, with the damage that's been done in Central, I'm not sure if . . . "

Russ was interrupted by the red flash from the Security Priority screen. He thumbed *acknowledge* and tapped to tie it in to Praeger's line.

One of Russ's technical investigators came onto the priority screen. It was Faid, a tech-intelligence officer who'd come to the Colony from the People's Republic of Palestine; he'd been one of Russ's own men before Praeger brought the SA in. He was one of the few left from the original security roster. "Right, we have source of water leakings in Corridor C, Chief. Martinson is having it for you, what?" That was just the way Faid talked. "He is made determination."

"Put him on."

Martinson's lean black face came on the screen. "The valves are auto-operated by the Tertiary Life Support System. The computer opened two of the unconnected valves. It simply opened them and increased water pressure in them. Whoever programmed Tertiary . . . " He shrugged.

"Must've been. Thanks. The water shut off?"

"Shut off and permacapped. They're draining for recycling now. And that's all we've got for you."

Russ nodded and cut the transmission.

"Why are those men still in the field?" Praeger asked.

Russ was caught by surprise. "Uh—Faid? Martinson? Why?"

"According to the new personnel guidelines, they should have been replaced. Especially this Faid person. He's culturally contraindicated for Security."

"Because he's an Arab? Sir, he may be a . . . a wog . . . but he's a damn efficient one. You saw how fast he got on top of—"

"Replace him!" Praeger barked. "And when you find out who programmed Tertiary, let me know."

Praeger cut off, and Russ stared at the blank screen where his image had been. There was an ugly taste in his mouth. Damn Praeger, that arrogant, bigoted son of a bitch!

But after a moment he muttered, "Nothing I can do about it."

Faid would have to go, maybe Martinson too. It was stupid, but it was unavoidable.

He ran the check himself on the programmer for Tertiary Life Support. It was Kevin Brock. Kevin *Brock*? Brock was SA! Hell, he was one of Praeger's toadies.

Russ shook his head in wonder. Had someone turned Brock? Converted him to a radical saboteur? Fat, middle-aged, overpaid, bigoted *Brock* had become a revolutionary?

Bullshit.

Someone unauthorized had gotten into the computer somehow. Life Support computers were triple-protected against unauthorized access and tampering. How had it been done?

The valve control tampering, the image of Rimpler—none of it should have been possible.

It was as if the computer itself had it in for them. Which wasn't possible, either. Was it?

• • •

Somewhere on the Island of Malta.

Steinfeld had ordered them out for assault exercises.

The Maltese Army was holding exercises on other parts of the island's coast.

NATO, and hence the Second Alliance, knew about the Maltese exercises. With luck they'd be camouflaged amongst Maltese activities.

Today, one hundred and eighty NR were out in six boats, thirty guerrillas apiece. They were green US Army amphibious landing vehicles, creaky old buckets with the insignia painted out. Witcher had bought ten of them from war surplus, had them partially refitted, smuggled them here in one of his false-bottomed oil tankers.

And it was getting dark. It was nearly time to begin . . .

Claire and Torrence stood on the top deck with the coxswain, looking through the gloom at the rocky coastline. A soft wind coming up the coastline from the south carried the sweet rot of brine and the diesel reek of the other amphibious boats, obsolete old buckets that still ran on diesel. There'd been some real progress toward electric and hydrogen-cell powering before the war—but all that was stalled. The last oil reserves were being gutted.

The sky was a thin sheet of amber above the sunset; the sea was a heaving infinity of copper and verdigris. The engines rumbled; the wake hissed behind them as the boat carried them south, a quarter of a mile out from the coast. Claire could just make out the bulky shape of Steinfeld in the lead boat, hunched over a chart.

"I wonder if Steinfeld is lost," she said, for something to say.

Torrence took the remark seriously. "There are hardly any beaches on this island. He'll know it when he sees it. Everything else is rocks and cliffs."

She nodded and shifted her assault rifle to her other shoulder. It was getting heavy. Torrence looked at her as if he might offer to carry it. She could see him think better of it.

"What are you smiling like that for?" he asked suddenly.

"Nothing."

He shrugged and went down the gangway; Claire watched him go, wondering what she'd done to annoy him.

She'd seen him put up with grueling conditions of all kinds; with cold, hunger, wounds, and firefights to make a seasoned veteran piss his pants in fear—and he'd shrugged it all off. But say the wrong thing, hurt his feelings, and he sulked like a little kid. He had become a professional fighting man and at the same time he could sometimes be absurdly immature.

His immaturity was exasperating, but . . . it had a certain appeal.

And when he made love, he was as patient as he was passionate. Still . . .

Did she want to commit herself to him?

And then, silently, she laughed at herself. Worrying about emotional commitment as if she were some cow-eyed Long Island debutante. The chances were excellent that they were going to be dead in a month or less.

Even without the likelihood of death in the assault on Sicily, there were half a dozen other deaths incubating in the teeming corridors of possibility. The New-Soviets could move in on Malta, take it over, imprison them all, enslave or kill them. The SA could find them, bomb them in their hideouts, or send in commandos to slaughter them in their beds. Or she could find her way to the States—and Praeger's hirelings could locate her. Kill her. Or the Third World War could escalate into nuclear holocaust. A fire-storm death, or a slower demise from wind-carried fallout . . . or death by cold and starvation in a nuclear winter . . .

And with all that heaped on my plate, I'm thinking, Should I commit myself to Torrence?

She shook her head and told herself, *Bury those feelings. Feelings about anything long-term. The desire to make a home somewhere. Bury it deep, but don't kill it. Not yet.*

"You look quite thoughtful," Karakos said, coming onto the deck. He had a pleasant accent and a mild, unassuming expression. He'd been cleaned up, and in the week he'd been there, his face had filled out a little. It was not a handsome face but it was attractively masculine, mature, deeply etched with character, and sometimes his eyes showed just a hint of the suffering he'd been through.

He hadn't talked about what he'd been through, what he'd seen, except to say that most of the time he'd been in solitary confinement in a room too small to stretch out in. He seemed unable to talk about his imprisonment at the hands of the SA, and that was understandable.

He stood at the rail beside her, gazing into the gloom. "Stars are coming out," he said. "We get caught up in trying to stay alive, we forget to look at things like that." He glanced at her. Smiled. Boyish, that smile. "But I guess, Claire, you've had enough of seeing the stars, eh? Up there."

The Colony. The screw pinning her stomach to her spine bit another thread deeper. It showed on her face.

"I have said something that hurts?" he said.

He put his hand on her arm and smiled sadly, as if to say, *I'm sorry. There is enough pain.*

His touch felt good. It felt . . . she wasn't sure.

But she found herself looking up at the sky, wondering—as the screw tightened another turn—if in fact her father was dead.

"You look lost," Karakos said. "I, myself, am feeling lost. I'm wondering if I belong. "

She glanced at him. "You're tired of fighting," she suggested. "I don't blame you."

"It isn't that. It's . . . I feel as if Steinfeld doesn't want me here."

"Are you serious? You have a great reputation in the resistance. Steinfeld has nothing but respect for you."

"And yet—he has told me nothing about what our plans are. I'm participating in an exercise to prepare for a mission I know nothing about. I'm not used to that."

She hesitated. She was one of half a dozen people who knew about Steinfeld's plan for an attack on the Sicilian SA base. The others knew an action of some sort was planned, but they didn't know where and when. It was best that few as possible know. "Steinfeld's told almost no one. It's not that he doesn't trust the people he's not telling—it's his fear that they might be caught by the enemy before the assault."

Karakos snorted. "And he thinks I would talk?"

"All the willpower in creation won't help you against an extractor."

"Extractors! It is a myth that the SA has them in Europe! They are extremely rare, expensive devices!"

"How the hell do you know it's a 'myth'?" Torrence asked as he stepped onto the deck from the gangway.

He was staring at Karakos's hand, which was still on Claire's arm.

"One of their people confided in me," Karakos said briskly, removing his hand from Claire's arm. "I got him to talk . . . " He shrugged. "He said they spread the rumor they have extractors so that prisoners will talk freely, will assume it's hopeless to hold back."

Torrence spat over the rail into the hissing sea. "Bullshit!"

Karakos shrugged again and moved stiffly away, down the ladder.

Torrence looked at her expressionlessly. "What did he want to know?"

"What makes you think he wanted to—?"

"Claire—*what did he want to know?*"

She stared at him. "He was understandably concerned to know about Steinfeld's assault target."

"Was he. I don't trust that son of a bitch. Not with our plans, and not with you."

"Dan, you're being childish." She broke off as Lila came up the ladder. Lila was captain of their assault unit, a tall woman with night-dark skin, wearing gray-black cammie fatigues. They saw her starlit silhouette and the glitter of her eyes. Claire had often wondered about her. Lila could speak English, French, and Martinique pidgin fluently—but speaking was something she rarely did. She was one of those people who communicated more with the subtle posture of her body, her eye contact, her timing. She made Claire think of Yukio.

Lila was neat, compact in all her movements, graceful even when loading and firing a gun. She never seemed at a loss for something really useful to do; never distracted or spaced-out. When there was a lecture on strategy she listened raptly, not taking her eyes off the speaker. When there was work to do she did it vigorously and gave it her full attention. When she was done and there was really nothing more to do, she slept, just like that. She'd lie down, and she'd be asleep in seconds. She didn't even snore.

Claire had a vague urge to make friends with Lila. But in the two weeks she'd known her, she'd never seen her make small talk. Or talk about herself. Or smile.

Lila gave them each a headset. "We hit the beach in about twenty minutes. Torrence will be in charge of Platoon A for this unit, I'll be in charge of B; Torrence will also be under my command."

Torrence and Claire nodded. Steinfeld had already told them the chain of command.

"The objective is a ruined building. It used to be where they pressed olives. We are to blow it up with MPGs, then we secure what remains. A will be approaching first; B on radio command. Do not fire weapons without confirmation. The new code applies."

She went on for a few minutes more. Without stumbling on a single word, without a need for clarification, holding their eyes with the intensity of her gaze.

When she was done, Torrence nodded and went down into the troop transport deck area, to where the others sat on the benches, talking softly.

Lila turned to go—and then stopped, seemed to hesitate.

Claire watched her in fascination, relieved to see her showing some human uncertainty.

Lila turned to Claire and looked her in the eyes. She smiled.

She reached out, tentatively, and touched Claire on the cheek. She turned and went down the ladder. Claire stared after her, amazed.

She saw Lila talking to Karakos, below. Torrence on the other side of the boat, fairly glaring at them. What was with Torrence? *"I don't trust that son of a bitch,"* he'd said.

Claire shook her head and shrugged her rifle off her shoulder. She held it in her hands and prepared to rehearse a massacre.

• • •

The Caribbean. The Island of Merino.

"No," Alouette said. "It didn't hurt."

"How about now?" Smoke asked her.

"No. But it is making a little itch," she said, reaching up to touch the spot on the back of her head. But she drew her hand back, remembering she wasn't to touch the incision.

"The itch means it's healing up," Smoke said. He wasn't sure if that was really true but he wanted to reassure her. "But if it starts to swell or anything, you must tell the doctor."

They were sitting together on the examination table in the clinic. The miniblinds were halfway closed; the subtropical light slanted brilliantly to the cement floor, next to the white bulk of the magnetic-resonance-holography machine.

Across from them, in a locked glass cabinet, other silicon chips—actually, each was a matrix of many nanochips—were laid out on the black foam-rubber tray like a display of individual fish scales. The room was warm. Alouette wore white shorts. She had no top on, because the doctor had been examining her but she was far from budding breasts. Smoke was wearing an islander's white cotton shorts, and buttonless overshirt. They sat on the table, swinging their legs, waiting for the doctor to come back, each being brave for the other.

"Before they put it in, I understood this thing, this chip," she said. "But now I wake up and I don't understand it."

"You're having what we call cold feet, I think," Smoke said. "That's normal."

"Cold feet. Like . . . *de peur de un hoyo?*"

Smoke smiled. She'd mixed French and Spanish. The island had been colonized by the Spanish first, then the French, then the Spanish fought to take it back, then the French once more . . . wrested back and forth like a child between divorced parents. The result was a mix of French and Spanish, in the names and dialect of the islanders. *De peur de un hoyo.* The fear of a hole. An island expression; being afraid to walk about at night, for fear of falling in a hole. "Yes," he told her, "*de peur de un hoyo.* It's the same idea. Afraid to go forward because you're not sure what's there."

"I understand what's there. But . . . "

"But at the same time you don't? I know the feeling. It's to protect you, Alouette. The chip will use your bioelectric field to communicate with us. When you get a little older you can use it to help you think about problems. It could save you. Neural-interface chips have been tested for twenty years. I'm convinced that this one is safe . . . I didn't decide to give this chip to you overnight. It connects with your brain and—well, I was afraid it might be dangerous. But we are . . . " He hesitated. He didn't want to frighten her. But there was a war going on. There was a war within a war. And because she had been adopted by the NR, she was part of the war. Probably, she would see some of it. He had to prepare her. "We are all of us in danger. This will protect you against that danger, a little. Its risks are outweighed by . . . " He looked for a way to explain it in words she'd understand.

"We're in danger because of the Fascists?"

"Yes. And lately . . . I'm afraid the CIA is looking for us. We think they've been spying on the island with a satellite. They're very dangerous. They're working with the Second Alliance."

"CIA . . . ?" She frowned. "James Bond's friends?"

He blinked at her. "Who's James Bond?"

"They showed him on video night in the auditorium. He's a spy hero. He's from England. He has a friend named Felix who's from the CIA who helps him sometimes." She drew her feet up onto the padded table, crossed them, and scowled over a blister on her heel. She prodded it, squeezed it.

"Leave that alone," Smoke said. "You'll get it infected or something."

She turned and poked the foot at his stomach, laughing. He caught her ankle and held it, tickled her foot. She squealed and pulled it away, and almost fell off the table. Smoke grabbed her, his heart pounding. God. What if he lost her like that. Something stupid. Fall and hit her head.

She regained her balance, and lowered herself to the floor. She looked up at him gravely. "The CIA are trying to hurt us?"

"They're . . . not James Bond's friends in real life. They're a sort of secret government within the government of the USA. Every so often the rest of the government catches them at something they shouldn't have been doing and they, um, rein them in a little. Like a dog on a leash. But the dog gets away again eventually. And it has again."

"What did they do that they shouldn't have been doing?"

"Oh God. Maybe we'd better wait till you're older. It's complicated."

She gave him her chilliest glare. There was something very adult in it that made him laugh. "I'm not stupid," she said.

"I know. Okay. Well—I'll give you some examples. After World War Two the CIA recruited Nazis—like Klaus Barbi, a man who tortured and murdered a lot of people in France. They recruited them to be spies. Later on they helped them escape to Central America and South America. These were the worst kind of Nazis, too . . . Something else the CIA has done is . . . well in the past it has overthrown democratically elected governments."

A certain distance in her eyes told him he'd lost her on that one.

Smoke went on, "You know what democracy is. You know what elections are."

"Oh, yes." That glare again.

"I know, I know you know." He smiled. He put a hand to his right shoulder. Empty. The crow wasn't there. The surgeon wouldn't let him bring him in here. He was in a cage, poor fellow, for the moment. "Anyway, um, America pretends to approve when a country elects its own government democratically. But in the twentieth century the American CIA used covert operations—secret spy operations of a very ugly sort—to overthrow and assassinate some very decent democratically elected leaders. Like a man who was elected president of Iran. This was mid-twentieth century. He wanted to nationalize the oil industry, which wasn't convenient for American companies. So they pushed him out—they said he was a Communist, but he wasn't—and they installed the Shah instead and that led to a generation of torture and killing and repression, things the Shah did to people who disagreed with him, all with the help of the CIA, and *that,* the repression, that led to a revolution run by people who hated us. The Ayatollah. It was a big mess. And the CIA overthrew the democratically elected president of Guatemala—I think this was in the 1950s—ah, they overthrew him because he wanted land reform to help the peasants and that was not convenient for an American company called the United Fruit Company. They said he was a Communist and they got rid of him. He wasn't a Communist but they said he was. Then they set up a military dictatorship that tortured and murdered people for generations. They did this in Chile and a lot of places. There was always a big mess afterwards. They always made things worse for everyone. It was a question of protecting the interests of big American companies who had a stake in the . . . "

He let his voice trail off, seeing her distress. She was standing there with one foot on the other, chewing her lip, frowning at the floor. She hadn't been able to follow it all, and didn't want to admit it. He was relieved. He didn't want to have to tell her these things. She was just a little girl. He was afraid she would ask him about the torture. The murders the CIA had sponsored: the death squads. He didn't want to have to tell her.

And it was a relief to see the limits of her comprehension, the limits of her precocity, because he wanted her to be a little girl. His child, his daughter, his proxy retreat into innocence.

"You get the idea," he said gently. "The CIA pretend to be the friends of freedom but they're the opposite—or sometimes they are. So we have to protect you from them . . . And people like them . . . And the implant chips are going to change the world, and we have to get a sort of jump on that change, to use it for our protection."

She looked up at him, bobbing her head. "I know that."

"Good. I'm tired of waiting for the doctor. Let's go find him."

"Okay. I have to pee."

· 06 ·

NEW YORK CITY. GRAND CENTRAL STATION.

"The New-Soviet is losing the war," the man on the giant screen said. "They've been driven back to the old Warsaw Pact lines in Central Europe. They hold only a small corner of Afghanistan, and only unimportant territories in Iran. The orbital battlefield has been static for some time, with the US and NATO holding the important orbits; the New-Soviet Orbital Army's only advantage is its blockade of the Colony . . . "

Charlie was standing against the wall in Grand Central Station, just below and to one side of the enormous clock over digital advertisement signs. He glanced at his watch. Three-fifty. His contact was due at four.

The crowd in the vast, hangarlike spaces of the old train station wasn't large at this hour; but it was feverish. People walked by with single-minded haste, their paths criss-crossing in a perpetual chaotic meshing.

Opposite the clock, a big videoscreen, slightly washed out in the daylight, flashed through a series of gigantic images illustrating the remarks of the commentator. The screen was silent unless, like Charlie, you wore a headset tuned to the screen's sponsor station, on which you'd now hear the commentator continue, *"While it is true the New-Soviets control the key shipping lanes in the Atlantic, their 'superior' sea power is already beginning to show its weaknesses; ships in greater numbers simply do not make up for inferior technology. War is primarily carried out through orbital drop and remote controlled 'smart' tech—at which the Allies excel. The great risk now is this: If the New-Soviets feel they are losing, they may assume we will take the initiative and invade Russia itself. Rather than abandon their way of life and their independence, they may attempt a nuclear first strike."*

"Jesus," Charlie said.

"No, it's Angelo," Angelo said, walking up to him. "'Lo, Charlie, 'sap, my man."

"Angelo! You're the . . . ?"

"Yeah. Fuck the passwords. I forgot 'em, anyway. But it's me. They didn't tell you?"

"Shit, no, I thought it'd be some Pakistani in shades or something. Damn!" They clasped hands.

Charlie had known Angelo for twelve years, since they were kids. It was Angelo, four years before, who'd recruited Charlie into the NR.

Angelo was small, thin, pale, but his curly hair and eyes were dark. He had a wide mouth that split into a big, luminous grin at almost any stimulus at all. He wore an old black leather jacket and beat-up jeans, black tire-rubber boots. His eyes flashed around as if he were walking into a party and expecting to see someone he recognized. He was like that no matter where he was.

"That guy," Charlie said, nodding toward the screen, "claims the New-Soviets have lost the war. You think so, or is that propaganda bullshit?"

Angelo looked at the screen. "Naw, that guy's a liberal. Not one of the Administration's flunkies. If he says they losing, they probably are."

"He says they might panic and first-strike us."

"Fuck it. Out of our hands. You got a tan, Charlie. You look stupid with a tan. Come on, we gotta go right to class."

"*More* classes. About what?"

"Video animation. Digital pix. You know anything about it?"

"Programming basics."

"This goes way, way beyond. This stuff is classified. Public doesn't even know it exists."

"What's this crap about a senator?"

"Don't talk about that in public, man. Don't even think about it."

"Shit! Look at that!"

Charlie pointed at the videoscreen. The program had changed. Now it showed the Arc de Triomphe, the image rocking as if it had been shot from something moving erratically toward the arch. It swelled in the screen as the camera got closer and closer.

Charlie turned up his headset and heard, " . . . *video obtained from an assault vehicle of some kind, possibly a Jægernaut, shortly before the destruction of the arch last month. This video would seem to refute NATO claims that the arch was destroyed in aerial bombing carried out by the New-Soviets.*"

"So what about it?" Angelo asked.

"Smoke told me about that—he got it to Judy Cotz at Cableview and damn if she didn't get it out onto the Grid! Shit, I'll bet it gets shut down, and fast. See that, those guys on top of the arch? You can see the muzzle flashes. That's *our guys!*"

"Fuck, Charlie, keep your voice down."

But the station was raucous with train announcements, music blaring, the perpetual rising and falling drone and drumroll of people talking and walking.

As the camera got closer to the Arc de Triomphe, a contiguous mike picked up noise generated from the arch's top: the structured squeal of an electric guitar and the chilled-out rhythm of programmed percussion.

"Man!" Angelo said. "That's *Rickenharp!*"

Charlie nodded. Both of them stared up at the screen, awed by the video of Rickenharp's final minutes. As the commentator said, "These two resistance martyrs—one of them has been tentatively identified as former download-recording artist Rick Rickenharp—drew the SA's attention to the arch in order to provide a decoy so that other important Resistance operatives could escape. Using a porta-amp, guitar, a mini-PA system, and sheer defiance, they drew not only the fire of the Second Alliance troops but the devastating attention of the Jægernaut . . . "

They heard Rickenharp shouting over the music, "Hey, you, with the machine gun! Come on, give me your best shot!"

. . . and Rickenharp, a tiny figure up there, almost unseeable. But hearable. His voice and his guitar, kicked through those mean little Marshalls, was audible even over the gunfire. Some original tune now . . . you couldn't make out the lyrics but you knew what it was about . . . you'd heard a thousand permutations of it. It was an anthem, and it was about being young. Maybe it should have been called Youth.

And then the Jægernauts rolled in from the east and west, two of them converging on the arch. They came like the neo-Fascist war machine itself. They came on like mortality. Looking from below like five-story spoked wheels, the spokes digging into whatever was in the way. There were clouds of dust, showers of smashed stone. The Arc crumbling. The neo-Fashes scattered, cheering. Yukio kept sniping at them from the shrinking top of the Arc . . .

The echoes of his gunshots rolled like bass lines for Rickenharp's electric wailing. Rickenharp had cranked the amps all the way up; he could be heard over the squealing of the oncoming Jægernauts . . .

The two Jægernauts converged on the arch from opposite sides, began to grind away at it, spinning in place at first, then crunching down as the microwave beams took the fight out of the stone. Yukio's bullets whined off the blue-metal scythes . . . metal bit down on stone with a screaming that was another kind of heavy-metal jamming with Rickenharp's final chords: fat blue sparks shot out from the machine's grinding spikes; cracks spread like negative lightning through the huge monument . . . the arch's great crown bent, buckled inward . . .

"Holy shit," Angelo breathed as they watched the Arc de Triomphe implode into a cloud of dust, boulders bouncing, gravel raining.

A final furious and defiant guitar chord and a burst of gunfire from the arch's top, and then the arch fell into itself—and was replaced, for a moment, by a great pillar of dust and a monolithic silence . . .

"The sacrifice of these two men was more than a means of decoying the enemy from their friends. It was a symbolic act," the commentator said. *"It was their way of saying no to the SA's unquenchable brutality . . . "*

"You hear that?" Charlie breathed. "That's fucking *great.*"

"No way the government's going to let 'em show that stuff again," Angelo said.

"I don't know. This goes out over the Internet too—someone for sure'll hit *copy.* It'll be distributed there for starts. Maybe if enough people saw it, they wouldn't dare repress it . . . I mean, check it out, some of them were paying attention . . . "

Here and there, around the station, a few of the people wearing headsets were staring up at the screen, looking into the dust cloud surrounding the wreckage of one of the wonders of the world. They'd heard Rickenharp's final chords. How many more had heard?

Charlie and Angelo looked at each other. Till now, they'd always felt, privately, that the NR's struggle was a hopeless one; was more of a gesture than anything else. But now, that look, that silent exchange . . .

Hope.

•••

FirStep: the Space Colony. Security Central.

"I've got to be wrong," Russ muttered, rereading the personnel lists. "Praeger wouldn't go that far."

It was 8:10 a.m. Originally the Colony had gone by military time—0800, 0900—but Professor Rimpler had seen the need for "Earth homey" touches. So it was nine in the morning. And the light in the street-wide main corridors had a gray-blue tinge, like early-morning light, from six till eight. By now it was yellow. The few "cafés" still open along the Strip would be exuding the smell of eggs and bacon—though both were artificially made, artificially scented—and the vents would be pushing a brisk morning breeze along the corridors and through the shrubbery of the Open.

Russ wished he were there, in the Open, where you could see real, though reflected, sunlight; where you could see the grass wave in the air-conditioned wind . . .

But he was sitting in his tomb of an office, drinking ersatz coffee that tasted like sawdust mixed with thrice-used coffee grounds, and frowning at his work-screen's list of personnel for the day's outer-hull repairs.

It was routine, since the sabotage had begun, for Russ to approve all personnel lists for in-space repair. And he recognized twelve—count 'em, twelve!—names on the morning's list for Repair Module 17. They were all names from the Security Risk list. And they all belonged to blacks or Jews. And Praeger had already approved the list.

It didn't add up. Praeger had made it clear to hiring agents that blacks, Jews, Arabs, and Pakistani/Indians were to be hired minimally, if at all. He claimed they were Security Risks who couldn't be trusted on the outside. And now he'd approved a whole shipload of them. The only Caucasian personnel were people like Carl Zantello, an Italian . . . and a notorious radical.

Must be some mistake. Praeger's assistant must have approved the list for him, without really looking at it. Something.

Unless . . . maybe Praeger had magically gotten himself some political savvy. Realized that he was only making trouble for himself by refusing work assignments to minority groups and radic technickis.

Forget it. No way. Praeger was too pigheaded to see that racism was counterproductive.

What was he up to?

• • •

Less than a quarter of a mile from Russ Parker's office, Kitty Torrence was wondering more or less the same thing. She was thinking, What are they trying to do?

She and Lester were in the Open. They each had about forty minutes before they were to report for work, and they'd decided to use up one of their last passes to get into the park. It was much less crowded at this hour, and in the "mornings" the breeze, carried on the badly filtered ventilator systems, was only faintly tinged with putrefaction.

They stood on a low hill, looking up into the circumscribed sky, talking. Lester's scowl surprised her; she'd expected him to be happy he'd gotten a work assignment that day.

But she understood when he told her about Billy Glass. A white co-worker.

"Billy didn't know what it was," Lester said. "They told him they were forming a new technicki union, and that if he went, he stood a better chance of getting some work. But they hassled him about how he felt about things, about the dark brothers and the radics. He wanted the work, so he played along. He felt bad about it. Anyway, he went to their meeting, and there was nobody there but white technickis except there were guys he figures are undercover for Security. The Security spies talked technicki. Said it was the radics who were screwing up for the rest of us. Said they were in league with the New-Soviets, and the New-Soviet blockade is what's put us on half rations. Said the blacks and the Jews were working together to vandalize things. They pointed out that three of the prisoners in Detention for Life Support Endangerment are black. They asked Billy and the others to take a vow: If armed conflict comes up, they got to take up arms against the people of color and reformists. Billy got freaked out. Went out the back way, came looking to warn us . . . "

Lester and Kitty stood in silence for a while after he finished his explanation. Lester sullenly watched a helmeted guard walking by on the path below the hill. Kitty looking up at the swirl of clouds, like a hurricane's eye, at one end of the immense green-furred tube that was the Open, wondering if Admin was really doing what it seemed. "Well, anyway," she said, glancing at her watch, "in ten minutes you'll have some real work."

"Yeah. I got RM17. Lot of my friends going out on this one. Guess this is the token nigger mission."

"Mmm . . . what they got you doing?"

He shrugged. "Going out to repair meteor damage. Pinhole stuff. They got me maintaining video comm with Repair Central. Which is kind of weird, because Judy Forsythe is going, too, and she's the same rating. I don't know why they need two comm techs. I'm surprised they need one." He reached over and patted her stomach. "They won't let you work much longer. Maybe if my job works out, you can quit right away."

"Lester, I . . . " *No, don't tell him.* But it came out on its own, all in a rush: "I'm scared to keep going to work. I'm afraid one of the supervisors'll start thinking about the pregnancy and check to see if I'm on Parenthood Monitoring. They'll make me go to PM, and PM'll tell me the baby's a risk from the radiation here or something and they have to abort it and . . . " She broke off and looked at Lester a little sheepishly.

He was looking at her like he couldn't believe it. "Christ—I never thought about that. But—they wouldn't do *that*—not with a baby that far along! Would they?"

"They did it to Betty Carmitzian. Her husband's Lebanese. A Muslim. They said the baby was deformed, but . . . "

"But maybe they murdered it because its daddy was a wog?" Lester looked so grim, it scared her.

She touched his arm—and quickly withdrew her hand. He was trembling with repressed fury. "If they touch our kid . . . " he said softly, his eyes, glassy with rage. "If they touch you . . . I'll abort their fucking Praeger right out the fucking air locks."

She threw her arms around him. "Don't get all worked up, Lester," she whispered. "You'll get in a fight or something. They'll throw you in Detention."

She felt some of the tension draining out of him as he put his arms around her. "We're gonna get out of this shit can, baby. I promise you. Safe and sound . . . "

She nodded into his shoulder.

"Hey," he said softly. "I got to go to work. You too. Don't push it, huh? Take it easy when you can."

They took one last look around at the trees, the grass, the half-finished condo housing in Rimpler Meadows, the mist of sky, and, beyond it, the curve of more of the inside-out land overhead.

Kitty stretched. It felt good on the hill. The gravity was less here, and it was easier on her pregnancy-burdened back. She sighed and took Lester's hand. Together they walked back to the passageway that led to Hollywood Boulevard: Corridor A.

As she went, she got heavier; her belly hung ever so slightly lower; her back began to ache . . .

• • •

Russ had been trying for thirty minutes, off and on, to get Praeger on the line so he could verify the RM17 worker list, and he just couldn't get through. Have to step up to his office and see him in person, maybe.

Damn screen was fuzzing over. They were having near constant interference on the comm lines. Maybe it was the saboteur again . . .

On an impulse Russ turned to his Security console and punched for Suspect Check, asked for the transcripts of the surveillance vid: The "Echelon-style" scans.

He scrolled through the transcripts for a while, scanning the high-lighted stuff Praeger's men felt indicated "incriminating conversation." It was mostly ordinary grousing. Like, "Fuckin' Admin's playin' games with us again; they're moving us around. Kate and I got moved to a fucking lower deck unit, thing smells like the sewage recycler . . . "

And another, *"Libish triguttusser sinker ginny—"*

Russ punched *TFT* for translation from technicki. The computer translated, *"The Lying Bitch will try to get you to sink [i.e., betray] your own grandmother."*

Big deal. Russ shrugged and scrolled onward, stopped at the transcript of a conversation between Kitty Torrence and her husband Lester.

"Okay, we ought to stand up to them, but . . . but don't you think it'd be more, um, powerful . . . that it'd give us, you know, a better chance, if you waited till the blockade was over? So they don't just use it as an excuse to come down on you? They've got to lift the martial-law alert eventually . . . "

"Maybe . . . maybe so."

Russ frowned. He scrolled up, scanned through the parts he'd missed.

He stopped at a remark the marginal notation attributed to the woman. "If they're fascists, they don't have any conscience about hurting people—maybe even *killing* people . . . "

Russ's gut contracted.

Well. There it was. A woman, a pregnant woman, soon to be a mother. Warning her husband about the storm troopers.

And he, Russell Parker, was one of the men she was talking about.

He'd taken an interest in Kitty Torrence. Maybe because when he'd questioned her, she made him think of his wife, who'd died eight years back. A plain woman, like Kitty Torrence, but as sweet and pure as mountain snowmelt.

Russ had intervened. He'd checked up on her, found they were going to send the Parenthood Monitoring officers around to bring her in for a mandatory abortion. He'd scotched that and managed to slip it past Praeger. For now. The baby wasn't really safe till it was born . . .

Was it safe even then? Her Lester was a troublemaker, all right. Smart, leadership qualities, and a radical. Bad combination.

But if he could help Lester and Kitty, he would.

And Lester was scheduled to go out on RM17.

Thinking about RM17 made him shift uneasily in his seat. RM17 had been chewing at the back of his mind for almost an hour now.

He stabbed a finger at General Communications and this time got through.

"Bucher here," said the face on the screen. "Rear Launch Deck. Can I help?"

"This is Russ Parker, Security. I want you to hold that RM17 launch for . . . ten minutes."

"You got it, Chief."

Russ changed frequencies and punched for Praeger's office.

Praeger's image, scowling, appeared on the screen. "Yes?"

"Hey, how yuh doin' there . . . "

"Cut the corn pone and get on with it, Russ. I'm in conference."

Russ cleared his throat. *Keep your cool.* "I've been checking the passenger list for RM17. Must be some kind of mistake—you check this list personally?"

"Yes, what of it?"

"It's almost all Suspects and High Risks. Blacks, radics, you name it. I thought you wanted . . . "

"You wanted me to give them more work, did you not? 'Defuse their anger,' I think you said. Well, I've done it."

But Russ didn't buy it. There was something more. Even in the two-dimensionality of the videoscreen he could see it in Praeger's face. "Just exactly why . . . "

He broke off, cursing as the screen fuzzed over with snow.

And then, gaping, he stared at another face forming in the visual white noise . . . a face forming out of the boiling field of white flecks. *Rimpler.* Old man Rimpler.

Russ had the uncanny feeling Rimpler was looking out at him. At him, personally. Was seeing him, was that instant staring back . . .

"Russ . . . " A small, raspy voice from the speaker.

Startled, Russ leapt back, overturning his chair. He fell on his ass.

The screen laughed. "Russ!"

Russ got to his feet. "What the hell!"

"*Russ!*" It was Rimpler's voice—but Rimpler was dead.

Russ hit the reset button on the console. The screen flickered. The snow returned. So did the face, a face of white-on-white, with empty eyes.

Russ went to the door, thinking, *Get help.* Part of him wondering, *Help against what? What are you scared of? A glitch on a monitor?*

But he slapped the open panel on the door. It didn't open.

He swore and pulled open the access box in the wall to one side of the door, reached in, threw the emergency open switch. The door slid aside.

He started to step through—

The door slammed shut on him, pinning his chest, wedging him in, crushing. A vertical bar of hot pain in his chest. He yelled and tried to push the door back. The door's mechanism whined.

One of the guards came into the hall outside his office, stared for a second, then ran up to help him. Together they pressed the door open. Suddenly it switched off. It was as if it had stopped trying. It slid meekly into the wall.

"What happened, sir?"

"I don't know. My whole damn office went haywire. Get tech security up here."

"Yes, sir." The guard loped away.

Russ turned to look back into his office. He saw that one of his wall cameras had moved. It was a camera used by his comm system to pick up his image for transmission—and it had shifted toward the door. The camera moved only when it was electronically commanded to. He had given it no such command. So why had it moved?

To follow him, when he'd gotten up to go through the door . . .

To follow him so that someone—whoever it was—would know when to slam the door on him.

He rubbed his chest. It was bruised. It stung. Was the attack a practical joke? Or had someone really tried to kill him?

• • •

On the Colony's rear launch level, A-Deck, the deck foreman looked at his watch. Russ had said ten minutes. It was now fifteen.

His screen pulsed, and Praeger's image appeared there.

"Bucher!"

"Yes, sir?"

"What's the delay?"

"Chief Parker said . . . "

"He's out of line. Launch it now!"

"Yes, sir."

Bucher turned and looked out the foot-thick tinted glass window into the Launch Deck area. The seventy-foot graymetal bulk of Repair Module 17, roughly beetle-shaped, was sitting in its deck collars, its pilot windows lit up, its launch lights glowing red.

Bucher hit a button, and the launch lights went green. He hit another button and spoke into a mike extending from the wall. "Clearance, 17."

"Copy," crackled from the speaker.

The enormous air-lock doors slid aside. There was no whoosh of air: the launch area was already pumped airless. The collars unlatched from the beetle's legs, and it drifted up. Small jets on its aft sent it sliding neatly into space.

It became a black insect-shape snipped out of the field of stars, and then slipped like a shadow to Bucher's left, out of sight, as it followed the curve of the hull back to where the temporarily sealed punctures were.

As the doors were closing behind it, Bucher saw something odd.

There was a two-man EVA module, just a bucket shape with clawlike arms extended in front of it, drifting by the doorway, from Bucher's right. It looked as if it were following the RM17. That was odd, because it didn't appear on his duty charts.

He switched on his extra Launch Deck cameras and saw a flattened image of the RM17 drift by. And then, thirty seconds later, the EVA module, coming close on the RM17's heels.

• • •

Russ stormed into Praeger's office, pushed past the secretary—and stopped short when he saw Praeger looking up at him. He felt his courage draining away, leaking through the holes Praeger's glare made in him.

"You have a reason to come barging in, Russ, you'd better give it to me *fast.*"

Russ's mouth was dry. He could talk about the door's attempt to crush him—but what really bothered him was the RM17. It was hard to put into words, though.

Sitting next to Praeger was Van Kips. Her normally immaculate flaxen hair looked a little mussed. Something odd about the way Praeger was sitting behind that desk too. And the room was dialed to dim illumination. It was almost dark in there. Could they have been . . . ?

No, ridiculous. Not in here, not now.

"Well," Russ began. "My com was down and I wanted to talk about that personnel list of the . . . " He stopped, his attention caught by the screen across from Praeger's desk. It showed a TV image of the outer hull of the Colony, curving away like a metal plain. Four things crawling over it. No, two things, and their shadows. Repair Module 17—he could see the big numbers painted on the side—closely followed by a two-man EVA bucket.

"It's already been launched?" Russ asked, his voice sounding hollow in his ears.

"Yes." Smugness in Praeger's voice. "Yes, why shouldn't it? I was just monitoring it because . . . " Parker could feel Praeger pause to make up a lie. Praeger went on: " . . . ah, as you had expressed some concern about it. It seems to be just fine."

"Isn't it unusual for an EVA bucket to work so closely around the RM series?"

"Yes," Van Kips said hastily. "We just put in a call to it. We couldn't get through. That crazy interference again."

"Well, we'd better try again . . . "

Van Kips and Praeger exchanged glances. "Oh, leave it alone, Russ," she said.

Russ started to tell them about the "glitch" that had trapped him in the doorway . . . but nothing came out of his mouth. He was staring at the image on the screen. The EVA module was moving in closer—moving in on the cylindrical fuel tanks on the underside of the RM17.

The arms on the EVA bucket extended, and punched through the metal of the fuel tanks.

A crackle of electricity along the arms, a billow of gas from somewhere on the front of the bucket . . .

The RM17 exploded.

• • •

It was eleven o'clock and Kitty's supervisor had sent her home early. She was riding in one of twelve small, rubber-wheeled cars pulled by something resembling an oversize golf cart. It made her remember being a little girl riding in a "train" not so different than this one at the Bronx Zoo, past a lot of tired, dull-eyed patchy-furred animals.

She sat across from a boy who held a smartfone on his lap. He was watching rock cartoons.

The people in the street-wide corridor—"Hollywood Boulevard"—were of all kinds. Unsmiling and dull-eyed, most of them, but there were people laughing here too. There was a group of boys wearing real-cloth jackets, covered with technicki patches, using markers to leave their gang tags on the walls. She couldn't read the stylized graffiti writing. The train swept past them, rocking as it turned a corner, and she winced as the inertia chased a snake of nausea up through her. She'd almost collapsed at work today. The supervisor had said, "You're past the time you can do this kind of work."

It seemed her super could no longer pretend she didn't know Kitty was pregnant. Kitty wondered if she'd reported it. They were supposed to report it in case the parents didn't.

She sighed. She closed her eyes. She hoped Lester was behaving himself.

Her eyes snapped open when the device on the boy's lap broke from its mindless minimono yammering to announce: *"Special news report from Colony Central. A repair module working outside the Colony has exploded, with all hands lost. However, no major damage to the Colony's hull was done. Although not yet Admin-confirmed, RM17 was reportedly destroyed by an accidental collision with a drone EVA module. A list of casualties will be . . . "*

"Jeez," the kid said.

• • •

Russ sat on his bunk, in the darkness, listening to an audio called "Night Noises in the Desert." Smelling the fragrance disk he'd put in the scent player: sage, wood smoke, mesquite. He was sitting on his hands. When he didn't sit on them, he tended to pound them against his temples, and that hurt, so he had to sit on them.

This is stupid, he told himself. So he took his sweaty hands from under his haunches and tucked them into his armpits for a while.

Goddammit. Goddammit son of a *bitch*.

They did it, all right. They had all the answers way too soon. Too pat. "Guidance mechanism on the drone EVA bucket poorly insulated, misdirected by RM17's computer navigation signals." They had it twenty minutes after the thing exploded.

He squeezed his eyes shut but still saw, against the darkness of his unlit chamber, the white flash, the fireball quickly snuffed out in the vacuum, the expanding ring of debris—

And twenty minutes after the RM17 exploded, Praeger was printing out a statement for release at 1800. The statement talked blandly of a poorly insulated guidance mechanism; the EVA bucket sent out to assist the RM17 was simply the wrong one, was the one that should have been in repair dock.

Some equipment dispatcher would get the blame. Maybe someone the SA wanted to get rid of. Just to put the cherry on the sundae. Get rid of one more, after killing all those men and women on RM17. All those troublemakers.

No, Russ told himself. No one's going to take the fall for Praeger. Not that he could accuse Praeger. Yet. Too risky. Praeger would have him removed from his job before the accusation could become public. Praeger's people—under Judith Van Kips' supervision—censored all the Colony's media now. Nothing went on the air or into printout without Van Kips' approval.

Removed from his job? Praeger wouldn't stop there. If Russ fought him, Praeger would simply have him killed.

And most of the SA guards were loyal to Praeger.

There had to be a way . . .

• • •

Someone tried to talk to her. She was walking down the narrow corridor, in the dorms section where most of the technicki lived, seeing only what she had to, hearing nothing.

Kitty was trying not to think; to perceive as little as possible; to feel nothing. Because if she let herself feel the pain, it would fall on her like gasoline on a man smoking a cigarette; she'd be a human torch with it, she'd run howling with it . . . where? Where would she *go*? To her parents? How many thousands of miles of interplanetary space was she from her parents?

What else was there? Some peaceful spot on Earth where she could let herself feel, let her surroundings heal her. The state park her parents had taken her to, one of the only parks not ruined by the acid rain or global warming drought. How many thousands of miles of radiation-charged vacuum between her and that park? How many air locks and bulkheads and men with guns?

But still she felt the pain moving in on her, unreasoningly implacable.

The baby. Oh, Jesus. Living here *alone* with the baby. Oh, shit; she wished she were religious. The baby. Without Lester.

(Faces drifting by, like shapes in smoke. Voices speaking to her in a meaningless string of syllables.)

If she killed herself, she'd be killing the baby. Maybe that'd be better. It was only going to get worse and worse here, under the Fashes. They might kill her baby, anyway, because it was Lester's.

And, of course, she knew they'd murdered Lester.

(Her hands moving automatically to tap the coded sequence on the lock unit, opening the door.)

It might be a blessing to the baby if she killed herself. At least then it wouldn't be the Nazis (stepping into the apartment) who'd killed the baby, it would be . . .

He was sitting on their bed.

"Hi, babe," Lester said sadly, sitting up, yawning. "Damn, can you believe I missed out on that job? I got back from the Open too late, couldn't get through the crowd around the assignment center, foreman said they'd overhired, weight limit wouldn't let them put anyone else—hey . . . what's the matter, Kitty? You okay?"

She moved across the room in a dream. *Touch him.*

She touched his lean, muscular arm. He was real.

She melted onto him. He threw his arms around her. "Why you cryin'—oh, the job, yeah, well, I'm sorry, babe, I just . . . "

"Lester, you didn't hear about the RM17?"

"No—what the hell happened?"

"Lester, I heard there's a way to get off the Colony. The New-Soviets let one ship through every two weeks. It's almost impossible to get on it. But there must be a way. Lester, let's get off this thing, please. I don't care if we don't have any money left. Let's go back. Please. Please."

"What happened to the . . . "

"You won't run out and start something if I tell you?"

"No." But his face went hard. "Tell me."

• • •

Russ lay on his back, smelling sagebrush, listening to the maracas of desert insects, the fluting of the desert owl.

And seeing two things in his mind's eye, alternately. First, the explosion on the screen. Ball of white fire, expanding ring of char. Second: Van Kips leaning over Praeger, the light from the screen image of the explosion lighting up their faces in that dim room . . . exposing, somehow, a febrile delight in Praeger's face . . . and Van Kips' hand moving under the table. He couldn't see what she was doing, but . . .

Van Kips had her hand on Praeger's crotch. Was fondling him while the two of them watched the explosion.

They were that . . . what was the word? *Perverse? Demented? Inhuman? Efficient?*

Yes. (Russ laughed bitterly.) *Efficient. Extract the maximum from everything. Pleasure, too.*

And, Jesus forgive him, he was one of them. He was on their side.

And he had to be. Sure he did.

Or, anyway, he had to sit back and let it all happen. He had to try to get involved as little as possible.

But he remembered something his mother had said: "If you don't choose a side, the side will choose you."

• • •

THE ISLAND OF MALTA.

The ship is my best opportunity, Karakos thought.

The ship would have a sat-link he could use. In all the confusion, he could slip away from the other hijackers, get to the radio room.

Ten p.m., and they were in one of the top-floor bedrooms of the old manor house. It was an old, mildewy room, with peeling rose-patterned wallpaper, an empty wooden wardrobe standing open beside the wall's single decoration: a framed, yellowing photo of a droopy-mustached man in front of the Maltese capitol building in Valletta.

Eight guerrillas were seated in a semicircle around Steinfeld, shifting to ease the discomfort of the wooden seats, as Steinfeld tapped the map. He talked of currents, sea lanes, New-Soviet surveillance routes, the probability—or improbability—of interference from New-Soviet or NATO submarines, the temperature of the Mediterranean this time of year, and the projected route of the target ship.

"The ship will be coming from Málaga, on the coast of Spain, then east along the North African coast and through the Strait of Sicily, rounding Sicily on the eastern coast," Steinfeld had said. "It will be unescorted and without cannon, so as not to draw the attention of the New-Soviets, but it'll be accompanied by at least twenty-five SA infantrymen. They'll be heavily armed."

It wouldn't be easy for the NR to hijack the ship, Karakos thought. During the skirmishing there might be time to radio the location of the NR stronghold to Watson.

Doing it aboard the ship was risky. But he wasn't authorized to use the NR's radio, and there was always someone on radio watch. Fone transmissions were barely workable, in Europe now, and the few that went out were easily noticed and traced. He'd decided against trying to get access to another shortwave elsewhere on Malta. It didn't seem possible without drawing attention to himself. If he was caught wandering around the island alone, trying to locate a radio, they'd become suspicious. And there wasn't a land line he could use: the international fone links had been destroyed by the New-Soviets, just before they pulled out of the area.

Karakos felt odd when he looked around the circle of faces. He felt . . . constricted. As if something were tugging in his brain and tightening in his throat.

But it was not as if he'd lost his resolve. Not at all. He knew that the only way to truly liberate Greece was to unite his homeland under a one-party nationalistic rule. Nothing else would render Greece strong enough to survive its endemic factionalism, the incursion of Communists, the predations of the New-Soviets and the Turks, the sedition of the Jews. And the only means to ensure a strong nationalist state in Greece was the Second Alliance.

Watson had shown him by direct brain transferral—had poured truth into his brain electronically and electrochemically—and it had been as if someone had turned on a light, blazing away the fog of ethical and political gray areas, leaving only the stark clarity of a single steely principle: "Strength is Security. And the Alliance gives strength."

But still . . .

Sitting here with the others—including Danco, who'd fought beside him in the first campaign against the SA (incredible now to suppose he'd actually fought his homeland's greatest benefactors!); the woman Lila, surely the finest woman soldier he'd ever met (impossible not to notice the way Lila was looking at this Claire Rimpler); Willow; and the others—the ghost of the old camaraderie made him tingle, made him shiver, just a little. It was as if his new conviction was an upright edifice, a tower of stainless steel in the expanse of his mind. But it was a haunted tower . . .

Steinfeld was talking about techniques for ducking the ship's radar, avoiding its infrared scans. But this man Torrence wasn't fully listening; he was staring at Karakos.

The Yank suspects me, Karakos thought.

Karakos gazed back at Torrence with wide-open, clear, guileless eyes, smiling like a big brother.

He could see Torrence's jaw muscles clenching.

"The ship is the *Hermes' Grandson,*" Steinfeld was saying.

And Karakos thought, *It's a sign. The messenger of the gods will be my messenger to the SA . . .*

And he must do something about the hijacking, of course. The *Hermes' Grandson* was carrying supplies of all kinds to the SA. He could not permit it to fall to the Resistance.

"Ship-assault training commences at 1600 tomorrow evening," Steinfeld was saying, rolling up his charts.

The others were going out. Except Torrence and Claire; Torrence waited to talk to Steinfeld. "How about we assign Claire shore correspondence duty for the assault on the ship," Torrence was saying. Claire turned a glare at him. He ignored her. "I don't think she's ready to go back into combat just now. She's had too much too soon."

"Who the hell do you think you are, Torrence?" Claire demanded.

"The question of Torrence's personal sense of identity is moot," Steinfeld said dryly. "I had already decided that you are to do shore correspondence that night, Claire. Torrence's suggestion was unnecessary. You've got good comm training, you'll be most useful there."

He tucked his satchel of charts under his arm and beat a hasty retreat, hurrying out into the hall.

Karakos pretended to follow. But he lingered in the hallway. He could hear very well from there; the door was not quite closed.

"Be realistic," Torrence was saying. "You're sick of killing, Claire; you're not even sure the killing is the right thing to do. Those nightmares . . . when you're shaky like that, you risk the other people."

"Torrence"—her voice wavered between outrage and tears—"I don't need you to tell me that I'm not ready for a mission right now. I know when

I'm ready and when I'm not. And this stuff about risking other people is bullshit. You're doing it to protect me."

"Come off it!"

"I know you, *Hard-Eyes*." Saying his nickname with that sneering undertone that meant the name carried some sort of objectionable freight of machismo. "I know your condescending, paternalistic bullshit."

"That what you call caring about someone?"

That slowed her up for a moment. Two moments. But not three. "I'd be lying if I said I didn't want you to care about me. But I don't want you to make my decisions for me. You could at least have discussed it with me before going to Steinfeld."

"Now you're being childish. There's a chain of command here."

"Fuck that, it has nothing to do with you being a captain. You took it over my head because you like being in charge of me—of your girl-friend."

"Fuck you, then," Torrence said coldly, evenly. "Take care of yourself. You aren't going to like it."

He started through the door.

But Karakos had sensed that the argument was peaking. He was on his way down the stairs, thinking, *Maybe this woman Claire Rimpler is the way.*

• 07 •

The New York City subways hadn't changed much. They were still rackety, grimy, graffiti-ugly, plagued by aging equipment and vandalism. They were still undermaintained; they were still dangerous.

Corte Stoner was riding the subway that night for all those reasons.

The noise would cover conversation; the danger and discomfort kept most potential eavesdroppers away.

But Stoner was worried. He was worried about the two guys he was meeting here. He could see them through the window in the door to the next car down, two men lurching with the swaying of the rocketing train.

The husky black guy in the real-cloth gray suit was Stu Brummel, his wife's brother (a leftist for a brother-in-law, for God's sake!) He could understand the suit; it went with Brummel's cover. He was a lawyer. But did he have to wear something so expensive? Real cloth? Was that even politically correct?

The little Spanish guy in the blue printout was the Nicaraguan, whom Stu referred to only as Lopez. Stoner had found him in CIA Domestic files, though: Carlos Lopez. Supposedly working in the SA, ranked lieutenant.

Brummel had told Stoner the rest: The NR had its Second Alliance moles. Despite all the SA's promises, none of the Hispanics would become influential in the organization

The NR's mole cultivated Lopez's resentment and fanned it into outright rebellion by letting Lopez in on the Second Alliance's long-term plans for Central and South America: complete subjugation.

Lopez was flipped, had changed sides, but the NR had kept him in place in the Second Alliance; he worked as an intelligence funnel for Smoke and Steinfeld.

Brummel wasn't New Resistance. He was a "post-Maoist," a believer in a democratic socialism who borrowed some of Mao Tse-tung's theory—the kind of guy, Stoner thought, Mao would have purged.

Brummel considered the NR politically tainted, suspect, to be contacted and used only when necessary. Which is why he'd contemptuously told Stoner too much about Lopez.

But, hell, Brummel could be up to anything. Maybe he was going to deliver Stoner into the hands of men who'd take Stoner hostage, demand money from the government for his release. Maybe he was a cold motherfucker who'd decided that his sister—who didn't approve of his activities, after all—had to be sacrificed for the revolution.

Or maybe he was on the level. Maybe . . .

As the train roared around a turn in the tunnel, racing to meet the line of lights in the ceiling, Brummel and Lopez came into Stoner's car, looking around.

It was after midnight; they were alone.

They stood close together in the center of the cold, trash-strewn, otherwise empty subway car, holding on to the grimy chrome stanchions, forced by the train's motion into an absurd, jerky dance, lurching to the percussion of the wheels, shouting to be heard; shouting what would get them arrested in other places.

Stoner looked at the two men and felt a long, slow, sickening wave of disorientation go through him. Something in him shrieked silently, *What am I doing?*

And he told himself, *I'm doing it for Janet. For Cindy. And because I have to survive.*

But still he felt like he was two men inside and one of them hated the other one.

"You sweep your house again?" Brummel asked. His expression was always the same: sullen amusement.

Stoner nodded. "Found a bug in each room. And I've picked up a tail. Pretty sure I lost him today."

Lopez, a fox-faced man with shiny, short-clipped hair, small eyes, and a way of snapping his head around to look eagle-intensely at each man who was talking, said, "But you are not completely sure?"

"Sure as anyone can be. Which means, not completely."

"We're okay here, Lopez," Brummel said. "You bring it, Stoner?"

Stoner snorted and shook his head. "I'm not going to hand files over to you guys till I know what I'm getting in return."

"How we know we trust you?" Lopez asked, smiling, raising both shoulders in an exaggerated shrug. "Could be you want to penetrate us. You could be a plant for CIA Domestic."

Brummel nodded. "Possibility exists."

Stoner gave Brummel a look of exasperated appeal, said, "Come on, I'm your sister's husband. She'd never set you up."

"But you might *use* her to set us up, man. Maybe your career ain't going so well. Maybe your bossman don't like you being married to a nigger—so you got to prove yourself. You could be using extractors on her, twisting her mind around. CIA scumbags capable of anything. No, man. You got more to prove than we do."

Stoner hesitated. It seemed he had to give them something . . .

Maybe he ought to blow this whole thing off. Grab Janet and Cindy, head out on his own somewhere.

The Company would find him if he tried it on his own. He needed an underground route that someone had already set up.

The decision hovered on the edge of his will, just out of reach. And the lights on the train went out.

The three men ignored the blackout. The lights went out on the subways all the time. Light from outside strobed the windows as the train shot past the tunnel lamps, flickering Brummel's face in and out of darkness. On, off, on, off; light, dark; trust and no trust; trust and no trust; on, off . . .

Then the train's interior lights came back on.

Stoner made up his mind. "I'll get you something that no plant would give you," Stoner said. "They've taken me off the SA/NR stuff, but I can still access the files on library console; I've still got high clearance. I'll get you something . . . "

But not his ace in the hole. He'd keep that back till he really needed it: the fact that there was an Second Alliance agent planted in the European NR. Someone close to Steinfeld himself. He'd hold on to that as a final bargaining chip. Maybe never have to tell them about it at all. It went against his grain, his years of training, to give them even an iota of classified stuff. And he was going to have to give them a hell of a lot more than an iota.

It made Stoner feel sick inside.

He had no naïve ideas about who the good guys were. The SA had basically taken over the CIA; the Second Alliance yobbos were racists and true fascists. But that didn't mean their opposition was "good." Working for an intelligence agency, you got real skeptical of anyone who thought they could clearly identify the "good guys."

"You bring us something we can really use," Lopez said, "we get you out of the country, set you up good."

Stoner nodded. The train screeched into a station.

"We'll be in touch," Brummel said, turning toward the opening door.

But both doors leading out onto the platform were occupied. There were eight men standing in the doorways, four in each. And there were knives in their hands.

Men? Almost men, mostly boys. Eight black teenage boys in fragments of military uniforms, bits and pieces, trophies stolen from some of their prey. A drunk serviceman on leave makes an easy victim. Air Force flight jackets with Orbital Army patches, Naval Moonbase patches; fatigues, khakis, dress trousers incongruous with combat boots; goggles, diver's masks, Army-issue medinject units; Marine Corps ties worn as sashes. Helmets from five services; cunt caps and sailor's caps. One green beret. The tougher the service, the more prestige in taking the trophy off a serviceman.

As if choreographed—maybe they rehearsed it to scare us, Stoner thought—the eight gang punks stepped left foot first, into the car. *Stomp:* Their boots came down together. The subway car hooted, and the doors closed behind them. The train began to move.

Stoner thought, *I'm stupid.*

He'd followed instructions, which meant he'd come unarmed, and it was going to end stupid. *Caught up in a scheme to ditch CIA Domestic and you don't watch where you're going, you fall into bullshit like this.* Like a man running cross-country from bloodhounds, looks over his shoulder, doesn't see he's blundering into a barbed-wire fence. Tangled, slashed, bled to death. *Stupid.*

The one in the stolen green beret was brandishing his Navy Seabee knife. Blued seven-inch blade, leather-banded grip, iron end-knob. Bluing worn off the blade's razor edge, catching light where it had been recently honed; small nick four inches up the blade.

The details of the knife were forever imprinted in Stoner's mind.

Run? He glanced over his shoulder at the door into the next car.

"Forget it," the guy in the beret said. The knife in his hand waved in the air with a sawing motion imparted by the swaying of the car. The train hissed and grumbled and cracked.

Stoner said, "What we got, you can have. This is your turf and we respect that."

"Then why you bring this suck-ass nigger in the suit whichoo?" Green Beret asked. His head was tilted a little to one side.

The other gang punks moved into an orderly semicircle around the three men.

"I don't like no suit-nigger on my train."

Stoner glanced at Brummel. Brummel was impassive. He wasn't going to bring up the Brotherhood. Rub them even more the wrong way with that. *Ohhhh, he's political, huh? Thinks he's more righteous than us, zat tight, huh?*

"Take money," Lopez said, digging into his wallet.

"Money isn't enough," Green Beret said. His pupils were expanding, shrinking, expanding, shrinking, in waves . . .

Which drug was it? Stoner wondered.

"Money onna outside, money onna inside," said a boy in goggles, holding up a polished surgical scalpel.

"Organs pay better," said a guy in a Marine Corps helmet, grinning. He held up a satchel clinking with jars. The satchel was open, and Stoner could see the bluetinged organs glistening in their preserving syrup.

Stoner felt cold and hollow, like he was a fire-gutted tree cooled to fragile ash. Kick the gutted tree and it falls over, crumbles.

Janet. Cindy.

And then a number of things happened, way too quickly.

The door to the next car banged open behind Stoner; someone back there pushed him aside and ran at the gang; someone else behind the first someone, following close, and Stoner saw them both as he fell back against the vibrating metal wall: two Second Alliance cops, hired by the Transit Authority to patrol the cars, both in armored suits of gray-black cloth, flat black, striated armor reminding Stoner of fencing vests and mirrored helmets, RR sticks upraised, the one in the lead with his machine pistol out, amplified voice booming from his helmet: "YOUR CHOICE IS STOP WHERE YOU ARE OR DIE. I REPEAT, STOP OR WE *WILL* SHOOT YOU SICK LITTLE ASSHOLES!"

The gang scattered, turned to run, one of them pulling a pistol, firing over his shoulder, the sound of the gunshot lost in the screech of the brakes as the train pulled into another station; the round catching the cop square in the chest but even at close range ricocheting from the armor, smacking through an ad in a ceiling panel that read, *The only security is full security!*

The cop returned fire with a machine pistol spitting three-shot bursts; the gang punk went spinning and falling; another kid running, dropping the organ satchel, jars rolling, smashing, freeing a kidney, a bladder, a heart, all nice and fresh, the organs skidding nasty wet across the floor to slide into a heap of grimy paper and plastic cans, vital human body parts becoming just more trash; the SA cop swinging the RR club down on the boy's head. Recoil Reversal stick splitting the kid's head open like a burst organ jar; his brains splashing, Stoner gagging, kid crumpling, cop catching the others, firing at their backs, running after them into the next car as the train pulled up . . . second cop cornering two other boys, smashing their faces into their cranial cavities . . . bodies slumping, cop straightening over them . . .

It was quiet for a moment as the train paused in the station . . . and as the cop turned with bloodied club toward Stoner and Brummel and Lopez.

A faceless cop, his head hidden in the helmet; a distorted reflection of the interior of the subway car in its visor . . .

Stoner got to his feet, turned to follow Lopez and Brummel toward the door. Lopez made it through, but Brummel had to stop when the cop pointed a machine pistol at him and boomed, "HOLD IT, NIGGER, OR YOU'RE DEAD!"

Brummel said mildly, "I look like I'm a teenage kid wearing gang colors, officer?"

"YOU LOOK LIKE A NIGGER AND MAYBE YOU WAS HERE TO SELL 'EM DRUGS. NOW TURN AROUND, PUT YOUR HANDS ON THE FUCKING WALL, OR YOU'RE DEAD!"

Stoner muttered, "So it's gone that far now . . . "

"Yeah," Brummel said. "A long time ago."

"SHUT UP, NIGGER. FACE THE WALL, HANDS BEHIND YOU."

With a practiced motion the cop used his free hand to replace his stick on his belt and unhook handcuffs from the belt, almost in the same motion, opening them for Brummel.

Stoner's heart was banging, his mouth papery, but he managed, "He's—he had nothing to do with them. He's a lawyer—"

The cop's enigma-chilled visor turned toward Stoner, the muzzle of his gun coming Stoner's way too. Stoner thought, *Oh, no, don't do it, Brummel!* when he saw Brummel reach into his coat, draw the little gun It looked so small, like a cap gun, it couldn't possibly penetrate that armor, he was a fool . . .

But then Brummel's gun hissed and a tiny hole appeared in the belly of the cop's black-armored outfit and Stoner thought, *Explosive bullet with armor-piercing Teflon coat.*

The cop screamed, the gun in his hand spitting fire but the shots going wild, smashing out windows. And then his armored uniform ballooned outward, swelling in a split second to an almost spherical shape, grown five times bigger with his blood and the force of the explosion that was going off in his gut . . . blood spurting in a thin stream from the hole in the suit . . .

Stoner ran behind Brummel, out of the car and up the stairs, thinking, again, *So it's gone that far . . .*

• • •

A SUBURB OF CHICAGO, ILLINOIS.

"First of all," the walleyed prizewinner said, "it's a feeling of power like you never had. I figure that's especially the case here, see, because it ain't like you're doing it in self-defense, or in a war where it's in a hurry—you got time to, you know, think about it first . . . "

Spector was watching the walleyed guy on Internet TV. The guy was tubby, was wearing a stenciled-on brown suit, one of the cheap Costco printouts where the tie blurs into the shirt collar. And green rubber boots. Spector puzzled over the green rubber boots till he realized they were intended to look military.

A ghost image of another man's face, ragged-edged, began to slide over the AntiViolence Contest winner's; the new face was bodiless, just a face zigzagging across the image with kitelike jerkiness. A punky face, a rocker; leering, laughing. His tag rippled by after his face like the tail after a comet: *JEROME-X.*

It was video graffiti, probably transmitted from a shoplifted minitranser.

Annoyed, Senator Spector hit the switch on his armchair, turning off the console. The thin screen slotted back into the ceiling. In a way, the program was his responsibility. He'd felt bound to take stock of it. But watching it, the gnawing feeling had begun in his stomach again.

Spector stood up and went to the full-length videomirror in his bedroom. It was time to get ready for the interview. He gazed critically at his fox face, his brittle blue eyes. His black crew cut was shaped to hint at minimono styles—to let the youngsters know he was hip, even at fifty.

He wore a zebra-striped printout jumpsuit. It'll have to go, he decided. Too frivolous. He tapped the keyboard inset beside the mirror and changed his image. The videomirror used computer-generated imagery. He decided he needed a friendlier look. Add a little flesh to the cheeks; the hair a shade lighter. Earring? No. The jumpsuit, he told the mirror, would have to be changed to a leisure suit, but make its jacket stenciled for more identification with the average American. He'd never wear a stenciled suit out to dinner, but just now he needed to project a man-of-the-people image. Especially as the interviewer was from the underGrid. Both Spector's Security adviser and his media secretary had advised him against giving an interview to an underground media rep. But the underGrid was growing, in size and influence, and it was wise to learn to manipulate it—use it, before it used you.

He tapped out the code for the suit, watching it appear in the mirror, superimposed over his jumpsuit. A cream-colored leisure suit. He pursed his lips, decided a two-tone combination would be friendlier. He tapped the notched turtleneck to a soft umber.

Satisfied with the adjusted image, Spector hit the print button. He shed the jumpsuit and waited, wondering if Wendy had contacted his attorney, Heimlitz. He hoped she'd hold off on the divorce till after the election. The console hummed, and a slot opened beside the glass. The suit rolled out first—flat, folded, still pleasantly warm, smelling of chemicals from its fabrication. He pulled it on; it was high-quality fabricant, only slightly papery against his skin. He used PressFlesh for his cheeks, tamping and shaping till his face conformed with the image of a friendlier Senator Spector, the 'Flesh appearing to blend seamlessly with his skin. Cosmetics lightened his hair, widened his eyes a fraction. Then he went to look over the living room. Shook his head. The room was done in matte black and chrome. Too somber. He had to take great pains to avoid anything remotely morbid or sinister, because of the AntiViolence Laws issue. He dialed the curtains to light blue, the rug to match.

The console chimed. Spector went to it and flicked for visual. The screen lit up with the expressionless face of the housing area's checkpoint guard. "What is it?" Spector asked.

"People here to see you in a van fulla video stuff. Two of them, name of Lerman and Baxter, from a channel called UNO. Citident numbers . . . "

"Never mind. I'm expecting them. Send 'em up."

"You don't want a visual check?"

"No! That would offend. And for God's sake, be friendly to them, if you know how . . . "

He cut the screen, wondering if he was being cavalier about security. Maybe—but he kept a .44 in the cabinet beside the console, as a security backup. And there was always Kojo.

Spector rang for Kojo. The Japanese looked small, neat, harmless as Spector issued his instructions. Kojo's official title was secretary. He was actually a bodyguard.

Flawlessly gracious, Kojo ushered the two underGrid reps into the living room, then went to sit on a straight-backed chair to the left of the sofa. Kojo wore a blue printout typical of clerks and sat smilingly with his hands folded in his lap; no tension, no warning in his posture, no hint of danger. Kojo had worked for Spector only two weeks, but Spector had seen the Security Agency's dossier on him. And Spector knew that Kojo could move from the bland aspect of a seated secretary to lethal attack posture in under a quarter of a second.

The "alternative programming" reporter wore "rags"—actual cloth clothing, jeans, T-shirt, scuffed black boots. Silly affectations, Spector thought. The interviewer introduced herself as Sonia Lerman. The big black guy, Baxter, was her techi. A silver earring dangling in his left ear; his head was shaved. Spector smiled and shook their hands, making eye contact. Feeling a chill when he met the girl's eyes. She was almost gaunt; her dark eyes were sunken, red-rimmed. Not a happy woman. Thin brown hair cut painfully short. But she and Baxter seemed neutral; not hostile, not friendly.

Spector glanced at Kojo. The bodyguard was relaxed but alert.

Take it easy, Spector told himself, sitting on the sofa beside Sonia Lerman. His body language, carefully arranged, read friendly but earnest; he smiled, just enough. Baxter set up cameras, mikes, fed them into the house comm system for transmission to the station.

The girl looked at Spector. Just looked at him.

It felt wrong. TV interviewers, even if they intended to feed your image to the piranhas during the interview itself, invariably maintained a front of friendliness before and after.

The silence pressed on him. Silence, the politician's enemy. Silence gave people time to think.

"Ready at your signal," Baxter said. He looked *big*, hulking over hand-sized cameras on delicate aluminum tripods.

"Now, what shall we talk about?" Spector asked before the cameras were turned on. "I thought perhaps—"

"Let's just launch into it," she broke in.

He blinked. "No prep?"

She smiled thinly. Baxter pointed at her. She looked at the camera. Serious. "I'm Sonia Lerman, for the People's Satellite, interviewing Senator Henry Spector, one of the key architects of the AntiViolence Laws and an advocate of the AVL television programming . . . "

For a while the interview was standard. She asked him how he justified the AntiViolence Laws. Looking at her solemnly, speaking in an exaggeration of his Midwestern accent (the public found it reassuring), he gave his usual spiel: Violent crime began its alarming statistical growth trend in the 1960s, continued to mount in the 1970s, leveled out in the 1980s, dropped in the 90s for a few years, and then feverishly resurged in early twenty-first century. Columbine. No respect for law. Countries that had serious deterrents had less crime. Long-term incarceration and lots of appeals wasn't serious. And . . . so on.

"The AntiViolence Laws are a heck of a deterrent," Spector said. "Violent crime is down sixty percent from five years ago. It continues to drop. In a few years the Security checkpoints and the other precautions that make modern life tedious—these may vanish entirely. Oh, yes, because of our sped-up judicial pace, a few people a year are perhaps unjustly convicted. I've insisted on full funding for DNA testing—in the cases where a DNA test is possible. But there will be a few unjust executions—that's the price we pay. The majority of the people are better off, and it's the majority we must administrate for."

"Even accepting that people are better off," Sonia Lerman said, "which I don't, how does that justify the barbarity of the executioner's lottery, the AVL TV?"

"First, it's more deterrent. If it's barbarity, well, that's why it works. The humiliation and the awfulness of being executed on TV—well, if criminals see it every day, it scares them. Also, the program gets the public involved with the criminal justice system so that they identify with society and no longer feel at odds with policemen. And it acts as a healthy catharsis for the average person's hostility, which otherwise . . . "

"Which otherwise might be directed at the State in a revolution?" she cut in, her neutrality gone.

"No." He cleared his throat, controlling his irritation. "No, that's not what I meant, as you know."

He was even more annoyed by her interruption, and her tone, when she broke in. "The phrase 'healthy catharsis' puzzles me. Lottery winners are winning the right to beat or execute a convict on public television. Ever actually *watch* the program '*What It's Like*', Senator?"

"Well, yes, I watched it today . . . "

"Then you saw the way people behave. They giggle when they're getting ready to hang the convict. Or shoot them. They'll give out with a happy whoop. A man or a woman, gagged in stocks; the winner blows their brains out . . . and they cackle over it. And the more demented they are, the more the studio audience cheers them on. Now you call that *healthy?*"

Stung, he said, "It's temporary! The release of tension . . . "

"Two of the lottery winners were arrested, tried, and executed for *illegal* murders, after their participation in 'AntiViolence' programming. It seems fairly obvious that they develop a permanent taste for, killing, reinforced by public approval . . . "

"Those were flukes! I hardly think . . . "

"You hardly think about anything except what's convenient," she snapped, "because if you did, you'd have to see that you, Senator, are no better than a murderer yourself."

Her veneer of objectivity had cracked, fallen away. Her voice shook with emotion. Her hands clenched her knees, knuckles white. He began to be afraid of her.

"I really think you've lost all . . . I don't think you're thinking about this calmly. You're hysterical." He said it as coolly as he could manage. But he felt fear turning to anger.

(Feeling, in fact, he was near losing his own veneer, his cool self-righteousness, feeling he was near snapping. And wondering why. Why had all the skills he'd developed in years of facing hostile interviewers suddenly evaporated? It was this fucking AVL issue. It haunted him. Nagged him. At night it ate away at his sleep like an acid . . . and the damned woman went on and on!)

"Everyone who has been killed, Senator—their blood is on your hands. You . . . "

Some inner membrane of restraint in Spector's consciousness flew into tatters, and anger uncoiled in him like a snapped mainspring, anger wound up by guilt. (Fuck the camera!) He stood, arms straight at his sides, trembling. Shouting. "Get out! Get *out!*"

He turned to Kojo, to tell him to "escort" them to the door . . . and saw Baxter stretching his right arm toward Kojo; in Baxter's hand was a small gray box like a garage door opener. And Kojo had frozen, was staring into space in a kind of fugue state.

Spector thought, *Assassins.*

Kojo stood and turned toward Spector. Spector looked desperately around for a weapon.

Kojo came at him—

—and ran past him, at the woman. A wrist flick and he was holding a knife. She looked at him calmly, resignedly, and then she screamed as—his movements a blur—he closed with her, drove the slim silver blade through her left eye. And into her brain.

All the time Baxter continued filming, showing no surprise, no physical reaction. Spector gagged, seeing the spurt of blood from her eye socket as she crumpled. And Kojo stabbing her methodically, again and again.

Spector stumbled back, fell onto the sofa.

"Kill Spector after me, Kojo!" Baxter yelled. Baxter turned a knob on the little gray remote-control box, dropped it—and the box melted into a lump of plastic slag. Spector stared, confused.

Baxter stepped into the cameras' viewing area, closed his eyes, was waiting, shaking, muttering a prayer that might have been Islamic—then Kojo rushed him, the small Japanese leaping at the big black man like a cat attacking a Doberman guard dog. Baxter just stood there and let Kojo slash out his throat with one impossibly swift and inhumanly precise movement.

Kill Spector after me, Kojo.

But Spector was moving, ran to the cabinet, flung it open, snatched up his .44, turned, and, borne on a wave of panic, shot Kojo in the back.

Kojo would have turned on Spector next, surely.

But in the pulsing silence that followed the gunshot, as Spector looked down at the three bodies, as he stared at the big, red oozing hole his bullet had torn in Kojo's back . . . seeing Kojo's own PressFlesh had come off, exposing the puckered white scar on the back of his head, a scar from recent brain surgery . . .

Looking at that, Spector thought, *I've been set up.*

And the Security guards were pounding on the door.

• • •

"Today on *What It's Like* we're talking to Bill Mitchell, from Vendorville, Pennsylvania, the first man to participate in an actual *legal duel* with an AntiViolence Laws convict. Bill, you wanted to execute the man 'in a fair fight,' is that right?"

"That's right, Frank, I'm a former US Marine, and I just didn't want to shoot the man down in cold blood, I wanted to give him a gun, and of course I'd have a gun, and we'd, you know, *go at it.*"

"Sort of an old-fashioned Wild West gunfight, eh? You're a brave man! I understand you had to sign a special waiver . . . "

"Oh, sure, I signed a waiver saying if I got hurt, the government couldn't be held responsible."

"Bill, we're running out of time. Can you just tell us quickly what it was like for you, Bill Mitchell, to kill a man."

"Uh, sure, Frank, killing a man with a gun has its *mechanical* aspect, like, you got to punch a hole through the guy, and that causes damage to internal organs, so they're no longer workin', and of course loss of life-givin' blood. Now, what *it feels* like to do that . . . oh, boy. Well, you almost feel like the bullet is, you know, a part of you, like you can feel what it would feel, and like, you imagine the bullet nosing through the skin, pushing through muscles and smashin' through organs, bustin' bone, flyin' out the other side of 'im with all that red liquid . . . just blowing the bastard away. And it feels good knowing that he's a criminal, a killer, that *he deserved it.* And you feel a kinda funny *relief* like . . . "

"Bill, that's all we've got time for now. Thanks for letting us know . . . *What It's Like!*"

• • •

THE CHICAGO CITY JAIL.

The cell they'd moved Spector to that morning was significantly smaller than the first one. And dirtier. And there was someone else in it, wearing a bloodstained prison shirt. The guy was asleep, his back turned, on the top bunk. The cell had two metal shelves that passed for bunks, extending from the smudged, white concrete wall, and a lidless, seatless toilet. They wouldn't tell him why he'd been moved, and now, looking around at his cell, Spector was beginning to suspect the reason, and with the suspicion came the stink of fear.

Don't panic, he told himself. You're a United States senator. You've got friends, influence, and the strings sometimes take a while to let you know they've been pulled. The defense contractors and the Pentagon need you for that military appropriation bill. They'll see you through this.

But the cell seemed to mock all reassurance. He looked around at the cracked walls; the water stain on the white concrete near the ceiling looking like a sweat stain on a T-shirt; the bars in place of a fourth wall, dun paint flaking off them. The graffiti burned into the ceiling with cigarette coals: *Julio-Z 2019!!* and *Whoever UR, yer ass is Fucked!!* and *At lease you a* TV *star!! Once??*

Spector's stomach growled. Breakfast that morning had been a single egg on a piece of stale white bread. They were going out of their way to show they didn't treat him any differently than anyone else. The media scrutiny had seen to that.

His legs were going to sleep from sitting on the edge of the hard bunk. He got up, paced the width of the cell, five paces the long way, four the short.

He heard a metallic rasp and a clang: echoey footsteps in the stark spaces of the hallway. Trembling, he went to the bars. A middle-aged, seam-faced man wearing a real three-piece suit, carrying a gunmetal briefcase, was walking up behind the guard. He walked as if he were bone-tired. Some lawyer from Heimlitz's firm, Spector supposed.

The bored, portly black guard said, "Got to look in your briefcase there, buddy." The stranger opened his briefcase, and the guard poked through it. "No machine guns or cannon in there," he said. A humorless joke. He unlocked the door, let the stranger in the cell. Locked it behind him and went away.

Spector looked at the sleeping figure on the top bunk. Still snoring, out cold. No need to ask for a private room for the conference with his lawyer.

"Senator Spector," the man said, extending his hand. "I'm Gary Bergen." Bergen's hand was cold and moist in Spector's.

"You from Heimlitz's office? It's about time."

"I'm not from Heimlitz," Bergen said. "I'm a public defender." Spector stared at him. Bergen looked back with dull gray eyes. "Heimlitz is no longer representing you. They formally withdrew from the case."

Spector's mouth was dry. He sank onto the bunk. "Why?"

"Because your case is—well, the word 'hopeless' was used. And your wife is in the process of seizing your assets, garnishing your bank account. She refuses to pay an attorney."

Spector suspected that Bergen was taking some kind of quiet satisfaction in all this. He sensed that Bergen didn't like him.

Spector just sat there. Feeling like he was sitting on the edge of the Grand Canyon, and if he moved, even an inch, he'd slip and go over the edge and fall, and fall . . .

He conjured some motivation up from somewhere inside him and said, "Senator Burridge's committee will provide the money to . . . "

"The Committee to Defend Senator Henry Spector? It's been disbanded. Public opinion was overwhelmingly against them—and they had to think of their careers. Frankly, Senator, the public is howling for your blood. For the very reason that you are who you are. The public doesn't want to see any favorites played. And they're sure you're guilty."

"But how can anybody be sure of that? I haven't gone to trial, there's only been a hearing—and by now they should have streamed the video. That should've vindicated me. I've been waiting to be invited to a court screening . . . "

"Oh, they've streamed it . . . Someone leaked it digitally to the Internet. Went from there to Grid-TV news. Everyone's seen it—apparently everyone but you. They saw you holding that gray box, pointing it at your bodyguard, making him attack those people. A close-up on your face as you shouted, 'Kill them!' The autopsy on Kojo turned up the brain implant that made him respond to the prompter against his will . . . and we saw you pulling that gun, shooting your bodyguard in the back—to make it look as if he'd gone mad and you'd killed him to protect yourself." Bergen was enjoying this. "Too bad you didn't have time to get rid of the video."

Spector was unable to speak. Finally he managed, "It's insane. Moronic. Why would I go to that much trouble to kill Sonia Lerman, a woman I didn't know . . . "

"Your wife says you were obsessed with her. That you watched Sonia's editorials and they incensed you. You babbled that Sonia deserved to die—and so forth." He shrugged.

"The bitch is lying! That's perjury! I never saw the Lerman woman, on TV or off, before that interview! My 'wife' . . . " He snorted. "God, I had no idea she hated me so much. Wendy's lying so she'll get everything. The video. The video—it can't have shown me saying 'Kill them.' I didn't say it!"

Bergen nodded slowly. "It may surprise you to know that, actually . . . I believe you. But the video contradicts you. Of course, they were at the UNO station for twenty-four hours before the police picked them up. The whole thing was transmitted from your place through your comm system to the UNO station and recorded there."

"They tampered with them!"

"Possibly. But try to get the judge to believe that . . . " And he smiled maliciously. "You'll have two minutes for that at the trial."

"The brain implant—whoever set me up had to have arranged that! We could trace Kojo's recent past, find out who his surgeon was when he . . . "

"Before your defense committee disbanded, they tried that tack. Kojo had cerebral surgery just after you picked him out from the body-guard portfolio at Witcher Security. He was to have an implant inserted to improve his speed and reflexes. The technicki who provides implants for the surgeons was contacted by someone by fone. The man he saw on the screen offered to transfer fifty-thousand newbux into the technickis' account if he'd consent to some unauthorized 'adjustments' to the implant. He consented, and the implant's 'adjustment' turned out to've been one of the army's attack-and-kill mind-control instruments. Remote-control. Experimental. But apparently it works."

The guard came back, waited impatiently. Desperately, Spector said, "The man on the screen must've been . . . "

"It was you, Senator . . . the technicki recorded the transmission . . . it's pretty damning evidence. But I'll tell you what . . . " His voice creaked with mockery. "I'll see if I can get you off with a 'mercy execution.' You know, death by injection, sedative overdose. I think you'll prefer it to being clubbed to death on television. Well, good afternoon, Senator."

The guard opened the door, let Bergen out, locked up behind him, and Spector was alone.

Except for the guy climbing off the top bunk. The guy looking at Spector and chuckling. "Hey, Spector, man, that guy's really got a hard-on for you, you know? Public defender! Shit! Unless you get a Special Pardon—and I can't remember the last time anybody got one—you're fucked but good, man. Screwed royal. They ain't gonna give you special treatment just because you're a senator. That's the PR cornerstone of the AntiViolence Laws, man: *Everybody* gets screwed—equally."

He was a wiry little dude with a yellowed, gap-toothed smile, flinty black eyes, and the spiky color-shifting hair of a Chaosist. It was hard to get a real handle on what he looked like, though, because of the bruises, the swollen tissue, and crusted cuts on his face from the public beating. Still, he looked familiar.

"You almost recognize me, man? Jerome-X. At your service, home-bro."

"Jerome-X," Spector muttered. "Great."

Jerome-X gave that slightly brain-damaged chuckle again. He was pleased. " 'At's me, my man. Yeah. Yeah. I got the hot trans 'n' they know it up 'n' down the freak-en-seize. I do some music too. I got a band now—shit, why not? I got the style. I got the name. I got . . . "

"You got *caught.*" Spector observed.

"Hey, pal—thas better'n bein' *set up.* You were right, man—sure as shit, they tampered with those vids. Not editing, pal—image reconstitution. You're talking to the VideoMan Hisself. I know. Computer analyzes a digital image of a man, right? Gets him moving, talking. Then codes its analysis digitally. Samples it. An' generates an image of the guy you *can't tell* from the real thing. Uses, like, fractal geometry for realistic surface texture. And they can animate you to do whatever they want. Sample your voice, synthesize it to make you seem to've said whatever they want . . . "

"But that isn't . . . "

"Isn't justice?" Jerome-X shook his head. "You're too much. I didn't think justice was high on your list of priorities, man. I seen you on TV, Spector—I know about you . . . hey, how many people who 'committed robbery' or 'murder' were people who were annoying to the local status quo or the feds—or the Second Alliance? Especially the SA. So they're videoframed. Convicted on the evidence of some security camera that just happened to be there . . . *ri-ight.* How many people died like that, pal, huh? Hundreds? Maybe thousands. About half the people convicted go down for videod evidence these days. That's a lot of lucky cameras. Sure, maybe if there were more time, you could prove the tampering—but *you,* big shot, you've seen to it you got *no time* and no chance for appeal. . . . "

"Videoframing . . . I don't believe it."

"Hey, you *better* believe it. But most people don't know about it, so it's no use tryin' to tell the courts. The up-to-dates on computer-generated images is kept under lock and key. They want the public to think it's really crude, see . . . and all the people involved, the government, the networks, no one wants to believe anything like that about it because, hey—this thing is a *moneymaker!* People got all jaded about violence from the last few generations of TV and movies, right? So they need it in big doses now—and the ratings are great on these shows so the advertising revenues are orbital, just sky-high, so the government makes big bucks off heavy-taxing that revenue and the networks—you get what I mean. No one wants to rock the boat . . . fuck it . . . me, I'm gettin' out in the morning, already got my beatings for pirate transmissions, videograffiti . . . but you . . . they're gonna splash you all over the studio, pal. 'Cause you're the Case now. And you're Big Ratings . . . "

• • •

NEW YORK CITY.

"What you say, Charlie boy?" Angelo tapped the table with his credit card, meaning he'd pay.

"No, it fucks me up. The next day I always feel like shit." They talked loud, and in Standard, to hear each other over the music.

"Come on, you're not gonna get hung up on it, you're not where you can get at it most of the time. Come on, I don't like to do Room alone. And this is the best fucking Room in New York, absolutely bar none, no shit."

"You're a big help, Angelo. You know that?"

Charlie and Angelo were in a dark place that was splintered with light. On the private club's stage, four nearly naked blacks and two Puerto Rican girls, all of them direct-wired to the muscle synthesizers, shimmied out a black sound that was something like sexy bagpipes and electric alto sax over salsa percussion; and the light came from behind the band, lasers and colored spots backlighting them, ricocheting from their sweat-shiny skin to dazzle the black ceiling, but lost in the deep dourness of the smoky club. Black walls, black floor. Sitting at a black table beside the black wall; one side of Angelo's face in darkness, laser jitters making an expressionist painting of the other side.

Charlie and Angelo were playing a game that was like sexual coyness. It was drug coyness. Charlie wanted to score some Room, but he was scared to get started doing that again, knew it wasn't responsible to the NR. So he needed to be able to tell himself that Angelo had talked him into it.

And Angelo sensed that. Angelo knew that the best way to get Charlie to do Room was to play to his guilt, cultivate his depression, hold something over him he'd need to get out from under. Saying, "Hey, it wasn't like it was your fault. It was Spector's. No one responsible but him. "

But just mentioning it was telling him the opposite. Because Charlie felt funny about his part in setting up Spector. You watch a guy for days, you get a little sympathy for him, whether he deserves it or not. And he'd done more than watch Spector, he'd filmed him from behind the two-way in the panel truck when he moved around in public. They'd checked out the stock video of Spector talking to the public—but that wasn't close enough, sharp enough for an animation-matrix.

The stuff Charlie got when Spector was walking around, was arguing with his wife in that café, that was something Charlie and the others could work with. Build up a computer data template of realistic movement style, speech style, grist for the animation . . .

"What you let it bother you for, Charlie? The guy's an asshole. A hypocrite, a Fascist. Not SA himself, but he plays ball with 'em all the time. The AntiViolence Laws were an SA project, man."

"Yeah, I know. I just hate the TV execution stuff so fucking much, it gets me so upset—and now we're slotting somebody into it. I know all the reasons to do it. But it still . . . " He shrugged. "And then Sonia. And Baxter. Kojo. Killed real nasty."

"Shit—Kojo was SA. Sonia and Baxter volunteered for that, no one talked 'em into it. Sonia tried to kill herself twice because her girlfriend Coochie got busted and snuffed on TV. You know Coochie? Sonia was fucking out of her mind, anyway. And Baxter, he was, like, into fanatic martyrdom stuff."

"Yeah, but maybe we shouldn't've played along with their sick problems for this."

"Otherwise they woulda been destroyed for nothin', without us. Look, you gotta get your mind off it. We do some Room, that'll take you right out of your head. And into the Hollow Head, right?" He grinned. "I mean, fuck it, right?"

Charlie played hard to get for a while longer. But finally he said, "Okay. I got to make a report to Smoke, and then . . . I'll meet you there."

• • •

THE CHICAGO CITY JAIL.

Sometimes it's possible to bribe a man with *promises* of money. And Spector used all his politician's skill to persuade the guard. *Get a message out, friend, and you'll be rewarded in a big way. I'm still a senator, right? In with the in crowd, right?* Wrong, but the guard didn't know it had gone that far.

Gave the guard a letter telling Burridge about the computer-generated evidence; and telling him to work on it seriously—or Spector's news-release what he had on Burridge: the death of a girl named Judy Sorenson and just where she'd got the goodies she'd OD'd on.

Three days later, nine a.m., the guard came to Spector's clammy cell, passed him an ear-cap, winked, and left. Spector put the capsule in his ear, squeezed it, heard Burridge's voice: "Henry, there's a method of digital analysis that'll tell us if what's on the video was genuine or computer-generated. First we'll have to subpoena the digi-vid. Of course, as you've already been convicted, that'll be hard. But we're pulling some strings . . . we'll see if we can get your conviction overturned in the next day or so. A Special Pardon. In the meantime don't get panicky and mention that mutual friend of ours to anyone."

But a week later Spector was being prepped for his execution. He sat on a bench, chained to five other convicts, listening to the prison's TV program director, Sparks.

The videotechs called Sparks "the animal wrangler." He was stocky, red-faced, with a taut smile and blank gray eyes. He wore a rumpled blue real-cloth suit. The guards stood at either end of the narrow room, tubular stun-guns in hand.

"Today we got a man won an execution-by-combat," Sparks was saying. "An EBC is more dignified than the execution in stocks, so you fellas should be glad of that much, anyway. You'll be given a gun, but of course it's loaded with blanks."

And then the chain connecting Spector's handcuffs to the man on his right jerked Spector half out of his seat as the small black guy on the other end of the bench lost it, just lost it completely, ran at Sparks screaming something in a heavy West Indian accent, something Spector couldn't make out. But the raw substance of it, the subverbal message in the guy's voice—that alone spoke for him. It said, *Injustice! Innocence!* and it said, *I've got a family!* And then, it could say nothing more because the stun-guns had turned off his brain for a while and he lay splayed like a dark rag doll on the concrete floor. The guards propped him up on the bench, and Sparks went on as if nothing had happened. "Now we got to talk about your cues, it'll be a lot worse for you if you forget your cues . . . "

Spector wasn't listening. A terrible feeling had him in its grip, and it was a far worse feeling than fear for his life.

At home—the condo his wife had sold by now—he'd opened his front door with a sonic key. It sang out three shrill tones, three precise notes at precise intervals, and the door heard and analyzed the tonal code and the interval code, and opened.

And the voice of the man who'd tried to fight, the small, dark man . . . his voice, his three shrieks, had opened a door in Spector's mind. Let something out. Something he'd fought for weeks to lock away. Something he'd argued with, silently shouted at, again and again.

He'd pushed for the AntiViolence Laws for the same reason that Joe McCarthy, in the last century, had railed at Communism. It was a ticket. A ticket to a vehicle he could ride through the polls and into office. Inflame their fear of crime. Cultivate their lust for vengeance. Titillate their own repressed desire to do violence of their own. And they vote for you.

And he hadn't given a rat's-ass goddamn about the violence problem. The issue was a path to power, and nothing more.

He'd known, somewhere inside himself, that a lot of the condemned were probably being railroaded. But he'd looked away, again and again. Now somebody had made it impossible for him to look away. Now the guilt that had festered in him erupted into full-blown infection, and he burned with the fever of self-hatred.

That's when Bergen came in. Bergen spoke to the guards, showed them a paper; the guards came and whispered to Sparks. And Sparks, annoyed at the disruption in his scheduling, unlocked Spector's cuffs. Glumly Bergen said, "Come with me, Mr. Spector." He was no longer Senator Spector.

They went to stand in the hallway; a guard came along, yawning, leaning against the wall, watching a soap on his pocket TV. Voice icy, Bergen said, "I have an order to take you back to your cell, pending a reopening of your case. You're going to get off. A Special Pardon. Rare as hen's teeth. Burridge has proof the vid was tampered with. It hasn't been made public yet, and in fact, the judge who presided at your trial is out of town, so Burridge arranged a temporary restraining . . . "

"Why is it you sound disappointed, Bergen?" Spector interrupted, watching Bergen's face closely. When Bergen didn't answer, Spector said, "You did everything you could to sabotage my defense. You were with them, whoever it was. Whoever set me up. I can feel it. Who was it?" Bergen stared sullenly at him. "Come on—who *was* it? And why?"

Bergen glanced at the guard. The guard was absorbed by the soap opera; tiny television figures in his palm flickered through a miniature choreography of petty conflicts.

Bergen took a deep breath and looked Spector in the eyes. "Okay. I don't care anymore . . . I *want* you to know. Sonia, Baxter, and I—we're part of the same organization. Sonia did it because her lover, a girl she'd lived with for eight years, was videoframed. She was very dependent on her. Baxter did it because he was part of another organization too: the Black Freedom Brotherhood—they lost their top four officers to a Second Alliance videoframe-up. Me, I did it—I planned the whole damn thing because I saw one too many innocent people die. We thought if you, a senator, were videoframed, condemned, publicly killed, afterward we'd release the truth, we'd clear you, and that'd focus public attention on the issue. Force an investigation. And something else—Simple revenge. We held you responsible. For all those people railroaded into dying."

Spector nodded like a clockwork toy. Said softly, "Oh, yes. I am responsible . . . and now I'm going to get off. I'll go free. And it'll be blamed on your people, your organization. They'll say it was an isolated incident, the only incident of videoframe-up. They'll pressure me to shut up about it. And once I was on the outside, where things are comfortable, I probably would."

And the realization came at him like an onrushing wall of darkness; it fell on him like a tidal wave: *How many innocent people died for my ambition?*

"Yes," Bergen muttered. "Congratulations, Spector, you son of a bitch. Sonia and Baxter sacrificed themselves for *nothing . . .* " His voice broke. He went on, visibly straining for control. "You're going free . . . "

But the gnawing thing in Spector wouldn't let him go free. And he knew it would never let him go. Never. (Though some part of him said, *Don't do it! Survive!* But that part of him could speak only in a raspy whimper.) "Bergen—wait. Go to Burridge. Tell him you know all about the Sorenson incident. Repeat it back to me."

"The Sorenson incident. What . . . ?"

"And tell him you'll release what you know about her, about Sorenson, if he tells anyone about that vid before tomorrow. Tell him this came from me. He'll stay quiet."

"But the restraining order . . . "

"Tear it up. And come with me—you've got to explain to Sparks that your paperwork was wrong. That you were mistaken about something . . . "

• • •

Spector walked out onto the stage, just glancing at the cameras and the studio audience beyond the bulletproof glass. He pointed the pistol loaded with blanks at the grinning man in the cowboy hat at the other end of the stage and walked toward him, toward the big gun in the man's hand.

He walked right up to a gun that was loaded with real bullets. And Spector smiled softly, thinking, *This is the only way I'll ever go free . . .*

• • •

NEW YORK CITY.

You could smell the place, the Hollow Head, from two blocks away. Anyway, you could if you were strung out on it. The other people on the street probably couldn't make out the smell from the background of monoxides, the broken battery smell of acid rain, the itch of syntharette smoke, the oily rot of the river. But a user could pick out that tease of amyl para-tryptaline, thinking, *Like a needle in a haystack.* And he'd snort, and then go reverent-serious, thinking about the needle in question . . . the needle in the nipple . . .

It was on East 121st Street, a half block from the East River. If you stagger out of the place at night, you'd better find your way to the lighted end of the street fast, because the leeches crawled out of the river after dark, slug-creeping up the walls and onto the cornices of the old buildings; they sensed your body heat, and an eight-inch ugly brute lamprey thing could fall from the roof, hit your neck with a wet *slap*; inject you with paralyzing toxins and when you fall over, its leech cronies drain you dry.

When Charlie turned onto the street, it was just sunset; the leeches weren't out of the river yet, but Charlie scanned the rooftops, anyway. Clustered along the rooftops were the shanties.

New York's housing shortage was worse then ever. After the Dissolve Depression, most of the Wall Street firms moved to Tokyo or the floating city, Freezone. The turn of the century boom in Manhattan deflated; the city couldn't afford to maintain itself. It began to rot. But still the immigrants came, swarming to the mecca of disenchantment till New York became another Mexico City, ringed and overgrown with shanties, shacks of clapboard, tin, cardboard protected with flattened cans and plastic wrappers; every tenement rooftop in Manhattan mazed with squalid shanties, sometimes shanties on shanties till the weight collapsed the roofs and the old buildings caved in, the crushed squatters simply left dying in the rubble—firemen and emergency teams rarely set foot outside the sentried, walled-in havens of the midtown class.

Charlie was almost there. It was a mean motherfucker of a neighbor-hood, which is why he had the knife in his boot sheath. But what scared him was the Place. Doing some Room at the Place. The Hollow Head.

His heart was pumping and he was shaky, but he wasn't sure if it was from fear or anticipation or if, with the Hollow Head, you could tell those two apart. But to keep his nerve up, he had to look away from the Place as he got near it; tried to focus on the rest of the street. Some dumbfuck pollyanna had planted saplings in the sidewalk, in the squares of exposed dirt where the original trees had stood. But the acid rain had chewed the leaves and twigs away; what was left was as stark as obsolete TV antennas. Torchglow from the roofs; and a melange of noises that seemed to ooze down like something greasy from an overflowing pot. Smells of tarry wood burning; dog-food smells of cheap, canned-food cooking. And then he was standing in front of the Hollow Head. A soot-blackened town house, its Victorian facade of cherubim recarved by acid rain into dainty gargoyles. The windows bricked over, the stone between them streaked gray on black from acid erosion.

The building to the right was hunchbacked with shacks; the roof to the left glowed from oil-barrel fires. But the roof of the Hollow Head was dark and flat, somehow regal in its sinister austerity. No one shacked on the Hollow Head.

He took a deep breath and told himself, "Don't hurry through it, savor it this time," and went in. Hoping that Angelo had waited for him.

Up to the door, wait while the camera scanned you. The camera taking in Charlie Chesterton's triple-Mohawk, each fin a different color; Charlie's gaunt face, spiked transplas jacket, and customized mirrorshades. He heard the tone telling him the door had unlocked. He opened it, smelled the amyl para-tryptaline, felt his bowels contract with suppressed excitement. Down a red-lit hallway, thick black paint on the walls, the turpentine smell of AT getting stronger. Angelo wasn't there; he'd gone upstairs already. Charlie hoped Ange could handle it alone.

The girl in the banker's window at the end of the hall—the girl wearing the ski mask, the girl with the sarcastic receptionist's lilt in her voice—took his card, gave him the Bone Music receptor, credded him in. Another tone, admission to Door Seven, the first level.

He walked down to seven, turned the knob, stepped through, and felt it immediately; the tingle, the rush of alertness, the chemically induced sense of belonging, four pleasurable sensations rolling through him, coalescing. It was just an empty room with the stairs at the farther end; soft pink lighting, the usual cryptic palimpsest of graffiti on the walls.

He inhaled deeply, felt the drug imbued in the very air go to work almost immediately; the pink glow intensified; the edges of the room softened, he heard his own heartbeat like a distant beat-box. A barbed wisp of anxiety twined his spine (wondering, *Where's Angelo, he's usually hanging in the first room, scared to go to the second alone, well, shit, good riddance)*, and then he experienced a paralytic seizure of sheer sensation.

The Bone Music receptor was digging into his palm; he wiped the sweat from it and attached it to the sound wire extruding from the bone back of his left ear—and the music shivered into him. It was music you felt more than heard; his acoustic nerve picked up the thudding beat, the bass, a distorted veneer of the synthesizer. But most of the music was routed through the bone of his skull, conducted down through the spinal column, the other bones.

It was a music of shivery sensations, like a funny-bone sensation, sickness sensations, chills and hot flashes like influenza, but it was a sickness that caressed, viruses licking at your privates, and you wanted to have an orgasm and throw up at the same time. He'd seen deaf people dancing at rock concerts; they could feel the vibrations from the loud music; could feel the music they couldn't hear. It was like that but with a deep, deep humping brutality. The music shivered him from his paralysis, nudged him forward. He climbed the stairs.

Bone Music reception improved as he climbed, so he could make out the lyrics, Jerome-X's gristly voice singing from inside Charlie's skull:

Six kinds of darkness
Spilling down over me
Six kinds of darkness
Sticky with energy.

Charlie got to the next landing, stepped into the second room.

Second room used electric field stimulation of nerve ends; the metal grids on the wall transmitting signals that stimulated the neurons, initiating pleasurable nerve impulses; other signals were sent directly to the dorsal area in the hypothalamus, resonating in the brain's pleasure center.

Charlie cried out and fell to his knees in the infantile purity of his gratitude. The room glowed with benevolence; the barren, dirty room with its semen-stained walls, cracked ceilings, naked red bulb on a fraying wire. As always, he had to fight himself to keep from licking the walls, the floors. He was a fetishist for this room, for its splintering wooden floors, the mathematical absolutism of the grid patterns in the gray-metal transmitters set into the wall. Turn off those transmitters and the room was shabby, even ugly, and pervaded with stench; with the transmitters on, it seemed subtly intricate, starkly sexy, bondage gear in the form of interior decoration, and the smell was a ribald delight.

(For the Hollow Head was drug paraphernalia you could walk into. The building itself was the syringe, or the hookah, or the sniff-tube.)

And then the room's second phase cut in: the transmitters stimulated the motor cortex, the reticular formation in the brainstem, the nerve pathways of the extrapyramidal system, in precise patterns computer-formulated to mesh with the ongoing Bone Music. Making him dance. Dance across the room, feeling he was caught in a choreographed whirlwind (flashing: genitals interlocking, pumping, male and female, male and male, female and female, the thrusting a heavy downhill flow like an emission of igneous mud, but firm pink mud, the bodies rounded off, headless, Magritte torsos going end to end together, organs blindly nosing into the wet receptacles of otherness), semen trickling down his legs inside his pants, dancing, helplessly dancing, thinking it was a delicious epilepsy, as he was marionetted up the stairs, to the next floor, the final room . . .

At the landing just before the third room, the transmitters cut off, and Charlie sagged, gasping, clutching for the banister, the black-painted walls reeling around him. He gulped air and prayed for the strength to turn away from the third room, because he knew it would leave him fried; yeah, badly crashed and deeply burned out. He turned off the receptor for a respite. In that moment of weariness and self-doubt he found himself wondering where Angelo was. Had Angelo really gone on to the third room alone? Ange was prone to identity crises under the Nipple Needle. If he'd gone alone—little Angelo Demario with his rockabilly hair and spurious pugnacity—Angelo would sink and lose it completely . . . and what would they do with people who were overdosed on an identity hit? Dump the body in the river, he supposed.

He heard a yell mingling ecstasy and horror coming from an adjacent room, as another Head customer took a nipple. That made up his mind: like seeing someone eat making you realize you're hungry. He gathered together the tatters of his energy, switched on his receptor, and went through the door.

The Bone Music shuddered through him, strong now that he was undercut, weakened by the first rooms. Nausea wallowed through him.

The darkness of the Arctic,
two months into the night
Darkness of the Eclipse,
forgetting of all light.

Angelo wasn't in the room, and Charlie was selfishly glad as he took off his jacket, rolled up his left sleeve, approached the black rubber nipple protruding from the metal breast at waist height on the wall. As he stepped up to it, pressed the hollow of his elbow against the nipple, felt the computer-guided needle probe for his mainline and fire the ID drug into him.

The genetic and neurochemical essence of a woman. They claimed it was synthesized. He didn't give an angel's winged asshole where it came from, right then; it was rushing through him in majestic waves of intimacy. You could taste her, smell her, feel what it felt like to be her (they said it was an imaginary her, modeled on someone real, not really from a person).

Felt the shape of her personality superimposed on you, so for the first time you weren't burdened with your own identity, you could find oblivion in someone else, like identifying with a fictional protagonist but infinitely more real . . .

But oh, shit. It wasn't a her. It was a him. And Charlie knew instantly that it was Angelo. They had shot him up with Angelo's distilled neurochemistry—his personality, memory, despairs, and burning urges. He saw himself in flashes as Angelo had seen him . . . and he knew, too, that this was no synthesis, that he'd found out what they did with those who died here, who blundered and OD'd: they dropped them in some vat, broke them down, distilled them, and molecularly linked them with the synthcoke and shot them into other customers . . . into Charlie . . .

He couldn't hear himself scream over the Bone Music (*Darkness of an iron cask, lid down and bolted tight*). He didn't remember running for the exit stairs. (*And three more kinds of darkness, three I cannot tell*), down the hall (*Making six kinds of darkness, Lord, please make me well*), out into the street, running, hearing the laughter from the shantyrats on the roofs watching him go.

He and Angelo running down the street, in one body. As Charlie told himself, *I'm kicking this thing. It's over. I shot up my best friend. I'm through with it.*

Hoping to God it was true. *Lord, please make me well.*

Bottles swished down from the rooftops and smashed to either side of him. And he kept running.

He felt strange. He felt strange as all hell.

He could feel his body. Not like usual. He could feel it like it was a weight on him, like an attachment. A weight of sheer alienness. He was too big, for one thing. It was all awkward, and its metabolism was pitched too low, sluggish, and it was . . .

It was the way his body felt for Angelo.

Angelo wasn't there, in him. But then again he was. And Charlie felt Angelo as a nastily foreign, squeaky, distortion membrane between him and the world around him.

He passed someone on the street, saw them distorted through the membrane, their faces funhouse-mirror twisted as they looked at him—and they looked startled.

The strange feelings must show on his face, and in his frantic running.

Maybe they could see Angelo. Maybe Angelo was oozing out of him, out of his face. He could feel it. Yeah. He could feel Angelo bleeding from his pores, dripping from his nose, creeping from his ass. A sonic splash of—*Gidgy, you wanna do a video hook-up with me?* Gidgy replying, *No, that shit's grotty, Ange, last time we did that I was sick for two days. I don't like pictures pushed into my brain, couldn't we just have, you know—have sex?* (She touches his arm.)

God, I'm gonna lose myself in Angelo, Charlie thought. Gotta run, sweat him out of me.

Splash of: *Angelo, if you keep going around with those people, the police or those. SA punks're going to break ya stupid head.* Angelo's voice: *Ma, get off it, you don't understand what's going on, the country's getting scared, they think there's gonna be nuclear war, everyone's lining up to kiss the presidential ass cause they think she's all that stands between us and the fucking Russians*—His mother's voice: *Angelo, don't use that language in front of your sister, not everyone talks like they do on TV—*

Too heavy, body's too heavy, his run is funny, can't run anymore, but I gotta sweat him out—

Flash pictures to go with the splash voices now: *Motion-rollicking shot of sidewalk seen from a car window as they drive through a private-cop zone, SA bulls in mirror helmets walking along in twos in this high-rent neighborhood, turning their glassy-blank assumption of your guilt toward the car, the world revolves as the car turns a corner, they come to a checkpoint, the new Federal ID cards are demanded, shown, they get through, feeling of relief, there isn't a call out on them yet . . . blur of images, then focus on a face walking up to the car. Charlie. Long, skinny, goofy-looking guy, self-serious expression . . .*

Jesus, Charlie thought, is that what Angelo thinks I look like? Shit! (Angelo is dead, man, Angelo is . . . is oozing out of him . . .)

Feeling sick now, stopping to gag, look around confusedly. Oh, fuck: Two cops were coming toward him. Regular cops, no helmets, wearing blue stickers, plastic covers on their cop-caps, their big ugly cop-faces hanging out so he wished they wore the helmets; supercilious faces, young but ugly, their heads shaking in disgust, one of them said: "What drug you on, man?"

He tried to talk, but a tumble of words came out, some his and some Angelo's, his mouth was brimming over with small, restless, furry animals: Angelo's words.

The cops knew what it was. They knew it when they heard it.

One cop said to the other (as he took out the handcuffs, and Charlie had become a retching machine, unable to run or fight or argue because all he could do was retch), "Jeez, it makes me sick when I think about it. People shooting up some of somebody else's brains. Don't it make you sick?"

"Yeah. Looks like it makes him sick, too. Let's take him to the chute, send him down for the blood test."

He felt the snakebite of cuffs, felt them do a perfunctory body search, missing the knife in the boot. Felt himself shoved along to the police kiosk on the corner, the new prisoner-transferral chutes. They put you in something like a coffin (they pushed him into a greasy, sweat-stinking, inadequately padded personnel capsule, closed the lid on him, he wondered what happened—as they closed the lid on him—if he got stuck in the chutes, were there air holes, would he suffocate?), and they push it down into the chute inside the kiosk and it gets sucked along this big underground tube (he had a sensation of falling, then felt the tug of inertia, the horror of being trapped in here with Angelo, not enough room for the two of them, seeing a flash mental image of Angelo's rotting corpse in here with him, Angelo was dead, Angelo was dead) to the police station. The cops' street report clipped to the capsule. The other cops read the report, take you out (a creak, the lid opened, blessed fresh air even if it was the police station), take everything from you, check your DNA print against their files, make you sign some things, lock you up just like that . . . that's what he was in for right away. And then maybe a public AntiViolence Law beating. Ironic.

Charlie looked up at a bored cop-face, an older, fat one this time. The cop looked away, fussing with the report, not bothering to take Charlie out of the capsule. There was more room to maneuver now, and Charlie felt like he was going to rip apart from Angelo's being in there with him if he didn't get out of the cuffs, out of the capsule. So he brought his knees up to his chest, worked the cuffs around his feet, it hurt . . . but he did it, got his hands in front of him.

Flash of Angelo's memory: *A big cop leaning over him, shouting at him, picking him up by the neck, shaking him. Fingers on his throat . . .*

When Angelo was a kid, some cop had caught him running out of a store with something he'd ripped off. So the cop roughed him up, scared the shit out of Angelo, literally: Angelo shit his pants. The cop reacted in disgust (the look of disgust on the two cops' faces: "Makes me sick," one of them had said).

So Angelo hated cops, and now Angelo was out of his right mind—ha ha, he was in Charlie's—and so it was Angelo who reached down and found the boot knife that the two cops had missed, pulled it out, got to his knees in the capsule as the cop turned around (Charlie fighting for control—*dammit, Ange, put down the knife, we could get out of this with—*) and Charlie—no, it was Angelo—gripped the knife in both hands and stabbed the guy in his fat neck, split that sickening fat neck open, cop's blood is as red as anyone's, looks like . . .

Oh, shit. Oh, no.

Here come the other cops.

•••

THE ISLAND OF MALTA.

Same night, another time zone, another variety of darkness.

Daniel "Hard-Eyes" Torrence walked through a vast, wind-scoured darkness, unable to see his feet or his hands in front of his face, guided only by the distant swatch of light ahead of him.

It was near dawn in Malta. Torrence had just gone off watch on the approach road to the safe house. Danco, yawning and cursing, had replaced him, was making himself ersatz espresso in the little shack by the dirt road.

A cold wind blew the rich scent of the sea from the coast, a quarter of a mile south. Sounds seemed eerily detached and lucid out here. He could make out the smack and rumble of breakers carried on the sighing wind; his rifle creaked softly on its shoulder strap; his booted feet made grumpy trudging sounds.

He felt as if none of it had anything to do with him. At any moment the wind might blow his soul right out of his body.

He was glad when he got to the barn, walked blinking into its well-lit interior. Two choppers sat there, looking glassy and bulbous and out of place, as foreign to the dusty wooden walls as flying saucers, their blades folded back on hinges overhead. Torrence nodded at the guard lounging in the cockpit of the compact chopper by the stairs. The Italian, Forsino, an old-fashioned long-hair, a *hipz* in Stateside terms, looking put-upon and bored.

Torrence took the open stairs up to the dusty attic, hearing the old wooden barn creak in the wind, wondering if tonight was the night it would fall over.

Lila was on the radio in the attic, monitoring the military bands and anything else she found of intelligence interest, keeping a frequency open for communications from Witcher and New Resistance affiliate groups. Wires ran to the next room—an old olive storage bin—where sat-link antennas, looking like miniature radar scoops, angled out an open window, listening to the babbling emptiness . . .

An electric light bulb burned naked in a white porcelain socket overhead; moths ticked at it, and it dimmed now and then when the wind blew particularly hard. Wearing a headset, Lila was seated at a table piled with a lot of arcane metal boxes that looked as out of place as the choppers in the rustic backdrop.

Lila was clear-eyed and alert, evidently ready for anything, even at this hour. She was so efficient it was maddening, Torrence thought. She took off the headset and looked at Torrence questioningly.

"I thought Claire was on tonight," Torrence said.

Was there a flash of displeasure in her face? "I have relieved her. An hour ago."

"Nice of you to relieve her early."

Lila said nothing. She seemed to be studying the dust-heavy cobwebs overhead; they shook when the wind thumped the barn.

"Hear anything interesting?" Torrence asked, nodding toward the radio.

She shook her head.

He turned away, hesitated, then turned back to her. "Was she here alone, when she was on duty?"

Lila didn't reply for a full three beats. She looked at him blankly and said, "Karakos. He was here talking to her when I came."

Torrence felt a chill. He went to the table, flipped open the comm log, looked down the list of dispatches, messages received and sent for the week . . . nothing at all for that day. "Karakos didn't transmit?"

"No."

"You sure?"

"Any transmission has to have written clearance from Steinfeld. Claire would not have let anyone use the radio without clearance. There are only four people cleared to do comm duty, and Karakos is not one of them. Claire knows that." A touch defensive on Claire's behalf.

"What did Karakos want here?"

"Probably couldn't sleep, wanted someone to talk to. How am I to know?"

"Okay." He turned away. She seemed hostile to him, in a subdued way. Why?

He went down the creaking stairs, dust rising with his every step, thinking hard, wondering if his feeling about Karakos was simply jealousy. *Or is it what I think?*

In forty-eight hours they'd hijack the *Hermes' Grandson.* Karakos was to go along.

He stepped into the windy night, crossed to the house, called out the password at the back door. Someone shined a flashlight in his face. He blinked irritably till they were sure of him, and went into the house. It was quiet; most of the others were asleep. But there was a steady creaking noise from upstairs.

Moving on sheer impulse, not thinking, borne along by some inner charge of urgency, he climbed the stairs, went to Claire's room—since their argument, she'd taken her own room. He knocked once, and before she'd finished calling out, "Who is it?" he opened the door and went in.

She and Karakos were huddled in bed, a candle fluttering romantically in a draft from the door. The two of them naked in the soft golden light.

Somehow it was the candle that hurt most.

"It won't be tonight, Karakos," he heard himself say, "but next time she's on the radio, that's when you'll talk her into letting you take it over for a while, right? That it?"

"I'm surprised it's the radio that's on your mind," Karakos said with a small laugh. "But what about it?"

"Dan, get out of here." Claire's voice was flat, dead.

He looked at her. A dozen bitter remarks rose up in him, vying for his voice, but all he said was, "Okay. Sure."

He left, seared inside, thinking, Just jealousy?

Just jealousy? Just jealousy? Just jealousy?

He didn't sleep that night.

And as soon as it was light, he carried his rifle to the beach for target practice.

• 08 •

THE SPACE COLONY. BITCHIE'S AFTER.

Kitty Torrence was squatting with her back against the wall, in Bitchie's After. The room was dimly lit at her end, brighter at the other where the meeting was going on. The walls were metal patchy with posters and faded porn, stitched with graffiti.

Bitchie's was an illegal after-hours club, in a double-unit that also functioned as a brothel on certain days. The back room was thirty feet by twenty, the floor space taken up by foam-rubber mattresses. She would have liked to lie down. Not here, though. The mattresses stank; she was careful not to touch them with anything but the bottom of her shoes. She wished they'd pick another place to meet—but Bitchie's was one of the few places Lester's loose organization of radics felt safe. Admin tolerated Bitchie's as a brothel; they didn't suspect it as a meeting place for reformists.

Lester and the new New Resistance rep and Hasid Shood and Ben Vreeland were sitting cross-legged in a circle, talking. Kitty could have taken part, but she felt like hanging back, staying out of it. She got upset when she took part in the meetings. Chu, the NR rep, was a serious, brittle-mannered Chinese woman in a dull blue Pilot's Aide jumpsuit. She had short, glossy black hair, no makeup, a single silver hoop earring; carried a blue canvas pouch, zipped half shut, and she kept her right hand always on it. Somehow the pouch made Kitty nervous.

"If we call for an investigation, as a group," Chu said dolefully, "we'll tip our hand; they'll know about us a group. If we demand an investigation as individuals, they'll know about us as individuals."

"They already know about us as individuals," Lester said. "Russ Parker called me in. They been watching me."

"They know about you, and maybe about Shood, but probably they don't know about Vreeland yet, or about me. I have been very, very careful." Her voice was almost a monotone. But there was an underlying intensity that kept Kitty's attention riveted when the woman talked.

"I dunno," Vreeland said. "I don't think they got me ID'd. Unless maybe because Sonny was my brother . . . I dint get involved in nothing before now." He was a great chunk of a man, short-legged but thick, wide-shouldered. He wore a ship tech's white jumpsuit, grease-stained with insulation fluid, and a flattop crew cut divided into three technicki signification colors for his earth-home, profession, and seniority. He spoke Standard badly and laboriously. His brother had died on RM17.

"It takes not long," Shood said. "They will identify us eventually. Me they maybe know, for Silla was very much loud in the Union . . . " He swallowed hard after mentioning Silla. Shood was a compact, dark Pakistani with mournful black eyes, wearing a paper suit of tacky red and yellow stripes, faded from two days' wear. He was a computer programmer, and "sharp as a razor," Lester said. He'd lost his wife to the explosion on RM17.

And I came so close to losing Lester, Kitty thought. And why? Because Lester went to meetings like this one.

"The longer we stay unidentified as activists, the better," Chu said.

Lester shook his head. "That's why they got away with murdering everyone on that repair module. Because most of them weren't publicly declared. So not enough people smell a rat. Well, a lot of people suspect, but most of 'em aren't sure it was murder because they aren't sure the people on the ship were anti-Admin. If the people who were killed had declared their stand publicly, the Second Alliance wouldn't want to kill them; they'd be afraid it'd cause more riots."

"Perhaps. But for what we have to do," Chu said, shrugging, "secrecy is the only way. It is hopeless to 'demand an investigation.' Nothing will come of it. And the SA will take note of who is doing the demanding. No. There is only one way: *to take power.* We know the Second Alliance plans for the Colony. The SA plans to man the Colony with their people only. The rest of us will be deported or . . . who knows? If the New-Soviets surrender to NATO—and it seems possible that soon they will either launch a first strike or surrender—the fascists will transform the Colony into their headquarters. Rick Crandall himself will come here. It will be his . . . his ivory tower. He will tolerate nothing less than complete dictatorship here. We must prevent that or we lose it all. We begin like this: to stock arms—with great secrecy, with caution—and to make plans to use them. And then to use them, when they are not expecting it. We must take control of Admin Central. There is nothing else to do."

Shood looked at Chu and then, to Kitty's surprise, he nodded. "We must take by force."

Lester looked uncomfortable. He glanced over his shoulder at Kitty. Then looked at Vreeland. "What you think?"

Vreeland said, "It's suicide. But standing up to 'em *any* kinda way is suicide too. So fuck it. They gonna pay."

"Yes," Chu said. "Standing up to them in any way is equally dangerous. Suicide? I think not, not if we plan very carefully. It would take very few people placed in the right nerve centers to take over the Colony. Getting there is the hard part. But once we're there, once we have control of Computer Central and Life Support, the people will rally behind us."

"What if they don't?" Kitty said, standing. Her legs were going to sleep. Her back ached. She did a few knee bends, grimacing. "What if . . . what if everyone's too scared. They won't know who you . . . " Who *you* are? Or who *we* are? Diplomatically she chose the latter. " . . . who we are. If people think we're terrorists, they won't trust us at the Colony's control system. The people won't back us."

"It's a risk we must take. One of many. I take a risk coming here at all, meeting with Lester and Shood. I risk my cover. But *I must* risk it now."

Lester said, slowly, as if thinking aloud, "I think they'd back us."

And as he went on, Kitty thought, *God damn you, Lester, we have to get out of this thing, not get locked up in it deeper! We have to get out for the baby!* But aloud she said nothing.

"People are pissed off," Lester was saying. "A lot of them suspect the explosion was rigged. And we haven't got the housing reforms they promised. And the air's getting bad in the technicki section; it's still fairly clean in the Admin section. The food's been shitty, and there hasn't been enough of it. The curfews—people are going stir-crazy. Claustrophobic. New-Soviet blockade's preventing Earth visits, and the curfew's keeping them in their units during off-time. We almost got busted coming over here . . . "

Chu looked sharply at him. "Almost? How?"

"A guard stopped us. We had a permit to go to medicenter for Kitty, so he let us go. But he did it like he didn't want to."

"Did he run an ID check?"

"Yeah, I think he did. But he let us go . . . "

Chu stood. "You are a known agitator. Your permit is for your wife; they would not have let you go, too, at this hour, unless . . . " She looked at the door, spoke with brisk authority. "We must go. Everyone go, quickly. I will be in touch."

They stood, everyone suddenly uncomfortable, as she got up and walked hastily across the mattresses to the door, stooped, and stepped through. They heard the outer door creak and clang shut behind her. She was gone. Just like that.

"She spooks easily," Lester said.

"Maybe we better go, too," Vreeland said uneasily.

Kitty's stomach churned with tension. Nausea welled up in her. "Lester, I think I'm gonna be sick. Is there a toilet here?"

"They took it out. You got to use the public down the hall. Go ahead, babe, I'll be there in just a minute."

She moved across the mattresses toward the way out, staggering a little on the soft and uneven walking surface, went through the door. Bitchie was sprawled in the next room, alone, his makeup smeared, his paper dress in dingy tatters. His face was drawn, hollow-eyed, pasty with pancake. His hair was a stack of dirty yellow coils. He was loading the little medinject unit attached to his leg with his black market Demerol-amphetamine mix; she could see his genitals, like a droopy white snail, under his printout skirt. He'd been a pilot, once; he had this place by contract for two years, and his two years were almost up. He hadn't worked at anything but collecting rents from whores for a year. He couldn't stay off the drugs, and when he was on them, he couldn't stay out of drag. Drag queens are not generally considered the Right Stuff.

She looked away from him—the sight of him made her stomach writhe even more—and went out the half-open door into the back hall. Chu hadn't even closed the door. Kitty's stomach contracted again, and she nearly threw up on the floor of the narrow metal hallway.

She was running by the time she got to the bathroom. She went in and, with not a second to spare, threw up in the vacu-flush.

She felt better almost immediately, then embarrassed. God, she must be unattractive this way, all puffy, throwing up half the time. No wonder Lester was ready to—Oh, don't be silly, that's not why he's doing it.

But she went to the sink, looked in the mirror, grimaced, tried to pretty herself up a little.

Five minutes later she gave up. She rinsed out her mouth and went out into the hall.

And saw two SA bulls dragging Lester away, down the hall . . . up ahead of Lester, three other bulls were shoving Vreeland along; he was resisting, and they jabbed him with shock-prods, making him tense up and stagger. Where was Shood?

But . . . Lester. They had Lester.

His hands were trapped behind him in permaplastic handcuffs, and he was bleeding from the back of his head, and she thought, *Chu was right.*

She started after them, but the bulls stepped into an elevator. The doors closed on them, and on Lester.

And that was it, that was all: he was gone.

• • •

New York City Jail.

Charlie was alive and Angelo was dead.

Angelo was gone. Charlie had sweated him out, metabolized him out, pissed him out. Burned him out.

But Charlie was here because the neurological Angelo, using Charlie, had stabbed a cop. Dead, Angelo had put him here.

It was an autonomic cell, robot-guarded, one of the newer cells; Charlie didn't rate a human guard. He was in the cell with another guy, a short, taciturn, spike-haired Chinese in a bloodied JAS who'd come in that morning from an AntiViolence beating. His face all patchy with red welts, bruises.

Charlie had been in the cell alone, awake all night, till just after the pathetic breakfast, when they brought in the Chinese. Charlie tried not to stare at the Chinese when the trash-can escorted him in. But he couldn't help looking at his battered face, wondering what they'd leave of Charlie Chesterton's face if that cop died. Or even if he didn't . . . Stabbing a cop. Great.

You're screwed to the max, Charlie.

The place was cold and echoey and unyielding. It was a great, slow-moving mower machine you were caught in.

Charlie paced around the little plasticrete cell. There was just enough room for pacing to *be* pacing. Moving around hurt, because when the cops saw he'd stabbed one of their buddies, they got him down and kicked him, maybe ten times; Charlie had just managed to cover his head with his arms. Before they did anything more than bruise the hell out of him and crack a few ribs, the sergeant came in and stopped them, told them, "He'll get all that's coming to him." So, right, it hurt to move, but he was too restless and scared to sit still, and anyway, it was cold in there.

The Chinese guy was sitting sullenly on a bunk and following him with his glare as Charlie paced. Past the two thin bunks, ripped-up platforms coming out of the wall; past the seatless toilet. Naked white walls on three sides marred only by dinge and a word someone had smeared in feces: *ShitPigs*, in ocher.

On the fourth side were bars floor to ceiling. Square-edged bars, not even comfortable to put your hands around. Some drugged jackass about two cells down was braying with maddening regularity, about every ten minutes, "*Yermasuxen sh'piz'n'hurb'd!*" Technicki, over and over. Your Mama sucks everyone, shit-pigs, and I hurt bad, your mama sucks everyone, shit-pigs, and I hurt bad, your mama . . .

"*Fuck off!*" Charlie screamed back after an hour of it. Adding in technicki, "*Yotta basherbruh awl cuzzabrufugznay!*" You ought to bash out your brains on the wall, 'cause your brains are fucked, anyway. The jackass paused his braying to laugh cretinously, then went back to "*Yermasuxen sh'piz . . .* "

"Shit pigs," Charlie muttered as the brain-damaged jackass bellowed for the three-hundredth time. "Now we know who was in this cell before us." Nodding at the smear on the wall. "You take the wrong designer drugs, mix 'em with video-direct, and you end up like the shit-pigger over there."

That's when the Chinese guy said the only thing he said the whole time he was in with Charlie.

"More likely," the Chinese said hoarsely, "he got brain damage from the beatings."

Charlie winced and closed his eyes.

How long before they came for him? According to the AntiViolence laws, he had to be in front of a judge and sentenced within seventy-two hours because he was charged with assault with intent to kill. A couple days left till the deadline. But he'd stabbed a cop. Hurt him bad, maybe killed him. In a case like that they'd give him priority. And because he'd attacked a cop, they'd probably sentence him to death, with the new laws, even if the guy lived.

Sure, maybe since the senator had gotten himself snuffed, and since the NR was going to make sure the public knew the senator had been railroaded, Congress would have to re-examine the AntiViolence Laws. A few months down the line, they might even suspend them.

But it'd be too late for Charlie.

They'd given him his one call. He'd tried to call his NR contact—but the fucking fone had rung buzzed times before someone had answered, and before he even had a chance to tell them where he was the operator cut in with "Please recredit fifty newpence," and his time was up and the cops were dragging him away from the fone and . . .

The NR didn't even know where he was. Didn't know what had happened to him.

He heard the squeak of the trash can's wheels at the bars.

Charlie looked over, thinking that maybe the Resistance had sent a lawyer in for him, or maybe they were going to bribe his way out, or . . .

But the trash can said, "Charles Chesterton, you are required for arraignment, judgment, and sentencing. Come with me." Its polite, characterless male voice was a little warped from wear.

The robot was about the size and shape of a standard street-side trash can, except it was on wheels, and it had the camera eye and the speech grid and the two nozzles. One nozzle for tear gas, the other for some kind of of knockout shot. The robot guards were heavy little fuckers, and even if you managed to knock one over before it put you under, the gates to the hall outside the cell block were always locked, and there were flesh-and-blood guards out there with guns and RR sticks and prods. And if anyone fucked with the trash cans, the devices instantly transmitted an alert to Control, and alarms went off, and your ass was on its way to being shredded.

So when the robot transmitted to the lockbox on the cell and the barred door swung open, Charlie did as he was told.

"Come out of the cell, proceed to your left at a brisk walking pace," the trash can said.

Charlie went out of the cell, his stomach twisting as he thought about sentencing. The trash can backed away, whirring, till Charlie turned left and walked on. It followed, out of arm's reach, behind him. The cell door rang shut.

A camera on the wall, near the ceiling, swiveled to follow his progress as he walked to the gate. A guard let him through, and Charlie screwed up his courage and asked, "Uh—did he die?"

"Not yet. But it don't make no never mind to you, asshole. Come on, turn around, bracelets time."

Not yet.

Twenty minutes later he was in the bedroom-size courtroom and they were showing the video of his attack on the cop, whose name turned out to be Arthur Anthony Gespeccio. The camera in the ceiling over the arrival chute for the prisoner capsule had been whirring away, and they hadn't had to enhance the images. But at first Charlie couldn't believe it was him on the video, sitting up in the capsule like a vampire in a coffin. Stabbing in that convulsive movement. Looked like, well, like somebody else. Moved like Angelo.

Physically it was Charlie Chesterton, and the judge knew it. A dyspeptic, matronly judge whose wrist was probably sore from banging the gavel, *the court so orders,* she sighed and shrugged when he tried to explain he'd been out of his mind; she murmured barely loud enough to hear—as if he weren't worth the breath—that the law no longer recognized insanity pleas no matter what the insanity was "by reason of." And she gave him the standard sentence for assault with intent to kill, compounded by a drug felony. Adding that he was also culpable for complicity with Angelo's death. Something he'd never thought of. The gavel said *bang.*

Death, to be preceded by public beating.

He was led out of there dazed, his throat too tight even to yell at them . . .

And then it sank in: He was to be beaten before being executed. That meant they'd give you a short rest in a hospital so you looked good, or anyway, so you didn't look persecuted when it was time for your public execution the following week.

The hospital stay. Prison hospital. But maybe in transferring he'd see a chance for escape. *Grab that hope. Hold on to that. Flimsy, almost nonexistent, but grab it and hold it.*

Hold on to that, he told himself, as they took him into the videotaping room with its blank walls and its sear of lights; as they attached his cuffs behind his back to the metal ring in the wall. "Whatever you do," one of the cops told him, "don't puke. Makes him *real mad* if the guy pukes." Then they left him there. He hated them, but he didn't want them to go, to leave him there alone. They went out, closed the left-hand door behind them.

There was another door, directly across from Charlie. Charlie stared at it.

The door opened. The big man in the mirror helmet came in, hefting the rubber club. Charlie thinking, *Mirror helmet. I'll have to see my own face as the guy wrecks it.*

"You fucking sick voyeurs!" Charlie screamed at the hidden cameras. Knowing they'd cut out anything he said that wasn't penitent.

"Try to relax," the guy in the helmet suggested softly. That's all he said. And then he began.

• • •

LANGLEY, VIRGINIA.

Corte Stoner tried not to look around as he went into Records, Classified, with his access chit. Got to look like it's all part of an ordinary day's work . . .

Records was a vault when the doors were shut and sealed, and despite the harsh lighting and cool waft of air-conditioning, the windowless place always felt claustrophobic to Stoner. There were two clerks behind the counter, Etta and Frank, and two lines. Shit. He wanted to put his request in through Etta. The line for Franklin was noticeably shorter. If he got in Etta's line, it would look wrong. The people who watched through the ceiling camera noticed anything odd that went down. It was their job to look for things that seemed out of place. Little anomalies. Maybe Unger was looking over their shoulder right now . . .

But it had to be Etta.

Stoner got in Etta's line, behind fat-assed Springsdale in one of his imitation tweed suits. Franklin glanced over at Stoner. Franklin was one of those prissy young men who look old and wizened before their time; he wore a newly printed flatsuit and a gaudy gold watch. He'd noticed Stoner's choice of lines. Maybe he took it personally. People who took little affronts personally made improportionate trouble for you. Snooty little bastard.

Stoner looked up the line to Etta. She was bent over her console, muttering to herself as she punched codes with arthritic fingers. She was eighty-four, had worked here since a ways back in the twentieth century. Stick-thin, pallid, silly excess of makeup; thick glasses; globe of blue hair. Quick, birdlike movements. Round-shouldered, almost hunchbacked from osteoporosis.

She was long overdue for retirement, but she was a tradition at Langley, the CINs concession to its roots. And she was still good at her job.

She was also one of those people who did favors for friends. She wasn't afraid of the Company.

He had to get into the Blue Classification files on the SA. Lopez and Brummel wouldn't take anything less. Class Blues couldn't be accessed through the outside computer lines; they were issued in noncopyable chip that were to be read by top-clearance personnel only. He'd lost his top clearance, thanks to Unger, four days before.

"Hey, Kimosabe," Unger had said, "you get my memo?"

"Sure. But, uhhh . . . " Stoner had feigned obtusity. "I'm still not sure what it is you want me to look for. I mean, all you said was, 'Keeping in mind our talk, look for evidence of Security Risks in these personnel' and then there was that endless list . . . "

"You don't know whereof I speak, Kimosabe?" His oily gloss of humor rubbing thin now, the cold metal threat showing through. "I think you know what I'm talking about. I'm talking about team players. Telling them from the others. And there's an easy way to tell them apart."

Stoner had lost touch with his common sense and replied without thinking. "Well, it looked like you wanted me to pick through the files and find excuses to downgrade and even prosecute everyone in government who was black, wog, Jewish, or liberal, but I know I couldn't have read you right, that couldn't be right, that isn't our standard criterion for risk . . . "

"Stoner, the criterion for risk changed when we opened our eyes to what was happening in this country."

The change in Unger's tone made Stoner regret not playing along. Hell, he could've played the game, pretended to, long enough . . . until he got safely out. Too late, he tried to snow Unger into thinking he hadn't meant it the way he had. "I'm talking about repercussions, man! For God's sake, some of these people are congressmen."

"Those people are on their way out. They won't be alone." And then he'd walked out of Stoner's office.

The next day, Stoner had found his clearance reduced. They made excuses about why it'd happened. Claimed it was because he wasn't working on Blue-relevant cases now, hence they'd decided to limit access for the sake of efficiency. Just efficiency, Stoner, that's all. Crap.

And now he was waiting patiently in Etta's line, Franklin glancing at him with pursed lips. Etta finished with Springsdale, Springsdale turned, saw Stoner, winked at him, and walked past.

Hey. What had the wink meant?

Forget it. You're getting the shakes. Springsdale gives that bogus wink to everyone.

"Hi, Etta." Stoner said, stepping up to the counter. Fingering his chit. Hoping the cold sweat on his palms didn't smear it.

"How you doing, Cowboy?" Etta didn't smile, but there was a lightness in her manner that said she found Stoner a relief after Springsdale. "You still listen to that twangy stuff?"

"Sure. You listen to that Hank Williams album I gave you?"

"Once or twice. Wimpy stuff." She cracked her arthritic knuckles. "You know me: give me rock 'n' roll anytime. It's maybe archaic, but not as archaic as that stuff you listen to. When I was in my thirties, I discovered Bruce Springsteen, and I'll never forget . . . "

He let her ramble through her memories for a while. He glanced at Franklin, a few paces away. The Priss was frowning over someone's access code on his monitor, had forgotten about Stoner. But he was close enough to hear, if he were paying attention . . .

There was nothing else for it. Lopez had insisted.

"What can I do you for?" Etta asked, smiling at her own ancient joke.

"Oh, uh—got it right here." He passed her the chit. Leaned over the counter just a little, enough for the merest shade of confidentiality. "I'm not exactly on for that." He didn't whisper it. Franklin would notice a whisper. "The clearance. Blue. But it's a lot of red-tape hassle, and I was hoping to seduce you into letting me slide so I can get what I need before they get around to changing my classification back to where it oughta be." That was it. It was up to her. He hadn't pushed for a favor from her before. If he was right about her . . .

He was. "Why, shore, cowboy. I'm headin' out to pasture in a month, what I care."

"You retiring, really?"

"Going to the elephant's graveyard in Florida. The part that ain't underwater from that global warming thing. I'm kinda skinny for an elephant. More like an ostrich." All the time punching through his request using her own access code. "Is there an ostrich's graveyard?"

"Stop thinking so morbidly. People are living to a hundred-forty-something now all the time."

"People who can pay for the treatments. I pay for my son's hospitalization half out of my own pocket. Maybe we should pull the plug, but I never could . . . Don't think I want to live to a hundred anything, anyway. Here you are." She went to the chute, which discharged a minidisk, and she brought it to him.

"Thanks. I owe you."

"Careful where you ride your horse, cowboy," she said, looking him in the eye.

She was on to him. She knew he wasn't supposed to have this file, and not only for reasons of technicality. She was warning him.

His mouth dry, he said, "I will. Don't take up surfing in Florida without lessons, okay?"

He walked numbly back to his office, feeling Franklin watching him go.

In his office he opened his desk, found the bottle, poured himself a shot of peat-cured Glenfiddich.

Then he got up and locked the door.

It took only about five minutes to attach the recording filter to the screen of his word processor. It was a transparent square that fitted neatly over the screen. It might've passed for an antiglare filter if not for the telltale wire trailing from a lower corner to the little gray metal box. The Second Alliance files were supposed to be noncopyable, but the filter read anything that was on the screen the way his eyes did and "drank" the light pattern.

He accessed the minidisk, began to read.

Same old stuff so far. The Second Alliance: World's biggest international private-cop outfit, its own sizable army, antiterrorist action, CIA-affiliated interrogations, et cetera, scroll ahead, more et cetera, go on to the next batch of info. And the next. Fresh reports from SA's European theater of action, cross-referencing with CIA on Socialist or partisan activists who'd oppose the SA's policing authority. Three of these people liquidated in France, two in Belgium. Harassment from the NR, retaliation against them, et cetera again, ho-hum stuff. Next. CIA endorsement of the Self-Policing Organization of European States.

What? What the hell was *that* all about?

The next section was in deep code. Only three people had that code, and Stoner was one of them. Which meant Unger was a step behind him.

Stoner punched in the decoding sequence and waited.

The section decoded, and he felt like someone had slugged him in the gut.

SPOES was "the multination framework for a single centrally authorized European State." It was to be a dictatorship operated by the Second Alliance, using nationalist leaders as puppets. Europe's several social democratic governments would be dissolved, not allowed to rebuild after the war.

Stoner was a hidebound capitalist, not enthusiastic about Socialism even in the watered-down form of social democracy. But SPOES would eliminate all choice in the matter. And it would systematically eliminate anyone who militated for a choice.

And: "A realistic assessment of Western Europe's racial situation leads us to conclude that minority races represent a threat to political and economic stability . . . " It went on to endorse a policy of rounding up blacks, Arabs, Indians, leftist Jews—it stopped short of endorsing the proscription of all Jews—and other "chronic problem races" for expulsion or something called "labor realignment." Which Stoner read as *slavery*.

Identified security risks were to be liquidated.

He stared at the word. *Liquidated.*

The Second Alliance estimated that forty percent of each "subracial community" were Security Risks.

Forty percent? They're going to liquidate forty percent of the non-Caucasians in Europe?

And why quit there?

He scrolled ahead, his hand shaking on the keyboard. He found what he was looking for. Progress reports.

Eighty percent success in stage one, all secured areas.

Stage one was the business of rounding up and isolating "risk groups" and the liquidation of priority troublemakers. Anyone they had confined whom they'd identified as an active, organized rebel had been killed.

Stage one was bad. Stage two would be worse. But it was stage three that left him scared.

• • •

Somewhere in Sicily.

Watson had made a resolution to get caught up on his reports that night. He was beginning to regret the resolution. But when he thought of shelving it, he remembered the look on Crandall's face . . . the look that said: *"You're expendable now, Watson."*

Watson was sitting in the Comm Center of the SA's Sicilian HQ, monitoring reports from around Western Europe, yawning, swilling coffee that didn't seem to help, fighting the fatigue that had dropped onto him at ten p.m. like a guillotine.

The consoles hummed. The lights overhead buzzed. It was almost midnight, he was alone except for his bodyguard, of course—and his eyes were aching from staring into monitors. The facts were beginning to lose their meaning; he had to repeat them to himself mentally.

Forty thousand fresh Second Alliance troops from the training camps had successfully deployed in four European capitals. Another four hundred Partisans had been arrested in Rome, three hundred more in Athens. All of them tagged for execution. Jews and Moslems in Dresden and Rouen impregnated with radio-traceable IDs and remanded to isolated sections of town. Reports from the NATO front, New-Soviets moving back across the Warsaw Pact borders, one last push, especially in Germany, piercing through Belgium and into northern France. Significant deployment of tactical nukes but none in use yet. Speculation from observers that this was the New-Soviet's last-ditch effort. If this failed, they'd surrender. Or turn to nuclear weapons.

But the NATO lines were frayed from sheer attrition. Maybe the New-Soviets wouldn't fail.

Watson's mind wandered. He found himself thinking about Crandall, wondering, *How long before Crandall becomes confident of his own safety?* Supposing it happened, supposing there was a way to get an assassin through to Crandall—what about Crandall's extractor team? They routinely rifled the brains of anyone who was to come physically near Crandall.

But there was a new technique the bloody damn albino had just developed—a technique that would make it possible to lay down a smoke screen in a man's brain. The extractor team would search the three layers of the man's mind. But what if you added a fourth layer? A false bottom to the wetware; a neurological subconscious, an access point at which a man could be programmed, without his own knowledge, to kill Rick Crandall when the moment came; a moment Crandall wouldn't know about till it arrived.

Watson would need an American, martially trained. Someone he could have access to here, where his own extractor team was. Better if it weren't someone established here. The camouflaging layer would change him, and his old cronies would know something was wrong. It would have to be someone else.

An American soldier, Watson thought. One who would be thought MIA if he disappeared. And a lot of them were in northern France now.

Very well. He'd go to Rouen. He was overdue for inspecting facilities there, anyway. Oh, there was a great deal he could do there.

Crandall had ordered him to remain in Sicily. The trip would be risky. But he was committed to taking risks now. One had to risk all to win all.

• • •

SOMEWHERE IN THE MEDITERRANEAN SEA.
Waiting in the Bullshit Belly.

Torrence was sitting on a metal bench in the half-darkness, smelling rusting metal and raw petroleum, watching Karakos.

There were forty of them in the hold of the tanker *Daniella*, in a gymnasium-sized compartment with a thin metal ceiling beneath a camouflaging layer of oil. Against the back wall of the compartment, roped down, was a two-man minicopter, on wheels.

The ship's engine droned in the background. Danco and Willow sat near Torrence, their faces picked out eerily in the yellow of electric lanterns near their feet; Carmen was sitting close to Willow.

She wore only fatigues, boots, and, over her bare breasts, a flak vest; she was nervously reassembling her Enfield. It was a "light support weapon," the combination of a rifle and a light machine gun she'd found on a British corpse in an overturned armored car, outside Paris. Standard NATO 5.56 ammo, lightweight, semi- and full-automatic firing modes, less recoil than most LMGs. Torrence envied it. He was carrying an ancient FN-FAL assault rifle, and an old Smith & Wesson .45 pistol. Danco and Willow were talking softly, their voices echoing tinnily in the great blank spaces of the hold.

"This Bullshit Belly," Danco said, "it's like that story *en la Biblia*. Jonah in the big fish." He said Jonah *Ho-nah*. He set his old, slender Sterling 9-mm submachine gun on the floor; the *clack* echoed like the snap of a whale's jaws.

"Jonah right enough, I'm bloody digesting in 'ere," Willow said. "What's it been? Seven hours, then?"

"More like five," Torrence muttered. "We'll be there in about half an hour." Across from him sat Lila and, lined up along the wall, a couple dozen more guerrillas. He found himself watching a pale blond guy, Farks, no more than nineteen, who was talking uneasily with Helmut Kelheim, an experienced German mercenary. He was big, dark, and confident; Farks was slim, pale, and clearly scared. Scared of not measuring up, scared of getting killed, scared he'd made the wrong decision in joining the NR. A decision made out of idealistic impulse, without the gristle of real anger—and anger was an important component of dedication. Kelheim had personal reasons for hating the SA.

Too late now, kid, Torrence thought. *Your pride won't let you turn back, and we need fighters too badly to just up and send you home.*

Torrence wondered what Claire was doing now. He hoped she was scared for him. As soon as he hoped it, he felt like a jerk for hoping it. But he kept on hoping.

He glanced at the steel door that would open out onto the sea when the time came.

The eight black-rubber zodiacs were stacked, inflated, beside the door, each with its small noise-suppression engine, no bigger than a lawn mower's. Coiled up beside the rafts was the magnetic climbing gear, the grapples and fiberlon rope ladders.

All neat and prepared over there, Torrence thought. And it worked on the training hulk. But the training hulk had been undefended . . .

And there was Karakos. Sitting with his face in the darkness thinking anything, God knows, anything at all.

"I think he's a risk," Torrence had told Steinfeld and Levassier. "I can't prove anything, but we shouldn't let him go if there's even a . . . "

"I've known Karakos for more years than you've had hair on your balls," Levassier told him, in French, the stump of his missing arm lifting as if he wanted to shake the vanished fist at Torrence in anger.

"If we get too paranoid, follow every little feeling up," Steinfeld had said, "we'll get lost, we'll splinter with the pressure. Karakos has had experience assaulting ships. We need him on the *Her*."

"We're making a mistake taking him along," Torrence had said.

"You're crazy from jealousy," Levassier had snorted, saying what everyone thought.

And now Karakos was sitting over there with his face in the darkness.

Willow caught Torrence staring at Karakos. "Chasin' ghosts again, 'ard-Eyes?"

Torrence ignored him. He didn't answer to the monicker.

"I think I'm getting another fucking bladder infection," Carmen said, pressing her knees together. "No fucking place to pee in here."

"Pee in Willow's ears, there's room where his brains oughta be," Torrence told her.

Nobody laughed.

The ship's engines coughed, sputtered, fell silent. The ship was coasting along in a current, angling to intercept the *Hermes' Grandson*.

Fuck it, Torrence thought.

He slapped a clip into his assault rifle.

• • •

A Trojan horse, the *Daniella* drifted, wallowing slowly, in a current that would carry it west, toward the *Hermes' Grandson*. The Second Alliance ship, coming from their base in the Spanish Mediterranean port of Málaga, was steaming steadily east. At 0110, an hour and ten minutes after midnight, the radar of the *Hermes' Grandson* took note of the approaching bulk of the *Daniella*. Radar watch informed the duty officer, who radioed the *Daniella* and asked for its ID number. The *Daniella* gave an ID number, which checked out with a registered oil tanker. According to the computer's registration search the tanker was American-made but now owned by a Spanish company that imported oil from the Persian Gulf.

The *Daniella*'s first mate explained by radio that the ship had been on its way to the Persian Gulf when it experienced engine trouble arising from a short in the ship's electrical system. The short not only froze the engine but also the electrical controls for the ship's gigantic anchor. It could neither move aside nor drop anchor. And it was squarely in the way of the *Hermes' Grandson*. However, it expected to get its electrical system working again in short order.

The duty officer on the *Hermes' Grandson* was under orders not to alter course except in emergency, since there were believed to be mines in the waters off-course. The captain would not consider this an emergency. So the *Hermes' Grandson* would have to pass close to the *Daniella*.

The ship churned yet closer to the *Daniella*. And now, turned sideways relative to the SA ship, it was directly in the way. It wouldn't be necessary to change course drastically to avoid the *Daniella*. They'd be a bit close together for a while. That was all. The SA duty officer swung starboard twenty degrees. The two ships slipped past each other in the dark. The *Daniella* was a squat black bulk against the starlight-tinged cobalt of the sea.

The duty officer of the *Hermes' Grandson*, who was young and over-confident, almost forgot about the *Daniella*.

• • •

Torrence chewed his lip as they rode another swell. He wondered if the SA ship would slip out of reach after all. The ship was in no hurry—but the little engines on the rafts were even slower.

They'd pushed off from the *Daniella* while the two ships were still parallel, the guerrillas' faces and weapons blacked, swallowed in the inky night.

Now they saw the great light-edged bulk of the enemy's ship ahead, looming like a cliff . . . blinked saltwater spray out of their eyes, heard the grind of the target ship's engines, and felt its wash slapping the rafts as they plowed toward it with painful slowness.

Torrence could just make out Steinfeld in another raft, saw him looking over his shoulder at the *Daniella*. The sharpshooters, with their infrared sights, should be in place by now . . . and the minicopter should be taking off.

• • •

Aboard the *Hermes' Grandson*, the duty officer was reaching for a cup of coffee when the call came. The deck sentry, his voice crackly in the intercom speaker, was yelling something about men in rafts.

What? the duty officer asked, Did he want men in rafts, or was there someone adrift out there, in a raft?

"No, dammit, sir, there are men in rafts with . . . " The sentry broke off in the middle.

"What? What did you say?" the duty officer demanded. No reply.

But he got another call, from radar, about a small helicopter. "Well, where is it?"

"Directly overhead, sir."

The duty officer punched the alarm button.

• • •

The sharpshooters had taken out three sentries, and the copter's crew had landed on the deck, fixed four ladders to the rail, lowered them—the upper sections of the ladders adhered to the hull magnetically, but the loose bottom rungs were whipping along behind the thrust of the ship, jumping at the waterline in the trough of the wake.

Danco, at the raft's little motor, opened the throttle, urging the raft within six feet of the ladder. It was dimly visible through darkness and spray. Torrence, rifle strapped to his back, said it for the second time that night: "Fuck it." And jumped for the polymesh ladder.

He fell short, cold seawater closed around him, and he wished he hadn't been too damn *cool* to wear a life jacket. He had a monstrously lucid image of himself lost at sea, treading water and spectacularly alone in the cold vastness with only minutes more to live before exposure and exhaustion dragged him under.

But his fingers closed over the synthetic smoothness of the rope ladder's lower rung as it dragged in the wake, and he pulled hard, feeling as if he could feel the whole dark breadth of the sea sucking at his legs as he struggled up onto the ladder, nearly wrenching his arms from their sockets.

Then he was somehow several rungs up, clinging, gasping. He heard Steinfeld yell. He got his footing on the ladder, turned, caught the rope Willow threw him. Tied the rope to the ladder. The other end was tied to a raft. He swung over to the next ladder, caught another rope, tied another raft on . . . gunshots and sirens from above.

Bullets whipped up the waves and pocked the rafts in places, emptying raft compartments but not yet sinking the little crafts. Answering gunfire rattled from the *Daniella* as the guerrillas scrambled up the ladders. Torrence saw Karakos going up one of the ladders, all eager-beaver, damn him. He forced himself not to think about Karakos. *Just keep the paranoia out of your head, you've got a job to do.*

And he and Danco and some of the others were almost up the railing.

There was a good chance he'd get to the top—and somebody'd blow his brains out the instant he stuck his head above the railing.

He moved past the scuppers, saw the gray-painted gunwale up ahead, getting closer. Wished he could climb and get at his rifle too. Maybe the seawater hadn't damaged his .45.

He paused just long enough to tug the pistol from his jacket and clench it in his teeth. He continued upward, expecting that any second someone above would pick him off the rope with an SMG burst. His wet clothes were raspy and heavy and cold.

He reached the rail, put one hand on it, took the gun from his mouth with the other hand, and dragged himself up.

Below the sharp electric lighting of the superstructure was an expanse of gray deck, and four sprawled bodies, and a man pulling himself along in a welter of blood. The minicopter was there, too, with bullet holes in its windshield; one of its crew was slumped, nodding his head monotonously from pain.

Torrence climbed over; hit the deck the same moment as Willow, who was coming off one of the other ladders; and ducked when he saw a muzzle flash from the corner of the cane-shaped top of a ventilation shaft. He dodged left, toward the bow, wet clothing making him move sluggishly, firing wildly with the pistol toward the muzzle flash just to keep the guy down.

Unslinging his assault rifle, Torrence reached the corner of the steel superstructure, out of the vent gunman's line of fire. He tucked the pistol in his coat, checked his rifle, and stepped out, around the corner.

Twenty-five feet away, a man in an SA regular's uniform, but without his shoes, stepped out of a steel hatchway, spotted Torrence coming at the same moment.

Willow was circling the guy at the vent, Danco making him duck back with rifle fire. Willow came up behind the SA regular and shot away the back of his head . . . as other guerrillas poured over the gunwale, hit the deck, ran for position. Lila shouting orders at her team; somewhere else Steinfeld yelling commands. Gunshots cracked and ricochets whined from metal.

The Second Alliance guy without his shoes looked scared as he fiddled with the submachine gun in his hand, trying to get the clip into it properly—and then he saw Torrence, and the scared look became terror. The guy's crotch went dark as he wet it. Torrence hesitated, imagining himself in this guy's place, the clip going in wrong, an enemy coming with a gun and no way to defend yourself and knowing at this range that your enemy couldn't miss.

Don't stop to think, idiot! And he made himself level the assault rifle at the guy—

"Wait!" the guy squeaked.

—and squeeze the trigger, the burst catching the soldier square over his heart, slamming him back against the bulkhead; he slid down the steel wall, leaving a long, vertical smear of blood like a gravemarker above him.

Torrence turned away and went on; felt a revolting combination of elation and horror as he shot two more men.

They'd lost the advantage of real surprise, but they still had the edge, had the initiative, and they had Steinfeld's leadership.

Torrence paused at a gangway leading up the superstructure to the bridge and drew his headset from its watertight pouch, put it on. He heard Steinfeld's voice, strident in the little earphones: "Teams two and three, regroup at the main deck aft gangway. Teams one and four, secure the forecastle and fantail."

An explosion and a ringing ran through the deck as one of the other teams tossed a seismic grenade through a hatch. Most of the enemy were still below, and Steinfeld was trying to contain them till the ship's controls and its captain were taken.

Torrence waited in the shadow under a large metal fixture he couldn't identify, across from the hatch. His team started showing up; Carmen and Farks and Kelheim and Willow, a little bent over as they ran, Farks looking white from fear, his chest heaving. *Asshole kid's going to hyperventilate.* And then Torrence caught a motion out of the corner of his eye from somewhere above; looked up and saw a big guy in an armored SA uniform, complete with helmet, leveling an M-30 at Kelheim and the other guerrillas. Torrence yelled, "Up there!" and squeezed out his last six rounds at the SA bull. They knocked the bull back but failed to penetrate his armor—and at the same moment the bull opened up with his M-30, directing it sloppily as he staggered.

Willow ran up, fired at the bull on the upper deck—making him keep back—

Farks screamed and Kelheim cursed. Torrence looked, saw Farks lying on his side, bending double and straightening and bending, opening and closing like a mealworm on a hot rock, gut-shot. Mewling. Kelheim was on his knees clutching at his own inner thigh and looking panicky. Torrence was surprised to see Kelheim react so strongly to a thigh wound till he realized the German was afraid for his genitals.

Torrence took a clip from his belt pouch, slapped it into his rifle—and it went in crooked. It was stuck partway, he realized, as he glanced up to see a grim-faced middle-aged guard come at him, raising an automatic rifle.

He saw in his mind's eye, again, the guy who'd got his clip stuck, the look of fear in the man's eyes, the whimper of *Wait!*

He had just time enough to think, *At least I'm not going to pee my pants—*

When Carmen ran up and shot the guy through the head with her side arm, two neat rounds, no hesitation. As Torrence cleared his clip, pushed it in.

Thinking, *But I almost did pee my pants . . .*

Willow was firing at the guard above them again as Carmen hissed, "Keep him pinned, I got the only piercer." She ran around the corner of the superstructure, fired at someone Torrence couldn't see, on her way to the gangway. She had to get closer to the bull for the armor-piercing round to work—and Torrence wondered if she'd gotten shot.

Then the bull fired down at him, missing with that burst; Torrence could see the armor's helmet, a glinting arc in the light from the bulkhead. A round scored paint from the cowl Torrence crouched under, making him jump a little. He returned fire, saw sparks jump as his short burst sang off the bulkhead—and then Carmen was there, padding up from the left, raising one of the little guns that fired armor-penetrating explosive bullets. The bull saw her, turned to aim his weapon. She fired; he fired. He missed; she didn't. His armor ballooned and he screamed, fell back.

Young Farks was lying still now, and Torrence couldn't keep himself from thinking the inevitable: *What a waste.*

Kelheim sprayed sealant on his thigh and then stood up, turned to shout a question at someone, trying to adjust his headset—and Kelheim's head exploded between his hands. One moment he was standing there shouting, his confidence back, once more part of the fight—the next his skull had flown apart under the impact of a round from an assault rifle fired from the lower corner of the superstructure. An SA regular, a stocky Hispanic carrying an M-18, was there, looking around.

Torrence stepped out to get a clear shot at him. Avenge Kelheim. The Hispanic SA—holding his rifle braced under his arm—was leveling the gun at Torrence.

One of those moments. The worst sort. When you can see the man you want to kill and the man you want to kill can see you, and you aren't under cover, and you aren't far from each other, and the outcome, your life or death, was contingent on a lot of factors, some of them out of your control. Not just a question of who shot better and faster. Could have just as much to do with who happened to have light shining in his eyes; who happened to be lined up best for a shot.

Who was simply more lucky.

They fired at the same moment. Bullets slashed by, Torrence expecting with each millisecond to feel the sickening crunch of impact. But the other guy was spinning, going down.

Torrence stood there for a moment, his bowels clenching, his heart hammering, hands shaking. *Get it together.*

But a wave of relief went through him as the call came over his headset, Steinfeld's voice through the fuzz of static, "All teams: The bridge is secured. We estimate half the enemy personnel dead. Hold your positions, and if you have enough people, send someone to the bridge to report. I believe we've got her."

Torrence took a deep breath and felt some of his calm return.

Until the thought hit him. Where was Karakos?

• 09 •

FirStep, the Space Colony, L-5 orbit.

Kitty stepped off the lift at Level 3, Corridor C13, and saw the SA bull waiting on the other side of the glass wall.

Was it glass or some kind of plastic or what? She wasn't sure.

She hesitated outside the elevator, looking at the big man in the padded gray-black suit, his face completely hidden behind the mirrored visor. She couldn't tell if he was looking at her or not, and that bothered her. He stood there with his legs braced apart, his hands locked behind him, motionless. He might be asleep in that helmet, or leering at her, or his face might be angry or . . . anything.

She wanted badly to see Lester. But she was scared of the guards. *Go on,* she told herself, *Security gave you a visitor's pass, what are they going to do?*

She walked over to the glass wall. She yelled, so he could hear through the glass, "I'm Kitty Torrence."

The guard pointed to an intercom grid in the wall. She heard his amplified voice. "May I help you?"

Surprised by his politeness, she stammered a moment till she managed, "I'm, um, here to see . . . " Then she remembered the pass, which would explain everything. She took it out of her pocket, pressed it to the glass.

The guard touched something on the wall to his left, and the glass lifted into the ceiling. "Go ahead on back. You'll see a door on the right says D5, the guard there'll escort you."

"Thank you."

Kitty walked by him with a little ripple of anxiety, half expecting him to turn and grab her from behind. Don't be stupid, she told herself. But she jumped a little at the noise of the glass wall coming down behind her. Hum, click.

She walked down to the hall, looking at door numbers. Her belly had grown a lot lately, making her back hurt, and making her feel awkward when she walked. She found D5, touched the door panel, and it slid aside. She went into a small gray metal room and spoke to a young, bored guard, plump and blond, sitting at a metal desk—this guard was, thank God, without a helmet. He looked at her pass. She saw him glance at her pregnant belly. He shrugged, took her handprint, then said something into an intercom. He listened, then nodded to himself and said, "Come with me, please."

They went down a long, narrow hall to a door stenciled D5, visitors. The guard used a code-key to open the door. She went in first; she was uncomfortably conscious of the guard behind her; she was afraid he might grab her from behind. Maybe there was a warrant out for her now.

It was a small room, harshly overlit, featureless except for a number of metal chairs along the walls and a vent. Sitting in one corner, a tearful Asian woman was talking earnestly, in Chinese or Korean, to an Asian man in a detainee's numbered blue printout. Paper pajamas, they called them. The opposite door opened, and Lester came in, trying to look proud in his own blue paper pajamas, a guard behind him. "You folks sit anywhere, you've got a half hour," Kitty's escort said.

Lester looked around sullenly till he saw her. He smiled and strode to her; she met him halfway and hugged him. She heard him suck his breath in quickly, and she asked, "I hurt you, huh? They bruise you pretty bad?"

"Ribs a little cracked, is all. They taped 'em up." He put his arm around her, and they went to sit in the corner opposite the other couple. The guards stood together at the visitors' door, talking in low voices about a glider race in the Open.

Kitty and Lester sat with their knees together, holding hands. They kissed. For a few minutes they looked at each other and Lester told her not to cry. But it was Lester whose eyes were filling.

When they spoke, it was in technicki.

"They beat you up since you been here?" she asked in a whisper.

"No. Just before they brought us in, if we even twitched a little. Here they mostly treat us like they're dogcatchers and we're the dogs. Dogcatcher doesn't beat the dogs, but he ain't nice to 'em, either."

"She was right." Meaning Chu. Kitty didn't want to say her name here. "They haven't got her yet. They . . . interrogate you?"

"Twice. Real politely the first time. Second time I think they were gonna use electricity, maybe drugs, but then Russ Parker came in, told them to send me back, he'd oversee an interrogation at 'a later date.' They didn't like that. It's like . . . " He glanced at the guards, lowered his voice further. " . . . like there's some kind of feud between the SA security and the old security. Which is, you know, kind of interesting. Maybe we could . . . "

"Lester . . . " She made a sound of exasperation. "I can't believe I'm doing this—I mean, I'm getting into this thing where the woman tells the man, 'Please don't do it, darling!' I don't like getting stuck in those archaic female roles, Lester. Don't make me have to plead like that, okay?"

She was angry, and she wasn't sure if it was at Lester or the Second Alliance or both. She was buzzing with it, and it was too much to handle; it made her want to cry.

"Well, babe, what you want me to do?" he asked, patting her baby-big belly.

"I want you to play their game. Play Uncle Tom if you have to. We've got to get off this thing. Out of the Colony. "

She glanced at the guards and saw with a chill that both of them were looking at her.

She wanted to spit in their faces. But she turned back to Lester and whispered, "They piss me off, too, Lester. But they have the guns and we don't. They know about you. And—the others."

He took a deep breath and closed his eyes. One of the tears that had been waiting there was freed to slip past his nose. He laughed softly at himself and wiped it away. "Crying. I'm a wimp, huh?"

She shook her head, feeling close to tears now herself.

"Thing is," he said, his voice breaking, looking at the floor, "there's no way they're going to let me out of the Colony, even if the blockade drops— maybe not even here. They don't want people on Earth talking them down. They got politics to worry about. I mean, you know where I am, here? I'm in a jail within a jail inside *another* jail. I'm in the lockup, and I'm jailed by being black here, and I'm jailed by being in the Colony at all, nothing but vacuum around us." He shook his head. "No way out. Nothing to lose."

"What about this?" She took his hand, put it on her belly.

They both felt the baby move. He smiled.

"How is he?"

"He? It's going to be a girl!"

"You had ultrasound? I thought we were going to be surprised."

"I just know . . . "

"Bullshit, it's going to be a boy."

"A girl."

"A boy."

They laughed a little, and that felt good. Then she started to cry for real.

He took her in his arms and whispered, "I don't know. Must be a way. This guy, Russ Parker . . . maybe you could talk to him. I can't see him, they won't let me. I already asked."

She drew back from him to ask, "What about an attorney?"

"They're all appointed for you, and they all belong to SA. And even if they're sympathetic, they can't do shit because of the emergency-martial-law thing."

She shrugged. "I don't think they'd let me see Parker."

They embraced again, but then the guard who'd given her that look came over and tapped her on the shoulder. "Come on, time's up." He had halitosis.

"It hasn't been a half hour," Lester said, and she could see him working hard to control his temper.

"I don't care. I can't stand looking at this unnatural relations here no more—"

Lester stood up, drew his arm back, shouted, "What'd you say, motherfucker?"

And the guy hit him with the RR stick he had ready in his hand. It happened too fast to see where he'd hit him; she didn't see any blood, but Lester went to his knees, stunned, and Kitty—sobbing, "Stop it!"—pushed between them, bent to put her arms around him.

The other guard came over. "That's enough, lady. Come on, he'll be all right." He took her by the elbow, dragged her firmly out the visitor's door. She yelled something and the guard ignored it and . . .

A few minutes later Kitty was in the elevator, going back to the dorms alone, shaking and holding her heavy middle, trying to control the sobbing.

But as she passed Admin's level, she punched for stop and reset the elevator. She went back up to Admin. To see Russ Parker.

• • •

ROUEN, FRANCE.

It was another wet day in Rouen, and Watson was tired of the place. The old quarter of town had a certain charm, with its narrow, cobbled streets, its rococo eighteenth-century buildings. But he'd come now to the abandoned supermarket they were using as a detention center; it was in the "new" quarter, which was already dilapidated, the high-rises dreadfully ill-kept, and the streets choked with debris.

It was nine a.m. He'd had a meager breakfast of stale croissants, orange juice going off, and excessively sweet coffee, and he was still hungry. The rain had been sputtering all morning; it returned as he stepped from the SA staff car to the cleared path that led between heaps of soggy trash and wet rubble. The barren supermarket building looked markedly truncated between two high-rises. They'd left ten-foot heaps of rubble around it as a defensive bulwark against guerilla attacks.

Watson wore his most elaborate uniform, just to cut back on red tape, and a shiny billed cap he himself had designed. Rain dripped off the bill as he stepped up to the metal doors and showed the helmeted guard his ID. He was ushered quickly inside.

It was more like a cattle barn than a supermarket now. The shelving had been removed, replaced by rows of pens to one side, wire fences between them, guards on the walks between fences. The pens were crowded and it was sickeningly obvious that some of the chemical toilets were overflowing. He must see that they had the prisoners clean them out, as they presented a health hazard for the guards.

High on the wall to the right was a glass mirror panel that housed the offices and once had provided a vantage for spying on shoplifters.

He went to the steps leading to the offices. He was looking for Chilroy.

He found him in Interrogation 9, at work. He was a trim, muscular young man, keen on dieting and working out; brisk, friendly, eager to please, generally considered on his way up. Watson disliked him for his cheerful willingness to impress everyone by overworking, never letting you forget he was overworking; and for his insincere geniality. He knew that some of his dislike was fear of Chilroy's ambition.

"Colonel Watson!" Chilroy said brightly, making sure his face lit up as he registered recognition of his superior. "This is an honor, sir!"

"Hullo, Chilroy. Bang at it as usual, I see."

"I've cut back, sir. Never more than fourteen hours a day."

It was a small room, perhaps once used for detaining shoplifters. The walls were institutional green. There was a doctor's examination table in the middle of the room. On it, strapped down under a dangling light, was a nude, pasty-skinned, Hasidic Jew, bearded, with the curls behind his ears, the classic nose right out of one of the old German propaganda posters. Watson made a face. This was the most demonstratively Jewish of the Jews. The man was shaking his head from side to side, muttering in what sounded like a mixture of French and Hebrew, bloody foam trailing from the corners of his mouth. The leather restraints creaked with his convulsive movements as Chilroy applied a smoking, white-hot electric instrument to the Jew's twitching skin, talking as he did it like a video metal-shop teacher demonstrating a soldering iron. "Some of them just seem to have the wrong brain chemistry for the extractor, and the damn thing is so expensive to use, we've fallen back on old-fashioned techniques."

"What is it you're trying to find out here?"

"Ah . . . " Chilroy looked nonplussed for a moment.

Watson enjoyed that. He'd forgotten why he was torturing the man!

"Oh, ah," Chilroy said, "we're trying to ascertain the whereabouts of his Rabbi. The Rabbi's an activist, a partisan."

"His Rabbi? Do I have the file on this man?"

"Yes, sir, we sent it to you by wifi. I just hope it gets through with the other material we've sent along. The New-Soviets have been scrambling again."

"Mmm. Not important for the moment. Don't spend too much time on him. He isn't worth it."

Not that Chilroy knew fuck-all about interrogation, anyway. He was too young for the job. He had no subtlety. He was a sociopath, with the requisite inability to feel empathy, and in that department he was ideal. He'd grow into it. Eventually Watson would have to see to it he learned the fine points. The shortcut to a man's secrets was the destruction of his sense of self-worth. Psychologically undermine him with humiliation, force him to identify with his interrogators. Physical torture did that, of course, for a time. But psychological torture was more effective in the long term. Watson had learned both techniques from CIA interrogators.

But it was hopeless to try to pass it on to Chilroy now, though Watson had the fatherly impulse to try, despite his dislike of the boy. One takes a pleasure in teaching the young the skills of adulthood. Later, later. Just now, something simpler . . .

Watson said, "You know, Chilroy, the technique you're using is time-consuming." Watson looked at the welts and blisters on the Jew's skin. "And a man can steel himself against it with some success. Much faster to bring in their family, play with the children a bit; these Jews have strong family instincts." He glanced at his watch. "I wish to see the American."

"Certainly, sir. This way."

They went down the hall to a padlocked double door. Chilroy opened the lock, removed the chains, and drew his side-arm. "The man is dangerous. He's under sedation, and he's handcuffed to a pipe, but . . . "

Watson nodded. Inside, they found an emaciated American soldier named Hayes sitting on the floor, cuffed to an iron pipe that ran floor-to-ceiling, staring at the barred window of the old storeroom. His left hand was bandaged; he'd lost several fingers. His eyes were red-rimmed, his hair thatchy. He twitched.

"His name is Hayes, sir."

"And the Army doesn't know where he is?"

"Not so far as we know. He's AWOL."

Watson said sharply, "Hayes!"

Hayes looked at him. Then at his cuffs, then back at Watson.

Watson could guess what Hayes was thinking.

"I see why you drew your gun," Watson muttered.

"Yes, sir. He's a killer. He's from one of those drug-enhanced units. He's quieter now that we took him off the amphetamines and hormones the American military had him on. But . . . "

Hayes murmured something—not to Watson or Chilroy or to himself, but, it seemed, to the shaft of light angling down from the window.

"He talks to a bird, Colonel. An imaginary bird. A parakeet. One of our patrols found him wandering the streets, talking to this imaginary bird, in English. We ID'd him with the DNA tag."

"I see."

He might be too far gone to use. But it would take a while for the drugs to really wear off completely. A better diet, a detoxification program, and probably something could be done with him.

Looking at Hayes, Watson felt that, indeed, something could be done. They'd have to rebuild much of his personality, in any case. And, of course, he'd need a new face.

Colonel Watson felt a queasy *déjà vu*, a sense of destiny unfolding. This man was to be his weapon.

Hayes growled deep in his throat like a whipped cur that had never been broken.

"I think he'll do nicely," Watson said.

• • •

Karakos walked moodily into the barn, past the men rolling the small, bullet-scarred copter back into place. He climbed the rickety wooden stairs to the radio room, hoping to find Claire.

But it was this man Bonham who was on his mind.

"I talked to Pierce before he died," Bonham had said that morning in the hold. "I was helping out in the infirmary and . . . I was the last one to talk to him. You look surprised. You thought he was dead, right? You were in a hurry to get to that radio, seems like, so you were sloppy. He told me: You shot him. There could only be one reason for that." He lowered his voice. "You're Second Alliance, my friend."

"I ought to kill you for that insult."

"Don't play the game with me, Karakos. Pierce wasn't delirious. He was sure. So am I. But it's okay. You think I like this cornball operation of Steinfeld's? I don't care about politics, man. I'm sick of this scene."

Karakos waited, listening. Wondering if he could kill this man here, make it look like an accident. No one would mourn him much. Bonham was a skinny, flabby, rat-faced man—what he had become had made him more rat-faced, somehow, than he would have to be—and he was easy to dislike.

"I'm sick of being held prisoner," Bonham said. "I want to go back to the States. I figure you can help me. Get me a pass from the SA, a guarantee of safe passage. In exchange I can give you some information they'd love to have: I know who the top New Resistance people are on the Colony. Only

Steinfeld and Witcher and Smoke know that, besides me. You help me and I'll help you, tit for tat, and I'll keep my mouth . . . "

"Shut it now," Karakos had whispered, looking up at the square entrance to the hold in the metal ceiling. Torrence had appeared up there.

There was still time to decide about Bonham. The man was dangerous, untrustworthy. But the information about the Colony could be very useful indeed.

And SA headquarters, speaking to Karakos aboard the *Hermes' Grandson*, had said, in essence: "Take your time, observe, learn what you can about this upcoming assault of theirs; learn about the NR's infrastructure, especially about their undercover operations in Europe, the States, anywhere. Gather more information about the Maltese base. We will destroy it when the time is right—you'll have plenty of warning."

And perhaps now Claire could be induced to give him something about the assault Steinfeld was planning.

She was there, in the radio room. With Lila.

The two women looked up from the decoder as Karakos came in. Lila put the decoder on hold and blanked the screen. *Does she suspect me?*

"Hello," Karakos said. He looked at Claire. There were rings under her eyes, and she was pale. She hadn't slept yet, either.

"Hi," she said, and pretended to look over something in a notebook.

There was a moment of silence; the only voice heard was the wind's, singing mournfully in the eaves.

Then Karakos asked, "Can I speak to you, Claire?"

She hesitated, then shook her head. "No, I—I've got some new stuff in. I've got to get it ready for Steinfeld."

Just an excuse. She didn't want to talk to him alone. So that was the way of it. She was having an attack of guilt over sleeping with him. Or perhaps this Lila, who was looking holes through him, had turned her against him.

He could wait. Claire was useful to him; she misdirected the others so that they couldn't take this Torrence seriously.

He would have her again in time. She was the hard type who wanted very much to let go and be soft, and that sort of woman was easy for him. She put herself in his hands like a gun, and it was a gun he would use.

• • •

THE ISLAND OF MALTA.

A windy morning on Malta. The three men stood on a tarmac dock in a Maltese shipyard: Steinfeld, Torrence and Danco. The cliffs of metal hulls rose on both sides; loading cranes, like the skeletons of abstract dinosaurs, reared over them.

They stood in the center of the dock, in a narrow patch of sunshine between shadows from the ships. They were warm from the sun and cold from the wind, by turns.

On Torrence's right the *Hermes' Grandson* was half-concealed by derricks and tarps and other dry-dock devices Steinfeld had used to camouflage the craft from spy satellites.

A number of still-mysterious crates and the prisoners had been removed from the ship, taken to storage and incarceration.

Torrence was exhausted. He hadn't slept in—how long? Thirty-six hours? Forty-eight? He wasn't sure. The sunshine hurt his eyes, but it felt good on his neck. He looked down the dock, hoping Claire would show up and ask for him. Maybe she was already with Karakos.

"You look like you need some rest, Dan," Steinfeld told him.

"What was Karakos's assignment during the assault?" Torrence asked, massaging the bridge of his nose.

"Radio room," Steinfeld said wearily. "Why?"

"Did he ask for it?"

"Yes, he said he thought he knew where it was."

"Did he go alone?"

"No, of course not." But Steinfeld looked uncomfortable.

"Who was it?"

After a moment's hesitation Steinfeld said, "Pierce and Griem."

Torrence said, "And both men were killed."

"Killed by the SA."

"How do you know?"

Danco snorted. "Torrence, Karakos is a freedom fighter, the real thing, a man fighting from patriotism—something you would not understand."

Torrence glared at Danco. Danco only grinned back him.

He wanted to hit Danco right in his grinning mouth. But Torrence held back. He had become increasingly alienated from the other NR lately— alienated both ways. *Don't make it worse.*

Torrence turned to Steinfeld. "This morning I was working on the deck, near the hatch where Karakos was. He was down in the hold . . . "

"I wondered why you insisted on working there. So you could keep an eye on him, eh?" Steinfeld shook his head in exasperation, his beard whipping in the wind.

"Anyway, this time I heard him talking to Bonham."

"What was Bonham doing there?" Danco broke in with maddening irrelevance.

"Steinfeld sent him over to help unload," Torrence said impatiently. "I couldn't hear most of what they said. But Bonham was offering some kind of deal to Karakos. And Karakos said he'd consider it. What I want to know is, what has Bonham got that Karakos would be interested in? What has Karakos got that Bonham could use?"

Steinfeld took a deep breath, expelled it in a long, sighing expression of irritation. "And you said yourself you couldn't hear them clearly. You could've heard what you wanted to hear."

"Steinfeld, Karakos is your old friend. You don't want to believe something's not right with him."

Steinfeld said, "Torrence, your judgment on the matter is even less objective than mine."

Torrence remembered that candlelit room, Karakos holding Claire naked in his arms.

Torrence said, "Maybe. But maybe not, too."

He turned and walked away from them. Wondering tiredly: *Are they right? Am I seeing things out of jealousy?*

He made up his mind to forget his suspicions. If he could.

• 10 •

THE SPACE COLONY. SECURITY.

Russ Parker was staring at the blank videoscreens, wanting to call the security checkpoints but afraid to use the fone. Afraid of what he'd see on its screen.

They got it out, he told himself. They said it was some kind of sabotage program one of the radics had worked into the system somehow. Despite all the safeguards. The door that had tried to crush him, the breakdowns . . . yesterday the lights going off and coming on and going off . . . fire sprinkler systems shooting off at random around the Colony . . . laughter coming from the intercoms but traceable to nothing. The images of old Rimpler, cackling dementedly.

All part of the hypothetical sabotage program.

And they promised to reprogram the system by one. It was two in the afternoon. It should be done. So go ahead. Turn on the screens . . .

He took a deep breath, reached out, flipped the switch. The screens lit up. "Type in access number," said the luminous green words. Parker let out a long, relieved breath and tapped the number for Security Checkpoint One.

A thing with gills appeared on the screen.

It was a sort of head, made of shiny black stuff, like glossy rubber; there were gills or vents on its jowls, corrugated tubes running from its nose and curving into its cheeks; pus running from the bright red, piggish eyes; bald head studded with black knobs. Mouth made of flaps within flaps, each one leaking a separate bright color of viscous fluid.

It was hideous, alien. But it was, viewed as a whole ensemble, weirdly recognizable. Just squint a little and the parts resolved into a distortion of . . . Professor Rimpler.

The screen's speaker gave out a sound that was pure mockery, a squawking like the noise made by one of those novelty-shop laughing boxes. Manic, mechanical laughter.

Revolted, Russ switched off the screen. The image faded.

Then, impossibly, the screen switched itself back on.

The rubber face, the squawking.

He reached behind and jerked out the power cord. The screen blanked. He sat back in his chair, trying not to hyperventilate. He stood up and went to the door. He didn't want to be alone in there.

He went to get the repairmen, and then to the commissary.

• • •

While Russ was out, Kitty Torrence came to his office.

"He's not in," the secretary told her.

"I'll wait."

"I'm sorry, but you'll need an appointment, and he's just not seeing anyone right now."

Kitty shrugged. "I'm not leaving."

The secretary pushed the call button. Two guards came into the office almost immediately.

That's when Russ returned, pausing in the outer offices to ask if the repairman had come for the viddycom.

He stopped when he saw Kitty Torrence. The guards were turning her away.

She was crying, shouting she wanted to see Russ Parker.

"Wait a minute," Parker said. "I don't recall having been asked if I'd see this woman. I told you I was coming back."

His secretary reddened. "Well . . . we thought, you know, you being so busy . . . "

It's Praeger, he thought. *He's told them to insulate me from the technicki.*

"Send her in," he said firmly, glaring at the receptionist. He was glad of something to take his mind off the black rubber thing on the screen. And he was scared to be alone in there.

He went into his office. Kitty came in and sat down in the only other chair. The door closed.

Her cheeks were streaked, her eyes puffy, but she'd stopped crying. She hadn't brushed her hair in a couple of days.

No preliminaries. "They beat him over the head just now," she said, "for nothing."

He knew who she meant, of course. "I'll look into it."

The words came out of her in a rush. "That's not enough. Let him go. You have the power to let him go. All we want is to go home to Earth. We can't cause trouble for you if we're not here. Let us go."

His mouth was dry. "I . . . it's not in my power to let him out or to let you go back to Earth. The space on the few ships the New-Soviets will let through is for emergency purposes only—administrative purposes." He realized he'd put that wrong.

"Administrative! Yeah, for Admin! You guys can leave whenever you want!"

"That isn't true." Oh, God, no, it so wasn't true. "And as for letting him out of detention—it's not in my hands. It's in Chairman Praeger's hands alone, and I don't think you'd find him a sympathetic listener. At any rate, there's strong evidence your husband was directly involved in sedition. It's only at my insistence, frankly, that you're not in jail, too."

Kitty Torrence closed her eyes. Her fists balled. "All we want is to go. To leave you all alone to your little war."

"Look, I doubt you'd get flight clearance for Earth even if I could arrange for you to go—you might lose the baby during G-stress on reentry. And, anyway, it's a big risk for anyone. There's a world war going on out there—not just on Earth but in orbit, too. If the military situation changes, the shuttle could be shot down. I'll tell you something more: There's a good chance the whole thing will blow up into nuclear war. In which case the safest place to be is right here."

"I can accept anything, even staying here, if Lester's with me."

He shook his head. "I haven't got the authority."

She leaned forward and said, "You think we don't know about RM17?"

He couldn't speak for a moment. He saw a flicker of triumph in her face. It made him angry. But he knew she was only doing what anyone would do, in her place.

He glanced at the door. "I don't know what rumors you've heard, but it's all . . . "

"Murder is murder."

"Now look, Mrs. Chesterton . . . "

"Murder is murder. Murder is . . . "

"All right. That's enough."

He sagged back in his seat. "Look, the damn Colony is falling apart.

Colony maintenance is at an all-time low. Especially since the explosion. Maintenance supplies are trickling through the New-Soviet blockade so slowly ... we've got just enough to keep going. We're getting sabotage like you wouldn't believe. Vandalism. We've got random violence—people are getting stir-crazy. I just don't have time to take your problems on."

"Murder is murder. You people are going to have to murder me, too, if you want me to shut up about it. Unless you let him go."

He opened his mouth to tell her not to threaten him, that there hadn't been a murder. But he couldn't say it. It was as if his voice box just wouldn't work. Not for that particular lie.

He thought, *Jesus, Son of God, I'm listening. Tell me what to do.*

He didn't expect an answer. But the strange thing was ...

He suddenly knew what he had to do.

He said, "I don't think I can help you." But he was writing something on a pad, keeping his body between it and the office's wall camera. "Here's a special pass to see him whenever you want."

When he handed it to her, he could tell by her suddenly guarded expression that she'd caught it; that he'd given her *two* documents. A pass and, under it, a note. She looked at him; he looked at her. She nodded and left the office. Probably wondering how she could trust the chief of security. And realizing she had no choice.

The note read, *My office is bugged. I'll contact you and we'll meet in the Open, at the Monument. Let you know when the meeting will be. I'll try to help you. Destroy this, after you get home.*

He watched her go, thinking: Now I'm in it deep.

But, hell, he'd made a choice. He'd chosen sides.

• • •

Faid was a wiry, nut-brown man with a droopy mustache and large, excited eyes. He wore a rather battered Japanese action suit today, tiger-striped, and he added a large smile when he saw Russ. "This is one funny place to meet," Faid said in a rather thick accent. "It's all broken here, rather." He'd learned his English in London, and he mixed Britishisms with his bad Standard.

Russ said, "Hell, it ought to be useful for somethin'." They were in one of the closed-off cafés on the Strip, the small section of the Colony that had been designed as the recreational center for its technicki population. The shops and cafés and spas were closed now; there were no supplies to keep them open. Russ, as Security Chief, had a key to all the silly little units on the arcade.

The place was dusty—more proof that the air filters were working badly in the Colony. Normally dust was precluded wherever possible, since it increased wear on the LSS equipment. Dust was a life-support risk. The windows were blocked-off paperboard; the only light was from the electric lantern Russ had set on the table.

"Shall we be sitting down, then?" Faid asked, gesturing toward a table. "I think the service will be slow, what?"

Russ smiled. He shook his head. "Can't stay long." He took two passes from his pocket, handed them to Faid. "You're security, you know how to use 'em."

"I *was* security, bloody not security anymore . . . "

"I know. I'm sorry. That's Praeger's doing. But take these. It's up to you if you want to actually use them—the situation is like this: I'm going to be taking some risks. I'm going up against Praeger. Chances are I'll be arrested. If you help me, there's big danger in it for you, and maybe not much else. But I thought you might want to, anyway."

Faid nodded. "You bloody well are knowing me too good, Russ!"

Russ pointed to each of the passes. "This one gets you into any place in Security Section; this one can be used to transfer prisoners. When the time comes, I'll want you to get this man out of detention and hide him." He gave him a piece of paper with the name and prisoner number of Kitty's husband. "I promised someone about him. And if he's loose, he just might do Praeger a dirty, which'll please the bejeezus out of me. Only, not yet. I don't want to do it that way except as a last resort."

Faid wagged a finger at Russ, saying, "You are knowing me too good!" And then he grinned and stowed the passes in his pocket.

• • •

A SHOPPING MALL IN WASHINGTON, D.C.
"We each get a copy, Stoner," Brummel said. "That was the deal," he added, as Lopez accepted the manila envelope from Stoner.

Stoner said, "They're both there." He was looking out the window of the cafetamine shop at the glassy maze of the lower levels of the capitol mall.

It was almost ten at night, and the shops lining the corridors of the vast subterranean mall were mostly closed. Some of the cases were dark, some were lit up but forlornly motionless; they displayed clothing and mindtoys and designer medinject units and ninja gear and sporting goods and vidinserts; the glass of the cases reflected one another, so the goods were layered in reflection, collaged with skewed squares of shine; one case mixed by reflection with another, a jumble of enticements; like a premonition, Stoner thought, of the coming time when the stuff ends in the city dumps, jumbled together again.

He felt empty and hopeless tonight; he felt bought and sold. Passing information to the enemy.

Think of the family.

Lopez slurped at his Styrofoam cup of speed-spiked ersatz coffee as Brummel looked at the little datastick in the envelope. Which was stupid; it wasn't as if you could tell anything by looking at some loose stick. Stoner shifted in the hard booth, rested his elbows on the synthetic white tabletop, his chin on his meshed fingers. A waxy cruller, made of God knows what, sat untouched on a paper napkin in front of him.

Stoner asked, "When do you get me out of the country?"

"After this stuff is looked at good," Lopez said.

"Work on your grammar," Stoner said. "How about we find a booth, I pay for the computer time, you read through it quick right there?"

Brummel looked at him. Perspiration glazed his dark skin. "You got a reason to worry?" He glanced at the corridor, then over his shoulder at the shop. It was empty, except for the Japanese kid behind the counter.

Stoner hesitated.

The three men sat bolt upright in their seats as the room shook with a sudden roar, the windows and tabletops vibrating; the Korean boy had switched on an iPod, blasting the heavy-metal squeal of a neopunk band. The lead singer was jeering:

Let's bring the war home
We deserve to suffer like the rest of the world
Yeah, bring the war home
Bring the killin' home
Build a brand new
Refugee dome
Yeah bring the war home

Stoner winced. "Yeah," he told Brummel, "I always got reason to worry. I don't think anyone's on me tonight. I don't see how they could have us under voice surveillance here when they didn't know—and we didn't know till ten minutes ago—where we'd have our meeting. But you're stupid if you don't worry."

"Come on, please, let's get out of here," Lopez said.

They left the shop, walked down the echoing corridor together, past a crowd in front of a cinema octoplex, Stoner asking, "What about the booth?"

"If we can find one with a working drive," Brummel said, nodding.

A bald man in a saffron robe was ranting at the octoplex lines. "Those of us who know these are the last days of man," he shouted, "demand that the suffering of innocents cease! Today I make another sacrifice, my flesh for their flesh, one ounce of flesh a week until the war is over!" He held up an arm and used a hunting knife to pare off a chunk of the heel of his hand; blood ran down the blade, twined his wrist; he screamed but completed his cutting; some of the crowd groaned in revulsion; others laughed.

Someone yelled, "You're not really serious unless you cut off your dick!"

The man in saffron opened his robe, took his penis in hand. An SA cop on a jitney rolled around the corner, pulled up next to him . . .

Stoner, Brummel, and Lopez turned a corner, hurrying away from the scene. Behind them there was a piteous scream.

They found a number of "Grid-in" booths at an alcove in the next corridor. There were twelve—seven were vandalized, scored with graffiti, their cables hanging out.

One of the booths worked. Stoner tapped its keyboard for "isolated reading" and then entered the stick files. He stepped aside, let Brummel and Lopez go through it, knowing he was taking a chance. They could always take the stuff and ditch him, leaving him twisting in the wind. Or kill him.

"I have something else, of course," he murmured, "something I'm keeping back till I'm safe and out of the country. Something very useful to the NR."

"It looks all right," Brummel said, stepping out of the booth, not concealing his excitement very well. "It—" He broke off, staring past Stoner at the bend in the corridor.

Stoner turned to look. A Second Alliance bull, this one without a helmet, was staring at them. He raised his arm, spoke into his wrist. Then turned away, was gone around the corner.

Just a routine check, Stoner told himself. He said, "When do we go?"

"We'll be in touch. I'll contact my sister," Brummel said.

Stoner held Brummel's eyes. "Soon."

"Soon as we can make it."

"How soon is that, dammit?"

"A few days."

"*Sooner*," Stoner barked. He moved off toward the escalator leading to the parking structure.

In the parking lot he started his Guatemalan Rapido and drove out into the weirdly abstract, arrow-marked lanes between cars. Seeing a light in his mirror. Another car starting

Just someone going home from the mall. Everyone goes out the same way, after all.

But when Stoner was out on the street, he turned at the next corner, and the car behind him turned too: A Ford Hydro Shuttle hanging back but tailing him. He took another turn, arbitrarily, watching it.

The stranger turned too.

They weren't bothering to hide that they were tailing him. Which meant they wanted to scare him—or they were about to come down on him.

He sensed somehow that they were going to take him. Now.

He pulled up at a crowded restaurant and bar, doubleparked, went inside as calmly as he could, going from deserted dark street into brassy lighting, noise, laughter.

"Yes, Sir, are you here for dinner?"

"I'm meeting someone in the bar," Stoner said.

He tried not to run, managed to keep it down to a trot, as he hurried into the bar, past it to the credfone booths. He slid his card into the fone slot, and the screen lit up. Stoner punched his home number, waited breathlessly, glancing over his shoulder. No one was following him in yet—but they could have put a bird's eye on him.

His wife's worried face appeared on the screen. "You okay?" she asked.

"Yeah. But . . . anything going on at home?"

She shook her head.

"Okay. Your sister there?"

She nodded.

"Okay. I want you to make that little trip to see your mom."

Her eyes widened. "Okay."

He cut the line. She knew what to do. She'd arranged it with her sister. Her sister would put on her clothes, get in the car, drive out of the garage as fast as she dared, drive off to Falls Church, where her mother lived. They'd think she was going to her mother's. The sister wasn't a twin, but she looked enough like her from a distance that it might work. The surveillance crew, with luck, would follow the sister.

His wife and daughter would go out the back, through the neighbor's yard to a friend's house, call a cab. They'd meet at a certain motel in Baltimore.

If it worked. If the Company was fooled. There was a chance: God knows CIA Domestic could be fooled.

Stoner went to the men's room. The window was nailed shut. He took off his coat, balled it around his fist, smashed the window glass, hoping the noise from the bar would cover it. He broke out tile jags from the window frame, climbed on a sink, wormed through the frame onto slimy asphalt, expecting someone outside to grab him as he came out. No one there. A wet, trash-gunked alley.

He got to his feet—saw headlights swinging into the alley to his right. He turned down a narrow walk between the restaurant and the next building, feeling his way along in pitch darkness; moving back toward the restaurant's front. Smelling urine, garbage. He emerged onto the sidewalk. The Ford Hydro was gone; it was around back. And there was a cab just letting a young couple out in front of the restaurant. He ran to it, got in before they closed the door, slid a fifty-newbux note through the slot to the driver. "Go anywhere, fast!" he yelled. The driver saw the bill, and the car squealed away from the curb.

Stoner watched through the rear window. He didn't see the Hydro. The dumbshits were still looking through the alley. The cab turned a corner and he felt a ripple of relief. Ditched them for now. Unless they had a surveillance bird on him too. He glanced up at the sky. No telltale silvery fluttering. But the birds were small; you never knew.

He'd have to contact Brummel directly, somehow. Tomorrow, if he got through the night alive.

• • •

THE NEW YORK COUNTY JAIL.

There were forty beds in the county jail's hospital room. Charlie was lying in the bed nearest the door, trying not to hear the shouts and babbling and jeering of other patients—other prisoners.

He gave up trying to get comfortable on his back, moved to his right side. That hurt too. He shifted to his left side. After some more experimentation he found that if he remained on his left side and tucked his knees up near his chest, bunched the sheets up under his sore kidney, he could minimize the discomfort. Now and then he reached under his sour-smelling, grimy pillow and let his fingers play over the plastic cigarette lighter he'd found in a refuse barrel. Some guard had thought it empty. But chances were there was a light or two left in it.

The prison infirmary was bigger than he thought it would be; danker, darker, more foul-smelling. It was shaped like an enormous Quonset hut, walls curved into ceiling. The only windows, shaped like quarter-moons lying on their straight sides, were near the ceiling; they were metal-meshed, flyspecked, never opened—probably never could. The light from the windows and the ceiling fluorescents was a sort of milky glare. There was no screen, nothing to read except the heap of printout magazines over by the door. The old metal beds creaked at one another constantly, as if groaning for the infirmary patients, and the patients—or prisoners, or victims, or stray animals—complained and cursed. Half of them were tied to the beds with plastiflex restraints; the orderlies came rarely, so the prisoners were forced to foul themselves and to lie in it.

The place was bedlam, and the shouting, the groans, the idiotic hoots and the weeping—everyone here in pain, most everyone condemned to more pain and death—the noise of the place scared Charlie. He found himself reverting to a kind of infantile state of terror, the fright only an infant can feel, a fear primordial in its depth, all-consuming. He was caught in the

State's garbage disposal; the noise of this place was constantly grinding away, and the sound of it was the sound of the gnashing steel teeth of the State, its teeth gnashing bones and flesh.

Charlie was trying to screen it all out. Think of it some other way, he told himself. Think of it as the noise of a storm.

He lay on his side with his eyes screwed shut.

His mind was busy. It cut his situation into segments, and cut the segments into smaller segments, and parsed the little segments into sorted heaps.

He could blame the Hollow Head. The place that was a drug. That's why he was here. Because of what the Place had done to Angelo and to him.

No. It was his own weakness. His psychological original sin. His own tendency to . . . what had the school psychiatrist called it when Charlie was in seventh grade? Disassociative neuroses? The need to disassociate his mental focus from himself and things around him. Drugs worked best. It was old news: he'd done drugs because they freed him, blew away his problems and anxieties.

And the Hollow Head, of course, was more than a drug. It was living drug paraphernalia; instead of you swallowing the drug, the drug swallowed you. All-encompassing. Real disassociation, internal and external at once.

When you left the Hollow Head, you were exhausted, sick, maybe greasy with self-disgust. Vowing never to go back. Same old story, same old hard reality.

Because you always found excuses, your feet turning toward the place without your thinking about it.

When you realized you were going to cop a buzz, you argued with yourself. Maybe only so you could say to yourself, "I tried, I fought it." But with never any real conviction in the fight.

Sure, it scared you. You'd seen the burnouts. You'd heard the stories of things happening like what had happened to Angelo. You were scared of the place, of the addiction.

Drugs, and the Hollow Head. The cycle had been eating him alive. So he'd gotten into the Resistance. He'd joined them, he knew now, more to escape from drugs than for ideological reasons. He believed in the Resistance passionately. But deep down he was there because he'd thought it would save him.

It hadn't saved him. The drug thing was like one of those movie monsters you thought was killed—and it rises up again and again. Out of water and out of flames, neither drowned nor incinerated.

And he'd shot Angelo into himself; he'd gone mad for a while; he'd killed a cop. He was judged and convicted. The sickening thing was, he understood the conviction very well. He didn't even have the consolation of feeling that he was an innocent wronged. He'd walked a tightrope over a vat of shit, and he'd fallen into it.

There was no appeal. He was here only till he healed up just enough to participate in the circus they'd make of his execution. Every day the doctors would examine him; treacherously, his body would repair itself, and with every improvement he was a little closer to his execution show. There were cameras in the ceiling, and the men in restraints were mostly the ones the cameras had caught mutilating themselves to put off their executions. He had a few days, as much as a week, and then they'd execute him.

The NR didn't know where he was. It probably couldn't help him, anyway.

He had an absurd image of his mother coming in, shouting at everyone, straightening it out, taking him away from here. *I'll be good, Mom. Just get me out.*

Shit. He didn't even *like* his mother.

The only way out of here alive was escape.

His hand closed over the lighter again. It was sweat-glossed with his touching.

Sometimes the guards came in and searched the beds for improvised knives, drugs, anything. Fouling your bed wasn't enough to keep them from searching it. They just made you clean it up first.

Next time they searched, they might find the lighter. Stiff as he was, now was the time.

He rolled onto his stomach, pulled the rancid sheet over his head and over the pillow, as if trying to blot out the light so he could sleep. He lay still for a while, smelling himself, sour but reassuring, in the gray semidarkness, hoping anyone watching on the ceiling cameras would think he'd fallen asleep.

Twenty minutes, till he was sweaty from being under the sheet, and then he reached under his pillow, found the lighter. He put it between the palms of his hands and began to rub it, warming it up with friction and body heat so the small amount of gas that was in it would expand, rise to the nozzle.

He pushed his head under the pillow, making a little hump under it so there was enough air for the lighter.

He decided he'd rubbed the lighter long enough. He flicked it, watched the sparks breathlessly.

There: a translucent, blue-white flame, as faint as a burnt-out freebaser's rush, but there all the same. Enough to set the pillow on fire.

And the pillowcase caught.

He jammed the lighter into the waistband of his prison-blue pajamas and jumped up onto the bed, shouting, "SHIT! WHICH ONE OF YOU IDIOTS TOSSED THAT FUCKING BURNING BUTT ONTO MY FUCKING PILLOW? SHIT, YOU CAUGHT IT ON FIRE!" And he convulsively tossed the burning pillow one way, the burning pillowcase the other, onto the heap of magazine printouts. The torn pillow's ticking floated in a burning cloud like moths of fire over the three beds nearest him; prisoners yelled and cringed away, others laughed, flames rose from the burning printouts, smoke darkened the room.

A Hispanic kid was spreading the fire around, laughing and setting fire to sheets, blankets.

Coughing from the flames, Charlie backed to the door, stood to one side of it, thinking, Maybe it won't happen the way I thought it will; could be they'll all burn to death because of me.

It didn't matter. They were better off that way.

And there was a certain exultation seeing the flame reaching with thin yellow spires toward the ceiling; it was as if all the bound-up anger of the patients was manifested in the fire, was dancing, restoring animation to this groaning repository of the good-as-dead.

The door burst open; guards with fire extinguishers came rushing into the infirmary. No ceiling extinguishers here.

They did what he hoped: In their haste they left the door open behind them. Not thinking anyone was back there, not seeing him.

He went through the door behind them, trying not to cough till he got far enough down the hall. He went down the blank hall, looking for a way out or a place to hide. Now what? The fire hadn't been out of hand; they'd have it out in a few minutes.

He turned a corner, came to a door. It was open. He stepped through and found he was outdoors—on the top landing of a metal stairway zigzagging down the outside of the building, four stories down into the unused concrete exercise yard below and to his left. It was gray and chilly out. Beyond the exercise yard was a high wall crested with concertina wire, cameras, and a guard tower. Charlie turned right, along the metal catwalk. Two men came out of another door, just in front of him. He saw his own face, reflected in a helmet visor. The SA was a private outfit. What was SA doing in the public police station? Were they that far infiltrated into the System?

"That's him," the man behind Charlie's face said, and Charlie's heart sank.

The other guy was a wide-shouldered, swag-bellied black guard—ironic that he should be working with the Second Alliance. He had a shotgun in his hands, its blue metal mouth open to Charlie's middle. "You going for a walk?" the black guard said, grinning.

Charlie said, "Trying to get away from the smoke, is all."

The SA shook his head. He had a plastic breast tag on his armored suit: SECSPEC. He was a security specialist. Highranking SA hired by the city—or by classified defense contractors, or airlines plagued by terrorists—to bring a special expertise to making security airtight. He'd seen Charlie on the cameras, known what he was doing.

"I've got a feeling about this young man," the SECSPEC said, approaching, slapping his RR stick in his gloved palm, his voice all crackle-edged from the helmet amper. "He thought it out very well. We checked your DNA imprint, Charlie. Just now. You were taken in two demonstrations. Leftist demonstrations. You're an organized rebel with a political bent."

"Got us a terrorist, huh?" the guard said.

Charlie backed away and came to a jarring stop against the rainwater-beaded metal railing around the landing.

"I think we're going to have to apply to the judge for an extractor order for this young gentleman," the SECSPEC said dryly. "Unless you'd like to confess your political affiliations now, Charlie?"

Shouts and smoke from the corridor to Charlie's right. To his left, a wall. Behind him, a four-story drop.

And ahead of him: the extractor.

Oh, no. Cold metal on his back. Concrete building. Metal catwalk. Concrete exercise yard below. Hard metal things in the hands of the men approaching him, the guard taking out a chromium pair of cuffs.

All the hard things, concrete and metal and barbed wire and guns: part of the trap. The hard-edged, hard-walled, unyielding concrete-hard trap. All the planes of metal and concrete contracting in on him, rushing toward him, bearing with them an inflexible conclusion: He had to die.

Right now.

If he let them take him, they'd use the extractor, dip into his brain, pluck his knowledge of the NR. Down to the approximate location of the HQ; the island, Merino. Smoke. Witcher.

He had a half second to make up his mind. *It's your fault, you did the Hollow Head, risked the NR doing it, face the responsibility for once, you asshole. Do it!*

"Stop him!"

He felt the gloved hand on his arm, but he wrenched away, turned, flung himself over the railing head first, angling his body vertically, throwing his legs back, hands gripping his hips; angling to fall head down, to make sure he landed on his—

• • •

The two men on the landing looked down at the body in the exercise yard. Red splash at one end of the body. "Mushed his brains out," the guard said. "Hell, you ain't gonna extract nothing from *that* mess."

"God *dammit*," the other man said; adding with a touch of admiration, "The son of a bitch beat us."

• • •

THE ISLAND OF MALTA.

Claire wasn't at all sure why she'd done it. Why she'd slept with Karakos. Why *really*.

Except that perhaps it had been a way out of the pressure.

She was sitting with Lila on a little window seat, looking out to the north. It was dusk. The tangerine light reached from the west to tinge the twig tips of the trees; the trees did slow shimmies in the wind. The sky to the north was violet. The house creaked in the sighing wind.

Lila was cleaning her gun, an H&K autopistol, but doing it with placid absentmindedness, the way a woman from an earlier time would do needlepoint.

Lila stole glances at Claire now and then; Claire, wearing only a robe, a little cold but not wanting to move and break the quiet spell of the moment, pretended not to notice Lila's glances. But she enjoyed them.

Enjoyed them as she thought about someone else entirely. Torrence. He pressured her without even trying. She wanted him, wanted his lean, hard, angular body pressed against hers. But sometimes when she looked at him, she saw one of the man-animals of her nightmare.

Karakos had finessed her with just the right amount of fatherly teasing, joking, and protectiveness; never assuming too much, but accepting the relationship as the most natural thing in the world. And he'd wept unashamedly in her presence. Wept at the horror he'd seen in the SA prisons. She'd put her arms around him, to comfort him . . . and the pieces fell into place, the chemistry took them from there.

She wondered, for a moment, if she'd fallen for what her father would have called "the oldest trick in the book." But Karakos had seemed, like her, honestly sick of the killing. Psychically wounded.

Torrence, on the other hand, despite admitting to having been afraid, never *showed* it, and if he was hurt by what he'd seen, he kept the hurt hidden.

His reluctance to *genuinely* open up, to show her his hurt . . . it frustrated her, made her feel excluded from real intimacy with him.

Torrence's protectiveness, too, had made her angry. Had she slept with Karakos partly out of anger?

The thought made her cringe. How had she gotten into this silly emotional maze? She looked at Lila, wishing she could be more like her. Always busy with something. Totally committed. Unruffled. Never tangled with men.

Before coming back to Earth, Claire had been celibate for two years. It was as if being on Earth (mental image of an earth goddess) had opened a hillside spring of sexuality in her.

Her only significant Colony affair, more than two years earlier, with Mouli, a Persian life-support-systems stress analyst, had discouraged her hugely. Mouli had been relentlessly cerebral, except in bed—when he became mechanical. She'd had a ferocious crush on him, though, till she realized that despite all his earnest pretense of listening to her, and despite his serious conversation about Colony politics and futurological projection, Mouli didn't give a damn about her, the real Claire Rimpler. The mental relationship was a sham; she was just pussy to him.

She knew she meant something to Torrence. And she seemed to have answered some deep need in Karakos (wondering with a vague unease, Was Karakos manipulating her, as Torrence implied? His emotional openness was almost too good to be true). But when you got involved with men, you became absurd. Unimportant things seemed significant; you became stupidly *girlish*. It was embarrassing. It was beneath her. Sexism was unfashionable with men like Dan Torrence—and Karakos. But somehow it was alive and well in them. As soon as you became involved with men, regardless of the best intentions of both sides, you became subsumed to them. Co-opted.

Still . . . the tension in her, the sense that she should be doing something to make up for abandoning her father, was maddening. And sex was an effective release from it.

She looked at Lila, the twilight's gloom making her dark skin look, in profile, like a black velvet cutout. She was laying her reassembled gun aside, wiping oil off her hands. Carefully not looking at Claire.

"You never seem to get rattled, Lila," Claire said on impulse. "You never seem to need to . . . to get drunk like the others sometimes do, or . . . I mean, even Steinfeld needs to get drunk about once a month. You never get drunk, never get involved with men. You don't . . . " She shrugged. "How do you do it?"

"There's something I do," Lila said, looking uncomfortable.

Claire was embarrassed. Afraid the woman was about to confess that she was in love with someone, like Steinfeld; that she masturbated wildly and fantasized about him.

"This is what I do," Lila said. She took a little brass pipe from a pocket on her fatigues, and a piece of tinfoil. "But only once a month—that's all I allow myself. To, um, *let go,* no? I find it does not impair my efficiency the next day so much as, um, getting drunk."

"What is it?" Claire asked.

Lila was opening the foil. Inside was a little brown lump of hardened mud. Or something that looked like it. Lila glanced at the door, as if to be sure that it was closed, and said softly, "It is hashish."

"Oh!" She'd read about it. "It's carcinogenic, isn't it? Lung cancer."

Lila smiled. "Perhaps this is so if you smoke it every day. Once a month it's much less risky than breathing the air in a city. And I only allow it to myself once a month." She broke a piece of the hash off, rolled it into a taffy lump, and pressed it onto the screen in the little brass pipe. She put the pipe in her mouth, gripped between her straight white teeth. She took a steel-gray New-Soviet cigarette lighter from her pocket and ran the flame over the hash, sucked on the pipe, making the tarry lump bubble and glow. The coal lit her face with a fan of soft red light. The blue-white smoke drifting up from the pipe was aromatic.

Claire was only a little short of amazed. Lila, a drug user!

Lila inhaled, held the smoke for a moment, then let it gush out and said, her eyes faintly sleepy now, "It's a very mild hashish." And she offered the pipe to Claire.

"Oh, um, no thanks."

"A guerrilla has to know the world from every—how would you say— from every window. From every direction. This will show you a new . . . "

"A new angle on things?" Claire smiled.

"You have been so tense. I've seen that. This will help."

Claire found herself accepting the pipe. The guerrillas sometimes smiled at things Claire said, as if they thought her just a little ridiculous. As if she were a naif because she'd lived most of her life in the Colony. She didn't want Lila to think of her that way.

But her stomach contracted with fear as she put the pipe in her mouth. Would she hallucinate? Would she think she'd turned into a sea gull and try to fly from the window and fall to her death?

She inhaled. "I don't think it's affecting me."

Lila giggled. "You inhaled before it was lit. I have to light again. Put it in your mouth . . . yes, hold it still . . . good . . . now suck on it to inhale . . . good, inhale . . . "

Claire felt a hot sandpaper hand jab sharp fingers into her lungs, and she gagged, coughed, almost dropping the pipe. Lila was making a strange sound. Something like *tee hee.* Astonishing!

"Well, I am guessing you got some that time, Claire. Beautiful Claire. Now I will have some more . . . "

Lila took another puff. A long one. She didn't cough.

Claire felt pleasantly distant from things, mentally. But physically she could feel the window seat's cushions under her; the fabric of her robe under her hand; air currents sliding cool past her throat.

Her lungs still burned from the first hit of the hashish, but she found herself wanting another.

They traded the pipe back and forth twice more, Claire coughing both times but caring less with each lungful of the hot, dark fragrance.

"It smells like incense," she said dreamily. "But a little more . . . a little edge to it . . . "

"It makes me sleepy," Lila said, "but not like I want to really sleep. Just to lay down and dream but with my eyes open."

"You mean . . . you hallucinate?"

"No, not that kind of dreaming. My mind goes wherever it wants."

She walked to the bed with an odd combination of floaty grace and stoned dislocation. With a soft cry she sank onto it, began to undress.

Claire stared at her, thinking she should leave. Lila was going to sleep, or wanted privacy to lie there and dream. But it was so fascinating to watch her peel her clothes off. She'd never realized before what odd things clothes are, what peculiar, soft encrustations they were. And Lila was so slender, smooth; watching her limbs move was like watching the flow of a dark river at night; just enough moonlight on the river to make out the contours of currents and ripples.

"You're so beautiful," she blurted.

A flash of white teeth in the near darkness. "Come and talk to me, Claire."

"I should . . . let you sleep, or . . . "

"I'm sad, Claire. I get sad when I smoke hash sometimes. Please don't leave. Come and talk to me." She was a woman-shaped pool of soft-edged shadow on the silvery silk bed. The bed didn't look like a bed; it seemed like a sort of great soft cake, as if you could reach out and push your hand into it and scoop moist chunks of bedcake.

Claire stood, swayed with a momentary dizziness, then walked toward the bed. It took so long to get there.

But in a moment she was lying on the great rectangular cake beside Lila, lying on her back, her robe fallen open, feeling the cool air whisper over her skin, one of the currents warm as it cupped her left breast and drew on her nipple, stiffening it.

Oh: It was Lila's mouth . . .

Claire stared at Lila's dark head moving on her chest, her large, lustrous eyes looking up at her . . . felt a connection, a bolt of wet lightning between her breast and her vagina. The electric wetness emerging there so she could feel the lubricants cooling in the slit where they met the air.

There was a glass pane of resistance in her, telling her: *This is perverse, this is a bad idea, shouldn't get involved like this because Lila will get attached and I'm not gay (am I?), and anyway, Dan will freak out* . . .

But the tide of sheer yearning rose up in her and pushed mightily at the glass pane, which turned out to be ice because it didn't break but melted in warm, salty sensation. As Lila slithered onto her, pressed succulently large lips over hers, ground her pubis onto Claire's—not too hard, the way a man will when he's clumsily trying to turn a woman on, but with firm tenderness and a suggestion of suction so that labia sucked on labia. They rocked together, and Claire basked in the ecstatic surprise of heightened sensory input as she drank Lila's skin with her own, letting her hands skate the impossibly perfect engineering of the feminine curvaceousness of Lila's back, the supple fullness of Lila's ass. With her eyes shut, she seemed to see what she felt, a synesthesia of tactile sensations translated into the visual, Lila's elegant arcs abstracted into swirls of ruby mist and exquisite ellipses of mouse-fur gray. Their tongues, entwined, were translucent, comma-shaped bubbles that became one another and then writhed happily apart and came together again with impudent stickiness . . .

A fulsome ache came into her stomach. Lowering itself into her groin.

As if sensing the ache's arrival, Lila moved off her—a sense of fleeting tragedy; wash of sweet, cool air—and knelt beside her, exploring with her fingers, chasing hot fish of sensation up from their dark caves. And then dipping to meet them with her mouth.

Oh, Claire thought, *no. I couldn't do that.*

Lila didn't insist. But after a while Claire found herself turning onto her side, pressing her head between Lila's smooth thighs, probing for the wet, warm place between the petal-shapes of wool. And after a time, a gong shivered, shivered, shivered . . .

It seemed like years later but it had been only an hour when the door opened and someone stood there, backlit in the yellow hall light.

Lila and Claire had rested. They had just begun again. Somewhere, sometime, they'd had another pipeful. And they'd begun kissing again, exploring each other's breasts with the satisfying slowness of the utterly relaxed.

And then someone had opened the door. Claire looked over. It was Dan. Hard-Eyes. Torrence. Staring.

Staring like he couldn't believe it had happened to him twice. And maybe because he couldn't believe it was Lila this time.

"How many times," Claire murmured vaguely, "is he going to walk in on me with people? This is ridiculous. Doesn't anyone *knock* in this place?" She sank back on the bed, giggling.

After a moment Torrence closed the door and they heard his footsteps recede.

"Poor Torrence," Claire said. Suddenly feeling cosmically sad for him. Lila comforted her.

• 11 •

MERINO, SOMEWHERE IN THE CARIBBEAN.

"The files Stoner turned over are essentially the stuff of allegations," Witcher said. "It's useful though. It'll help. Of course, the CIA can claim we fabricated the files. But *this*"—he tapped the screen—"this they can't deny."

"They can claim it was computer-generated," Smoke said. "But we can provide video for independent analysts. They'll analyze it and see it wasn't computer-fabricated, prove it's authentic. Along with the general impact of Kessler's propaganda spotters and the stuff Stoner gave us, it should wake up the media."

"Like a beehive in their beds," Witcher agreed. "That is—the media the SA doesn't control . . . "

Smoke and Witcher were in the briefing room, standing together at the blackboard-size instruction screen. It was a cool night on Merino, almost eleven p.m., but the island was quite awake. They could hear the clank of rifles on buckles as sentries walked by to relieve the guards at the rear fence. Mosquitoes whined in bloodthirsty frustration at the window screen. From the distance came the dulled thud and blurred chant of music as someone got in their R and R.

Smoke wondered what it was like to relax at a party and, well, to *dance*. To laugh and slap friends on the back and dance and feel at one with a party without trying. He'd never been able to do that sort of thing, and he envied it. He thought about Alouette, sleeping now, and he missed her.

His mind swerved hastily back to priorities. He turned to look again at the screen; the crow, on his shoulder, made a raspy caw and fluttered his wings at the motion. Smoke and the crow gazed thoughtfully at the stilled image on the big, inch-thin videomonitor.

It was an image of the president of the United States. President Anna Bester, America's own Maggie Thatcher, out in a snowy field, in tan overcoat, brown pantsuit, and high gold rubber boots, walking with a fat man in a tentlike white mackintosh; she was talking earnestly to him. The president had none of her usual charismatic composure, was missing her look of it's-all-under-control-and-I'm-sanguine-about-the-future-despite-the-gravity-of-the-situation. She was scowling. The scowl showing the lines of her late middle age in spite of her face-lift.

The fat man was Sackville-West, Head of Security for the Second Alliance International Security Corporation. The SA's Head Inquisitor, Witcher called him.

Witcher hit the button, and the vid began to play again; as if responding to a choreographer, the president and Sackville-West began to move, walking in matched stride. The image was a little unstable; it drew back for a wider angle that took in two Secret Service men, expressionless and wearing shades as they had for generations—old-fashioned dark glasses had become their totem of office, like the archaic costume of a British Beefeater.

"It's amazing they didn't spot the bird's eye," Smoke said. The crow made a creaking sound in its throat, as if in agreement.

Witcher spread his hands and put on a comical expression of false modesty. "My outfit makes the best surveillance equipment on the planet. And on the Colony. Anyway, the sky was with us, the cloudy backdrop, the diminished light, not much reflection. The surveillance bird is treated with something we call chameleon spackle, blends in with the backdrop. Also, the snowfield dazzled them some. And we were simply lucky. For example, the two Secret Servicemen were watching the woods almost exclusively. They were thinking assassins, because she was so out in the open, not surveillance. They really have become embarrassingly incompetent lately. It's a national scandal."

Witcher rewound the video a little and turned up the volume. They heard bits and pieces of the conversation, perhaps forty percent of it.

"Shame about the sound," Witcher said. "They spoke softly. There was noise from the wind and boots in the snow."

"There's enough," Smoke said.

As they heard Sackville-West say, "Madame, the Fourth Estate, to put it bluntly, is the enemy of this enterprise. The media must be kept under strict rein. We . . . " Garble. "If the Emergency Powers are . . . " Garble. " . . . intolerable situation unless we take strict . . . " Garble. " . . . bottom line is this, Madame: To paraphrase Pastor Crandall, 'In order to take control, one must first take control!'"

The president's scowl vanished; she actually laughed out loud.

Then she became grave once more. "Possibly I will be granted some power of control over the media, by Congress—there is precedent, after all, in World War Two the media was more controlled than people know—and in the Iraq War media access was strictly controlled. And we *are* at war. If I'm granted the powers to control the media, I'll use them, and once I have them, I see no reason to have to relinquish them. But in order to establish police control, we'll need coordination with your . . . " Garble. " . . . not sure of the timetable. In the meantime we'll eliminate . . . " Garble.

Smoke froze the image again. "It'll shake things, and nicely."

"Your people deserve the credit, really," Witcher said

"How many meetings did he have with Bester?" Smoke asked suddenly.

"Four, over two months. We've got proof of them all. This is the only one with dialogue, the others were indoors and were very top secret."

"Our writers in the media will ask, '*Why is the president meeting this man in secret?*' to start—and then we'll reveal the latest, the dialogue . . . "

"Yes, that'll work, I think."

An undercurrent in something Witcher had said began to tug at Smoke. He looked at the older man. " 'Your people,' you said. 'The NR,' you said. You don't think of yourself as NR. Is that snobbism because so many of us are technicki?" Smiling to defuse the implied criticism. "Or because you think of them as a . . . as a tool?"

Witcher shrugged. His lips pursed. The faint narrowing of his eyes, the way his hands tucked into his pockets as if to force concealment and control on them, indicated one of his little bursts of paranoia coming on. "I just can't see any reason to keep up this prying into my motives, Smoke. Don't look a goddamn gift horse in its dentures."

He turned and walked out, banging the screen door behind him.

The crow squawked softly, as if to reproach Smoke. "You're right," Smoke muttered. "I've been unsubtle."

But he thought he began to see, almost intuitively, why Witcher funded the New Resistance: The Second Alliance's political plans were in Witcher's way.

It seemed Witcher had his own plans for the world.

• • •

THE SPACE COLONY, SECURITY.

When the SA bulls came to his quarters, it was officially three in the morning, and Russ was lying in bed, wide awake, arguing with himself about sedatives. *You start using them, you could get dependent on them,* he told himself. To which he replied, *That's your tight-assed Southern Baptist upbringing. Hell, give yourself a break.*

And then the chime, and he'd answered the door, found the bulls there.

So they've come for me, he thought wearily. *It's my turn.*

But one of them said, "Sorry to wake you, sir. Chairman Praeger would like you to come to an emergency meeting of the council."

Not fully awake yet, Russ started to ask why they hadn't simply used the screens, and then he remembered that the screens were down because the Face was still thrusting itself onto them.

"Okay," he said. Not as relieved as he should have been that he wasn't being arrested.

He printed out a preset suit, put it on still warm, and followed them to the council room.

They were sitting at the conference table, which was shaped like a backward S; the room was lit thoroughly but softly, from nowhere apparent. Praeger sat in the center, Judith Van Kips beside him as always; beside her was Dr. Tate, the Colony's chief psychiatrist. Even Tate looked tired, despite his rebuilt, unnaturally regular features, his surgical affectation of youth, some of his true age showing through the mask of a thirty-five-year-old.

Ganzio, the Brazilian, sat across from Van Kips. He was a slim, black-eyed man with a pencil-thin mustache and a penchant for gaudy real-cloth suits, and now (yes, even at three in the morning!), he was resplendent in a double-breasted suit of sky blue, with blue-trimmed ruffles. He tugged on his lapels to straighten the lines of his suit, glancing at the camera, near the ceiling, that was supposed to be recording all the council meetings for the Colony's appraisal. He was unaware that Praeger had long ago had the camera disconnected.

Messer-Krellman, the technicki's union rep—nontechnicki himself and generally regarded as the Boss's lickspittle—sat to Ganzio's right. He was a ferret-faced man with an air of boredom.

There was much talk around the table as Russ opened the door. When he came in, the talk died out. They all looked at him, smiling in polite welcome.

Russ remembered the meetings with Professor Rimpler and his daughter, Claire, and how subtly at first, and then more and more clearly, the Rimplers had been excluded from the diffuse cronyism that characterized Admin's inner circle. Russ, then, had been one of that charmed circle. Now he felt the chill. He was officially, to an extent functionally, still part of the council. But in fact, he was on his way to becoming an outsider.

Feeling a queasy combination of fatigue and wired anxiety, Russ took his seat on Ganzio's left, asking, "Anyone going to clue me in on why this graveyard shift was necessary?" There was a pot of ersatz coffee on the table, and Styrofoam cups. Russ poured himself some, sipped it, regretted it.

"We have had the results of the comm system and LSS analysis," Praeger said, sighing the words, "and we've been forced to conclude that . . . " He hesitated, folded his hands on the table, stared at them for a moment. Van Kips looked at him questioningly. He went on, "That the majority of the recent sabotage and the comm system imagery interference has not been caused by radic involvement. Has, in fact, somehow been induced by Rimpler himself."

Russ felt sweat start out on his palms.

So now it was said. What everyone had been trying not to think.

And no one actually said, out loud: *But Rimpler is dead!*

"Evidently," Praeger went on with a weary dryness, "there's some sort of . . . " He glanced questioningly at Dr. Tate.

Tate shifted uncomfortably in his seat and said, "It's a sort of psyche-gestalt presence maintaining the dynamics of Rimpler's personality despite the fact that we, uh, technically cut his personality away when we removed a large part of the brain tissue we're using to direct some of the electronics. We can only speculate, at this point, about what psychic mechanism has been engaged. But I'm fairly sure some rather base, almost infantile portion of Rimpler's personality has survived as a kind of subtle electromagnetic field, which, by a sort of, ah, cyber-telekinesis, seems to be exerting its influence over the contiguous LSS computer control systems. The, ah, ghost in the machine, as it were . . . "

"Holy shit," Russ breathed.

"Yes," Praeger said. "We've accrued enough parts to replace the life-support computer system without using cerebro-interfacing. We can . . . dispose of Rimpler's brain. But we're not sure we can get to it. We sent some people in to try to shut him down—he overrode the door sensors, locked our people out. Rimpler seems to have accessed computer security systems. He's been opening and closing the detention cells at random, for example. The guards have kept the prisoners in place but . . . " He shrugged. "Obviously, if he can do that, and if he's truly aware of us—as he seems to be—he can block our access to the LSS using its security backup systems. Electrification, paralysis gas—even drawing the air from the access corridors."

Russ swallowed. "And you want me to find a safe way through."

"You're the Security specialist, and you know the Sec systems like no one else."

Russ looked from face to face, repressing an urge to shout at them. He stared at their emptied coffee cups. "You were having the meeting long before I got here. You didn't bring me into it until you had to."

"This is no time to harp on esoteric rules of procedure," Van Kips said sharply. "This is an emergency. Can you help us with it or not?"

Russ thought, *I'm more on the outside than I thought.* It seemed Praeger had decided he was a radic sympathizer—and therefore expendable. In that case, with all the usual irony that attends politics, he'd have to be a radic sympathizer to survive. *No more putting it off. I'll have to make my move. Soon.*

He rubbed his damp palms on his soft paper trousers. Then, annoyed at himself, he looked down and saw that the sweat had blackened his palm with print-dye. "I'm not sure I can be of much help. Seems to me, if we try to blowtorch into the place, he may retaliate by opening air locks here and there."

Everyone reacted. Sharp intakes of breath, faces going pale, eyes staring as they imagined it. The Colony's nightmare. The void, the cold vacuum, always waiting outside . . .

"There might be one way," Russ said slowly. "Shut down power around the Colony except for battery-survival minimum for each section. While the main power lines are shut down, Rimpler can't control the doors, air locks, anything. We can waltz in and shut him down easily."

"Battery-survival minimum doesn't provide for Security or for comm systems," Van Kips said in her most brittle tone.

Praeger nodded his agreement. "Judith is quite right. We would be unable to seal off Admin with any effectiveness, unable to communicate with the Security Forces, and unable to maintain surveillance in the technicki dorms. It would be the ideal time to mount another rebellion. We'd be all but helpless."

Russ snorted. "We'd still have most of the weapons, the armor, the trained guards!"

"It's not enough," Praeger insisted. "We're too badly outnumbered. No. Absolutely not. We can't risk dropping Security envelope. We'll have to find another way in."

Russ took a long, slow breath. He exhaled it even more slowly. Then he said, "Okay. I'll try. I'll play it by ear, see what we've got, try to break in. But if he . . . "

Tate put in, "In my opinion, he thinks of the Colony as part of himself. He *has* gone mad—he seems to be willing to be, in a way, deliberately incontinent, to foul and mutilate himself. But he won't kill himself."

"You'd better be right, Tate," Russ said.

• • •

Kitty sat uncomfortably on the stone bench under the Monument, in the Open, looking up through the branches of the eucalyptus trees, smelling their menthol fragrance, wondering if she was being set up in some way.

She looked up at the statue. The Monument—a man in a pressure suit, sans helmet—created by an artist using a 3D printer, memorialized the EVA workers killed working outside the Colony. They were almost forgotten now. And the hypocrites would have to put up another monument for RM17.

The statue's arm was raised, hand outreaching, his face exaggeratedly expressive of awestruck yearning for the stars. Bogus, Lester would say.

It was "noon," so the mirrors and filters at the Open's enormous circular windows, at both ends, diffused the park with a homogenous golden sunlight. The air here would have made a visitor from Earth gag, but to Kitty it smelled clean, after the dorms and the corridors. The Colony was choking itself; it was an organism whose liver and kidneys were failing, whose lungs were too clogged to filter out poisons. The foul air seemed fouler in the background of social tension: the persistent rumors about RM17; the latest cuts in food rations; the arrests. And the vandalism—the insane old man's face that came and went on the comm system; the power failures and burst pipes.

She saw Russ coming a hundred yards away, cutting across the soccer field that no one was allowed to use at the moment—public gatherings of more than three were forbidden until Admin saw fit to lift the state of emergency—and she felt like running.

How could she trust the Chief of Security?

But Chu had surprised her. "Go see him," she'd said. "There are strong indications he's on the outs with Admin's Council. He's had several conflicts with them. The danger is, maybe he wants to flush us out through you, to regain their favor. But I have studied the man, and I don't believe this is the case. He may be our best hope."

She got to her feet, but it was too late to run. "Hello, Kitty," Russ said, smiling wearily. He stepped onto the path and stood there awkwardly, hands in pockets, looking at his shoes, so she almost laughed at his "aw-shucks" posture. But then she realized he was staring at the grass stuck to his shoes. It was dried, yellowed. "Grass is dying out there," he said. "They watered it this morning, looks like, but it maybe came too late. Maybe not pure enough water." He looked up at her. "How you getting on?"

"Okay." Then she shook her head. "No . . . not okay."

He nodded and moved toward the bench. "Let's sit down, talk."

"Not there." (Chu had advised her.) "I prefer to walk."

He smiled sadly. "You think the bench is bugged? I could be wearing a bug, for that matter. But hell, let's walk."

They strolled down the path toward the Admin housing project. "Here's the story," he said in just above a whisper. "The Colony can't go on this way. If we leave things the way they are, it'll get worse before it gets better. There's something happening here I couldn't even describe to you . . . You'd think I was making it up. But it means that Admin is distracted now . . . and that could help. Now I'll tell you something about RM17. You're right about it. I trust you, Kitty. I don't even know why. I do, though. I don't trust the other radics. Maybe I trust you because the way I read you—I could be wrong—you aren't politically motivated, not really. You just want decent treatment, a fair chance. So you're not a radic, per se—I know your husband is, but . . . the way I see it, you're a person willing to fight, but you don't have any axes to grind ideologically."

She wasn't following him. "What about getting Lester out?"

"Sure, well, I'm comin' to it." He glanced around. "I fooled with the surveillance cameras, reassigned the guards out here, but all this open ground still makes me nervous. Damn, it looks empty. Seems a shame."

"Hard to get permission to come out here lately. Kids are getting stir-crazy."

"I know. That'll change, too, if . . . okay, listen. What we're going to have to do is to organize a counterforce, our own security outfit, and disarm the one that exists. But I'm going to need commitment from the technicki underground that they'll coordinate with me. Move where I say, when I say. If they'll do it, we'll pull the rug out from under Admin. You'll be my liaison with the underground. That way I don't know who they are, so they aren't threatened. The thing will happen in stages . . . You look like all this's thrown you a bit."

"I . . . God." She shook her head in amazement. She hadn't come prepared for this. Having a full-scale rebellion dropped in her lap. A complete takeover! "But how will you keep control of it after Earth finds out?"

"We'll worry about that when we come to it. I think I can establish that Praeger's Admin was guilty of murder, for one thing."

"I—this is too much. I thought you were going to smuggle me and Lester out or something."

"I can't get Lester out until the Second Alliance thugs are disarmed. Those people are not under my command anymore, except for the simple day-to-day assignments. If I told them to disarm, they'd turn me into Praeger. They're not the Colony's security anymore—if they ever were. They're SA."

She stated it flatly. "They're Nazis. Or something close."

He sighed. "I'm beginning to think so too."

They didn't say anything for a while. Finally she had to say, "I'm scared."

He nodded. "Yeah."

• • •

Cloudy Peak Farm, Upstate New York.

Hayes was inside out, scraped clean.

Sometimes he almost felt like he was shining.

Hayes was standing in the Media Center. It was at the southern edge of Cloudy Peak Farm, an annex on Crandall's private wing of the overgrown log cabin. On three sides were screens, and gear for bringing the screens alive. The fourth side was a filtered glass wall, which Crandall usually kept dialed to opaque. But it was a sunny morning near the end of March, and Crandall's doctors had insisted—so far as they'd dared—that the sunlight would be good for the leader's health. He'd let them dial the wall to transparency.

Hayes was the door guard, standing against the room's only bare patch of nonglass wall; the door to his left, the screens to his right, transparent wall directly ahead. And Crandall, with Rolff and Ben, between him and the see-through wall.

Hayes liked to know where everything and everyone was. It was more than that he *liked* to; he'd been made that way. Made recently. (If he tried to think about how he'd been made that way, he came to an impenetrable membrane, and he had to turn back.)

He was supposed to keep track of things spatially, like a chess player visualizing the board. Because . . .

He didn't know why. He knew it was for something. Anyway, it felt good.

Crandall was sitting in an electric wheelchair, still wearing pajamas and a robe. Looking frail. Hard to believe a man that sunken, that frail, had so much power. Behind him, on either side, Rolff Getzerech and Ben stood bodyguard.

"*Guards right outside the building,*" Hayes had told Rolff. "*Guards patrolling the grounds, in guard towers, on the fences, patrolling the area in helicopters and jeeps. Guards in the hall, at the door. Radar to watch for missiles. And with all that, he needs two more guys standing behind him all the time?*"

"All those guards," Rolff had said in his soft accent, "and yet the NR shot him and killed his sister. For a long time he would not come out from behind the bulletproof glass in his bedroom. He saw people with cameras. Even now he carries a gun on him. Even with the two guards."

Now Rolff stood there with unflinching patience, wearing a short-sleeved Special Guardsman's uniform, his big, meaty hands clasped like an altar boy's over the brass SASG buckle with its chrome "iron cross" inset. Rolff was Klaus's brother: Klaus Getzerech, the bodyguard and factotum for Colonel Watson. Rolff had Klaus's delicate red lips, incongruous with the craggily chiseled face, the massive chest. His hair was so blond it was almost white; his eyes a blue so pale, they were almost silver. On his hips were a Browning machine pistol and a walkie-talkie.

Ben wore glasses, but he was as big as Rolff, his brown hair clipped into the classic Mid-American choirboy's haircut. He had a dimple in his chin and small, empty brown eyes. He was dressed like Rolff. And like Hayes too. But Hayes hadn't yet earned the privilege of attending church services in dress whites, like Rolff and Ben, even with the fake SA background Watson had created for him.

They were an impressive sight coming into the little chapel under the oaks with Crandall, in their honor-guard dress uniforms, modeled on Marine Corps dress but red and white. Mostly white.

Outside the glass wall, a guard in an armored uniform and mirrored helmet walked by, his visor making semaphores of sun-glint with his movements.

Hayes felt a strange unrest. *Flashing lights.*

His hand went to his gun.

But the guard walked by; the flashing went with him.

Hayes felt as if something had been taken from him just now. Like a section of his stomach had been pulled out like a drawer. He tried to think about what it was, but he felt the membrane again. So he simply took his hand off the gun, and the unrest went away.

Crandall was using a complicated remote-control box he held in his lap to switch on the screens. The big one across from him, first—most of the smaller screens to Crandall's right were conference screens, for talking to the regional commanders and other high-ranking personnel. And for watching SA christenings, initiations, rites of all kinds.

At ten, Crandall was to watch a graduation presentation by the boy, Jebediah—the boy Crandall called "the living destiny of my church." Just a precocious kid, as far as Hayes could tell. He'd seen him onscreen a few times. Smart, articulate, schooled in the Three Fundamental Ideas and all the ideological underpinnings. Even better schooled in it than Hayes, who knew Crandall's Corrected Bible by heart, though he couldn't remember ever reading it. The kid, Jebediah, seemed to *understand* it better. Give him that.

On the big screen there was yet another report about the war. The anchorman claimed the New-Soviets were retreating. "Unilaterally in retreat, their offensive splintered," the guy said. There had been some increase of New-Soviet mobilization in orbit. Some analysts wondered if the orbital mobilization could be in preparation for a first strike—a plan to knock out our antimissile satellite weapons. *Maybe it's finally coming.*

People should be more optimistic, Hayes thought. Look how marvelous the world was, really. *Those Gridscreens, themselves. We take 'em for granted, but, hey, they're amazing. Screens dancing with light. Sunlight outside the glass. Look through the glass out into the world. Look into the screens into other avenues of the world; the televisions were windows into the world.* Nice thought. Made him feel shining. Positive, optimistic. Accent the positive in things. Screens were windows, windows into some big unknown mind, and all it's thinking, each channel a train of thought—

"Smoke," Crandall said, the sharpness of the utterance interrupting Hayes's rumination. "That's Jack Brendan Smoke."

Casting about for a morning news program, Crandall had stumbled on someone all too familiar. Crandall's jaws were clamped, muscles bunched in them.

'The New Racism has deep, complicated roots," Smoke was saying on the big screen. He was sitting in a pastel talk-show setting of some kind, with a talk-show interviewer nodding patiently to his right. One of the public-television types, judging from the fact that he didn't interrupt with a lot of stupid, sensationalistic questions. Smoke was looking well-groomed, quietly confident. "Some of its growth is the accident of circumstances, and some of it has, I think, been cultivated by coalitions of highly organized racists."

Crandall grunted at that and shifted in his chair.

Smoke went on. "There was a certain amount of backlash to civil rights legislation and racial quota hiring practices in the 1960s, 70s and 80s. But something even more important to the New Racism emerged in the 1990s, and continuously thereafter. The influx of non-European immigrants, especially Arabs, Persians, Pakistanis, people from India, from the Caribbean; Israelis, Japanese, Koreans, and Vietnamese—all these people began to seem sort of overwhelming to the average American and the average Caucasian in Western Europe. The immigrants tended to create their own well-defined cultural environments in the urban settings, changing the looks of neighborhoods, threatening the standard American religions, altering the type of service available, and so forth. But the turning point came when immigrants began to organize for political power. Each one of these various new ethnic communities became a political force to be reckoned with. Most Americans could accept Caucasian European immigrants, even Hispanic immigrants—they were at least Christian—but not this other massive influx of unusually alien aliens. White Americans felt that their cultural traditions, their very identity as Americans, were threatened."

"If I understood your latest writings . . . " The interviewer held up a copy of a printout's cover page and read off the title: "*Wave of Darkness: The New*

Racism by Jack Brendan Smoke, published by Penguin Printouts . . . uh, if I understood it correctly, you link the reaction against immigrants to an increase in racial prejudice against blacks, native Americans, and Jews."

"I do. I think this xenophobic reaction, this inflammation of the territorial instinct, if that's what it is, grows and feeds on itself once it's set free. Racism against one group leads to racism against another."

"What are the social and environmental factors that bring this reaction about in people?"

"There's some evidence that sociobiological factors may be at work. For example, population density. Up to a certain level, high population density promotes a kind of adaptive acceptance of many kinds of people—but there's a breaking point. After the breaking point of population density is reached, people feel constantly threatened by other people. They tend to group with their own ethnic and cultural types increasingly in an instinctive search for protection. All this is aggravated by poverty, lack of opportunities, depression, a general sense of frustration. People look for someone to blame for all this, and they naturally blame groups of people who're obviously different, like other ethnic groups. They tend to be perpetually scanning for differences in other people that might represent a threat.

"Another factor is the breakdown of useful family structures, the ephemeral quality of families, a trend that developed at the end of the last century. This combined with pervasively ephemeral cultural trends to produce 'wandering self-image.' People became vulnerable to identification with mass-marketed imagery. They began to feel reduced to pixels on a TV screen themselves. In the immensity of society—an immensity shown them every day in the Grid—they felt insignificant. So they turned—and were led—to excessive identification with their own race to give them a handle on identity."

"You've intrigued me by saying that people are 'vulnerable to mass-marketed imagery,' that they're being 'led.' What exactly . . . ?"

"There are organizations at work who recognize these trends as useful to them. They use them to build political power, or more accurately, to *seize* political power. In part two of *Wave of Darkness* I demonstrate—with plenty of evidence—that the Second Alliance and Rick Crandall's Second Circle church organization—these days they call it 'His Church'—are conspiring to promote racism in the United States, in order to facilitate their own political ends, and that they are instrumental in a new Fascist power grab in Western Europe. I have new information that has not been incorporated into the current *Wave of Darkness*. Proof that this racist organization has the ear of the president of the United States. That they are—to put it bluntly—working very closely with her to scrap the Constitution, and *take power* here."

"Take power." The interviewer looked almost disappointed. As if he'd decided Smoke was just another crank.

Crandall snorted with pleasure. "Go ahead, tell 'im another one."

"I have brought proof," Smoke said. "I propose to show that proof here, on this program, for the first time anywhere." He opened a briefcase, took out a tiny datastick, and handed it to the interviewer, who gave it to a technician.

Crandall sat up straight in his chair. He swiveled to his right, punched a button on his remote-control unit. A face appeared on one of the screens in the stack to Hayes' right.

"Yes, Reverend?" the face asked. A woman, that's all Hayes could tell from where he stood.

"Get me Chancelrik at Chicago Worldtalk. Fast!"

Smoke was saying, " . . . hard to say where the SA's insinuation into federal government began, although it seems to have been in partnership with the CIA for many years. Last year they exchanged their own new techniques for submarine-silencing to the Department of Defense in exchange for participation in Defense planning committees and other projects . . . " Then Chancelrik came onto Crandall's commline.

Hayes heard him say, "What can I do for you, Rick?"

"You monitoring channel fourteen?"

"No. I was . . . "

"Never mind. Monitor it *now*."

"Gotcha. Okay, I've got it. That's what's-his-name, Smoke, isn't it?"

On the screen Smoke was saying, " . . . were photographed covertly by operatives of the New Resistance."

The screen showed the president of the United States walking through a snowy field with a fat man Hayes didn't recognize. "Sackville-West," Smoke called him.

After the vid ran, the interviewer and Smoke came back on. The interviewer looked shaken. "Of course it has been analyzed for falsification?"

"It has. And it's available to anyone for that same analysis. It'll be out on the Internet, every corner of the Grid."

"Holy fucking shit." Chancelrik's voice.

"There's more," Smoke said.

"God in heaven," Chancelrik said.

Another image came on the screen. Swarthy-looking men were opening crates in what was probably the hold of a ship. Harsh lights brought in for the filming. Smoke's voice-over: "Here we have video provided by the Israeli

Mossad of the inspection of cargo of a ship called the *Hermes' Grandson*. The Resistance intercepted the ship and turned its contents over to the Mossad. This is a Second Alliance ship—here you see SA prisoners—and it's packed stem to stern with artillery, illegal devices for interrogation, antiaircraft missiles." One by one the items were shown as Smoke ticked them off. "And *this* carton contains nerve gas. We found two tons of nerve gas on the ship. The SA's legal presence in Europe is as a peacekeeping and police force. It would have no legitimate use for nerve gas, missiles . . . And if they are confiscations why didn't they tell anyone they confiscated these things?"

"We can claim the New Resistance stocked the ship, made up some of its own people to look like SA troops," Chancelrik said.

"Shit," Crandall said. (Making Ben look at Crandall with surprise.) "If it was by itself, we could make it look like it was bullshit. But along with the video of Bester talking to that incompetent tub of lard and the damn book . . . well, do what you can. Make this go away—or I swear I'll make you go away, my friend."

He cut Chancelrik's connection and cut into another line. "Johnston?" Head of Second Alliance International Security for the United States.

"Yes, Reverend?"

On the screen, Smoke was talking about CIA files that had come to his attention recently. He was talking about a man named Kupperbind. He was talking about a campaign to purge the ranks of CIA Domestic of blacks and Jews. He was talking about files—he admitted they'd been stolen from the CIA—that discussed the CIA's part in the initiation of a European apartheid.

Crandall was saying, "Johnston, Jack Brendan Smoke. *Tagged.* Quietly as possible—but kill him! Try to make it look like he was killed by . . . radicals. A power grab or something. And tell Sackville-West I want him here by tonight. Here, *in person!*" His voice breaking, almost weepy with anger.

Tagged. Make it look like an accident or like someone else did it.

"Smoke entered the country under heavy guard two days ago, recorded some interviews yesterday, and left this morning, Reverend. By private jet. The jet was bound for Mexico City. We followed by satellite recon to Mexico City, but after that . . . Witcher's people are in control of the airport there. Smoke changes planes in Mexico City and we lose track of him. Mexican immigration so far has either been recalcitrant or too inefficient to . . . "

"No excuses! Find him. Make him *dead*—but make it look good."

• • •

THE ISLAND OF MALTA.

"Recon post Seven is about sixty-five miles southeast of Iraklion," Steinfeld was saying, tapping the coast of Crete on the map. "The post is the SA's key

Mediterranean reconnaissance center. It coordinates satellite surveillance, it monitors transmissions of all kinds, collates information from their various outposts in Europe. SA troops there number—if the Mossad is right—less than a hundred. Artillery and missile defense is minimal. So it's underdefended, it's vulnerable. The Greek government—or the SA occupation government, to be more accurate—has about three hundred men stationed within an hour of Post Seven. But by the time they're mobilized to give Seven assistance, we'll be well away."

Karakos, Torrence, Danco, Lila, Levassier, and the other officers were sitting in a semicircle around Steinfeld. The briefing room was lit only by the map lamp. The back part was in darkness. Sometimes Karakos imagined things moving out of the corner of his eye back there. But when he looked, it was always gone. Sometimes he still felt the strange pressure, and the impenetrable places in his mind, the membranes beyond which he could not pass. He tried not to think about it. He tried to think about Greece. Its Nationalist salvation.

He noticed that Bonham was not there. He was never permitted at the planning sessions. They didn't trust Bonham.

Maybe, Karakos thought, *I shouldn't trust him, either.*

Bonham had given Karakos the names of the NR operatives on the Colony. Time would prove whether the names were real or not. To test that, he must once more get to a radio. And, of course, there was the matter of reporting the assault on Post Seven.

Steinfeld went on to describe his strategy for their assault on Post Seven; some part of Karakos's mind was absorbing Steinfeld's briefing, but thoughts of this Torrence were like dogs locked in some mental outbuilding, fighting and snarling in there, distracting him.

The bastard was doing nothing, saying nothing about Karakos. But Karakos could feel him watching, even when he didn't seem to be. Torrence must be working against him somehow. Otherwise, why was it that Karakos still had not been told when the real assault against the SA would commence? Why was he still in the dark about its target? It had to be Torrence. He had planted the seeds of doubt in the others, and despite all their denials, they told him nothing. This business of the attack on Post Seven was minor, just a warm-up for the April Assault.

But he didn't dare press anyone for information. That would make them suspicious. He would find a way.

"The destruction of Seven will set the stage for the April Assault," Steinfeld was saying.

And then he looked at Karakos. Expressionlessly. But looked right at him.

• • •

Torrence resented the night. It was balmy and the air was sweet as he left the house to take his turn at the sentry shack by the road. He could smell the sea, and the mosquitoes seemed to be on vacation. His mood demanded a stormy night, or at least a driving rain, and as much discomfort as possible.

Torrence was stepping off the porch when someone in the darkness came toward him from his right. He swung his assault rifle around.

"It's me." Claire.

He slung the rifle onto his shoulder. The weapon seemed heavier than it should have.

"You want to talk about it?" she asked softly.

His eyes began to adjust to the dark. Her face materialized like a ghost. He tried to not say it, but he couldn't stop. "You going to sleep with everyone else? Who's next?"

"That's not talking about it."

"I didn't say I wanted to talk about it. Christ, I don't know. I'm just ... I'm human. Shit, Claire ... "

She touched his arm. He trembled at her touch and felt stupid about it, so he stepped back from her, and she misinterpreted him.

"You decided you want no contact with homosexuals?"

"You're not a homosexual. You might be bisexual. But you were feeling things, real things, with me." His tone challenged her to pretend it wasn't true.

"Of course I did. I don't think I'm gay. But she . . . she's very tender and . . . in some way it's what I need right now. I don't know for how long."

"Should I take a number?"

"Fuck you, Torrence."

"I'm sorry. I shouldn't have said that. I'm sorry."

"I know."

"Yeah, you always say that. You know me. I don't know you. You accused me of not opening up more than once, but I *don't know you*." He looked up at the stars. After a long moment he said, "Maybe that's my fault."

Her silence acknowledged that maybe it was.

• 12 •

BALTIMORE, MARYLAND.

Stoner was running—even when he was motionless.

They'd changed motels twice in two days, Stoner making light of it, pretending for Cindy that he wanted one with a Gridfeed screen so she could see her cartoons. And then wanted one with a Gridfeed screen *and* a pool. Trying to hide from his little girl that he was moving them out of simple fear.

But he couldn't hide it from Janet. Stoner and his wife sat in a window seat overlooking the skating rink of the underground mall their motel was in, sipping weak cocktails in squeaky plastic cups sent up by the automated room service. Janet was sitting there rigidly, staring out at the gliding figures on the skating rink, her eyes tracing the blades that etched off-white lines into the chalky ice below them; Cindy was watching the Japanese reactive cartoon, *Roboboy*. Cindy had the interaction box in her hand; the screen was set to receive the various *Roboboy* interactive programs, and Janet had booted Cindy's name into the flexible sound track. "Uh-oh!" Roboboy was saying. "Stoned Dr. Drugmaster has shot a hypnotic into Designer Dan! What should I do, Cindy? Should I try to find an antidote, or should I go to the Garbage Marsh to rescue my pal Lowtech without Designer Dan's help?"

"Find an antidote!" Cindy said, pushing the button for Option A.

"Well, hell," Stoner muttered, "I wish Roboboy'd rescue us from the Garbage Marsh." He watched Janet's face, hoping she'd smile.

But her lips compressed, whitening as she tried to keep from crying.

He glanced at his watch. *Eight.* It would be dark up above. But here, at the underground motel and rink, it might be any time of day. The walk between the motel and the rink was still busy with shoppers and browsers moving like bees gathering pollen at the shops around the rink. On the far side a Silent Radio strip formed marching letters for newsblurbs and ads:

DEPARTMENT OF DEFENSE REPORTS NEW-SOVIETS CONTINUE WITHDRAWAL IN EUROPE BUT INCREASE ORBITAL PRESENCE . . . PRESIDENT BESTER DENIES SECOND ALLIANCE PLOT ALLEGATIONS CALLS FOR INVESTIGATION INTO "ANTI-PATRIOTIC PROPAGANDA SOURCES" . . . SECRETARY OF INTERIOR SWELL REAFFIRMS NEED FOR EMERGENCY PRESIDENTIAL POWERS, WILL NOT RULE OUT MEDIA CENSORSHIP, CITES WAR EMERGENCY, HISTORIC PRECEDENCE . . . ACID RAIN CONCENTRATED IN TORNADOS BLAMED FOR TOXICITY DEATHS IN MISSOURI . . . COURT FINDS COMPLETE VINDICATION FOR LATE SENATOR SPECTOR. SPECTOR WAS KILLED DURING ANTIVIOLENCE LAWS PROGRAMMING; GRAND JURY NAMED FOR VIDEOFRAMING INVESTIGATION . . . IN SPORTS, THE HOUSTON ORBITERS SHOT DOWN THE . . .

Stoner looked away, shrugging. And saw Lopez, standing by the railing of the rink, looking up at him.

"There he is," Stoner murmured.

"Where?" Janet asked breathlessly.

"He's coming into the motel now." Where was Brummel? Stoner wondered.

Lopez came to the door. Stoner let him in, glancing at Cindy. She hardly looked up. She told Roboboy, "Apply for new memories, Roboboy!" and pressed a button.

Lopez went directly to Janet, still sitting in the window. He was wearing a brown overcoat, speckled from rain.

"It's raining up there?" Stoner said.

Lopez took off his soft plastic fedora, held it in his hands in front of him, and said softly, "Mrs. Stoner, I'm sorry to tell you, your brother he is dead, or . . . he will be soon. He was stop at a checkpoint and he lost his temper with a policeman, he pull a gun. They hit him and take the gun away, took him to be questioned and . . . they put him under extractor. So . . . they know what he does. Under the antiterrorist section of the AVL laws . . . well, I am sorry. We cannot help him."

He said all this quickly, and with a sympathetic gentleness that surprised Stoner.

Janet covered her mouth, squeezed her eyes shut, rocked in silent pain. Stoner went to stand beside her, put his arm over her shoulder. And then the implications hit him like a chilled spike: *Brummel, extracted.* Which meant that Lopez would soon be under surveillance.

Lopez, looking at him, saw it on his face and nodded. "We have to hurry. And I will be coming with you. They know about me now."

Twenty minutes and they were all down in the lobby, bags sloppily packed, on the carrier beside Stoner, who was waiting at the desk for the Pakistani clerk to bring his credit card back. Wondering if maybe there was an APB out for him with a credit freeze tagged to it, which would mean the clerk's credit reader would refuse Stoner access to his funds. And would alert the police.

Cindy was crying because she'd seen her Mommy cry; she clung to Janet's legs, and Janet was trying not to cry, and shit, the clerk was taking too long to come back with that card. Why had he taken it into the next room, anyway? He'd slotted it into the desk reader, said it wasn't working, he'd have to take it to the back room.

Oh, Lord. Stoner looked at Lopez. "I think there's . . . "

"Yes," Lopez said, "we'll have to leave the bags."

Stoner bent, took the small blue Tourister off the stack, handed Janet her night bag, said in a low voice, "That's it, I'm sorry, honey, but that's it. Come on." She followed her husband, and Lopez across the lobby to the glass doors, looked over her shoulder at the bags they'd left. Just once. "Mommy, we have to take our bags," Cindy said.

"Someone's going to send it for us," Janet told her, lying with an admirable cheeriness as they went out the doors onto the walk with its skating rink schmaltz music, the generic mockery of crowd sounds.

A neopunk boy in a fatigue jacket, an orange flight suit, and spiked boots approached Lopez. He had a pallid, longnosed face and needled eyes, and he wore a headset communicator. He said loudly, "Hey—ya moneyman, slide me a one forra train, huh?"

Stoner expected Lopez to brush him off and hurry on but he made a show of taking out his wallet, poking through it as the neopunk "panhandler" whispered, "Armando called down, says a Fed copter landed on the roof and a bunch of guys who look too much alike got out of cars and ran into the mall upstairs—about a minute ago."

Lopez swore in Spanish, handed him a bill for appearance's sake, and then said, "You find the way?"

The boy nodded and jerked his head: *Come on.* They followed him through the crowds to the door of an office with a dull black plastic sign, mall security. Lopez glancing at Stoner with that look of inquiry. *Betrayal?*

But they went past the door, around the corner into an alley littered with waxpaper cups, the wall graffitied: *Jerome-X wins when he loses.*

A small three-wheeled truck was parked there, the words mall security patrol on it in the mall's colors, gold on dun. Another kid was in the driver's seat, his zigzagged haircut looking odd under the Security guard's cap. He wore a brown uniform.

Lopez, Stoner, Janet, and Cindy were ushered into the little truck—a van, really—and Janet gasped. Stoner looked, saw a man in yellowed briefs tied up in the back of the van, turned to the back door. Hands cuffed behind his back; ankles cuffed together. Breathing but gagged.

"Mommy . . . ?"

"It's okay, honey, he's a . . . a bad guy. But they're not going to hurt him, they'll let him go soon."

"Lay down in the back," the driver said, a teenager's voice.

God, we're in the hands of children, Stoner thought.

They lay down side by side, Lopez at the rear beside the subdued guard, Stoner turned away from him, toward his wife, the two of them holding Cindy between them. "It's really a kind of game, Cindy," Janet said, inevitably making Stoner wince. Because he knew that Cindy wouldn't fall for it.

She pretended to fall for it. She nodded and closed her eyes as the truck started moving. She was a good girl.

Hearing the electric motors droning, vibration coming through the floor; thinking that it was his fault they were here, undergoing these absurd contortions, he should have stayed out of it for his family's sake or left them, the Company probably wouldn't have . . . yes, they would have. They'd have picked up Janet in case she knew where he was. Maybe to use her and Cindy as hostages to get him back. To shut him up.

But somehow this was his fault. Dragging his family through this, making them feel like wetbacks lying on the floor of a truck. Maybe in the trunk of a car next, for God's sake.

And this absurdity was made worse by its probable futility. They'd probably be busted; any second cops or CIA Domestic would stop the car, dourly smug faces would look through the front windows at them.

He felt the van descending a ramp of some kind, turning; he and Lopez nudged by inertia against one another, Cindy whimpering, Janet clutching her tighter, trying to smile at Stoner.

Maybe they'll simply execute the lot of us. Cindy too.

The van was leveling out, probably in the underground parking lot.

The van stopped. Men's voices. Stoner wondered if it would have helped if he'd brought a gun.

"If I knew where, I wouldn't be out looking for them," the kid driver said to someone.

Don't come close enough to look in the back.

The van was moving again. Stoner realized that Cindy was squeaking with pain because he was holding her so tight. He loosened his grip, whispered, "Sorry, sweetie."

Lopez hissed, "*Silencio!*"

The van hummed along for ten minutes, and Stoner realized, *We must be out!* and as he thought it, the light shifted its quality, became streetlight, harsh blue-white. They were on the streets.

Ten minutes more and then the kid driver said, "Checkpoint. Lay still no matter what."

The van grumbled and stopped. Clipped voice of a young by-the-booker who sounded like he'd just finished his stretch in the service. "You got a pass to—what the hell is that? In the back. Get out of the . . . " Then a rattling hiss. A bubbling *uh-uhnk* sound from the guy who'd stopped them. The van was moving again before Stoner realized . . .

It was Janet who said it aloud. "Oh, God, no," Janet said. "He . . . "

"You must be quiet!" Lopez said.

"Oh, shut up, Lopez," Stoner snapped. "Doesn't matter now."

There'd be a patrol car after them in minutes. The van wasn't fast, maybe wasn't even street-legal, was designed for trundling around the walkways of the mall. It stopped.

"Change vehicles fucking *fast!*" the kid driver yelled, banging the side door open.

They were up and moving. Glimpses of an industrial park, Cyclopean red light atop a tower, and then they were in a bigger van, thirty years old, its sides painted with surfer myth imagery, a bulging window blurrily shaped like an arrow on the side above a god-sized curl that never breaks. In the back, they sat on the metal floor.

Sirens.

"Oh, shit," the kid driver said, putting the van in gear. A lurch and a growl, the van burning rubber. "Oh—he's not on our road . . . I don't think . . . just a mile to our airstrip."

Stoner was certain that any second they'd come up against the roadblock or a Police Assault Van forcing them over, maybe taking out the rear tires with a neatly placed 20-mm shell.

But then a long, long curve as they turned off the industrial park road, down a utility road. Gravel crunched under the tires till they reached the tarmac of the airstrip. Stoner sat up, peered past Lopez, saw the Lear and thought, *No, really?*

Really. Thirteen minutes and they were aboard, the little jet taxiing down the runway, Janet, laughing with relief as a steward—no kidding, *a steward*—saw to it they were strapped in, and they were in the air.

Stoner and his family were the only passengers except for Lopez and the kid driver (what happens to the guy they left in the van? The cops would find him), the kid throwing the oversize guard's cap in the corner, then beginning work on his acne, squeezing pimples methodically as they talked to Lopez.

"You heard they got Charlie Chesterton? Not sure how. But he snuffed hisself, probably so they couldn't brain drain him."

Stoner glanced at his daughter and changed the subject, "Where we going?"

"South," Lopez said. "The Caribbean."

The kid adding, "Little island you got to call home for a while. It's comfortable, almost like a resort. It'll be okay."

Will it be prison? Stoner wondered.

He still had a bargaining chip. He knew about the mole in the European NR. They might subject him to the extractor, of course. But he had a feeling that wasn't their style. So he had something to bargain with. Maybe he'd have to bargain with them for his family's freedom.

Maybe he'd have to give them the SA agent who'd penetrated Steinfeld's base on Malta.

• • •

CLOUDY PEAK FARM, UPSTATE NEW YORK.

"Satelex from Colonel Watson," Johnston said, coming into the room. "He's on his way here." He showed the printout to Crandall, who was in his office, sitting at a WorkCenter; he'd been scowling over some statistics on the monitor. The scowl deepened as he scanned the satelex. Hayes was at the door as usual, watching and listening but not seeming to. It wasn't like he was *spying*. But it kept him amused, kept him from mentally roving up to those disconcerting membranes that cut him off from certain channels of free association. He listened because he wanted to feel like a part of the place. He believed in Crandall, admired him.

"Watson's coming here?" Crandall said. "I didn't order him to come here."

It was Sunday afternoon. They'd just come from chapel, where Crandall had preached on the security channel, for Initiates only. Fresh from church, Ben and Rolff were in their dress uniforms, standing beside Crandall's chair.

Johnston was in a real-cloth Sunday-go-to-meetin' suit, blue serge and subtly cut. He had the sturdy, brown-haired, blue-eyed, enlightened-young-cowpoke looks that Crandall liked to surround himself with. Early twenties, very serious. Johnston stood by in case Crandall wanted to send a reply.

Crandall seemed to consider it, then shook his head. "Wouldn't get to him, anyway. Well, he'd better have a hell of a good excuse. He's supposed to be gettin' squared away to clean the chimney, sweep those little greasers out of their nest."

Meaning the NR, Hayes guessed.

Hayes found himself watching Rolff. He looked a little pale. He was staring at the satelex print. Rolff looked up and looked directly at Hayes, almost like he wanted to say something to him. Then he dropped his eyes and cleared his, throat. "Sir . . . "

Crandall muttered, without looking up from the computer screen, "Yes?" He'd gone back to picking through statistics.

"Permission to use the bathroom."

"Sure, Johnston's here, he can stay till you're back."

"There's something else, sir," Johnston said with a little hesitation. "I don't know if I should report on it till I'm sure . . . but I've got a good feeling about it."

"What's that?" Crandall asked, glancing up at Johnston.

Rolff was moving toward the door, but slowly, as if he wanted to hear what Johnston was going to say.

Johnston said, "The Secur-search data base has put a red star next to an island in the Caribbean. Place called Merino. Dinky place, sir. Military installation there we thought belonged to Costa Rica. Set up to look like it's part of Costa Rica. Camouflaged that way, I think. But there are a number of irregularities. Civilian jets from Mexico City landing there with unusual frequency, and we've identified the owner of one of the jets, sir. *Witcher.*" Edge of excitement in his voice. "We think we might have a major NR stronghold. Maybe Western HQ."

"Lordy. Who all knows about this?"

"Just me and you, sir. In accordance with your directive."

"Good. I'm feelin' funny about security again. If it leaks that we know where they are, they'll run and hide again."

Rolff wasn't listening to them, Hayes realized. He was standing in the doorway, staring. At Hayes. Just looking at him, a little to his right. One hand resting on his gun butt. The other, his left, remained in his pocket. The hand in his pocket made a movement. Hayes saw it through the cloth, and then lights flashed. The ceiling lights. Flashing on and off, over and over, in a pattern and—oh, God, but Hayes had a roller-coaster feeling inside. The room got all tunnel-dark, except for a corona of light around Crandall and Johnston, and they were moving in slow motion, looking up at Hayes, Johnston reaching into his coat, Crandall throwing his arms in front of his face. Why were they reacting that way?

And then Hayes saw that there was a gun pointed at Crandall (the lights flashed—oh, no) and the gun was in Hayes's hand, his own gun. *I'm pointing a gun at Rick. What am I doing?*

Slow motion went to fast motion as he squeezed the trigger again and again, not even having to sight in, his hand doing it for him. He heard shouting, and then Crandall's head exploded, and the gun was tracking up to Johnston.

Johnston had his gun out now, and Ben had his leveled. Something kicked into Hayes, right through the middle of him. He saw Johnston falling, knew that he'd shot him, felt another kick in the side of the head where Rolff had shot him.

He heard a long squealing sound, like metal wheels braking, the sound accompanying a white light, a white light that bore down on him like a train's headlight, and when it hit him it made everything into white light.

And then silence.

• • •

"The lights flashed," Ben said, "like a signal. And the new guy shot Rick. That Hayes guy." Ben was crying, big guy like that blubbering.

Klaus, standing behind Watson, snorted and shook his head.

Watson turned to Rolff. "What was Johnston there about?"

"About your satelex," Rolff said. "And about something he'd found. I didn't catch what. I was . . . Hayes seemed to be acting funny so I was pretty focused on him . . . " Rolff glanced at Ben. "I didn't move fast enough . . . "

You're a bad actor, Rolff, Watson thought. But fortunately Ben was too upset to notice.

Rolff went on, "I didn't catch it. You get it, Ben? What was it Johnston wanted?"

"Something about a satellite picture," Ben said, his voice breaking, nose running. They were in the dark-wood living room, sitting on the black leather couch, Ben with his head in his hands.

Crandall was only three hours dead. Watson felt . . . what? Mostly a kind of dreamy detachment. *Crandall was dead!* Unreal. And Watson was tired, jet-lagged, but the adrenaline of the trip—never quite sure if the New-Soviets were going to let you through—still had him jacked up. "I don't know," Ben said after a moment. "I didn't pay attention because I was noticing how Rolff was looking at Hayes and . . . " He shrugged. Then he looked at Rolff. It made Watson uncomfortable to look at Ben; such a big man, a muscle rippler, with his face tear-streaked like a five-year-old who'd scraped his knee. "You shouldn't have shot Hayes in the head, Rolff," Ben said. "That was stupid. We can't extract now."

Not that extraction would show much. But then, perhaps Rolff had done well: an experienced extracting tech might realize that Hayes had had his brain rearranged by an extractor before. Conclusions could be drawn from that. Yes, Rolff had good instincts.

"And you," Ben was saying, looking at Watson. "Hayes was sent over by your people."

A shame Johnston had been there. That had confused Hayes's cerebral reprogramming. He'd been programmed to shoot Crandall and the man standing with Crandall, which should have been Ben. But Johnston had been there with Ben . . . so Ben was alive and might be suspicious.

To kill him, though, pretend he'd been killed at the same time as the others. That would alert Sackville-West. "This came in just ten minutes ago," Watson said. And in saying it committed himself to letting Ben live. He handed Ben a satelex. It read:

Arrest Special BG Hayes instantly. Repeat: Arrest and hold now for extraction team. The following is text of Hayes's letter to newspaper *International Herald Tribune* . . . "I have decided to terminate the life of Rick Crandall, a pious hypocrite whose distortions of God's Teachings are an embarrassment to all real Christians. St. Peter has come to me in a dream and asked me to do this, and I want the world to know why I'm doing it. By the time you get this, I will be a part of history. I will have killed the Antichrist."

"So that was it!" Ben said. "He was crazy!" A little relieved, for some reason. "But why couldn't this have come just a little earlier . . . It isn't fair . . ."

Watson nodded with a believable look of sympathy, thinking: The ground had been prepared; false background on Hayes, which Sackville-West would be allowed to unearth, made it look as if Hayes had converted to "Christ's Army" fanatics, the Christian equivalent of Muslim militant fundamentalists, dead set against Crandall. "He'd decided that Crandall was the Antichrist."

Ben put his face in his hands. Rolff and Klaus looked at each other; Klaus rolled his eyes. Rolff smiled.

"Rick was important to you, wasn't he, Ben," Watson said.

Ben nodded into his hands.

"He was important to all of us," Watson said. "He was the heart and soul of the Second Alliance and its Church. We can't let him die. Our people, our movement . . . all of us, we need him too badly."

Ben, red-eyed, looked up at him. "You can't revive him. His head . . . "

"We can revive . . . what he symbolized. And we can revive Crandall as a symbol. Not as a martyr. Not yet. In time. But for now, we need Crandall himself. Or . . . an image of him. We'll computer-animate him. A generated image of him will go out on the channels, will continue giving orders, lectures, insights. Just as he would. We'll be . . . arranging it."

Ben shook his head in disbelief. "That's . . . it's not respectful!"

Watson went to sit on the coffee table directly in front of Ben, so close that their knees were touching. He looked into Ben's eyes and said with all his earnestness, "It's what Rick would have wanted. He would want whatever's best for the Church. He was the glue that held it together. We have a world to make, Ben. A sacred war to fight. We need him for the morale of that war's soldiers. Do you understand?"

After a moment Ben swallowed and nodded.

• • •

FirStep, the Space Colony, Life Support Central.
The Colony's survival mechanism was operated from right here. This was the Colony's autonomic breathing apparatus, its bodily thermostat, its immune system. And at the top of the spine that made the system work was a brain. It had been an electronic brain; it was now an uneasy collaboration between electronic and biological brains. *Rimpler*. His brain,

his pared-back mind, crouching in the center of that webwork of wiring like a spider of gray matter.

Since the system was of priority importance to the survival of the Colony, it was multiply protected. It was equipped with an air lock to give it a buffer should meteor damage—or a missile—evacuate the air in the surrounding sections and out into space. It had its own temperature control units, special layers of insulation. And there were protections against sabotage . . .

Russ could feel Rimpler watching him.

The security cam near the ceiling was whirring. Refocusing on Russ and Stedder as they entered the air lock between the access corridor and the Life Support Systems Primary Computer housing. Then the camera tracked down to look at the plastiseal box Russ carried. Did Rimpler know what was in the box? Did he guess that it was his electronic replacement?

Stedder wore an electrician's yellow-paper jumpsuit, freshly printed out so that it rustled as he moved, and he carried a stainless-steel briefcase of tools and testers; he was a darkeyed, compact, muscular, deeply tanned German mechanic and elec-tech who was also the Colony's low-grav wrestling champion. Most of his free time he spent training or soaking up solar radiation in the sun rooms. He was said to be gay. He had an air of perpetual boredom whenever he was at work, as if he were only putting up with this sort of thing until his shot at the Olympics came around.

He went into the air lock first, Russ right behind him. It was a rectangular room with a door on each end; the room was about the size of a walk-in closet, military green on the metal walls, ceiling, floor. Near the ceiling, to one side of the camera, was a ventilation grate. It made Russ think uncomfortably of the gas chamber he'd seen once when he'd done consultancy work.

The first door closed behind them with a hiss, and its locking wheel spun. *Clack:* locked shut.

Some of Stedder's air of boredom vanished as he turned to look at the door.

"It does that automatically," Russ told him. And there were two SA bulls on the other side who could open it from there for them, if necessary.

"Oh, yes. Yes, of course," Stedder said. "I was just startled by the noise." He turned to face the door into the Primary Computer housing, frowned, studying it. "You couldn't get in?"

"We tried the lock about twenty times. It just won't accept the combination. Rimpler's over-ridden the . . . " He broke off as Stedder looked at him, eyebrows lofted at the name *Rimpler.* Stedder didn't know about Rimpler's brain; the interface.

"It's too hard to explain," Russ said. "The main thing is—can you get us in?"

"I don't know till I try." Stedder examined the seals on the double-thick air-lock door. He pointed to a panel in the base of the door. It was bolted shut, the bolts the smooth kind that could only be removed from this side by force. "I could drill out those bolts, open the panel, try to trigger the door from inside."

Russ nodded, and Stedder opened his case, squatted down to work.

Russ glanced down at the blue plastic box under his arm, then up at the camera. Wondering if Rimpler knew. Rimpler could monitor the whole Colony from here; might know that the New-Soviets had let them bring in another subsistence shipment. He might have listened in on the shipping clerk's report on the cargo.

Stedder's drills whined; tiny, spiral worms of metal sifted into small heaps on the floor beneath, and Russ thought, *I'm thinking of that thing in there as Rimpler. But is it Rimpler? It's a portion of his brain, conceivably a portion of his consciousness.* It seemed they'd cut out everything but cunning, hatred, and a sense of humor so reduced, it was imbecilic. It seemed to have some memories. It had motivation, initiative. Is that enough to make it someone? Is it *Rimpler?*

But what am I anymore? Used to be sure of myself, of what I was, what I believed in, who I believed in. Not now.

"There it is," Stedder muttered, withdrawing the drill. He took a flat tool from his case, began to pry on the edge of the metal panel in the door.

"If we get in," Russ said, "you're going to have to help me remove something and put something else in. You might be a little . . . well, you might not like what you see. When you see it, don't ask me why it's there. It was a stupid idea. It's incredible to me that Admin put it into effect."

Stedder snorted, and, frowning with concentration as he worked on the creaking panel, surprised Russ by saying, "Ja, but you know worldly people have stupid ideas and carry them out all the time. There are very educated people who think that a real nuclear war is something a person can win . . . That the atmosphere, the ecology, that these things would absorb any amount of poison and everything would be fine."

With a sulky rasp, the panel came free and fell on the metal floor with a rattling clank. He glanced up at Russ and again surprised him by grinning. "You have a look on your face that says you did not think I would speak that way, like a man who thinks, eh? You're very much one of the Admin to think that, Russ Parker." He took another tool from his case, looked into the panel, murmuring, "So we're going to find one of those kind of stupidities in here? The intelligent person's stupidities. That's what I came to the Colony to get away from." He bent to look deeper into the panel, put a hand on the door to steady himself. "Things like . . . "

He screamed and went rigid, his neck cording, lips drawing back to show his teeth in a skull's grimace, his whole body shaking. The smell of burning flesh, a wisp of smoke.

Russ kicked at Stedder's hand, hard, with his rubbersoled boot. It clung, smoking, to the wall, seemed as immovable as the root of an old tree. But he kicked it again, as hard as he could, and Stedder's hand came free of the panel.

Stedder stopped shaking. But he toppled onto on his back, face contorted, eyes staring. And the death's-head grin was permanent.

Russ tried artificial respiration, tried to pound Stedder's heart into re-starting. But it was like trying to revive a mannequin.

He stood up, shaking, and looked at the door to the computer housing. It was sealed with some nonconductive synthetic. The floor wasn't electrified. But the door was wired for electricity. There shouldn't have been enough voltage to kill a man. But Rimpler had seen to it that there was.

Russ bent, looked into the open panel. A cryptic tangle of wires. Some of them metal-cased. They could be electrified. Russ didn't know anything about electronics. No way he could open the door on his own.

He looked up at the camera near the ceiling. Saw its lens, irising as it focused on his face. Maybe there was enough Rimpler left to reason with. "You . . . you built this colony, Rimpler. It is a legacy to you, man. Little by little you're destroying it. Stop it. Give it up. Let me in. Let me help you ."

This is crazy, Russ thought. It's not as if Rimpler could reply.

But Rimpler did reply, in a way. With a hissing sound from up near the ceiling. The sound of air being sucked out of the air lock.

Russ stared at the ceiling gate, dumbfounded.

Rimpler was draining the air out of the room.

"Stop it!" he shouted. "This is . . . you're . . . " Hopeless to try to talk to him. To *it*.

He turned to the door behind him. Tugged on the wheel.

"Oh, no." Unbudgeable.

Already he felt pain in his ears, an ache in his lungs, headache as air pressure dropped. He took a deep breath, filling his lungs, and held it, afraid his lungs would collapse. He heard a pounding in his temples, felt the tautness in his chest become a strangling sensation as he turned, snatched up a wrench from the tool case, used it to bang on the door, frantically. Waste of energy.

Explosives. Had Stedder brought explosives? No, dammit, the council had vetoed that idea: blowing the door could damage the Life Support equipment behind it, send the whole Colony haywire.

The damn entry door was thick; the guards on the other side might not hear him. Hell, they might be gone.

Because maybe . . . maybe it wasn't Rimpler who was pumping the air out. Maybe it was Praeger. Using this chance to get rid of him, lay the blame on Rimpler.

In which case he was a dead man.

Bang on the door. Can't hear the sound of my own banging anymore. But keep banging.

My breath. Got to take a breath. Don't. You'll lose pressure in your lungs, they'll collapse. Hold it.

The hissing had almost stopped. In its place was a high-pitched hum. Some effect of losing air pressure on his ears. God, the pain in his eardrums was unbearable. Something was going to burst.

Metal squealing and a cloud of darkness closing around him.

• • •

Rush of cool air on his face. Feeling cold. Then hot, a hot flash. A series of hot flashes rippling through him. He opened his eyes.

"Chief Parker?" the man in the helmet asked him. Directly overhead, looking down.

Russ took another deep breath. "I'm okay. You guys heard me bangin', huh? Jesus Christ, you took your time."

• • •

They were in Praeger's office. Russ, Praeger, and Van Kips. The two of them on the other side of the desk from Russ. A desk built for two, it seemed. The room well lit this time . . .

"We have no choice," Russ was saying.

Praeger said, "A team of technicians, working at it for a while. Insulated equipment, pressure suits . . . "

"Not enough. I've been looking at the security setup for the LSS. There's more he can do. But what worries me is what else he'd do to the rest of the Colony."

Russ remembered her touching Praeger, arousing him while the RM17 exploded on the screen, and a surge of nausea swept him.

He shook himself and took a printout from his pocket, passed it across the desk to Praeger. "It happened about the time Stedder was drilling through the door. A pipe exploded over the day-care center. Two kids nearly drowned in sludge. He meant that as a warning to us. He won't let us tinker with him. He won't give us time to break in the way you want to.

He's got the capability of killing us a section at a time or the whole Colony almost at once. I think he's probably self-destructive."

"Dr. Tate disagrees with you," Van Kips pointed out, her voice silkily contemptuous. "He's the psychiatrist, not you."

"That thing—or Rimpler, if you want to call it that, he . . . it . . . it's too unpredictable to take chances like that. We have to cut the power down to local battery units. Emergency minimum. He can't operate on that. Life Support will hold out long enough for us to break in, and he won't be able to stop us."

"And the radics will use the blackout as an opportunity to run rampant." Praeger put the tips of his fingers together. "You'd like that, wouldn't you?"

Russ stared at him. "What?"

"We have a report of a rumor you're collaborating with the radics."

"That's bullshit." Russ's hands were suddenly clammy with cold sweat. "There's always a hundred stupid rumors."

"What you've proposed suggests to me that this particular rumor isn't 'bullshit.'" He pronounced the word in mocking imitation of Russ's southwestern accent.

Van Kips was smiling, looking at the door.

Fucking hell, Russ thought.

"I'm under arrest?" he said.

The door hushed open behind him. He felt the guards standing there.

"What are you going to do about Rimpler?" Russ asked.

"Work with a team. Protect them."

"There is no protecting them, because they're part of the Colony, and the Colony's at Rimpler's mercy."

"Rimpler won't endanger the Colony. His survival instinct will prevent that."

"He's too fucking crazy to have a survival instinct. Shit, for all you know, you cut out that part of his brain."

"I doubt it," Praeger said. "Anyway, we're going to prepare carefully to make sure the operation goes as swiftly as possible. He won't have time to do much damage."

Russ snorted. "Not much. Just the acceptable casualties, right? A few hundred people, maybe. But what's that, after sacrificing everyone aboard RM17? What's a few hundred more ?"

Praeger rocked back in his chair, smiling faintly, unaffected. "Take Russ, here, to detention," he told the guards. "He's no longer Chief of Security. He's unemployed now."

"Yes, sir."

There were two of them. Big, confident, quiet. Russ went between them down the hall, passive. But at the core he buzzed and shook, like Stedder dying.

They walked past his office. Russ stopped. "Any objection if I stop in, just send a note out on my line to let 'em know I'm out of commission? I had some meetings set up, and I don't want to hang anyone up."

The guards were mirror-helmeted, as they always were when they were busting someone. But their body language spoke hesitation. They turned to one another and spoke on their helmet radios, without external volume. Then one of them nodded. "If it's quick."

If he'd been anyone else but their former boss . . .

He nodded, palmed his office door; the door slid aside and he went in. The guards waited politely outside. The light came on, and Russ sat at the console, typed out a quick message to Faid—a message he was instructed to take to Kitty Torrence.

He sent the message, then he went outside, and they took him away and locked him up.

• • •

THE ISLAND OF CRETE.

There was no one around, but Torrence felt closed in. It was dark out, but Torrence felt as if bright lights were shining on him.

He and Danco were the point of Steinfeld's assault, moving up the cracked, one-lane road, a quarter of a mile inland from their beachhead on the rocky shore of Crete. The assault teams were in four units of nine each, moving toward the Second Alliance Post Seven on foot. They were moving in a fairly tight column now; when they reached the outer defenses of the post, they were to split into four squads, each with its own fire mission, for the attack on Surveillance Post Seven. Torrence and Danco were at the head of the column, each carrying an auto assault rifle.

The darkness was thick on the ground, and in the olive orchard to the right and left; the olive trees were shadows in shadows, their tops faintly glazed by starlight.

It was a mild, moonless night, windless, cool but not cold. "It's so damn quiet, Danco." Torrence whispered. "Not even crickets."

He looked over his shoulder and could just barely make out the man coming behind them in the column. Not a man: it was Lila. There was supposed to be someone beside her. He wasn't there. Torrence dropped back beside Lila.

"Where's Karakos?" Torrence asked softly.

"He said he was going to the rear to speak to Steinfeld."

Something out to the right caught his eye. Torrence stared into the darkness of the olive orchard. There: a small red star, just a wink of minute light, and then it was gone. As if hastily extinguished. A match. Someone lighting a cigarette in the orchard in the middle of the dark night. Someone stupid.

Torrence hissed, "Danco! Lila—freeze where you are!" The word went down the line; everyone stopped moving. He took his rifle in his right hand; with his left he put on his headset. "Squad One to Four, do you copy?"

A crackle. Steinfeld's voice: "Torrence? What's the delay, everyone's stopped . . . "

The air split open, humming. Bullets ripped it open. Muzzle flashes alternated in the orchard, bringing the thud and rattle of gunfire. Lila screamed. Someone else behind them yelled in pain. Torrence felt something smack his left hand and he spun, lost his headset, staggered; and suddenly his hand was slick with wet warmth. A wave of dizziness and nausea whipped through him. He went down to his knees and shouted unnecessarily, "Ambush—we've been ambushed. Pull back!" He tried to take his rifle in both hands, but his left hand was numb, like there was a lump of frozen meat between his wrist and the gun; he couldn't hold it up that way. So he planted his left knee on the ground (the air whining, humming as rounds whipped past him), propped the rifle barrel on his right knee, fired from the hip into the orchard, spraying at the muzzle flashes, probably not hitting anything, wanting to suppress them so the others could get back (wanting to run, his bowels vised with fear). He emptied the magazine—just as he saw a shape loom up in front of him.

He dropped the rifle, fumbled for his pistol—but it was Danco.

"Torrence, what you doing, come on!" Then the two of them were up. Torrence stumbling along behind Danco, feeling a stab of guilt even through the throbbing ache traveling up his arm and the nausea and fear: *Left my rifle behind. We don't have enough guns.* But the air was still flying apart, humming with invisible bees; bees whose stings killed and maimed.

Torrence almost fell across Lila. Lying sideways across the road (it was funny, he could *see* better now, maybe it was some adrenaline reaction).

Torrence said, "Danco, it's Lila . . . "

Danco's reply was lost in the rattle of gunfire and someone's scream.

He bent and found her arm, felt it move under his fingers. She was alive. He gripped her upper arm with his intact right hand, tried to lift her. It was hard. He was already weak from blood loss.

"Danco!"

Danco cursed but took her other arm. Between them they half dragged, half carried her to the ditch that paralleled the road. They stumbled down into the ditch, four feet deep, used it for partial cover as they dragged her through the darkness, back toward the sea. Stopping so Danco could put a belt tourniquet on Torrence's left arm—the tourniquet, after a few moments, hurt more than the wound. And they stopped again so Torrence could vomit.

They went on, carrying Lila, coming across three more bodies, each completely inert, slipping in puddles of blood more than once. Steinfeld had set up protective-fire units here and there down the road to try to cover their retreat; they'd fire a few bursts, retreat a few steps, go into position, fire a few more bursts . . .

Torrence felt a wave of weakness kick the pins from under him; he stumbled and fell to his knees. Lila drooping to the ground between him and Danco. "I can't carry anyone," he muttered, disgusted with himself.

In broken syllables filtered through the gunfire, Torrence heard Willow shouting at Carmen to get back to the beach.

Danco yelled, "Willow! Are you hit?"

Willow scuttled up to them, Carmen beside him, ignoring him when he told her to go back. "It's Lila, she's alive," Torrence said. Surprised at how hard it was to talk. Such a small wound, a shot to the hand, funny how it could make you feel.

Carmen and Danco took Lila, and feeling weightless now, Torrence trotted on ahead, back toward the beach. Behind, the gunfire continued but more sporadically now.

Once he paused and held his injured hand up to silhouette it against the sky. Two fingers were gone. The little finger and the fourth finger. Stumps a quarter of an inch above the palm. His stomach lurched. He went on.

Somehow his pistol was in his right hand. Someone was running at him, and he raised the pistol, then lowered it, recognizing the bearish silhouette. They crouched down to talk. "Steinfeld . . . where's Karakos?"

"I don't know. Maybe hit. He was at the point with you."

"No. Just before the ambush, he went to the rear."

Torrence knew by Steinfeld's silence that he understood.

Torrence said, "How bad is it, do you know?"

"Not so bad. You stopped us right before we walked into the worst of it. The bastards are on the beach, too, of course, but I've shifted to the alternate beachhead. Radioed the boats to pick us up there—head for the alternate and try to make sure everyone else does too. And listen: No wounded stay behind. If they look like they're not going to make it, then it's a matter for triage. Because of extractors."

Which meant: *Kill anyone who wasn't likely to make it alive.*

Thank God Claire was out to sea, on the ship's comm station.

Torrence said, "Yeah." And moved out, dizzy, but feeling more together now.

After a while, with a crude bandage on his throbbing hand, he was trudging down a beach road with three other NR; the sea hissing to one side, a rocky field to their left; the SA ambush was well behind them. The road was blue-black against gray, stony sand.

Someone was lying by the side of the road up ahead. Face-down. Torrence knelt beside him, found a penlight in his belt. It was Ali Mubarak, one of the Egyptian immigrants to France they'd rescued from the camps. A quiet little man, always eager to please everyone; someone who would've liked to have had more friends. Torrence had always meant to get to know him better.

Now he had to shoot him.

Ali was murmuring, and sometimes he'd try to weep a little, but that hurt, so he'd stop weeping and gasp. Torrence turned him enough to see that he was gut-shot; the movement made Ali cry out in Arabic. Torrence could see that the guy's belly was ripped open, sternum to groin; it was a boiling mass of blood and ragged entrails. Torrence pictured Ali stumbling to this spot, holding his gut closed with his hands, trying to make it to the alternate rendezvous. Collapsing here. He wouldn't survive the trip back. And Torrence couldn't wait with him till he died—he'd be killed or captured. But if the enemy found Ali, they might put him in an oxygenator, keep his brain marginally alive. A dead man's brain could be subjected to an extractor if you kept it oxygenated. The SA had been waiting for them here; they might have an extractor waiting too. Torrence had the .45 pistol in his hand. He pressed the pistol to the back of Ali's head.

"Don't," Ali said in English.

Torrence looked up at the stars. He tried to pretend that someone else was pulling the trigger.

• 13 •

FirStep, the Space Colony, Brig.
Russ Parker sat in a clean white room on the bench that folded down from the wall, staring at the clear, unbreakable plastic panel that blocked the doorway.

He sat there, rocking slightly, wondering if Rimpler would kill them quickly—the walls would sunder, the Colony would be sucked into the void and death—or if he might simply shut down the systems bit by bit, destroy the water supply, turn off the heat, and let the cold of interplanetary space make thousands of crystalline corpses floating in the dead shell of the Colony.

Remembering the insanity-twisted face on the monitors, Russ was certain that Rimpler would eventually kill them all. He was only waiting for the provocation.

The provocation that Praeger was going to give him.

And Russ had to sit there and let it happen. The detention cell was a mockery; the walls were solidified laughter. He boiled inside with the need to *do something,* and what he could do here was pace, piss, and pout. That was just exactly all of it.

He blinked. Something interrupted the line of his unseeing stare. There was someone standing in the doorway. An SA bull in a mirror helmet.

The doorway hissed into the wall, and the bull gestured.

Russ thought, *Maybe I'm going to an air lock. To join the crew of RM17.*

He stood up and walked like an automaton to the door. The guard stepped aside and gestured again; Russ put his hands behind his back; the guard put the plastiflex cuffs on him. Then Russ preceded him down the hall. They passed other cells, these with at least four people apiece in them. Kitty's husband Lester watched them go, shaking his head slowly. In the next cell down was a woman alone, an Oriental.

They passed through two electronic checkpoints, a door opening for them at each one, before they got to the admitting office. The young, helmetless SA sitting at the desk said, "Let me see that transfer pass again." He had a reedy voice that didn't go with his affectation of great authority.

The bull took a pass from a velcro'd pocket and handed it over.

Russ looked at the guard who'd escorted him from his cell. He was smaller than most of them. And his uniform didn't fit very well.

The desk guard asked, "You don't want another escort?"

"No." The bull's voice came filtered through the helmet PA.

"Okay." The kid shrugged. "Take him to Praeger directly."

But they didn't go to Praeger's office, They went to Russ's. The guard unlocked the door with a card-key and said, "Inside."

Russ went in, expecting to find Praeger there. But the office was empty. Except for an empty SA armored uniform draped over his chair—and a helmet sitting on the chair's seat. Russ turned in confusion to the guard—and froze.

The guard had come in and closed the door behind him; had taken off his helmet. It was Faid. Grinning. "I'm sorry. You wanted the passes to get that other man out, right, mate, but I couldn't leave you there. And anyway, this is what we decided to do."

"Who's we?"

"You sent a message to Kitty Torrence, what? She is contacting the NR.

All the NR but one have been arrested, two hours ago. They are take our leader, Chu, bloody damn, because there is a message from some ruddy bastard on Earth. Everyone NR arrested but me."

"You!"

"You would not have give me the cards if you knew I was in the Resistance, what?"

"I'm glad you didn't tell me. So you went to the SA dorms, got a couple of spare suits . . . this one for me?"

"Yes, mate. There are two hundred technicki rebels waiting for you to tell them to move—they are not NR, but they are allies. This is through Kitty Torrence. She is talking to everyone about the RM17, don't you know. Everyone, they are angry. And yes, suit is for you. A good idea or not one?"

"A good one."

• • •

Praeger, Judith Van Kips, and Dr. Tate were staring into a console screen, looking at diagrams. Probably of the LSS Computer housing. Praeger looked up in irritation as the two guards came into his office.

"Well, what do you want?" Praeger demanded. "Why didn't you announce yourself on the . . . " He broke off as the taller of the two guards pointed a gun at him. A .357 autopistol.

"If you call anyone in here," the taller guard said, "I'll shoot you. I guarantee it." He removed his helmet with his free hand. "Have you begun on Rimpler already, Praeger?" Russ asked. He tossed the helmet onto the table.

Praeger said, "This is very stupid, Russ."

"Answer the question."

"No. We have not."

"Mighty pleased to hear it. Faid, take Praeger into that room there. Don't let him say a word. If I give you the signal, or if it sounds like there's trouble in here, you shoot him in the head. You understand?"

Faid nodded. He drew his gun and gestured with it.

Praeger's face was flushed; his lips trembled with fury. But he walked stiffly into the next room. Faid followed and closed the door behind them.

Russ smiled easily at Judith Van Kips. She looked at him like an angry Barbie doll. Russ said, "You're the new Security Chief, Van Kips. That's what I hear."

"What of it?"

"You're giving the orders now, and the men know it. This is what you're going to do: Tell all SA units they're to meet at the ordnance center. Tell them it's for disbursal of new equipment. They'll be getting new armored uniforms and new weapons which just came in on the shuttle. They're to line up and wait. They'll be called in one by one. Once inside, they'll undress, and, one by one, in a separate room, hand over the old gear and . . . " He smiled crookedly. "And then we'll give them something new."

"You'll kill them?"

"Don't be absurd. This is going to be a bloodless coup. Or it will be if you let it be. We'll cuff them, gag them, take them out into the maintenance corridor and into storage. One of our people will put on the armor. And one by one we'll have them. They'll be put in Detention Brig."

"You'll never take Ordnance. It's well-guarded."

"We already have. They trustingly let Faid and me in, and we threatened them with high explosives. They gave us their guns and we've let our friends in. Two hundred of them."

"But I won't play along, you know that. I'd rather you killed me."

"Would you rather I killed Praeger?"

She became a thing of wax, still and pale. Then she laughed, almost explosively. "I know you. You have an overblown ego that supports an overblown sense of ethics. You'd never shoot a man down like that. Just execute him."

Russ went to the door into Praeger's chambers. "Faid! You're going to hear a gunshot! Don't do anything to Praeger even when you hear the shot, unless I tell you to!"

"I understand," Faid called.

Russ turned to Tate. "This thing with Rimpler is as much your fault as anyone's." He pointed the gun at Tate's chest. Van Kips backed away from Tate.

Much of the missing age returned to Tate's unnaturally young features. He stood up and took a step backward. "I don't think you'll do that," he said after a moment. "After all the hours I spent trying to help you."

"And reporting on me to Praeger. Yeah, I know about that. But you're right. I'm not a natural killer. I don't know how to do this without getting sick."

Russ squeezed the trigger; the gun leapt in his hand. Tate's chest burst open, sprayed red onto the console. Tate spun and fell. Blood dripped down the computer's monitor screen.

Sure enough, Russ was sick to his stomach. He took deep breaths and turned to Van Kips; he managed, just barely, to keep from vomiting.

"Judith!" Praeger called. Then, to Faid, "That redneck has shot her!"

"She's all right, Praeger. I shot Tate."

Van Kips moved to the seat and sat down. She stared at the wall, hugging herself. "You'll be convicted of murder."

"Maybe. We'll see. Anyway, you can tell I'm committed now, I guess. Wipe the blood off the screen and call your people. Tell them what I told you to. And no one else will have to get hurt."

She looked at the door to Praeger's chambers. "I believe you'd do it."

Russ nodded.

She took some tissues from a drawer and thoughtfully cleaned the blood off the screen.

And then she did as she was told.

•••

THE ISLAND OF MERINO, THE CARIBBEAN.

On a hot afternoon, and on the island of Merino, in a small, air-conditioned bungalow with cool blue walls and wicker furniture, James Kessler, Julie Kessler, Stoner, and his wife, Janet, were sitting on a wide sofa and in wicker chairs, watching satellite television. Cindy and Alouette were on a field trip with the NR's day-care unit, collecting seashells.

Attached to the media console was a Media Analysis microprocessor, booting up Kessler's Media Alarm System. On the smaller monitor next to the big wall-screen, arrows, exclamation points, and capsule analyses flashed as the system interpreted Worldtalk's propaganda.

"How many of these did you send out?" Stoner asked.

Kessler said, "Witcher sent out more than three million media-alarm software disks. Spent three or four fortunes doing it. But it's having its impact. Congress has been inundated with letters and emails and tweets and even actual demonstrators, in person . . . ." Kessler said it with a quiet satisfaction. Julie reached over and squeezed his hand. Her other hand lay on her pregnancy-swollen belly.

On the big screen, the Worldtalk-produced drama *Ghetto Cop* paced itself through a series of archetypal confrontations. The blond, blue-eyed hero was confronted with a dull-witted spectacled higher-up who tried to mitigate the cop's macho dynamism—in short, a Liberal—and the hero plowed right through his boss's misgivings and went out to kick some ass; the hero was confronted with drug addicts and whores who were reluctant to give up information on the doings of a Zionist terrorist ring hiding in the ghetto, and the hero beat the truth out of his informants, plowed right through them to the next obstacle where the hero was confronted with the miscreants, who were reluctant to give up their sniping positions, and the hero kicked down their doors and . . .

The media-alarm system went ping, and the propaganda analysis appeared on the little monitor screen:

THE FOLLOWING IDEAS ARE PROPAGATED BY THE STORY IN THIS EPISODE OF *Ghetto Cop.*

• Liberals are dupes.

• Terrorists, no matter what their color, typically hide in ghettos, implying collusion with ghetto residents.

• Ghetto residents are mostly whores and junkies.

• Ghetto residents know where terrorists are hiding and what they are up to, implying that the nonterrorist residents are somehow part of the conspiracy.

• Terrorists plan to blow up a white grade school, therefore terrorists hate white children and wish them harm.

• Terrorist sees news report of new New-Soviet invasion, remarks, "Time we did our part," implying that all terrorists are in league with the New-Soviet.

• Terrorists are Jews (or Arabs or blacks).

• Violence with no holds barred efficiently eliminates terrorism.

THE FOLLOWING BACKGROUND DETAILS FOUND IN THIS EPISODE OF *Ghetto Cop* COMPRISE SUBLIMINAL SUGGESTIONS APPEARING WITH A FREQUENCY THAT ADDS UP TO NINETY-SIX PERCENT PROBABILITY OF DELIBERATE INSERTION BY THE PRODUCERS.

• During scene in which terrorists make plans to blow up white middle-class grade school, there are seven objects arranged in the background of their hideout to form subliminal shape of the Star of David.

• During the scene in which the hero confronts the liberal demagogue the tides of books on his office shelf all have one word which is larger than the others; the large words taken from each title and reading left to right are:

DEATH
FOR
YOUR FAMILY
BLACK
SUPREMACY
and
JEW
SUPREMACY
LEADS
TO
YOUR POVERTY

The titles are too small to be picked up by the conscious mind.
• In the scene in which the hero breaks into a whorehouse, a
TV screen in the back of the whorehouse's living room, behind
the main action, shows the following images, almost too small
to see:

A BLACK MAN RAPING A WHITE WOMAN.
AN ARAB KIDNAPPING WHITE CHILDREN.
A HASSIDIC JEW

"You get the idea," Witcher said, as he came into the room. He turned off
the air-conditioning and stood in the back of the room, rocking nervously
on the balls of his feet. "What you say we switch channels. Smoke should
be coming out of the hearings about now. Yeah, there it is."

Kessler'd switched to a news channel. Smoke was standing on the
steps of the Senate building with several congressmen. Stoner recognized
Senator Harold Chung and Senator Judy Sanchez, who were there with
Smoke for a quick news conference after the Senate hearings. Smoke had
given testimony on the SA.

Senator Sanchez was reading from her notes. "We feel there is strong
evidence that the Second Alliance has been involved in an active conspiracy
essentially to do away with the Bill of Rights; to eliminate SAISC enemies
through the courts and the AVL laws by means of an illegal video evidence
tampering which fabricates false evidence for use in court; there is, further,
substantial evidence that Worldtalk Public Relations Inc., which is owned
by the Second Alliance International Security Corporation, deliberately
and willfully inserted illegal subliminal ideation into television programs
of their production; that the SAISC repeatedly violated conflict-of-interest
laws by using their influence to place their operatives and cronies within
the ranks of the CIA, CIA Domestic, the FBI, and the police departments
of every major city in the United States. We further feel there is indeed
strong evidence that the Second Alliance conspired with Anna Bester, the
president of the United States, to devise a plan eliminating congressional
decision-making power and freedom of the press, under the cloak of
declaring a State of Emergency . . . "

Cameras flashing, as if the flashes were the light given off by the awe
and amazement of the reporters; gasps from Mr. and Mrs. Kessler and
Stoner, who were astonished the investigation had gone that far.

"It's Smoke," Witcher said. "People took him seriously because he
won the United Nations Literary Committee prize, used to be a major
figure in the academic world. He's been pushing things in the underGrid,
sending vids and interviews and programs to the underground stations

till he could get it on the networks. I guess it just built up in a sort of groundswell . . . "

Smoke stepped to the microphones to make a statement. "There can be no mistake. If we don't act quickly, we're going to lose the United States of America—and not to the New-Soviets. The New-Soviets are a danger, but there's a more immediate internal danger."

A confusion of sudden movement on the steps behind the people at the portable podium, a *bang,* a rush of men in uniforms . . .

Smoke was no longer at the podium.

The image wobbled as the camera turned around, the commentator yammering confusedly. A crowd of people bent over someone on the steps. The crowd parted just enough to give Stoner a glimpse, as someone ran to call an ambulance . . .

Smoke was lying there, his chest bloody.

"Oh, Jesus," Julie said. "God, I'm glad Alouette isn't here."

"Oh, no," Kessler said.

Witcher said, "Stupid." He snorted with contempt. There was no grief in his voice, but it creaked with anger. "Stupid bastards. They shot him, and that makes it worse for them."

Stoner said, "You see the guy who shot him? I couldn't see him. Oh, fuck. I need a drink. You see him? Was he black? I figure they'd set up a black guy or an Arab, maybe, to do it."

Kessler said, "The public won't fall for that. The SA's stupid to do it now, in public."

Hands shaking, Stoner went to the bar to pour himself a drink. "Chances are the order went out to kill him before the investigation went public. They failed to contact their man to pull him back in time. Stupid is the word, all ri . . . "

"Shush!" Julie said. "They're going to say something."

A flushed, wide-eyed woman reporter came onto the screen. "Uh, I can definitely confirm that Jack Brendan Smoke has been shot while speaking at a news conference—we are told that he is alive but 'critically wounded,' but we have no definite word on his . . . his status . . . as yet . . . Stay with us as we report on this tragedy . . . "

•••

THE ISLAND OF MALTA.

Torrence shook his head in disbelief. "Satellite reconnaissance. That's how you explain the ambush—satellites? You must be kidding."

Steinfeld said, "I don't see what's so unlikely about it. They could have spotted us coming, set up the ambush."

"What horseshit. You're suffering a massive case of denial, man!"

Torrence was surprised he'd shouted at Steinfeld. It didn't seem possible. They didn't speak for a moment.

They were in the little back bedroom that Steinfeld slept in. The room was monkish, dusty, almost bare. The morning light was diffused to a blush by the window shade. Steinfeld sat on his cot. His face sagged; his eyes were ringed with sleeplessness. Torrence was pacing around the room. He paused to look sullenly at his maimed hand. With only three fingers, it looked like the paw of an animal.

Staring at the stumps of his fingers, Torrence said, "They knew we were coming. We lost a fourth of our people and we achieved nothing." He turned to Steinfeld. "For the sake of the people that we lost—the people who are dying now . . . for Lila . . . Lila's dying. Steinfeld, we've . . . we've got to . . . *to assume* . . . "

Steinfeld said, "But to start a witch-hunt now when morale is so low . . . "

A soft knock on the door.

Levassier came in, carrying something in his remaining hand. He handed it to Steinfeld, all the time looking at Torrence's own disfigured hand. Then he smiled at Torrence and shrugged as if to say, "Not so bad, really."

Steinfeld read the printout twice, and then looked at Hard-Eyes. "I don't want you to take this as a confirmation of what you've been saying—it isn't necessarily Karakos. But apparently we've had a defector from the CIA. A man named Stoner. He says we definitely have an SA mole. Right here on Malta . . . "

Torrence slumped against a wall in relief. "We'll move out of here?"

"Yes." Steinfeld turned to Levassier and made it an order. "Now. Contact the Mossad, ask them about Haifa. Just get us off the island . . . "

"I have to bring more news," Levassier said, looking at the shaded window. "Our Lila is dead. She died . . . " he shrugged " . . . a few minutes ago, in the Valletta hospital."

Torrence felt the rage turn in him; it turned inward. He was angry at himself for feeling just the faintest streak of relief that Lila was dead.

Steinfeld put his head in his hands. "She was, perhaps, our best."

Torrence nodded. Then he said, "What about the mole—what about Karakos? You do understand that it must be Karakos . . . "

Steinfeld looked up, hesitated. Then, slowly, he said, "I don't know. I don't know who to believe. Anybody could be a traitor, Torrence. With the extractor. Even you. For all I know, all this harping on Karakos—is your way of hiding."

• • •

FIRSTEP, THE SPACE COLONY.

The Colony was blacked out. Dark. It looked like a dead thing hanging in space. Even the New-Soviet blockade ship, orbiting a spare twenty miles away, called in to Colony Comm Center to ask if the Colony was in danger.

But the Colonists were there, alive, sitting in the darkness and semi-darkness. The only illumination came dull red from the emergency panels glowing over the doors.

Russ had switched off the Colony's power. Only the emergency battery power remained, the bare minimum to sustain Life Support. And only for two hours.

Russ moved down the ladder in the eerie silence of the maintenance access shaft, his rubber-soled boots making almost no sound on the rungs. He wore a hard hat with a light on it, and where he looked, a blob of colorless light pooled on the wires, tubes, and microprocessor boxes lining the curved walls.

Russ saw LSSCH LEVEL stenciled on an oval hatch. He stepped onto a metal grid under the door and swayed, almost losing his balance on the narrow ledge. The black throat of the shaft yawned behind him. He clutched at the door, his fingers found the wheel, and he hung on; felt the shaft suck at his back, felt sweat tickle his neck.

He took a deep breath and got his footing. Then he turned the wheel and opened the door, climbed through. He was in front of the air lock that led to the LSS Computer housing. The door was open. It was dark in there, except for the faint, malevolent shine of a small, round red emergency light like a demonic eye.

He couldn't go in.

If he went in, the door would slam and the air would suck away, and this time no one would come.

Rimpler can't slam the door, can't draw out the air, Russ told himself. He hasn't got the power to do it anymore. You're safe. Go on in.

Russ took a step toward the door—and stopped when his lungs seized up, an ice giant's fingers closed around his chest, tightening. He wheezed and shook with a surge of fear that was like an electric current.

There's air here. He forced himself to breathe, and take a step, and another, and he was inside, committed. The icy hand went away, and the electric feeling, replaced with a dull ache of fear. *He can't do anything now! He's shut down!*

Russ saw the open panel on the door across the chamber and, in his mind's eye, saw the tanned, confident German crouching there, reaching into the door and shaking with electrocution. Only his toolbox and the

LSS Computer replacement unit remained, on the floor where they'd left them.

Russ said, "Come on, now." He took the printout diagram from his pocket and bent, diagram in hand, beside the door. He looked at the diagram and matched it up with what he saw in the panel. He reached in. *Don't touch it. Electrocution.* But he found the lever for the emergency manual over-ride, something that wouldn't have worked while Rimpler was still powered, and pulled it down. The door clicked and moved out a quarter of an inch from the jamb. *If I put my fingers in it, he'll slam the door shut, smash them.*

Using up his reserves of willpower, he pushed his fingers into the margin and pulled the door back. It slid easily into the wall.

The little room beyond was all convoluted arrangements of component shelves, consoles, dials, numbers. He was dazzled by its cryptic intricacy.

Should have brought a tech with me, he thought. *I'm lost.*

But he'd elected to come alone because of what had happened the last time he was here. A man had died. This way, he risked only himself. *Stupid. An act of guilt.* He had felt that, being Admin Security, he had some culpability in the death of all those aboard RM17.

After twenty minutes of looking and staring at the second page on the diagram, he found the unpretentious metal box containing the LSS Computer guidance unit, and what was left of Rimpler's brain.

He unscrewed the panels, opened it. Inside was a black metal box that was sloppily soldered where it interfaced with other units. It looked jerry-rigged.

That was it. A big portion of a man's living brain was in there, in that small box. And all that remained of the man. An ambition, a dream, and an irrational rage.

He clipped the wires, removed the box, his hands shaking. "I'm sorry, man," he said. *Had* to say it. "Rest in peace."

Russ put in the purely electronic unit, following directions on the diagrams.

Then, carrying the cybercerebral interface box, he found his way out and back up to the power station. An hour later the Colony lit up like a Christmas tree.

•••

Russ took the box containing Rimpler's brain to a jettison air lock. He thought he could feel impotent fury tingling from the box into his hands as he carried the thing into the air lock, but of course he was imagining that . . .

He left it there, in the air lock, and went back to the control chamber. He told the jettison tech, "Seal it." The air lock sealed off. Then Russ closed his eyes, said a prayer ending in, "Ashes to ashes, dust to stardust. Be part of it forever." And then he nodded at the tech, who pressed a button, opening the air lock so that the atmosphere in it, and the little metal box, were sucked out into space, and gone.

•••

THE ISLAND OF MALTA.

Karakos could feel Torrence glaring at him as he came into the room. He saw Torrence from the corner of his eye, standing by the window.

Steinfeld was lying on his cot, staring at the ceiling. Levassier was sitting on the edge of the cot beside him, staring at the floor. They looked comical that way, one looking up, the other looking down.

Karakos felt the tension in the room like a bubble, pressing him back, so he stayed in the doorway. "They said you wanted me, Steinfeld."

"Lila died."

"Oh, Lord. God, no."

"Yes."

"The ambush was a terrible thing. I was almost shot myself, many times," Karakos said. "I was lucky."

"Yes."

"Well . . . I am deeply sorry to hear—"

Steinfeld interrupted. "I am telling you this because I want you to take Claire's radio duty. She was very close to Lila. I don't want someone distracted by . . . well, I prefer she rest now. So report to the—"

Torrence had crossed the room, was standing by the cot, staring at Steinfeld, pointedly not looking at Karakos. "This is . . . " He shook his head as if he couldn't believe it. "It's stupid. You're going to let *him* on radio call? He knows we're pulling out."

Karakos looked at Torrence. "What?"

Steinfeld snorted. "He *didn't* know. But I was going to inform him, true. Yes, Karakos, we're moving out. In just under two days. The entire HQ staff. We'll establish a new base in Italy. We'll be leaving here in forty-eight hours."

Karakos struggled to maintain his mask. He wanted to shout, *Damn you, no! That'll be a day too soon.* But he said only, "Italy? Where?"

"Steinfeld . . . " Torrence said warningly. "There's no reason to tell him, especially when he's going on radio . . . "

"Shut up!" Steinfeld snapped, glaring at Torrence. Steinfeld had the look of a man who's angry from weariness. "This man has worked with me for years. I know more about him than I know about you. I want no more of this idiotic divisiveness in our ranks."

Torrence turned angrily toward Karakos, who stepped aside, and Torrence shoved roughly past him, stalked away down the hall.

Steinfeld said, "We're moving to somewhere near the town of Bari on the coast of the Adriatic."

"Bari!" Karakos was surprised. Bari and the entire coast around it was supposed to be an SA stronghold. The man Tellini whom they called The Cutthroat was in power there, an SA major who was said to disdain gas and the other mass-killing methods as being economically wasteful. "*You bring them to the sea, you cut their throats, you push them off the cliffs, one-two-three, no messy mass burials, no expensive gas chambers, simple, effective, and fast.*" The Cutthroat tolerated no rebellion within shaking distance of Bari.

Steinfeld smiled wanly and said, "You look surprised. You've heard the stories about Tellini. I'll surprise you some more: Tellini is *our* man. The SA are not the only ones with extractors; we have one, just one, in Rome . . . Tellini was extracted by Witcher's best man, put under extractor post-directive. Now and then he does things we want him to and doesn't remember doing it. He will protect our base without knowing he's doing it. The SA could put him under an extractor and find nothing. But the postdirective is in there." He stood and put a meaty hand on Karakos's shoulder. "I'm telling you this because . . . I want you to know I trust you. Because you have been with me so long. You are like part of me. I would sense it if there was anything wrong . . . " He turned away.

Karakos was surprised by the warmth of the gesture and the tears in Steinfeld's eyes.

Karakos clapped Steinfeld on the shoulder. "Thank you, my friend. You will not regret it." And then he went to do his radio duty.

• 14 •

FirStep, the Space Colony.
Russ sat on the desk in the admissions area of Detentions and felt a foolish shiver of vicarious happiness as he watched Lester coming through the door, running to embrace Kitty Torrence.

Praeger was right, Russ thought. I'm too soft for this job.

Other prisoners were emerging. A group of women now: Judy Assavickian, Angie Siggert, an Oriental woman—Chu, or something—and the black twins, Belle and Kris Mitchell, hugging one another, crying with relief. Belle and Kris looking as if they'd been routinely beaten about the face.

A group of men came out, and then Faid, walking up to Russ in a tentative way, almost on tiptoe, and Russ knew he was carrying bad news.

"Chief—" Faid's voice broke. "There are being only half as many prisoners as there should be . . . "

Russ went cold inside. "Did you talk to the guards who were here?"

"Not yet, but the prisoners say the bloody bastards took people away every day for the last week and they never came back and, chief, I don't thinking they are letting them go—"

"No. No, I don't think they did either."

• • •

"I wonder," Praeger said, "if you have even the slightest inkling as to what's going to happen to you, Russ, eh?"

Russ leaned against the wall of Praeger's cell with his hands in his pockets. Praeger looked small and pink sitting in the corner of his white-walled cell. A guard in full uniform—except, they didn't wear the helmets now—stood at the door. He was one of Russ's people.

Russ said, "I can't believe you did it."

Praeger acted as if he hadn't heard. "UNIC won't stand for it. NASA won't stand for it. The European Space Agency won't stand for it. The American government."

"We've been getting transmissions again. The American government has big problems of its own right now. The president of the United States is going to be impeached."

Praeger laughed softly. "A silly rumor. Nothing will come of it."

"They seemed pretty certain about it, friend. How did you do it, exactly? Did you put them alive and kicking out into space, Praeger? Did you at least kill them with sedation first? Twenty-seven men and women taken from the cells and vanished."

Praeger shrugged and said offhandedly, "I told them to do it the way they thought best. I know the bodies were jettisoned."

"I feel like hitting you. Just holding you down and hitting you." The desire to do it was a buzz going through him. "But what I'm going to do is, I'm going to try you for the murder of the people on the RM17, and for the murder of the prisoners in your charge, and, if the jury agrees, I'll execute you. And Judith. A *technicki* jury. I think they'll go for it."

Praeger stared at the floor. He swallowed so you could see it, and said, "You're getting yourself in deeper and deeper."

"I was in deep a long time ago."

"Not Judith, Russ."

"Oh, yes. If anything she's worse than you are. But the Second Alliance bulls, all of them, will be considered on a case by case basis. The SA leadership is going to be prosecuted in the US, it seems. If that happens, I'll ship them down."

"Chances are none of this will happen," Praeger said rather distantly. "The New-Soviets will . . . ah . . . "

"They're withdrawing. Most people think they aren't going to fall back on nukes. We have too many missile-carrying submarines. They lost too many subs in the war. And anyway they're scared of nuclear war as much as we are."

Praeger said nothing.

"We're overcrowded with prisoners, so I'm going to have some put in here. With you."

Praeger shot him a look of pure venom.

Russ chuckled. "The idea of being in with the hoi-polloi repel you? Yeah, you'll have to crap in front of them too."

"This making you feel better, Russ? You think you can take this thing over and the people on Earth will shrug? Russ—the colony belongs to Earth. It belongs to those nations. They won't take this."

"Sure they will. We were about to go into the black, before the shit started coming down. We're a moneymaking proposition. If we're unanimous, if we're united here, we'll be making them an offer they can't refuse. They need us, more and more they need us economically. Asteroid mining is beginning to really take off. And we'll tell them what the Admin did. We'll tell them about RM17 and about the other murders. And I think they'll understand."

" 'If we're united here?' You're a Communist!"

"You say that like you mean I fuck my mother. No, I'm not a Communist. But I'm making Kitty Torrence and her husband the technicki reps. He for electrician ratings, comm ratings, and mechanics; she for the other labor levels. And *they're* lefties. Me, I ain't a lefty but I guess I've gone a ways to the left. And that's *your* fault, Praeger, you did it to me, you pushed me to the left. I don't like it over in the left: it's cold over here." He went to the door. Stopped just long enough to say: "And Praeger? You asked if jugging you with the scum was going to make me feel better? You know—I think it is."

And then he left Praeger alone with his thoughts.

• • •

When the NATO spacecraft came onto the screen, gliding sedately into position, Russ was almost disappointed. It looked sluggish and about as impressive and threatening as a tugboat. It was a cylindrical thing with a lot of spokes at one end. The New-Soviet ship was moving, too, jets firing here and there as it jockeyed about.

Russ was in the Colony Comm center, surrounded by banks of screens showing the Colony inside and out and views from the tethered satellites extending miles from FirStep's hull. All the small views of various other environments in and around the Colony added up, on the banks of screens, to one collective video environment, a chamber of video swatches, checkerboard patterns of shifting grays and electric-whites and misty greens and the Bible-black of space; the room a place made of other places.

Faid and Lester sat beside Russ in bucket-seated swivel chairs. They were all a little drunk. The occasion seemed to call for it, so Russ had broken out his treasured fifth of Kentucky bourbon and they were sipping it from plastic cups.

"They really going to do it?" Lester asked, his voice slurring. "They going to fight it out?"

"Hell yeah," Russ said. "And with this fight we're either fucked or we got it made."

They watched as the ships approached within two miles of one another. They saw the ships on separate screens, monitored their positions with instruments, Faid muttering, "If that ships are blow up, bloody 'ell, some debris could come here and be smashing us, mate."

Russ nodded. "Or a stray missile . . . "

With comical but inadvertent simultaneity, they took another sip of bourbon. All thinking: *Good chance we'll be dead in five minutes.*

The conflict took less than five minutes. Less than *one.* The ships seemed to be just looking at one another. Lester raised their radio frequencies, and they heard a babble of Russian and fragments in a Missouri accent (" . . . we've got alignment but no . . . [crackle] reads five-seven-oh [crackle] . . . good thing you can't smell anything through . . . you're going to owe me that shortcake . . . ") and then there was a flash, just a little flare on the NATO ship on screen 6, a matching flare on the New-Soviet ship on screen 7, and a pencil of light on screen 6 as the eight-megawatt Fluorine-based laser, near infrared and showing red tinged, lanced out and caught the New-Soviet missile. They couldn't see the missile, but they saw the wink of light as it exploded.

And then a crackle and a confused shout on the New-Soviet frequency and a big smear of white filling screen 7. And, on the New-Soviet frequency, a nerve-wracking squeal. Four seconds of noise that expressed the murder of the New-Soviet ship's electronics; implying the murder of more. Then static-edged silence.

Lester said, "Jesus. All those men are dead now. Just like that. Poof. *Shit.*"

"Blockade's over," Russ said. "Just like that, poof."

Lester was looking at the instruments and the screens. "We're okay. No debris coming our way. Nothing to speak of."

Russ drained his cup and sloshed some more in. In a drunken mock of a high moral tone, Faid said, "We should not drink more, mate, now that we know we are not going to die, what?"

"We don't need that excuse," Russ said. "Hell no. We got plenty more reasons to drink. We'll drink to the New-Soviets who died on that ship. Who called and asked if we were okay when our lights went out."

"I'll drink to that," Lester said.

•••

It was almost midnight on Merino, and they were still watching the television. Stoner was bleary eyed and blurry brained, from TV and from drinking, but they were afraid to silence the big flat screen. Too much was happening.

The Stoners and the Kesslers—Cindy asleep on the couch with her head on Janet's lap—were slumped here and there about the dark room, looking ghostly in the blue light of the TV screen.

They couldn't look away from the war news; the sense that it was either going to end, or detonate into nuclear holocaust. The announcements of the arrests and indictments; the demolition of the American SAISC. The calls for the president's resignation. NATO's promised investigation into the European Second Alliance. The announcements of a new administration in the Colony and the arrest of Colony SA. The assassination attempt on Smoke. The announcement that he was off the critical list. (They'd sent a messenger to tell Alouette, with a note for her handwritten by Smoke.) The editorials, the interviews, rehashing all of it. The New-Soviet defeat in orbit, the New-Soviet withdrawal from blockade positions under renewed air attacks from NATO.

There couldn't be anything more, Stoner thought. Time to try and sleep.

On the screen a political analyst was droning about the likelihood of the opposition candidate's winning the next presidential election. Comparisons with Watergate, the Iran/Contra affair, the failed attempt to oust Clinton. "But of course this is something far worse: what we have here, at least in the minds of many, is treason on the part of the president herself . . . "

Stoner was just getting up and stretching, ready to go, when the political analyst was pre-empted, and an excited young announcer came on and told them . . .

" . . . The New-Soviet Union has expressed its desire to call a ceasefire to the war in order to negotiate a peaceful end. Secretary of State Carnegie has said, and I quote, 'We feel that the end of the war is at hand. The New-Soviets are indicating they are ready to surrender.'" The newscaster cleared his throat. "Ladies and gentlemen . . . " His voice choked with emotion. For once the cookie-cutter newscaster was gone, the man behind the glossy image emerging, moved by the emotional electricity of the moment. "Ladies and gentlemen—ladies and gentlemen, *the Third World War is over.*"

• • •

Cloudy Peak Farm, Upstate New York.
"The crisis is very real," Watson said, "and it's going to mean drastic retrenching. But it's only a setback on one front."

Sackville-West shook his round head so that his jowls waggled. "It's not a *setback* on this front. It's a *complete defeat.* The president will be forced to resign. Our American bank accounts are already frozen. CIA Domestic is under investigation by the Justice Department and our enemies in Congress—and our people who were in the Justice Department are under arrest. American public opinion is ninety percent against us. Even the Fundamentalists. They're pretending they're horrified, had nothing to do with us. Worldtalk's assets frozen. Worldtalk Grid projects seized. Indictments and more indictments. The Colony fallen, Praeger taken. Most of it happened through the media, the underGrid, social media, the networks . . . "

"You sound bitter," Watson said coldly, "and that's ironic."

There were four men in Cloudy Peak Farm's comm center, in person, including Carlton Smith, the SA's Special Education Coordinator, tall and bushy-browed, with short, receding brown-blond hair; always the pipe and the faint smile as if the biggest problems were just a matter of father and son talking it out. He was the father of Jebediah Smith.

Watson and Sackville-West were there, and Klaus; as Watson's bodyguard, he went everywhere with him. Klaus was slated for a major promotion . . .

There were others on the video conference lines, four SA chiefs in various parts of the country, and in various states of panic and disgust.

Watson, Smith, Klaus, and Sackville-West were seated around a small, round conference table Watson had brought in.

Watson went on. "I mean, Sacks, you really sound as if you're angry about all that's happened. As if you're angry with other people. But you, Sacks, you were in charge of security, you were the one who allowed yourself to be recorded in conversation with the president, recorded and photographed discussing a very sensitive matter. You were the one who let Stoner get away. So you won't be surprised when I tell you that you are being replaced."

Sackville-West's head jerked up. Jowls jumping again.

His eyes went piggish, his skin vermilion. "Replaced by whom?"

"Klaus, here. I have looked at the matter from every angle. He has been extractor-approved. He has an extensive background in security." He added a lie: "He was in charge of my station security in France."

Sackville-West turned to the screen. "Gentlemen—the buck is being passed here, I am a . . . a scapegoat for . . . for . . . " But after that, all that came out was inarticulate fragments and sputters. Perhaps because of the way the men on the screen were looking at him. Watson went to the door and called, "Ben."

Ben came in and stood behind Sackville-West's chair. The young man seemed mildly embarrassed. "Sir. Come with me, please."

"And where might that be?" Sackville-West demanded.

"Debriefing," Watson said smoothly, sitting down. "And retirement. Ben . . . ?"

Ben nodded. He put one hand on his gun and the other on Sackville-West's shoulder.

The old man shuddered and sat there a moment, breathing through his mouth, sweat glossing his forehead. Then he stood up, upsetting his chair, and walked with a kind of roly-poly dreaminess out of the room, Ben close behind him.

Ben shut the door behind as they went out.

Watson sighed, rubbed his hands together, and said, "Now. The New-Soviets have removed their blockade from the Atlantic ports. They're talking ceasefire and negotiation, and all this is generally being taken as a sign they are close to surrender. Thanks to the crisis here it behooves us to remove ourselves and our projects from the US, to take them overseas." He smiled at Smith. "Yes, even the people of Colton City. And all the kids in your charge. We'll transplant the town to Britain. We're strong there now, and, after all, the roots of the Caucasian Prime are in Europe. In a way we'll all be going home. In a month, we'll be ready to announce the formation of the Self-Policing Organization of European States."

He paused dramatically, looking at Smith and Klaus, and looking into the camera that conveyed his image to the men on the screens.

Watson wasn't as good at this sort of thing as Crandall had been, but until the new Crandall was video-fabricated, he'd have to deploy all the leadership faculties at his command.

"Rick is in seclusion, as you know, but he has asked me to be his spokesman—I believe you all got his signed statement to that effect—and I have the joy to inform you that we have some very good news indeed to offset all the bad news that's plagued us lately. The good news is: Europe is essentially ours, though NATO is withdrawing its support. We will get no more help or credibility from them. But it doesn't matter a bit. We are being incorporated into the military infrastructure of our adopted European nations. The government of every European nation where we maintain a presence is a government we have established. And in a month they will announce SPOES, essentially a 'united states' of Europe, united for reasons of defense, and by philosophical alignment. But not a democracy. Anticommunist, anti-immigrant, nationalist-central and of course a strong advocacy of racial purity. And yes, it's that simple."

Tamping his pipe, Smith nodded, like a TV father hearing Abraham Lincoln quoted. But he said, "If we could hear it from Rick, I mean, in person . . . " He lit the pipe; its aroma slithered through the room.

"You will, shortly. He'll be taping an announcement. He'll be announcing the retirement of Sackville-West, Klaus's stepping into the job, our move to Europe, and the formation of SPOES."

" 'Formation of SPOES,' " Jaeger said. "You do make it sound very easy." Jaeger spoke from his screen. He was a stocky, pug-nosed, thin-lipped man, an ex-football player who'd failed in three bids for the US Senate. His munitions company had designed the Jægernauts.

"Resistance on the legitimate political level is almost nil," Watson said. Not a lie but surely an exaggeration. "And as for the fringe groups, like the NR—well, they're being taken care of. Klaus?"

Klaus cleared his throat and threaded his fingers together. He wasn't used to having to deal with people this way. "Yes—it is all coming together very nicely." Klaus rumbled. "Our man in the NR, on Malta, has warned us that they are about to relocate, so we have moved up the date of our surgical strike against them." He glanced at his watch. "Twelve hours from now, the majority of our Sicilian air unit will carpet bomb the area. Our troops will move in by helicopter to do the mopping up, I think you call it. We expect the strike to destroy Steinfeld himself and the core of the NR leadership."

Smith nodded. The smile was still there, but he was pale, and the hand bringing the pipe to his mouth was leaving a crooked trail of smoke. "I see. And as for the relocation—you feel we will be, um, allowed to leave?"

"We've got a lot of friends still. They're lying low, of course," Watson said, "but they'll help us. Friends in immigration, customs especially. We'll get everyone, ah, significant out. And most of Colton City. You can be sure we're going to take good care of Jebediah." He smiled at Smith. "You should be very proud of that young man. He's our future. I can tell you that Rick is thinking of Jebediah in terms of his successor. One day, ten years from now, after he has been properly prepared . . . "

Smith's smile became genuine. He fairly glowed.

Watson congratulated himself on winning Smith over. The others seemed ready to go along. They were desperate, after all . . .

Things were going badly, in one sense. But in another way, everything was falling into place.

• • •

Watson and Klaus were alone. The screens were blanked. Smith had gone to call his family in the privacy of the guest room.

Watson leaned back in his chair in the silence, and wondered how long he could keep the rest of them from knowing that Crandall was dead. And wondering who he should tell.

Klaus lit a cigarette and said, "This SPOES State . . . Jaeger is right. It's not going to be so easy. There is probably going to be a reaction, a resentment against the new governments by the regional nationalists. They will know that the figureheads are being manipulated by foreigners. You think the Basques in Spain were a problem—just wait. Many new such organizations will emerge. And there are still opposition parties, still political resistance, especially in Germany and Italy . . . "

"Italy is always fighting itself. Its internal chaos will make it easy for us. Within our organization, there is no chaos. But I suppose you should know there's another method . . . a bigger picture . . . "

Klaus looked at him expectantly. Watson wondered how much he should tell him. Well, Klaus was really and truly inner circle now. Still, he mustn't tell him everything.

Watson went on, "I've been in conference with the Worldtalk people. We are going to create our own national leaders much the way we're re-creating Rick Crandall. We'll use video animation and computer-designed psychiatric models to create for each country a kind of . . . well, a false idol, the ideal demagogue for that country. He'll look and sound like that country's ideal leader, incorporating in his speech and mannerisms all the cultural characteristics of the quintessential Frenchman, Brit, Dutchman, German, Greek, Belgian, Italian.

"Of course, people have been doing this for years but not so literally. In America the political PR specialists do something equivalent, packaging their candidates, so their candidates seem to have all the right qualities for the average American's taste. In public our man will only be seen in the distance. For security reasons all interviews will be done via screen. We'll have to invent a private life for him. In one case we'll be co-opting the public life of a certain national favorite—we'll alter the man's image to suit our needs. And the man himself will be entirely under our control. Extractors are marvelous things . . . we're just beginning to explore their potential."

Klaus shook his head in amazed disbelief. "It'll never work."

"Klaus, you underestimate the power of the Grid. The media is powerful—it's what wrecked our work here in America, and in a remarkably short time. People will believe in our creations. They *believe* the men they see on TV and the Internet—and most of them never see them in person, really know very little about them."

Klaus sat in silence for a moment. Then he said, "Yes. Perhaps you're right. Still, we're going to be observed: we want to eliminate the mongrel gene pools, the lesser races. But Europe is sensitive to genocide."

"Much of it will be done . . . " He hesitated. This was too sensitive to tell Klaus about yet. The virus was a very serious matter indeed. When you are contemplating the extermination of millions, you must be more careful than anyone has ever been before. "We will talk about that later. When the time comes . . . "

• • •

THE ISLAND OF MALTA.

At three a.m., Karakos stepped out the back door of the villa, closing it carefully behind him. The sentry was on the other side of the house for the moment. Carrying his satchel, he turned, stepped into the darkness, took only one step toward freedom and safety. And then the darkness grew the shapes of men.

They moved in all around him, and he froze as one of them shined a light on him. It was Steinfeld. "When are they coming, Jean?" Steinfeld's voice came out of the darkness above the glare of the light. The hurt in that voice was unmistakable.

"Who? What is—I was going to Valletta, to . . . well I have private matters . . . "

"And you needed the bag you're carrying? We'll have a look in that bag. Please, Jean. Tell us when they're going to come." The light angled up to shine in his eyes. He looked away—but the other men switched flashlights on, to shine in his face, so many he could feel the heat of the beams.

"This is insane."

"The SA has arrested Tellini." Torrence' voice. "We told you he was NR to see if he would be arrested. He was. They didn't try to salvage him with extractors. I guess they bought the bullshit about our extractor techniques being too subtle to detect. They took him away and shot him, in front of his men. He was loyal SA. He was never really our mole. That means you told them our story about him."

"I see," Karakos said. "Disinformation." His own voice sounded very far away to him. "And you acted your part very believably, Torrence." There was a strange kind of relief in him, and it came as a surprise. He closed his eyes against the light, but opened them when Steinfeld said:

"I must insist you keep your eyes open, Jean. So you used the radio to tell them about Tellini and our people in Bari saw them take Tellini the Cutthroat away. And that is some good to come from this, anyway. And you've told them we're going to Italy—so they'll be here sooner. How soon?"

"It doesn't matter if you know—you'll leave in time, I'm sure, anyway. They are coming in two hours from now. Just before dawn. Now please. My eyes hurt."

Steinfeld lowered his light, so the others lowered theirs too.

"Put the bag down, Jean."

Karakos thought of running. Useless. He dropped the bag. "I won't make any more transmissions for you. They have made me so I will not knowingly do anything against them."

"Yes. The extractor." Steinfeld was silent for a few moments. They could hear the sawing of cicadas, the muted rumble of the sea. "I had hoped to take you back to the States, perhaps restore you to yourself with our own extractors. But we could never be sure of you—we couldn't know for sure we'd taken out everything they put in. So . . . "

"I understand." Karakos felt airy, distant from things. No fear at all.

Steinfeld came toward him and took his arm, and they walked off into the night together.

"Where will you go?" Karakos asked.

Steinfeld told him, because in a few moments it wouldn't matter what Karakos knew. "Now, we go on the assault. Sicily. While most of their forces are here, attacking our empty base. Afterwards, Haifa. Israel. The Mossad have set a base for us up there." Steinfeld sounded as if he might cry. But his grip on Karakos's arm was like a beartrap. "You know, I hate these extractors, Jean. Look what they force us to do. And what do they leave us—what are we to believe in? We can't even believe in our enemies. There is no trust at all now. And can I even trust myself? Who knows, maybe someone put me under an extractor once and told me I believe what I believe. If beliefs are so malleable, then we are nothing but computers in flesh, and that is a very ugly thought, Jean."

"I think . . . I think there is something more. Even when I do the SA's work—and I admit I could never have done anything else, once they changed me—but even then, there was a . . . a kind of shadow of something. Maybe cast by my soul. A taste of regret, of longing for . . . I don't know."

"It is a great relief to hear you say that, my friend." Steinfeld stopped walking. They stood together in the middle of a field, and Karakos looked up at the stars. He heard Steinfeld cocking his pistol. Steinfeld said, "Thank you for restoring my faith in the soul, Jean. Thank you, and I'm sorry . . . "

Then came the father of all thunders, and the starry night up above them poured icy cold down into the hole Steinfeld's gun made in his friend's head, and filled his mind with forever.

• • •

Torrence found Claire sitting in the kitchen, sipping from a little porcelain bowl of tea she held in both hands. She was wearing her fatigues and boots, her rifle leaning up on the table beside her, ready to go. They were short-handed; no one would be staying behind this time. She didn't look at him when he came in. He stood awkwardly in the doorway. He looked at the night-blanked windows, and then at the bulb over the wooden table, and then back at Claire. She still wasn't acknowledging him.

"Claire . . . I'm sorry about Lila."

She sat the bowl down hard enough to make it slosh onto the table. "Is Karakos dead too? Was that the shot I heard?"

"Yes. Ask Steinfeld. He was . . . "

"I know!" She glared at him. "And you told me so."

"Look, that's not what I'm . . . "

"Bullshit. You're glad she's dead. And he's dead."

"You really rate yourself highly. Glad Lila's dead? She was one of the best. We'd be better off losing *you*."

The words had come out of him on a wave of anger, and he regretted them.

She went red. But her shoulders slumped and her face crumpled. He went to stand beside her and she turned and she was in his arms like a stone falling into a well.

"I'm sorry, Dan. She was hard to lose."

• • •

The shouting of the NR and the droning of helicopters brought Bonham awake. He sat up in fear—sounds at night did that to you when you lived with these bastards.

He went to the window; there was an iron grating over it. Bonham had been arrested earlier that night, and brought here and given a sedative. They had insisted he take it. And they locked him away. He was still muzzy from the sedative but it had nearly worn off and all that noise . . . and now he saw what made it. A number of big helicopters and two cargo trucks. They were just slamming the doors on the trucks, which went grindingly away almost immediately. The NR were getting into the copters . . . and Claire was with them.

Bonham pulled on his clothes, then went to the door and tried to open it. Still locked. There was a piece of paper on the floor, a corner of it still under the door. He picked it up, turned on the light and read the message penned in big block letters on the ruled paper. It was from Claire.

We are leaving you here. The SA is coming. Try to break out and you might survive. Some of us wanted to execute you, so this isn't so bad. The people you betrayed on the colony are free now, and you were never one of us, and you don't know anything else that could hurt us so Steinfeld said you could live. Good luck.

Claire

"Good luck," he muttered. "Thanks, bitch."

He looked around the room. The bedframe was all there was to use. He pulled the mattress and boxframe off, disassembled the metal frame, and took one side of it in his hands. He began to batter at the door.

• • •

The Island of Sicily.

The Israelis were committed. "Everything short of declaring war," they told Steinfeld. "And yes—your request for back-up in a preemptive strike has been granted. We can give you eight Z-90 fighter-bombers and two escort air-to-air fighters."

The Mossad's surveillance satellite had given them the details of the SA's European HQ. It was shaped like a skewed four-leaf clover. ("Or an iron cross," someone said), with four broad approaches, between the ancillary buildings, to the main operations building. It was eight miles east of Palermo on the Tyrrhenian Sea; was protected with radar, and with satellite surveillance, and with missile emplacements; with cannon and a no-man's-land of mines and concertina wire.

The SA's aviation unit sent its squadron out at four a.m. The Israeli radio listening posts picked up the departure codes identifying the copters accompanying the jets. And the radiomen of the six NR transport copters accompanying the Mossad's complement of fighter planes knew those codes. The six transport copters had been repainted to resemble SA copters. As they approached the base, the SA radar techs demanded they identify themselves. The transports gave the SA code.

"You're back early," one of the SA radiomen said.

"Yeah, we're ahead of schedule."

The helicopters moved in at five hundred feet; the fighter bombers were behind them but rapidly catching up. Two minutes more. More questions from SA control. A visual check confirmed the copters were the right type, but the planes seemed to have the wrong configuration. And they couldn't be *that* much ahead of schedule. Still, they'd had the right code.

"No," said the XO, hearing all this a little too late, "that was the departure code. The return code was . . . "

But by then the bombing had already begun.

• • •

MALTA.

Another island, other bombings. The SA hitting four places on Malta where the NR had been an hour before; buildings that were lit up as if they were occupied. Inviting themselves to be targets . . .

Empty buildings.

At one of those places, the old villa, Bonham ran from the building, his hands bleeding, seeing the VTOL jets coming in to strafe, the bigger jets diving and letting missiles go that sang neatly into the barn—the barn throwing itself into the air in a fountain of fire.

Bonham screaming, waving his arms, "You idiots, don't! Don't! I'll work with you, I'm not one of them—you morons, you cretins, you jerks, there's *no one here!* This is a *decoy!*"

A chopper was coming in, swinging its minigun toward Bonham. Bonham ran toward it, waving his arms, shouting hysterically, "There's no one—"

The minigun round that caught Bonham in the center of the chest was big as his thumb, and coming hard at a range of only forty-eight feet. So his chest quite literally exploded under the impact, and he was dead before he could mouth another syllable.

• • •

SICILY.

They were descending into flame. They came down into a sea of molten air, churning with cinders, swirling with the orange and red and yellow fires.

Dan "Hard-Eyes" Torrence jumped from the chopper, fell six feet to an ankle-jarring impact on the asphalt of Entry Three, and turned to shout at the others, getting them off and running, leading them onto the road and into the tunnel of roaring light.

Weapons in hand they sprinted between sheets of flame that sucked the oxygen away, flame bannering and billowing from the windows of the big square barracks and wooden office buildings and pressboard mess halls and computer bunkers; flame reaching above them in sheets four stories high, rearing like some mythical entity, a god of the elements. At intervals parts of the buildings were smashed, flattened outward in rings of embers and burning timbers where concussion and incendiary bombs had struck.

Torrence looked over his shoulder, saw Claire and Danco, Willow and Carmen and four others running behind him, gasping, firelight tiger-striping their faces. He turned and, running, carrying his assault rifle with his maimed hand—the finger stumps aching—fumbled in his shirt for his dark glasses, unfolded them and put them on. It didn't help much. Entry Three was a forty-foot strip of asphalt, melting on the edges, running straight to the heart of the SA's European HQ.

They ran down the middle but the heat sucked the perspiration off them, made their skin ache and rasp in their clothing; successive walls of smoke left them choking, gagging as they ran, inhaling cinders, feeling their nostrils coating with ash, beginning to cough up blood, lungs searing with every white-hot breath.

Dizzy, wobbly on their feet from oxygen deficiency, Torrence yelling into his headset, "Steinfeld—not enough air, we can't—there's no one alive here anyway. Do you copy?"

He pressed the little instrument to his ears; it was hard to hear over the blustering of flames and the rolling booms of explosions, but he made out, "Keep going . . . clear up soon, we couldn't reach . . . "

Static.

They came to a place where the road was nearly blocked by flaming timbers and burning sections of ragged wall. There was a narrow path between the fallen building on the right and the burning structure on the left. Torrence turned, mimed *Hold your breath!* and led them onto the path, flame on either side sucking the air away, roaring . . .

Torrence glanced back, saw Claire staggering, her knees buckling, her head down, hands over her mouth. She was a red silhouette against a backdrop of yellow flame. He ran back to her, took her by the arm, and they stumbled on, lungs bursting. He thought they'd fall but they emerged into the open road, ran through a wall of smoke, into a wash of cool air.

Gratefully drawing lungfuls of cleaner, cooler air, they threw themselves flat, slapping rifles into firing position. Bullets sang overhead.

They were forty yards from the central building—where the gunfire was coming from. It was a rectangular five-story concrete building, utilitarian-brutish, unpainted, its windows shuttered with metal slitted for gun muzzles. Muzzle flashes strobed at those windows. Other NR teams were emerging from the other Entries, coming at the building from the four points of the compass. The frayed ends of smoke and the distortion of heat waves refracting massive firelight gave them partial cover. Up ahead, parked at an angle, was a small armored car, its front doors showing the SA cross, a Christian cross with the iron cross at its center; it was abandoned but it looked intact.

Torrence squeezed Claire's arm, yelled over the roar of flames and the crack of gunfire, "You okay?" She was still coughing but she nodded. He shouted hoarsely, "Get behind me when I start moving, and stay low!" He signaled to the others to stay directly behind Claire. He laid his rifle down beside her. "Hold on to that for me."

And he ran in a crouch—keeping the armored car between him and the HQ Central—up to the side of the car, looked in. Empty. He opened the driver's side door, got in, keeping below the dashboard. Someone had seen him: machine gun rounds struck sparks from the hood of the car, gouged the asphalt beside him. Squatting behind the car, the others in his team returned fire.

Using a knife, Torrence set to work on the car's ignition: His hands shook, but at last the car started. He put it in gear, got it moving forward, wedged the knife against the accelerator at an angle that would keep it moving about ten MPH. He peered over the dashboard, angled the car for the machine gun emplacement, behind sandbags, where the front door had been . . . Torrence shouting into his headset, asking for suppressive fire from the Mossad chopper moving in overhead . . . the chopper opening up at the windows with its miniguns . . .

Torrence opened the door, slid out, running alongside—feeling a giant's hail of machine gun rounds hammering the door. Closer—now just thirty feet to the doorway. Twenty-five. Torrence let the car slide on ahead, took a grenade from his bandolier. He pulled the pin with his teeth while opening the gas tank's cap with his free hand—working clumsily with the three remaining fingers. MG rounds whistled around him as he dropped the grenade into the tank and ran behind the armored vehicle, shouting out a warning. His team flattened, everyone throwing themselves face down. Torrence threw himself down, flattening with his face buried in his arms, as the car plowed into the sandbags . . .

The explosion slapped the sky with a wave of heat; the hair on the back of Torrence's neck incinerated and he winced with the pain of the shock wave. But less than a second later he was up, catching the rifle Claire threw him, turning to fire past the yellow flames, the burning hulk of the car, into the building—

"Shit!" Carmen's voice. Torrence saw her dragging Willow into the cover of the building, under the windows. But it was useless. The side of Willow's head was missing. He was dead.

A rocket from the helicopter blew in one of the ground-floor windows, near the corner, forty feet down from where Carmen was hugging Willow's body. Torrence ran past her, shouting, "Come *on!*" and she followed, they all followed, they climbed into the smoking socket of the window, burning their hands on the edges, coughing, firing bursts at anything that moved. Two men went down.

Carmen shot a woman in a dress—she was probably only a secretary. Then a man in armor stood in the doorway, firing.

Torrence and Carmen and Claire ducked behind a desk. Rounds from the gunman in the door chewed the fiberglass desk apart. Danco whooped as he came through the window only to be knocked back out as he was hit. Torrence jumped up, firing at the figure seen dimly in the smoke. The guy staggered but his armor held against the assault rifle's rounds.

Carmen shrieking, "FUCK YOU FUCK YOU FUCK YOU!" Running at the door while the armored SA paused to reload; Carmen with a hand grenade in her teeth, jerking the ring, tackling him, the grenade between her and the SA bull (Torrence thinking: FUCK NO!), the grenade booming, shaking the floor, ripping them both apart and killing another SA around the edge of the doorway . . .

Torrence and Claire stood up, slapping fresh clips into their rifles, ran to the smoky doorway, coughing, firing, trying not to look at what remained of Carmen, firing at men who came around the corner in the hall, coughing again, rifles jumping in their hands. Gutman, behind them with a grenade launcher, took out another guy in armor at the end of the hall, Torrence and Claire reeling back from the shock wave, coughing, getting their footing, firing again and again toward the muzzle flashes, the blurred shapes of running men; trying not to see Carmen's bloody grin, her severed head . . .

Torrence holding back hysterical laughter, coughing, sprinting down the hall, jumping over bodies, firing, firing . . .

After a while, no one fired back.

• • •

FirStep, the Space Colony.

"You don't want to go back," Kitty said. "Be honest."

"I promised you we would," Lester said, shrugging. "We will. But you're just not in shape to take a shuttle trip till after the baby's born."

They sat in the grass, basking in reflected sunlight beside the Open's playing field; they were watching a touch football game, listening to the music from the Colony's folk quartet over the PA that Lester and Russ Parker had set up. Russ himself was quarterback on the Admin team, which was taking the worst of it, losing 44 to 12.

The Open was thronged, the crowd around the playing field dancing, drinking wine from Admin's formerly private stock, laughing. Admin with Technicki; a multicolored crowd shifting with restless energy, making Kitty think of a World's Fair she'd been to as a girl, with her brother Danny. Where was Danny Torrence now?

Lester laughed. "What's so funny?" she asked.

"The looks on the face of the storage officers when we came in and Russ told them he was turning Admin stores over to the technicki—for a party! 'A party, sir?'"

They both laughed. And she felt better than she had in months. "Oh, hell, Lester. The blockade's down. Russ's offering you an important job. A job like that on Earth . . . " She shook her head. "Lester, let's stay."

He slipped an arm around her. "I knew you'd come around if I kept my mouth shut."

• • •

HAIFA, ISRAEL.

The brassy light of Israel.

Gold domes, great swathes of white walls, a maze of narrow streets, ambience of the ancient . . . beyond the domes and tile rooftops, the heartbreaking blue of the Mediterranean. A furious sun was baking it all, trying to cook it back into the sand.

Torrence turned away from the window, disoriented by the shadowy, air-conditioned room, the row of consoles and print-out gear and screens against the right-hand wall. Three men and a woman sat on the dark wooden chairs, watched over by the portraits of generations of Israeli politicians on the walls, a gallery of bitter smiles and restrained optimism. And there was an old-fashioned pendulum clock, the sort with springs and hands pointing to the hour, that said *tick tick tick tick . . .*

Bensimon, the Mossad's military attaché, sat behind the brown metal desk. He was a bearded man with deepset black eyes. He wore an Israeli military uniform and gold and red embroidered yarmulke. There were pipes in a rack on the desk but he made no move to smoke. He seemed a little in awe of Steinfeld.

Steinfeld and Witcher sat across from him, Claire sat between them.

"Will Captain Danco not be coming?" Bensimon asked.

"No," Steinfeld said, shifting in his chair. "He was wounded. Rather badly. But he's expected to live. With luck he'll be at the next meeting."

"Good." Bensimon looked at Torrence, gestured toward a chair that stood empty to Steinfeld's left. "You do not wish to sit, Captain Torrence?"

Captain Torrence? "No, thanks," Torrence said. Amenities. Weird. "I was sitting for hours on the helicopter and the ship. Let's get started."

Bensimon shrugged. He put his hands together, cracked his knuckles, and said, "We did quite well in Sicily. It is a great victory for you, Steinfeld. Their records, perhaps half of their European leadership—all wiped out. Colonel Watson, however, apparently survives. He is believed to have recently arrived in Rome. Crandall is somewhere extant. Now as to the next step: I have been in touch with a friend at the American embassy.

The new president makes great noises about the SA in Europe, but will not consider moving against them militarily, for a variety of political reasons which come down to this: the American public is sick of war, and it is hard to disentangle the targets from the people they are hiding behind. To attack the Second Alliance the US would have to attack Italy, France, Britain, all the countries where . . . " He made a dismissive gesture. "You see the problem. But our intelligence tells us that the pogroms are ongoing. The European apartheid proceeds. Israel also cannot yet declare war. But we have committed everything short of war to helping you. Especially intelligence, logistics, and recruitment. Some air support. But we are already weathering accusations from Italy about the attack on Sicily . . . "

There was more talk, much talk of specifics and talk of money. And then Bensimon invited them all to lunch at "a very nice place not far from here."

How strange, Torrence thought, considering what they were used to, to be invited to lunch. At a "nice place."

Witcher said, "I'm sure we'd all be delighted—I wonder if we could have just five minutes alone here. And we'll join you downstairs. There's something we need to discuss . . . "

Bensimon nodded, and stood, smiling. "Of course. I have something to do anyway. Downstairs in five minutes." He smiled and went to the door, paused, and turned to them, a little embarrassed. "Ah, please permit me to . . . to express my admiration." Steinfeld nodded. Bensimon left the room.

Witcher turned to Claire, and said, "I have some news for you, young lady."

Torrence thought: And how weird to hear her called "young lady." Everything seemed strange today.

"The Colony?" Claire's voice was small, tentative. Which was also weird.

Witcher nodded. "I understand there was some doubt about your father's . . . about what happened to him. There isn't now. I'm sorry to tell you he's dead."

Claire swallowed, and after a moment said, "Go on."

"The Colony has been taken—you've heard that. The technicki control it and a few rebel Administration personnel, specifically a man named Russ Parker."

"He's with Praeger."

"Not anymore. In fact, he's arrested Praeger. It's very probable that, by now, Praeger has been executed. Evidently he had a number of people murdered."

"Do you know who?"

"I don't have a list. You can find out for yourself."

"What?"

"Our people are now on the, uh, ruling council, whatever you call it, of the Colony. The Colony is effectively an NR enclave. In fact, we believe the SA may know about our retreat in the Caribbean. Everyone in our Caribbean headquarters—everyone who wants to—will be removed to the Colony. Once things are stable there."

"But if the SA find out—"

"We're not going to advertise it. And if you do your part, the new board of UNIC, NASA, and the US Orbital Army will be working to protect the Colony. It'll be one of the safest places in existence."

"What do you mean—my part?"

"They want you to take over as Chairperson. As the new Colony Chief. You're the daughter of the man who designed the place. You have experience in Admin Council. You're someone UNIC and the NASA people can relate to. They'll accept the new order there with you in charge."

"Me in charge . . . ?"

"Yes. And we want you there." He smiled. "Because you're NR." After a moment he said. "Well? What do you say?"

She turned and looked at Torrence. Then she looked at Witcher. Then she looked at the floor and frowned.

No one said anything. Except the clock on the wall that said *tick tick tick tick . . .*

• • •

"I feel different about a lot of things," Torrence said.

He was sitting up, holding Claire in his arms, in the hotel room's double bed. The bedclothes had been thrashed onto the floor; the sheets were rumpled like a great carnation around them. Moonlight from the double glass doors onto the balcony silvered them.

"I was childish about Lila and Karakos," Torrence said. "I wasn't thinking of what you went through. I wasn't really *seeing* you, then . . . Claire, don't go back."

"I decided."

"Claire . . . "

"I have a responsibility to it. To my dad, too. Steinfeld and Witcher both said it's the best work I can do for the NR. I'm going."

She reached up and touched his face and her fingers were shocked by the tears on his cheek. But she didn't change her mind.

• • •

Washington, D.C.

Across an ocean, Smoke lay partly propped up in a hospital bed, feeding crusts to his crow. The crow sat on a perch in a square brass cage, the door of the cage wide open, on a table to Smoke's left.

Beside the table was a cot, on which Alouette slept, curled up. She had insisted on sleeping in the same room with him, supposedly to keep him company. The TV was on, but Alouette could sleep through anything. It was because of her—because the nurses could deny her nothing—that the hospital had grudgingly allowed Smoke to keep the crow here, though the bird was supposed to be in the cage.

To the right of his narrow bed was a machine that fed him through a tube in his right arm. There was a bandaged hole in his chest, just under his sternum. A TV on the wall across from him chattered happily about peace negotiations. The New-Soviets. The new president. The disappearance of key American SA personnel. Not a word about the European SA. It was like the Iran/Contra hearings in the last century; then, too, the investigators had looked just so far and no farther. The Iran/Contra investigators ignored the evidence linking the president. It was now as it was then—as if they didn't want to see certain things. Didn't even want to think about them.

On Smoke's lap was a clipboard and a letter he'd scrawled to Steinfeld. He wondered who he could trust to take it . . . so that Witcher wouldn't intercept it. Witcher wouldn't like the last paragraph:

I'm worried about Witcher. Did he ever give you his lecture on World Government and why it's the next step? He has it all worked out, or so he thinks. He doesn't like the SA's notion of a world government. He prefers his own ideas. His personal vision of One World. He doesn't even hint about his part in it. But I think we should both be worried about him.

Smoke tore the sheet off the clipboard and stared at it. Then he tore it into many small pieces and let them drift to the floor.

He sighed. He no longer ached all the time, no longer felt feverish. But he was tired. Needed to rest. After he got out of the hospital, there would be work. There would be no rest for the handful who felt the chill; who acknowledged the shadow of the Eclipse.

The Puerto Rican nurse came in and said, "You want me to turn off the TV? You look tired."

"Yes please. I've lost the remote." He closed his eyes and lay back. "Turn it off."

THE END OF VOLUME TWO

A Song Called Youth
Book Three:
ECLIPSE CORONA

John Shirley

The author wishes to thank the following people for research assistance and other kinds of help, some of it difficult to define: Corby Simpson, William Gibson, Bruce Sterling, Jude "St. Jude" Milhon, and Michelina Shirley

• • •

Blessed is the match consumed in
kindling flame
Blessed is the flame that burns in the
secret fastness of the heart
Blessed is the heart with strength to
stop its beating for honor's sake
Blessed is the match consumed in
kindling flame
—Hanna Szenes,
Jewish Resistance fighter;
written the night before she was
executed by Nazis.

• Prologue •

A tooth in a star.

It looked like a broken tooth; a molar broken off near the jaw. The shattered remains of the Arc de Triomphe in the center of L'Étoile, where the great avenues of Paris come together to form the arms of a star. Men in dirty orange worksuits labored in the Arc's rubble, clearing, preparing, following the terse directions of the engineers and artisans operating out of the little aluminum trailers around the site. The laborers were men with sunken eyes, sallow skin, filthy beards, and the shaky movements of the malnourished. They worked under the unceasing watch of the mirror-helmeted soldiers in black cloth armor who stood guard over them. They worked as men thousands of years before had worked; as the slaves who'd moved stones for the pyramids had worked; as the Bronze Age men who had labored on Stonehenge: without gloves or cybernetic assistance. Hands bled on sharp edges of stone; knees bled from stumbling. There were two bulldozers, in another part of the site, for less delicate clearing, shuddering plastech machines that coughed and hummed. Around the worksite, guns gleamed in the dull sunlight. The Arc would be rebuilt. Or anyway, as one of the engineers had muttered, "A low-rez architectural scan."

The Second Alliance—the twenty-first century's neo-Fascists, operating under cover of a private international police force—had destroyed the Arc after Rickenharp and Yukio captured it for the New Resistance. An overzealous American SA commander with no comprehension of politics or French history had ordered the destruction of the Arc, that day, to get at the NR mice who'd hidden within its crown. To him the Arc was just a big heap of fancy stone used as a refuge for the enemy. That enemy's bones had been found by the workers clearing debris, and tossed in the small-rubble bin.

The truth had been transmitted to the rest of the world through the Grid, the international media network; especially through that part of the Grid called the Internet, with its social media. But now there was an information blackout in SA-held Europe. The French knew what the neo-Fascists told them: The Second Alliance claimed that so-called New Resistance Terrorists had destroyed the Arc de Triomphe. The French mourned the monument, but few asked questions. The destruction was just more of the prevailing madness of the Third World War. There were just too many questions; the answers were one more thing being rationed to the survivors . . .

The Third World War had not been a nuclear war. After a Central Committee coup by KGB hard-liners ended what had been begun by *perestroika* and *glasnost,* the New-Soviets and NATO had squared off over Western Europe. But the New-Soviets lacked the technology and the infrastructure to win; fortunately they also lacked the will—or the irrationality—to choose the nuclear option.

The internal tumult brought on by a war going badly drove the New-Soviet hard-liners into hiding. Under a new Party leadership, the New-Soviet Republic retreated—and surrendered. But not unconditionally. Their vast nuclear arsenal precluded any unconditional surrender. They still remained in control of the NSR and some of the Warsaw Pact countries— though they had lost Poland, Czechoslovakia, Bulgaria and Yugoslavia. They agreed to pay reparations and to open their borders. Their society slid into a ferment of upheaval as reformists with a strong base of military support jockeyed for power.

Nuclear war had been sidestepped. But the conventional war had been devastating enough. And the crypto-Fascists, in the guise of an international police force in place "to keep order" in the chaos behind the lines, had seized the moment. Had put their puppets in place, contrived the illusion of a nationalist movement in a squirming handful of European states; had taken control of France, Spain, Italy, Belgium, Austria, Greece; were seizing the reins in Britain and Germany. "A wave of nationalism sweeping Europe, strangely similar, from nation to nation, in its ideological foundation," one American observer had said. Observers were few in media-darkened Europe, and those few were not permitted to see the pogroms, the European apartheid, the rounding up of Jews and Asians and the dark races; of anyone vocally outraged by the new ghettoism, the new "processing centers."

The Second Alliance's power had foundered in the United States, for the most part, thanks to Jack Brendan Smoke, and other NR activists. But it had consolidated in Europe; was consolidating further, now, through the wonders of technology . . . and psychology. And it was for psychological reasons that the new French Fascists had given priority to reconstructing the Arc.

The Arc de Triomphe was a monument to the ego of Napoleon Bonaparte. It was the embodiment of his power; of the strength of his armies. A concretization of megalomania. On pretext, it was built to honor the French army; in reality, it stood for the ambitions of the man who'd directed that army to conquer Europe. Who had sent hundreds of thousands to their deaths as a sacrifice to his vanity. The Arc was begun in 1806; not completed until 1836. A hundred and sixty-four feet high, a hundred and forty-eight broad, more massive than any other European monument of the time; both florid and martial in its design, like a pompous architectural Goliath wearing both his armor and an effete, intricately embroidered cloak.

It was the symbol of French military might and that made it the symbolic backbone of nationalism; it was irrefutably masculine, structured as solidly as an empire.

There was an irony. It had been, for a while, also the symbol of the New Resistance; an outline of the Arc sewn on the NR flag. But that flag had been rarely seen, and the Fascists had again taken the initiative, retaken the symbol, like land retaken in a battle, co-opted it and, in a way, inverted it for their own use.

The New Resistance would find another symbol. It was about to raise a new banner, a banner neither red nor black, and certainly not the white of surrender. The flag was simply blue. The blue of an open sky.

PARIS, FRANCE. JUNE. DEEP INTO THE TWENTY-FIRST CENTURY.

Dan Torrence knew the look; knew how to wear it. A walk that conserved energy; a hunching over, just a little, with hunger. Not stumbling or belly-gripping but sheltering the hollowness in your stomach, and the weak fire that still burned there, as if you were trying to protect it from going out in the thin rain of this lusterless spring day. It was the camouflage he adopted as he moved slowly but stolidly around the edges of the crowd filling the Place de l'Hôtel de Ville.

He'd seen the look often enough in the last few months; could now simulate it effortlessly. Here it was repeated in the crowd like an expressionist's motif: the distorted posture, the gaunt faces, the pasty skin, the expressions of deep waiting on pallid faces.

He glanced with studied disinterest at the high, ochre insta-mold and raw-wood stage newly set up on the other side of the square, festooned with banners in the colors of the French flag; colors gone dull under the lifeless, aluminum-gray sky. The clouds shrugged out a little rain, and a fitful wind made Torrence hunch deeper into his green plastic slicker. Suddenly, the Marseillaise blared and echoed around the square, pumped from stage speakers as, behind the podium, French soldiers, every one of them Caucasian, in full dress replete with berets, tugged white ropes, to ceremoniously raise an enormous French flag as backdrop for the stage. The flag drooped like a man with a bent back until, pulled taut, it snapped into display as if the man straightened to bare his chest. The crowd reacted with a smattering of applause and a shudder of skeptical muttering. Everyone quietly aware of the forty Second Alliance bulls, the men in soft armor and mirrored helmets, carrying rifles and Recoil Reversal sticks, standing at parade rest, in formation, to either side of the stage . . . They were part of the array, as well as protection for the new president of France . . .

The flag blocked out a large section of the Hôtel de Ville—the City Hall of Paris, in its latest incarnation. Built first in the sixteenth and early seventeenth centuries; burned by the Commune in outrage against the excesses of Napoleon III in the nineteenth century, rebuilt in a foggy imitation of Boccador's somewhat extravagant wedding-cake conception, looking now Victorian and called by the French an example of *Belle Époque*. The Second Alliance had chosen it for this event, Torrence supposed, because it was one of the few intact government buildings left in Paris.

The square had been the Place de Grève until 1830; a place of celebrations and official functions, which sometimes combined when there was an execution. In this square, so Levassier said, Ravaillac, the man who'd assassinated Henry IV, had his dagger hand burned off; his torso torn open with sharp tongs, and the wounds filled with boiling oil. Then, while he still lived, his body was pulled asunder by horses . . . And in this *Place,* other criminals, and supposed criminals, had been "broken on the wheel," their bones crushed by an executioner wielding a heavy bar; others were simply hung or axed or guillotined, events reliably attended by great crowds of the rich and the poor, enjoying the spectacle.

The spectacle had arisen again, like a ghost who returns on lunar cycles. But today there would be no executions. *Except perhaps one execution,* Torrence thought: *Truth,* Smoke would probably say, *will be guillotined here today.*

They raised the instrument of that particular execution: a television monitor big as a movie screen, humming upright on the back of the sound truck parked to the left on the stage. On it, almost immediately, was an image of the Arc de Triomphe, unfurling in pixels like an electronic flag.

Daniel Torrence, whose *nom de guerre* had been Hard-Eyes, looked at the scene through the shutters of apparently hunger-blurred eyes, seeming to see only the podium, the flag, the image of the erstwhile Arc: the symbols. Some other observer behind the shutters of his eyes saw the blank boxes set up to one side of the stage: holographic-shading projectors camouflaged as sound equipment.

And, without looking directly at them, he saw that Danco and Lina Pasolini and Charles Cordenne, looking as drab and inconspicuous as Torrence, were in position in the crowd. They stood at points diametrical to him, facing the stage.

The guards slid the paper-thin antiprojectile styrene into place in front of the stage now; stuff so thin and transparent and glare-resistant you couldn't see it from most angles. It would stop bullets; it wouldn't stop the interference projector hidden under Torrence's rain slicker.

Torrence didn't understand the inner mechanisms of the projector. To him it was a harness of plastic and conductive ceramics, the narrow ceramic cone of the projective nozzle strapped around his upper arm. Switch it on and point your arm and it killed . . .

It killed images. Only images. But the victim was to be the image of a politician, the image a creature with a life of its own; and to destroy it would destroy the politician, in some sense.

Now Louis Cambon, the mayor, was stepping up to the podium. The cameras moved like eels out from their electronic warrens, telescoping sinuously through the air, just a lens on the body of a metal snake. They froze in an almost floral array like stamens around the jowly, balding figure of Cambon, crook-shapes angling back to stare at him. One of them gradually moved farther out, to the brink of the transparent shield, hooking back toward Cambon for a full-face shot, as he intoned the amenities and began his introduction of Larousse, " . . . the elected president of the Republic." Torrence nearly laughed at that.

Someone was cutting a swathe through the crowd, angling toward Torrence: a drunk, wobbling out of kilter with the collective body language. There was nothing much to eat in Paris, except what was tossed off the back of trucks at the relief stations, but somehow there were always determined men who managed to find alcohol, Torrence thought. It was a superhuman talent.

This one wore a long black coat smeared with mud from sleeping in some damp park; his beard was caked gray with filth and his eyes were lost in squint as he bellowed at the stage, *"Voila! Le Maire de Quoi! Le Maire de Quoi!"* The streetside nickname for Cambon: *The Mayor of What?*

The mayor of ruins, came the unspoken reply.

But aloud, there was only a nervous ripple of laughter in response. Cambon didn't pause. None of the SA bulls, in their armor and armament, came to carry the drunk away. Not yet. But other, camouflaged cameras were at work. They'd have him computer-identified already. He was marked. He wouldn't live out the night.

Four men dressed in the white jumpsuit of sanitation workers, here ostensibly to clean up after the crowd (which in any event had nothing to discard), came grinning and chuckling toward the drunk, surrounded him with a semblance of jokey reproach, good-naturedly herding him out of the crowd, slapping him on the back and winking at everyone. Just civic-minded city workers going to take the man home, they told the crowd, get him to his bed, let him sleep it off.

Removing him as casually as wiping a cinder from the eyes. No show of force. That wouldn't do.

But the others, the ones who'd mutter *Maire de Quoi,* only under their breaths, knew the drunk would never be seen again. And they were the ones intended to notice his absence.

The crowd grew, swelled to fill the *Place,* to overflow it. Torrence was now in the midst of the crowd. Cambon was winding up his introduction of Larousse. Torrence hadn't mastered French, but had enough to make out the phrases . . . like the mythical Phoenix leading us out of the ashes . . . the hope of France . . . I present: Frédéric Larousse!"

Ringers planted in the crowd started enthusiastic applause; the others reflexively followed suit.

Larousse and Cambon exchanged hugs, kisses on both cheeks, and then Cambon stepped to the rear and Larousse began to speak, and there it was, the little telltale: when he stepped up to the podium he seemed, impossibly, to come a little more into focus. As if Torrence had just put on a pair of glasses, corrected a nearsightedness. A change in the way Larousse looked, something you wouldn't notice if you hadn't been told about it. You might think: I never noticed before what sheer *presence* the man has . . .

The holographic correction of Larousse's natural image had taken hold. He was transfixed and airbrushed by the hidden projectors, as he pointed to the image of the Arc in the huge screen. "This," he said in French, "is a relic of the past. But it is also a monument to tomorrow. It will arise once more, prouder than its first incarnation, crystallizing an unbroken link to the past. Symbolizing a revitalized future."

Work to rebuild the Arc had already begun. At first, the few opposition voices had grumbled of the waste of manpower and resources that should go to housing and hospitals and obtaining food for the city's legions of homeless; thousands on thousands were living in ruined buildings, in refugee shelters and tent cities, and in the open streets, flotsam on the tide of war.

But Larousse's Unity Party, a descendant of Le Pen's National Front, had shut down the grumblers, had pressed on to rebuilding the Arc de Triomphe. The Foundations of Nationalism needed a symbol grounded in French history.

It wasn't yet rebuilt. British neo-Fascists had crushed it with their Jægernauts, and everyone knew it.

How would they square that contradiction in the minds of the suckers? Torrence wondered.

A moment later, Larousse answered him. " . . . the Communist terrorists, the so-called NR, destroyed the Arc by hijacking Second Alliance demolition devices. Their perfidy has not cast its shadow on the French people, however—it was engineered by the New-Soviets, who connived to undermine our resolve . . . "

Simple as a lie.

Communist terrorists. There were people in the NR, guerrillas who were believers in the true French Republic, who would wax apoplectic hearing themselves called Communists. There were Communists in the NR; there were also anarchists, Libertarians, Christian Democrats, and every manner of conservative.

Torrence watched Larousse and felt it himself: a subtle summoning, a tug at his identity. Something about Larousse, something in his cadence, his gestures, his visual presence—something manufactured by the mind-control program designing the holographic enhancements of his image—that something called out to a visceral need to *belong*. To trust and follow and rage with him at the racial injustice that had slung chaos and poverty on all of them . . .

Torrence had to look away. But he knew his cues: he raised his arms with the crowd, which was now swept up in genuine enthusiasm that needed no ringers, and he chanted, *"Pour la France!"* with the others when Larousse gave out with some particularly stirring phrase. But he kept his eyes focused elsewhere. He waited for the signal.

• • •

Colonel Watson and Dr. Cooper walked down the chilly, antiquated hallway of the Hôtel de Ville, and stepped into the Administrative Media Room. Watson had found the ornate interior of the other rooms overbearing; this stripped-down, utilitarian nerve center was a bit of a relief. There was no insolent historical presence here. Its ceramic-white consoles, unfailingly steady TV monitors, and humming mainframes were a kind of electronic continuity for Watson, a connection to the nascent Empire that was his dream and his life.

Watson, head of the Second Alliance's European operations, was a tall, bulky Englishman in late middle age, florid and balding but energetic, his movements as brisk and crisp as his flat-black SA uniform, his demeanor authoritatively cheerful, the upbeat of a calculated achiever . . .

The milk-haired Cooper was a droopy, pallid contrast: a slender, thirtyish albino, by turns dyspeptic and then feverishly animated, wearing a dun Tech's uniform: a rumpled, stained short-sleeve outfit at least half a size too big for him.

Watson firmly believed that poor tailoring bespoke the inner man. The two men bore their mutual dislike like a yoke when they walked together: stiffly cooperating but laboring under it.

Watson visibly unbent as he moved away from Cooper, shaking hands with the security chief, Klaus, the other techs and officers working at the consoles; accepting a cup of tea in a Dutch-china cup, exclaiming over it, exchanging banter, backslaps, and the changeless one-liners. "Welcome back, Colonel! Couldn't bear that Italian food, or did those wop rosies tire you out?"

"I exhausted that lot weeks ago, Chas!"

Cooper watched this display of spurious *bonhomie* with clinical detachment until at last Watson handed his empty tea cup to an orderly and returned, his smile fading. "Right, Dr. Cooper. What's the status?"

Watson was fresh from the armored limo that brought him from Orly.

He'd flown in from Sicily, where he'd been weeks overseeing the new security measures on the rebuilt SA Communications Center and Central European Headquarters. He was out of touch with developments here. Klaus, Spengler, and the Board had approved the testing of Larousse's public-image modifications. But Watson was skeptical.

"It's worked out lovely in Rome with Serro," Cooper was saying, lacing his bone-white fingers over his crotch; lacing and unlacing them again. "And you can see we're getting a crowd response in the upper seventies-plus for Larousse."

Watson glanced at the crowd-response readout. The graph jiggled up and down as the readings vacillated, but it never went below seventy-five. "Short-term success is very heartening, but sustaining it, especially with the vulnerability to sabotage . . . " Watson took a deep breath as if preparing for an overwhelming task.

"Well, Klaus thinks he's got any open ends for sabotage quite under wraps," Cooper said, fluttering his hands at the security-cam monitors. "And as for long-term responses . . . Colonel, a crowd, once it's primed, will react consistently. A crowd is an entity unto itself, don't you know, especially one this big. It has, well, a general mood to it, a, ah, collective attitude." Cooper's stare slipped into the middle distance; he rocked on his feet, riding one of his enthusiasms. "There are streaks of dissent, but most especially a crowd which has come to see someone for patriotic reasons is a trainable entity. You understand, we're monitoring the crowd responses on a nanodigital grid, unit-by-unit. We're literally missing nothing. Every twitch of a muscle in their faces; every blink—and blinks are very significant, don't you know; every shrug, every glaze of an eye, every modulation of tone and throat clearing. We wrap it up into the Receptivity Signals Factor and it is simply a very consistent output—especially with RSF Enhancement."

"People in a crowd often act as they're expected to," Watson objected, "not as they really feel."

"It's how they *really* feel I'm talking about," Cooper said, flicking dust from a console with a finger that, if you didn't look closely, seemed white-gloved. "I barely touched on the signals we monitor. Body-heat levels, exhalation rate, body language in forty-two modalities, bioelectric fields collective and individual, perspiration and the hormone traces in its evaporation—that's one of our very best indicators. We're really quite thorough." His tone carried a dry dash of rebuke.

"The cost just doesn't justify the potential, to my mind," Watson said.

"It saves money in the long-run." Cooper's voice was becoming a little shrill. He blinked rather frequently in his closeted anger, as if he were personally modeling a Response Factor. "Saves money, don't you see, because it predicts changes in public mood and allows us to suppress or manipulate them before they become militarily costly. The RSF monitor models out the sum total of the RSF factors and does a ninety-eight percent sociological/sociobiological projection." He sniffed. "We anticipate the crowd's mood swings—and by extension the public mood swings—well before they come to fruition."

Watson knew the general principle. Certain RSF readings correspond to strong latent desires in a crowd. To the desire for expression of hostility against outsiders; to the desire for a ritual of racial unification (which might be as simple as a group salute to the flag); the desire for group violence; the desire for reassurance by an appeal to sentimentalism; the desire for paternalistic reassurance; a volatile range of suppressed and psychologically encrypted needs.

Decrypted, RSF readings could warn the speaker, through implants or hidden headsets, when he's gone too far, if he's not energetic enough, if he's said the wrong thing—even before the crowd had seemed to react at all. Cued second-to-second, he's got the edge, time to compensate, say just the right thing to bring the audience back under control, this right thing calculated by a computer interfaced with "human resource specimens": high-level speechwriters pressed into service for the Second Alliance, maintained in semiconsciousness, extractors working in their brains to add the human creativity factor to the computer's notion of charismatic speaking—the computers having analyzed thousands of speeches, correlating crowd reactions.

Larousse was the focus of all this, a dancer on unseen puppet strings. His public appearance was holographically altered, a thin veneer of image superimposed on the real Larousse, or more precisely on his bioelectric field, an image reconstituting, according to computer models and sociological studies, the look and mannerisms of the idealized French Nationalist leader. Instant charisma.

Watson shook his head. "Surely when he moves he'll go out of phase."

Cooper sighed theatrically and led Watson to a large screen on the opposite wall; he thumbed a tab, and Larousse's profile fizzed onto the screen. Larousse was describing France as a great tree, an ancient and primeval tree that reached up into the heavens. But parasites, vines, and insects were sapping the tree's strength, cutting off the flow of its vitality at the roots. And it is at the roots that this disease must be stopped . . .

"His movement cues," Cooper said wearily, "are given to him via small metal nodes implanted just under his skin. They cue him with tiny impulses, little jolts of sensation timed a millisecond ahead. At first his response to this, his movements, were jerky, unnatural, imprecise, but we made it a matter of life and death for him to respond smoothly, and after a few weeks of training it became second nature. It's all in the head, you know, the attitude. With our enhancement, right down to voice shaping, he's quite irresistible. I'm overcome by him myself now, when I listen, don't you know . . . " Cooper smiled thinly; his almost colorless lips vanished. "He's come to enjoy it, rather. He imagines it's all his own invention, the Larousse persona . . . And he's quite disoriented when we take him off the cues. That's all backstage, of course . . . It's essentially a new stage of 'virtual reality' technology . . . "

"It would seem simpler just to project a holo onto the stage and animate that—"

"They just don't look real enough. And he can't always be appearing on television, not exclusively. There's something about the physical presence of a man, maybe even something . . . " Cooper broke off, frowning. Stopping short of suggesting a psychic connection. Crandall didn't approve: psychic phenomena was the province of demonology.

But Watson knew what he meant. Hitler had been effective in newsreels and would have been effective on television. But for the core of their movement, they needed to get in touch with something animal, something tribal, atavistic, at the heart of the best fascism. And that required physical presence from time to time, however dressed up it might be. "And the cameras are filtered against telltale holo shifts?"

Cooper had had enough. He turned sharply to Watson, snapped, "Ask your man Klaus. He's made quite sure of every bloody detail. If you'll excuse me . . . " And did his best to stride in manful outrage from the room.

Watson snorted as Klaus walked up, chuckling, looking after Cooper. Klaus was a bigger man than Watson, even massively muscled, his hair cut flattop, his short black beard clipped with equal geometric severity, his eyes onyx glittery. He wore the jet uniform of Security staff, and on his shoulder the chrome insignia of its chief: A Christian cross topped with an eye.

Klaus was effectively the second most powerful man in the European Second Alliance. Not that, at this point, there was any single publicly defined leader . . . except for Crandall. And Crandall, though he made daily appearances, was quite dead. His death was something few people knew about.

"I'm afraid Dr. Cooper feels I've been breathing down his neck," Klaus said. "But there are so many ways this . . . this false presentation could go wrong. I feel the same way about it as—"

Watson raised a hand for silence, glancing at the techs at their control consoles, then turned to go into the conference room. Klaus followed. Watson shut the door behind them. The room was soundproofed and, except for a table and chairs and a blank comm stack, almost featureless.

They sat at the table facing the door, and Klaus went on, "I don't like it either. It's not—It seems so clumsy, so indirect, manipulating people this way."

Watson nodded. "One would think the cleverer thing to do would be to find a natural charismatic, train him, and set him up. In a sense, he'd already have all the necessary software . . . "

"The Committee is very high on Cooper. They want to plug this thing into the Grid eventually. And in a way, it works with Crandall. He's a Larousse without the warm body beneath the image."

"Larousse worries me. A holographic, computerized persona is just too fragile in a public place."

"Mmm . . . Do you want to see this afternoon's transmission? 'Crandall' was quite impressive." Klaus opened the table controls and punched in the code. One of the screens blinked on showing Rick Crandall, midway through this afternoon's "little talk with my friends and neighbors."

Crandall smiled out at them, his gaunt, Lincolnesque features faintly numinous with some inner light, and said, "I'm convinced the Good Lord wanted us out of North America for a very sound reason. Same reason he wanted the Israelites out of Egypt. To escape the unclean, the persecutors. We're going back to the roots of the Aryan race, to drink from the wellsprings of our genetic heritage. It's an Exodus of renewal. We are the true Israelites—those cast out from Israel, falsely replaced by the vermin who occupies that land now, the Jew. The difference between the Jew and the True Israelite should be obvious to anyone not blinded by the Zionist conspiracy. As some of you know, my research indicates that the true Israelite in fact originated in the mountains of Austria . . . "

Watson shook his head in quiet amazement. Crandall was, of course, quite dead. Assassinated. But only a handful of people knew it. They had re-created him as a holographic computer program—and since it said whatever Watson and Klaus wanted it to say, it was the ideal leader.

"The program's wandering a bit in its logic," Watson said with approval. "That's uncannily like Crandall. His way of almost seeming to make sense, weaving that gloriously superficial illusion in logic . . . "

Klaus glanced at him. "You do not believe the origin of the Great Race is Austrian? That the Jews are impostors?"

Watson suppressed a smile. "Oh, I have no doubt of it. I'm just very pleased we've re-created such a lifelike Crandall . . . The animation is flawless and the charisma is there, too. Perhaps that vindicates Cooper, goes to show just how very artificial charisma is . . . How did the staff react to this little presentation?"

"Warmly. It was like liquor for them."

"Good." Watson struck the table with the flat of his hand, a sign he'd made a decision. "Right. We'll give Cooper's latest project a bit of a chance, and if it doesn't work out, 'Crandall' will have every excuse to can the program." Watson sighed happily. "It's such a relief to have the little bastard's ghost working for me . . . " He was aware of the pressure of Klaus's gaze, and turned to him, adding quickly, "And for you, of course, Klaus."

• • •

The crowd was like a hysterically happy dog greeting its long-lost master, as Larousse thundered into the climax of his speech. The enormous screen beside the stage flashed through fabricated images of a reconstructed France, intercut with .005-second subliminal flashes of Larousse himself holding in his arms a baby wrapped in a French flag, shots of Larousse offering the viewers food, money, love.

"The purification of the French race means the survival and the *triumph* of the French race!" Larousse boomed. Each syllable masterfully timed, masterfully intoned. Torrence again had to fight himself, feeling the mob immersion in the Fascist fantasy sweep over him like a drug-rush. The man had, literally, an aurora, a faint divine shimmer, almost unseeable . . .

Everyone in the crowd reaching out to Larousse as if in invocation . . .

Torrence looked away and put a hand into his left sleeve, pressed the activation stud strapped to his forearm. It sent a signal to Danco and Cordenne and Pasolini. Together, at four widely separate points in the crowd, they raised their arms as if joining in the adulation, reaching imploringly to the distant figure of Larousse, and the harnesses began to transmit.

• • •

"And how is our Anomalous Crowd Movement?" Watson asked as he stepped up behind Klaus, who was seated at the main security console.

Not taking his eyes from the screen, Klaus said, "They haven't moved, Colonel. Four of them, almost symmetrical, rooted to the spot while the crowd shifts around them. They picked their positions and stayed in place. It's as if someone painted the footprints for them to stand in. RSFM projects sixty-eight-percent probability of a planned disruption from those four. Smaller possibility of an assassination attempt. "

"Larousse is shielded against rocket launchers, grenades, hoverbirds, all that sort of thing, is he? As well as bullets?"

"He is. And the NR knows it . . . Ah, there we are. Our people are moving in."

• • •

There was so far no effect on Larousse's image. The harnesses would try a broad range of frequencies. To try to disrupt it, try to make it ripple and warp so the crowd would see him as a fake. An agitprop attack. So far the SA's filters held. It could take time.

But the time was past. Torrence saw the men in white, the "sanitation workers," moving toward him, elbowing expertly through the crowd, this time carrying RR sticks. And SA bulls in full armor moving in around the edges. Other figures in white moving toward Danco, Cordenne, Pasolini.

It was all over. *Blown.*

Torrence reached into his sleeve, hit the stud, signaling the others: *Get out.*

He didn't wait around to see what became of them. As of this moment, they were on their own. He turned and plunged into the crowd, recklessly violent, trying to create a stumbling block of turmoil in his wake. He jabbed ribs and stomped insteps and tripped people; they shouted at him, cuffed him as he passed, but no one took their eyes from Larousse for long.

The men in white came steadily on, slowing but never getting entangled, like antibodies searching him out. Torrence pulled the slicker off over his head, stumbling once doing it, nearly falling, catching himself. He fumbled for the plastic suction grenades on his bandolier as he reached the edge of the crowd and plunged into the street, sprinting for the Metro station. It was boarded up, the Metro was defunct, but some of the tunnels had been selectively unblocked by the NR.

An SA bull loomed up, running ponderously to cut him off at the corner, his mirrored helmet flashing dull silver with the afternoon light, his amplified American voice booming and bouncing, "STOP OR YOU'RE DEAD MEAT!" The last word echoing: *MEAT-EAT-EAT.* Torrence sailed the flat disc of the suction grenade at the bull, like a miniature discus. It hit the Fascist soldier in the chest and sucked itself flat against his armored sternum, whirring as it drilled with its tiny iridium-tipped drills. The SA bull shrieked, "FUCK *NO!*" Echoing *NO-WOH-WOHHHHH . . .*

As the drills dug through and the grenade charge went off with a muted *whumpf,* driving its drill bits into skin and flesh and bones so that blood sprayed around the disc's flat edges . . .

Torrence heard another explosion, much louder than it should have been; he glanced over his shoulder and saw that the Pasolini woman had tossed a couple of standard grenades into the crowd—*oh, god*—and people were screaming . . .

Damn her damn her damn her damn her.

He saw Cordenne running along the fringe of the crowd, heard gunfire spurt, Cordenne's gut erupting red as he went skidding into his own puddle, giving out a sort of sobbing laughter.

Torrence glimpsed a silvery whirring out of the corner of his eyes not far overhead: a bird's eye, a small thing of featherlight metal and glass, flashing on plastech wings to follow him. He imagined the image of himself—a small, desperate, fugitive figure—transmitted to some Security Center TV monitor. The boarded-over Metro was just ahead (bullets spat chips of street asphalt at his ankles) and the bird wouldn't follow him down into the metro station because it wouldn't be able to transmit from underground.

Bullets whined past his ear as he reached the seemingly boarded-over Metro, felt the soft warmth of an aiming-laser kiss the back of his neck. And as he dove through the paper of the false-boards the NR had left here, submachine-gun rounds parted the air where he'd been a half second before.

He slipped in his rush, fell down the stairs of the subway station—striking heavily on his shoulder, cursing with the pain, somersaulting down the steps quite without control, nose bloodying, lip splitting on concrete edges.

Up, instantly, at the trash heap on the bottom of the stairs. Up and running into darkness. Because it was get up and move, or die.

Running into darkness, thinking: *That fool Pasolini played right into their hands . . .*

• • •

"Did you get that clearly?" Watson said. "The NR operative—the woman—tossing a grenade into the crowd?"

"We got it," Klaus said.

"Let them try to pretend they're not terrorists when we get that about!"

"Here's the fourth one . . . He looks familiar . . . "

Klaus tapped the keyboard, the image on the screen zoomed: a compact man with dark hair; a Spaniard probably, though not dark enough to evoke notice in the crowd.

"That's the Spanish fellow," Watson said. "We haven't got a name for him."

His name was Danco.

They watched the monitor. On it, Danco struggled in the grip of four men in white jumpsuits, who were dragging him to the building. The New Resistance guerilla thrashed like a worm on hot stone, Watson thought.

The Spaniard bellowing something. Watson caught a few words, " . . . Cowards if you don't kill me . . . spineless cocksuckers!"

Danco was trying to provoke them into killing him, of course. Knowing the extractor would pick his brain; knowing there was simply no way to resist an extractor.

Klaus reached for a toggle, spoke into his headset, "San Simon, get down there and tell them to search him before they—" And then he swore in German.

Danco had wrenched an arm loose, found the explosives strapped under his slicker. Klaus shouted, "No, no, you idiots, get it away from him, don't run—we need him—!"

But they'd instinctively flung themselves away as Danco thumbed the detonator on the plastique, a cylinder no bigger than a perfume bottle that exploded into a fireball, engulfing Danco and the SA bull running up to him and two of the unarmored security men . . .

"Bloody hell!" Watson burst out.

Danco was reduced to pulp, the second one would be too long dead to extract, and two others had so far gotten away . . .

"We need to wire those tunnels," Klaus murmured.

"Yes, obviously, naturally, but there are miles of them. And it could cause whole streets to collapse if we blow them. Move over, please."

Klaus stood, and Watson sat down at the console, feeling as if he'd drunk a gallon of espresso, his pulse racing with fury and frustration. He ran back the images of the two who'd gotten away. They had a clear shot of the woman. But the man was harder. Every angle was half blocked by someone, or he'd been turning the wrong way. There—when he looked back over his shoulder, after the grenade went off in the crowd—a grainy shot of his face. Rather too much range for the cameras . . . He seemed to be missing most of an ear . . .

Watson punched for computer enhancement and magnification. The image rezzed onto the screen. A man's face. A strong, simple, sharply chiseled face. Eyes with an almost psychotic intensity. Maybe that was just the fear, the danger. Still, Watson shivered with a faint sense of déjà vu. He'd looked at that face before . . . and not in a glossy CIA file photo. He'd seen it somewhere digitally, like this. Where?

He punched for a facial match-up search in the videofile. On a hunch, he specified May 12. The evening of the Le Pen assassination . . .

Watson remembered it with toothache clarity . . .

The Palace of Versailles. The fantasy of the Sun King. The embodiment of absolutist royal power. The austere and vast chateau to the west of Paris, its fanatically symmetrical array of gardens now overgrown and pocked with shell holes; the North Wing partly caved in. The South Wing, though, mostly intact.

Le Pen had weathered criticism from the neo-Fascist ranks for making Versailles his base of operations. It was not a state building, it was just a vast, oversized museum. A monument to Louis XIV's aloofness; his disdain for the stinking, starving masses of the great city. But Le Pen's intent was obvious to the man on the street; the symbolism shone like fireworks in the sky: imperial power was returned. Kings had been chosen by bloodline, and genetics was the axis of power in the new state.

Le Pen began holding televised nationalist fêtes in the South Wing, and for the latest had arranged to bus a thousand white middle-class Parisians—returned to Paris at the announcement of the war's end—to the dowdy grounds of Versailles. They waited for him lined up to either side of the formal walkway approaching the Petites Écuries; a shield stood between the crowd and the walkway where Le Pen was expected. The impenetrable transparent plastic shield had been erected in a tunnel shape from the entryway out to the podium in the gardens where Le Pen was to speak. He was always thoroughly protected. And with equal thoroughness he had directed that the carvings over the arch of the Petites Ecuries be restored for the occasion: the masterpiece by François Girardon, *Alexander Taming His Charger Bucephalus.* Alexander the Great (Alexander the unapologetic tyrant!) astride the raging horse, with two trained chargers holding the rebellious mount to the course. The damage from the war to Versailles was relatively minor: the breast of Bucephalus had been cracked, was partly fallen.

A team of workers from Paris had seamlessly replaced the horse's chest with a clever cosmetic plaster, tinted to suggest age. The repair was complete when the president of Fascist France, Jean Le Pen, grandson of the founding father of the Front National, stepped out of the entry between the cheering crowds . . . The crowds waved and shouted on the other side of the temporary plastic shielding . . . Le Pen took one long stride toward the podium, where he was to announce the formation of the Unity Party and its alliance with SPOES, the Self-Policing Organization of European States . . .

And the breast of Bucephalus burst open. A stream of Teflon-coated bullets ripped through Le Pen and his bodyguards and his minister of defense.

Le Pen had been killed by a small, remote-controlled machine-pistol lovingly hidden in the ornate carvings over the archway of the entry to the Petites Écuries rotunda. Hidden there by NR operatives two days before. They'd waylaid the repair crew and taken their places. The plaster over the barrel of the gun was paper-thin.

Now, Watson ran the video of the assassination, again and again, zooming in for crowd close-ups. They'd rounded up everyone in the crowd, or so they thought, debriefed them all, extracted them one by one: they found two Jews pretending to be gentiles, and sent them to the "Processing Centers." But they found not one NR operative, not one assassin. Well, someone could easily have slipped away from the crowd in all the confusion after the shooting.

He scanned the faces, not sure what he was looking for. And then saw him. Half turned away. His hands in his pockets, perhaps activating the remote control on the weapon hidden in the sculpture . . . If you didn't look closely at the eyes, the assassin looked vacuous, smiling vaguely, happily confused. Putting on the expression of a starved half-wit. His eyes, though, didn't match the rest of the expression. They were focused, intent, predatory.

It was *him!* Missing most of an ear, the man in the Larousse crowd just now. The one who'd gotten away in the Metro tunnel (Gotten away? There were still soldiers in pursuit, combing the tunnels. But he'd have his escape route carefully planned, so yes: Gotten away.)

A cross-check with CIA files told Watson the subject was a man marked by the CIA for termination with extreme prejudice. A terrorist.

One Daniel Torrence. Aka "Hard-Eyes."

"You filthy little rotter," Watson said softly, staring at the man on the screen. "You buggering bastard. You stinking little turd Jew. You ugly little wog. You're the target now, fancy boy. You're it. You especially. *We're coming after you, Danny boy!*"

• 02 •

Los Angeles, California.

Nine a.m., and Jerome-X wanted a smoke. He didn't smoke, but he wanted one in here, and he could see how people went into prison non-smokers and came out doing two packs a day. Maybe had to get their brains rewired to get off it. Which was ugly, he'd been rewired once to get ofs Sink, synthetic cocaine, and he'd felt like a processor with a glitch for a month after that.

He pictured his thoughts like a little train, zipping around the cigarette-burnt graffiti: "YOU FUCKED NOW" and "GASMAN WUZZERE" and "GASMAN IS AN IDIOT-MO." The words were stippled on the dull pink ceiling in umber burn spots. Jerome wondered who GASMAN was and what they'd put him in prison for.

He yawned. He hadn't slept much the night before. It took a long time to learn to sleep in prison. He wished he'd upgraded his chip so he could use it to activate his sleep endorphins. But that was a grade above what he'd been able to afford—and way above the kind of brain chips he'd been dealing. He wished he could turn off the light panel, but it was sealed in.

There was a toilet and a broken water fountain in the cell. There were also a few bunks, but he was alone in this static place of watery blue light and faint pink distances. The walls were salmon-colored garbage blocks. The words singed into the ceiling were blurred and impotent.

• • •

Almost noon, his stomach rumbling, Jerome was still lying on his back on the top bunk when the trashcan said, "Eric Wexler, re-ma-a-in on your bunk while the ne-ew prisoner ente-e-ers the cell!"

Wexler? Oh, yeah. They thought his name was Wexler. The fake ID program.

He heard the cell door slide open; he looked over, saw the trashcan ushering a stocky Chicano guy into lockup. The robot everyone called "the trashcan" was a stumpy metal cylinder with a group of camera lenses, a retractable plastic arm, and a gun muzzle that could fire a Taser charge, rubber bullets, tear-gas pellets, or .45-caliber rounds. It was supposed to use the .45 only in extreme situations, but the robot was battered, it whined when it moved, its digital voice was warped. When they got like that, Jerome had heard, you didn't fuck with them; they'd mix up the rubber bullets with the .45-caliber, Russian Roulette style.

The door sucked itself shut, the trashcan whined away down the hall, its rubber wheels squeaking once with every revolution. Jerome heard a tinny cymbal crash as someone, maybe trying to get it to shoot at a guy in the next cell, threw a tray at it; followed by some echoey human shouting and a distorted admonishment from the trashcan. The Chicano was still standing by the plexigate, hands shoved in his pockets, staring at Jerome, looking like he was trying to place him.

"'Sappenin'," Jerome said, sitting up on the bed. He was grateful for the break in the monotony.

"*Qué pasa?* You like the top bunk, huh? Tha's good."

"I can read the ceiling better from up here. About ten seconds' worth of reading matter. It's all I got. You can have the lower bunk."

"You fuckin'-A I can." But there was no real aggression in his tone. Jerome thought about turning on his chip, checking the guy's subliminals, his somatic signals, going for a model of probable-aggression index; or maybe project for deception. He could be an undercover cop: Jerome hadn't given them his dealer, hadn't bargained at all.

But he decided against switching the chip on. Some jails had scanners for unauthorized chip output. Better not use it unless he had to. And his gut told him this guy was only a threat if he felt threatened. His gut was right almost as often as his brain chip.

The Chicano was maybe five foot six, a good five inches shorter than Jerome but probably outweighing him by fifty pounds. His face had Indian angles and small jet eyes. He was wearing printout gray-blue prison jams, #6631; they'd let him keep his hairnet. Jerome had never understood the Chicano hairnet, never had the balls to ask about it.

Jerome was pleased. He liked to be recognized, except by people who could arrest him.

"You put your hands in the pockets of those paper pants, they'll rip, and in LA County they don't give you any more for three days," Jerome advised him.

"Yeah? Shit." The Chicano took his hands carefully out of his pockets. "I don't want my cojones hanging out, people think I'm advertising—they some big fucking cojones, too. You not a faggot, right?"

"Nope."

"Good. How come I know you? When I *don't* know you."

Jerome grinned. "From television. You saw my tag. Jerome-X. I mean—I do some music too. I had that song, 'Six Kinds of Darkness'—"

"I don't know that, bro—oh wait, Jerome-X. The tag—I saw that. Your face-tag. You got one of those little transers? Interrupt the transmissions with your own shit?"

"Had. They confiscated it."

"That why you here? Video graffiti?"

"I wish. I'd be out in a couple months. No. Illegal augs."

"Hey, man! Me too!"

"You?" Jerome couldn't conceal his surprise. You didn't see a lot of barrio dudes doing illegal augmentation. They generally didn't like people tinkering in their brains.

"What, you think a guy from East LA can't use augs?"

"No, no. I know lots of Latino guys that use it," Jerome lied.

"Ooooh, he says *Latino*, that gotta nice sound." Overtones of danger.

Jerome hastily changed the direction of the conversation. "You never been in the big lockups where they use these fuckin' paper jammies?"

"No, just the city jail once. They didn't have those motherfucking screw machines either. Hey, you're Jerome—my name's Jessie. Actually, it's Jesus"—he pronounced it "heh-soos"—"but people they, you know . . . You got any smokes? No? Shit. Okay, I adjust. I get use to it. Shit. No smokes. Fuck."

He sat on the edge of the bed, to one side of Jerome's dangling legs, and tilted his head forward. He reached under his hairnet, and under what turned out to be a hairpiece, and pulled a chip from a jack unit set into the base of his skull.

Jerome stared. "Goddamn, their probes really are busted."

Jessie frowned over the chip. There was a little blood on it. The jack unit was leaking. Cheap installation. "No, they ain't busted, there's a guy working on the probe, he's paid off, he's letting everyone through for a couple of days because of some Russian mob guys coming in, he don't know which ones they are. Some of them Russian mob guys got the augments."

"I thought sure they were going to find my unit," Jerome said. "The strip search didn't find it, but I thought the prison probes would and that'd be another year on my sentence. But they didn't."

Neither one of them thinking of throwing away the chips. It'd be like cutting out an eye.

"Same story here, bro. We both lucky."

Jessie put the microprocessing chip in his mouth, the way people did with their contact lenses, to clean it, lubricate it. Of course, bacterially speaking, it came out dirtier than it went in.

"Does the jack hurt?" Jerome asked.

Jessie took the chip out, looked at it a moment on his fingertips. It was smaller than a contact lens, a sliver of silicon and non-osmotic gallium arsenide and transparent interface-membrane, with, probably, 800,000,000 nanotransistors of engineered protein molecules sunk into it, maybe more. "No, it don't hurt yet. But if it's leaking, it fuckin' *will* hurt, man." He said something else in Spanish, shaking his head. He slipped the chip back into his jack-in unit and tapped it with the thumbnail of his right hand. So that was where the activation mouse was: under the thumbnail. Jerome's was in a knuckle.

Jessie rocked slightly, just once, sitting up on his bunk, which meant the chip had engaged and he was getting a readout. They tended to feed back into your nervous system a little at first, make you twitch once or twice; if they weren't properly insulated, they could make you crap your pants.

"That's okay," Jessie said, relaxing. "That's better." The chip inducing his brain to secrete vasopressin, contract the veins, simulate the effect of nicotine. It worked for a while, till you could get cigarettes. High-grade chip could do some numbing if you were hung up on Sim, synthetic morphine, and couldn't get any. But that was Big Scary. You could turn yourself off for good that way. You better be doing some damn fine adjusting.

Jerome thought about the hypothetical chip scanners. Maybe he should object to the guy using his chip here. But what the Chicano was doing wouldn't make for much leakage.

"What you got?" Jerome asked.

"I got an Apple NanoMind II. Big gigas. What you got?"

"You got the Mercedes, I got the Toyota. I got a Seso Picante Mark I. One of those Argentine things." (How had this guy scored an ANM II?)

"Yeah, what you got, they kinda basic, but they do most what you need. Hey, our names, they both start with *J*. And we both here for illegal augs. What else we got in common. What's your sign?"

"Uh—" What was it, anyway? He always forgot. "Pisces, I think."

"No shit! I can relate to Pisces. I ran an astrology program, figured out who I should hang with. Pisces is okay. But Aquarius is—I'm a Scorpio, like—Aquarius, *qué bueno*."

What did he mean exactly, *hang with*, Jerome wondered. Scoping me about am *I* a faggot, maybe that was something defensive.

But he meant something else. "You know somethin', Jerome, you got your chip, too, we could do a link and maybe get over on that trashcan."

Break out? Jerome felt a chilled thrill go through him. "Link with that thing? Control it? I don't think the two of us would be enough."

"We need some more guys maybe, but I got news, Jerome, there's more comin'. Maybe their names all start with *J*. You know, I mean—in a way."

In quick succession, the trashcan brought their cell three more guests; a fortyish beach bum named Eddie, a cadaverous black dude named Bones, a queen called Swish, whose real name according to the trashcan, was Paul Torino.

"This place smells like it's comin' apart," Eddie said. He had a surfer's greasy blond topknot and all the usual Surf Punk tattoos. Meaningless now, Jerome thought, the pollution-derived oxidation of the offshore had pretty much ended surfing. The anaerobics had taken over the surf, in North America, thriving in the toxic waters like a gelatinous Sargasso. If you surfed you did it with an antitoxin suit and a gas mask. "Smells in here like somethin' died and didn't go to heaven. Stinks worse'n Malibu."

"It's those landfill blocks," Bones said. He was missing three front teeth, and his sunken face was like something out of a zombie video. But he was an energetic zombie, pacing back and forth as he spoke. "Compressed garbage," he told Eddie. "Organic stuff mixed with the polymers, the plastics, whatever was in the trash heap, make 'em into bricks 'cause they run outta landfill, but after a while, if the contractor didn't get 'em to set right, y'know, they start to rot. It's hot outside is why you're gettin' it now. Use garbage to cage garbage, they say. Fucking assholes."

• • •

The trashcan pushed a rack of trays up to the Plexiglas bars and whirred their lunch to them, tray-by-tray. The robot gave them an extra tray. It was screwing up.

They ate their chicken patties—the chicken was almost greaseless, gristleless, which meant it was vat chicken, genetically engineered fleshstuff—and between bites they bitched about the food and indulged the usual paranoid speculation about mind-control chemicals in the coffee.

Jerome looked around at the others, thinking: at least they're not ass-kickers.

They were crammed here because of the illegal augs sweep, some political drive to clean up the clinics, maybe to see to it that the legal augmentation companies kept their pit-bull grip on the industry. So there wasn't anybody in for homicide, for gang torture, or anything. No major psychopaths. Not a bad cell to be in.

"You Jerome-X, really?" Swish fluted. She (Jerome always thought of a queen as she and her, out of respect for the tilt of her consciousness) was probably Filipino; had her face girled up at a cheap clinic. Cheeks built up for a heart shape, eyes rounded, lips filled out, tits looking like there was a couple of tin funnels under her jammies. Some of the collagen they'd injected to fill out her lips had shifted its bulk so her lower lip was lopsided. One cheekbone was a little higher than the other. A karmic revenge on at least some of malekind, Jerome thought, for forcing women into girdles and footbinding and anorexia. What did this creature use her chip for, besides getting high?

"Oooh, Jerome-X! I saw your tag before on the TV. The one when your face kind of floated around the president's head and some printout words came out of your mouth and blocked her face out. God, she's such a *cunt*."

"What words did he block her out with?" Eddie asked.

"I think . . . 'Would you know a liar if you heard one anymore?' That's what it was!" Swish said. "It was sooo perfect, because that cunt wanted that war to go on forever, you *know* she did. And she lies about it, ooh *God* she lies."

"You just think she's a cunt because you *want* one," Eddie said, dropping his pants to use the toilet. He talked loudly to cover up the noise of it. "You want one and you can't afford it. I think the Prez was right, the fucking Mexican People's Republic is jammin' our borders, sending commie agents in—"

Swish said, "Oh, God, he's a Surf Nazi—But God yes, I want one—I want *her* cunt. That bitch doesn't know how to use it anyway. Honey, I know how I'd use that thing—" Swish stopped abruptly and shivered, hugged herself. Using her long purple nails, she reached up and pried loose a flap of skin behind her ear, plucked out her chip. She wet it, adjusted its feed mode, put it back in, tapping it with the activation mouse under a nail.

She pressed the flap shut. Her eyes glazed as she adjusted. She could get high on the chip-impulses for maybe twenty-four hours and then it'd kill her. She'd have to go cold turkey or die. Or get out. And maybe she'd been doing it for a while now . . .

None of them would be allowed to post bail. They'd each get the two years mandatory minimum sentence. Illegal augs, the feds thought, were getting out of hand. Black-market chip implants were good for playing havoc with the state database lottery; used by bookies of all kinds; used to keep accounts where the IRS couldn't find them unless they cornered you physically and broke your code; the aug chips were used to out-think banking computers, and for spiking cash machines; used to milk the body, prod the brain into authorizing the secretion of betaendorphins and ACTH and adrenaline and testosterone and other biochemical toys; used to figure the odds at casinos; used to compute the specs for homemade designer drugs; used by the mob's street dons to play strategy and tactics; used by the kid gangs for the same reasons; used for illegal congregations on the Plateau.

It was the Plateau, Jerome thought, that really scared the shit out of the feds. It had possibilities.

It was way beyond the fucking Internet. It was even beyond the Grid.

• • •

The trashcan dragged in a cot for the extra man, shoved it folded under the door, and blared, "Lights out, all inmates are required to be i-i-in their bu-unks-s-s . . . " Its voice was failing.

After the trashcan and the light had gone, they climbed off their bunks and sat hunkered in a circle on the floor.

They were on chips, but not transmission-linked to one another. Jacked-up on the chips, they communicated in a spoken shorthand.

"Bull," Bones was saying. "Door." He was a voice in the darkness; a scarecrow of shadow.

"Time," Jessie said.

"Compatibility? Know?" Eddie said.

Jerome said, "Noshee!" Snorts of laughter from the others.

"Link check," Bones said.

"Models?" Jessie said.

Then they joined in an incantation of numbers.

It was a fifteen-minute conversation in less than a minute.

Translated, the foregoing conversation went: "It's bullshit, you get past the trash can, there's human guards, you can't reprogram them."

"But at certain hours," Jessie told him, "there's only one on duty. They're used to seeing the can bring people in and out. They won't question it till they try to confirm it. By then we'll be on their ass."

"We might not be compatible," Eddie had pointed out. "You understand, compatible?"

"Oh, hey, man, I *think* we can comprehend that," Jerome said, making the others snort with laughter. Eddie wasn't liked much.

Then Bones had said, "The only way to see if we're compatible is to do a systems link. We got the links, we got the thinks, like the man says. It's either the chain that holds us in, or it's the chain that pulls us out."

Jerome's scalp tightened. A systems link. A mini-Plateau. Sharing minds. Brutal intimacy. Maybe some fallout from the Plateau. He wasn't ready for it.

If it went sour, he could get time tacked onto his sentence for attempted jailbreak. And somebody might get dusted. They might have to kill a human guard. Jerome had once punched a dealer in the nose, and the spurt of blood had made him sick. He couldn't kill anyone. But . . . he had shit for alternatives. He knew he wouldn't make it through two years anyway, when they sent him up to the Big One.

The Big One'd grind him up for sure. They'd find his chip there, and it'd piss them off. They'd let the bulls rape him and give him the New Virus; he'd flip out from being locked in and chipless, and they'd put him under Aversion Rehab and burn him out.

Jerome savaged a thumbnail with his incisors. *Sent to the Big One.*

He'd been trying not to think about it. Making himself take it one day at a time. But now he had to look at the alternatives. His stomach twisted itself to punish him for being so stupid. For getting into dealing augments so he could finance a big transer. *Why?* A transer didn't get him anything but his face pirated onto local TV for maybe twenty seconds. He'd thrown himself away trying to get it . . .

Why was it so fucking important? his stomach demanded, wringing itself vindictively.

"Thing is," Bones said, "we could all be cruisin' into a set-up. Some kind of sting thing. Maybe it's a little too weird how the police prober let us all through."

(Someone listening would have heard him say, "Sting, funny luck.")

Jessie snorted. "I tol' you, man. The prober is paid off. They letting them all through because some of them are mob. I know that, because I'm part of the thing. We deal wid the Russians. Okay?"

("Probe greased, fa-me.")

"You with the mob?" Bones asked.

("You'm?")

"You got it. Just a dealer. But I know where a half million nfootageewbux wortha augshit is, so they going to get me out if I do my part. The way the system is set up, the prober had to let everyone through. His boss thinks we got our chips taken out when they arraigned us; sometimes they do it that way. This time it was supposed to be the jail surgeon. By the time they catch up their own red tape, we get outta here. Now listen—we can't do the trashcan without we all get into it, because we haven't got enough *K* otherwise. So who's in, for fuck's sake?"

He'd said, "Low, half mill, bluff surgeon, there here, twip, all-none, *who* yuh fucks?"

Something in his voice skittered with claws behind smoked glass: he was getting testy, irritable from the chip adjustments for his nicotine habit, maybe other adjustments: the side effects of liberal cerebral self-modulating burning through a threadbare nervous system.

The rest of the meeting, translated . . .

"I dunno," Eddie said. "I thought I'd do my time, cause if it goes sour—"

"Hey, man," Jessie said, "I can *take* your fuckin' chip. And be out before they notice your ass don't move no more."

"The man's right," Swish said. Her pain-suppression system was unraveling, axon by axon, and she was running out of adjust. "Let's just do it, okay? Please? Okay? I gotta get out. I feel like I wish I was dogshit so I could be something better."

"I can't handle two years in the Big, Eddie, and I'll do what I gotta, hodey," Jerome heard himself say, realizing he was helping Jessie threaten Eddie. Amazed at himself. Not his style.

"It's all of us or nobody, Eddie," Bones said.

Eddie was quiet for a while.

• • •

Jerome had turned off his chip, because it was thinking endlessly about Jessie's plan, and all it came up with was an ugly model of the risks. You had to know when to go with intuition.

Jerome was committed. And he was standing on the brink of link. The time was now, starting with Jessie.

Jessie was *operator*. He picked the order. First Eddie, to make sure about him. Then Jerome. Maybe because he had Jerome scoped for a refugee from the middle class, an anomaly here, and Jerome might try and raise the Heat on his chip, make a deal. Once they had him linked in, he was locked up.

After Jerome, it'd be Bones and then Swish.

They held hands, so that the link signal, transmitted from the chip using the electric field generated by the brain, would be carried with the optimum fidelity.

He heard them exchange frequency designates, numbers strung like beads in the darkness, and heard the hiss of suddenly indrawn breaths as Jessie and Eddie linked in. And he heard, "Let's go, Jerome."

Jerome's eyes had adjusted to the dark, the night giving up some of its buried light, and Jerome could just make a crude outline of Jessie's features like a charcoal rubbing from an Aztec carving.

Jerome reached to the back of his own head, found the glue-tufted hairs that marked his flap, and pulled the skin away from the chip's jack unit. He tapped the chip. It didn't take. He tapped it again, and this time he felt the shift in his bioelectricity; felt it hum between his teeth.

Jerome's chip communicated with his brain via an interface of nano-print configured rhodopsin protein; the ribosomes borrowing neurohumoral transmitters from the brain's blood supply, re-ordering the transmitters so that they carried a programmed pattern of ion releases for transmission across synaptic gaps to the brain's neuronal dendrites; the chip using magnetic resonance holography to collate with brain-stored memories and psychological trends. Declaiming to itself the mythology of the brain; reenacting on its silicon stage the Legends of his subjective world history.

Jerome closed his eyes and looked into the back of his eyelids. The digital read-out was printed in luminous green across the darkness. He focused on the cursor, concentrated so it moved up to ACCESS. He subverbalized, "Open frequency." The chip heard his practiced subverbalization, and numbers appeared on the back of his eyelids: 63391212.70. He read them out to the others and they picked up his frequency. Almost choking on the word, knowing what it would bring, he told the chip: "Open."

It opened to the link. He'd only done it once before. It was illegal, and he was secretly glad it was illegal because it scared him. "They're holding the Plateau back," his brain-chip wholesaler had told him, "because they're scared of what worldwide electronic telepathy might bring down on them. Like, everyone will collate information, use it to see through the bastards' game, throw the assbites out of office."

Maybe that was the real reason. It was something the power brokers couldn't control. But there were other reasons.

Reasons like a strikingly legitimate fear of people going mad.

All Jerome and the others wanted was a sharing of processing capabilities. Collaborative calculation. But the chips weren't designed to filter out the irrelevant input before it reached the user's cognition level. Before the chip had done its filtering, the two poles of the link—Jerome and Jessie—would each see the swarming hive of the other's total consciousness. Would see how the other perceived themselves to be, and then objectively, as they really were.

He saw Jessie as a grid and as a holographic entity. He braced himself and the holograph came at him, an abstract tarantula of computer-generated color and line, scrambling down over him . . . and for an instant it crouched in the seat of his consciousness: Jessie. Jesus Chaco.

Jessie was a family man. He was a patriarch, a protector of his wife and six kids (six kids!) and his widowed sister's four kids and of the poor children of his barrio. He was a muddied painting of his father, who had fled the social forest fire of Mexico's civil war between the drug cartels and the government, spiriting his capital to Los Angeles where he'd sown it into the black market. Jessie's father had been killed defending territory from the Russian-American mob; Jessie compromised with the mob to save his father's business, and loathed himself for it. Wanted to kill their bosses; had to work side by side with them. Perceived his wife as a functional pet, an object of adoration who was the very apotheosis of her fixed role. To imagine her doing other than child-rearing and keeping house would be to imagine the sun become a snowball, the moon become a monkey. Jessie's family insistently clung to the old, outdated roles.

And Jerome glimpsed Jessie's undersides; Jesus Chaco's self-image with its outsized penis and impossibly spreading shoulders, sitting in a perfect and shining cherry automobile, always the newest and most luxurious model, the automotive throne from which he surveyed his kingdom. Jerome saw guns emerging from the grille of the car to splash Jessie's enemies apart with his unceasing ammunition . . . It was a Robert Williams cartoon capering at the heart of Jessie's unconscious . . . Jessie saw himself as Jerome saw him; the electronic mirrors reflecting one another. Jessie cringed.

Jerome saw himself then, reflected back from Jessie.

He saw Jerome-X on a video screen with lousy vertical hold; wobbling, trying to arrange its pixels firmly and losing them. A figure of mewling inconsequence; a brief flow of electrons that might diverge left or right like spray from a water hose depressed with the thumb. Raised in a high-security condo village, protected by cameras and computer signals to private security thugs; raised in a media-windowed womb, with computers and vids and a thousand varieties of video games; shaped by TV and fantasy rental; sexuality imprinted by sneaking his parents' badly hidden cache of brainsex files. And in stations from around the world, seeing the same StarFaces appear on channel after channel as the star's fame spread like a stain across the frequency bands. Seeing the Star's World Self crystallizing; the media figure coming into definition against the backdrop of media competition, becoming real in this electronic collective unconscious.

Becoming real, himself, in his own mind, simply because he'd appeared on a few thousand screens, through video tagging, transer graffiti. Growing up with a sense that media events were real and personal events were not. Anything that didn't happen on the Grid didn't happen. Even as he hated conventional programming, even as he regarded it as the cud of ruminants, still the Grid and TV and vids defined his sense of personal unreality; and left him unfinished.

Jerome saw Jerome: perceiving himself unreal. Jerome: scanning a transer, creating a presence via video graffiti. Thinking he was doing it for reasons of radical statement. Seeing, now, that he was doing it to make himself feel substantial, to superimpose himself on the Media Grid . . .

And then Eddie's link was there, Eddie's computer model sliding down over Jerome like a mudslide. Eddie seeing himself as a Legendary Wanderer, a rebel, a homemade mystic; his fantasy parting to reveal an anal-expulsive sociopath; a whiner perpetually scanning for someone to blame for his sour luck.

Suddenly Bones tumbled into the link; a complex worldview that was a sort of streetside sociobiology, mitigated by a loyalty to friends, a mystical faith in brain chips and amphetamines. His underside a masochistic dwarf, the troll of self-doubt, lacerating itself with guilt.

And then Swish, a woman with an unsightly growth, errant glands that were like tumors in her, something other people called 'testicles.' Perpetually hungry for the means to dampen the pain of an infinite self-derision that mimicked her father's utter rejection of her. A mystical faith in synthetic morphine.

. . . Jerome mentally reeling with disorientation, seeing the others as a network of distorted self-images, caricatures of grotesque ambitions. Beyond them he glimpsed another realm through a break in the psychic clouds: the Plateau, the whispering plane of brain chips linked on forbidden frequencies, an electronic haven for doing deals unseen by cops; a Plateau prowled only by the exquisitely ruthless; a vista of enormous challenges and inconceivable risks and always the potential for getting lost, for madness. A place roamed by the wolves of wetware.

There was a siren quiver from that place, a soundless howling, pulling at them . . . drawing them in . . .

"*Uh-uh*, wolflost, pross," Bones said, maybe aloud or maybe through the chips. Translated from chip shorthand, those two syllables meant. "Stay away from the Plateau, or we get sucked into it, we lose our focus. Concentrate on parallel processing function."

Jerome looked behind his eyelids, sorted through the files. He moved the cursor down . . .

Suddenly, it was there. The group-thinking capacity looming above them, a sentient skyscraper. They all felt a rush of megalomaniacal pleasure in identifying with it; with a towering edifice of Mind. Five chips became One.

They were ready. Jessie transmitted the bait.

• • •

Alerted to an illegal use of implant chips, the trashcan was squeaking down the hall, scanning to precisely locate the source. It came to a sudden stop, rocking on its wheels in front of their cell. Jessie reached through the bars and touched its input jack.

The machine froze with a *clack* midway through a turn, and hummed as it processed what they fed it. Would the robot bite?

Bones had a program for the Cyberguard Fourteens, with all the protocol and a range of sample entry codes. Parallel processing from samples took less than two seconds to decrypt the trashcan's access code. Then—

They were in. The hard part was the reprogramming.

Jerome found the way. He told the trashcan that he wasn't Eric Wexler, because the DNA code was all wrong, if you looked close enough; what we have here is a case of mistaken identity.

Since this information *seemed* to be coming from authorized sources—the decrypted access code made them authorized—the trashcan fell for the gag and opened the cage.

The trashcan took the five Eric Wexlers down the hall—that was Jessie's doing, showing them how to make it think of five as one, something his people had learned from the immigration computers. It escorted them through the plastiflex door, through the steel door, and into Receiving. The human guard was heaping sugar into his antique Ronald McDonald coffee mug and watching *The Mutilated* on his wallet TV. Bones and Jessie were in the room and moving in on him before he broke free of the television and went for the button. Bones's long left arm spiked out and his stiffened fingers hit a nerve cluster below the guy's left ear, and he went down, the sugar dispenser in one hand swishing a white fan onto the floor.

Jerome's chip had cross-referenced Bones's attack style. Bones was trained by commandos, the chip said. Military elite. Was he a plant? Bones smiled at him and tilted his head, which Jerome's chip read as: *No. I'm trained by the Underground. Radics.*

Jessie was at the console, deactivating the trashcan, killing the cameras, opening the outer doors. Jessie and Swish led the way out, Swish whining softly and biting her lip. There were two more guards at the gate, one of them asleep. Jessie had taken the gun from the guy Bones had put under, so the first guard at the gate was dead before he could hit an alarm. The catnapping guy woke and yelled with hoarse terror, and then Jessie shot him in the throat.

Watching the guard fall, spinning, blood making its own slow-motion spiral in the air, Jerome felt a perfect mingling of sickness, fear and self-disgust. The guard was young, wearing a cheap wedding ring, probably had a young family. So Jerome stepped over the dying man and made an adjustment; used his chip, chilled himself out with adrenaline. Had to—he was committed now. And he knew with a bland certainty that they had reached the Plateau after all.

He would live on the Plateau now. He belonged there, now that he was one of the wolves.

• • •

PARIS, FRANCE.

At the broken heart of Paris is the Île de la Cité, an island in the River Seine. On the easternmost tip of the island is a memorial to the Jewish victims of Nazi occupation. The current government did not keep it in good repair. The Cathedral of Notre Dame on another tip of the island was also in ill repair, as the Unity Party had no great liking for the Catholic Church, which did not support its racist agenda, and blocked the Vatican's access with a thousand bureaucratic obstacles. North of Notre Dame lay the ruins of old buildings in the Rue Chanoinesse, the Rue Chantres, and the Rue des Ursins. On the Rue des Ursins was a war-damaged police station, a *gendarmerie*, long since abandoned. Though not thirty yards from it was an official rationing station, where, every day, the disenfranchised lined up, sometimes for days, to receive pathetically inadequate government rations of freeze-dried and canned goods and petrosynthetics. Groups from a mere cluster to a crowd could be expected here at any time, so it was good cover for the New Resistance. An NR operative approached the rationing center as if he were part of the crowd waiting for a handout; simply entered the ruined building next door, as if to find a spot for a quick pee. He passed through several woebegone, debris-cluttered rooms, and then into an alley, blocked at both ends. Here was a boarded-over back door to the erstwhile police station. The door swung aside if pulled just right. And if the NR operative made the appropriate hand signal as he entered, the guard wouldn't blow his brains out.

Best to be updated on the hand signals.

If you make it past the guard, you go down a clean but unheated drab-blue hallway to a metal door opening on a row of cells. If you said the right words at the metal door, the guard behind it wouldn't blow your brains out, either.

Instead, she'll slide the door open for you, and you'll go to the cell where your debriefing takes place.

• • •

Steinfeld, Pasolini, Dan Torrence, and Levassier sat around an old Formica table in a chilly metal room, formerly a big holding tank used mostly for drunks. There was a sat-link terminal in the corner, gathering dust, because they didn't have a secure way to use it just now, and there was a plastic flagon of hot coffee on the table. There were rifles stacked against the wall. There was the smell of dust and sewage: the toilets didn't flush. Sewage had to be carted out in buckets.

Torrence was sitting on a wooden bench that rocked on its uneven legs whenever he shifted his weight. His hands clasped the tin coffee mug for warmth.

He felt like shit.

"Danco is dead, Cordenne is dead," Torrence said, "and that's bad. But I'll tell you what's worse. Six civilians were injured, three are dead." He turned to stare at Lina Pasolini. "And the fucking Fascists have a major propaganda victory. We go from being freedom fighters to being terrorists."

Lina Pasolini was dark, her black hair cut short, her thick eyebrows two bars of black emphasis over her hooded eyes. Her face was carved out of deep shadows and strong planes, a handsome face that hid its sensuality under a burden of quiet suspicion. She wore khaki trousers, sneakers, a grimy sweatshirt. There was a .44 stuck in the waistband of her pants. She didn't need it here.

She lit a stubby Russian cigarette and looked at it, caught like a pointer between her thumb and forefinger, as she spoke in her careful, trained English. "Showing they have the will to kill anyone necessary has worked for many guerilla groups. The crowd was in support of the fascists . . . And—you know—bad propaganda can be good propaganda if it is followed up, redirected." She'd grown up in Sardinia, but she had a master's in international poli-sci from Columbia, and more than once Torrence had heard her speak of having lit a cigarette with the burning diploma.

Torrence thought she was dangerously certain of herself and, worse, unbearably pretentious. And as if to confirm that, she went on:

"Terror is the only statement that, once heard, is never forgotten." Her voice was deep but without much inflection; her Italian accent was almost imperceptible. Torrence thought of Italians as noisy and assertive. But Pasolini was always laidback, maddeningly calm, methodical. As if she was absolutely certain that everything she said was inarguable fact.

"You're saying you did it on purpose?" Torrence asked. "You meant to kill civilians?"

"Not precisely—there were fascists after me, I was trying to kill them. But if it happens that we sacrifice so-called civilians—if there is such a thing—it becomes part of our statement. A declaration of commitment, you see." She gave him a gauzy look from somewhere deep inside herself. "There really are no civilians, 'Hard-Eyes.'" A little mockery in the use of his long-discarded *nom de guerre*. "Everyone must be in this war, children and adults, women and men, and if I knew how to bring their dogs and cats in, I'd do that too."

Torrence looked at Steinfeld, who was combing his graying beard distractedly with the blunt fingers of one work-grimy hand, shifting his heavy bulk in his chair. His curly black hair had grown shapeless, was streaked with white. His black eyes were sunken; his face had been round, was sagging to jowly. He had been working, that afternoon, on one of their old FRG Army trucks, in frayed grease-spotted overalls and a yellowed T-shirt. His Mossad-issue Damazi machine rifle leaned against the wall.

Steinfeld said at last, "I understand your thinking, Lina. War is not simple. But the New Resistance has a policy. The policy sustains our ability to work together despite differing political backgrounds." He almost never used the term "New Resistance"; usually he'd say, "We." His use of it meant this was some sort of official ruling. "The policy makes a strict distinction between civilians and our enemy. We do not kill non-combatants."

"What was Le Pen? You killed Le Pen—or did I dream that?"

"He was a commander in chief," Torrence snapped. "Not a civilian."

Steinfeld said, "There are better examples you could use, Lina. This Mengele of theirs, so to speak, this Dr. Cooper—he's a civilian. I would gladly kill him if I could. We tried to kill Crandall. He was a civilian. But those are false civilians. They are worse than collaborators. We know the difference most of the time. People killed at random in a crowd, now . . . even people cheering for the enemy—I mean, after all, who knows how they were pressured into being part of that crowd . . . " His voice trailed off, his eyes roamed some dark inner landscape.

There was a moral weight in this work, Torrence knew, a weight you had to carry; a weight that grew. And Steinfeld was feeling it. Torrence felt it too.

It would be easy to become like Lina Pasolini and never feel uncertainty. It would be a relief.

"I think we should take Pasolini here off of armed duty," Torrence said, looking at Steinfeld, taking the tone of one administrator to another.

She stiffened, just a little. It was good to get some kind of reaction from her. "I got you people back into Paris," she said softly. "Me."

"The Mossad got us in," Torrence shot back.

"That is shit. I was on the inside, I led the team that cleared the tunnels, I organized it. They were postmen for the move only. And you need *soldiers*, not people to sew uniforms." She smiled vaguely at Torrence. "You are a very tired man. You do this because you needed something to do, and because you like to fight, and maybe you are one of those people who simply like the feeling that comes in a fight. Something to chase away the depression, no? And you are here to find a reason for it. A . . . justification. Me, I am not tired. I do not fight because I don't know what to do with myself. I fight because I'm angry. This anger never sleeps."

Torrence felt his face go hot. "You—" He couldn't finish it. He turned to Steinfeld, swallowed the cold stone that had risen in his throat, and said, "You know your people. If I'm not motivated, if I don't believe in this thing, then get me a fucking ticket home. Send me back through Israel. Which is it?"

Steinfeld made a fly-shooing gesture. "I have no doubts about you at all." He hesitated, then nodded slowly. "She's right about one thing, I can't take her out of combat. We're too short."

He turned to Pasolini. "But Captain Torrence is also right. We do things one way. We distinguish between civilians and the enemy, and when there are exceptions, *I* make them. Not you."

She stood up, abruptly, so that Torrence flinched a little in his chair. She smiled at that. "I'm on watch."

"Not yet," Steinfeld said. "Take a meal."

"Our stomachs are too delicate here for eating. I'm going on early."

She drifted from the room, closed the door very gently behind her.

Torrence said, "Steinfeld, you ever wonder about the kind of people this kind of thing attracts?"

Steinfeld shrugged. "That's what she said about *you*."

• • •

PROCESSING CENTER 12, A FEW MILES NORTH OF THE CITY LIMITS OF PARIS, FRANCE.

"It's not so different, this place now, than it was before the war," Gabrielle was saying. She was a black French woman, with a dirty blue scarf on her bald head—the SA shaved them all to make the lice manageable. Or to make them into human ciphers. She wore the dull-orange pajamalike detainee's uniforms they all wore, and sandals made of tire rubber. Roseland wore the same.

Roseland was an American Jew, had been working on a kibbutz in

Israel. He'd volunteered to help on an unauthorized airlift to take food to Jewish refugees in France, the airlift had been shot down, and he was one of two who survived the crash outside Paris. The other one, a woman named Luda, had been murdered by the SA thugs for screaming when they dragged her out of the wreckage, the bone splinters driving her mad with pain . . . So they shot her and left her body there.

And now Abe Roseland, a pale, gangly boy of twenty-one with slender feet and hands and a faint look of weary amazement, kept his mouth shut and survived to sit here in the "exercise yard" of Processing Center 12. Roseland had been a performance-art critic and programmer in the States for an interactive digital-TV channel. A life that seemed as far away as the planet Pluto now. He'd been a cynic politically, essentially apolitical, but interested in his cultural roots, feeling an itch to do some sort of Judaic walkabout. Which led to the kibbutz, which led to the airlift, which led here: looking out at the Philips LHD 11377 microwave fence. The gray metal posts beaded moisture in the misting rain, the boxlike transmitter/receivers quivered with strangely symmetrical patterns as water beads rearranged to electric fields. A thin precipitation did a little shimmy as it passed the microwave beams, as if running over warped window glass. You could almost hear the fence humming. The metal posts had been recently cemented into the street, and Roseland wondered, with all the dampness, if maybe they hadn't really set very well. Maybe they could be pushed over if you—

No use trying. Any interference with the posts and the guns went off overhead, one spraying the area indiscriminately, the other computer-aimed. He had seen it happen.

Some part of Roseland's mind was thinking about this. The rest was thinking about food and trying not to think about food. Rations had been reduced again.

Don't think about the protein package in the old sofa.

He hugged himself, rubbed his upper arms in the cold, and moved a little closer to Gabrielle on the steps. The cold got to him more lately. Maybe it was anemia.

The exercise area was a sort of courtyard between two high-rises. They were low-income housing, chiefly for Algerian and Arab and Persian immigrants, before the war. Badly built and under-maintained and vandalized, in some sense sabotaged by the disappointment and despair of the prior inhabitants, the high-rises had become crumbling eyesores, cracked and rust-streaked and smirched with graffiti. The SA hadn't cleaned the concrete apartment buildings before making them into Processing Centers 12 and 13. Around the outside of the foundations was a collection of trash and debris, furniture thrown from the gutted apartments, garbage of all kinds: "Like the filthy panties of a whore down around 'er ankles," one of the Brit SA guards had said. "And these wogs are the crab-lice 'appy to live in it."

There were two thousand detainees upstairs, crammed into the windowless rooms; some of the walls had been knocked down between apartments, but there wasn't space for everyone to lie down. That had to be done in shifts. They had stopped allowing them baths, and the open sewage tubs were rarely emptied, so the stench was unspeakable and lately there was cholera. They had no medical treatment, and sometimes the dead lay in the rooms with the living for days before they were allowed to carry them out. Roseland's stomach lurched, remembering the guards holding a detainee's head under the sewage, dunking him again and again as punishment for prying a breathing hole in the blocked-over windows.

Roseland took a deep, grateful breath of the open air. Only forty detainees were allowed outdoors at any one time, twice a week. It was Gabrielle and Roseland's turn, with thirty-eight other "processing detainees" on the front steps or poking listlessly about the eighty-foot-wide compound.

He looked across the courtyard compound at PC 13, the almost identical high-rise, with another almost-identical group of detainees on its steps, huddled inside their own microwave fence perimeter.

(How remarkably alike they all became, at least to look at, after they were here for a while, Roseland thought. The same expressions, and the uniform imprint of hunger and sickness on their faces . . . And now he himself was beginning to perceive them all as alike as white mice or cockroaches. That was the triumph of the ones who had put them here: they were molding his own perceptions of himself, and the others.)

Roseland shivered, and coughed, and looked back at the microwave fence.

The microwave beams weren't strong enough to hurt a trespasser on their own; they were triggers and orientation devices for the dual system of the Chubb CCTV surveillance cameras fixed on the sides of the two high-rises, and the contiguous Saab-Scania Datascan microprocessor system that controlled the aiming and firing of the four FN 7.62 mm sharpshooter's machine guns, two on each building, mounted on 180-degree turrets . . .

There were SA guards too, three in an office on the second floor, usually playing cards or cursing the bad reception on their little satellite TV; wearing their armor but not their mirrored helmets. Sometimes taking one of the women in, sharing her around. Beating the ones who complained, beating the prisoners who protested.

There were two more guards supposed to be in the instabunker across the street, as often called out on scavenging errands, hustling wine and

cheese to supplement the rations of the officers housed in the old pensione
down the way. Just about half the time the bunker was empty.

But the Philips/Chubb/Saab-Scania security troika was never turned
off, never took a break, never looked away—and it never made mistakes,
as far as Roseland knew. It was smart enough to distinguish between SA
and prisoners. An Iranian whose name Roseland had never known had
tried to cut the power cables to the camera/gun turret. But the camera had
stored power in it, and kept working, and the microchip-controlled gun
across the street tracked over and shot the Iranian fifty times, as well as a
woman who happened to look out a window nearby.

"You think there's going to be another transport today?" Gabrielle
asked. She'd learned English at the Université de Lyon and in America
before the war. Her family had owned a string of *patisseries*, which had
been seized by Le Pen's people as "stolen property": her parents, the
SPOES government said, had "stolen business opportunities from native
Frenchmen." She had watched as her mother and father were taken away
in the trainlike semi-trucks; a huge tractor-truck pulling six separate
trailers, each with its microprocessor-controlled steering keeping it on a
computer-imagined train track.

"Yes," Roseland said, "they'll be by again for more. They'll take me next
time, I think."

"Do they take people to gas chambers?" She asked it lifelessly, as if
asking whether there was a toll booth on a bridge ahead. After the guards
had used her the vibrancy had gone out of her voice.

"No," he said, "I don't think there are gas chambers this time. I think
they take you to work." They'd taken her parents, so he didn't tell her the
rest: that they worked you to death. Literally to death, like a bar of soap
(that inescapable irony) used to scrub—to scrub what? A prize pig?—used
till it dissolved into nothing, was washed away and gone. And he didn't tell
her that some were taken for medical experiments; that all died, eventually,
one way or another. That by now her parents were surely dead.

"Maybe the work—it's better than here." She didn't sound as if she cared
if it were better or not.

He thought about that. Maybe he should pretend to her that it was
better. So she'd feel all right about her parents. But maybe not: then she'd
try to get on the trucks and go, and she'd soon be dead.

"It can't be better," he said. "To tell you the truth, I think it's death."

"*Ma mama et môn papa*, they are dead, I know, but maybe it is better
than here."

He hated the flatness in her voice. Like one of those old computer toys
that talked to you when you pressed its buttons.

He swallowed. It was wet and clammy out, but his throat was so dry.

As a teenager, he had read about the Holocaust. The horror had been difficult to bear, so he hadn't read widely in the subject, and he hadn't tried to remember the details. To remember the event, the historical fullness of it, that was enough, he decided. That would not be forgotten.

But later he had read something else: that there were people claiming the Holocaust had never happened, claiming the exterminations had never happened, the monumental brutality had never happened. And there were people stupid enough—or politically opportunistic enough—to believe it, or pretend to believe it. And he had learned that the young in most countries, even those countries involved in the Second World War, were learning almost nothing of the Holocaust, and many didn't believe it had happened at all . . .

The enormity of this stupidity, the insufferable amorality of this abdication of responsibility, this abandonment of history, had left the young Abe Roseland breathless.

He had gone back to the library and delved into the details of the Holocaust, so that he, at least, would remember.

He had read about the camps, and wondered what a great many others had wondered: why had there been so few rebellions?

The Nazi guns? Yes. But so few guns, relatively, and so many prisoners. Why not rush them, en masse, when you found out you were all going to die anyway, otherwise?

Now he knew the answer. *Hunger.*

Hunger became weakness and weakness was passivity. It was hard to think things out, hard to work in unison with others when you couldn't think. Hard to make a decision and hard to find the strength to carry it out. Hunger was more effective than a thousand guards.

And the degradation, too, the shaving and the uniforms and the cattlelike herding and the random punishments. Techniques that worked on men and women like coring tools on apples. They cut the pith out of you.

They left you with nothing, or at best with a ghostly hope that something would break down, the Americans would get wind of it, Israel would come, the NR would come, or the Second Alliance and SPOES would realize it had gone too far and it would stop, or perhaps you could finesse your way into a servant's job somewhere if you waited one more day, just one more day . . . Better to wait . . . better than rushing their guns . . .

It wasn't better.

He said it aloud. "It's not better."

He stood up and said it again. "It's not better." And he said something else. "Not this time. Not again."

Gabrielle didn't even look up at him.

(How many months had he been here, trying to tell himself that it wasn't what it seemed? That it wasn't happening again? But he knew, some part of him knew, from the first day. The denial had died out in him about the same time the strength and the will for rebellion had drained away. Realization and resignation, coming together. So what had brought him out of it now, so suddenly after all this time? Was it Gabrielle? Yes.)

After the first rush of anger, Roseland felt weak in the knees, dizzy. Legs wobbly. He had a package of protein paste saved, thinking if ever the chance for an escape came, he'd need strength. He'd hidden it selfishly, back when they'd had the children with them; had watched children go hungry and hated himself, but he'd kept it hidden.

Now he made a decision. He would need the food now, for the strength to talk. The day's ration would come soon, if it came at all, and he had to talk before the ration came. He had to talk to everyone.

He moved to the heap of trash to the right of the steps, where there was an overturned sofa whose synthetics, churned by acid rains, had collapsed into a gummy, shapeless mass of shit brown. He knelt behind it, reached into the plastic frame, felt for the package. Panicked. It was gone. Stolen! He bent over, stuck his head in the mildewy, soggy stuff, clawing it away from his eyes . . . saw the glint of shiny plastic wrapping. There. He drew out the little rectangular transparent plastic container, with shaking fingers hit the open-tab. Its top peeled itself open, and he ladled the stuff into his mouth with his fingers. Tasted of vat-chicken and mold.

Maybe his great decision was a sham, was just an excuse to eat the food, he thought.

He felt the warmth and mood-lift of the sugars, the proteins roll through him, lifting him inside like a summer updraft, and he sucked it from his fingers and thought: *Now*.

He turned and began to run to Gabrielle, thinking he'd share the last of the paste with her; then told himself: don't run. Conserve your energy. He strolled to her, glancing at the camera on the opposite building, knowing the guards could be monitoring him. Hidden food was contraband. He saw foxfaced Dindon watching him sharply, eyeing the plastic box. "Give some me, or I tell the guards," Dindon said.

"Fuck off," Roseland said. "You say anything, I'll kill you in your fucking sleep. No, I take it back. I'll wake you up first." He felt positively eloquent now.

He hunkered next to Gabrielle and offered her the food. She just stared at it. He took her grimy hand and dipped her fingers in it; he put her fingers to her mouth. After a moment she sucked the paste away, and kept sucking absently on her fingers. He took her hand from her mouth and fed her the rest of it, except for a thin coating around the edges of the tin. He tossed the package to Dindon, sensing that Dindon and the sallow Lebanese guy beside him were going to jump him for it anyway, and then went into the building. Someone said, "If you go in, the guards won't let you come back out again."

He didn't reply. He took Gabrielle's arm and dragged her after him, went into the all-consuming stench of the place and gagged a moment—you could smell it more when you had strength—and then he climbed the stairs and went into a room, and everyone looked up. He paused, looking at them, overcome by an unexpected amazement: it was as if he was seeing them for the first time. Sagging faces, dull eyes, pallor, cueball heads, misery shared between them with stunning uniformity. He knew that he looked just exactly the same. And he began to talk. After a while, urged by Roseland, Gabrielle fell into the rhythm of translating. The urgency, the mood, the insistence they took from his tone; the sense from Gabrielle's affectless translation.

At first no one really listened. They were faces emptied of volition, like a room full of cancer-eaten children watching cartoons—children bald from chemotherapy, sunken from disease—turning incuriously, briefly, to see who was at the door of their terminal ward. But in about an hour, near dusk, the guards came with the ration pail, and prisoners had a little strength after that, they were adults again briefly, enough to listen, to stand, to consider, as—once the guards had gone—Roseland kept talking. Driven by the rage of six months' confinement and degradation, driven by a sacred memory—the Holocaust—he kept talking. Articulating their feelings for them, talking their feelings alive again, like breathing CPR into a drowned man, bringing him back. He talked, and he kept moving, even after he felt his strength ebbing, adrenaline spurring him on from room to room. He spoke of dignity. He spoke of slow, degraded death and quick glorious death; he said, "Who will die with me today? Who will die in freedom? Who will die with me so that they see us as we are? Who will die so that our people remember us? Who will go with me now?"

Some of them followed him up to another room, and another, and he kept talking. The SA hadn't bothered to wire the rooms; they could talk all they wanted, if they had the strength, and he used that luxury, used it up, kept talking, talking till he was hoarse and then mute . . .

But by then the others were talking, saying things that had been said before but never acted on. Only now Roseland was the activating spark, and they felt a conflagration growing in them, a burning strength in the mutuality of their choice and their conviction. They felt it all around them, charging the air, growing toward a Moment.

The Moment came when two SA guards came to the first room downstairs and shouted, "What the bloody 'ell is all this noise? No more talk! Lights out!"

And then the call went up from hallway to hallway, stair to stair, room to room, *"Maintenant! Now!"*

And the surge began, a lava eruption of people from the volcanic recesses of the high-rise, the first two guards borne down and disarmed, their armor pried at till it came away and they lived only long enough to kill twice and to shriek once apiece. All the while the others surged past them and down the stairs and out the doors, chanting, a chant led by Roseland, *"Jamais plus! Jamais plus! Jamais plus! Jamais plus!"*

Never again! rolling endlessly and raggedly from two thousand parched throats as they poured from the building.

Some of them slung offal at the cameras, trying to block the lenses, and partially succeeded, but the guns found their targets anyway, guided by the sensors in the microwave fences.

The mass of starveling detainees surged across the microwave barriers, setting off the sirens; the cameras swiveling, the guns barking like startled dogs, people screaming, others remembering what Roseland had drilled into their heads: *Don't turn back when the shooting starts, because they'll only kill us all anyway. No matter what, don't stop. Die with me today.*

Your sister falls beside you, shot in the back: don't stop.

Your husband stumbles and falls: don't stop.

Your best friend spits blood and screams for help: don't stop!

"Don't stop!" Roseland bellowed in the midst of them, dragging Gabrielle along beside him, *"Jamais plus!"* Never again!

The dying words of a hundred people, two hundred, three hundred, mowed down by thundering guns equipped with hundreds of thousands of rounds . . . machine guns with computer guidance, guns unceasingly fed, capable of aiming themselves and firing for days if necessary . . .

Roseland was distantly aware that detainees in the other building were watching, across the compound, from cracks in the sealed-over windows and from the front steps; a few making tentative motions as if to join the rebellion—until they saw the lake of blood spreading out from the fallen . . .

Roseland kept going, past the empty bunker, dragging Gabrielle along, hearing bullets whine past his head, hearing her scream.

Turning to see her brains flying out her mouth.

Letting go of her. Choking with grief—but, *Don't stop.*

The machine guns never pausing, cutting methodically and almost flawlessly, rows of men and women falling like harvested wheat . . .

The security system was flawed: the machine guns were programmed to concentrate their fire at the compound's perimeters; if they'd concentrated their fire on the building doorways, almost no one would have escaped.

As it was, of fifteen hundred who'd run, some four hundred won past the guns; leaving eleven hundred dead and dying, a reservoir of carnage, of suffering and blood. As the buildings shook with the whoops of sirens, the yammer of guns, almost drowning out the screaming and the chanting. *Jamais plus.*

Then came the IS vehicles, Internal Security Vehicles, three anti-insurgency Mowag Roland units: six wheels apiece, olive-drab armored cars shaped like thick ax wedges, their prows equipped with dozer blades, turrets that fired gas or grenade rounds or bullets, the operators watching everything on screens inside; up-angled deflection skirts all around against mine blasts. Electrically charged exteriors.

Suddenly the ISVs were wheeling around the corners, plowing into the four hundred survivors, grinding them under, driving them back, shunting them like human mud. Booming out commands in a voice so amplified it cracked the eardrums of those standing near: *DO NOT MOVE AND YOU WILL BE UNHARMED. RUN AND YOU WILL DIE. DO NOT MOVE AND YOU WILL BE UNHARMED . . .*

"Don't stop! *Jamais plus!*"

Roseland kept shouting, kept running. Running through a cloud of exhaust smoke as an IS vehicle smashed past him and crushed a dozen men and women under its dozer blade; as another opened up with a barrage of explosive rounds to his rear . . .

Then he felt the ground shake. He paused, looked back to see the crystallized-steel Gargantua arching its metal scythes over the horizon: a Jægernaut, ten stories high, this one, a spoked wheel without the rim, a giant steel swastika, a skyscraper-size Rototiller ripping up anything in its path, brought here through the ruined buildings near the high-rises. Converging on Roseland's high-rise, biting down on Processing Center 12, the five hundred who'd remained inside crushed between the floors as they accordioned flat . . . he could hear them screaming even from here . . .

Making an example for the ones across the street, in PC 13. And for the ones who'd hear about it later in other parts of the city.

A mountainous geyser of dust rose where the building had been, swirling around great scythes of metal that cut through the night sky.

It was an act beyond murder. Murder was too small a word.

I should have died with them . . .

But when he heard the ISVs rumbling down the street, searching him out, he began to run once more.

Running blindly. Or perhaps some part of his mind made decisions about where it was running to. Or maybe it was dumb luck.

But thirty minutes later, when the strength went out of his limbs, he collapsed into the high weeds of a vacant lot, letting a fresh rain wash over him. Wash some of Gabrielle's blood from him . . .

He found that he was alive. Alone. Intact.

• • •

It was almost five hours—hearing IS vehicles, now and then, roar obliviously past him—before Roseland had the strength to move.

He sat up and retched. The world spun.

When the spinning stopped, he saw that the clouds had parted and there were stars. He sat there, very still, cold, muddy, not moving in the yellow grass that reached up to his chin. The smell of the wet grass was overpowering.

Was he the only one who'd made it?

Oh, please, no. Kill him if it was so. Someone kill him if that was true.

Another thought, then. It wasn't in words, at first. Just a picture, a blurry peripheral image of people exploding from gunfire all around him. After a while, there were words to go with it: *I led a thousand and more to their deaths. I led them into the slaughterhouse.*

He waited for the guilt to come. Gabrielle was just one of more than a thousand dead. He was guilty of leading her and the others to death. The guilt would come down on him like a hammer from the sky.

He waited. Not moving.

Nothing.

Feel it. Face the guilt: Maybe they should have waited. Maybe someone would have come to save them. Maybe . . .

No. This was better.

He felt another kind of remorse. He had survived: he should have died with Gabrielle, with the others. Not because he led them into a shower of bullets, but simply because he was one of them. There was no fair reason he should survive and they shouldn't. No justice in it.

He sat completely inert, balancing precariously on his spine, thinking he'd fall forward or back if he tried to move. Thinking: *All that death. Most of them gone.*

It was still better.

He went into a gray study. Stopped thinking at all.

A little while later, something ran over his leg.

He moved only his eyes, some instinct priming his fingers, waiting . . .

Again. Motion. Something moving toward him. Investigating him. Thinking he was food. A rat.

Moving up his leg.

All by itself, his hand moved. He watched his own hand with amazement as it struck like a rattler and grabbed the rat. Squeezed it dead and tore it open. He closed his eyes and let his hands and mouth do their work.

After a while, Roseland could move again. He was on his feet, staggering south, toward the city.

Just after dawn, as he crouched in a doorway somewhere in Paris, he saw a woman spraying a wall with a glue can, then slapping up a poster. Translated, the poster said, *THEY'RE LYING TO YOU. LIES MAKE SLAVES. WAIT FOR THE RESISTANCE.* Above the words was a picture of a sky-blue flag.

Moving quickly, the woman put up two more posters, then hurried away.

He trotted after her. "Hey! *Hey!*"

She froze on the street. He could see she was about to break into a run. She thought he was police. He shouted hoarsely, "Please! I need . . . I ran away from the processing center!"

Just as he said please, she'd started running. But now she stopped. He could see by her body language, her silhouette against the dawn-lit backdrop of blue morning mist, that she felt she was taking a chance as she turned, slowly, to look at him. She walked toward him—then suddenly ran to him, grabbed his wrist. A faint expression of revulsion flickered over her face as she looked him over.

She led him into an alley, into another street, and into a debris-choked entrance to a Metro station. After much worming and climbing and walking in darkness (all the while Roseland feeling he would die if he took another step, but somehow always taking another step), they came up in a ruined building, and she took him through some doors. There was some argument at the doors in French, but they went through.

They were brought to a lean man missing an ear. A man whom Roseland knew immediately as an American. Knew without knowing how.

"Monsieur Torrence," the woman said, introducing the stranger.

Roseland said, "My name is Abraham Roseland. Give me a gun. Give me a fucking gun."

And then he collapsed.

• • •

MERINO, AN ISLAND IN THE CARIBBEAN.

Jack Smoke, a tall man with a hawk nose and sharp black eyes, walked on a long-legged drooping gait across the tarmac to the transport plane; he was walking more slowly than he would have liked so that the little girl carrying the crow could keep up with him. Her name was Alouette; she was about ten. She was the color of a polished coconut shell, her wavy black hair tied up under a sky-blue scarf. Smoke wore an identical scarf around his neck. Both of them wore short-sleeve white shirts, shorts, and sandals.

"You said we could go swimming again before we took the plane," she said. She made it sting by saying it matter-of-factly.

She had too many of the adult tricks, Smoke thought. There are advantages to having a gifted child, and disadvantages. But he'd never regretted adopting Alouette.

"We're not taking this plane yet. We will go swimming before we leave the island," he promised, glancing at the sky. It was a warm day, but the subtropical island was sheeted over with a thin cloud cover, and there was a brisk wind. Weather report said a storm was coming; he hoped it would take its time, and not make him a liar. "We're going out to this plane to see the reporter from MediaSat."

"Oh. You could've told me before."

"You were too busy bragging about your chip access level."

"Wasn't bragging."

"You were too."

"No, wasn't." She took his hand and kissed it. The crow, nestled in the crook of her other arm, made a crotchety caw. "Hush, Richard," she told the crow. "We're going to see a television man."

Hand, the digital-TV man. Smoke had seen Witcher's file on him. Hand's real name was Nguyen Hinh. Rising young muckraking our-man-in-the-field for the relatively new MediaSat, an Indie that had taken advantage of the big Worldtalk shakeup to carve out a broadcasting niche. Hinh was known to his ratings share as Norman Hand.

Nguyen Hinh. US citizen. Father was Vietnamese, mother American, thirty-two years old. Got his degree at NYU in media studies, was a member of the Democratic Party with a history of voting for party moderates. Nice head of hair, vocationally color-streaked for that streetside identity cachet. Mostly round eyes, pretty blond skin, boyish, said to be gay but not remotely effeminate, at least on camera. Suits were printouts but not stenciled. High-quality designer prints, the kind you get in your clothes printer only if you're a platinum-card subscriber. Hinh was chic but not snobbish enough to wear real cloth.

Highly ambitious. Probably not interested in the New Resistance story for partisan reasons.

Hand was posed in the shade of the forward-swept wing of the fat-bellied blue and white jet, talking intensely into the little fist-size camera standing on a thin collapsible tripod. His black technicki cameraman hunched over the viewfinder, making minute adjustments.

Behind Hand, islanders directed by a Witcher employee loaded plastic crates from a luggage tractor onto a portable conveyor belt carrying them into the plane. A swaying robot arm whirred from the plane, grasped the crates in its immense tri-fingered metal hand, and hoisted them into place. The crates swung precariously in the robot's grip, but somehow were snugged exactly into the optimum packing configuration. Muscular backs bare and sweat-glossy, the human laborers worked in concert with the cybernetic laborer as comfortably as rice farmers with a water buffalo.

Smoke gestured for Alouette to be quiet, and the two of them waited behind the cameraman for Hand to finish his taping.

"What you see," Hand was saying, "is a small piece of an exodus; the final preparations for an exodus from an island—an island which must remain unspecified—which has been a haven for this intriguing band of guerrillas, now on the run from, so they allege, an illegal international force of crypto-Fascists. Their destination: somewhere distant and secret; their timetable: immediate and desperate." His voice was deep, resonant, and utterly confident.

He paused and then spoke to the gray-jumpsuited technicki. "Go to the sound bite."

"Gah," the technicki said. Meaning, *Got it.* He made an adjustment and said, "Go."

"NR guerrillas—getting out, and fast. In a hurry like Moses' people, but this time it's the supposed Fascists playing Pharaoh's Army. Where are the rebels headed? We don't know where, but we know when. *Now.* In a helluva hurry."

He paused, then nodded to the technicki, who tweaked the mouse. "Down," he said, nodding.

Smoke knew the drill. One recording for the upperclass public-TV seg, the smallest demographic slice, known as the C viewers; then the sound bite for impatient, hungry middle America, the A viewers: the biggest slice. The last for the semiliterate, the technickis, the B viewers. Other variants would be computer-dubbed in Cantonese, Japanese, Spanish, German, Farsi, Arabic, Ebonics.

"NuRillas," Hand was saying in Technicki. "Gedouwf, hidgoodn'gone, s'pose fash hanimerdown—dunhu buhwheh. Hup."

Hand paused, then nodded at the technicki. "That's it." He turned, smiled at Smoke, widened his smile for Alouette. Behind him the loading machinery went whir, click, clack. "Mr. Smoke. Good to meet you in the flesh." His voice off-camera was higher, daintier.

"Likewise. That was recorded? You're not linked, I trust?"

"Right. Your people'd scotch it anyway." He winked.

Smoke smiled. "We'd sure try. You can send it when we're home free."

"You ready for that interview?"

"We could do a preliminary here, but I'd like to do the bulk of the thing in our media center, so you can see what we've got."

Hand seemed to consider, then touched a corner of his jaw, spoke into his implant. "You got that, anchor? Yeah. Yeah. Okay, well no, we're not going to let them stage a—Right. No, there's no ER." His eyes flicked at Smoke; Smoke knew what ER meant. It wasn't Emergency Room, it was Editing Rights. He was going to have to take whatever they dished out and hope it looked good. That was the deal. MediaSat was the only overGrid outfit interested in covering the story. Too much of a downer, too unprovable, and too rhetorical, was what the others said. The lefties from the underGrid covered them, but who cared? They had the ears of a tiny slice of the populace. The Internet stories of an ongoing New Holocaust in Europe, after all, were countered by the authorities, were dismissed by most people as hoaxes. "Okay, just get that comparison segment ready so we can—yeah." He tapped his jaw joint again, walked toward Smoke, hand out, his smile like a cool breeze as he went to Alouette. "Lead the way, young lady!"

She shook his hand, staring at him. "Your voice changed," she said.

"When I was sixteen," he said, winking.

• • •

Only a few monitors and the linkup mainframe remained in the comm room of the Merino NR headquarters. Hand's technicki had interfaced with the linkup system so they could intercut NR video as needed. But the camera wasn't on yet. Smoke sat across from Hand, who was trying to soften the chill that had set into the room after Hand had let slip this was going to be only a fifteen-minute segment and not the hour special he'd hinted at.

"You can't make people understand in fifteen minutes that they've lost a continent to Nazis when they weren't looking," Smoke said. "It's too big to comprehend, too big to believe without proof. People have this blind faith in the Grid, in media—if their media hasn't told them it's happened, then they believe it hasn't happened. There's this myth that everything is 'covered', everything is reported on, that free media is everywhere. It's been a myth since the last century. And everyone believes the myth. In the face of that—we need at least an hour to get even close to proving it. Lord, just to lay the groundwork."

"You'll have a basis for starting," Hand said. "A springboard. It'll prompt more media interest . . . "

"Bullshit," Smoke said. "The president slithered out of impeachment.

She saw the country through a war so they don't want to hear about her connections to a bunch of right-wing extremists. Okay, they tell us, so she got a little panicky and went too far, World War Three was on, could happen to anyone. So let's put this nasty talk of Fascists behind us and look to the sunny future and . . . the whole schtick. I've heard it two hundred times."

"Maybe they've got a point?" Like a psychotherapist, putting it as a gentle question.

"More bullshit. It's just denial, Hand. American media and American foreign policy hide from the truth because they're tired of conflict and maybe because they're hoping the bastards'll take care of the Third World émigré problem for them—"

"That comes off pretty paranoid. The Second Alliance corporate people were jailed or deported or had to jump the country, Smoke. It's hard to believe they're much of a threat. I'm giving you the benefit of the doubt and we'll cover it from your angle, but—"

"'Much of a threat!' They're running France. Germany now. Italy. England soon "

"England? I was just there. Travel lines are beginning to open, I didn't see any jackboots. Certainly no concentration camps."

"In England, it's just beginning. Why do you think no outsiders can travel in France, Italy—"

"They say it's because of the aftermath of the war. No functional airports yet, cholera, various other diseases, bands of hungry desperadoes—"

"Since when did those kinds of restrictions ever stop media coverage before? What happened to 'fearless war correspondents'?"

"Look, we're wasting a lot of good material here. We should be getting this on camera. Let's see where it takes us, okay?" Hand's most open, winning expression. It bounced off Smoke like a bubble, and Hand let it slide. His face went blank. "Yes or no?"

Smoke snorted. "Let's do it. Maybe you'll see . . . "

Hand nodded to the camera technicki, then raised a hand for a pause. He took out a hand mirror, checked his media-flesh and his makeup, put the mirror away, then pointed at the camera.

"Go, " the technicki said.

Hand conducted the interview in a soft combination of phrasings for A and C viewers. "Mr. Smoke, the public relations division of your organization claims that"—he glanced down at a printout on his lap—"there's an ongoing apartheid throughout Western Europe fast becoming a genocidal Holocaust." He looked up at Smoke. "World War Two Redux?"

"It's not a replay of World War Two, obviously, except in the genocidal sense—and even there it's different. Its ideological foundations are more a distortion of sociobiology than what we knew as old-style Fascist racism. Then again, to some extent it's rooted in an extreme form of Christian fundamentalism. And as for its execution, it's enormously broader. It applies to vast numbers of Arab and Persian and Pakistani immigrants, to Hindus and Muslims from India, to blacks and gays and Jews. Of course, more people than Jews were persecuted by Nazis during the Second World War, but the scale—"

"Whoa, chill out long enough to explain to us how something like this could go on unreported under the noses of the governments and media of Western Europe, of American forces who are still stationed along the front of the war—and most of all, Israel—"

"It hasn't gone on unreported. It's there on the alternative stations, on social media, a great many places. Mainstream media is treating it as a conspiracy theory. But that's not what it is. We've got statements from hundreds of soldiers, including fifty-two officers, complaining of the 'apartheid methods' of the Second Alliance and SPOES . . . "

"The 'Self Policing Organization of European States . . . '"

"Yes. Second Alliance sympathizers in the NATO high command suppressed the reports, saw to it they never reached Congress or the UN. Censorship is easy to justify in those conditions."

"A media blackout over a whole continent? That's a little hard to swallow."

"It's not necessary over the whole continent. What was the last communiqué you saw from France that wasn't from the US military or, say, from the Larousse government? Most of the lines of communication are down. Unauthorized sat-transers were destroyed, cables cut, and fone relay towers down. Travel is still restricted 'until order is restored.' And the question is, what *kind* of order will be restored?"

"And Israel is just standing by as Jews are rounded up—"

"Israel has repeatedly demanded investigations into the stories of new death camps and these so-called 'refugee processing centers.' It's hard for them to go in alone and establish the truth without violating international law. They are assisting us on a certain level. They may well go further . . . "

"We have a new US senator," Hand put in, referring to the printout again, "Senator Jæger, who says, and I quote, 'These NR people are trying to foment a dangerous postwar hysteria, and if you ask me, the whole thing is a leftist fund-raising device.' How about that? I mean, isn't it in your interest to convince people for fund-raising reasons that there's another Holocaust going on, Jack?"

Smoke bit down on his temper till it stopped writhing to get free of his mouth. Finally he said, "It's in the interest of stopping the Holocaust, *Norman*. Senator Jæger's company manufactures the Jægernauts used by the SA to destroy the homes and lives of thousands of innocent people. He's hardly an objective opinion. Why hasn't the UN been shown the charter for SPOES?"

"Ah, right. They're more or less like Interpol was, I believe—"

"No. It's a military alliance which I believe is the blueprint for a single Fascist state uniting Western Europe."

"If I remember rightly, their 'charter' is to locate terrorists and collaborative saboteurs—"

Smoke ground his teeth in frustration. "That 'collaborative saboteurs' chestnut is a smoke screen, an all-purpose phrase they use whenever they want to get rid of anyone. The 'saboteurs' who supposedly helped the Soviets in their invasion are—just by coincidence—always Jews, Muslims, Socialists, anarchists, or the wrong kind of intellectual. The SA arrests anyone it wants with—"

"Now, whoa again. You keep referring to the SA as if it's the same organization that was policing the war zones a few months ago. To the best of our information, the SA is now just an ordinary private-cop outfit."

Smoke looked at him in amazement. "You really believe that?"

"Our information is—"

"Let me run the scenario down for you in its simplest terms," Smoke snapped. "Western Europe has been through hell, and its people are hungry for the kind of orderliness promised by SPOES. But the European countries who are part of SPOES are puppet governments run by the same people who ran the SA. The SA has become a police-action arm of SPOES. They're talking about dissolving their NATO ties in favor of the SPOES charter. Now each SPOES military force is on the surface commanded by nationals from the country it occupies, and most of its troop strength are local people— except for the SA, which functions more or less as the SS did for Hitler's people—but the orders come from outside the country. Each country thinks it's developing a new nationalism, but in fact it's selling its soul to a greater European Fascist state. There are dissenting voices, but—"

"Do you have evidence for any of this? This talk of puppet governments—"

"We have video testimony, affidavits, some of our agents you can talk to. But I'd like to start with the most pressing issue, the images of ongoing apartheid and genocide . . . " Smoke turned and hit a button on the bank of monitors; the technicki recorded the vid for later intercutting. Hand turned to watch the monitor.

The image was sometimes focused, sometimes not; it was apparently shot from waist height, and it wobbled. But they could make out a room packed full of detainees—heads shaved, filthy uniforms, starved. One of them clearly dead. An SA bull suddenly stepping into the shot, grabbing a young girl by the throat, dragging her aside, someone rising to protest, beaten down by an RR stick wielded by a second guard, whose back blocked the cameras. "This video was shot by one of our people who penetrated a processing camp . . . Here's a shot of the SA rounding up 'detainees,' as they call them, into a transport. You can see there are whole families here, old people who can barely walk, children, people herded like animals, hardly a raid on a terrorist camp—"

"Now, this material looks very convincing, and it could be what it appears to be. It could also have been staged, or mixed with computer-generated imagery," Hand said. "You have to admit you have the resources. And we do have some contradictory video from these processing centers." Hand signaled the technicki, who ran the video on another monitor. "This came to us from the French minister of foreign affairs . . . "

Another kind of processing center. Happy, well-fed people in their own clothing in a comfortable dormitory, waving at the camera. A guard handing a doll to a small girl, who hugged him and then kissed the doll . . . Interviews with the 'refugees.' In French, dubbed in English. A man wearing a yarmulke: "I was worried when they asked us to move to the processing center, but when you get here you understand, we have food here, we have safety and warmth—we didn't have any of this at home. They did it to save us from the terrorists. God bless them."

Smoke stared at the screen. "You are going to show this patently obvious fake to the American public?"

"We have to show both sides—"

Smoke turned and pointed a trembling finger at him. "If you don't see for yourself, you're a fake yourself. Come and see for yourself, or you're no reporter. I can get you into Europe. Our lines of transportation are open. It's dangerous, but I can get you in. I challenge you to see for yourself."

Hand glanced at the technicki, who was watching him, curious to see what he'd say. Smoke said, "You can edit this out, you can edit all of this. No one has to know I challenged you to see for yourself. But you'll know, Hand. *Nguyen Hinh* will know."

The two men looked at one another. Hand swallowed. "Set it up. I'll go."

A tall, black Witcher guard in fatigues and boots, pistol strapped to his hip, banged in through the door from the next room. "Intercepted this maybe thirty seconds ago." He passed Smoke a printout. Smoke read:

PD 5
REPORT TYPE IS 0370
!FDC 8/2621 FDC PART 1 OF 2
CARIBBEAN FLIGHT ADVISORY . . .
DUE TO PUERTO RICAN INSURGENCY DANGEROUS
ENVIRONMENT IN LESSER ANTILLES/ PUERTO RICAN
CARIBBEAN ZONE . . . US NAVAL VESSELS AND AIRCRAFT
OPERATING BETWEEN 20 DEGREES NORTH AND
15 DEGREES NORTH ARE PREPARED TO EXERCISE
APPROPRIATE MEASURES. IT IS STRONGLY ADVISED THAT
ALL AIRCRAFT/ FIXED WING AND HELICOPTERS/MAINTAIN
A LISTENING WATCH ON 121.5 MHZ VHF OR 243.0 MHZ UHF
WHEN OPERATING WITHIN THESE AREAS. SPECIAL CAUTION
ADVISORY: AIRSPACE ISLAND OF MERINO.

PD 5
REPORT TYPE IS 0370
!FDC 812621 FDC PART 2 OF 2
CARIBBEAN FLIGHT ADVISORY . . .
MILITARY AND CIVIL AIRCRAFT UNDER ATC CONTROL SHOULD
IMMEDIATELY ADVISE ATC OF ANY CHANGE OF HEADING
AND, IF APPROPRIATE, DECLARE AN IN-FLIGHT EMERGENCY.
FAILURE TO RESPOND TO REQUESTS FOR IDENTIFICATION
AND INTENTIONS, FAILURE TO ACCEPT RECOMMENDED
HEADINGS, FAILURE TO RESPOND TO WARNINGS, OR
CONTINUING TO OPERATE IN A THREATENING MANNER
WILL PLACE AIRCRAFT FIXED WING AND HELICOPTERS AT
RISK BY US COUNTER INSURGENCY AND/OR DEFENSIVE
MEASURES . . .
END OF PART 2 OF 2 PARTS

Smoke passed the printout to Hand, who scanned it and gave it to his technicki. "Get a shot of this." He looked at Smoke. "If that's okay."

Smoke nodded. "You know what it means?"

"It means there's some kind of guerrilla action involving aircraft on Puerto Rico—"

"The revolutionaries on Puerto Rico have no aircraft at all," Smoke interrupted tiredly. "These 'counter insurgency measures' are part of a CIA operation, working through the NSA. They're going to claim the Puerto Rican Communist guerrillas were constructing some kind of military base on Merino. They'll claim the Communists are launching an air attack from there. With aircraft that doesn't exist. They know we're here, which is why we're leaving. And they know we're leaving. They don't intend for us to get away. I'm afraid you visited the island at a rather unfortunate time, Norman."

• 03 •

PARIS.

"St. Zoros," Father Lespere was saying, as he slapped a clip into the assault rifle, "is one of the most important examples of the Flamboyant style of architecture in Paris." His accent was thick, though his grammar was good. Roseland and Torrence had to listen carefully to make out the words. Words like flamboyant and important, spelled the same in French and English, Lespere pronounced the French way. Roseland listened raptly as Father Lespere took aim at the firing range's target. "The south side of St. Zoros, on the cemetery—the decoration is marvelous." He pronounced this roughly mar-vay-you. "The traceries on the gables, the pinnacled buttressing, all the best saints in sculpture, and some very fine gargoyles. These gargoyles, creatures of real character, you understand? Not these banal, bland gargoyles one sometimes sees . . . " He switched off the laser-sighter, which he regarded as unsportsmanlike for target shooting and not much use in a firefight (he was wrong about that, Torrence maintained), and opened fire on the target, a riddled and splintery outline of a man with a mirror-visored motorcyclist's helmet stuck on the top to resemble an SA guardsman. The helmet was quite intact until he opened fire from seventy feet; Roseland jumped a little at the racket of the gun in the narrow, low-ceilinged stone chamber, and the helmet spun on the stump of the neck. When it stopped spinning, its back side was turned to them: shot through, shattered.

Roseland had spent ten days recovering in the NR's chilly, badly outfitted infirmary. But the dingy infirmary was a franchise of heaven, after the processing center. He'd eaten twice a day, and bathed, and shaved, and they'd given him imitation vitamins and blue jeans, boots, and a soft blue plastic jacket.

Now they were a few hundred yards from the abandoned police station that was the NR's regional headquarters, and about thirty-five feet below the nave of the church of St. Zoros, in what had been a wine cellar for the manor that had stood here before the church. The wine racks were long gone; there were only stone flags, stone blocks, a chemlantern, and two battery-powered floodlights for the gallery; the target at the far end of the room stood like a war-disfigured scarecrow against a thick backdrop of bullet-pocked fiberboard and mattresses.

Father Lespere was a man of pale skin and very dark hair and eyebrows; he had a long nose and hands as precise in their movements as in their manicure. He wore the traditional black cassock; his hair was tonsured, but only by middle age, balding at the crown. "And the tower of Elizabeth de Bathory," Lespere went on, sighting in on the belly of the target. "I will show you myself. The art is late Middle Ages, very fine, nothing damaged in the war at all. The interior of the church is splendid: remarkable vaulting—" He fired, stitched a line of bullet holes across the target's middle. He spoke with luxuriant pleasure in the description as he aimed the weapon again: "The vaulting of the side aisles and ambulatories, delicate columns that flow up into the vaults, into ribs like fans, you must set them—Joris-Karl Huysmans compared them to a palm forest." He sighed. "I should have remained in the study of architecture." He passed the gun to Torrence and turned to Roseland. "You will forgive me my enthusiasms, but I have not belonged to St. Zoros very long . . . I was a priest who was really only a kind of tourist guide at Notre Dame, and then when there were no tourists to guide, a priest who was really only a custodian. Do you like our place for target practice?"

"I'm no connoisseur of target shooting, Father," Roseland said. "They can't hear it on the street?"

"No." Lespere watched critically as Torrence fired a burst through the helmet, spinning it on the stump again. "You are pulling the trigger too hard, Daniel."

"I hit it, didn't I?" Torrence said, shrugging a little too briskly. He could be defensive, Roseland had noticed.

"Some of the rounds hit and some did not," Father Lespere replied. "Enough for now. Come on." His cassock whisked softly on the stone floor as he switched off the floodlights, plunging the bullet-crucified target into darkness. He picked up a chemlantern and led the way from the room.

Torrence tossed the gun to Roseland, who caught it clumsily and followed them down a damp, dark, low-ceilinged corridor of irregular stone blocks. There was a faint smell of sewage, with dissolving minerals. And gunpowder.

Lespere bent near Torrence to speak softly, probably intending that Roseland not hear him; but the whisper carried with eerie lucidity along the echoey stone shaft. "The news for you is not good. Apparently you have been identified. They do not know where to find you, but they know who you are. What you look like. They have connected you with the Le Pen assassination. Perhaps it's time you . . . " He hesitated.

"I can't leave," Torrence said. "If I do, people like Pasolini . . . " He didn't finish it, merely shook his head.

"I was not going to suggest you leave. We cannot spare you. I suggest, instead, that you change your face."

"Those kinds of surgeons are in short supply."

"It is your decision, but . . . you need not use those kinds of surgeons."

Roseland felt his gut contract at the suggestion. This Lespere was one hardassed priest. Christ! Basically, telling Torrence that disfigurement was a viable option . . .

Torrence said, "If it comes to that." His voice very flat.

Lespere shrugged. "Do you really suppose it matters how pretty you are? None of us are likely to live a year."

Hearing that, now, didn't bother Roseland at all. It was perfectly, entirely appropriate. (A flash of memory: the Jægernaut arching over Processing Center 12 . . .)

Lespere went on, "You must understand: Klaus is sending *The Thirst* after you. He will do things. This man The Thirst is a German, raised in Argentina and Guatemala—his great uncle was an SS officer. His grandfather a Hitler Youth. His name is Giessen, but they call him The Thirst, and he will *do* things . . . "

Open space swelled around them. They were in a vast, dimly lit room. Their footsteps took on a different sound here. The room was big, very long, two stories up to the pipe-clustered ceiling; it was subterranean but not a cavern; its walls were hidden by strips of exposed insulation, veined with wire; its floors were piled with plastic crates, and cryptic machinery: old-time dynamos and factory presses. The insulation and metal surfaces and crates were sloppily starburst with red and yellow. Paint splashes, splattered with impact bursts. "What's all this?" Roseland asked.

Torrence gestured vaguely, perhaps thinking, Roseland guessed, about the kind of man who could earn a nickname like The Thirst. "Underground storage for the downtown system of fallout shelters," Torrence said. "The crates are mostly filled with loose plumbing parts. They've forgotten all about it."

"Please, take a little stroll, look at this place," Lespere told Roseland gently.

Why? Roseland wondered. But he took a few steps farther into the chilly, shadowy room, looking around. He strolled into the maze of junk, peered into the shadow-wrapped dimness. It reminded him of a big train station in a way, "What are we going to do with this place?" Roseland asked. "Some kind of, um, hideout or—"

Men sprang into view all around him, rifles clicking smartly. Aiming at his chest, or head. They'd been hidden behind crates and machinery, not more than six feet away.

Roseland was paralyzed, impotently clutching the rifle.

"To answer your question," Torrence said, walking up behind him, "we use it for training." He nodded at the guerrillas. They lowered their weapons. "You're going to train with these people."

•••

THE ISLAND OF MERINO, THE CARIBBEAN.

"Someone at the State Department fumbled the ball," Witcher said. Smoke had difficulty hearing him over the whine of the jet. "They couldn't know Hand is with you. They must know that if they bomb an installation with a hotshot American TV journalist in it, it's going to look pretty bad."

"Not necessarily," Smoke said. He was sitting beside a very nervous Norman Hand in the cargo plane's little passenger compartment, talking to Witcher on a fone. He kept the fone screen on the seatback blanked, so Hand couldn't see who he was talking to. "They'll pull some strings, whitewash it, say that Hand was covering this imaginary 'Puerto Rican Communist guerrilla air attack.' Same old bullshit. It'll be worth it to them, to get us." There was a staticky pause before Witcher's reply. He was talking via satellite, a continent and an ocean away, safe in his Kauai estate. "Suppose you're right. We'll try to call them on this one . . . But it'll be too late to—Whoa . . . A trace. Got to go."

Smoke glanced at Hand, saw the reporter's knuckles were white on the arms of his seat. Hand peered out the scratched window; Smoke looked over his shoulder. The airfield was near the beach, and out to sea the picket of American destroyers was visible, gray notches against the horizon. "Why don't we take off? I should've called that damn chopper back—"

"It wouldn't have come," Smoke told him, not for the first time. "They're . . . civilian. They won't ignore the aircraft advisory."

He was thinking of Alouette, glad he had gotten her out ahead of the others. He worried about the islanders. They'd gone into hurricane shelters, a long way from the NR base, but American naval artillery was notoriously inaccurate; its smart missiles so poorly made—by the contractors who routinely ripped off the Pentagon—they weren't so smart . . .

"Why don't we take *off*?" Hand demanded again, his voice a little shrill. Across the aisle, his technicki smiled in quiet satisfaction.

As if in answer, the plane lurched into movement.

The pilot's voice crackled from the fone. "We're getting a stay-down warning, Jack. They claim we can surrender peaceably."

"Accept!" Hand burst out.

Smoke shook his head. "It's a lie. This isn't a military operation, this is CIA. They might or might not take us alive, but eventually we'd all die in their hands."

You they might just put under an extractor and erase your memories of the whole thing, Smoke thought.

He wasn't going to tell Hand that. It would be an acceptable option to Hand. Unacceptable to Smoke.

"See if you can stall them, tell them we're thinking about it," Smoke told the pilot. Feeling sweat stick his back to the seat; hearing his heart hammering in his ears.

There were seventy others with them in the passenger compartment. A few were muttering; no one crying, no one panicking. Every one of them NR; every one of them ready to die.

Their silence touched Smoke, made his throat contract with emotion.

The plane took to the air; two others, almost simultaneously, took off in other parts of the field, carrying the entire NR base. The island was at the end of its usefulness to the NR anyway, Smoke reflected. Most of their work was in Europe now. And on FirStep. They'd divide their operations between the space base and, probably, Israel. A springboard to Europe.

On some level, he was conscious that he was thinking of these things, making these mental preparations, to cover the fact that he was scared as a son of a bitch. He was trying to convince himself he had a future to plan for.

The US Navy, lied to by the CIA, was going to try to shoot them out of the sky.

Of course, Smoke had tried to talk to the ships on radio. He was presumed to be an American radical sympathizer, lying to protect Puerto Rican Commie compadres.

The plane was angling up as steeply as the pilot dared. "We're for it," Hand said. "They'll use hunter-seeker missiles. Exocets, whatever. Blow us out of the fucking sky."

"Quite possibly," Smoke said. He wondered if Alouette was taking good care of his crow.

Smoke looked at Hand, wondering if he was going to become hysterical. Hand sat there rigidly, staring out the window, watching for a missile. Obviously not the war-correspondent sort of reporter.

Trying to broaden his résumé, Smoke thought, and look what it got him.

Finally, Hand took a deep breath and relaxed. "Whatever happens, happens," he said hoarsely, shrugging.

Smoke nodded, then held on to the seat as the plane banked sharply, its engines roaring now. "If it's any comfort, this plane is augmented for defensive actions." He could feel the inertia trying to pull his spine one way and his rib cage another. "Might surprise them."

"Ohshee, cheh'dow," the technicki said, staring out his window, his voice cracking.

Smoke looked over. The plane had banked so that the port wing was pointed almost straight down at the island. Alongside a surfline of blue-white butterfly-wing delicacy, a line of fireballs huffed, threw tons of sand into the sky. The sound and muted shock wave rolled through the plane, which shivered and rattled. Smoke saw the next wave of artillery shelling hit the NR's little airport tower, blowing off its top and splitting it down the middle.

"Neb'zah?" the technicki asked.

Smoke shook his head. "No, nobody there. Evacuated in good time."

"What the hell are those?" Hand blurted. "Look like flying saucers . . . "

Smoke didn't have to look. "They are, sort of. Saucers about two feet across. They fly, or glide anyway, down behind us. We just let go a cloud of them."

"Pulse camouflage," the technicki said, saying it in standard English.

Smoke nodded. "Some of our defensive augmentation. They put out an electromagnetic pulse that distracts the missiles—"

"We got past two of them," the pilot said.

"Two what?" Smoke asked.

"My guess is Patriot Fourteens. Very nice missiles with Multiple Target Capability. The defense industry's finest. But that's not saying much."

Irony in the pilot's voice. You deal with it how you can, Smoke thought.

"We lost them with the pulse cammies?" Smoke asked.

"Looks like. But we've got SPVs coming after us . . . "

"Stop with the goddamn acronyms!" Hand snapped at the intercom.

"Self Piloted Vehicles," Smoke translated. "Drones. They can do things no human pilot can. Sometimes they make mistakes no pilot will, too."

"They're turning off for . . . " the pilot said. "Oh, waitaminnut. Here comes another, and it's not taking the bait. Well, shit."

Smoke closed his eyes. Assuming the pilot had seen a missile getting through to them. He waited for the impact, the noise, the crushing and tearing and screaming. The pain.

A dull, distant *whud*. "They got Number Two." The pilot's voice was almost too soft to hear.

Smoke opened his eyes, relief and horror leapfrogging in his gut. He saw the fireball through the window. Trailers of vapor left by pieces of the disintegrating passenger plane, making it into an exotic flame-red and smoke-black flower against the sky. Sixty-four NR operatives, dead in an instant. Shot out of the sky. To the American media, it would be sixty-four Puerto Rican Terrorists shot down while en route to a bombing run over San Juan.

"Holy shit," Hand breathed, face pressed to the glass. "Fuck. We're next."

Smoke shook his head, feeling tears on his cheek. "No, we're probably out of range by the time they get their RPVs back in line. They haven't got any human-Piloted vehicles." He felt like he was locked up in a flying steel jail, while some fake Smoke was outside the jail cell, chatting with the warden.

"Are we really going to make it?" Hand said. "Get away scot-free?"

Smoke winced. Scot-free. Dozens of his brothers and sisters blown into meat scraps. Scot-free.

Smoke felt like he should have died back there too. Glad he didn't and disgusted that he didn't. Both.

"There's a good chance we're away," he said, clearing his throat. "We . . . If we hadn't got the jump on them, we'd be dead by now . . . "

"So where to now?" Hand asked. "What happens to me?"

"We're going to a place in Mexico," Smoke said distantly. Still seeing, as if projected on the blank screen in front of him, the chrysanthemum of fire and smoke as the second NR transport blew up, like the centerpiece of a funeral's floral arrangement. "You can go on your merry way or go with us, see some things," he said dully. He should try and talk Hand into going along. But he didn't have it in him to say a word more than he absolutely had to.

He felt the old wrenching come back, the uncertainty about what was real and who was important and who he was; seeing, not so far away, the brink: beyond it, the madness that had held him at the beginning of the war. He had been fractured when the SA goons had taken him, tortured him; fractured still deeper when he saw the new Nazis tearing like jackals at the dying corpus of European civilization. Steinfeld and Hard-Eyes had saved him, welded him back together. But the fracture was still there, like a badly welded crack in a steel post. Maybe there was too much pressure on the post. Maybe it was going to break again.

Several of the others were sobbing. Some had lost friends, lovers, maybe relations on the exploded jet. Some simply wept after seeing sixty-four people expunged like flies in a cloud of insecticide. Instantly snuffed out, like pests.

Smoke got out of his seat. There was an NR doctor sitting two rows back; a stocky Filipino woman in glasses, a white dress, and anomalously, a flak jacket. She'd just finished throwing up into a vomit bag as Smoke labored up the aisle to her. Straining against the inertia of the accelerating jet, Smoke leaned against a chair back and said, "Give me something."

(Steinfeld wouldn't ask for a tranquilizer, Smoke thought. Steinfeld wouldn't show his pain, not like this. He'd be moving around, comforting people, helping them get over this. He'd be tougher, more caring; he'd be what we needed now. I'm not Steinfeld.)

The doctor nodded, folded the bag up, dabbed her mouth, wiped tears from her eyes. She took a bottle of pills from her coat pocket, popped one herself, and gave one to Smoke. "Don't take it if you have to do something in an intelligent way."

"Who the hell knows what's intelligent?" Smoke muttered, popping the pill and sitting down.

• • •

From the Second Alliance psych evaluation report on Patrick Barrabas, aged twenty-one, Citizen of the United Kingdom:

Barrabas has the usual British obsession with class issues. He is perhaps more obsessive about it than most. Angry about class barriers—cited the appeal of Nazi Party's promise to dissolve society into one class of grass-roots Caucasians. Hypocritical about class: Seems to have been Cockney, worked hard to eliminate the lower-class accent, manages most of the time to sound upper middle class. Clear-cut and steerable convictions about the lesser races, but maintains: "Not that I believe in genocide, none of that. Repatriation, that's my idea for them." Probably salvageable aggression curve . . . Grew up in a poor London neighborhood where several ghettos intersected, was persecuted by a black gang: good resentment foundations there . . . two years with the National Front "skinheads," for the sake of street protection at first, then politicized firmly. Gave up video technology vocational school after two terms due to inability to pay tuition. Minor digi-vee editing job experience at VidEx before the company became a war casualty: possible use in battlefield video-journalism but deep motivation speaks well for counter-insurgency assignment. No neuroses that are not utilizable. Recommendation: recruit for SPOES enforcement, front line.

[WITCHER FILES NOTE: The American psychologist who conducted the interview and composed the preceding report was recently stripped of his standing by his colleagues for his racist papers on what he called "The Sociobiological Foundation of the Caucasian Imperative."]

• • •

SWINSHOT, ENGLAND.

Patrick Barrabas was marching through a ground fog with twelve other men. They were marching in close formation behind their American trainer. Barrabas was a short, muscular young man. At five foot four and a half, he was a bit touchy about his height. He had good looks: bright blue eyes, wavy red-brown hair, pretty but masculine features—"You should have been a digi-star," his last girlfriend had told him. That had salved his ego a little. He wore a flat-black SA trainee's uniform with infantryman's green plastic boots, carried an SA/Jæger Mark 3 assault rifle, one of the new "smart" rifles, with its special ordnance launcher and microprocessors for aiming and heatseeking and warning you when it was overheated or dirty. But it didn't yet have a battery—or ammunition—more's the pity.

Barrabas was beginning to feel at home in Swinshot, decrepit though it was. Swinshot was the flesh-plucked skeleton of a rural village northwest of Southampton. The New-Soviets had made only tentative forays into England, low conventional bomb runs over military installations. Either confused military intelligence or bad aim made harmless, bucolic Swinshot the target of a carpet-bombing raid. As if synchronicity had arranged another delicious irony, the few surviving buildings were the only ones with any strategic value: the post office still stood, and the city hall, and the police station. The school and the clinic and the old people's home and most of the houses in Swinshot—all were devastated. One of the chapels still stood, only half-caved-in. The village's survivors had been relocated by the government.

The intact buildings were unoccupied, except the chapel, and City Hall, which had been turned over to the company that had been given unofficial-and-yet-official use of the Swinshot area: the Second Alliance International Security Corporation.

And Patrick Barrabas had worked for them, training here . . . how long now? He totted it up in his head as he did a smart about-face, making the mist churn. About eight weeks now. Work? It was more like boot camp, he thought. But he had come to like it.

They were strange people to work for. Clever people, the way they'd put it all together—a security company, a political movement, a religion rolled into one. The SAISC was in hot water in the States, it was said, but in England the corporation openly advertised its services on the BBC like any other company.

When Sparky put him up for the job, he'd thought he was going to be a security guard somewhere. Something dull. But then come to find out there were wheels within wheels, in the SAISC . . .

You couldn't just apply to work for them like any other company. Which was strange as well, because there was a shortage of able men to work in the U.K. after the war, and most companies had people stopping you on the street to hand you an application—but not the SAISC. And there was no SAISC personnel office. You had to know someone on the inside. And then they talked to you till you thought you were going to drop from exhaustion. Made you talk to a shrink. And they put you under the extractor thingie, and maybe they said yes, and if they did, well, here you were.

Marching in a bloody private army, through the rubble.

He'd missed NATO military service with his high lottery number, but he'd have gone, eventually, if the war hadn't ended. When it ended he'd felt a stab of irrational disappointment. A war like that, chances were you'd get yourself killed. Hundreds of thousands had. But afterward, you didn't feel quite a man if you hadn't gone, stupidly trite as that was. It was a feeling you couldn't quite get away from.

He felt better about it now, tramping in step through the morning fog. The sun rising to the east was burning mist off the broken roof of the old chapel. Off to the south, beyond the fallow rye field, a mistletoe-choked oak woods looked grimly dark, as if it were still night within its hoary confines.

"Barrabas, dammit!" McDonnell bellowed at him. "Keep your eyes straight ahead! Did I tell you to gawk at the fucking landscape?" The red-faced, pig-eyed American trainer with his buzzcut hair and almost lipless mouth was tramping along side by side with Barrabas now. Barrabas savored it. He was perfect, even his ugly face. Just like a Marine D.I. in the movies.

Barrabas snapped his eyes forward, suppressing a grin. He liked this "job," he definitely liked it.

"You are working as part of a fine-tuned machine, Barrabas! You can't do your part without paying attention, fuck-face! What do you think we are, here, eh? A lot of individuals? Like fucking Bohemians? Like bloody anarchists? You're just a part of the outfit! We're all one unit or you end up dead, shot in the back by guerrillas!"

• • •

"We're never quite one unit here," Torrence was telling them. "We work together, but we have to be as autonomous as possible, too, partly because we often get separated. There aren't very many of us. Your determination to complete your mission has got to come out of something personal in you, you know?"

Roseland nodded to himself. It felt right.

Roseland and the other guerrilla trainees—mostly French Jews, some Algerian immigrants, a couple of Americans, an Israeli who'd been stranded here, and a Dutch woman—sat on the cold floor in the ring of the lantern light, in a semicircle around Hard-Eyes. Rifles leaned against the dusty crates behind them; the weapons, gathered piecemeal from here and there, were as variegated as the nationalities of the trainees. Ammunition that'd work for everyone was a perpetual problem.

"Certain fundamentals of our overall strategy will be kept from you, though," Torrence went on. "And information about the whereabouts of some safe houses, weapons, observation posts, people who work with us—that is, you know only about the ones you have to know about. Because of the extractor. An extractor extracts information directly from your brain, electrochemically, whether you like it or not. Extractors are expensive—they don't always have one, not right away. And then there's torture, when they don't have access to an extractor, or if your brain chemistry is extractor-resistant. Some people seem to be. But no one is immune to torture. Everyone, eventually, spills whatever they know under torture. Don't kid yourself." He paused to sip weak coffee from a blue plastic mug. "We keep what we can from you, but you already know a lot that can hurt us. You know about Lespere. He's a valuable man. He's got them convinced he's an enthusiastic collaborator. A racist, an enthusiast for the National Front and the Unity Party. He's got the confidence of Larousse himself. And yet you know about him, about what he really is, because he's part of your training. You're not to speak of him outside this circle: not everyone in the NR knows about Lespere—you do, because you're the Point Cadre. Lespere will be using you, directing you—Lespere and I both—for special actions. You've been chosen for your strong motivation . . . "

Why, Roseland wondered, did Lespere have to be part of training? If he was so important, they should leave that to someone else and keep his complicity a secret.

Roseland, thinking about Lespere, suspected he knew. There was a sense of release about whatever Lespere did with the guerrillas; a sense of tensions easing. As if he were letting go, acting out something he needed to get out of himself.

Roseland figured that Lespere insisted on taking part. It was how he kept his sanity after having to chum it up with Nazis, maybe even take part in their genocide in some way. Lespere was a deeply humane man. His conscience led him to the undercover work for the NR; his conscience led him to become a monster.

The pressures these people work under! Roseland thought with awe.

There was a terrible beauty in their sacrifice and in their contradictory mutuality. Roseland was an American Jew. Lespere was a French Catholic priest. Others here were Muslim; the historical conflict between Muslim and Middle Eastern Jew was still hot in their racial memories. But these Muslims, these Catholics, these Jews, were utterly convinced of the spiritual necessity of their work together. They were brethren in a moral imperative that plumbed a humanity deeper than all their differences.

Roseland felt an exquisite pain thinking about it. He was moved, and saddened for them all. Because what had brought them together was horror, and loss. He closed his eyes, seeing Gabrielle's pretty mouth spitting blood and brains . . .

He made himself listen more closely to Torrence. "What all this means," Hard-Eyes was saying, "is that you're on your own in a lot of ways. If you're captured, we probably won't be able to help you. If you escape, you may not be able to find us again—because when someone is captured, someone who knows where home base is, we move on to another. And since you know about Lespere, we'd have to take him out of place, evacuate him. We'd lose him as an intelligence source. And there are other things you know, unavoidably, that we don't want the Nazis to know. So . . . I can't order you to do it, but . . . " He paused a beat, meeting their eyes, his own eyes smoldering with emotion. "Danco . . . Danco was the heart and soul of the Point Cadre. And . . . "

Danco had killed himself on capture, Roseland knew.

Slowly, Torrence unbuttoned his coat. He opened it, and they saw the explosives taped to his chest. "You have a choice. You'll all be issued these. We don't wear them constantly. It depends on the risk of capture. If I'm captured, I'll use mine. Whether you use yours . . . " He shrugged. "We're not the kind of people to indoctrinate you so much that you can't make choices. You'll always be able to think in the NR . . . "

• • •

SWINSHOT.

"The best thing is if you never have to think!" the American told them. McDonnell shouted the words, hammering the verbs with window-shaking authority. "You shouldn't have to make choices most of the time. Your training will make them for you. You'll be so thoroughly trained, you'll know what to do or who to defer to in each situation."

The town hall was very old, with a blackened stone fireplace and a warped wooden floor. All but one of the windows had been dashed out by the bombing shocks and were boarded over. Butter-yellow sunlight, hinting seductively of fragrant summer fields and flower-lined roads, poured through the remaining window, but Barrabas was careful not to look that way. He was turned slightly away from it, in his wooden desk, third row back from the portable instruction screen McDonnell had set up. The screen was like one of those old blackboards that came in a wooden frame and on wheels. But the frame was aluminum, and a wafer-thin TV screen replaced the blackboard. McDonnell moved a control mouse and the video-animated outlines of men shifted obediently. McDonnell's blaring declamation gradually broke down into an instructor's drone. "Suppose the guerrillas are fanned out around us in these derelict buildings. Twenty of them, well spread out. They may or may not be communicating with headsets. Our patrol moves in here in an orderly column. The guerrillas open fire. Some will have armor piercing rounds. Your patrol captain gives you the Ambush Seven command, and you break up into four units of five men each, two units to each side of the street. You've got your helmet filters on; the gas operative has laid down the smoke-and-choke screen and you're rushing the buildings; your unit's APD operative does an AntiPersonnel Device sweep for mines, trip wires, as the rest of you lay down suppressive fire on the high ground. You enter the building behind the designated point man. Should the designated point man be injured and unavailable, the designated *replacement* point man will take his place." The cartoonish SA soldier shapes moved across the screen into the down-angled view of the maze of buildings. "You're communicating on your designated helmet frequencies, using the designated code of the day in case the enemy is monitoring you, so that you move in tandem with the other three units. It's important for each unit to know as accurately as possible where the other units are at any given time for reasons of strategy and the avoidance of 'friendly fire.' Entering the building here, we see a scenario requiring that Unit Man Four and Two move to the right and left and One and Three move down the middle of the room, firing as they go . . . "

• • •

PARIS.

Roseland was scared of getting shot, and felt foolish for it, considering what he'd been through at the detention center. He'd been shot once already that afternoon, right in the heart. And it had stung, too. But it had left just a little welt—the round was only a wax ball containing red soap-liquid, fired by a C02 gun. It was just to mark you, so you knew for sure if you were "dead."

But he'd stood there, marked "dead," looking down the barrel of the grinning Arab trainee he'd stumbled across, then looking at the wet red smear over his heart. And he'd felt his legs go rubbery. He'd had to clutch at the wall to keep from falling. A Jew—shot through the heart by an Arab.

The Arab had slapped him on the shoulder and said, "You'll learn, you're a smart one, I see that!" And offered him a smoke. But Roseland had been spooked ever since.

Alone now, his own CO_2 rifle in his hands—they had about a dozen of them, scavenged from a bombed-out sporting-goods store—he moved down the corridor of dusty crates, squinting into the thick shadows. He paused to wipe sweat-fog from the inside of his goggles, then moved on. Froze at the sound of a scuffle, paint balls smacking some plastic surface about fifty feet away. Someone swearing, someone else laughing.

They're just paint balls, he told himself.

But his mouth was bone dry as he went on, in a half-crouch, air rifle slipping in his sweaty fingers.

They'd been skirmishing for days like this, running short of paint balls. Roseland wondered more than once if all this meant anything in the real battlefield. The guys who wore the white armband were playing SA, but they didn't have armor. A lot of the SA had armor though SA regulars went without much protection. The stuff was expensive. They kept it back for "elite" search-and-destroy and for sentries, who were vulnerable to snipers. But if you did come up against a squad in armor, what did you do when your bullets bounced off them? Laugh sheepishly and back away?

There were ways of getting past the armor, Torrence claimed. They'd get to that part of the training. But still, the odds were in favor of the armored soldier . . .

Next time, real guns. Next time, the SA. Next time, the stuff won't be soapy goo. It'll be warm and red, and there'll be more of it.

•••

SWINSHOT

The kid speaker was a special treat, they were told. Something inspirational. But he was getting on Barrabas's nerves. Maybe it was an aftereffect of the drug.

They'd told Barrabas the Second Alliance didn't use medication-spigots on their soldiers, as some of the NATO forces did. They didn't drug them into kill-consciousness. Barrabas wanted none of that. He'd seen a bloke in a pub, ex-infantryman back from the war, strangle a barkeep into unconsciousness for calling Time. He'd seen the infantry bloke's glazed eyes, the way he'd clutched at the spot on his thigh where the spigot used to be.

Not for Barrabas, thanks all the same. But now they were giving him a "harmless variant of vasopressin, just a memory kicker" so he could "soak up the tactical reflexes." McDonnell had said it throwaway like that, like he was offering a cup of coffee.

Only, the stuff in the inhaler made Barrabas tense and vaguely headachey; it made his eyes itch and his nose dried out. Affected the way things looked to him, too.

Might be that was why the chapel looked like something from a bad dream. Or maybe it was the little blighter with the glittering blue eyes. Their speaker.

They had chapel every morning right before lunch. A bit of the C. of E. chapel was missing, part of the wall and ceiling, at one corner, crumbled in, behind the altar. You sat in the pew and at the end of the sermon, when the sun had moved around the sky some, you squinted against sunlight coming through the break in the wall. Somehow it was appropriate; the wounded church symbolized their sacred struggle, they were told, their sturdy faith still standing despite a crumbling world.

They'd left in the old stained-glass windows, those that had survived, but they'd put in a Second Circle cross on the altar. A big steel Christian cross, with the hologram attachment down at its base.

The boy Jebediah, with his two armored bulls for bodyguards, stood beside the cross, talking softly to the roomful of recruits; softly, but to Barrabas, somehow, the boy could almost have been whispering directly into his ear. The kid was like some toy action-figure in his scaled-down, immaculately tailored uniform: A flat-black uniform with black gloves and wide black belt; the Second Circle symbol on his arm patch: the eye over the cross. Jebediah had brown hair and deep-set glittering blue eyes, an almost girlish face and a voice that hadn't changed yet, telling them, like a perfect little angel, "When I met Rick Crandall, everything changed for me, and I had the wonderful fortune to see what many adults never see." Reciting it, but he had the trick of making it sound as if he'd never said it before. "I saw God's divine plan for us. It's all in one word. *Purity.*" A dramatic pause. "Purity is cleanliness, and if you're not clean, you're in sickness. As we've seen in the last several years, the world is in great sickness. What we have before us is the job of doing more than a little tidying. Purifying is a very strong word, and Rick means it in its absolute sense. He *means* the word to be strong!"

The kid was the Second Alliance's idea of a kind of USO show, supposed to go around to all the troops and cheer them up. "Psyche you up good," McDonnell had said. "So listen up." Up, everything was up. Up the White Brotherhood.

Barrabas glanced around at the others. They were rapt; the kid had them in his soft, rosy little palm.

But to Barrabas, the kid seemed less like a sending from God. To Barrabas he seemed like a well-oiled robot. And maybe a bit around the bend. What ten-year-old kid could talk like this with such conviction and still be in his right mind?

Finishing, the kid said breathlessly, "God has put his sacred blueprint in each and every one of us. Behold." The boy switched on the hologram.

Humming faintly, a three-dimensional representation of a DNA molecule shimmered into being around the stainless-steel cross. Above it floated an eye. "This is the configuration"—the kid, to Barrabas's satisfaction, had a little trouble saying "configuration"—"of genes which can be found as part of the DNA chain of each and every man in this room. It is the distinctive DNA marking of the Upper Caucasian race. And as you can see, God watches over it. And in our own smaller way, it's our job to protect it too . . . " And that was it. The kid led them in a hymn: "Racial Purity Is Thy Will." Then he smiled shyly and turned off the hologram.

McDonnell, tears in his eyes like a little kid himself, prompted the recruits into a standing ovation and a hymn as the boy, carrying his hologram box under one arm and Crandall's Corrected Bible under the other, was escorted from the chapel.

The service ended. Barrabas shook his head, walking out into sunlight. What had happened? That morning he'd been feeling good, feeling like a part of something bigger than himself, and loving it. Feeling strong in it.

But something—maybe the drug, maybe the sight of the self-righteous little prig talking about the genes . . .

Maybe that was it. All that talk of genes was too close to talk of breeding, which sounded like aristocracy. Class stuff. You had to stick with white people over the wogs, but this stuff about genes, that was right in line with notions of royalty. Set his teeth on edge.

"Barrabas!" McDonnell said, stepping up beside him. He took Barrabas by the arm and led him off to the side of the little group lining up for lunch. Barrabas was shaken: How had McDonnell known the treason he'd been thinking? Was it written on his face?

But it wasn't that. "You're getting your orders early," McDonnell said, handing him the papers. "You're going to Lab Six, up by London somewhere. They're not giving out the location. Sending someone to pick you up."

"What?" Barrabas blinked at him.

"You've got some kind of camera skills?"

"I did some video work, is all—"

"It's that and they've decided you've got the right attitude or something. I didn't get the lowdown." He was a little apologetic. "You'll see action later, you can count on it. They want you to vid some kind of experiment . . . He shrugged, and clapped Barrabas on the shoulder. "Good luck."

He walked away. Barrabas stared after him.

He wasn't going to Paris. He was going to . . . Lab Six?

He looked at the papers. Yeah. Lab Six.

• 04 •

THE OUTSKIRTS OF PARIS, FRANCE.

Dan Torrence sat in a rotting easy chair with his feet up. Roseland glanced at Torrence, could see only his Hard-Eyes in a bar of harsh light coming through the slat. Roseland was hunched on a wooden box beside him. They were hunkered down in a blind made of trash. It looked like the rest of the roof: a trash heap, stuff thrown from the taller, adjacent building by some errant Soviet shell the previous year. Sheathed in damp cardboard, black plastic sacking, ancient broken rooftile, and a half-gutted mattress matted with a rain-gooey beard of stuffing, they watched through the shaded slats as the guards changed at Processing Center 13.

The night was almost warm, but it was damp in the blind and reeked of mildew. Roseland bent and peered through the lower slat, watched the Second Alliance bulls, seven stories below, gathered in a knot of high-tech body armor, talking, laughing. One of them had his helmet off, was smoking a cigarette. Roseland could just make out the coal of his cigarette, faintly pulsing as the guard inhaled. "They're more armored than they were before," Roseland said softly.

"Your breakout shook 'em up," Torrence said.

Behind the glare of floodlights and beside the mound of rubble that had been PC 12, Processing Center 13 was shaped like a stubby high-rise made of rectangular shadows. Only one light was visible, at the guard's office, second floor.

"You know, we'd never get tower evacuation before their reinforcements come," Torrence said.

Roseland swallowed, a painful scraping in his dry throat. "There's got to be a way." He had to say what he'd been thinking, and had tried not to say, for too long. "You waited too long already. I mean—didn't you guys *know?*"

"There aren't very damn many of us," Torrence said defensively. "Some of us sprang a work camp, up in Belgium. Four hundred refugees were killed. We lost *forty* fighters, man. We're hoping that . . . well, we've got some people working politically. Trying to get the pressure on to stop this shit from the outside. While we concentrate on what Steinfeld calls pressure points." There was a shrug in Torrence's voice.

"We can't let this go on anymore," Roseland said.

Torrence nodded. "We're risking it all, but . . . " He sighed. "There's a way, maybe. We've got a man who thinks he can get into a Jægernaut. We could use it to block the reinforcements, give us a chance to move the others out . . . " He shrugged. "I dunno . . . "

A Jægernaut. Roseland's heart revved at the thought. The justice of it. *Go with it, sell Torrence on the idea.* "That'd work. It'd be a propaganda victory, too . . . the Jægernauts are a symbol. And hey, you got to understand, you'll triple your recruits after this, at least," Roseland pointed out.

"Most of those we rescue won't be capable of fighting," Torrence said. "They'll need medical help. Getting them to safety once we break them out is a logistical nightmare. We're gonna try to get them to the NATO hospital and hope they're believed . . . "

"So what do we do at this end?"

"Get them at shift change. They do it all at once—so we'll do it that way too. All but two are together, then. We get most of them at once, with armor piercers, and they don't hole up anywhere. We can't handle a siege situation; we've got to get *in*, fast."

"What about the two upstairs?"

"Have to hit them with an RPG."

"Blow the office from out here? That'll take out maybe half the floor above them, kill some prisoners."

"I don't think it can be helped." Torrence's voice had no apology in it. "We haven't got time to do it any other way. We've got all those people to move out . . . "

"They're going to be scared," Roseland said, "and an explosion'll scare 'em worse." He felt lame saying it. It sounded trivial, but it wasn't. Only, it was hard to explain how it wasn't. "They saw what happened to PC 12 . . . "

"They'll come with us; they won't have a choice," Torrence said.

Roseland nodded. *None of us have a whole lot of choice,* he thought.

He realized, then, that he was scared of being killed in this raid. Breaking out of PC 12, he hadn't been scared of dying. That was living death. He'd seen people die every day. He'd seen people spiritually murdered, too. Death had seemed a strangely viable option.

Now he was ashamed to realize he wanted to live again; ashamed because of what had happened to Gabrielle; to the children he had seen dragged away, and beaten, or dying of cholera with not even an aspirin to soothe them.

His gut churned with the wrongness of his own survival. He thought about his mother, and remembered that she'd let herself die after his dad had gone. She'd been healthy, but then she mostly refused to eat, and wasted away. She had let pneumonia get her. She'd known what to do.

"I'm sorry," he muttered.

"About what?" Torrence asked, glancing at him, his Hard-Eyes going into shadow when he turned.

"Never mind," Roseland said. "Thinking aloud."

He stared out the blind at the Processing Center . . .

Torrence stared at him for a few moments. "Let's get out of here before they do heatseeker check. They send up those fucking birds sometimes, spot checking."

"Let's do it."

They crawled out the back way, through a tunnel of trash.

• • •

JUST OUTSIDE OF TIJUANA, MEXICO.

Jerome-X was sick of being cooped up. This was almost as bad as the fucking jail.

Not that there was anything appealing outside the building. I mean, fuck it: Go ahead, go outside. He'd seen it, coming in on the plane. In the distance, maybe four miles from here, was the outskirts of Tijuana. Junkyards, abandoned resorts, shantytowns. Around "the ranch" was just desert—a tarantula-haunted, scorpion-infested, ugly brown dusty desert. Cactus and twisted little gray trees, and along the cracked, empty concrete highway the occasional rusty car pocked with bullet holes.

Not even a goddamn cantina around the ranch.

The ranch. An old therapeutic spa for bogus cancer cures, purchased by Witcher and converted for the NR.

Jerome-X sat in the air-conditioned, cinder-block lecture room in a wheelchair. That was what they had to sit in, old, motorless wheelchairs, with rusty spokes. They came with the ranch. "If you aren't crippled before you sat in this thing," he mumbled to Bones, "you will be afterward."

Bones—gaunt, zombie-phlegmatic, ghetto-black Bones—shook his head at him once, smiling but reproachful. Meaning: Shut up and pay attention.

There were seven students, counting Jerome-X and the little girl, and there was the instructor, Bettina: a three-hundred-fifty-pound (Jerome's chip calculated) black woman with Rasta'ed hair; she was close to six feet tall, sweating despite the air-conditioning, wearing a printout shift. It was a pink Tuffpaper dress, a cheap brand that used the same patterns for its line of paper towels. As the day wore on, her sweat would make the dress deteriorate, bit by bit, under her arms, crumbling its edges into little pink worms of synthetic paper-cloth.

The floor shuddered faintly as she strode back and forth in front of the holographic illustrator, tapping factors into place with her fingernail cursor, explicating the computer underground in her hoarse New Orleans drawl.

The holustrator had been an object of fascination for Jerome-X the first few days he was here. When it was turned on, it looked like an astrolabe of translucent neon lines, hovering in the air about six feet across. The 3D cursors moved about in the faintly reticulating globe like fireflies in geometric formation; formations that split into contrary asymmetries as luminous, floating numbers flickered by. "Computer viruses," Bettina had explained that first day, "and yo' so-called computer 'tapeworms,' were de pests of de end of de twentieth century . . . "

And despite advances in decryption and the use of hard partitioning write-protects, the only thing that reliably resisted the predatory viral programs was the cybernetic immune system provided by parallel programming. The "clean" system of the secondary and tertiary computers interlinked with the primary mainframe to watch over the primary programs. "But—dere are ways: A smart enough virus can redirect de code traffic to fool de guardian computer. And if we git ourselves parallel progammed—lotta brain chips working together—we stand a better chancea outsmartin' de guardian. We use de holustrator to practice dat cooperation. We learna be awarea one another as on-line processing factors . . . "

They were here to improve their chip-to-chip communication for underground information dispersal. And for one other, more trenchant reason . . .

To learn to be human computer viruses . . .

It had all seemed very romantic at first, when Bones had pitched it at him. Bones, it turned out, was New Resistance. The NR was a brotherhood, Bones said, a brotherhood that transcended race and nationality. And it could be a refuge, too. After the jailbreak, Jerome needed a home. He was on the run. And even internally, Jerome felt homeless and fugitive. Seeing himself in cybernetic summary, with unwanted objectivity; seeing his own shallowness.

I've been jerking off all this time with video graf, he told himself. I've been playing with the toys of the ego.

The New Resistance was in line with his own political convictions, his mistrust of the Grid, the power structure. Like Bones, he was convinced that the Second Alliance's attempt to take over the US wasn't isolated. He'd heard too many stories through the hacker networks about the repression overseas. Like Bones, he believed that the New-Soviets had been *pushed* into their aggression, forced into World War Three, by the economic machinations of the multinationals. Big Business had wanted a conventional military confrontation and now it wanted a Fascist power structure in order to further roll back the threat of communism. Jerome was no enthusiast for communism, but he understood its provenance: the people at the bottom of the pyramid were tired of holding up the ones at the top. They wanted a fair share.

Bones's offer had seemed like serendipity. Join the Resistance. Travel, meet interesting people, all expenses paid; try not to get yourself tortured and murdered by Fascists. Okay, there were drawbacks, the likelihood of getting killed was one of them, but . . .

But it had seemed like just what the doctor ordered then. Now it seemed like a trap.

He felt their hands on his brain in some sense, molding him. He felt himself molded into a tool for their political imperatives.

Maybe all that was just the perception of a man with cabin fever, he thought. Too many days in this room. Staring at the bare cinder-block walls, or into the headache-maker—the holustrator. Watching Bettina thunder back and forth, her enormous breasts tweaking his libido while her thick, collapsing ankles made him wince. But then, he'd always had this weird *thing* for, ah, heavyset girls . . .

Stop evaluating the woman on those levels, Jerome. Take another deep breath and give it a chance. Bones was a right guy . . .

Bettina was saying, " . . . and Jerome, you focus on yo' factor and work wid Alouette."

Jerome-X sighed.

Bettina paused, turned to him. "You got a problem with dat, honey?"

"Uh-no." But he did. The little girl, Alouette, was smart, some kind of genius and a natural with this stuff. But he knew her; she'd run off into playing with cellular automata and leave him holding the processing bag. He glanced at her and saw her pouting. Little kids don't hide that stuff. "No, she's good, but . . . "

"She good but what?" Bettina asked. "Hell, she faster on de uptake den you are."

"It's just that . . . " He glanced at Alouette. The little black girl, sitting with her feet dangling, looked as if she was going to cry. She was too damn young for this. How could they do this to her?

Most of the time, though, she loved working with chips. She seemed happy, except that she missed her dad. The one they called Smoke . . .

She was happier here than Jerome was. "It's just that I'm burnt out, is what it is," Jerome burst out. "I need a fucking break—" He glanced apologetically at the little girl. "I need to get out of here. I mean, for a day or—or something."

Bettina checked the time blinking in a corner of the holustrator. "Shit. Dat's it for today." She tapped the foot switch with a toe, and the shimmering globe vanished. "We do dis set in de morning. I guess it time to break out de recreation. We got a video to show, and you can each hab two Tecates. Except Alouette."

Alouette's pout deepened. "I can't see the video and drink beer?"

"No. You can hab a Dr Pepper. And you can get on de bus." Bettina grinned at her. "Mario's going take you to de Tijuana Sheraton to see a man."

"Smoke! It's Smoke!" The little girl flashed a smile like sun-washed seashells. "Can I take Richard?"

"Yeah, sho, what I care you take de crow."

Alouette made an excited motion with her hands, as if she were patting down invisible dough. And then she sprinted through the door. .

There goes one of my classmates, Jerome thought. Gnarly.

"Go on now, alla you," Bettina said.

Gratefully, Jerome got out of his desk, stretching. The others moved toward the door and he started to follow.

"Not you, Mr. Burnout," Bettina said, blocking Jerome's way. "I wanna talk to you."

He groaned inwardly. *Another ideological pep talk.* As the last of the other NR students filtered out of the room—Bones glancing back with a funny, rueful expression on his face—Jerome said, "Hey, Bettina, I know what you're going to say. I hear it every night from Bones. I got to either get my motivation together or get out."

Bones closed the door behind him. Jerome was alone with Bettina.

"You got to get some shit in perspective." She put her hands on her hips and took a step toward him. Like the rolling of a great soft wave, coming toward the beach. "You tired of twelve-hour days, workin' every day, little holustrator headaches? You going to go up against a cybernetic mind got a computing capacity dat compares to you like Einstein to a Chihuahua. You wanta hack into de SA's computers, some of de mos' sophis'icated around, you got to be committed to *work*."

"I know that, I just—"

"Besides which, who de hell *you* to complain?" She took another step toward him. He could smell her. Salty, meaty, sweaty, and female. Not unpleasant really, if a bit overwhelming. "Dere's thousands of people under de fucking jackboot in Europe, women and children, sufferin', starvin'. Dyin'." She shook her head, came closer. He moved back.

"I wasn't complaining. I was . . . well, making a suggestion, like. This is creative work. I do better creative work if I get a little, I don't know, R and R and maybe some, uh . . . "

She took another step toward him. He stepped back, looking into her big brown eyes. Trying not to think about her big brown . . .

He swallowed.

"Maybe some what?" she said. "Some *pussy?*"

"Uh . . . "

"You think I don't see you watching me?"

"Well, I . . . "

She had him pressed against the wall now; she radiated heat: she was a pliant, dusky sun; her great, barely confined breasts were puddles of sensation on his chest. They seemed to suck at him. He could almost feel the gravitational pull of her mass: a delirious heaviness. He felt a rustling at his crotch; his erection, bent like a bean sprout in his pants, struggling to reach her nurturing warmth.

"Come here, skinny little white boy."

She enfolded him then, and a few moments later there was the sound of paper ripping.

● ● ●

KAUAI, HAWAII.

How long have they been with me now, Witcher asked himself, looking at Marion and Aria and Jeanne. Three years? Four? Something like that. He was becoming dependent on them. As he got older, he found it harder and harder when he had to go away from them. They were a tonic, as his father would have said.

Pretty girls pretty girls pretty girls with guns. Arrange them in the room like flowers in a vase.

They were in his bedroom at nine o'clock on a sunny, crystalline Hawaiian morning. They'd all slept in the bedroom, Witcher on his single bed with its lacquered mahogany backboard, the girls on the big, very big, round bed across from his. Where he could see them, if he woke in the night.

One wall, curtained with white silk now, was a mirror. The other held Witcher's professional awards, citations and certificates, framed and mounted. He hadn't received one in years, had become too reclusive for the bonhomie of the business world. Another wall held the doors to the walk-in closet, with the girls' vanities lined up in them, their video mirrors, and the Jacuzzi.

The seafront side of the room was all silver-curtained glass doors; the doors were closed, but from somewhere he could smell the sea breeze.

Sometimes he felt a little guilty, in his comfort. But his foresight had made it possible. The western world was mired in war, the residue of war, and poverty; he had invested in the East. His money was all about China and SE Asia.

Aria was doing her calisthenics, wearing only her bikini panties. The tall, Amazonian fullness of her; the ripple of her exaggerated extreme-body-builder muscles; the Swedish gold of her hair, her skin. The gold-plated Walther autopistol strapped to her thigh put an edge on her erotic appeal. Those jiggling golden breasts; those deeply set jade-green eyes . . .

He was pleased she hadn't taken off the weapon before doing her exercise. She knew he liked to see it shine beside the other shininess of her perspiration. (He did hope, though, that she showered soon. She also knew he disliked anyone getting their bodily effluents on the furniture.)

And Jeanne. Lying on the bed, on her tummy, nude but for the prescription dark-blue sunglasses, reading Bataille's *Historie de l'Oeil*. Small, this creature, small-breasted and only five two, but full-hipped, softly dimpled all around. Straight, Cleopatra-cut raven hair, bangs over her tinted glasses like the fringe in a funeral limo's window. She knew he sometimes liked to see her wearing only the blue glasses.

And her skin. He never tired of it. Alabaster, touched with rose pink here and there. Her black hardened-plastic carbine—plastic but quite real, quite lethal—leaning against the bed, within reach. Jeanne.

And Marion. Watching a rock TV show without the sound on. As usual. Half Puerto Rican. Short and busty. Heavy kohl on her brown-black eyes. Two little rings in one nostril, gold wire stitched up and down the edges of her ears. Short auburn hair, spiky, each spike tipped with a different color. Made him nostalgic for the college-circuit punk shows he'd gone to in his early twenties. Long time ago. All that shared and hopeless anger . . . Marion wearing a black neoprene bikini—amazing that she could sleep comfortably in that thing—and a black lace brassiere. You could see nipples through it the color of dried blood. Spike heels that looked as if they'd been carved of volcanic glass. Black painted finger- and toenails. She was, culturally if unconsciously, a part of her own little demographic tribe. Her submachine gun, one of those transparent jobs that showed off its bullets, lying across her knees, under her hands. Her hands reposing like black-beaked doves on it.

Sometimes he thought: *Maybe I should do it. Actually make love to them. Physically do it. Maybe they're disappointed I never actually do it. That I just like to have them there to look at, play with, pet a little.*

Probably not. They were hired escort-bodyguards, expensive ones; courtesans who could fight and shoot. They were his own secret service and, in an austere way, his companions. They were professionals, and to them it would be just more work if he wanted to actually have sex with them.

He was having sex with them, after his fashion. Just watching them move about. Knowing that he *could* fuck them if he wanted to. They were available. Profoundly available. They were there for him, eternally waiting. Sometimes he made them strike poses. Spread their legs, torquing this way and that. Jut their bosoms, tease him with their expressions. Sometimes he put his face close to them, so close he could feel the body heat of the girl on his lips. Sometimes he'd put on the freshly laundered silk gloves and pet them a little. He'd order them to make love to one another; combine and recombine them as he watched from a chair by the bed. They were all bisexual. And he paid them breathtakingly well.

So they didn't mind if he chose their clothing and their unclothing; their perfume and their bath soap; their makeup and their cold creams. Their lingerie and their weapons.

He was convinced that if he actually had sex with them, it would be a let-down. Any one of them, he didn't doubt, was quite proficient. But the act itself had always been a disappointment to him. The excellence, the exquisite essence of sex, for Witcher, was in the contemplation of it. The anticipation. The almost. The allure. *That* was the high. His refinement of voyeurism was an esthetic achievement, really, an art form that he was proud of. Was he making them into objects? Sex objects? Partly. Making them into art objects, more truly, with his mind the gallery for his art. That's how he felt about it. Arranging them around him like the parts of a living erotic collage.

But sometimes . . . he felt oppressed by their mocking nearness; near and yet far. Their availability and tenderness—but underneath it, they always maintained an emotional distance.

How could he expect anything else?

He couldn't. And sometimes that depressed him.

It helped to get away from them for a while when he felt that way. As he was beginning to, now.

"I'm going to have breakfast in the main office," he said. "Need to talk to old Lockett. He gets flustered when he sees you. You want your breakfast on the balcony?"

"Yes, please." Jeanne didn't took up from her book.

"Thanks, Dad," Aria said, as she did her t'ai chi.

"That's be great, Dad." Marion absently reached over, toyed with Jeanne's ass.

They called him Dad, and he encouraged it. He wasn't sure why.

"I'll have it sent down. Then take a patrol around, check out the grounds, will you?"

"Sure thing, Dad."

"You got it, Dad."

"We got it covered, Dad."

• • •

Witcher's isolated beachfront estate on the Hawaiian island of Kauai was watched over by a dizzying variety of reconnaissance devices; by satellites and motion-assessment cyber-eyes; by vibration sensors and overflight recon birds; by a variety of cameras and human guards. Aria, Jeanne, and Marion were just three of fourteen bodyguards.

But it was Witcher who saw the thing first, just looking out his window.

"It can't go on," Witcher's accountant was telling him, shortly before Witcher saw it. "It simply can't go on!" Mincing through the sentence. Lockett—who was on a video display, his image sat-shot from New York—pursed his lips in his prissy way, and as usual Witcher thought of Lockett's closing lips as the shutting of a clutch purse. "Your capital outlay is just not matched in the—"

"There are other issues here besides financial convenience," Witcher said. He was standing at his breakfast bar, picking at the remains of his morning's organically grown fruit salad, gazing absently out the window as he talked to Lockett. The sea was restless today. Thin clouds skied ahead of the wind, and below the clouds a single aircraft flecked the azure. "The NR is an important step in the direction that I . . . "

Witcher's voice trailed off.

The aircraft had birthed something out of itself. It was too far away to make it out clearly. But it was growing . . .

"Jesus!"

He ran for the hurricane cellar.

"Now, look . . . " Lockett was saying from the monitor behind him. "You can't pretend it's going to go away . . . this kind of debt . . . "

The voice diminishing, lost as Witcher half dove, half ran down the steps—then grabbed at the railing as the world roared and the building rocked around him.

A missile. He couldn't believe it. How dare they.

He watched a crack make its way across the concrete basement wall ever so slowly. *Crick. Crick-crick.* He waited for the building to come down around him.

But the crack stopped spreading; the building quieted down. Whatever was left of it was going to stand.

Slowly, on wobbly legs, he climbed the stairs, into smoke and shouting, flickering light. A few shards of glass tinkled from the crust remaining in the frame of the picture window. Flame licked down the hallway; gray smoke collected under the cracked ceiling. The monitors were blacked out; two of them cracked, one caved in.

Maynard, his new chief of Security, a whip-thin black man in a sky-blue jumpsuit, came in wearing a gas mask but coughing underneath it. Witcher felt his spine freeze, and asked, "Did they nerve-gas us?"

Maynard shook his head. "No, I'm wearin' the mask against smoke." He pulled it off, and his face was sheathed in blood from a cut on his forehead. He was gasping, leaning against the tilted breakfast bar. "You okay, Mr. Witcher?" When Witcher nodded, Maynard went on. "There were two more missiles, but we got those, they went down in the ocean. The one that got through hit the sun veranda, took out the whole south wing. The aircraft is gone. We didn't get a clear make on it. We'd better get you out of here."

"You'd better run a check for antigens, especially viral agents."

Maynard looked around nervously. "Germ warfare?"

"Chances are slim, but check." They wouldn't have used one of the viruses; they wouldn't want to tip anyone off about them. They didn't know the New Resistance was aware of their viral program; and they didn't know about Witcher's contact in their lab. At least, last he knew they didn't . . .

Witcher had to wet his mouth, working up saliva, before he could talk. "Anybody hurt?"

"Your whole kitchen staff. Most of them dead."

Witcher shook his head impatiently. "I mean *the girls.*"

"They're okay, they were out on the grounds, on the other side. They're checking the fences now."

"Okay. Get on the fone in the limo, get some paramedics out here, then get the chopper warmed up. We'll risk the sky. I want out of here fast."

"Where to?"

Witcher hesitated. The Second Alliance was behind the attack, of course. They had decided to take the offensive. They were tired of playing with his intermediaries. His funding was the lifeblood of the resistance. They were trying to slash the artery.

He had to get way out of range.

"Book me on a shuttle to FirStep. "

Maynard blinked. "The Space Colony? Seriously?"

"Seriously. Have the girls go to my suite in The Waikiki till I send for them. Tell Russ Parker I'm coming out. And get yourself bandaged up. See a doctor when he comes."

Maynard turned to go.

Witcher called after him. "Maynard—make that shuttle ticket a one-way."

• • •

JUST WEST OF LONDON, ENGLAND. LAB SIX.

It had taken Barrabas all morning and half the afternoon to get clearance for Lab Six. Interrogation, extractor mind searches, more psych profiles, sheer bureaucratic suspicion. He was afraid they might have stumbled onto his misgivings about the Second Alliance, his dislike of the boy Jebediah, and his mistrust of their reverence for aristocracy. But they hadn't followed up the right chains of associations, it looked like, because here he was at last, walking into Lab Six with the albino.

"It's such a relief to be back in England after Paris," Cooper was saying. "You can't get a proper biscuit there, and they have no understanding of heated housing."

"Oh, yes?" Barrabas said, thinking he was expected to say something. He was tired from all the interrogation, from trying to defend himself without being defensive. It was like balancing on a narrow tree limb in a wind.

Both men were wearing white lab jumpsuits. They walked down a hallway done in dull-green tile and soft lights, with a temperature so exactingly controlled you never felt even a fractional change in temperature from the mean. Cooper, with his one pink eye and one blue eye, his dead-white skin and wispy thatch of white hair, had startled Barrabas when he'd first seen him. Naturally Barrabas had tried to conceal that reaction.

"I understand that you, ah, were slated for another kind of work for the Alliance," Cooper said, superficially apologetic. "But the war, you see, has created a shortage of available technicians. We have to make do . . . "

Make do? Insulting, that was. But Barrabas shrugged it off as Cooper unlocked the double locks of the editing room.

"All this security is so tiresome," Cooper said. "It really is an impediment, don't you know."

Digital editing equipment, white plastic consoles, and chromium interfaces filled most of the small editing room. A wall-size video screen stood beyond it. "Here's your workstation," Cooper was saying. "If some of the equipment is unfamiliar, we'll try to get hold of the appropriate manuals."

"I know the main unit here, but this other stuff . . . " Barrabas shook his head. "It's like I tried to tell them, I had a year of video tech voccie and I worked about two weeks at VidEx before they went belly-up. I'm not real experience—"

"Oh, we'll soon get you up to form. I've been doing some amateur editing myself, and I can operate the main unit. Some of the other stuff is a bit, ah, arcane . . . " He activated the machinery as he spoke, tapped rewind. "I was just going over the recordings when they called and said you were here, so we've got wizard timing, anyhow. We're really not supposed to leave this material in the machines when we're out of the room, but I locked it up and, ah, I only popped out for a few minutes. I doubt we've been infiltrated by spies in the last five minutes, eh? But Klaus and Colonel Watson aren't much interested in common sense . . . Ah, here we are."

He hit the play button and the screen rezzed up a slightly blurry image of the detention pens in the experimental center near Lyon. It was a down angle on three pens of wretched-looking prisoners, divided up along racial lines. Brown, black, white. "I suppose you've been briefed?" Cooper asked. "As to my, ah, work, I mean."

"Well, no, not really. That is, a little. Psychological warfare against mongrel terrorists, they said."

"Yes, ah, something along those lines. Amongst other things. I'm a social geneticist, you see. In this experiment we're attempting to prove that racism is instinctive—not so we can tell the world, but so we can activate the instinct where needed and bring people around to our, ah, *cause*, don't you know. Here we used increased survival-stress factors to promote racism between the three groups . . . I enjoy using the fast forward here." He chuckled. "Watch." He hit the button, and the video fast forwarded through several days of prisoner millings and interaction, so that the figures, seen from above, surged around and betwixt one another like beans in boiling water; whirling together, bouncing apart, a feverish human Brownian motion. "If you watch closely, you can see the pattern superseding over time, a kind of rhythmic surge, back and forth, between the pens, as they move in slow waves of aggression that gradually build up till we remove the barriers and they come together in Secondary Aggression—an outbreak of violence." He slowed the images down so they could see the detainees in combat, race against race, maiming one another with teeth and fists and feet.

Barrabas's stomach lurched. *Be a man,* he told himself.

"Of course," Cooper went on, "these racist instincts are usually well under control in most people—it's possible to condition them out entirely. And some people are resistant to them—they may lack that particular behavioral gene. You can see some of them hanging back."

"What's my part in all this?" Barrabas asked.

"You'll be editing this recording with me, and some others, for presentation to the Inner Council. And to certain select individuals. Also, you'll be helping me review video—we have some prisoners we regard as salvageable, if they're racially appropriate. We check through the vid for the right bone matrices, the other indicators. A winnowing process, don't you know . . . " He was switching feeds, going to another vid.

Barrabas watched with mounting discomfort as Cooper showed him studies of "degenerative behavior in Detention Center prisoners"; the "degrees of resistance and the submission points, in reference and contrast" as Jewish and black and Oriental and homosexual prisoners were tortured (one of those made him gag, something Cooper ignored—Cooper understood the need for workplace acclimatization) using techniques developed by the CIA and perfected by Chilean and Guatemalan secret police; experiments in "efficiency-execution of prisoners"; nerve-gas tests on prisoners; experiments in mind control on children separated from their parents under enhanced-trauma conditions and "undergoing behavioral reprogramming with negative/positive stimulus." And then the last recording . . . of the squirming pink things.

"Blimey!" Barrabas burst out. Backsliding to old speech mannerisms in his shock. "What the bloody 'ell!"

Cooper was shaken himself, for, a different reason. "Not supposed to be on here. You weren't supposed to . . . " His finger hovered over the off button. But then he shrugged and drew his hand back. "Well, you've, ah, seen them. You'll have to see them eventually anyway, although we'd planned to do some further extractor work with you—we can always erase your memories later, I suppose."

On the screen were half a dozen semi-human creatures. Squirming, wheezing, hairless pink things, rather like shaven puppies standing on their hind legs. But with flattened, slightly warped human features. They had hands too big for their arms, double-length fingers, receding foreheads—the skulls of chimps behind human faces—and shrunken human genitals. No nipples. They were a bit bigger than German shepherd puppies. As Barrabas watched, one of them defecated on itself, then scooped the stuff up in its fingers and smeared it on another creature's back in a spiral pattern . . .

"These are our darling little subhumans," Cooper was saying. "S-Human 6. Our sixth generation. I call them Puppies. People Puppies. They *are* rather like puppies, aren't they?"

"What are they?"

"The work force of the future. Or, anyway, an early model of it. A proto-type. They're genetically engineered for certain characteristics . . . We've not got all the kinks out of the old DNA spiral, as you can see, but we're working on it, coming along nicely. These are rather stunted, it's true. Once the mongrel races and the otherbloods are eliminated, these subhumans will be needed to fill a certain, ah, economic niche. In a way they're idiot savants—they're animal-stupid on one level, bred to be entirely obedient, but on another they're capable of being trained to do some kinds of skilled labor, like bricklaying, assembly-line work, plastic molding, garbage reclamation, even electrical work. They're too mentally handicapped and passive to ever cause us any trouble. They can understand language up to a point, enough to take orders—but they can't *use* language. They're almost living robots. These, now, are rather stunted. They tend to die young, and they have faulty lungs, but they have a good attention span for instructions when they're motivated with an electric prod. By the seventh or eighth generation—available in about three years, we hope—the subhumans will be workable. And one day the world will be divided between the Ideal Race and the Subhumans. There will be no other races. And this lot will never be capable of rebellion—not a bit. They're marvelous, really, don't you think?" Cooper turned to look at him.

Barrabas marshaled all his self-control and parrotted, in a rasp, "Marvelous." He cleared his throat. "Um—will I be . . . working with them . . . in person?"

"Oh, but of course!" Cooper said cheerily, hitting the fast forward button. "Now that you've seen them." The squirming pink things scurried around their filthy little pen like hyperactive maggots on legs.

Barrabas stared at the screen and took deep breaths, and after a while thought, *Okay. I can go through with this.*

But deep down, he wasn't so sure.

• • •

FirStep, the Space Colony. Interplanetary space.

From the outside, the six-mile-long Colony looked like a cylinder that had swallowed something too big to digest . . . The bulge at its middle was a Bernal sphere, itself a mile and a half in diameter. The concave interior of the sphere was to have been the main inhabitable area of the Colony. It was Pellucidar, the Hollow Earth: the landscape stretched away to an inside-out horizon, curving up when it should have curved down. The colony's cylinder was pointed toward the sun, and reflected sunlight glowed from filtered, circular windows at the sunward end . . . The colony rotated once every five minutes, creating a subtle centrifugal artificial gravity for the thousands of people who lived in it, working at refining ore brought from the asteroids; working in the lowgrav areas on lowgrav specialty products; working on finishing the floating city in space—though it was a vast artifact designed to be never quite finished . . .

• • •

Claire Rimpler knew that something was wrong with Witcher when she shook hands with him. She could feel the telltale rubberiness of a sheath on his hand: a sort of condom for the hand, much tighter than gloves, nearly invisible, difficult to feel. And even with the sheath, he drew his hand back faster than was quite civil.

They stood in the Colony Administration conference room, beside a wall-size videoscreen and a table shaped like a backward S, making small talk as they waited for Russ Parker—actually, they were sizing one another up.

Witcher looked about forty, but he was much older; he had the slightly glossy look of a man who used cosmetic surgeons and glandularists, enzymologists, RNA retoolers to slow the aging process. He'd allowed a little silver into his long, neatly clipped brown hair and his small, geometrically perfect beard. He was a compact man in what looked like an astronomically expensive tailored suit of soft maroon leather.

Claire Rimpler was not quite diminutive, but nearly; she had, large, hazel eyes, short auburn hair, lips a little too large for her doll-like face. It was an appearance that might have made her seem a soft person, someone of negligible force—but she came across as the opposite. *What I heard was, she's no kill-virgin,* someone had said when she'd come back to the Colony to take over the administrative reins; she had killed, and seen killing, seen enough to fill the lives of three generals, in the service of the New Resistance; her father, who had designed and run the Space Colony, had been first murdered and then cerebrally violated, portions of his brain used to interface with a colony computer, until the disastrous consequences.

Claire had left her lover, according to Witcher's files on her—an NR operative whom Witcher knew slightly, Dan Torrence—left him back on Earth, to come here and take charge. And she was smart as a whip.

And much of that hard past, that lethal competency, was subtly present in her body language and her expression.

But when she smiled, you heard wind chimes.

She smiled at Witcher now and said, "It must be a comedown, your quarters, after what you're used to. When Russ came back from your place on Kauai, he had palm trees in his eyes."

"It's kind of comforting here, actually, the smaller rooms," Witcher said. "After someone has fired a missile at your house, you want to go to ground." Adding distractedly, "And I'm close in where the gravity is light; it's refreshing." He was looking at the door as Russ Parker came in. Behind Russ came Lester and Stoner and Chu.

I was right about Witcher, Claire thought, watching him. The man was some variation of paranoid. It was like sitting with your back to the wall, being here, for Witcher. *He doesn't know how fragile the place really is . . .*

Russ Parker was a stocky, red-faced middle-aged guy wearing real blue jeans and a blue printout shirt. It was gauche, supposedly, to mix printout and cloth clothing, but it was like Russ to be oblivious to that.

Lester, the technicki rep, sat at the table with Stoner and Chu, talking softly. He was a large man, black as the space between stars, wearing a comm tech's gray zippered jumpsuit. His wife, Kitty, was a nondescript white woman who turned out to have enormous wellsprings of character. Chu, the brisk, intense Chinese woman who was now administrative secretary, was an NR organizer who had found out that Kitty was Dan's sister: Dan Torrence's *sister!* The coincidence was a little eerie. But maybe not so strange, really. In her way, Kitty was a fighter. She had fought for Lester. She had fought for her baby. She had fought for Russ Parker's conscience, and she'd won it.

And Dan, as of a few weeks now, was an uncle. She'd have to get word to him somehow, she reflected, as they all sat down. Dan needed cheering up. But it was hard to get word into Paris. There was a Mossad line of communication that could be used sometimes. Witcher could set it up for her perhaps.

Claire ached to talk to Daniel "Hard-Eyes" Torrence. Every morning, charging into her workday, she told herself she should forget him, let her feelings for him die on the vine. He was a guerrilla in a hotbed of fascism. It was like being an active resistance partisan in Hitler's Berlin. His chances for survival—especially with extractors around to help ferret him out—were microscopic. She'd probably never see him again. Thinking about him, worrying about him, took her out of focus here.

So every morning it was, *Today I forget about him.*

But at night she curled up, fetuslike, around an ache shaped like his name.

She felt not only lonely for him, but guilty for having left him to take this job. She'd been the only one he could open up to. Without her, he had to stay in that hard shell all the time. Emotionally claustrophobic . . .

Unless he had already found someone else. There were other women in the resistance—and New Resistance women didn't waste any time; they went after what they wanted.

Chu broke into Claire's thoughts as she read the minutes of the last meeting, then went directly to the major topic for this one. "Security. Mr. Witcher has some concerns."

"We've all got some concerns in that direction, I think," Stoner said. He was a paunchy, wide-shouldered man with thinning grease-slicked hair and a face that was bland except for bright blue eyes. He wore an antique cowboy shirt with mother-of-pearl snaps and cowboy boots. He'd had to flee the CIA when the agency's racist collaboration with the SA had "stuck in his craw." Stoner and Russ Parker had hit it off despite some fundamental contrasts. Parker was a Christian and Stoner wasn't; Stoner was a family man, come here with his black wife and child, and Parker was a longtime bachelor; Stoner was a northerner and Parker a southerner. But both were older men with a nostalgia for the middle twentieth century, and the somewhat mythical values of the American West.

And both of them had turned their lives upside down for the sake of conscience. Russ Parker had left the employ of the SA, staged a successful mutiny that had overthrown the Fascists who had wormed into power at the colony; Parker's coup had become an administrative *fait accompli*. UNIC—the United Nations Industrial Council, a multigovernmental consortium that oversaw the Colony from Earth—accepted the unauthorized transfer of power. The Colony coup coincided with the discrediting of the Second Alliance International Security Corporation in the United States. UNIC perceived it was saved some political embarrassment. Parker had kept the *putsch* quiet.

"I've been debriefing Percy Witcher here," Stoner was saying, "and it appears that there's been a recent attempt on his life." He went on to outline the missile attack on Witcher's Kauai stronghold.

Chu said, "I don't wish to seem inhospitable, but . . . the Colony is in some respects a fragile thing. If they want to get to him badly enough, they might be willing to sacrifice the Colony's inhabitants." She shrugged. "They're willing to exterminate half of Europe if we let them. Why not the few thousand we have here?"

Russ pointed out, "Mr. Witcher is a major Colony stockholder, as of just about one month ago today, and without him the New Resistance just would not have gotten a single foothold. He's been protecting us, and to me it's pretty damn obvious it's the good Lord's will that we reciprocate." His faint Texas accent was charming, Claire thought, but the reference to his Christianity embarrassed her. Primitive stuff.

Claire said, "The Second Alliance is well aware that the Colony is resistance-sympathetic now. We're their target either way, I'm sure."

"Anyway, I don't think they've made him here," Stoner said. "He covered his tracks pretty well. Used fake ID, arranged decoy 'appearances' in New York while he was at the launch site in Florida . . . "

"I've got confirmation about an hour ago: they're still looking for me in New York and Boston," Witcher said. "They don't know I'm here."

"They will find out," Chu said. "But it is true: we are quite possibly targets anyway."

"The Colony is not a balloon," Claire pointed out. "If you puncture it in one spot, it won't all burst. My father built it with section integrity, so that if one section loses air pressure or becomes a danger in some other way, it's sealed off. It would take a large nuclear device to really devastate the Colony. It could be crippled, though, in other ways—if someone hacks into the life-support system." She paused, feeling a tug as she remembered the strange, posthumous sabotage her father had wreaked on the Colony. The others knew what she must be thinking about, and respectfully said nothing till she cleared her throat and went on. "It's expensive, attacking us up here—from the outside."

Stoner nodded sharply at the implication. "You got it. What we got to worry about is internal. The SA wants to get us, it'll be from the inside."

"What you need," Witcher said flatly, "is a freeze in hiring. For starts."

"That suits the union," Lester said. "Except in external repairs—they're shorthanded, after the RM17 thing . . . "

"They'll have to make do," Parker said. "We can't risk bringing in anyone new right now."

"How many have you brought into the Colony in the last month?" Witcher asked.

"Maybe a dozen," Claire said.

"How about tourists?"

"We aren't letting them through yet, till we've finished repairs."

"I recommend you don't let them through at all until the SA problem is . . . resolved."

Lester blinked. "T'ers!"

Witcher grimaced with impatience. "I really don't speak Technicki."

"Sorry. I said, it'll take years!"

Witcher shrugged. "It's the only safe course. And not just safer for me."

"I reluctantly have to agree," Stoner said. "No tourists—no stopover people . . . "

Claire shook her head. "It's not realistic. We can't control who the Lunar Mining Corporation hires. And their people have to stop in here when they make the trip."

"Then we'll have them interrogated, and watched." He hesitated, looking at Witcher. "Extractors might—"

"No!" Claire snapped, hitting the table with the palm of her hand. "Those things are the tools of fascism."

"Both sides use them," Witcher said.

"It doesn't matter! The NR shouldn't use them! It's inviting fascism when the Resistance uses them! It's laying the groundwork for a future fascism. It's just wrong for any government to have access to a machine that can . . . can violate your inner thoughts, your memories! The right to privacy is the right to freedom, my dad used to say. Extractors ought to be outlawed everywhere."

"They might be usefully employed by psychologists," Chu suggested tentatively.

"Psychologists will just have to get by without them, if it's up to me. No, I won't have them. I'll resign—"

"Whoa, slow down, honey," Russ said hastily. "No one's put in an order for an extractor."

Claire had been doing an awe-inspiring job as administrator; no one wanted to lose her. She'd facilitated rapid repairs on the damage done to the Colony during the rebellion. She'd smoothed the transition to a redress of the balance of power so that technickis, the Colony's working class, were able to move up without much resistance from the Admin minority. She was a general and a politician both.

"Then we'll do it with camera surveillance and maybe a buddy system on visitors," Stoner said. "But we have to do it."

"Fine," Claire said, telling herself to cool down. "You and Russ work up a brief on that for me." Witcher was scowling now, she noticed. He wanted extractors. Maybe he wouldn't be happy till he was on the Colony alone.

Chu went on to the next item, pay raises and improved housing for technickis.

Lester leaned forward. "Admin is falling behind on the timetable for reform."

"We just haven't got the resources to raise pay any further," Claire said. "We're cutting Admin paychecks considerably, as it is, in order to be able to afford—"

"Administrative positions are easier in some ways, and should not rate a better pay—" Lester began.

"Lester, I realize that you and Chu are 'Reds.'" She used the slang term without denigration, saying it almost affectionately, the way an outsider would refer to the Amish. "But we are not all painted with the same brush here. I am just not a socialist. I believe that you need an incentive system for people to work hard."

"When was the last time since the overthrow that you promoted a technicki?" His face had gone stony.

"There haven't been any posts open. Be reasonable. It's only been a short time. Trust us for a year, okay? Housing is improved—we have technickis moving into the Open almost every week."

"But there is still a predominance of Admin people living in luxury in the Open housing projects—"

"I can't just evict those people. The damage to morale . . . those people have children."

"So do technicki families."

He might have said, *So do I.* Claire admired Lester because he'd refused to move into a house offered him in the Open though she knew he longed for his wife and child to have a comfortable home. He wouldn't go "till all technickis have decent housing."

"We're *building*, Lester, as fast as we can. There's an ecological balance in the Colony's parklands, and there are quality-of-life considerations—we don't want to overdevelop. We're building as much as we can, and we're going to build a new section onto the Colony this year." He opened his mouth to object again, and she broke in, "I'll tell you what—I'll meet with the union personally, offer them a better timetable for reform, and we'll vote on it, set up a two-year schedule. It's what we should have done anyway. We'll find the middle ground."

Lester held the hardness in his expression for two more beats. And then let it soften into a sardonic smile. "I guess I just been finessed. But okay."

"I didn't finesse you, Lester. You'll see." She turned to Chu. "Anything else pressing? I've got to get to the Comm center."

"Nothing else."

"Class dismissed!" Claire said, standing.

She hurried, out, feeling she couldn't wait any longer: she had to contact Dan. Thoughts of Dan Torrence had distracted her too often. She needed to discharge them in some way so she could concentrate on her work.

Stoner caught up with her at the elevator, stepped on with her. "Hey," he said when the doors closed. "You going to message Haifa?" Meaning their Mossad contacts in Israel: the message conduit to the New Resistance in Europe.

She nodded, and he handed her a datastick. "I was going to get permission from you for a message—could you transmit that for me and then erase it? And listen—before you scramble it, read it when it comes up on the screen. I thought maybe you should know my thoughts . . . No real emergency, but—I wanted to keep you up to speed."

"Sure, okay. But what's it about?"

"Just . . . read it. The whole thing."

He got out at the next floor. Thoughtfully, she watched him go. He had seemed to be saying something more than he was saying out loud.

In the Comm Center, she booted up the message file Stoner had given her and read it. Intelligence reports, none of it really arresting. But at the end, she found what he'd been talking about; something earmarked for Smoke and Steinfeld:

> Witcher keeps popping up with blank spots. He's covering something from me, and being pretty cagey about it. It's nothing I can call him on. I don't think it's any kind of special relationship with the other side. His hostility for the SA is almost pathological. But some of his own operations (including Orange County Research operations) are still opaque to me. Also, he says things that worry me. I quote verbatim: "The trouble with the world is there are too many people on it to manage. It could be a utopia, it really could, a place of racial harmony, all the races living in peace and complete equality, if there were only, say, a few million people to administer . . . " The guy means: a few million people on the whole damn planet. I don't know, maybe it's just paranoia on my part. Maybe it's nothing . . .

• 05 •

PARIS. PROCESSING CENTER 13.

"So, where's Steinfeld?" Roseland asked.

"He's in Egypt, trying to get us some backup," Dan Torrence said.

"He's not going to be here for this?" Roseland said. "Christ!"

" 'Christ'? Some Jew you are."

"Okay, okay: *Moses!* You happy? Me, I'm not so happy, I mean, this is delicate, isn't it? It's not that I don't trust you to—I—" Roseland fumbled for words.

"I know what you mean. I wish he was here too. We'll do all right, man."

They were crouched in the rooftop blind, close but not too close to the high-rise concentration camp, watching the skyline, ready to give the signal to the others. It was a warm, gently breezy night. Paper trash scraped and fluttered on the rooftop outside.

Some Jew you are, Torrence had said. His idea of a joke. Not a racist joke, just a weak one. Roseland's own sense of humor had only started to come back to him in the last week. You needed strength to make jokes. Torrence seemed to feel a little threatened by Roseland's humor, felt he had to contribute from time to time. An uncle of Roseland's, old Dave Meyers, used to say, "People without a sense of humor shouldn't try to be funny." And it was true of Torrence. Not much of a sense of humor. But you didn't tell "Hard-Eyes" things like that . . .

Anything, apparently, to avoid thinking about what was coming. Roseland dreaded it. Dreaded going to PC 13. Dreaded seeing the blood of the innocent mixed with the blood of the guilty.

Just do it, he told himself. Just do the job.

Torrence was looking fixedly through the slat. Roseland saw him tense; or sensed it somehow, in the dark. Heard him speak into the headset. "That's it, it's the change of the guard. Tourists, take your pictures."

There was a staticky snip of reply, and then Torrence's gun clattered against his gear as he moved out the back way. Roseland followed, his own rifle on its strap across his back, and in minutes they were climbing out through the first-floor window, into the little, narrow street behind the building where the others in the first assault team waited.

Pasolini was there, and Musa and Jiddah, and a French woman, Bibisch: a pale, lanky, long-faced woman who almost never spoke, but cared for her submachine gun lovingly. And others Roseland hadn't got to know much yet. There was a moment when they clustered on the corner, in the light from the full moon; they stood next to the window of a deserted butcher's shop, waiting for Torrence, who conferred with other assault teams on the headset. And in that moment Roseland found himself looking at his own reflection in the glass of the shop. Roseland had been eating modestly but regularly, and his face had filled out some; usually he looked almost healthy but not in this reflection. In the muted light, his reflection in the dark glass was hollow-eyed, cadaverous, his face a thing of shadows and sallow planes. As if he were looking out from the dimension where dead things dwell, he thought. The way he'd looked in the concentration camp they'd called a processing center.

He stared at himself, thinking: *That's me inside.*

He'd always had a deep empathy for children. And he remembered, when there were children in the Processing Center, how they had died of dysentery and cholera and malnutrition, shaking from spasms of endless diarrhea, puking when there was nothing left to puke, feverishly pleading for water; the dull anguish on the parents' faces when they gave up trying to explain about the water ration; when they had to accept: *I cannot help my child. I cannot even comfort the child.*

Someone had been shot one morning for giving away their own water ration; for no particular reason, giving away your ration was forbidden. And the children, dying slowly, had begged, as their parents hugged and rocked them, and one of the guards had become annoyed and shouted, "Shut that brat up or I'll feed 'er me boot!"

Roseland had seen what was happening that day in the Processing Center, and hadn't the strength, then, to fight. Couldn't say a word.

Maybe that was when his insides had shriveled to match his outsides.

He thought these things, staring at his sunken-eyed reflection, until Torrence said, "Here it comes. Let's do it."

Here it comes but still a ways off, between the buildings, the clean-edged, cold, crystallized steel arc of the hijacked Jægernaut, slicing up through the skyline. The distant, ringing thunder of its approach, coming through areas already war-ruined, or condemned.

They were in the prearranged positions in seconds, Musa and Jiddah and Bibisch and Roseland under Pasolini's command; Musa with his RPG; Torrence rendezvousing with a second group taking out the guards.

Torrence came out of one alley down the street, while a third team on a rooftop opened up on the guards with armor-piercing explosive rounds. The cluster of guards meeting for the change in shift had the new kevlar-7 armor, more resistant than the old SA bull outfitting, and the rounds tended to explode on the armor or on the ground near them, with little effect; but one high velocity round hit at just the right angle and penetrated the armor. The guard fell writhing while his armor ballooned with blood. The others were staggering with the small explosions, trying to bring their rifles into play, the so-called "smart" rifles, computer-enhanced, except they were stupid because you had to perform two steps, accessing the firing chip and rangefinder, to get them to fire, and by then Torrence was on them with three others, tossing the explosive disks at them . . . one of the disks deflecting, the other two sucking flat on the armor and blowing. The NR to Torrence's right going down, spinning, cut in half by a burst from a guard who finally convinced his smart rifle to defend him . . .

Roseland only glimpsed this in fits and snatches as he steadied Musa's RPG-8 and stepped out of the way. Musa had brought three of the vintage twentieth-century rocket-firing weapons with him when he'd slipped into Paris, and a small truckload of rounds: a masterful stage-magicking act of smuggling. A survival skill handed down through generations of Mujahedin.

The RPG hissed exhaust from its vents, and the rocket went *shuh-shuh-shuh* directly to the third-floor window. Roseland prayed it was the right window. The rocket punched through the plaster and fiberboard patch over the window, detonating, obscuring the socket with a fireball—

Almost simultaneously another guerrilla RPG on the roof ripped the security-camera-and-machine-gun system to shreds—

The horizon's battle-ax thundered closer—

The last of the outer guards went down, blown in half, his screaming amplified by his helmet PA system to echo around the street—

(There are *men* inside those mirror fishbowls, Roseland thought.)

A guard stumbled out of the front door of Processing Center 13, missing his helmet, coughing in the smoke that billowed after him, his face charred, but firing at them, bullets strafing up the street until Pasolini cut him down with a short, neat burst that punched his face into his skull.

Roseland couldn't move.

You're Point Cadre, he told himself. *Go!* But the monolithic bulk of the converted high-rise seemed to lean forward, as if poising to fall on him, to scoop him into itself, like some gigantic shell-creature eating a worm. *How could he have come back here?*

He looked at the tumbled ruins of 12, thought he could just make out a human skull and a yellowing, skeletal hand emerging from beneath the massive pinch of a boulder. Whose body?

Gabrielle's, bulldozed there?

Pasolini kicked him in the tailbone. It hurt like a bitch, like the bitch she was, Roseland thought, but it was a blow that could have come from the other, angry part of him, personified.

"Get moving, asshole!" she shouted, saying what he was saying to himself.

And he remembered Father Lespere telling them earnestly, "All of us are already dead. That is what you must accept, and then you can begin to do the work."

Jamais plus. Never again!

The dam burst and the rage poured through, carrying him with it, his rifle spitting fire and metal at the second guard staggering from the door. The bull's armor deflected the bullets, sparking, but the firepower's impact knocking him backward. Roseland was running at him, firing again, screaming something (What? Maybe it should have been: "Never again!" But it wasn't. It was: "Die, you ASSSSSSHOOOOLLLLLLLLLLLLESSSSSSSSS!") as the guy got to his feet, only to be knocked back again by Roseland's next burst. But still the guy got up, almost literally wading upstream against Roseland's gunfire. And then Roseland's clip gave out and his assault rifle lapsed into sheepish silence and the guy was firing back . . .

Pasolini shoved past Roseland, tossing a grenade, everyone flattening except the guard who reacted too slowly, the explosive flipping him through the air so that blood made a spiral against the wall behind him.

Roseland: Up and plunging into the building, running up the stairs, not allowing himself to think, not even stopping to reload (aware that Pasolini was yelling at him, cursing him in a mix of Italian and English), climbing over the body of a guard dying under a heap of imploded masonry. The guard's crushed body giving a little under the slab that Roseland clambered over; the guard screaming with pain—

Then Roseland was past, kicking down the door, and there they were.

They were being punished.

• • •

Outside, Dan Torrence issued commands, sending guerillas into the building to begin evacuating prisoners as the articulated truck Musa had stolen that morning backed up to the door. Torrence moved across the courtyard, checking the blockades, moving from one to the next as they were set up: stolen cars blocking the street.

Behind him, Pasolini dispatched the wounded enemy. Torrence had given her the job because she'd argued for the necessity of it the night before. Torrence had argued that wounded men are a burden on the enemy; leave their wounded alive and you slow them down and force them to use resources and time and personnel. But Pasolini pointed out the SA Army was relatively small and most of them were racist fanatics. A greater advantage was had in reducing their numbers than in inconveniencing them. If these wounded recovered, they were a political and military resource for the enemy.

But killing the enemy wounded is not a sound political move, Torrence had said.

Oh, but it is, Pasolini said. It underlines our commitment. We're more a force to be reckoned with . . .

She'd persuaded Steinfeld, and now it was done. Sometimes Torrence wondered if they hadn't skirted the real issue: that he simply wanted to spare lives, and nursed some guilt over the act of killing; whereas Pasolini enjoyed killing.

Crack: a shrieking soldier silenced.

More gunfire now, on the perimeter of the little square, as the vehicles the guerrillas had driven up to block the street came under fire from advancing SA. There were only about a dozen Second Alliance, so far. They were containable: Torrence's backup team were holding them back with rifle-launched grenades and firebombs.

The greater threat was from the north: Second Alliance reinforcements in large numbers were moving in with armored cars, maybe only blocks away.

But the Jægernaut was there: he felt the ground shudder under him, glimpsed a gargantuan shifting, as if a tower of steel were stretching itself after a long hibernation. Voices in his headset: "*Swineherd, we're making contact with the trotters.*" The Jægernaut hijack unit was moving the gargantuan machine into place.

What potential power there was in controlling a Jægernaut, Torrence thought . . .

He noticed Roseland running from building 13, white-faced. Panicked, maybe. Looked like he was going to lose it, after all. They might have to—

But then he saw Roseland rummaging in the cab of the evacuation truck, coming out with insulated wire clippers, swearing to himself as he turned and raced back into the building. Torrence went in to see what was holding up the evacuation.

Upstairs, past the rubble, he found Roseland in a large stinking room that had been made when the walls in the original apartments had been knocked down. He was using the clippers to cut away plastic restraints from the necks and wrists and ankles of the prisoners. Every one of them had been bound in the stuff, tied together, squeezed in so tightly there was barely room to move or breathe. Torrence recognized the hard but prehensile gray plastic, as sparks shot from the clippers, severing it. Restrain-o-Lite, it was called. Used by British cops to hold large numbers of prisoners after a riot; the stuff absorbed static electricity and gave it off whenever you moved. Sit still and it didn't hurt you; squirm and it gave you a nasty shock. The condition of the prisoners . . .

Torrence, who'd thought himself inured to horror, had to turn away till his stomach quieted down.

About a fourth of them had died in the restraints; were hanging there, rotting. Some had rotted free, slipped to the floor. The others were starved, bruised, cold, semiconscious, drained of dignity. Looking like plucked game birds hanging in a string.

And there were more, hundreds more on the floors above. Torrence took a breath and turned around, began to shout orders, commencing the evacuation. Glad Claire wasn't here to have to see this. And yet wishing she was at his side . . .

● ● ●

The Hôtel de Ville, Paris

Colonel Watson, Klaus, and Giessen stood at the monitors in the Security Center, watching the shaking TV image shot from the underside of the chopper approaching Processing Center 13.

"How did they get hold of a Jægernaut?" Giessen asked, not troubling to conceal his disgust. "That is supposed to be impossible—"

"I know it is," Watson snapped. "And I don't know how."

"How many gunships can you muster?" Giessen asked. "Air support will compensate for the Jægernaut . . . "

"Only about three, at the moment," Klaus murmured, as he stabbed a number on the fone.

"I'm afraid I cannot commend your planning, Herr Watson," Giessen said.

Watson turned to look at him, knowing he'd made a mistake in bringing Giessen in, and wondering how big an error it had been. Giessen—"The Thirst"—could have been a tax investigator. He was a prim, ferret-faced, sartorially elegant little man who had been, inexplicably, excused by Rick Crandall from wearing a uniform. He wore a real-cloth suit two hundred years outdated, a Victorian outfit, ludicrously anachronistic ("looks like a bloody actor in a Public School revival of an early Shaw play," Watson had muttered), modeled on an old tintype of a certain Dr. Gull, who'd been "seen on der fringes of der Ripper investigation." But Giessen's methods were very up-to-date. He'd patched into the Crime mainframe on the plane from Dresden, and fed in a collation program of his own design. Already he'd confirmed Watson's guess: that the assassin of Le Pen was most probably the New Resistance officer known as Daniel "Hard-Eyes" Torrence.

"You're not here to second-guess my planning or policing tactics," Watson told Giessen. He couldn't exactly upbraid him: Watson's post was something like an Internal Affairs officer. Watson didn't outrank him, or vice versa. Giessen's was a post independent of rank, but reeking of authority.

Watson saw digital-compressed mayhem from the corner of his eye.

"Bloody hell," he muttered, turning to the monitor in time to see the hijacked Jægernaut reducing a convoy of armored cars and I.S. vehicles to scrap metal. It simply rolled right over them. "How did they get it? Who did they bribe? Those men are supposed to be our most loyal . . . "

"There is a report of a black market in drugs," Giessen said, clearly making a conscious effort to control his accent.

Watson glared at him as Klaus foned in orders to the chopper to ignore the Jægernaut and concentrate on Processing Center 13. Why was this fetishistic lunatic maundering in non sequiturs? "There's always a black market in drugs!"

"Not always in der—in the military," Giessen said. "Sometimes ja, sometimes no. Now, we haf a—we have a trade in US Army experimental fighting-drugs. Oxycontin, stimulants, tranquilizers. I have reason to believe that some of our sentries are using them. I also suspect that these resistance terrorists are selling them under some sort of . . . cover. You see, there were sniping attacks on SA sentries around the Jægernauts and other installations. They seemed to reach a peak intensity about two weeks ago and then stopped when so-called 'street people' began coming around to sell zese—to sell these drugs."

Watson stared. The man had been here only hours! How had he found out so much? He must have had some preliminary studies done. Must have realized he was to be called in.

Watson cleared his throat and lied rather clumsily, "Well, of course . . . we knew about that."

Giessen allowed himself a self-satisfied smirk. "Yes, most certainly. The connection is clear: through the sniper attacks the resistance deliberately built up in the sentries a constant fear for their lives, then through intermediaries they offered them drugs, knowing they were very much ready for them. They introduced the addiction into the Army to poison it, to weaken it—and to obtain access to sensitive areas. A man becomes addicted to something, he will sell secrets, he will allow access—even to the Jægernauts, *ja*?"

Watson swallowed. "This is Steinfeld's doing. The man is devious."

Giessen nodded. "I have come to the same conclusion. He would be a better target than this Torrence—but, not likely to be as emotionally vulnerable."

Watson blinked. "You're going after Torrence through his emotions?"

"*They've got some kind of surface-to-air missile . . .* " crackled a voice on the emergency frequency. Chopper Two, at center 13. "*Evasive—*"

No good. The dancing digital image blanked out. The guerillas had blown the chopper from the sky.

"What about Chopper *One!*" Watson roared.

"Engaging a rooftop machine-gun emplacement," Klaus said.

"Get it away, that's a decoy! Deploy to the street, stop those bloody trucks!"

"The Jægernaut is on the scene, it's blocking the chopper. They're increasing altitude but—"

"*Microwaves—*" Chopper One. "*Microwave beam from the fucking Jæger—*"

Then a scream muted by transmission—and another monitor blotted out.

"Why not bring a second Jægernaut to bear?" Giessen suggested.

Watson spun on him, spraying spittle in his fury, taking his frustration out on Giessen. "Because, damn you, we have only one other here, and it's the bleeding wrong end of town! We can't run it through the middle of town! The French went half mad when one of our lads rubbled their bloody Arc de Triomphe. The Jægernauts are to be used to attack cities fully occupied by an enemy—they're a weapon of siege! We've had a cunt of a time doing damage control on that one, lying through our bloody teeth—we can't plow through the middle of town, those things destroy wherever they go . . . "

"I see, of course, they need a special route. It was a bad suggestion, Herr Watson." Giessen gave a thin, maddeningly patronizing smile.

Klaus was listening tensely on the fone; Watson could tell he was getting something nasty. "Well, what is it, Klaus?"

"Their trucks! The Jægernaut completely routed our boys and the guerilla trucks are away. They've quite escaped with their load of Jews and Negroes . . . "

• • •

Sometimes human planning lines up neatly with chance; sometimes synchronicity vibes sympathetically; sometimes there is serendipity.

When it happens, you have a holiday from fear, you can lie to yourself cheerfully about how it'll all turn out. (And sometimes, it does indeed turn out well. Sometimes.)

When Torrence returned to the safe house, he found he was resonating sweetly with things for the first time in a year or two. First there was a sense of relief: they'd taken the refugees to the meeting place where they were turned over to those who'd agreed to take in the stronger escapees—taken in by hundreds of decent Parisians who were among the NR's "auxiliary." The most grievously ill were taken by the "underground train"—carried on stretchers, through the old Metro tunnels—to the north of the city, where other partisans waited to take them to outlying hospitals and sympathetic doctors. It had taken a long, difficult while to organize, and it had gone off well, and they had been lucky.

Another serendipity: Smoke had been at the meeting place, an artillery-ruined square in the north of Paris where the evacuation trucks left off their long-suffering human cargo. Smoke, and an American newscaster named Norman Hand.

Hand and his technicki assistant had videoed the refugees, interviewed those who could talk. With enormous satisfaction, Smoke watched Hand's skepticism melt into horror.

Then had come the safe house, which seemed warm and snug after the "bullet weather" of the firefight. They had the space heater going, and the six male refugees they'd recruited were fed warm broth and a little rice—Roseland fed them, almost weeping from happiness and release—and Torrence thought: *If we don't accomplish anything else, we've made this difference. Hundreds freed from the Fascists. Among them, some children.*

He was just sorry they'd had to blow up the Jægernaut. He'd been tempted to try to get it to Second Alliance headquarters, use it to stomp them good, turnabout is fair play. But the Jægernaut would have crushed civilians, getting there. So, instead, they'd used it to mangle a couple of roads and railroad lines important to the Fascists, and then trashed it.

Now he sat in a corner near the rattling electric heater and ate his soup, his thoughts turning to Claire—and to his sister Kitty.

Kitty had a new baby, was working with her husband on the Colony; both of them happy with their promotions, proud of having come through hell together. Kitty was doing all right. That was something else to hold on to.

Claire's letter had come off affectionate, but also a little irrationally petulant. As if she was reproaching him for hanging around in her head when she was trying to get some work done. He would have liked the letter to have at least hinted at romance. Maybe she was deliberately forgetting their intimacy. She seemed to suggest that he should find some other . . . outlet.

When you have time, just live, she'd told him. *Try to feel some warmth, even though I know it's hard to do there. Try to get close to people. That's survival, too.*

He was still pumped up from the fight, the escape, the sight of the Jægernaut coming down like a slaughterhouse hammer on the swine at the Detention Center. He was almost high on the knowledge that they'd made a material difference . . .

It was hard to just sit here and watch the others; watch Smoke and Hand talking to the refugees and Pasolini cleaning her weapon—as she tried to be an example of the perfect soldier, another overcompensating female—and Musa and Jiddah, half-seen through the door into the next room, on their knees, praying toward Mecca. And Bibisch . . .

Who sat down beside him, dipping a bit of sourdough bread into her bowl. She glanced at him out of the corners of her eyes, then looked fixedly back at her soup.

Oh, he thought.

Well, she was pretty enough. Curly black hair, delicately elongated Frankish features, softly brooding gray-blue eyes; very handsome, her face, if a little dour. She wore shapeless clothes, as all the women here did, so it was hard to know if . . .

He winced, mentally imagining Claire telling him off for his sexist speculation. For wondering about Bibisch's tits and ass. Her legs.

Demeaning, Claire would say. And she'd be right.

But still, he wondered how those long legs looked in moonlight . . .

Synchronicity, serendipity: Bibisch suddenly turned to him and said, "Did you see the moon? It is so bright tonight. The clouds blow away, the moon come in, *c'est tres jolie.*"

"Yeah, saw it when I was coming in."

"You look . . . happy. This is abnormal for you, yes?"

He smiled. "Yeah, well, I'd be pretty fucking abnormal if I was happy around Paris nowadays, Bibisch."

"Your fucking is abnormal?" She seemed interested.

"That's not what I meant, it's just an—Forget it. You know, I didn't know you spoke much English."

"I am not very good on it, so I do not like to, you know . . . " She shrugged. Inconspicuously, she moved closer to him.

"Your English is better than my French."

"*Toujours*. Bad English is better than bad French. French, *c'est fragile*." She said it "frah-*sjheel*." The French pronunciation bringing onomatopoeia.

An outburst from Norman Hand distracted them. "I still can't believe this could be going on without NATO and, I don't know, without the UN knowing about it."

Smoke said patiently, "I've told you: they know about some of it. But there was a war on, Hand, remember? There are hundreds of thousands of refugees, there are destroyed economies, there is starvation in pockets all over the continent, there is pestilence, there are bands of paramilitary groups jockeying for power, factions fighting for control—the so-called international 'authorities' are dealing with all that, they can't sort out the SA-created suffering from the suffering that comes from the aftermath of war. They've got their hands full. They can't see the goddamn forest for the trees. We need you to bring this out where people can see it."

There were two rail-thin Oriental men among the group of refugees from the concentration camp; one of them tried to explain things to Hand in Korean, rattling it off arcanely for a full minute as Hand tried to tell him, "I'm not Korean! I don't understand! I'm Vietnamese!"

The other Oriental sat up excitedly. "Vietnamese! Me Vietnamese!" Then he reeled off a couple of feverish paragraphs in Vietnamese.

"I'm Vietnamese, but I don't *speak* Vietnamese!" Hand protested weakly.

The Vietnamese broke off, looked at him with raised eyebrows.

Torrence and Bibisch laughed. Bibisch leaned over against Torrence, as if simply to share a confidence, but he felt her linger over the casual touch, press a little closer than necessary. He felt his manhood harden. He was that pent up.

"I heard this Hand when he arrive," she whispered, "he is bitching about the quarters to stay in, no hot water, he was so jet lag, he want a good meal, this was like a kidnap almost, he said." And then she made a noise like a puppy whimpering.

Torrence and Bibisch laughed till tears came. Hand snapped a glare at them, sensing he was the object of some unheard drollery.

Torrence looked at Bibisch and stopped laughing. She looked gravely up at him. "You can see the moon," she said, "from the storeroom, if you open . . . I don't know the word: *la fenêtre* . . . "

He nodded. His throat was dry; the pants at his crotch were taut. "You want to, um, check out the moon?"

She stood, nodding, and went to the stairs. He followed her, aware that some of the others were trying not to stare at them. They climbed the narrow, winding, creaking stairway, two flights, to the top of the old police station. There was a storage room, dusty and smelling of mildew, packed with weapons in crates, and the single window. Ornate black bars over the glazed window, this side. Light streamed through the window; the rest of the room was a jumble of sharp-edged shadows. They crossed to the window, and he tried to open it. It hadn't been opened in years; wouldn't budge. He was a little embarrassed at being unable to open the window; then felt foolish at wanting to look strong to her.

"It's old," she said, "and the wetness, it makes the wood . . . "

She shrugged, looking at him. "But the moonlight is still here . . . " She motioned at the window with a tilt of her head, without taking her eyes from his. "The moon is there, but . . . "

He looked at the window glass. The moon was distorted by the glaze, was big and blurry, as if the moon's light had been evaporated into a milky spray, something to bathe in. *Her skin in the moonlight . . .*

"It's beautiful," he heard himself say. Clumsy at this kind of thing.

"*Mais* . . . I am cold here," she said.

He knew an opening when it was offered him. He put his arms around her and she came to him easily, dropped all pretense instantly, and kissed him, lingering only a moment on the lips, going quickly to a mesh of tongues, pressing her breasts against him, full enough for him to feel even through their clothes, and it went on and on. They kissed till they swayed from standing too tightly together, and then she took the initiative again and took one of his hands, guiding it up under her coat, under a sweater, into a good place, between flesh and the moist, welcoming, static-electricity itch of damp, body-warmed wool. She closed his hand over her breast. Closed it instructively, hard. To let him know her taste: she liked a hard grip, at least for now, she wanted aggression.

"Yes," she said as he squeezed, hard, felt the tissue give like a swollen sponge but exquisitely silken (blocking an image of Claire, forcing himself to concentrate on *now*—and it wasn't difficult to focus: the desire was roaring through him like a subway express).

"*Oui*," she said as his other hand gripped her ass and bruised it. "*Forte.* Harder. *Oui.*"

Following his instincts, he bit her full lower lip. Not quite hard enough to break the skin. "Oh, *oui, encore,* hurt me a little, tell me what I am . . . "

She taught him things. She directed him; instructed him to abuse her just a little, and both of them sensed that it was entirely appropriate for the two of them, it was in the pocket, it was *them*. Knowing full well she was a political feminist, Torrence himself a believer in absolute women's equality. And simultaneously: she asked to be dominated. And he fell into it with an almost frightening naturalness. Almost tearing off her clothes, not bothering to remove his own. He simply dropped his zipper (she liked that, too, this time) . . .

They lay on a bed of shed clothing, Torrence almost tearing into her, taking her, the first time, till he came, resting like a lump of slag on her, then hearing her whisper to him again, *Hurt me a little, hurt me a little . . .*

• • •

NEAR TIJUANA, MEXICO.

At the same moment, but during daylight: in the same instant that Torrence thrust himself into Bibisch, Jerome-X lay on his back in the very center of Bettina's double king-size bed, staring up at the Brobdingnagian folds of her flesh descending on him, her enormous, doughy-soft but powerful thighs, the great waddling smothering ebony pillow of her belly hanging down, almost covering the black and chocolate and glistening pink bifurcations of her vagina; the small, floral organ nearly hidden in folds of thigh flesh like the interior of some oversize Claus Oldenberg orchid; an orchid of swollen flesh and surreal excess. The smell of her soap and the smell of her musk and sweat and skin . . .

All of it coming down on Jerome like a sexual apocalypse.

"Take it," she ordered him. Obediently, he opened his mouth. She snapped, "What'd you say?"

"I said, 'Yes, ma'am.'" And the gratification of his submission made his cock even harder as she encompassed his face and very nearly, deliciously nearly, smothered him . . .

• • •

Torrence, afterward, holding Bibisch tenderly in his arms, kissing her eyelids, kissing her lips softly, stroking her head soothingly as she nestled against him. As if comforting a child frightened by thunder. "*Toujours,* I adore you," she said. "I never stop watching you." She sighed—and then stiffened a little, looked sharply at him. "You won't tell anyone what I ask you to be doing? OK?"

"No," he said. "I won't." The moonlight streamed over her white skin. "You look almost . . . " He almost said *made out of moonlight,* but stopped himself. "You look good in the moonlight, it fits you . . . "

Would he tell anyone? *Hell* no. He was amazed at the things he'd done, amazed at his own rapacity. He'd never done that sort of thing . . . role playing, sexual-discipline games, even talking dirty in sex. Never. He'd had no idea it would evoke such arousal in him.

God, am I that sick? he wondered. *Is that me, or has the war done it to me, made me this way?*

But he knew, even as he asked himself. Sexual dominance was deeply a part of him, and always had been. It had been closeted in him, till now. Maybe it *was* a sickness, but he had felt it shiver sympathetically in the core of him, and he knew it was integral to him.

But he also knew it wouldn't work if she didn't enjoy it. He was too empathetic to be a true sadist. He was just a little bent, apparently. Just a bit . . . kinked.

And he felt a little better about it when he reflected that Bibisch had led him through the whole thing. She'd begun it, instructed him in it, and in some sense it was really Bibisch, with a kind of sexual judo, who'd really been in control the whole time.

"Did you know," he asked, "that I'd get into, uh, this kind of thing?"

"Yes."

"*How* did you know? I mean—I didn't know myself. Am I . . . do I seem like I'd be a . . . "

"No, no! When you fight, you are very strong and beautiful and efficient, but you are not cruel, and you are very kind to everyone. Pasolini and some others, they think you are . . . "

"Soft?"

"*Oui.* But you are not . . . not soft. You are kind inside. I don't know how I knew that your sex was . . . I don't know. *C'est subtil.* Probably no one sees but me. I see because I am one too, from the other side . . . "

He nodded. Still feeling a little revulsion at himself, but some relief, too.

● ● ●

Jerome-X lay in Bettina's arms, serenely reposing in her great soft damp fullness. She stroked his hair soothingly, muttered sweet endearments, and he was happy. But something chewed a fusty little tunnel under the skin of his happiness.

Was he sick? He'd never done it this way before, and he'd been amazed at his own response. How had Bettina known he'd be complementary to her own dominatrix inclinations? Did he radiate some kind of sexual wimpiness? Doubtful. It had to be subtler than that.

He not only got off on being dominated by her—he got off on her obesity. Sexually, for Jerome, she was the Earth Mother, the Venus of Willendorf, the very incarnation of the fertility goddess, and she was a refuge he could explore for hours. He could sort of understand if someone found all that extra flesh unattractive but it hit him right in the basal ganglia—right in his sex. The more of her there was, the more lust it evoked in him. Bizarre.

Where did it originate in him? Was it Oedipal? Freud had been discredited, but still . . . Jerome had been alienated from his mother—no, that seemed too simpleminded an interpretation.

He shrugged. Probably he'd never know. He reflected that, in some strange way, he was in control when they made love. There was comfort in that.

"Dis time," she said huskily, "we gone switch on our chips, and get on de same frequency. I got a frequency no one listen on to. And we gone use a little augments for it, and I show you some stuff."

And in minutes, they were frequency-wired together, fucking electronically and somatically, and he saw the beauty and horror of her, saw her expanding in his mind's eye like a mandala from hell.

With the flick of a nanotech switch, Jerome was in love.

• 06 •

THE BADOIT ARCOLOGICAL COMPLEX, A QUARTER MILE BENEATH THE QATTARA DEPRESSION, EGYPT

Steinfeld's palms were sweating, though the room was almost painfully air-conditioned. Abu Badoit, seated across the low comma-shaped table from him on the confoam swivel chair, seemed centered and at ease, patiently watching the video on the table's fold-out screen: a vid of Second Alliance atrocities, and interviews with European apartheid victims. He watched it almost as if he were sitting through someone else's tedious home movie.

Why shouldn't Badoit be at ease? He was sitting in the center of his power base.

Steinfeld had just met Badoit for the first time; he wasn't sure the Arab leader was as unperturbed as he seemed. But his expression was as composed as his grooming. Badoit wore an immaculate real-cloth flat-black silk suit from Broad Street in London. He had been schooled at Harrow, which seemed to impart its gloss to his short, sculptured black beard, his impeccably clipped hair, and his onyx eyes. There were several platinum rings on the fingers of his right hand, one of them glowing with a big smoky diamond, and a rather incongruous gold-chain choker in his high collar. His was a dark, boyish face, but he was at least fifty, Steinfeld knew.

What did he know about Badoit? That Badoit was a *mutakallim* to some, an embodiment of the *Sanna* of the Prophets to others: Not thought to be divine but a man with a direct line to God.

Badoit, a good host, poured tea for them both, only flickeringly taking his eyes from the digi-viddy . . .

Steinfeld let his gaze wander out the polarized window of the Egyptian's office to the vast, fully illuminated, cluttered recesses of the underground Badoit Arcological Complex. A refuge from war, Jihad, and the ravages of global warming, the complex was one hundred seventy-five square miles of subterranean city, residence, clean industry, and hydroponic farming. It was built partly in a vast system of caverns underlying the lowlands of the Western Desert, and extending into man-made caverns carved into the bedrock. It was all lit by a mellow blend of electricity and reflected-sunlight shafts. Solar power, gathered on the Saharan surface, provided energy, driving toylike electric trams winding, underground, between the hulking blocks and opaque-glass pyramids of the complex; in two places the minarets of mosques broke the stark angularity with their ceremonious curves, spires, and intricate ornamentation. Nearer were swooping yellow-and-black banners with Islamic slogans declared in Classic Arabic lettering. The metal reinforced ceiling was just a hundred and fifty feet over the tops of the highest buildings. Now it looked like a mythical city under a metal sky that shone with a hundred small, strangely geometrical suns; in the evening, when they turned down the lights, it was a netherworld metropolis glowing softly under a perpetual lid of lowering cloud. Only, look close and the cloud became granite and plastic and metal. Huge, gleaming steel columns that were also elevator housings to the upper world stood at intervals for stability; the ceiling was triply reinforced against earthquake with a groinwork of high-tensility plastech girders.

When he'd first read about the Badoit Complex, it had made Steinfeld think of the Space Colony, FirStep. But now he thought Giza; of the sphinx, of the great tombs of the pharaohs, of the wonders of the ancient world. He was a little in awe of Badoit, who had created a quasi-secessionist Islamic state in the midst of the Arab Republic of Egypt—a masterpiece of quiet diplomacy, brilliant engineering, and relentless necessity. Egypt had been threatened with civil war between the Islamic extremists and the moderates; between the isolationists and the internationalists.

The political wisdom of creating a sacrosanct enclave for Badoit's brand of moderate-to-fundamentalist Islam had been obvious; the wisdom of spending billions developing the underground Arcological Complex had been more elusive for many.

But Badoit had insisted the Arcological Complex could not maintain true spiritual integrity without economic and military self-sufficiency. True economic self-sufficiency required agricultural self-sufficiency; but in North Africa, a land of droughts and desert, the only agricultural surety was in a greenhouse. And the only military surety, in a land of coups and factions and extremists, was in a bunker. And the only economic surety, in a land of struggle over oil sources, was energy self-sufficiency. And as for cultural integrity—it was hard to achieve in a world suffused with transmissions and travelers.

Badoit envisioned a grand solution: a combination greenhouse and bunker. The complex's location underground made television and radio transmissions highly controllable; the complex received only what it wanted to receive. Badoit's commission of cultural censors allowed more than Jamaat-I-Islami law would—Badoit did not forbid vids or lectures where women showed independence and dressed untraditionally, and, within the limits of decency, much "western" clothing was allowed—but the arcology disallowed excessive violence in media, explicit sexuality, homosexual imagery, and non-Muslim theology: Islam was taught as an inarguable fact in schools, and Mosques throughout the arcology proclaimed the *salat*. Badoit strictly forbade so-called "female circumcision" or violence against women on the basis of non-traditional behavior. Yet theft was still punished with hand-amputation, and traditional dietary restrictions, including a fixed prohibition against alcohol, were in effect.

Here, too, travelers could be restricted in a way that was impossible on the open borders of an overground city, preventing entry by terrorists from rival factions, as well as inhibiting the cultural terrorism of those who carried the decadent ideas of the corrupt West with them.

The underground deep-water sources were not quite enough, but Badoit had recently begun piping seawater to a desalination plant, and water perfusion was at last adequate and he was able to sell clean water to other states; Saharan solar energy seemed eternal; the hydroponic greenhouses, thriving on reflected and artificial light, never suffered drought or pestilence.

Here and there the austere cityspace was picked out with palms and other greenery in small parks. Broad panels in the ceilings glowed, reflecting sunlight from a baffle of shafts.

Craning his neck just a little to look down, Steinfeld could see people—in traditional Bedouin garb, up-to-date printout suits, or gowns and veils— milling past the view windows of a mall.

The place had captured the imagination of the Arabic world. As a city, it was called simply "Badoit." And Badoit, the underground city, was a second Mecca. Oil-rich Muslims from all over the Middle East had lined up to donate millions on millions to its construction, adding their largesse to grants from the governments of Egypt, Tunisia, Syria, Iran, the Republic of Palestine, and Saudi Arabia. In exchange, they received a place in Badoit, permanent or simply in case of emergency. A nuclear war had seemed close—this would be the only refuge.

It was a magnificent conception, Steinfeld thought. And he was a little shaken to be sitting beside the man—indeed, to be soliciting help from the man—who had built it all. This vista had begun as an idea and a commitment in this man's head; a vision had somehow superimposed itself over a hundred seventy-five square miles of Earth, had crystallized the local world into conformity with itself. There was no squalor here; no extreme poverty. There was no pollution—that would have been lethal—and there were up-to-date hospitals and vaccination programs.

But the Complex had its problems: the power drain from the constant necessity of recirculating air was enormous. The Arcology was growing faster than its housing, and was becoming crowded, in some sectors, so constant expansion was necessary—and expansion was costly. Immigration restrictions had become fanatically stern, for anyone not bloated with money. Despite its success at exporting pesticide-free produce, water, and highly refined metals, and despite Badoit's oil-founded personal fortune, the Badoit Complex wavered back and forth between solvency and insolvency. And perhaps the arcology's relative cultural insularity—its limits of freedom of expression, its absence of freedom of religion—were regrettable.

But still, Steinfeld reflected, in its realization of artifice and organization, of order from chaos, its economic fairness at all levels—this place was civilization distilled.

"That will do," Badoit said suddenly.

Steinfeld came to himself with a start, and hit the stop button on the digi-viddy. He looked at Badoit, who seemed thoughtful but wholly unsurprised. "If you have any doubts about the authenticity of this video," Steinfeld said, "you can run a check for computer animation. I can assure you that this information is accurate. If you wish to send some of your people back to look over the situation personally, I will be glad to provide them the coordinates—they will see that it's all quite true: Muslims are being persecuted systematically throughout France, Italy, Germany—"

"No, no," Badoit said, waving a hand impatiently. "I'm quite sure it is authentic. Don't you suppose my people *have* 'looked over the situation personally'? Naturally. We have wide-ranging intelligence sources. We have become aware that these Second Alliance devils are persecuting the European Islamic community—"

"Persecuting is too weak a word."

"Quite. We were not aware that it had gone this far—your material brings a certain immediacy to the issue. The problem is not that something needs to be done—it is to determine, precisely, *what* should be done." He paused and smiled distantly. "You do not care for tea, I notice. Will you take some coffee? It is always ready."

"Yes, thanks. Coffee."

"Splendid. Sixteen years in England; I picked up the habit of tea in the afternoon. But if tea is my habit, coffee is my vice." Badoit turned to an intercom, spoke a short sentence in Arabic.

Steinfeld wondered what was going on in Badoit's head. There was no hint in the man's neutral expression. Perhaps he would be dangerous to deal with. Could such a man ever be knowable, even to his intimates? He was a nation builder, a city builder, the president of a microcosmic nation he had created himself: a man who never questioned his course once he set it. A visionary, but a ruthless one. He would take an alliance very, very seriously.

Steinfeld was lucky to have got into this office at all. Steinfeld was a Jew—there had been relative peace between Jews and Muslims, since the Israelis had—at long last—accepted a Palestinian state. Badoit was relatively moderate, an advocate of rapprochement, even alliance with the Jews. Still it was difficult for a non-Muslim who was not a head of state to meet with Badoit in person. Badoit maintained contacts with the Israeli Mossad, as there were some Islamic extremist factions who opposed him. Those strict-Fundamentalist factions were security threats to Badoit, Badoit the city and Badoit the man, and the Mossad—the Israeli intelligence service—helped him keep tabs on them. In exchange, he had agreed to see Steinfeld, who was something of a Mossad ward, if not truly an agent.

"You come here asking me for military aid, for weapons and soldiers. It seems to me that you have undervalued and underused the political channels," Badoit said. "You have jumped the gun, quite literally, and gone right to a military solution."

"Most political channels are closed to us," Steinfeld said. "The UN will not hear us. We've tried. The media is restricted in Europe. Most American media regards us as cranks. Armed resistance, so far as I can see, is the only practical course. Naturally, we're trying to alert people politically, to raise consciousness, as they say, in America. To use political channels. To

interest the media—with only indifferent success. In the meantime, the
murder goes on."

"You are working on many levels," Badoit said, "but your efforts on
some of those levels are rather trivial." There was a touch of smugness
in his tone as he revealed the extent of his knowledge of New Resistance
activities. "You promote notions of divisiveness in the 'Self-Policing
Organization of European States.'" Saying the catch-all name of the new
Fascist state with heavy irony. "You spread discontent with stories that
the umbrella organization is bleeding the member nations for cash and
resources. You promote the idea in France that the German leaders of
the Second Alliance corporation are more influential than the French in
SPOES, and so will reroute resources to the German advantage. You use
television graffiti, Internet, pirate radio, leafleting, postering—you even
spread seditious jokes. 'How many Frenchmen does it take to make up the
French government? A thousand Frenchmen: five Frenchmen with French
accents and nine hundred and ninety-five Frenchmen with American and
German accents . . . '" He smiled, though clearly not amused. "You have
contacted the American media and international Grid sources, including
young Norman Hand." He shrugged disdainfully. "You have done *nothing*
politically. These efforts are . . . minuscule."

Steinfeld nodded. "We only do what we can. I'm in favor of political
effort wherever possible. But there simply is not time to wait for political
action on a larger scale—the oppressed are being *killed,* even as we speak.
Your people and mine."

The doors swung open and a coffee cart hummed into the room on its
own, a steward walking behind it. The cart paused by the conference table
and the steward poured thick, sweet coffee for them into small china cups.
There was also a silver tray of sweetmeats.

The steward discreetly withdrew as they sipped their coffee in silence.
The stuff made Steinfeld's cheeks flush and his head hum.

Leaning back in his chair, Badoit said at last, "I agree that military
intervention is necessary. But you propose that I do it under the auspices of
the NR. And indeed, I would feel the need to work within the framework
of some such organization—I do not want to send my people in cold. Just
getting them into Paris would be difficult without you. But . . . it would be
a political time bomb for me. Dealing with you; with, if you will forgive
the expression, infidels. There are people who would use this connection
to denounce me. I have much support, but . . . not from everyone."

"You can trust me not to—"

"Can we?" Badoit interrupted. "Can I trust you with my fighting men?
You know, you would have some authority over my soldiers—it would be a

very delicate situation. I would have to trust you. I cannot take the chance without investigating you somewhat more thoroughly."

"What does that mean, precisely?" Steinfeld asked.

Badoit spoke a brisk phrase in Arabic into the intercom.

Almost instantly, four heavily armed men came into the room. Abu Badoit turned to Steinfeld, rose, made an ironic variation of the gracious gesture offering accommodation, and said, "It means you're my guest, for a while. It is only a matter of attitude, really, the distinction between *guest* and *prisoner*—don't you agree?"

• • •

COOPER RESEARCH LABS, LONDON.

She said her name was Jo Ann Teyk. And, she said, that morning she'd found something in her brain that scared her.

She was here at the lab complaining that Cooper Research Labs had used her brain for some kind of "calculations," if he understood her rightly, and the stuff scared her. She wanted it erased. And Barrabas knew, almost instantly, that he fancied her. He wasn't sure why. She was at least ten years older than him, her curly blond hair in no particular style, just flouncing to her shoulders any way it chose; her eyes were pale blue and her features were, somehow, reminiscent of the Dutch. But her accent was American.

They were standing awkwardly in the waiting room of Lab Six, Cooper Research Labs, a waiting room that hadn't been used, till now, in all the weeks Barrabas had worked here. A lab technician had fetched Barrabas, because this Jo Ann Teyk woman was asking for Cooper, and Barrabas was the only assistant to Cooper currently in the building.

"Dr. Cooper isn't here," Barrabas said. "He's in Paris. He's coming back tomorrow, I think. I could try to get him on the fone—"

"Would you? This thing is really bothering me. The Brain Bank won't be held responsible, they say. They won't pay for the erasing time, and I can't afford to pay for it. I'm trying to save up to get back to the States. Flights to New York are just outrageously overpriced now because they haven't got the war damage at the airports fully repaired and . . . "

She was rattling on rather nervously, and he nodded in the appropriate places, but he was only half listening. He was staring at her, wondering why she was so attractive to him. She wasn't beautiful. He pictured her in one of those old-fashioned white cloth hats, almost like nurse hats, the Dutch women had worn. Nothing sexy about that. She was moderately pretty. Her breasts were small and her hips a shade too wide. But she gave off something indefinable. Energy. Need. Maybe something seen in the warm ghostliness of her glance, a subtle female vitality and . . .

Sexuality, yes, somehow, though she wasn't dressed for it. She was wearing a rather weathered charcoal-blue printout women's suit and blue transparent-plastic sandals. He was glad she wasn't wearing heels; she was already at least three inches taller than he was. He was glad, too, he hadn't had to wear his SAISC uniform to work in the lab. People sometimes reacted nastily to it. People on the street who saw you in an SA uniform seemed to either wink at you, give you a sort of illicit approval, or else they'd glare and you had a sense they'd like to tell you off but didn't dare.

" . . . I mean," Jo was saying, "you do see the problem, don't you?"

"Hmm? Oh, oh yeah—" He broke off and grinned. "Actually, no. I'm a bit muddled on this Brain Bank business. Had the impression they hired people to do calculations or something. You're a mathematician, or—?"

"No. No, I'm an artist, or was. I'm an American."

No kidding, he thought. Her American accent was like a trumpet declaring her nationality.

She went on, "I had a show over here when the war started, and I've basically been stuck in London ever since. My patrons all sort of . . . some of them are dead now. The others I can't find. The gallery was burnt in the food riots, all my work gone. Digital paintings."

"Really? I do some, uh, digi-vid work myself. Just a little editing, nothing artistic. We have a Sony Ampex system. Doing a sort of documentary."

Clam up, he thought. He turned to the video painting on the wall: a rectangle of wafer-thin glass playing a loop of collaged digital imagery, soothing pastoral scenes, pictures of rustic North Country villagers and the like, all bathed in a kind of halcyon ambience. He nodded at it. "What do you think of that one?"

She seemed annoyed at being distracted to make art criticism, glanced irritably at the videol painting. "I think it's a decoration meant to go with the furniture, not a painting. Not a real one. Facile interior design background stuff."

"Yeah, I see what you mean," he said, looking at it more critically. Although he didn't see what she meant particularly.

"Well, back on the subject: if you don't know what Brain Banks are . . . " She made a fluttery gesture of frustration, and then said, "It's a . . . essentially, they rent a portion of your brain, see. Companies who can't afford high-speed mainframe time. Or just trying to save money, cut some corners. So they hire a 'passive'—that's what I was, at this Brain Bank—and they attach a dermal contact socket and access your brain for computer time. And you just lie there and let them use it, let them do all the thinking with a part of your brain you don't normally use. You can be thinking of something else entirely, and all this stuff is buzzing around in the . . . in the *very* back of the mind. Sort of."

He blinked at her in confusion. "They . . . hook into your brain somehow?"

"Yeah. The human brain can do some things better than computers: holo-imaging, certain kinds of computer-model elaboration, and the kind of stuff they were trying to develop artificial intelligence for. Certain kinds of complex thinking, see. And if you interface with a biochip, the brain is capable of all these, like, remarkably complex calculations and storage in parts of the brain we don't usually use much. A 'passive', you know, rents those out to people. Sort of like transients selling blood to a blood bank. The pay is better, but not all that much."

"And you just sit there wired in, and the data . . . "

"It just flashes by in your brain. Too quick to comprehend, usually. You don't usually remember anything afterward, see. All you got left is this weird taste in your mouth and a headache. Normally. But I guess sometimes the operator is sloppy with the erase function—sometimes the stuff remains in your brain. And it can flash onto your conscious mind, see, and bug you. I mean, I'm walking down the street, and then all of a sudden I see about a trillion numbers flashing by instead of the cars, and I see these, uh, molecular models instead of buildings. It was so fucking weird. It was like the numbers were the cars and the molecules were the buildings. And I walk into a wall or something. It *blinds* me. And it wakes me up at night. It's like someone's talking statistics in your ear all the time. You can't sleep with all that—"

"And it was Dr. Cooper who rented this, um, brain-time?" Barrabas asked.

"Yeah."

"That's odd . . . " Cooper had a budget for access to a major-league mainframe. Why go to one of these cheapo brain-rental outfits? "Um—do you remember what sort of work your brain was used for?"

"I had a semester of molecular biology a few years ago. I recognize stuff from that. It *looks* like the models we saw of genetic engineering for microorganisms. Build-your-own-virus stuff. Except it's not the same kind of viruses, if that's what they are . . . " She shrugged. But the shrug wasn't really one of indifference. Somehow, he sensed she had an inkling what the research might be, and it worried her.

Barrabas felt a chill. The program she was talking about had to be the Second Alliance's biowarfare work. Not Cooper's project per se—its provenance was the molecular biology team—but Cooper was Head of Research, and all major computer time was approved by him. They'd have brought him the work, asked him to authorize it. Cooper had evidently decided to run it himself on another system. The one they usually accessed was secure—the SAISC used it for virtually everything. Dotty old bugger.

And now the stuff was churning around in this woman's head. The molecular breakdowns, indices, models. If she recited some of it to the wrong people—or had it read out on an extractor—it would all come out in the wash.

Barrabas shook his head silently. Personally, he was frightened of the whole project. He didn't know exactly what sort of biological warfare it was—a viral attack of some sort. He was only on the periphery, but still, he could be held accountable by a war crimes commission. He'd told himself they wouldn't really *use* a virus, it was just a deterrent device, just a club to hold over the heads of the enemy once the SA took power. That's what Cooper had hinted.

But the Second Alliance wasn't in power in England yet. They were close, but they still didn't have the reins. In the meantime, if this thing broke . . .

What the bloody hell had Cooper been thinking of? Why had he used a nonsecure calculation device? The brain of an American expatriate artist, yet.

"Do you think you could fone him?" she asked again. "Or maybe get authorization somewhere else to pay to have this stuff taken out?"

"Um . . . no. It'd have to be Dr. Cooper. I'll see if I can get him. Have a seat."

He smiled at her, saw her face soften a little as he agreed to try to help her. The softening let something else shine through: the attraction was there. She felt it too. What was it about this woman?

He went into the comm room, was relieved to find everyone else had already gone for the day. The duty officer was on break. He sat at the console and tapped out Cooper's "Find and Notify" code. Somewhere in France, Cooper's fone would be going off. He was probably in the HQ, not far from a fone.

The console's respond light flashed green. Barrabas sat back within clear range of the camera that would transmit his image to Cooper, and hit the receive button. Cooper's face, looking like an irritated ghost, appeared on the little screen. "Yes? Oh it's you, ah, Barrabas. What is it?"

He told Cooper what Jo Ann had told him. Barrabas wouldn't have thought it possible for the albino's face to go paler, but what little color there was in Cooper's cheeks made itself noticeable with a sudden absence. "Oh, Lord, it would have to happen this once," he muttered. He said something else, but a shash of static and snow blotted it out.

"I didn't get that, sir, there was interference. What did you say?"

"Nothing, never mind. Listen—I don't want anyone else taking care of this. All right? I'll do it myself. I'll be back in a couple of days. Tell her stiff upper lip, I'm on my way."

"But—"

"No!" Cooper's vehemence was startling. "No . . . I'll have to handle it myself, in person. You're to say nothing to anyone else about it. You work for me—show some loyalty, man!"

"As you say, Doctor."

"In the meantime—keep an eye on the girl. I don't care how you do it. Romance her if you have to. But make sure she doesn't talk to anyone else about this."

"Um—I'd have to take the rest of the day off in order to—"

"Yes yes, fine fine, just see to it!" And he rang off.

Barrabas returned to the waiting room to find Jo Ann staring into space, squinting as if trying to see something better.

Distract her. "The doctor will attend to the matter personally when he gets back. In a couple of days."

She blinked, then frowned at him. "A couple of days! I can't live with this stuff." She shook her head incredulously.

"Isn't there anything that, um, suppresses it?"

"Well . . . loud music. Drink. Stimulus of different kind . . . "

"Look, I feel responsible for you. I mean, it was our fault, and we really should be doing more to help you. How about if I . . . " He hesitated. This sounded pretty phony. But maybe she'd play along. "If I took you out to some places to ease it. Some clubs, maybe. Do you like minimono or angst or retro or bonerock or House Dada or what?"

She smiled ruefully, looked at him for a full five seconds. He felt his cheeks flush. Finally, she said, "Bonerock and House Dada, mostly. Minimonos are so reactionary. Can't stand 'em. I heard Jerome-X is in town. His first tour. Just doing a few dates."

"I don't know his stuff."

"He's pretty obscure. He had a kind of college-radio bonerock hit called 'Six Kinds of Darkness.' He was on the edge of hot in the underground for a while, and he was 'big in Korea,' and then he disappeared. Just now resurfaced. He only had one album, but I'm kind of a fan. I have some files of video graffiti he did, too."

"Oh, yes?" He tried to sound neutral, though he didn't approve of video graffiti. The bloody wog radicals used it. Never mind. "Right. It's my solemn duty to take you to see this Jerome-X cove. Tonight?"

"Okay. Tonight."

●●●

A NIGHTCLUB AMONG THE DOCK WAREHOUSES IN LONDON, ENGLAND.

"Sure, Brit Customs believed it," Jerome-X said. "But if the Second Alliance or M15 take an interest in us, we're fucked. They know we came overseas on a private jet. They know most of the jetlines aren't open yet. They know that some of the biggest bands in the US couldn't get over here and I'm like a *nobody* in the bone scene—"

"Hell no, boy, dey *don't* know that," Bettina said. They were sitting in his dressing room on the sagging, cigarette-charred sofa, waiting for his cue. They were in the London club, *Acid Burn*, once an Acid House nightclub now basically gone bonerocker. In the background, filtered by the cracked concrete walls, was the rumble, rattle, and hum as a band cranked on the stage, from here sounding like a thunderstorm approaching across a mountain range. "Yo' bein' paranoid." Her accent seemed to have thickened since coming to England, as if in defense. She was a three-hundred-pound New Orleans black woman; she was Jerome's contact in the Resistance; she was Jerome's lover; she was his computer-systems guru; she was the Sage. "You think dese cock-biting English prigs know anything about American rock?"

"Lots of 'em do, actually, but—You really think I'm just being paranoid?"

"You bet yo' skinny white butt. De jet was loaned to us by a guy who admires yo' music, is all. Dat's our line. A fan, is what we telling people. He got it registered under a different name. Ain't nobody knows it Witcher."

"I'm nervous, I guess."

She slapped his rump. "Boy, I guess so. Relax, kid!" She took his head in a playful armlock.

"Don't be doing this shit in public!" he wheezed.

"Just playin', son, don't get all—"

"Hey, I'm in charge of the stage biz, we agreed that, Bettina! Don't be doin' that shit to me here!" he protested, pulling free.

"We backstage now. Gimme a kiss." She crushed him to her, and he gave in. She broke it off herself, looking him in the eye, almost nose to nose. "You know de protocols?"

"I know the UNIX protocols. I know the systems call code to log on as a superuser. I know how to evoke the debug function. If they haven't changed the debug function."

"Dey probable haven't, 'cause dey using a rented system. High security, but rented. If dey have changed it, fuck 'em, we log off and dey won't be able to trace it to an aug chip. I think de back gate is still open on dis system—"

"Where'd you get it from?"

"De anarchist underground. Plateau subsystem bulletin board."

"Some of those Wolves'll give you fake codes just to get their rivals in trouble."

"Dese ain't Plateau Wolves, these are Plateau Rads. About de only people I met on the Plateau I trust. Dey got a guy used to be a hacker for SAISC till he found out what dey were into. He knows de system's back gates."

"The anarchist underground cooperates with the resistance? You'd think they'd say fuck off. The NR wants to re-establish the old European republics. That's not very anarchist."

"Anarchists hate de Fascists worse den de Social Democrats, worse eben den de Republicists. Dey scared, like ever'body else out in de cold, boy. One of my braid's comin' loose, can you—Ow! Don't be doing it so tight! De NR's got anarchists in it, along with everything else. Just get rid of de Fascists and den fight over de bones, I guess is—"

The rest was drowned out in a tidal-wave magnification of the careening noise from the stage as the door opened and the club's manager looked through. He was a weakchinned rocker with sections of his depilated scalp shaped into three-dimensional figures like those on ESP testing cards: wavy lines, star shapes, squares, circles—like little flesh antennae on his head, made of transplanted skin and collagen. "Scalping up" hadn't hit the States yet, and Bettina found the fashion disconcerting. Whenever the guy came in, she stared at his head, which pleased him enormously.

"Are you ready, then?" the scalp-up asked.

"Yeah," Jerome said, standing up, so the guy would think he was coming right that second. So he'd leave, thinking Jerome was going to follow. He left, and Jerome turned to his shaving kit, took out his shaver, took off the rotary heads and found the plastic-wrapped aug chip. Bettina got hers from a tube she carried in her vagina. At her size, she had to wrestle with herself to get it out.

Jerome took the chip from the plastic; wet it, opened the flap of skin on his head, and inserted the chip, activating it with his thumbnail mouse. In a way, it was like doing a hit of speed, only it was isolated in you; one part of you hummed with restrained power, and the rest paced itself normally.

He ran through the password code, ran a quick program to check that the chip had gone through Customs without being magnetically scrambled, and then, nodding to himself, headed for the stage, Bettina coming along behind him, moving like a sailing ship in high seas. "I'm not that much into the concert part today," he said over his shoulder. "I'm, like, totally out of practice, and I was forgetting about performing anyway when you guys thought this shit up . . . "

"Oh, yo' love it, yo' little ham."

"Sometimes I do, sometimes I don't. I was never in a band much. I used to do little concerts with digital and maybe one player, and the recording was all electronic, except for a couple of musicians I used in the studio and never saw after that. A band is such a hassle, it's like babysitting, I'm not really into it. But you can't get up enough crowd energy just using purely electronic backup, you got to have some other people, live . . . "

He was already picking his way over the gear on the stage, looking to see that everything was in place.

Bones was there, waiting, at the synthesizer. They called him Bones, but he couldn't stand Bone Music normally, calling it "neurological masturbation for bored middle-class white kids," and he could barely play the keyboards. It didn't matter much that he couldn't play well, though Bones didn't understand that. He was as nervous as a kid auditioning, running through the simple keyboard lines over and over, behind the polarized screen that was the stage's curtain. Club roadies moved equipment to either side of him.

Andrea, the guitarist, was dialing her tuner, and the wire dancer, a faggy Spanish guy named Aspaorto, was taping his wireless transers to the electrodes on Jerome's thighs and arms and calves and hips—Jerome-X used *some* of the minimono techniques—and the mikes were whining with feedback as the soundman turned them up. It was a live, noisy, electrically charged space, and that would help mask the aug signals, Jerome thought.

He sighed, and shook himself. His hands were damp. He wasn't in the mood for the music part. He wanted to break into the system, do the work, get it over with. Only, the way it was set up, it wouldn't be over with, in a sense, for a long time. A long, long time. Because they were infecting the system for now. Not destroying it. Bones had gone all stress case over this approach. *We oughta wipe it out while we got the chance, not fuck around,* he'd said. *It's taking a dumb chance.*

Steinfeld wanted it done this way, though. Slow infection.

Steinfeld could plan, long-term, Bettina said. That's why he was going to kick ass, she said, when the time came.

Jerome took a headset mike off its stand and slipped it on over his head. Heard his own breathing come back to him on the monitors.

Get into the mood, he told himself. These people paid their money, and there ain't much of that around London nowadays.

He was still invisible to the audience behind the black plastic screen, but he shouted over the mike to see if he could prod them in advance a little. "Maybe we shouldn't *bother* playing, nobody fucking *cares* anymore what *anybody* does!"

"Sod off, ya barstads!" someone shrieked in gleeful reply, and the audience set to whooping and howling. He could see them in foggy silhouette through the translucent screen, a gallery of faceless busts from here, joggling up and down. Some of them, he could see by their outlines, had scalped up: tombstones of cemeteries atop their heads was a favorite. Others were still in flare hairstyle variations, in multi-Mohawks, in retro spikes.

"Yeah, well fuck off, or we *will* play!" Jerome threatened.

"Uhgitta chezick!" someone in the audience yelled in technicki. Meaning, *I'm getting chillsick,* and the rest of the audience laughed, because it was a joke, a sort of pun. Bone Music gave you the chills when you heard it, very literally sent shivers through your bones, but between bands the club played music without the shiver frequency to give you a rest, otherwise the audience got sick, "chillsick," and to say you were chillsick while you were waiting for a band meant, essentially, *Don't bring 'em on, I'm sick of this shit already, especially when it comes to these blokes.* Which was in fact not really an insult, just affectionate mockery, taking the piss out.

Jerome laughed, liking it. He was getting some attitude on now. He had to slip into a kind of split subpersonality, a schizy character that was all authoritative punkiness, in order to pull off a concert. It didn't come to him naturally, not like some—not like, say, Rickenharp. Jerome had to work on getting the right attitude in a public place. It was a lot easier to do video graffiti at home alone with your minitrans and camera. He was a little embarrassed on a stage playing underground pop star. His boyhood idol had been Moby—and he found himself pretending to be Moby in his own mind. It was okay to be a pop star if you were Moby.

He checked that everyone was in place. He glanced at Andrea, who nodded to signify readiness, one spike-heeled boot poised over the sound-control box on the floor; she wore a video dress that was showing an old movie, *Apocalypse Now,* exposing her long, seashell-pink legs and tattooed shoulders; her bald head crawling with anima-tattoos. He could never quite follow the animation sequence; something about a grinning Jesus smoking a pipe and firing an AK-47. Andrea herself was smoking a glass pipe with an all-night THC/MDMA flameless-smoke capsule in it; tonight, a hot-pink smoke that matched her boots and belt. Her eyes glazed from the X-dope. She always looked as if she were going to fall over, but she never missed a note. She was a real find.

Jerome glanced back at Bettina, saw her glaring at him from hooded eyes, her silver-robed hulk of a body emitting an unexpurgated body language of angry jealousy. Evidently he'd spent too long looking at

Andrea. He grinned and mouthed, "I love you" at her, and she relaxed and grinned, put on her headset mike for backup vocals.

He nodded at Bones, who hit the program for the percussion, the shivery thuds rolled out into the club like stark milestones in a sonic landscape, and the screen rolled aside and Andrea hit the bass programmer with one toe while segueing into the guitar lead with her hands. Bones shakily skrilled out his keyboard part, frowning with concentration.

Jerome hadn't turned to the audience yet, he just stood there, back to them, looking over the band, like some kind of inspector, moving a little to the music but not acknowledging the crowd till he was good and ready. Bones was a pretty lame keyboard player, all right, but it was adequate, and when he missed, it somehow sounded like the deliberate "noise factor" that many bands used; much of it was masked by the undulating sheets of sound Aspaorto rippled out of his limbs, dancing music out of his neuromuscular impulses.

Jerome was chip-linked with Bones on the Plateau. He transmitted a readout to him that said: *Scan for surveillance.*

No shit was Bones's reply. Smartass.

Rather tardily, the soundman did the introduction, yelling "Jerome-X!" over the house PA, but that was washed away by the torrent of sound from the stage, and the audience knew who he was anyway, they were his small but intense London cult following, and they were already shivering to the sound . . .

As Jerome turned to them and bellowed,

The thing that lives in Washington
It's a kind of living stone
The thing that lives in Washington
Its makes the planet groan.

Jerome letting the shivers carry him, getting into it now, letting his pelvis tell him what to do. More vigorously, as he found the groove and delivered:

The thing that lives in the temple
The temple with five sides
The thing that lives in Washington
Takes children for animal hides . . .

The room itself shivered, and, on some secret molecular level, the walls themselves danced.

• • •

Bone Music always made Barrabas feel ill. But he tried to keep his expression from going sour as the shivers whirled around his stomach; as he danced with Jo Ann in a sardine press of people. Only now and then, through the churn of bodies, could he make out Jerome-X, a geeky American kid gyrating and bellowing, barely carrying a tune. A big fat Negress wobbled like jelly on a plate behind him, every so often punching through with some gospel-sounding backup singing. Something like,

Show me, show me, show me the way out
Oh show me, show me, Lord show me the way out . . .

Why'd they have to use these bleeding bone-shivering frequencies? Barrabas thought crabbily. He'd read about it, but he'd been in a bone club only once before. Some people claimed the vibrations could cause bone cancer; some people claimed it *cured* bone cancer.

Whatever, it reached into you, a subsonic current that carried the music like a kind of aural flotsam; carried it into you physically, so you felt the chords shivering in your bones, in your skull, in your flesh. Some people had Bone Music receptors implanted in their skulls, in pelvic bones, in their spines, receptors that picked the music up on special frequencies others couldn't hear, turning their whole bodies into antennas. Some people, lots of people, found it ecstatic. Sexual and hypnotic and all-involving.

"You okay?" Jo Ann yelled into his ear. Yelling loud, but he could barely hear her over the blast of the band. "You look like you wanna puke!"

"Not used to this bone stuff!"

"Come on, let's get a drink!"

She took him by the wrist and led him into the bar. He didn't much like being led around by girls, but he let her do it, anything to get out of that dance floor.

The bar had closed doors, the music was filtered, and the bone shivering was mostly gone in here. It was dark, like it was supposed to be, the only light coming from the bar itself, which was made of stained glass; murky, oddly shaped panels of blood red and wine purple and jade green and dull blue, some of them illuminated from within, shattering the shadowy, smoky room with random shafts of colored light. Barrabas sat on a stool in a shaft of purple; Jo Ann sat almost astraddle a beam of green, some of it streaming up her front to tint her gray eyes jade.

They ordered vodka martinis and sat hunched together between two groups of sweating, almost-naked men giggling over cocaine fizzes. Advertisements blinked up the cocktail straws; digital music groaned like a machine about to break down. On the walls, videopaintings re-creating scenes from medieval depictions of the Crucifixion and Resurrection flickered through sequence in doleful chiaroscuro; occasionally the images of Christ alternated with other figures, paintings by Paul Mavrides and other icons from the erstwhile post-Acid House era: Timothy Leary ascending into heaven, riding a CD like a flying saucer; William Burroughs and Laurie Anderson waltzing through a concentration camp while the starveling camp victims played Strauss on orchestral instruments; Kotzwinkle shooting skull-shaped dice with William Gibson; the minimono star Calais chained to Stephen Hawking's wheelchair; Philip K. Dick with an arm growing from his forehead, arm wrestling with an arm growing from Rick Crandall's forehead; Rickenharp falling into the rubble of the collapsing Arc de Triomphe; Ivan Stang adding twentieth-century paper money to the flames under the stake on which a grinning J.R. "Bob" Dobbs is being burned alive; David Bowie eaten cannibalistically by a demonic horde of twenty-first century pop stars; Iggy Pop having sex with Mrs. Bester, the president of the United States.

And back to the dead but numinous body of the scourged Christ, his head in Mary Magdalene's lap.

"That loose data bothering you here?" Barrabas asked. "The Brain Bank stuff, I mean."

Jo Ann shook her head. "Isn't room for it with all the input here. You feel better?"

"Much. I'm sorry about the dance. I'll get a few drinks in me and then—"

"Don't worry about it. It was too crowded to dance anyway. What is it you do for Dr. Cooper? Video stuff, you said?"

"Documentation, editing." He wanted to change the subject. She was frowning slightly.

Two guys behind him were talking over one another, yelling opinions that neither heard. He felt a nonmusical chill when he realized what the issue was. "The bloo'y SA Fascist barstads 'er in Parliament now, what yuh going to do, ay?" one of them, a white guy in dreadlocks, yelled. "There's no bloo'y way we can get the Nazi barstads out without a war, a blee'in' civil war, mate, ay?"

At the same time the other shouter—a black with a scalp-up shaped like a street scene, his home neighborhood—was saying, "Oi mean, these buggered right righ-cist barstads are everywhere, fuck me for a joke, 'ow you goin' to fight them, bloo'y 'ell you'd arv to bust in the system, righ'?"

And, Barrabas realized with a twinge, Jo Ann was listening to them. He wondered if she knew the lab she'd done brain work for was a branch of the SA. He wondered, too, if she was politically liberal. She was, after all, an artist. She answered his unasked questions, then, when she remarked, "The SA corporation really scares me, the way it's growing. Racism amazes me. It's like some old superstition, like believing the world is flat and the sun rotates around the Earth!"

"What, the sun doesn't rotate around the Earth? Go on!" he joked, hoping to kid her away from the subject.

She smiled fleetingly and then put on an expression that said, *But seriously* . . . "I mean—what can anyone do about these racists? That dude was right. They're a part of the system now . . . "

• • •

He was into the system. Jerome felt it before he saw it. He was *in*.

The computing work was done by the left brain—and the camouflage by the right brain. The right brain was singing. Singing the chorus to "Six Kinds of Darkness," while the other part of his mind worked with the chip. The right lobe singing,

> *Six kind of darkness, spilling down over me*
> *Six kinds of darkness, sticky with energy . . .*

The left lobe hacking:

London UNET: ID#4547q339. Superuser: WATSON.

The music was camouflage, cover for the mole-signals, the piggyback signals that used updated palm-pilot tech to reach out, to access . . .

The left lobe of his brain working with the chip, which emitted a signal, interfaced with a powerful microcomputer hidden among the micalike layers of chips in the midi of Bones's synthesizer; Jerome-X seeing the Herald on the hallucinatory LCD screen of his mind's eye:

London UNET, ID #, date, assumed "superuser" name.

Then he ran an e-mail program that was his encryption worm, executing his diabolic algorithm, overflowing the input buffers receiving the data, the overflow carrying him into the target computer's command center. Bypassing the passwords and security, now that he was in the computer's brain, and then commanding:

CHANGE DIRECTORY TO ROOT.

ROOT: Superdirectory of the system. Scanning, at the root, for the branch of the system he needed.

Scanning for: Second Alliance International Security Corporation: Intelligence Security subdirectory . . .

• • •

Watching from the audience, Patrick Barrabas remarked (and was unheard in the blare) that Jerome-X had a funny, contortionistic way of dancing as he sang. His eyes squeezed shut, his hands moving as if over typewriter keyboards . . . Not playing the "air guitar," but typing on the air keyboard . . .

• • •

Jerome was typing the commands out. Using a technique Bettina had taught him to implement more complex commands; sending through his aug chip by radio trans to a powerful mainframe; typing physically on a mental keyboard.

The chip fed him tactile illusions and read out his responses through its contact with the parietal lobe, reading the input from the proprioceptive sensors—sensory nerve terminals—in the muscles, and kinesthetic sensors , tactile nerves in the fingers: Jerome's movements translated into cybernetic commands. His rapport with the aug chip essentially creating a mental data-glove, a data-glove that materialized only in the "virtual reality" holography of consciousness.

As Jerome sang,

Darkness of the Arctic
Six months into the night
Darkness of the eclipse
forgetting of all light
Six kinds of darkness
Six I cannot tell . . .

Finding his way through the darkness in the forest of data. Taking cuttings. Taking information. Planting something of his own . . .

• 07 •

PARIS, FRANCE.
They were in Father Lespere's flat behind the church. It was in one of the old-fashioned Parisian stone houses, with its high, narrow, rusting-iron front door; a door so tall and heavy it could almost have belonged to a cathedral. The cracked walls were brown with age and, in streaks, sepia with water stains. They'd come through the rear building, up the narrow, winding stairs. The light in the clammy, echoing stairwell, in the parsimonious French manner, turning itself off after they'd climbed a flight. The place smelled musty; its spaces were glum.

Father Lespere's flat was a little more cheerful. It was cramped but high-ceilinged, done in off-white and pale yellow; there were some tasteful chandeliers, and an old rolltop desk, a few silk daffodils in antique Flemish vases. Lespere was one of the city's elite, which meant he had a gas fire and electricity, a console playing music. Mozart. The furniture was simple to the point of spareness. There was a crucifix, of course, and a Mother Mary, and a wall filled with books on theology and architecture. Many books, but nothing that would make SA visitors suspicious. He had long since purged his bookshelves.

Briand looked at them with a gentle amazement as they came in. Smoking a cigarette, Old Briand sat in an old wooden kitchen chair; his face was gray with grief and age and flecked with salt-and-pepper stubble; he wore the uniform of a street cleaner, his crumpled hat in his hands, a china bowl of coffee and a bit of bread on a white wooden table beside him.

Bibisch and Torrence were dressed as construction workers themselves, as if they'd been laboring with rabble-reclamation teams all day. They'd put dust in their hair and grimed their hands. Their machine pistols were well hidden in their clothing.

Father Lespere wore a cassock, as if he were about to take confession, and in a way he was.

They shook hands and drank a little coffee and complained of the drizzle outside. Through the window, through the attenuated slant of rain, Torrence saw the strange landscape of Parisian rooftops, looking to him, in his present mood, like the monuments of a cemetery, the humped gray tile roofs and attic stories like barrows and mausoleums, the chimneys like an endless vista of abstracted gravestones. Here and there were the blasphemous intrusion of dormer windows. The surfaces slick with water; the sky murky with it.

"*Et bien*," Lespere said, "if you are ready to hear the story, I will ask Briand to tell it."

Torrence nodded mechanically.

Working hard to keep his expression neutral, Torrence listened as Bibisch translated the old Frenchman's account. "They came in the morning, when everyone is a-sleeping. Not me, I work very early, I am alone awake in the building, happy that morning because I have some tea, *difficile* to get . . . Then there is a sound of a truck and a machine that smashes doors and the building shake, everything fall from the wall; and the men come into every apartment, take us out by the necks, we cannot see the faces because they have balls of glass on them. You know this kind of soldier . . . they take us to the street, everyone is looking from the other buildings. And they murder. That is all. They murder. They broke in—many times I have seen them break in and take people, and say that it is for France, it is for the Unity Party, it is for Security, and they had weapons so we will not argue—but this time they did not take someone to a prison, no. They kill them. They kill them there on the street. They say is reprisal. Is execution for . . . " She hesitated, then asked Briand to repeat the name. Briand did; said it quite clearly. Torrence felt a ghostly hand trying to choke off his breath.

Reprisal. For the one called *Hard-Eyes*. For the work of the terrorist Hard-Eyes.

Aka Daniel Torrence.

"How many are dead?" Torrence asked in a croak.

"*Quatre*," the old man said. "*Une petite fille.*" One of them a little girl.

Torrence let out a long, slow, shuddery breath.

"They do it with a child, too. *C'est psychologie.*" Bibisch told Torrence softly, squeezing his arm.

He nodded. "They're trying to play on everyone's feelings. Including mine. And it's going to work."

She shook her head. "*Non! Merde, c'est pas vrai!*" And then launched into a burst of rapid-fire French. Telling him off for letting this get to him, he gathered. The sound of her voice was loud in the room, but to Torrence it was a distant echo, the sound of a passing siren heard in the distance as you stand in a funeral chapel.

He envisioned strapping explosives about himself, breaking into SA HQ, blowing up The Thirst and Watson and as many others as possible . . . just taking them with him.

"Why did they pick your building, Monsieur Briand?" Torrence asked.

Lespere did the translation this time, as the old man wearily said, "Maybe no reason, or perhaps because someone in the building complained about the water. We had no water for two weeks, and the Unity government controls the utilities, and they said it was unpatriotic to complain because everyone must face shortages. Or perhaps for no reason, just a neighborhood where none of their own class live. I do not know, *Monsieur*."

Lespere turned to Torrence. "They probably picked one that had annoyed them, but it wasn't of great consequence. Their object was to attack you, Torrence."

The old man was crying now, with no change in his expression. He simply let the tears roll as he spoke. "Simone," Bibisch translated for him, "was my niece. The little girl. I have no one now." She added, in an aside, "Say he wants to die . . . " She shrugged.

"Then he came to the right place," Torrence muttered.

"You are feeling sorry for yourself?" Lespere asked him.

Torrence shook his head. Then, abruptly, he said, "Yeah. Yeah, I am. For me and everybody else that got stuck in this fucking thing."

"You leave the work of Christ to Christ. Sacrifice is required of you, but not martyrdom. It is just beginning. You have to be ready. It will be worse. The Thirst will bring people in and torture them to try to find you. But the truth is very simple: You are doing more good than harm, even if they take reprisals in your name, Daniel."

Bibisch nodded. "*Exactement. C'est ça.*"

Torrence felt like an urn filled with ashes. *Une petite fille . . . Torture them to try to find you . . .*

"More good than harm?" he snorted. "That's hard to believe."

"There is one thing I am especially equipped to know," Lespere said. "And that is: believing is always hard."

• • •

THE GLASS KEY CLUB, LONDON.

Barrabas and Jo Ann. It was the third club they'd gone to on their first date. The Glass Key was an after-hours place, rounding out things nicely because both of them were jacked up on MDE spritzers and couldn't have slept anyway. And the Glass Key was the kind of place you went when you felt that way and you were looking for a place to be in public and yet be alone . . .

They'd gone into the ambient-field of the sex club's back rooms by tacit mutual agreement, acting as if they were just looking around, checking the place out, but both of them knowing how it'd end up here, especially with the sexual momentum that'd been building up all night, and the drug-drinks.

The first time, they did it standing up; he pinned her to the wall, her skirt hiked up and her legs wrapped around his hips. The second time, on the mattress that covered the floor, and they'd even undressed, except he'd forgotten and left his socks on; she mercilessly teased him for that later.

The third time was very slow, and he never did quite come, but that was all right.

Afterward, though, the MDE was beginning to wear off, they were both tired and sore and, one of the after-effects of the drug, a little irritable. "I could just burn out the fucking Brain Bank excess with druggy brain damage," she said, "if I keep this up."

"Oi'd die for a pint o' bitters," Barrabas muttered. His birthright accent showing through his fatigue.

"Yeah, I could use a drink without any goddamn uppers in it," she said, awkwardly pulling on her panty hose. They dressed in silence after that, went out to the bar, and—it was closed.

"Shit!" they both said at once.

Outdoors, the morning sun had the cruel temerity to be breaking through the clouds, and Barrabas felt his head throb with the intrusion of light and street noise.

But the fresh air helped a little, and the walking flushed out their systems some, and after a few minutes of strolling to the tube station, looking wistfully at the black-snail humps of the electric taxis they could no longer afford, they held hands and felt a little closer once more.

They paused in front of some shop windows, where cameras took in their image, digitalized it, and projected it onto the blank-faced robot mannequins in the window—so that in the window display he was now wearing baggy pants and a coat-and-tails made of black leather, and a ruffled puce shirt, and she was wearing a skintight spiral-strip gown. Their exact faces appeared on the mannequins, which mimicked even their movements, like reflections in mirrors. They laughed when they saw it. "That's supposed to make me want to buy it?" Barrabas said. "Seeing myself in that I'll never go near one of them rigs." He gave it the finger—and the mannequin of himself in the black leather coat-and-tails and ruffled shirt dutifully gave him the finger back, his own exact face grinning back at him.

She laughed, and then held her head. "Ow. Don't make me laugh." They walked on.

"That was some exxy night," Barrabas said when they reached the image-crowded hoardings around the tube station.

They stopped, and she grinned at him. Some of the almost luminous vitality that had attracted him to her flared in her eyes again. "Yeah."

Four young Pakistani men, probably students on their way to university, burst from the tube station and shoved hurriedly past Barrabas and Jo Ann, one of them bumping into her. Barrabas scowled. The Paki who'd jostled her paused beside Barrabas to look her over. She was rumpled and mussed from the events at the sex club.

He grinned. "Sorry, miss. Wish I had time to apologize right. Looks like you're a bit o' fun."

Barrabas reacted instinctively. His hand snaked out, smacked the wog backhanded so that he staggered into his friends. In his most upper-crust voice, Barrabas snapped out, "You disgusting little wog. How dare you." Feeling a surge of pleasure as he said it. Thinking he was making points with Jo Ann, showing her he'd fight for her, keep the rabble off her. "Get the bloody hell out of here, you wanking wog bastard," he said. "Back to Packi-land, preferably."

The wog went all flint-eyed and started to sputter an answer, but the students laughed derisively at Barrabas to defuse the thing, and made obscene gestures, then dragged their angry friend away. Chiding him to ignore the Fascist oaf: "Probably an SA git."

Barrabas realized that Jo Ann was staring at him. The red of fatigue in her eyes could have been tailored for the cold anger in her expression. "I don't believe it," she said with slow and careful incredulity. "You had me fooled into thinking you were a human being. But you're a fucking Nazi. Aren't you?"

"What? Nazi? Bloody hell. No. No."

"You're a racist thug!"

"I just . . . I just want them out of England, the wogs. There isn't room. There isn't enough work or food, and we have our own effing way of doing things here."

"You really believe that shit? You ever think for yourself?"

"I always think for meself. What a load of bollocks—what do you know about it, you're a bloody American!"

"Yeah. Fine. Fuck off."

She turned on her heel and ran into the tube.

He wanted to go after her and couldn't.

There was a monstrous roaring in his head. But it was only a train, roaring by on the elevated tracks. Stopping on the platform, up the staircase from him. His train. After a moment, he dragged himself to it.

•••

Paris, France.

The Jægernaut crunched down the street, making the buildings shake, so that loose bricks and bits of cornices rained onto the sidewalks and Watson was glad he sat in the armored protection of a bus-sized Internal Security Vehicle. They had driven in only a minute ahead of the Jægernaut, and now they watched its approach on the monitors inside the ISV—cameras were safer than windows—and it felt something like watching a missile test in a military ICBM-launch installation: The monitoring equipment bleeping to itself, the impassive technicians wearing their headsets as they helped direct the Jægernaut and scanned for saboteurs. It was distanced just enough by the screens—watching it from the street nearby, exposed, was a little too awe-inspiring. Too unnerving. It was like watching a volcano erupt—or watching as some contorted, massive-girdered suspension bridge pulled itself up from its moorings and went for a vindictive walk . . .

The Jægernaut—this model remote-controlled—came on with the methodical pacing of automation, not gracefully but without hesitation, making directly for the old tenement building. Watson was glad they'd got the address right. It was a bit dismaying when they crushed the wrong house, since they usually killed several hundred of the wrong people. And that was perfectly awful public relations.

Some of the tenement's residents had felt the Jægernaut coming, and a few had made it out the door. But most of them hadn't had time.

Others came to the windows to look for escape. But then the hammer came down. The Jægernaut's smashing scythe of impervious girders, aided by a tight microwave beam to soften the building's stone, bit deeply into the roof of the tenement, crunching through tile and roof like a beak crushing the shell of a snail.

And the building's people were like the slugs that squirmed in snail shells, Watson thought. They stood in the windows, screaming and waving their arms as if that'd stop thousands of tons of crystallized alloy bearing down on them.

Bloody stupid of them, really. If you know you're going to die, Watson reasoned, die with a little dignity. What was the use of hysteria?

The Jægernaut bit more deeply into the building; Watson could feel the vibration of its impact as it shivered through the street, quivering through the ISV. In less than a minute, an eight-story building was imploded, a crushed shell, a spindly, collapsing thing in a hood of smoke and dust. The screaming was now drowned out in the steel-foundry roar of the Jægernaut's grinding progress. When the scythe rotated up, like the blade of a Rototiller coming around again, it was edged in dripping red.

Watson would have enjoyed this more under normal circumstances. But Giessen—The Thirst—was here, looking as usual for all his dramatic *nom de guerre*, like a prissy Royal Tax Accountant, and the bastard was spoiling Watson's fun.

They were sitting side-by-side in the cramped control deck, just behind the driver and to one side of the forward gunner, whose head was entirely concealed by the complex machinery of his video targeting ordnance. Watson sipped tea from a plastic cup; The Thirst drank coffee with a little schnapps in it. He was listening on a headset to the rooftop surveillance crew and the chopper.

"Anything?" Watson asked. Knowing full well from Giessen's expression that they'd come up with nothing, but wanting to needle him.

The Thirst shook his head. Nothing.

Watson smiled to himself. It was perverse to be pleased when the New Resistance didn't fall into a trap. But he'd told the fool it wouldn't work. Giessen's plan had been like a plot from a Dumas novel, or *Zorro*—in order to flush the guerillas, let them know you're going to carry out a reprisal on a tenement full of Arabs. They'd be there to defend them, to avenge them. They hadn't let anyone know which tenement it would be, or even what neighborhood—but they'd let them know it would happen. They assumed the New Resistance would watch the compound where the Jægernauts were kept, follow them to the attack site and then move in with Stingers or some other armor-piercing weapon—and hopefully this Torrence wretch would be there, directing the operation . . .

It hadn't worked out that way, of course. Steinfeld was no fool. And Torrence was no sucker. They would not be drawn so easily. Especially knowing that there was little that could be done against a Jægernaut. The reprisal against the building—said to harbor New Resistance civilian auxiliary—was useful in and of itself. That was the sort of thing they kept the Jægernauts for. Eventually, of course, they'd be used in warfare: advance phalanx when invading a city. When the time for expansion came . . .

Giessen took off the headset, shrugging. "I wasn't at all sure it would work. But I wanted to try a feint, see how they would react."

Watson seethed inwardly. "I told you how they would react. Your lack of regard for my opinion is hardly flattering. Security is after all my specialty."

"I have every respect for you, Herr Watson. But I have a need to explore this problem in my own way. My feeling is that some of the old-fashioned techniques will work. Executions in return for this Torrence's activities— that is an ancient, time-honored method, and it will eventually provide us with informers, as well as put pressure on this man, force his hand. I intend to use some newer techniques also. We have some new surveillance technology . . . something that will be very useful in these Metro tunnels and sewers they are using."

"What, precisely? Listening posts?"

"No. Bird's eyes."

"But they lose their guidance signal underground! And then they can't transmit!"

"The new ones are internally guided. They don't transmit, they record. They are equipped with infrared. They will explore the tunnels for us. They will find them."

● ● ●

Torrence and Roseland, assault rifles cradled in their arms, stood with their backs to a stack of moldering cardboard boxes filled with books, keeping an eye on the door. The room was dim, dusty, chilly, and smelled of piss. The old furniture that had been stored in it was coated with powder from the insulation in the ceiling, shaken down during the shellings of Paris. Their only light was a guttering chemlantern and what came through the basement window. They'd left the old van parked around the corner, but the SA could notice it, might realize it hadn't been there earlier. They might have seen them scramble into the building. They might be here any minute.

Torrence didn't think so—the SA's attention was focused on the buildings and streets closer to the one being demolished.

"We could have done something," Roseland said, his voice lifeless.

He had gone into his monotone phase, Torrence noticed. Roseland, when he was coping, would joke around, use funny voices, toss out the one-liners. Letting off steam that way—for himself and everyone else. But when the emotional pressure was there, when he looked right into the face of the monster, his voice and personality became affectless, monotone. It was as if he'd slipped back into some sympathetic variation of the typical Detention Center victim, voice and eyes flat from despair, his bitter assertions made in a voice colorless as tin. "We should die with them. We deserve it, sitting here watching them die."

"We couldn't have stopped it," Torrence said. "We didn't know what building it was. And they've got the whole area staked out. We'll be lucky if they don't track us in here."

He was, in fact, watching a handheld monitor that was supposed to show a blip if a bird's eye or some other electronic surveillance device was near enough. The screens weren't very reliable, though.

The building shook and a little white dust filtered down from the ceiling, as the Jægernaut made another pass over the tenement three blocks away.

Torrence glanced up at Norman Hand, who, with this technicki aide, was sitting on the back of an overturned sofa, which was stacked on another sofa, just under the basement window; they were getting digi-viddy out the window.

"You getting a good shot, Hand?" Torrence asked.

Hand nodded. His technicki was using a long-range, digitally enhanced camera scope. They didn't have to get in closer.

The reporter hadn't said a word since the demolition had begun. He was watching the little monitor in his hand, seeing, magnified, what the camera saw. Sometimes his jaw trembled a little.

Torrence was glad. Hand was affected by what he was seeing. He was seeing something that couldn't be denied, couldn't be shrugged off. With luck, he'd have the balls to translate his feelings about it into Grid reporting. He'd have the video as partial proof. Maybe they could round up some survivors to interview. At least the men, women, and children in that tenement hadn't died for nothing. They'd die again on the Grid, where there would be millions more witnesses.

But Torrence felt foolish and helpless when he thought about what was going on right down the street.

Roseland was fidgeting. "We could snipe some of the bastards, at least."

Torrence shook his head. "We can't risk this Grid project. This coverage is a way of attacking them, it's turning their own brutality against them, man. You know?"

"You're going to just vid this thing and go home."

"And use the images. Yes."

"People will say it's computer-fabricated stuff."

"It can be tested for that. And—it has . . . it'll just feel too damn real to deny."

Roseland's voice was especially flat when he said, "It isn't worth it. I'm going out, to kill some of them."

Torrence said, in the tone he'd learned since becoming a paramilitary officer, "No. No, you're not."

Roseland stood up and moved toward the door.

Torrence debated threatening to shoot him. He wasn't at all sure that a threat would work.

He might have to kill him.

"Roseland," he said.

Roseland put his hand on the doorknob.

"If you do it—"

Roseland turned the doorknob.

Torrence took the safety of his rifle off.

Then he said, "If you do it, I'll kick you out of the NR. We'll ship you to the States, and you can go live with your relatives happily ever after."

Roseland hesitated, then slowly turned to him. "I've proved myself."

"Sure you have." Torrence put the rifle aside. "But I'd have to do exactly that."

"You want to maintain your authority that much?"

"I want to keep the Resistance organized, Roseland. You do it and you're out. Gone. You won't be able to kill another Fascist. Not around here. And they'll just go on . . . "

Roseland stared at him. His eyes were lost in the shadows. He looked like the living dead.

Sounded like it, too, when he said, "Yeah. Okay."

He went back to his spot on the floor and sat down. He hugged his gun and stared into space.

The building shuddered again. Hand groaned and, shoulders shaking, began to weep. Torrence felt sick.

• • •

Lab Six, Cooper Research, London.

"What do you mean you lost touch with her?" Cooper's voice was stretched into a squeak with near-hysteria.

"Steady on," Barrabas said. They were standing in the editing room with the door shut. It was close and stifling in there. "This is a cock-up, all right. But she's going to get in touch with you. She needs us to pay for her erasure."

"You don't know that. She might have gone to the bloody radicals if she realized it was biowarfare stuff. To anyone."

"She doesn't know what it is." But he wasn't so sure.

"Right. This is what I want you to do for me—"

"Hang on," Barrabas interrupted. He had been thinking things over. "I want a talk first."

Cooper licked his cyanotic lips. "What, ah, did you want to talk about?"

Barrabas hesitated. It had occurred to him that he knew something about Cooper that could be useful leverage. He could get something in exchange for his cooperation in keeping it mum. Still, Cooper might not like being blackmailed, however subtly. He'd make a dangerous enemy. But Barrabas wanted the hell out of this project.

"I heard a bit of gossip, Dr. Cooper. To the effect you've been on balancers."

Cooper opened his mouth to deny it, then thought better of it. "What of it?" he grated. "I got started before anyone knew how . . . "

"How addictive it is?" Barrabas nodded. Balancers. Ironically named. A kind of drug spigot, an implant that doles out doses of stimulant in the morning, a certain amount of tranquilizer to take the edge off the stimulant, a high in the evening—sometimes a long, illegal rush of pure pleasure—and then a sedative. Keeping you stoned, feeling good, getting you off, but never giving you too much of one or the other . . . constantly balancing, with its micro bloodtesters, the levels of the drugs with your daily needs. Only, it didn't take into account tolerance beyond a certain point, and it got more and more expensive; was more addictive than any one drug, and left you so sensitive to neurological change you couldn't do without the implant for a minute, once you were used to it. And going without for even five minutes led to suicides . . .

So they made it illegal. Meaning the price went up, way up, and if you didn't want to rehab, you paid through the nose. Eventually you broke your financial back under the strain. Or learned, in Cooper's case, to embezzle.

"My guess is," Barrabas said, "you've been skimming the budget that's supposed to be for the High Security mainframe, diverting the cred to pay your illegal balancer bills, and doing the calculations yourself on the cheap through the brain borrowers. You had the basic calculation program . . . " Cooper's pasty tongue made another swipe over his blue lips.

"You're guessing. That's a serious accusation. The SA doesn't tolerate—"

"Right. Doesn't tolerate much of anything. Doesn't tolerate a cock-up that costs them money, most especially. Ay? And I'm not really guessing. I did a little . . . research." Barrabas was bluffing about that.

But Cooper bit. "Right, then. What do you want?" Whining now. "You know I've no money."

"I want a transfer. I want out. Transfer to some place . . . I haven't decided. I'll let you know. And a recommendation of a promotion. Those things you can get me."

"Yes, yes, I suppose so. Righto. But listen, mate—" He was all matey and conspiratorial now, talking in a manner he fancied appropriate to Barrabas's class. "You got to do a little something more for me. This has to get itself cleared up."

Covered up, he meant, Barrabas thought. "I'm with you, 'mate.' But if you want me to find the girl . . . " He shook his head. "Won't be easy. She and I, we had a falling out."

"Find her. Apologize. Do what you must. But find her and tell me where she is. Keep her there and I'll come and . . . talk to her. All right?"

Barrabas chewed his lower lip. Talk to her? Cooper?

"Yes," he said slowly over a churning in the pit of his stomach. "I'll find her."

• • •

TEN MILES OUTSIDE PARIS, NEAR ORLY INTERNATIONAL.
The refugee camp had gotten worse for some and better for others.

Torrence and Bibisch and Roseland and Hand were trudging along the rutted mud path winding through the camp, squinting in the unobstructed sunlight, talking softly. Summer had finally come to north-central France. They weren't dressed for the weather. Most refugees simply wore everything they owned. Torrence and companions dressed in the unwashed, haphazard clothing typical of the refugees: Roseland wearing a promotional sweatshirt for participatory movie-software, on his chest a grimed, grisly solar-activated videoprint touting *Psycho Sam, the Man With the Chainsaw Fingers*; Bibisch wearing a stained jogging outfit; Torrence wearing a thickly layered outfit of pieces of military uniforms, insignia removed, the whole too warm in the sunny afternoon but usefully concealing his weapons; Hand wearing a grungy blue sweater and torn khaki pants, mismatched Army boots.

They looked to be luxuriantly outfitted, Roseland thought, compared to the people squatting at the huts and shanties and tents around them. The starveling children, their faces dull as veal calves in an agribusiness pen, particularly depressed Roseland.

Children, he thought, were just adults that hadn't come into focus yet, and it was probably stupid to feel more sentimental about them than about the adults who suffered here. Suffering was suffering. But inescapably he felt a special empathic sense of violation when he saw the children in the camps.

And there were so many homeless children in Paris; everywhere in Europe, children either dying before they were twelve or becoming murderous with their determination to survive. They were a rootless nation within a nation; a nation of the disenfranchised.

The camp stank, of course. At first there had been chemical toilets, brought by the puny efforts of the Red Cross. But when the Red Cross witnessed SA atrocities and complained, it had been excluded from the camps. The few sanitary facilities were overwhelmed by the numbers of the refugees, who had taken to digging open pits as privies. The flies were terrible, big and blue-black and so ubiquitous they seemed somehow spontaneously generated by the stench. That was a medieval notion, but then, Roseland reflected, medieval notions were apt here.

The refugee camp itself was a patchwork that refused definition by the eye. It gave the general impression of thousands of human beings living in a trash dump, occupying it like sea gulls on a barge. The path had been muddied during the rains, then hardened by the sun into something footprint-pocked, rutted, and cement-hard. Torrence and the others picked their way along the road, swiping at flies and trying to breathe through their mouths.

And then they came to the giant digital video screen.

"I don't believe it," Hand breathed. "What the hell is that thing doing here? The fucking thing is two stories high!"

It was. Torrence pulled his floppy hat lower over his eyes, trying to obscure his face, as they approached the clearing with the giant TV in it. It was big as two billboards stacked one atop another, a TV screen several stories high and broad as a barn: an absurd anomaly in a refugee camp. It was a glassy, chrome-edged section of the Grid, set onto a girderframe that was held in place by rock-hard insta, with orderly rows of folding metal chairs in front of it. The chairs were empty, but for an old woman who cursed incessantly to herself and a ragamuffin child toying with his genitals as he gaped at the screen. Four Second Alliance soldiers stood guard around the giant screen, two in back and two in front, the legs of their armored suits well apart and locked in place so they could lean on the suits inside; the suits were air-conditioned, quilted Kevlar-backed black fabric, mirror-reflective helmets locking their heads into insect anonymity.

On the video monolith rearing two stories over them, the talking head of the president of France yammered about the Unity Party. Every so often images of the French flag superimposed over his shoulder, alternating with shots of the small sections of Paris the Second Alliance and SPOES had cleaned up and rebuilt.

Then came shots of happy Parisian citizens at work on the "Volunteer Rebuilding Plan," waving at the cameras and chatting companionably as they cleared rubble from shell-damaged buildings; as they replastered and repainted damaged walls, happily chatting, everyone cheerfully working without pay except for stamped coupons supposed to be good for food at a later date. Some unnamed later date . . .

Then came a short commercial for SPOES, with the Unity Party's endorsement of the alliance that would give France "a new national strength." Followed by a public service announcement warning about "anti-Unity Criminals." There were mug shots and digitized re-creations of some of the "criminal" faces; many of them Roseland recognized from the NR. Most of them were black or Arab or Sikh or Hindu. The last two were white—but one of them was Jewish.

They were Torrence and Roseland.

A jet of chill air played along Roseland's spine as he stared up at the two-story image of himself on the screen, running away from the processing center. The video computer had blocked out the people running on either side of him—people who were being shot down. There was just a profile shot of Roseland, and then full-face as he looked over his shoulder (he didn't remember doing that; maybe it was a computer modeling), and into the camera. The image froze, close up.

A criminal who staged a massive jailbreak, they said. *Watch for him. Report him. Or turn him over to a Citizen's Justice committee.* Which meant, betray him to the Fascist vigilantes, the brownshirts who roamed the street looking for scapegoats to brutalize.

They'd passed such a group on their way to the refugee camp. The brownshirts had looked at Hand as if they were considering kicking his ass for being Asian. But they were intent on some other mission. If they'd recognized Roseland from this video mug shot, they'd have jumped him, beat him to death.

But either they hadn't seen the video or he looked much different now. His face had filled out and he'd grown a beard and long hair. He was going to have to do more to disguise himself.

And now there were the computer-enhanced shots of Daniel "Hard-Eyes" Torrence. Who was staring up at the images of himself, the two-story high digital wanted poster; gazing up at it with something beyond paranoia; something more in the category of awe.

A "terrorist responsible for the deaths of many innocents, possibly including the murder of President Le Pen." A lunatic killer, they said. If you see him, don't try to take him prisoner: send someone for the Second Alliance police. He's highly dangerous.

Roseland was a little jealous of their special regard for Torrence.

Roseland glanced at Torrence, who was watching the video with no change in the expression he'd worn all day. It was a look of resignation and depression. He'd been like that since the Second Alliance had begun carrying out reprisals "for the activities of the terrorist Hard-Eyes Torrence." Reprisals that were the true "murder of many innocents."

Twice Torrence had made plans to turn himself over to the Second Alliance; twice Smoke and Roseland and Bibisch and Lespere had talked him out of it.

If Torrence turned himself in—or, more precisely, blew himself up on their doorstep—someone else would have to take his place as Steinfeld's field commander. Someone else would do the same job, and someone else would be picked as "the cause of reprisals." That's what they told Torrence, anyway.

And then of course there was the extractor to think of. But Torrence insisted that he could be prophylactically extracted in advance, if they could get him to the Mossad—they could take out his knowledge of Lespere, and the NR's safehouses.

Still Smoke said no.

Torrence muttered that the reprisals were something personal; Watson and The Thirst, the bureaucratic sociopathic Giessen, had it in for him in particular.

Hearing that, Father Lespere had called him a solipsist and a *mégalomane*.

They talked him out of turning himself in.

But looking at Torrence now, Roseland thought that perhaps the Second Alliance had already won. Torrence was going through the motions. But in some sense, he was beaten.

"Jesus and Buddha in bed," Hand swore under his breath, staring at the video mug shots. "That's—"

"Shut up," Bibisch hissed.

"They're going to see those two," Hand whispered. Visibly shaking.

"We're too far away," Roseland said softly. "The guards won't recognize us from here. They probably wouldn't, even up close. I've changed. Our boy Danny has his face pretty well covered."

Hand took a deep breath. Roseland could see him suppress the panic. "I can't believe this TV screen in the midst of all this . . . What the hell!"

The TV was showing an old movie. A French film about a heroic police commissioner's fight against Arab terrorism. A few people from the huts trickled out to watch the movie, shading their eyes against the sun.

"A movie!" Hand said. "I don't believe it! These people are half starved and living in huts that, as far as I can tell, are made out of *shit*, and they put *this* thing up! I mean, an installation like this is expensive."

"And there's a dozen of them in the city, and in the camps," Roseland said.

"Mind control's more important than housing and feeding people," Torrence murmured in a rather distant tone.

Bibisch told Hand, "*Mais*, they have given some housing to some people. They push Arabs and Jews and blacks out of houses, and give places to white people. Very simple housing plan. And on the other side of the camp it is different. They have metal houses—" She turned to Torrence. "What do you call it?"

"Quonset huts. With running water, chemical toilets, showers. Rations. Compared to tents or trash huts, they're pretty decent short-term shelter." He nodded toward the south; they could see the sun glancing off rows of gray metal humps on the far side of the camp.

"Well, that's not so bad, then," Hand said. "They're working on it."

"It's only for the white refugees, Hand," Torrence said wearily. "And only the loyal white people. The whites in the camp who aren't loyal to the SA and the Party at the start soon learn to be."

"Can we confirm that?" Hand asked.

Torrence nodded. "We'll take you to see it. Talk to a few of them."

"I'd like to get some video here . . . "

"We'll smuggle your procam stuff in after things cool down."

Hand looked nervously at him. "What do you mean, after things cool down?"

"I thought you wanted to see an NR action."

"*Today?* I mean, I thought we—Well anyway, I, yeah, I want to see one, but, you know, not from right in the middle of it. I was planning on shooting—camera shooting, I mean—from somewhere nearby. Somewhere safe. I'm a journalist, not a soldier. And I don't have my proper equipment, just my fone-cam."

Torrence looked at Bibisch, "I thought you said he wanted to come for this? Didn't you tell him . . . ?"

"Oh!" She pretended surprised remorse. "I have forgot. *Merde!*"

Torrence almost smiled. Roseland chuckled. Hand looked at Bibisch accusingly. "You set me up to get caught in this! This your idea of funny?"

She looked at him wide-eyed. She didn't like Hand. "I don't know what you mean!"

Torrence sighed and shook his head at her. "You shouldn't have done it. He's important to us. He can get the truth out."

She pouted a little. "It's okay—he's going to come out of it alive."

"Or if he doesn't," Roseland joked cheerfully, "we can prop him up in front of the camera, use ventriloquism, maybe work a few jokes into the act."

"That's not very funny," Hand said icily.

"Okay, I'll leave that joke out."

Hand turned with exasperation to Torrence. "What exactly have you got in mind? Am I going to get shot at?"

"With luck, no. Which is probably why Bibisch thought it was okay to drag you along. Come on, it's all set up and we can't waste it. They do a check of this place every so often and they might find it . . . "

Torrence set off into the maze of trash huts ringing the TV clearing, and led them to a sort of sod hut made of sections of sod covered with tarpaper and bits of plastic held in place with bricks and spikes of torn metal. It was bigger than most of the others. Two thin, shoeless men Roseland didn't know, men in rags who looked Pakistani or Indian, were hunkered in the doorway, loosely gripping homemade spears made of broom handles tipped with sharpened nine-inch nails. They nodded at Torrence and moved away from the door.

"Go ahead and take off," Torrence told them. They didn't understand his English, but they knew the gesture he made with it. They seemed poised to go, but didn't quite. Torrence reached into his coat, pulled out two US Army ration tins. "Almost forgot." The men took the rations and disappeared into the piebald complexity of the camp.

The entrance hole to the large sod hut was facing the back of the other huts. No one was watching as Torrence pushed the burlap flap aside, and they went in.

Inside, it was dim but for a slat of sunlight coming through a narrow airhole in the dirt ceiling. There was a portable video transer and some other equipment on the hard-packed earthen floor; Roseland didn't recognize most of it. It looked like a shortwave radio crossed with an old laptop. The Dell logo on the back of the display was smeared with dirt, or maybe dung.

The room was hot, and it reeked. Hand held a perfumed kerchief over his nose; Roseland wished he'd thought to bring one. You could get a bottle of expensive perfume fairly easily in Paris lately. It was much less expensive than a can of beans.

"Dammit," Torrence muttered, "this stuff ought to be camouflaged somehow. Covered up, at least."

"Should've been wrapped in plastic to protect it, too," Hand said, trying to be one of the guys.

"Easy to say," Roseland said, "but it was hard enough to smuggle this stuff in here. They probably didn't feel like sweating the details."

Bibisch squatted beside the equipment and switched it on. Its batteries were intact, it seemed. It hummed, and bits and pieces of it lit up with green light, including the small display screen. From his coat, Torrence took a datastick and handed it to Bibisch, who slotted it into the transer. She watched the readouts, made adjustments, tilted the antenna—which projected through a wall to look like a spike holding a bit of roofing in place—and said, "*C'est marche.*"

"What exactly," Hand asked, "are we doing here? If it's not too intrusive of me to ask."

"Going to do some pirate transmissions," Torrence said.

"Won't they trace whatever it is you're going to transmit? You know— trace it back to us?"

"There's an interference-signal generator that should confuse their ability to triangulate us without losing our signal." Torrence was talking distractedly as he watched Bibisch, trying to understand, Roseland supposed, the mystical rite of this technology. High-tech hands-on stuff was not Torrence's strong suit.

Suddenly Hand jumped up, hitting his head on the low ceiling, capering about, scrabbling at the back of his neck. Yelling, "Shit! Get it out!"

Bibisch laughed. Torrence impatiently plunged his hand down the back of Hand's sweater, plucked out a squirming cockroach big as his thumb, and tossed it out the doorway. Hand shivered, tugging his collar snug, and examined the ceiling. "This place is infested!"

"Most of them are in the little holes," Torrence said, squatting again beside Bibisch. "Just stay away from the little holes."

"What was that little dance you did, Hand?" Roseland asked. "La Cucaracha?"

Hand glared at him. Torrence said, "Stop being a pain in the ass, Roseland, and watch the back door. That's what you're here for."

Roseland was happy to follow the order. He could breathe cleaner air at the door. He hunkered in the open door, peering past the doorflap. No one around except a couple of little kids staring listlessly over the top of the huts at the giant digital video screen twenty yards away.

One of the kids gasped and pointed at the screen. Roseland stood up and peered around a corner at the screen that rose like a drive-in movie screen in the distance. The guerrillas' transer was working. They'd interrupted the signal with their own. It flickered from time to time, but held: images of Second Alliance thugs beating children; images of a Jægernaut crushing a building. People trying to get away from it, dying like bugs under a boot heel. While a recorded voice warned in French that the New Nazis were taking over Europe and must be resisted. The blue New Resistance flag waving. Another shot of a fascist atrocity . . .

That's when Roseland heard the autotank coming. He knew the sound, the high-pitched whine of it. He'd seen them in another action. There was no one in an autotank, and somehow that scared him more than facing an IS vehicle. The thing knew only how to hunt and kill.

The interference-camouflage Bibisch was using wasn't working. Maybe corrosion from exposure to the damp had got to it. Something, some damn thing: the Fascists had located them; had traced the signal.

Had to be. Because Roseland saw them now. There were two autotanks, converging from opposite directions. Coming straight for them.

● ● ●

LONDON.

After two days of watching the place, Barrabas found Jo Ann in the warren of junk shacks and shops crowding Portobello Road. She was trying to line up a cheap seat on a flight to New York—negotiating for the ticket in an antique shop.

It wasn't an antique ticket. It was black market. In the wake of the war, trans-Atlantic flights were still few and far between, and were mostly for the use of Officials on Official Business. Clerks in the Foreign Office could sometimes get seats when some O on OB had crapped out of the trip; the clerks sold tickets on the black market, it was said. Supposedly.

Barrabas stood at the edge of the crowd filtering up and down the sidewalks, watching from the shade of an awning as Jo Ann bargained with a gray-haired fat man who had tiny eyes and a great potato of a nose. Jo Ann was about thirty feet away, in the antique shop with her back to him; he knew she wasn't buying antiques, and this was the bloke rumored to be selling the black-market tickets. She'd mentioned, that drunken night at the bar, that if Cooper didn't come through for her she'd try to buy a black-market ticket. Looked like the price was too steep for her, judging from the way she was shaking her head, angrily spreading her hands.

It was a warm day, a Sunday, and the Portobello was experiencing a rebirth, the shoppers and strollers out watching jugglers and musicians, browsing through open-front shacks of merchandise and ancient shopfronts, window-shopping for goods ranging from the exquisite to trash-with-a-price-tag. For most of the war the Portobello had languished, doing poor business. Now the New-Soviets had been driven back over their borders and commerce was beginning to flow again. It wouldn't be long before the airlines were back, jets crowding Heathrow like cars on a rush-hour freeway. But Jo Ann, Barrabas knew, was sick to death of London. And of waiting.

She was opening her carrybag. Time to step in.

Barrabas plunged into the crowd, drew some sarcastic remarks as he elbowed through and stepped into the shop. Musty, dark, crowded, all of which meant old-fashioned; not like the new shops, where campy antiques were bathed in mellow stage lighting and arranged in postmodern, irony-pungent composition. This one had been here since the middle twentieth century probably, accumulating dust and questionable profits.

"I wouldn't, Jo Ann," Barrabas said.

She stiffened, then shot a glare at him over her shoulder. "Leave me alone."

"If you can afford the ticket, then the ticket's no good," Barrabas said. "They usually aren't any good no matter how much you pay for them."

"Now see 'ere," the man behind the counter said. "I've been in business 'ere for—"

"Shut your hole," Barrabas snapped.

Jo Ann turned to face him, her cheeks mottled from anger. "You still trying to impress me by bullying people?"

Wrong move, he thought, and told her, "You're right." He turned to the shopkeeper. "Sorry, mate. Been worried about the girl. Didn't mean to take it out on you." Thinking: I'd like to kick your fat arse up around your ears.

Jo Ann was looking at the ticket on the counter, frowning. "Goddamn you, Patrick." She closed her carrybag with an angry jerk of her hand and stalked past Barrabas toward the door.

"'Ere, now, miss!" the shopkeeper began.

Barrabas grinned at him. "Better luck next time."

He followed her into the street. She shouted something over her shoulder at him. A one-man band, clashing cymbals together with his knees, playing banjo, blowing a mouth harp on a rack, and banging a bass drum with his foot pedal, was adding his racket to the street's hum of electric cars and rumble of methanol lorries and hissing fuel-cell SUVs, and Barrabas couldn't hear what she was shouting at him. But he got the gist of it.

"Right, I'll fuck off, right out of your life, I promise!" he shouted, catching up with her. "If you'll just have a cup of tea with me. Maybe some chips. What d'you say? And then I solemnly pledge to be gone forever, if you still want. I'm sorry about what I did the other night. Please."

She stopped, turned, and shouted in his face, embarrassingly loud, "I don't truck with racists!"

"Look—it's just the way I was raised, you know? I mean, I've been thinking about it. You're right about all that stuff." He wondered if he was lying convincingly. And then he wondered if he was lying. "Just have a bite with me and hear me out."

She stared at him.

He added, "I can get that erasure you wanted. Come on. Cup of tea."

She tossed her head resignedly. "Okay. Just for a few minutes."

•••

THE REFUGEE CAMP, NEAR PARIS.

The autonomous weapon was drawing a bead on the sod hut, its cannon swinging around, the PA grid on its turret emitting a warning siren as the tank plowed through the shacks. The autotank was khaki-colored, on shiny stainless-steel treads, and it was shaped like a dull hatchet with a flattened, streamlined turret studded with electronic sensors. Refugees scrambled to get out of its way; children shrieked and hooted, some terrified and others elated at the break in the monotony. Their mothers simply grabbed them and ran.

The robot tank had an insignia showing the Arc de Triomphe, the new symbol of the Unity Party, on its armored front, and one of the symbols of the Second Alliance, the eye and cross, stenciled on its sides. An old man stood in its path, staring at it, gaping in hunger-dulled confusion till it simply ran him down, crushing him against a wooden shack so that blood fountained from his mouth onto the image of the Arc.

Seeing this, Roseland muttered, "Winning hearts and minds as always," as he worked his way toward the tank from its left side.

Flame strobed at the muzzle of the autotank's cannon. Thunder, and the shack just in front of the sod hut flung itself in four directions at once, as the shell exploded inside it. The ground quivered. Debris rained. Blue-black smoke billowed, then elongated in the faint breeze and drew itself over Roseland. He coughed, tasting caustic chemicals and oil. Shreds of tarpaper and chunks of wood were burning raggedly around him. The next round would hit the sod hut.

He heard Torrence yelling at some of the refugees, telling them to get down. Saw the sun blazing off helmets of SA guards approaching cautiously, in a line of six, well behind the first autotank.

Torrence was drawing off the second autotank, thirty yards to

Roseland's right, dodging through the shacks, firing short, innocuous bursts at the unmanned killing machine to get its attention. Roseland was moving toward the other autotank, thinking, *This is crazy, I ought to be running away from this thing.*

But they couldn't. They were surrounded. And Bibisch was busy with something vital . . .

Roseland was forty feet from the hulking robot vehicle now, imagining he could feel its camera watching him, feel the crosshairs of its machine gun sight in on his head. It shouldered through another shack, crunching and splintering, churning the debris with its treads, spewing dust, its machinery whining. He let go a burst from his Ingram autopistol at the tank, making a broken line of sparks across its beveled prow; accomplishing nothing except scoring the paint.

And making the thing notice him.

Its cannon and machine gun whirred smoothly around to sight in on him. He sprinted off to the left, farther from the sod hut. Heard a crack—and felt the air buzz—as one of the SA bulls took a potshot at him. He felt the faint pulse of the tank's microwaves bouncing off his chest, targeting him.

Roseland dived behind something metallic and rusty. *Thud.* The ground erupted where he'd been a moment before. He shivered as the shock wave rippled past and dirt pattered down over him. He'd taken cover behind an old Audi hulk, just the rust-pitted body of the car remained, half-filled with trash and scraps of cloth laid out in an oversize bird's nest for some refugee.

He heard the autotank whining toward the old car. Raising his head to look through the Audi, he saw the autotank framed in the farther car window. It was only about thirty feet away. Well beyond it, the SA bulls were hanging back, hoping the autotank would take the risks, do the work for them.

Halfway between Roseland and the tank someone was lying on an improvised mattress made of the front and back seats of the old Audi. The seats had been pulled from the car and dragged into the sun. It was a woman, hard to tell her age; all he could tell was that she was sick, maybe from cholera. Too weak to run for cover, just hoping the thing would pass her by. But Roseland had inadvertently drawn the autotank toward her: Whining, rumbling right at her, blaring its warning siren.

She turned and, mewling wordlessly, tried to drag herself out of its way. She didn't have the strength to get to her feet. She crawled.

It was picking up speed.

It'll go around her, Roseland thought. He was reluctant to give up the cover of the car.

It kept going, gaining on her—but looking for him.

It wasn't going to go around her.

The guards will stop it, he thought.

It kept coming, she was in its shadow now, and her mewling had become yowling. Screaming.

"Goddamn it to fucking hell!" Roseland yelled, jumping up and firing at the tank turret. He sprinted to the left, trying to draw it away from her. Too late.

Without hesitation, it rolled right over her.

It broke her back, and broke her head, and churned her up, and spat bits of her out the back. This wasn't some programmed-in cruelty, it wasn't punishing her; she was simply in the way, and the device was not going to be diverted even for an instant from its objective.

Roseland stopped moving, froze, staring at it. One of the SA soldiers fired at him, the bullet kicking up the dirt close beside his left foot, but he didn't move.

He stared at the autotank.

The autotank was the Second Alliance International Security Corporation. It was all fascists. It was all intolerance, all inflexibility, all racism, all xenophobia, all absolutism, all of it. In one machine. Programmed by the Fascists. Told to hunt down these guerrillas and don't slow up for the civilians in the way. Simply move in and eradicate the little pocket of resistance.

It was a thing of hard angles and unforgiving edges. It was implacable. It was murderous, it was efficient; it was murderously efficient. It was the mechanical embodiment of his enemy.

He saw again the processing center. The electronic fences. The gray, septic hours packed in the misery of Processing Center 12's little rooms. The breakout, the escapees mowed down as they ran. And her, Gabrielle, his friend: her head exploding.

He saw Hitler; he saw the Nazis. He saw the Holocaust.

All of it somehow compressed into this one machine.

Suddenly he was running at the thing, shrieking obscenities, firing past an oil barrel. The thing returned fire, the oil barrel catching its burst, *spang-spang-spang-spang*, bullets pocking the rusty metal. Roseland throwing his only explosive, a magnetized metal disk that stuck to the front of the autotank—*whump* as its cannon fired and *crack-thud* as his explosive went off. Its shells struck a shack just in front of him. Something picked him up and threw him down. Shrapnel raked his thigh and right arm.

Blank.

And then Roseland found himself on the ground in front of the autotank. Looking up through the smoke and dust as the autonomous weapon bore down on him.

The explosive hadn't stopped it—maybe confused only its sensors a little and dented its hull. But it kept coming.

He got to his knees. That hurt. Getting up was like climbing a ladder made of broken glass. He raised his gun to fire, trying to shout, to let the pressure out, but his mouth was gummed with blood.

He felt the pulse of its aiming device; knew its crosshairs were centered on him.

He spat blood and yelled, "Fuck *you*! I'll meet you in Gehenna, you brainless pigs!" And he fired. And it kept coming, aiming at him, and, he fired and—

It stopped.

Clank: *stopped*. Humming indecisively to itself.

He blinked and coughed in the smoke, staring at it. Had he hit something electronically vital with a lucky round from his pathetic little machine pistol?

Through the smoke he saw the silhouettes of enemy soldiers, coming at him. Half a dozen of them.

Suddenly, the autotank's turret whirred into an about-face, like an owl turning its head all the way around, looking behind itself. It fired its cannon three times in quick succession. SA soldiers were snatched clumsily into the air by fingers of chaos.

She did it.

Bibisch had interfaced with the Plateau. Found sympathetic wolves. Using the microchip unit in the sod hut. Got the access codes, the back door into the autotank's computer. Transmitted new programming.

The guardsmen were running. The tank was firing on its partner. *Wham*. Hit the other autotank dead center, kicked it onto its side so its treads dug uselessly at the air.

Torrence, grinning, was trotting up to him, coughing through the smoke. A fire was spreading through this section of the camp. "You okay?"

"Yeah. Bibisch do that?"

"She fuckin' *did* it!" Torrence crowed. "That's my *girl*!"

"How'd she get control of it so fast?" Roseland asked as they hurried back to the sod hut. The autotank was opening fire on more SA. Driving them back. Killing half of them. It was a beautiful thing to see.

"She's been working on it for a while, for days really—working with our people on the chips. Alouette—Smoke's little whiz kid—she worked it out, along with some others. So Bibisch sent an inquiry just now, like, did they have the dirt on the thing yet, and, yeah, they had it. We just lucked out."

"Hand probably pissed his pants."

Torrence laughed. "Yeah, probably." He'd needed this, to get his mind off the reprisals. Needed to "Dance with Mr. D."

The autotank met them at the hut, a different critter now. Like a big, friendly, domesticated rhino, waiting for another command. Its engine heat feeling like body heat. They heard the yawing whoop of approaching sirens, coming from the North.

Bibisch came out of the hut carrying the little computer unit. Norman Hand, pale and hugging himself, came out just behind her. He was talking into a little hand-held voice recorder. Something about, "The sirens of SA police approaching—"

"They're on the far side of the camp," Torrence said. "We're near the old refining plant on this side—it's about a quarter mile south of here. I think we can hide the tank in there, but we'll make 'em think we headed west." He was already putting on his headset, calling for a decoy hit off to the west of camp.

Roseland listened to the sirens. Sounded like Torrence was right. They had time. Just enough. It would take the SA commanders a while to figure out what had happened. They'd figure it out, though: much of war now revolved around strategies of signal transmission, signal interference, and electronic co-optation.

They climbed onto the back of the autotank, clinging behind the turret as Bibisch gave the autotank new commands and Hand babbled into his recorder. The tank whined and moved off, rumbling to the south, full speed.

Roseland smiled. They were going to keep this autotank, hide it till it was needed. And, oh yes, it was going to be needed.

In fact, they used it again as they fled the camp. On the way out, they told it to blow up the giant TV screen.

It did. And that was a beautiful sight, too.

• • •

PARIS, SA HQ

Jebediah dropped the videodisc into the player and turned to the small audience in the conference room. Watson, Giessen, Klaus, and a dozen lesser functionaries were seated around the table, facing the big screen. The room was white, windowless, lit brightly; it could have been any time of the day or night. It was ten p.m.

Our Jebediah, Watson thought, ought to be in bed, and not up here running the show.

He was beginning to fear the boy.

The screen flickered alive, making Watson remember the pirate transmission that had gone out to most of the functioning televisions in Paris via the unit in the refugee camp; and he remembered the stolen autotank that had shattered the giant TV screen. A lot of money down the drain.

Worse, the propaganda that had gone out on the pirate transmissions. The cheering when the resistance vermin had escaped . . .

The refugee camps were hotbeds of potential trouble. They had to be cleaned out. The wheat separated from the chaff, and storehoused; the chaff disposed of.

"The Reverend Crandall," Jebediah said, "has made an announcement that will shortly be sat-transed to the entire world." His voice reverent but confident. His uniform spotless. Remarkable poise, too, for a child. His father, Watson supposed, had drilled him in this little speech. "It is an announcement that will seem to some people to be only of scholarly interest. But other people will be very angry when they hear it. Eventually, everyone will see what it means: a change in the way we think about God and our place in God's Plan." He looked at them gravely, then hit the play button. "What you're going to see is a revelation from God."

As Crandall's image appeared on the TV screen, Jebediah went to stand respectfully to one side.

On the screen, "Crandall" was saying that thirty years of research by Church scholars had at last come to fruition. Through archaeology, documentation study, and a dozen other scholarly means, they'd come at last to the incontrovertible conclusion: the Bible, as we know it, is not truly the Bible. "We have positive proof," Crandall was saying.

No. Crandall wasn't saying it. In a power-grab, Watson and Klaus had murdered the real Crandall. Only they, of those in this room, knew that they were watching a lifelike computer animation; only they knew that Crandall was dead.

Watson had no interest in listening to Crandall's speech. He'd written it himself, he'd heard it till he was sick of it. He'd given it to Jebediah and his father, and was gratified to see the way they'd taken it to heart. At the same time, he'd been unsettled by the boy's fanatic conviction. His grasp on what "Crandall" was saying made Watson feel he was losing control, his project somehow co-opted by the boy.

Watson looked away from Jebediah, covertly watched the others to see what their reaction would be. Redesigning Christianity was an important step in the taking of power. They needed the philosophical reins, as well as the political ones . . .

"Jewish conspirators," the computer-generated Crandall was saying, "tinkered with the New Testament of the so-called King James Bible, and altered it to make it appear that Jesus was of Jewish origin. Further, they edited out those sections which confirm God's plan for genetic purification."

Giessen was reacting to Crandall's revelations with a flaring of nostrils, a dilation of the eyes, a slight twitching of the hands. Watching him, Watson felt a thrill at his own power over Giessen's mind.

"And now," said the stunningly realistic animation of Crandall, "I have something precious to give to you. A direct quote from Jesus himself that has been lost to us for two thousand years! This quote came to us from the Damascan Scrolls, which were discovered by a team of our Church archaeologists two years ago and only recently translated. I repeat, what you are about to hear is a direct quote from Jesus Christ Himself: 'I am the spark that lights the Flame of Purification. Let the miscegenists hide their faces from my light. Those who would interbreed besmirch the Divine Plan. Yea, verily I say unto you, those who do not recognize the Chosen Race are the whisperers of Satan, who would elevate animals to rule beside men. The Flame of Purification will burn away the tinder that is the Animal Races. Truly, the worshipers of false gods are those who would elevate animals; and those who would elevate animals are worshipers of Satan under another name. In my name, then, return them to God's Judgment with the Flame of Purification; give them to Death who gives them to Judgment. Verily, this is my word. Write it in your hearts.'"

There were gasps in the conference room—the gasps of believers.

Watson allowed himself a small smile of satisfaction. He had written those words, just as he had fabricated the Damascan Scrolls. Some would know it was a hoax, of course, and would say so, but the believers would believe anyway.

Crandall paused reverently, looking gravely out at them. "The teachings of our church are confirmed in the word of Jesus. In another passage, Jesus prophesizes of the Satan of the 'Dog-Men' who will be born in the southeast, in the place call Mecca . . . ' This man, whom he calls 'one of the five great Liars,' will poison much of the world with his false doctrine. Clearly, Jesus is speaking of the man called Mohammed. His warning is clear, and his admonition to us about the worshipers of false gods, and those who would elevate animals—in other words, the lower races—to the status of men, is quite clear. Deliver them, said the Lord Jesus, to Death, so that Death may deliver them to Judgment . . . Our task is obvious."

Watson glanced at Klaus. Saw the tension in the set of his jaw: Klaus was nervous about releasing the bit about Mohammed, the great Liar. "*We aren't ready for a holy war,*" Klaus had said. "*Chances are, the Muslims won't wait for us to carry out the 'word of God.' They'll come after us. We aren't strong enough yet.*"

"*The white Christians will close ranks around us,*" Watson had replied. "*This will polarize the world more, accelerate the whole process—we need the confrontation to knit us together, make people see their enemies clearly.*"

"*It's lunacy. It would get out of hand, Watson. Play that bit for our people, if you want, but don't release it to the general public . . .*"

"Inarguable documentation," Crandall was saying, "will be released in the near future to confirm the authenticity of these sources. In the meantime, I will be largely out of touch. I am going on Retreat to meditate on these revelations, and to ask God just how we are to realize these revelations in the world of men. In my absence, please regard Colonel Watson as my voice. I will be in close touch with him. God bless you all."

The recording ended. Watson carefully didn't look at Klaus. He could feel Klaus staring at him.

"You are going to release that to the public?" Giessen asked abstractedly, inspecting his manicure.

Watson said, "All but the last part about his retreat and my standing in for him."

Giessen looked at him. "Are you quite sure he wants the rest of it released?"

"Quite sure," Watson said coldly.

"But—this business about Mohammed. It is rather inflammatory. Bad politics . . ."

Klaus snorted as if to say, *For a sane man, it would be obvious.*

"And you are saying that the Reverend Crandall's interpretation of the Newly Revealed Scriptures is false?" Jebediah demanded, sounding more like a white-bearded old dogmatist than a boy.

"Not at all!" Giessen put in hastily. "He has confirmed what I always knew in my heart! But—it's a question of timing, of how and when it will be revealed—"

"That sort of concern is not your province," Watson said sharply. "You are essentially a police investigator."

"I thought that was your role as well," Giessen said, his voice flat.

"No longer," Watson said. "You have not been keeping up with developments."

He smiled distantly at Klaus. Who merely stared back at him.

I'll have to smooth things over with Klaus, Watson thought. And until then, I'd better watch my back.

"The world is changed," Jebediah said suddenly. They all turned to look at him. His eyes glittered like an eagle's. "Just as surely as it was changed when it rained for forty days and forty nights. Everything is new again. We have the word of God, the true word of God, for the first time."

Watson had a sinking feeling, hearing that. *Can I really keep control of this?*

But Giessen had clearly been moved by the boy's words. There was a mystical streak in Giessen that, in its balancing counterpoint to his punctilio and pragmatism, was very German.

Giessen—The Thirst—stood, and said, "I . . . I feel ashamed that I have done so little. While Rick Crandall is on Retreat, we must do his work."

"*God's* Work," Jebediah said.

Giessen nodded. "Yes. God's work." He smoothed down his coat jacket, tugged his tie into proper position and checked his watch. All signs he was about to launch into some sort of activity. "Truly God's work. There are prisoners I have not interrogated. I will remedy this now. One of them, I feel, will lead me to the animal they call Hard-Eyes Torrence."

He went briskly to the door, purposeful as the swish of a knife blade.

• • •

THE BADOIT ARCOLOGY, EGYPT.

When—a week after his first visit—Steinfeld was brought back into Badoit's office he had the feeling the meeting was continuing as if it had never been interrupted by his arrest. It was about the same time of day, the tea cart was there, Badoit wore more or less the same suit, and the same expression of friendly detachment.

"Please sit down, my friend," Badoit said. "I would like first to apologize for keeping you in 'house arrest.' We informed your people you would be delayed in returning, but I am sure it was a great inconvenience to you."

Steinfeld shrugged, and sat in the same seat he'd occupied before. "More like a vacation. I had a spa, movies, TV, a comfortable apartment, good food, and access to a swimming pool. And a masseuse."

"And then there was the indignity of subjecting your mind to an extractor search . . . "

"It's a painless process. I'd have done it voluntarily. I didn't mind. Because—I was prepared to open my mind, my heart to you, Shaikh Badoit."

Badoit smiled thinly as he poured coffee for them. "You are the very soul of politesse. Very well: I take it you have forgiven me. Let us put it aside. You passed the extractor test with flying colors. The extractor insists that you are quite sincere." He grinned, brief and bright as a flashbulb pop. "And not at all bent on sabotaging my organization from within. Some of my advisers had thought . . . well, no matter. The other investigations into your background confirmed everything you told me. You are really quite an honest man for a former Mossad agent."

"I am not a Mossad agent," Steinfeld said. He shrugged. "Hard as that may be to believe. I do some work in association with them. I am merely an antifascist organizer."

"Ah." He didn't sound convinced. "You mentioned the television." He passed Steinfeld coffee and a scone. "Did you see, on that television—about Damascus?"

"The announcement from the Reverend Crandall? The so-called Damascus Scrolls. Yes. Astounding. And this business about Mohammed—the gall of these people amazes me. They have made a great mistake. They've become overconfident. Arrogant. And stupid. They think the rest of the world is even stupider, apparently."

"Precisely correct: they have made a great mistake in this fabrication. And they make a mistake to malign the Prophet. They pushed me into commitment, my friend. You will have your freedom, and the help you require—up to a point."

"Up to which point, Shaikh Badoit?"

"To begin with, up to about four-hundred-thirty million in world currency, to fund your resistance organization. Or you may have it in securities, gold bullion, or bank transfer to any account you name." He sipped coffee. "Later I hope to double that amount."

• • •

FirStep, The Space Colony.

Russ Parker and Claire Rimpler stood on the podium platform under the inverted cradle of the sky—that was also the ground, if you walked far enough—and waited for the dedication to get under way.

The temporary platform was made of pressed recycled paper—the artificial-cellulose pulp they used for the printout clothing they wore—and it quaked a little under Lester's rather heavy tread as he crossed to them, shook their hands for the Colony TV station's cameras, and then went to the grass-blade-thin microphone taped to the podium. He spoke to the technicki crowd in Technicki argot; telling them that it was partly through Claire and Parker's efforts that the new technicki-staff housing project had been completed in the Space Colony's Open; that Parker had saved his life; that Claire Rimpler was a person who understood workers, who cared about them. That the housing here in the Colony's Open—the parklike space in the Bernal Sphere that held the inside-out biosphere, complete with fresh air and sunlight and beneficial fauna—was a symbol of the new respect Colony Administration had for workers on every level.

Parker didn't understand Technicki well, couldn't make out most of it. He heard his own named mixed in with a mush bowl of consonants and vowels, each sentence sounding to Parker like one long word. Parker felt embarrassed, knowing he was being praised, but happy, knowing something had been achieved. And he felt close to Claire just now.

Sometimes she intimidated him. She had come back from Earth with a real edge to her. She'd seen things there that had hardened her, sharpened her. But when she was happy, the *woman* shone out of her like Texas starlight, and man, he just wanted to . . .

You too damn old for her, Rusty, he told himself.

When Lester was done, Claire nudged Parker, and he went awkwardly to the mike, wincing at the paper noise as he unfolded his notes, read out his short speech in Standard. Claire, the show-off, did hers in Technicki. They cut the ribbon, strolled through the multidwelling units to drink punch at the reception in the project's Community Center.

Claire and Parker stood together, chatting with Lester's wife, Kitty; Lester strolled over and Claire muttered, "Uh-oh. He's got that *rhetoric* look in his eye." Kitty chuckled; Parker inwardly groaned.

"You know," Lester said, pinning Parker with his challenging stare, "we got some momentum going here, zeal for reform and all that, Maybe we should use it, keep going. Reform the economic infrastructure of the Colony."

"Lester," said Parker, "do you really think that if you put it up to a popular vote people'd vote for a socialist state in the Colony? Come on. Most technickis are more or less of Democratic Party persuasion, not radicals."

"Especially in light of the changes lately," Claire said. "Things are working for them as is."

"No," Lester said. "Things are *easing* for them. That doesn't mean that things are really fair. There's still a class structure here; there's still under-representation; there's still salary inequities. Admin's not treating them like indentured servants anymore—more like . . . like ordinary servants with a 'liberal' employer."

"Reform's ongoing," Claire said. "I'd like to see it go farther—Maybe we do need *some* kind of Democratic-Socialist structure. In a moderate kind of way. I think your health care should be completely subsidized and not come out of your paycheck; I think housing should be more broadly subsidized. But socialism per se is just too archaic for this kind of environment, Lester."

"Socialism isn't archaic any more than the principles of engineering are archaic—they get refined as people learn how to build things better, but the basic principles . . . "

It went on like that for a while, ending with everyone agreeing to think about it. Lester didn't seem angry that they hadn't jumped on his bandwagon, but he could be pretty inscrutable; it was hard to tell for sure.

After Lester's wife rescued them, dragging him off to help her with the baby, Claire said, "I've had enough politics for one day. Feel like taking a walk, Russ?"

Hell, yeah.

There was weather in the Colony. Understated weather, but weather still. Some of it was deliberately contrived by Life Support Systems, some of it was an accident of the Colony's design and internal cycles. There was some clouding and mild, misty precipitation in the Open; there was a little smog sometimes, from the imperfect air filtering. The rotation of the Colony, with changes in temperature as the solar wind basted its turning sides, led to breezes produced by shifting air-pressure. Today, with the windows adjusted to let in more sunlight than other times of year, and with the evaporation from this morning's irrigation, it was rather humid, making Parker think of Dallas.

"What I want right now . . . is ice cream," he told her as they strolled down the path through the thin woods, watching potbellied "Frisbee athletes" gliding plastic plates to each other on the grassy field beyond the treeline.

"Might give you some, you play your cards right," she said.

"You got ice cream? Since when did that ship in?"

"It didn't. I made it. My dad had a hand-crank ice-cream maker."

"And you've been hiding this from me! Boy, I tell you, there's nothing to this old-boy stuff among the Admin people if you're any example! Where's my damn share of your decadent perks?"

"You got to exercise to earn it. Ice cream's fattening. When it's humid like this, I like to go to the freefall rooms, do some air tumbling, work out a little. It's not much fun alone, though. You want to come?"

"Uh—sure. I guess. I haven't been but once . . . "

"Elevator for that section's at this end of the woods."

Parker followed her onto a crosspath, toward the curving wall, recently cleaned of most of its graffiti, where a transparent-plastic corridor, like an umbilicus stretching from the placenta-like Open, led into the intricately engineered uterus of the Space Colony.

She seemed a little pensive; that, and the fact that the freefall rooms were often used for sexual trysts, made him think: Maybe I'll get lucky.

No way. You're too old for her.

• • •

In the Colony's Admin Comm Center, Stoner was sucking Coca-Cola Nine from a paper carton and waiting for his call from Earth to come through.

He sat at the console, staring at the empty screens; three of them centered with the words "Transmission Wait."

Steinfeld came in first, from Israel, his image blinking onto the left-hand screen; then Smoke, from London, in the right-hand. The middle screen stayed blank, as Steinfeld said, "Our backer—" meaning Badoit "—won't do the videoconference. He's just too paranoid—or maybe just wiser than me. But he's with us all right. I've got the money to prove it. And I think he's going to lend us some troops for certain actions . . . "

With the transmission lags edited out, the rest of the conference went, "Smoke, you getting us both?"

"Right with you."

"Steinfeld?"

"Yes."

"Steinfeld, are you confident about the security of this transmission?"

"Unless someone's got a technological edge we don't know about. Always a possibility."

"Let's just do it," Stoner said. "I got something I need to talk about. Look—if our Backer's really there for us, then we don't need Witcher. Correct?"

Steinfeld hesitated. Some interplanetary interference, maybe a burst of solar radiation in a troublesome wavelength, made his image flicker and fuzz for a moment, as if the TV screen were acting out his uncertainty. Then it stabilized—and he nodded. "We can always use Witcher's support too, but we can now get by without it and still be effective, I think. It's gotten worse?"

"Yeah," Stoner said. "it's gotten worse. I'm pretty sure Witcher's making concerted efforts to keep intelligence from us."

"This doesn't necessarily mean he's hiding something from us for, ah, the wrong reasons," Steinfeld said. "It might be a need-to-know issue. Because of extractors."

"What extractors? Here on the Colony? I doubt it. Anyway—I've had an inkling what some of it's about. It's something he definitely should be sharing, you know what I mean?" Stoner paused, sucked thoughtfully at the Coca-Cola. These transmissions were expensive, the systems time shouldn't be squandered, but he had to think about how he put this. "He approached one of our technicians, offered him a lot of money to work for him in private. Setting up a transmitter controlled from his room. He paid the guy to do EVA work, set up a shortwave antenna to piggyback the signal onto our main beam after the transmission goes out, and receive independently . . . Well, the guy thought about it and came to Parker to see if it was okay. Russ Parker's the security chief, and assistant administrator.

And Parker brought it to me. I told him go ahead and install it, with some modifications . . . and Witcher doesn't know about the modifications."

"You've been spying on him?" Steinfeld said. "That was pretty risky. If he'd found out and we didn't have the backer . . . "

"Maybe. I couldn't resist the chance to find out what's going on with him."

"You're still CIA at heart, Stoner," Smoke said.

Stoner shot a glare at Smoke's camera. The remark hadn't been a compliment.

"It's done," Stoner said, "and what I got is some back-and-forth with his company vice president about some investigation his outfit's been doing for him. The SA's been hiring people with expertise in gen-engineering viruses. Witcher sent a transmission asking them to get him the specs . . . "

"To me, sounds like he's doing research for our protection," Steinfeld said. "We have worried about the fascists developing biowar materiel."

"But why all this secretiveness about the transmission? His transmission is no more secure than ours—except from me and Parker."

Steinfeld shrugged. "He's a paranoid, maybe deciding to look into it on his own, doesn't want to trust anyone else until he has to."

"It doesn't feel like that to me. It doesn't jibe with my experience," Stoner said. "And that *is* the CIA man in me."

Steinfeld said, "Okay, keep monitoring him. Investigate any way you want. The risks . . . "

"Maybe," Smoke said, "it warrants extractor interrogation—if it comes to that, we could talk about it."

"Are you serious, Smoke?" Steinfeld asked. "Witcher?"

"I've often felt he had some kind of . . . hidden agenda," Smoke said.

"He might be playing both ends against the middle," Stoner said. "NR against SA for some reason. Maybe just to benefit his company."

"No," Steinfeld said. "If you think that, you don't know him. He's a strange sort of idealist. If he's playing us against them, he has some other reason."

"So I can go ahead and look into it."

"Yes." There was regret in Steinfeld's tone, audible over hundreds of thousands of miles of void. "Look into it."

• • •

Women's liberation, Russ Parker thought, was a regional thing on Earth. It was widespread in much of the US and Europe, still a rarity in much of the Middle East and parts of India though the worst oppression of women had eased there. Lately it was doing surprisingly well in Africa, largely due to the efforts of the black woman who was the president of South Africa and the chairwoman of the African National Congress.

But it hadn't made a lot of headway in Texas. Not where Parker was raised.

It was one of those things that Parker believed in—but somehow found hard to live up to. So Claire's aggressiveness caught him off guard. Confused him.

That's not to say he didn't like it when she grabbed him in midair, kissed him hard on the mouth, and wrapped her legs around his hips.

There had, yes, been preliminaries. They'd talked a great deal on the way here. He'd talked about his ex-girlfriend back on Earth, and she'd talked about Torrence. Talking about past lovers was a way of laying the romantic groundwork without being too blunt about it, he supposed. And for her, maybe it was a kind of confessional—she felt guilty about Torrence. About thinking she needed a love life away from him. Talking about it, admitting the guilt, was some kind of expiation in advance, he supposed.

Talk had stopped ten minutes into their freefall time. The sound system was playing the Japanese composer Tanaka, sweeping expanses of synthesizer sound and sampled choirs superimposing the cathedralesque on the ethereal; beating with the soft, insistent pulse of longing, of subdued libido. He watched her turn in the air like an Eastern European gymnast in a slow-motion instant replay, no wasted motion, interpreting the music but without self-consciousness, without extravagance. He watched the ballet ripple of her breasts; the roundness of her movements in the air . . .

Then she'd grabbed him, kissed him, clasped him with her legs. They were spinning in a slow cartwheel through the big, roughly circular room, its lights dialed low. The padded walls wheeling by. Parker's stomach rebelled—he had less tolerance for anything that threatened his balance, the older he got—but his sex engorged, and strained at his trousers. He felt her undo his zipper, was briefly embarrassed when he felt the cold air at his crotch. She wriggled out of her clothes like some fantastic flying animal molting in the air. He undressed more clumsily, wishing the lights were dimmer to better hide his paunch. He reached out and stopped her spinning when they got near a wall; Claire seemed to accept that he needed anchored sex. He'd never done it in freefall; had heard it took training. But holding on to a wall strap, finding the center of gravity between them, in their interlocked genitals, they had the advantage of freefall sex without the disadvantages. It was rather like something he'd done on Earth once: making love in a swimming pool, holding on to the concrete edge. But there was no water to interfere with them here. Nothing interfered with them. The near-weightlessness seemed to cohere their flesh more completely, let their blood surge more freely. He penetrated her gravitational field, a gravity well it was called, and imagined they were like a two-planet system in space, like the Earth and the moon . . .

After he came, the semen escaped from her vagina, made opalescent pearls around them in the air, quivering with potential life.

Okay, he thought, holding her, the two of them floating slowly, reclining in one another's arms, drifting through afterglow . . .

She took his head between her hands and gave him a long, slow kiss.

Okay, she likes older men too . . .

• • •

PARIS.

"They know I'm here," Torrence said.

"Don't be stupid," said Roseland. "It's a coincidence."

Torrence sat with Bibisch and Roseland at a café table on Place Clichy. The place was crowded. They sat with their backs to the glass of the café windows, at one of the innermost tables, feeling the sunlight glancing off the window bring sweat out on the backs of their necks. Underneath the statuary in the midst of the square, across from the bombed-out shell of the old adult video store, the Unity Party soldiers were lining up the prisoners. More prisoners blinked in the sunlight as they were brought out of the backs of trucks. How many were they going to execute?

"They *must* know I'm here," Torrence said again.

"How could they know?" Bibisch said. "*Nous arrivons—*" She broke off when Roseland shook his head at her. She sipped her iced coffee with no sign of enjoyment.

They'd come to the café because she had heard that this one had real coffee. Now that the war was over, shipments of prime consumer goods were coming into Paris again, but the stuff was taking forever, it seemed, to reach the public. Maybe some of the corrupt U.P. bureaucrats had to take theirs off the top first, to make a last profit on the black market.

Forty, Torrence thought, as the soldiers slammed the rear doors of the transport truck. *They're going to kill forty people. They know I'm here.*

"They are the U.P.'s Soldats Superieurs," Bibisch whispered.

Torrence nodded dumbly. The government's new SA-trained elite troops of Racially Pure Frenchmen. Superior Soldiers. The Unity Party's SS. They wore armored kevlar uniforms of silver and flat black, the U.P.'s symbol sewn onto the shoulders: the Arc de Triomphe against a French flag.

"We will go now, Dan," Bibisch said. "Come on."

He shook his head. He couldn't move. A spiritual inertia held him rooted to his chair. A weight in his gut he couldn't possibly lift. He weighed about a ton and a half. About the weight of forty underfed people.

Some of the prisoners were dark-skinned, a few of them were Hassidim, several of them white French "subversives"; they milled in a small oblate crowd, blurred together, individuality lost in the commonality of their confusion at this abrupt consummation of destiny. The guards stood around them in a human chain, facing inward. A man Torrence recognized as Giessen, The Thirst, studied the crowd around the square. *Don't move. Don't run. Don't scream. He'll notice you.*

"I can't move anyway," Torrence muttered.

Bibisch looked at him. "*Quoi?*"

Torrence said nothing.

Giessen spoke softly to the FSS commanding officer, who turned to the crowd, announced that this execution of "criminal conspirators" was being carried out in reprisal for the crimes of the terrorist "Hard-Eyes." Then he turned to his soldiers, and barked an order. The soldiers aimed their machine pistols. Prisoners screamed, cringed. Some of the people watching screamed. The FSS officer opened his mouth with the command to fire.

Torrence stood up. Didn't know he was doing it.

He began to move toward Giessen, opening his mouth to shout.

But Giessen wasn't looking his way. Roseland and Bibisch took Torrence, one on each side, turned him away from the sight, Roseland covering Torrence's mouth with a hand, Bibisch hissing something in French at their waiter—a friend.

Roseland murmured, "Role-reversal time, Torrence. My turn to keep you from blowing it." He and three other men, shielded from the sight of The Thirst by the crowd around the square, dragged Torrence into the café. Into the back, out through a back door, up a stairs, into the building . . . down into a back street.

Torrence, voice muffled, was trying to tell them, *They must know I'm here anyway, so it doesn't matter. They're doing this to torture me, before they come and get me. They know. They know. This is punishment.*

"No, no," Bibisch said. "Hush."

Torrence heard the C.O. bark his final command.

But he wasn't there to hear the machine pistols' *sss, sss, sss* as the pellet-size explosive bullets were shot into the prisoners.

Torrence wasn't there to hear it; he wasn't there to see it.

But, somehow, he saw it over and over again, in his imagination, for a long time after that.

09

LONDON.

Cooper was acting strangely. And Barrabas began to worry he'd done the wrong thing in bringing Jo Ann back here.

They were in the video editing room; not for editing, but for talking in privacy. Cooper was sitting on a swivel stool, hugging himself, swaying a little, looking as if he might fall off at any second. His eyes were dilating and shrinking, dilating and shrinking.

He's stoned, Barrabas realized. *He's been tinkering with his balancer.*

"She's out in the lobby?" Cooper asked thickly.

"Yes."

"Go out and talk to her, keep her there. I'll have Security bring her around back. We'll have a car ready . . . "

Someone's footsteps sounded in the hall. Barrabas reached over, sloppily hit a switch, turned on the editor so the noise would cover their talk. It showed disconcerting images of the subhumans. Stumbling around, shitting themselves; living mockeries of humanity. Barrabas looked quickly away, trying to ignore the mewling sounds that came from the speakers.

"How much are you going to erase?" Barrabas said. "I mean—not all her recent memories? I don't want to be erased from her memory. Unless maybe selectively. Just the gen-engineering stuff or—?"

"What are you babbling about?"

"She's come to have that stuff erased—"

"That costs money. I mean, we can't erase that without causing a lot of questions to be asked . . . "

"What? I mean, what the bloody hell—"

"I'm saying, never mind any of it. Leave it to us." Cooper tried to smile reassuringly. It was like a ferret baring its teeth.

Barrabas stared. "You're going to kill her."

Cooper made a dismissive gesture. "Not personally."

Pink things, mewling, squirmed in video on the edge of his vision. "They're going to take her in the car and—"

"You're not really *involved* with this creature, are you? She's a leftist, quite possibly a Communist or an Anarchist. Leave her alive and she's liable to marry some great strapping Negro and have his children. Miscegenation of the worst order. Revolting. Put her out of your mind."

Barrabas blanked his face, and shrugged with resignation. "Right."

"Toddle along, now. Keep her out there till—"

"Right," Barrabas said again. He nodded, turned, mechanically opened the door, walked stiffly out and down the hall.

He found her in the lounge. Looking nervous, turning her handbag over and over in her fingers. "Did you get the approval for the . . . thing?" she asked. As if he'd been arranging an abortion.

"Yes. Yeah, uh . . . "

He heard voices in the next room. One of them was the chief of Security.

Barrabas took her firmly by the wrist. "Come on, I'll take you over there myself."

"Don't yank me around like that." But she went with him, out of the building. "What are you in such a fucking hurry for?"

He looked around, sorting through the traffic. It had just rained; the streets were damp and glossy, and the air was muggy as the pavement gave off the earlier heat of the day into the twilight.

There, parked in front of a pub, a hulking black taxi. The driver wasn't at the wheel—probably having a pint.

Barrabas dragged her through traffic, making cars honk at them and swerve. He pulled her into the pub. He looked out through the dusty window, saw the SA security men stepping out of the lab's front door. They were looking around, frowning. A beer lorrie pulled up in front of the pub, blocking their view. And traffic was thick. There might be time.

Barrabas found the cab driver at the old brass and wood bar: a squat, sallow bloke with a thin mustache and watery eyes, Southeast Asian maybe, sucking up the brown foam at the bottom of a pint. Barrabas took the width of the room in two strides, grabbed the driver's elbow, slapped a twenty-pound note down in front of him. Britain had never changed to the world currency—was still using the pound sterling.

"Break's over, mate. Bit of an emergency."

" 'Ere, I'm not giving up me dinner break for twenty quid—"

"You drinking your dinner? All right, here." He slapped down another twenty quid. It was all the money he had.

"Barrabas, what the hell!" Jo Ann started, angrily. Thinking he was bullying a wog again. "The guy is—"

"Trust me this once, love."

The cabbie was making a great show of his reluctance as he scooped up the forty and folded it, put it in his pocket. Then he unsteadily followed Barrabas out to his cab. Jo Ann trailed after, scowling.

The security men were on their way across the street as the lorry pulled away. They spotted Jo Ann as she and Barrabas got into the cab. The SA men shouted as the taxi pulled away, reaching into their jackets. The flow of traffic was with the cab and they quickly left the SA thugs behind.

"Where to?" the driver asked.

"Just . . . Picadilly." Till he could think of somewhere else.

She looked at him. "We were running from them?"

He nodded, leaned back on the seat, letting the tension drain from him. Feeling dizzy. He'd hyperventilated. He whispered, "They weren't going to erase the stuff—they were going to erase you, completely." He made a throat cutting motion across his gullet.

She gaped at him, shook her head in disbelief. "Why?"

"Just an erase extraction—Cooper'd have to do a lot of explaining—it'd come out how he'd been skimming money from the SA. See, he—" And then he saw the way she was looking at him. Realized what he'd said.

"The SA," she repeated. "The Second Alliance. That's who owns that lab?" Adding in a whisper: "That's who you work for."

"*Did* work for. It was—I just needed work." What was he ashamed of? He'd been proud of the uniform, the training. The mission. He ought to tell her to go to hell. But he said, "I saved your life. You know that, or not?"

She nodded slowly. "Risked yourself to do it. I know that. But you're one of them. They don't just hire people. What I heard, everybody's got to *believe*." She was staring at him, seeing him differently now. She asked him bluntly: "Do you believe in that crap? Their racist shit?"

He reached for the belief, for his pride, his conviction.

Then he saw the pink squirming things. The subhumans. The things in tank forty-one. And conviction was a wet bar of soap.

"I don't know. It's—getting harder to believe in." It was the best he could manage.

She looked out the window. "Why Picadilly?"

"No reason. Just wanted to get to another part of town. Got a better idea? My house or yours is right out."

"I ought to ditch you," she said, not looking at him. "But I guess . . . I guess I don't want to."

But she continued to look out the window. He wanted to take her hand, put an arm around her, but a certain compression of her legs together, a warning in the set of her shoulders, kept him back.

After a long moment, she added, "I got an idea where we could go."

"Some friends to hide with?"

"Yeah. Somebody, anyway, I know through a friend. Only met him once. But I think he'd help. I heard he was in town, over at Dahlia's. A guy named Smoke."

• • •

Barrabas had a sense of unreality when he saw Jerome-X and his enormous black Negress sitting on the sofa at Dahlia's.

No: Jerome wasn't on the sofa, exactly. Jerome was sitting in her lap.

Miscegeny, Barrabas thought. Expecting to feel the nausea of revulsion. All he felt, though, was a dull disorientation.

Jerome was wearing a black leather jacket, open to show a few hairs on his skinny, shirtless chest. Antique jeans, rather silly red plastic boots with bright yellow baby doll's arms on them in place of Mercury's wings. The black woman wore a big shapeless red house dress with electric-blue carnations strobing on it. No shoes. Barrabas was worried the couch would break under the bloody great bulk of her.

"Hi," Jerome said. "What's happenin'?"

Barrabas decided it was a rhetorical question used as a greeting, and only shrugged.

Jo Ann said, "We're looking for Dahlia."

"Right here." She appeared at the door to the dining room—a tall, gracefully long-necked black woman in an African robe batiked in red clay, copper, and silver; she wore silver contact lenses, white-blue lipstick, earrings that were dangly gold replicas of ancient tribal fetishes; cornrowed hair, each row glazed a different metallic color: copper, silver, gold, platinum, bronze, stainless steel . . .

"'Ello, love," she said, crossing to Jo Ann. Her anklets clinking; her bare feet slapping on the polished hardwood floor. She hugged Jo Ann, slowly and deeply. A little embarrassed, Barrabas looked around.

They were in a high-ceilinged sitting room, in the old Edwardian terrace house, beside a dusty marble fireplace. The room was busy with the sheer excess of its decor. The mantel was crowded with a collection of jade figurines. The late-nineteenth-century plaster moldings near the ceiling were ornate. On the walls, between the cheerfully painted woodwork, covering most of the faded, intricately patterned wallpaper, was a crowd of artwork; aboriginal art, with its assertive angularity, was mixed indiscriminately with the evocative blur of Impressionist paintings and the restless collaging of video paintings. African and Australian nature gods scowling out from between Seurat and Thaddeus Wong.

My God, where has she brought me to? Barrabas thought.

Dahlia came out of the giggling clinch and snaked out a long arm to Barrabas.

In a rather rummy voice, Barrabas thought, Jo Ann said: "Oh, Dahlia, this is Patrick Barrabas."

"'Lo." He took her hand. It was warm and moist.

"I guess you've already met Jerome and Bettina."

"Sort of," he said. "And we saw them perform the other night." Dutifully, he added, "Exxy show."

Jerome grinned. "Thanks."

Dahlia led Jo Ann to the Louis XIV sofa. Barrabas sat across from them in an antique chair of cracked brown leather. He tried not to stare at Jerome and Bettina.

Bloke looked like a bloody ventriloquist's dummy sitting on the great puddle of the black woman's lap, Barrabas thought.

Dahlia reached languidly to a remote on a mahogany end table. "Let's have some music," she said. Her accent was middle-class London, Barrabas thought, for all her African affectation. A wealthy family, like as not, judging from the expensive jumble of the furnishings. From a family of black immigrants, he told himself, come over a generation ago, taking opportunities that should have gone to white British natives.

Barrabas tried to work up some inner spark of outrage about it. But the flint found nothing to strike on.

The music swelled to thud and skirl on the high ceiling; Barrabas had expected recordings of "authentic aboriginal" music, or some such, but instead the music was an amalgamation of house music and dance electronica. Perhaps it was the contemporary equivalent of aboriginal music.

"I was hoping Smoke was still here," Jo Ann was saying. "I need to talk to him, if you think it'd be okay. I've got a problem. Some people—"

"Might be better to tell as few people as possible," Barrabas broke in. Smiling apologetically. "To protect them as well."

Jo Ann hesitated. "I guess so. To protect them."

"Oh, I *do* love the dramatic sound of all this," Dahlia said, yawning. "Not going to tell even poor Dahlia?"

"Um—eventually," Jo Ann said.

"They don't know if they can trust us," Jerome remarked, whispering it sotto voce to Bettina.

"Hell, I don' know if dey can either," Bettina said. "I don' know who dey are. I don' care about dis shit neither. Dying for some motherfucking dinner."

Jerome started to get up. "I'll get Smoke, maybe we can all cruise for something."

Bettina grabbed him, held him back. "You ain't goin' nowhere. Did I say you get up?" Looking at Jerome with narrowed eyes.

Not serious, Barrabas realized. Some kind of game.

"*Fuck* you," Jerome said, trying not to laugh, wriggling free of her. "I go where I please, bitch."

"Who you calling bitch—? Come here, I beat yo' skinny pink ass!"

But he was gone, laughing at her as he went through the door.

"Little white punk!" she called after him. "I make you sorry!" But shaking with silent laughter, big belly and the obese undersides of her arms quivering.

Weird, Barrabas thought.

"If you want Smoke's help," Dahlia said, thoughtfully clicking her long, gold-painted nails against the carved wood of the armrest, "then it's maybe some . . . political problem?"

"Yeah," Jo Ann said.

"You need Smoke's people too?"

"Yeah."

"Right, no reason not to talk in front of Jerome and Bettina. It'll come out, I reckon—they're part of it."

"Uh—" Jo Ann looking at Barrabas. Thinking, he supposed, of warning Dahlia not to say too much in front of him. She wasn't sure of his loyalty.

And he wasn't sure himself. But he said. "It's okay, Jo Ann. I'm committed."

She pursed her lips—but shrugged resignedly.

Barrabas noticed Bettina watching them; following the implicit message as well as the explicit one, in the exchange between Jo Ann and Barrabas.

He had an uncomfortable feeling Bettina knew exactly what was going on. Looking at her, just a quick glance into Bettina's eyes, he glimpsed the analytical whir of her mind; was shaken up by the hard glitter of intelligence he saw there.

Jerome returned with a stooped, lanky, hawk-nosed man in a rumpled, ill-fitting real-cloth suit of gray pinstripe. He was in his stocking feet. "This woman wanted to talk to you," Jerome said.

"Jack Smoke," the tall man said, crossing to them, shaking Jo Ann's hand.

• • •

The restaurant was crowded and close and smelled strongly of beer and beef. Yellowed prints of nineteenth-century opera posters on the wall almost vanished into the dim, dark-wood ambience. The low rafters were smoke-blackened from a time when smoking was allowed in restaurants. Barrabas, Jo Ann, Dahlia, Jack Smoke, and Jerome banged elbows in a hard wooden booth. Bettina sat grouchily on a chair at the end of the table. Jo Ann told her story, keeping her voice down for much of it so they had to strain to hear her. Finishing just as the food arrived.

"Only ting dey know how to cook in dis fuckin' country is roast beef," Bettina said, digging into hers with no further preliminaries.

Barrabas would have liked to have resented the remark, only it was uncomfortably correct.

"There's curries," Dahlia said. "And cous-cous."

Not British, Barrabas thought. Except by default.

"I've been taking cooking courses," Dahlia said. (Barrabas thinking: I was right about her, she's a course taker.) "North African cuisines. And it's had an effect on my paintings." (Barrabas nodding to himself.) She went on, "The spicier the food I cook, the more color I tend to use—it's a reflection of those energies, you know." And she went on, filling up the time talking about "her art" and "her music," as Smoke ruminated on Jo Ann's dilemma.

Finally, when they were drinking bitters and eating pudding, Smoke said, "Jerome. Bettina."

They looked at him expectantly.

He went on slowly, staring into his half-eaten pudding. Talking low, though the place was crammed with noise, "Can you check the Plateau, see if anyone we can trust has access to an extractor in London?"

Jerome-X and Bettina nodded, like a person with two heads.

And as one, their eyes glazed.

Barrabas felt a chill, looking at them. Like they were in a trance. Some kind of chip augmentation, maybe.

"Mickin," Bettina said.

"Cover," Jerome said.

"Hub?" said Jo Ann.

Smoke explained. "They're talking in a sort of aug-chip shorthand. She said that there was a microwave oven in use creating some interference; Jerome said he'd give her some transmission cover so she could get through."

"Oh."

"You wouldn't mind our using an extractor, Jo Ann?" Smoke asked. Politely but without any real concern for her dislikes.

"An extractor?" Jo Ann asked nervously. "Can you get the stuff out with . . . well, I guess you can."

Smoke nodded. "And we can record it. Find out what it is. Way you describe it, it sounds as if it would be of interest to us."

To us. It was then that Barrabas was sure. About who he'd fallen in with.

He was with the New Resistance.

He was hiding out with his own enemies.

• • •

They thanked Dahlia and sent her home. The rest of them cabbed directly from the restaurant to the London Institute of Neurobiology, where a sympathizer had access to an extractor. Getting into the cab, Barrabas was uncomfortably aware that the big black woman was standing very close to him; was, in fact, watching him. As was Jerome. They began keeping an eye on him directly Jo Ann told them about his involvement with the SA. He began to wonder if he would be separated from Jo Ann at some point, taken somewhere for interrogation. Afterward, his body dumped in the Thames . . .

They weren't going to just let him go, that was certain. He toyed with the idea of disappearing on his own. He was afraid to return to the SA, but he might hide out with relatives upcountry—or somewhere, anyway, on his own.

He couldn't bring himself to break away completely from Jo Ann, though. When he looked at her, a strange gestalt organized her face into someplace exquisitely restful.

Suppose he suppressed those feelings. Suppose he asked them to let him out of the cab, right here . . .

They'd never let him go. They didn't dare trust him. He could hardly blame them for that, really. There'd be an argument at least, quite possibly a fight.

No. He'd have to take his chances with them, at least for now.

By the time he'd decided, it was fair dark out and they'd arrived at the hospital.

They drove around the back. A nearly midget-size Paki doctor in a blue tunic was waiting for them, his arms clasped anxiously over his chest. He nodded briskly to Smoke, frowned at the others, but said nothing. The doctor led them into the clinical brightness and medicinal tang of the corridor, their footsteps echoing off the white tile walls. He took them hastily into a lab, through the lab to a little room filled with equipment Barrabas didn't recognize. In the midst of all the cryptic gear was a padded examination table. "Lie down, please," the doctor said.

Barrabas realized, with a chill, that the doctor wasn't talking to Jo Ann. He was talking to him. To Patrick Barrabas.

"I'll go first," Jo Ann said, seeing the look on his face.

"First?" Barrabas said.

"Lord, motherfucker can talk! I thought he was deef!" Bettina said.

"Keep your voices down, please," the little doctor said, almost squeaking it, looking through a window in the door. "We're not supposed to be in here, you know."

Smoke nodded and said softly to Barrabas, "We have to debrief you, find out how much we can trust you, how you stand on things, what you might know that can help us."

"For all I know, you might erase part of me," Barrabas said. "To protect yourselves. Or brainwash me."

Smoke shook his head. "Not going to erase anything from your head. Or plant anything. Just going to read it. We won't force you. But . . . "

But. Barrabas nodded. It wasn't a threat exactly. That wasn't the tone the man was using. More a mixture of regret and warning—that they might have to kill him.

Barrabas took a deep breath and said, "You are forcing me, in a way. But sod it." He turned to Jo Ann. "I'm going to do this for you." Maybe it was melodramatic; he didn't care.

He felt trapped. But, strangely, at the same time he felt set free.

He lay down on the table, and she held his hand.

• • •

Dover, Kent.

Dawn was breaking steel blue and aluminum gray across the Dover Straits. It was a windy morning, and the sea lashed against the pilings of the dock, making the big hover ferry rock at its moorings. Barrabas and Jo Ann and Smoke and Jerome stood on the dock at the back of the crowd, waiting for the all-clear to go aboard the hover ferry. Bettina was conspicuously absent.

To their right, drivers with permits to take cars to France were queued up, mostly in the cheap Brazilian methanol compacts.

Barrabas huddled into his coat and moved a little closer to Jo Ann. The sky was dull with clouds, and whitecaps tipped the jade peaks of the sea. "Fuckin' cold," Jerome-X muttered.

"That's England for you," Jo Ann said. "Supposed to be summer."

"It'll warm up," Barrabas said. "It's early days." He was looking around, trying to spot SA. "Wish we'd done a plane flight, though."

Smoke said, in just over a whisper, "The SA'll be on the airport for sure. They might not've come this far looking for us."

Barrabas said, "I don't know. I'm surprised they're not here. They want Jo Ann, and they mean to find her. I know 'em."

"Maybe they'll just have the cops arrest us," Jerome said. Looking over his shoulder; searching the street behind them for someone.

"They've got a relationship with the police—but they don't want them involved in this, I'm sure," Barrabas said.

Jerome looked small and sorrowful, almost lost in the oversize gray trenchcoat he'd borrowed from Dahlia.

Smoke glanced at him. "You sure about this, Jerome? Going with us?"

"Yeah." But Jerome looked over his shoulder again.

"You think she's going to come and talk you out of it?" Smoke said.

Jerome-X shot him a hard look. "Fuck you."

"Jerome—we've got Bones in Paris now. He's our connection to the Plateau there."

"I don't want to be a chip chippie. I want to fight."

"Your career is beginning to move in the States. If you were a celebrity, you could help us there."

"I don't fucking want a career. *I want to fight.*" Pouting, he huddled deeper into his coat.

Smoke said gently, "Jerome . . . "

"*What?*"

"There's more than one way to fight."

"Look—I saw something once. When I was linked. When we got out of jail. Saw myself. Like—a kinda personality animation thingie. It was sick, man. Need attention all the time. No belief in myself. Trying to be a performer because I want to get into the media. Like, I'm not a valid person unless I'm making records and on TV and stuff. That's bullshit, Smoke."

"This is what you were up all night arguing with Bettina over?"

"Yeah."

"She's got good instincts, Jerome."

"You trying to tell me to stick to what I know how to do? I can learn. I don't have to spend my life trying to be a fucking spectacle. It's childish. I got to get away from that."

"Yes. Rickenharp felt something like that. But it didn't change him. Everybody's got drives to be one way or another. You have a drive to be a spectacle—so what? Maybe there's a reason. You saw only the subjective gestalt. There might be some other reason you're a performer—if it's neurosis, well, maybe there's a higher reason for the neurosis. You only see a small thread on the tapestry."

"It's too fucking early in the morning to be mystical, Smoke."

"She's back there, Jerome, about a block down."

Jerome looked at Smoke, startled. "Bettina?"

"Yeah. Sitting in a rental car. I saw her. She doesn't want to come after you. She doesn't want to humiliate you that way."

"Be the first time."

"You should know her better than that. And yourself. You don't have to prove anything. I know you're ready to die for us. I just think you could be more useful to us going on with the other thing. Fight for us as an artist. Public relations, consciousness raising. Be yourself, Jerome. I know that hurts. It hurt me once."

Jerome stared at him, looking as if he was about to erupt with a *fuck you.* Finally, he grinned. And said, "Hey, it's a dirty job, but somebody's got to do it." He slapped Smoke on the shoulder, turned to the others. "Okay. I'm outta here. Good luck, you guys. Keep your head down."

And then he turned back to Smoke. "What kind of rental car?"

"One of those big Arabian saloon cars that uses lots of cartel oil in its gearbox. I think it was yellow or—"

"Never mind—I've got her on chip now."

He hurried away. Back to Bettina.

Back to his huge black mama, Barrabas thought.

Well, why the hell not.

Barrabas looked speculatively at Smoke. "You going to tell us what the extractor came up with? From Jo Ann, I mean? What was all that stuff they were buggerin' with in her head?"

Smoke said with flat authority, "No. I've got to confirm something first. Bones is in Paris, I'll talk to him first. He's got a lot of stuff about genetically engineered organisms stored up. When I know what I'm talking about, I'll talk about it."

He looked like something was eating at him, Barrabas decided. Like he's guessed what this Bones'll confirm for him. And it scares him.

Quietly scared.

Barrabas knew what it was like to be quietly scared.

"I wish I'd had time to arrange a private boat," Smoke said, peering southeast, toward the coast of France. Just across the channel, but not quite visible from here. "Anyway, Dahlia said she'd have some people here to cover for us."

Barrabas snorted. "Dahlia. Bit full of herself, that one."

Jo Ann shot him a look. "Are you going saying something racist? Because if you are—"

"No, no, no. But—"

"I know what he means," Smoke said, coming to his rescue. "She's always talking about herself, her little projects. She can seem shallow."

Jo Ann shrugged. "She had the crummy luck to be born wealthy. Her parents have a diamond wholesaling outfit. And she's an only child. Got everything she wanted, almost instantly. She's never been quite sure of who she was, because she had the freedom to be anyone she wanted. But she's always there for you. She's almost the only real friend I had in London."

Smoke nodded. "She's always there for us, too. She knows what she's risking, helping us. She'll grow up. And in the meantime, she has so many connections—she may surprise you, Patrick."

Barrabas shrugged. "I been surprised already." The Hover ferry's deck hands dropped the gate chain and the crowd began moving onto the vessel, sifting through the bottleneck a few at a time like grains of sand in an hourglass.

And then Barrabas saw the SA chief of London Security, and half a dozen others, all of them in plainclothes, but with hands on guns in their coats. They were getting out of the back of an unmarked green van.

"I see them," Smoke said. He looked at the ferry. Its gate was still about thirty feet away and there was a heavy crowd in front of them.

The plainclothes thugs started across the street toward them. Smoke reached into his pocket. Jo Ann dug her fingers into Barrabas's arm.

And then a score of howling teen thrashers on skateboards erupted from an alleyway.

And they made straight for the startled SA heavies.

The thrashers'd look ridiculous if they didn't look so frightful, Barrabas thought—and so kinetically in control. Their scalp-ups were molded into the sort of fins you saw on mid-twentieth-century cars. And they all wore those absurd mirrored goggles. Despite the chill, they wore nothing but skin-tight neoprene kneepants, no shoes. Every one of them was etched with lean muscletone, and gang-color tattoos. Chrome insignias from cars, from Fuel-Cell BMWs, Jaguars, Mercedes, Mitsubishi 999s, swinging, glinting, on glass chains around their necks. They skated on big, narrow translucent-plastic skateboards edged in super-glued broken bottle glass, patchy with decals; skating half crouched, heads forward, chromed teeth flashing.

Strapped to their calves, hook-shaped blades, razor sharp; spikes on knees and elbows.

And the same expression, like a kind of uniform, on every face: as wide and as evil a grin as human facial muscles are capable of.

Probably a result of their drug combination, their stoke-up rush: 2C-B mixed with methedrine and vitamins, he'd heard. Which was why they were up at dawn, raging and indifferent to the cold.

Some variant of thrash/acid-house, mixed special for the thrashers, whipped the air from a soundbox strapped to the leader's back as he led the gang into the thick of the SA thugs. The leader—the thrasher cap'n— pumped his legs on the skateboard, its wheels gimmicked to translate the pumping motion into kinetic energy so he didn't have to kick off from the street. The boys yelled cryptic war cries in the variation of Technicki that English street punks used, "Guhfee muh bleh outcher—"

"Arsebug uh shuva bya fook!"

"Ava gowan yehdir upa shuh!"

(Barrabas and Jo Ann and Smoke were carried on the surging tide of the crowd running from the gang, shoving brutally to get onto the Hovercraft. Barrabas watching the fight over a shoulder.)

What followed was a blur, like a cartoon animation of electrons whizzing around the nucleus of an atom; an atom undergoing fission, maybe, as blood spurted, men screamed, guns fired, all of it punctuated by the ugly thud-crunch of elbow and kneespikes ramming flesh.

"Uh killuhfuh meh me bloo'ole Yiby!"

Two of the thrashers went down yelling, one shot through the neck, another through the groin. A third with a bullet through his ankle rode away from the melee like a crane, one-legged on his skateboard.

The Second Alliance thugs were either on their knees—gashed, clothes like circus-hobo rags—or half running, half limping, back to their van. Their guns were mostly scattered across the street. Their security chief was stumbling backward, fumbling with his gun. The thrasher captain bellowed, "Gowasuckerteetsies yarble ya bollkscunts!" and smacked the gun to spin away in the air, grabbed the SA London Security chief by the neck, bent him back, kissed him openmouthed with tongue, bit off a chunk of his lower lip, spun him, and kicked him in the ass so he fell on his face. The security chief scrambled screaming in horror toward the van.

Doing all this, the thrasher captain never lost his balance on his skateboard.

And then came the seesaw sounds of approaching police sirens, and the thrashers whizzed back into their alley.

Smoke's party stumbled hurriedly onto the hover ferry.

The boat embarked with no delays. The street's vendors were there to give the story to the police.

But in the glassed-in café on the upper deck of the craft, Jo Ann was crying at the smudged window. "God, that was awful. Those men cut to ribbons! Two of those boys shot dead." Adding in a whisper, "Was it for us, Smoke?"

He nodded. "Dahlia sent them for sure. Probably bought them a month's supply of stoke-up, had 'em watching the place. And the thrashers don't like the fascists."

"Second Alliance security'll ring the SA in France," Barrabas pointed out. "They'll be waiting for us."

Smoke shook his head. "There's a boat going to come out and meet us before we reach the other shore. I've got it set up with a bosun on the ferry. The ferry'll 'break down' for a few minutes, about a mile out from France . . . "

Jo Ann wasn't listening. "God. Those boys are dead because of us."

Barrabas put an arm around her. Gave her a white plastic cup of hot chocolate. "Don't cry for those kids. They live for that sort of thing, love. They're dead already, most of 'em, from the neck up. Products of the war, in their way. Out of their effing heads."

She bit a lip and turned away from the window. "Oh, fuck, what did I do?"

Did she mean *What have I done? Or What did I do to deserve this?*

Barrabas decided not to ask her.

• • •

PARIS. THREE DAYS LATER.

The erstwhile drunk tank in the NR's safe house was crowded, and the sad thing was, Roseland thought, they were all dead sober. He could have used a drink.

Most of the top Paris New Resistance people were crowded into the room, sitting on folding metal chairs, on the floor, or leaning against the wall. The door was open, but the air was sticky. Steinfeld and Smoke sat at a small table with hard-copy printouts on it, at one end of the room; the others sat facing them, in ragged rows. Hand was there, taking notes at the back on a palm device.

"How close are they to using this stuff?" Torrence asked.

Smoke sighed. He glanced at the new people, the English guy Patrick Barrabas and the young woman Jo Ann Teyk. An American. "From what the extractor gleaned from Jo Ann the virus is deployable anytime they want to mass-produce them. They have the facilities. Once the thing is released, it'll thrive on its own for a while—not infinitely. It's designed to die out after a certain amount of time. But not before hundreds of millions of people die. They're still checking its efficiency—but that probably won't take long."

Roseland thought: I should be shocked, or bowled over, or shouting in outrage. Or something.

But he wasn't, because he wasn't surprised. A new Final Solution had to be part of the equation. Part of their mindset. He'd been expecting something like this. It made sense. A racially selective virus kills only according to your DNA codification—an efficiency the Nazis would have envied.

Father Lespere said, "I believe they have been testing some early variations of it in the detention centers in the last month. People are dying more rapidly than usual. Unusual symptoms . . . "

"Oh, *merde*," Bibisch said. Her eyes filled with tears. Torrence put an arm around her. All of them sat there for a few moments in silence, imagining the suffering.

"You have any trouble getting them out of the country?" Roseland asked, pointing with his chin at Barrabas and Jo Ann. He was mentioning it to change the subject. Right then he couldn't bear thinking about children dying of the virus . . .

"Some," Smoke said. "At the docks. There were SA thugs there. Out of uniform, but armed. They hadn't told the police anything about it." He gave a sickly smile. "The British kids have a big skateboard-revival thing going. Dahlia made a few calls, had a gang of 'em show up when we were about to board. The SA started to move in, and the kids came out of nowhere on their skateboards—"

Roseland blinked. "Skateboards? Are you kidding or what?" But he wasn't amused. Nothing was funny just now.

Smoke added with grim satisfaction, "SA tough guys cried like a lot of spoiled children."

The whole anecdote was told absentmindedly. They were all thinking of that looming Something Else.

Steinfeld said, "Jerome-X and Bettina and Bones . . . " He nodded at the cadaverous black man leaning, arms crossed, in a corner. " . . . broke into the SA computer, confirmed they've ordered the genetic raw materials to begin manufacturing the viruses. "

"I don't believe this," Hand said with a sort of desperation. He was sitting with his back to the wall, to Roseland's right, tapping at his palmer.

Steinfeld wouldn't let him record the meetings except for notes. And Steinfeld checked the notes. Just having Hand here was dangerous enough. Roseland hoped Smoke knew what he was doing . . .

"It's just . . . it's just too much to believe," Hand said. "They wouldn't go that far. That kind of genocide. Whole nations wiped out."

"You don't believe it," Torrence said, his voice lifeless. Face blank. Most of the time, he'd been that way since the massacre at Place Clichy. "You don't fucking believe it. You believed the processing centers. You saw the Jægernaut chew people up and spit them out. What difference do the numbers mean?"

Hand shook his head. He looked nothing like the slick, poised TV reporter he'd been when he came to Paris. He looked haggard, and ill, and haunted. "Probably they intend to . . . to hold us all hostage, *threaten* us with the virus . . . "

"You ever read about the Wansee Conference?" Roseland asked him. "Where the Nazis, in the 1940s, planned the extermination of millions? You have any idea how clinical they were, how calmly they went about it? A psychopathic ideology makes psychopaths of its believers, Norman. They'd use it."

"But the economic fallout—a collapse—it's just not practical even for . . . " Hand's voice trailed off, trembling.

"As to that," Smoke said wearily, "our new friend Patrick Barrabas has a tale to tell. They're developing a sort of home-grown labor force.

Genetically engineering a labor pool of stupid, obedient lumpen. *People Puppies*, I think they call them, with a sick try at a sense of humor. Semi-human things. Subhuman. Their own caricature of an 'inferior race' ... "
He grimaced. "Probably not going to work out the way they think it will. Anyway, Barrabas copied one of their video files, brought it along. We're giving it to you, Hand."

"How'd you get away with copying the file?" Roseland asked.

"Barrabas is a former Second Alliance operative," Smoke said blandly—electrifying the room. "He turned. He's with us now. He'd copied the file when he started having trouble with Cooper—thought he might use it to blackmail the bastards."

Barrabas was staring fixedly at his knees, probably aware that everyone else was staring fixedly at *him*. Anger twitched at the corners of his jaws.

"We put him under extractor, decided we could trust him. He's pretty disillusioned."

Barrabas snorted. "Disillusioned." His voice breaking. "Bugger it. Disillusioned. Shit. They're fucking *maniacs*."

Either the guy was a great actor or he meant it, Roseland decided. Barrabas knew the whole story now. Made him realize things—that people are people and death is forever. And that deep suffering *seems* like forever.

Roseland said, "Hey, Barrabas. Welcome aboard, man."

Barrabas reached out, slowly ... and shook the Jew's hand.

• • •

Torrence had come up to the storeroom to be alone. He sat by the window in the musty darkness, waiting for the moon to come out. Just to have something to wait for. He thought about viruses. Viruses to sicken computers; viruses to annihilate a people.

He thought about Giessen. About Giessen winning. Giessen and Watson and Crandall. If he turned himself in to them, had they won? Hell, no. They'd just snagged one self-important guerrilla. A self-appointed *Che* without even a people, in particular, to fight for. And then the reprisals would stop for a while.

He thought about Randy Maynard, a friend of his in high school. Pretty close friend, for a while, till he found out Randy was gay. And then he'd distanced himself from Randy, without really cutting him completely off. Well. Maybe he *had* cut him off.

Still, it'd been a kick in the head when he'd heard that Randy had AIDS-three. Every damn time they had a vaccine for the HIV virus, some other mutation of it cropped up, and the vaccine didn't work on the new one. AIDS-three killed pretty fast. Anywhere between three weeks to six months of coming into contact with it. It took Randy two and a half months to develop significant symptoms. They kept him going for a while with antiviral treatments.

And Torrence was thinking about something Randy had said when he'd gone to visit him at the hospital. "I open my eyes in the morning, and for a minute or two I'm just here, waking up in a bed, stretching, yawning, looking around. Thinking about, like, what do I have to do today. It's always a minute or two before I think of it . . . you know . . . remember that I'm dying . . . "

That's how Torrence felt, after a fashion. He could get involved in New Resistance planning, in resistance work. And in Bibisch. He could forget his personal doom for a minute or two. But the shadow was never far from him.

He still heard the screams at Place Clichy. In reprisal for the crimes of the terrorist Hard-Eyes.

He blinked away tears, and laughed bitterly, thinking: *Hard-Eyes*. What a fucking joke.

Some of them died quickly . . .

For the crimes of—

Some of them took a while.

The terrorist—

Fountains of blood . . .

Hard-Eyes.

"Dan?" The creak of the boards under her feet. "Danny?"

"Hey, fuck off right now, okay, Bibisch?"

"I don't like you to talk to me that way." She knelt beside him. "Don't cry. It's not your fault—"

"Just don't say that, okay?" Snarling it.

"You are making me ashamed with this sheet."

"This what?"

"Sheet. *Merde.*"

"Oh: shit." He laughed stupidly. "I don't care if you're ashamed. Leave me fucking alone."

"You are a . . . " She searched for the American term. "Wimp. Pussy."

"What kind of clumsy bullshit psychology is that? You think I'm insecure about myself? Call me what you want."

She changed tactics. "You kill those people. They die because of you."

"What?"

She slapped him. Grabbed his hair and jerked his head back.

"Maybe this time I spank *you*, 'Hard-Eyes.' "

He pulled loose. "What kind of stupid game—"

She lunged at him, knocked him on his back, straddled him. "Kiss this, you—"

He was a switchblade, triggered. She was flung against the wall.

He saw a flashing red light. (Hearing the screams at Place Clichy.) He struck out—

Then he saw blood—the blood on his hands. He looked at her. She was motionless, leaning against the wall, eyes closed.

"Bibisch?"

She opened her eyes and smiled sadly. "*Ça va.* I'm okay." Her lip had split, bled on his hands.

"Oh, Jesus, Bibisch, I'm sorry."

"It's okay. How you feel?"

"Me?" He felt relieved. He should be ashamed of feeling relieved, he thought. Self-disgust oozed like an oil slick over him. "Goddammit. Why'd you—God, I'm sorry. There's no excuse. It's wrong, hitting you. In a serious way like that. Your lip. I'm sorry—"

"You hurt me."

"I'm sorry—" His shoulders shaking with it.

"It is wrong to hurt me. To hit women like that."

"Yes." Shaking with the flood of released guilt. "True."

Torrence thinking: If Claire knew what he'd done just now. Hurt a woman. Not a little roughness in a sexual game. But he'd really hurt her, beaten her, taken out his rage on her.

Guilt seared through him like a lethal poison. Burning through him.

Purging him.

He sat up and stared at her. He was empty and tired. But suddenly, he felt some hope. "I . . . "

"You feel better."

"Yeah. You did it on purpose?"

"*Oui. Bien sûr.*"

"You liked it, then?"

"Ah, no. Not at all. It was far too much. It scared me. Hurt me. No, it was not . . . No, I didn't like it. But—" Her voice became husky and she looked at the window. "But—*Je t'aime.*"

And that's when the moon came out.

• • •

PARIS. SA HQ

"We think they're back in Paris," Rolff told Watson. "And there's something worse. We interrogated a man who says the NR have an important TV reporter. It is a global company with a lot of syndication in the United States. Norman Hand. They're going to try to get him out of the country—

apparently he has some very damaging video. We think they're going to take Barrabas and this woman along . . . " Rolff shook his head sorrowfully. "It's this idiot Cooper's fault."

"Is that whose fault it is?" Giessen asked, almost innocently.

Watson ground his teeth so hard he could feel them chip. He sensed Giessen smirking at the other end of the conference table—Giessen not even having to point out that Watson didn't have the city in hand. "Did you get a location?"

"No. We still don't know where they are . . . "

"We can't let this Hand get out. Or the others. It's just unthinkable. I suppose Cooper is useless now?"

Rolff sighed. "He's functioning. We've got control of his balancer. He babbled for an hour after he had his little breakdown . . . I'd like to kill him personally."

"We need him still," Watson said, adding absentmindedly, "but when we don't—be my guest." There was a moment of restless silence. Then Watson slammed a fist onto the table. "Bloody hell! Seal off the city!"

Rolff winced. "Just as things were getting back to normal here. The Party won't like it."

"The Party will do as it's told. *Seal off the city.*"

• 10 •

Torrence knew something was wrong when the train stopped suddenly and noisily between Paris and Charles de Gaulle International Airport. The usually quiet train sinking down off its electromagnetic cushion, banging down onto the track with a clang and a spine-shivering *scree-ee-ee . . .*

Clack. And it was stopped.

It was two a.m.; Torrence and Bibisch, leaning on one another in a front seat of the first car, woke and jumped up at almost precisely the same instant. Bibisch hissing, *"Merde, quoi—?"*

Both of them reaching for their weapons.

Torrence snatching up his beautiful, his pristine, his compact and cunning, his oiled and shined-up AMD-65. A Hungarian assault rifle, developed in the late 1980s, widely purchased by the Arab nations in the 1990s. Old ordnance, like most of the NR gear and yet almost unused. It had been in protective storage for a generation, in Egypt. Part of a shipment of weapons Badoit had gotten to them just two days before. Torrence had only had one opportunity to learn its intricacies and test it out—in Lespere's underground range. But he'd fallen in love with it immediately. It was a grenade-launching rifle, equipped with a shock absorber in the folding stock, forestock that reciprocated as the 7.62 x 39mm-caliber rifle was fired, and an optical sight. Torrence slung his knapsack on his right shoulder; it carried two antipersonnel PGR grenades and two antiarmor PGK grenades. Bibisch carried a Hungarian Spigon submachine gun—more importantly, she had charge of a US-made Stinger ground-to-air missile launcher.

All this probably wouldn't do them a bit of good, Torrence thought, because they'd been taken by surprise.

•••

Four hours earlier, Steinfeld had come into the attic of the old police station with Bones. Found Bibisch and Torrence there, naked, asleep in each others' arms. He sighed, annoyed, and shook them awake. "It's your watch, Torrence. Bibisch, go downstairs and clean up."

They dressed silently—Bibisch trying valiantly not to giggle—and went downstairs.

Then Steinfeld sat in the attic of the old police station with Bones. Who put on a headset that double-jacked him into the hidden transmitter on the roof.

Steinfeld and Bones sat in the dark room on two crates near the window, limned in diluted moonlight coming through the frosted glass. Bones was rocking slightly as he communed with the SA's Paris database: with a mind that was beyond morality, indifferent to the suffering imprinted in its bubbles of magnetism, its crystals of silicon; he was a wolf of the plateau. They sat there for twenty minutes, Steinfeld's lower back hurting with the tension. He wondered, for perhaps a second of that twenty minutes, if it would have been better if Jerome and Bones and Bettina hadn't broken into the SA's London database. If they hadn't got the code for the Paris database; for decryption and full access. They could have gone on in blissful ignorance, thinking they were making a difference. But some of the things they'd found out made them feel puny . . .

And then Bones sat up straight. "They've got a couple of our auxiliary people."

Steinfeld's mouth went dry. "Who? How?"

"The reprisals. This guy Giessen's behind it. Some of our boosters had some relatives shot in the reprisals. Others in processing centers. One of them came forward, just walked into Second Alliance HQ asking for Giessen . . . the other they caught in the tunnels. Giessen put out some kind of a night-seeing bird's eye that followed one of our people after an action at Montmartre . . . followed him home. Watched the place. Scooped up one of our cells an hour ago, there."

"*Who*, I said, damn you."

"Guy named DeBlanc."

"DeBlanc. I think he used to be with the Point Cadre—which means he knows—"

"Wait. Wait. It's coming up. He was Point Cadre—but he was one of those people with extractor-resistant brain chemistry. They couldn't extract him, so they tortured his kids in front of him . . . Oh, shit. It says . . . it says, *Confessed during interrogation of offspring.* Fuck. He just broke. I guess . . . The first one, French guy named La Soleil."

"*Not* Point Cadre."

"No. But he helped us get Barrabas and the woman into the city. He saw Hand there. Told them all that shit. Then the other guy DeBlanc cracked maybe . . . less than half an hour ago. Told them—" Bones seemed to listen for a moment. Stiffened. "Oh, motherfucker. Steinfeld, they know where we are."

• • •

Steinfeld had no time at all—but he had to make a critical decision. He found Hand sitting in a corner of the drunk tank that was now a think tank; Hand was cross-legged on the floor, taking notes on paper with a pen. He couldn't get batteries for his voice recorder and he'd lost his palmer as they'd fled the refugee center.

Nearby, Pasolini and Bibisch and four others standing in a group, arguing politics.

Steinfeld snapped to them, "We're getting out. Move everyone out through Exit Three, and—" He spoke directly to Pasolini. "After everyone's gone, see to it there's nothing much left for them to search through."

"But what—"

"Just do it! They're on their way!"

The group burst apart like pool balls at the break, as they raced to follow orders.

Hand stood up, licking his lips. "The SA? They're coming?"

"Yes. We're leaving here—some of us will be staying in Paris, some of us . . . " He stared at Hand. He had about one minute in which to decide. "Let me see your notes."

Hand hesitated, then passed them over. Steinfeld skimmed through them. Nothing damaging, no specifics, as arranged—Hand's general take on things. He frowned, reading snippets here and there:

SPOES continues to gain momentum. Distributes food, shelter, jobs to war refugees & homeless who have learned that the more nationalistic they are, the more supportive of SPOES racist policies, the better their treatment by authorities . . . The Refugees find ways to justify fascism to themselves. Not difficult, it can be very appealing in all this chaos. Unity Party offers order and jobs and a satisfying return to national IDENTITY. The war was humiliating, making them feel they were unimportant pawns of US and NSR . . . Crowds respond emotionally at Unity Party rallies; racists and jingoists in full throttle . . . continued reports of isolation and deportation to PCs of troublesome ethnic groups . . . U.P.'s Soldats Superieurs said to be brainwashed into ruthlessness in expediting orders . . . some key officials rumored to have been brainwashed w/extractors . . . NR's greatest enemy apparently global apathy, the "it can't happen again" mindset . . . I am unable to find non-native colleagues in Paris, offices of UPI and ITV et al. closed down . . . NATO & SA discourage close reporting here . . . NATO officials stonewalled me . . . American journalists evidently concerned with NATO's liberation of Eastern Bloc countries & terms of New-Soviet surrender . . . Smoke's reports mostly carried only in underGrid . . . big Grid, Internet, social media mostly indifferent or closed by (?) SA connections . . . Holocaust Virus story could blow Grid open for NR . . . Critical . . .

Steinfeld nodded briskly and handed him back the notes. Hand was okay. "We need you and Barrabas and his American friend to do some witnessing for us on the outside. We're going to get you out of Paris." Steinfeld smiled grimly. "Don't look so relieved. They've sealed off the city. It won't be easy."

• • •

They'd gotten out of the safe house with four minutes to spare. The fascist troops arrived and found the place empty—and on fire. Four minutes earlier, the last of the NR contingent got out through the abandoned building next door, down through a camouflaged tunnel, into the old Metro. They headed for the one functioning train station. Some of their people were already there, taking over a surface-track magnetic-cushion train.

Bones had tinkered with the enemy's database, used some of the computer-bug input Jerome-X and Bettina had planted through the Plateau. They had the train cleared as a special transport, supposedly for Colonel Watson. The city was sealed off—but they let the train through.

• • •

Only, a little too soon, someone noticed that Colonel Watson wasn't on a private train, he was in the Second Alliance Comm Room.

"*Fuck* me," Watson breathed when they told him. "They have to be on that train. How did they do it? How did they get clearance for it to get past the—Bloody hell. They had to have gotten into our computers. Take 'em all off-line before they—"

• • •

Walking, the two of them, Martha's small hand in Steinfeld's, through the peach orchard on the banks of the Jordan. Very early. Morning mists. Both hungry for breakfast but in the kibbutz, this time of year, with the fruit heavy on the trees, there is little time for lovers. She is so small, Martha, her hand like a mouse nestled in his palm, but he had seen her strength . . . Now she turned to him and said—

"—they know we've got in," Bones shouted, shaking Steinfeld's shoulder. On the train. Steinfeld had drifted off. "What?" The dream of Israel. Martha. How long had she been dead now? "What—what is it, Bones . . . ?"

"They know we—"

Then it sank in, and the last vestiges of the nostalgic dream dispersed. The time had come—perhaps they'd waited too long. There had been risk, in waiting before activating the virus that Jerome-X and Bettina had planted through the Plateau—it might've been discovered, rooted out. But it had made sense to wait for the strategic moment. The maximum advantage.

Maybe they'd waited too long. Maybe it was too late. Thinking all this, he was saying aloud only: "Then do it! Transmit! Tell the bug to spread!"

• • •

. . . And Watson had the report back in five minutes.

The computers were blanked—years of intelligence gathering, erased. Most of the Unity Party's banks wiped too. The Sicilian center's database— ditto. Erased.

It didn't matter. It was an inconvenience, but it was all right, of course, they naturally had everything on backup, copies in the Sicilian Intelligence Center.

And then his minitranser beeped.

The message was too long for the small screen; he tapped its little keyboard so it'd transmit to the printer. It was a transmission from Sicily asking why they'd been ordered to destroy the backups and hard copy. Virtually all their intelligence data, antisubversive information, everything on the NR and related groups, plus a great deal of logistical information. Gone for good. The incendiary bombs had been set off, the work was done, and they'd had two confirmations from the central computer that they were doing the right thing. But when the SA major in Sicily had tried to call Paris to ask, *What's going on?* there was some sort of restricted access to fone communication, the computers that made the connections wouldn't let them through, apparently. So they followed the orders that had come in over the computers, kept trying the fones. No soap—except, after repeatedly trying, they were able to send a call directly to his transer interface through the fone relays. And the message asked, essentially, *Why did we destroy the backups and documents? Are we about to be invaded here?*

"FUCK MEEEEEE!"

Watson in a rage, backhanding the aide who'd brought the printout, literally knocking him down, kicking him. "THEY'VE BUGGERED OUR FUCKING COMPUTERS! *FUCK MEE-EEE-EEE!*"

As behind him, Giessen said calmly to Rolff, in German: "It appears to be up to us. I suggest we stop that train."

• • •

The train track's electric power was shut down, and the track was blocked—and it was blocked by a Bell-Howell four-man Antipersonnel Forward Offensive Armored Vehicle equipped with 23 X 152mm automatic cannon, two 7.62 X 63mm H & K machine guns and a NATO heat-seeking missile launcher.

"That," Dan Torrence muttered, "is a problem."

So were the two hundred SA soldiers scrambling from trucks to the west side of the train. And there'd be more on the way.

The east side of the train was just seven inches from the concrete outer wall of a storage warehouse. There was no getting out on that side. The enemy had picked the spot carefully.

The train was not quite dark inside; the only light a red glow from the emergency-battery bulbs above the luggage racks. It was hard to make out faces. It could have been the inside of a wrecked submarine.

"Come on, Bibisch . . . "

Torrence and Bibisch found Bones in the next car back. Torrence ran up to him, gear clacking, shouting, "Bones—got some transmission for you! Bibisch has the transmitter if you can do the control and calculations. She'll give you the frequency. Basically aim the transmitter back the way we came . . . "

Leaving Bibisch with Bones, he ran to find Steinfeld.

Up and down the three-car train, the guerillas, with the train to themselves, were deploying weapons, taking up firing stations at the windows and door. Their faces were bleak. They expected to die here.

• • •

Steinfeld was up front, peering out a window like a commuter trying to figure out why his train was delayed—looking like that except for the Israeli carbine in his hands.

He was thinking how vivid the dream of the kibbutz had been; the dream of Martha. Maybe a kind of omen. He had come to believe in them. Maybe Martha, on the Other Side, saying that the transmission to the Badoit Arcology was going through . . . That they wouldn't have to die here . . .

He shook his head. Funny, the ludicrous things you think, right before you die . . .

An announcement through a bullhorn from a Second Alliance official with a German accent blared and rattled in the windows, his English largely unintelligible in its particulars, but clear enough in general:

You have two minutes. Surrender or we'll kill you.

• • •

"Two minutes," Torrence muttered.

Torrence hurried up to Steinfeld. "Where's Pasolini? She should be on radio call. We should be trying to—"

"She's in Paris. Left her in authority."

Torrence stared at him. *"Pasolini?* In charge of Paris—? Steinfeld, she's—"

"She's the most qualified, apart from you. And I need you. I've taken care of the radio call to . . . " He swore in Hebrew, hearing the sound of a helicopter gunship. "That's too soon to be our people."

Torrence looked back along the car. Everyone was crouched, guns at ready. No one was making a move to bolt. He didn't see Roseland. Probably left behind in Paris, in the old Metro station Steinfeld had picked as an emergency safe house. "I figure we've got maybe sixty people . . . " He shook his head, peering out a window. He could see them out there in the dull-red light from the train and in the headlight shine of the armored trucks behind them. And around them . . .

"Christ," Torrence muttered. "Flowers."

They were stopped beside a field of flowers. It was a flower farm. Rows of verdant red and yellow carnations—cultivated in straight lines till they came to the shell holes left from some New-Soviet assault on the area. The rows curved neatly around the shell craters. Tenacious farmers.

The Fascist soldiers were digging in, in beds of flowers.

The carnations' color seemed flat and dusty in the dim light. As he watched, the SA switched off the truck lights—after a moment he could make the troops out as gray silhouettes in the moonlight. A mix of Soldats Superieurs and SA armored troops. The French Soldats had carried Eagle-Feather Brand fences of foamed kevlar from the back of the trucks, set them up around the truck in seconds. They kneeled behind them, to aim their weapons through the gun notches in the white fences.

The stuff looked—and weighed—like Styrofoam, but deflected most calibers of bullet, once its grippers were dug into the ground.

Torrence wondered why Steinfeld hadn't ordered his people to open fire immediately. Now the sons of bitches were dug in behind their cheap bullet-proof walls. He looked at Steinfeld and guessed the reason. He'd needed time to get Hand and Jo Ann Teyk and Barrabas under cover. "Where's Hand?"

"Over there. Crammed down behind those seats. We put baggage around them, to protect them."

"Maybe we could . . . "

The rest was drowned out by the tympanic drumroll of the chopper gunship as it barnstormed the train, firing its 16mm Jæger-sevens to announce that the NR's two minutes were up.

The windows imploded. Glass made a jagged snow-flurry in the car. Someone's head vanished in a welter of blood.

Torrence instinctively shouted orders, firing a burst through the window to suppress the soldiers on his side. He tried not to worry about Bibisch.

The guerrillas fired at the soldiers, the SA/SS fired back. Exchanges of chaos; gunfire and ricochets making a wall of sound; the noise of a hundred iron foundries compressed into a few railroad cars. Bullets smashed through the windows on the west side, passed through the train, smashing through the opposite windows, pocked the concrete wall.

The resistance fighters took the worst of it. Once they were activated, the SXs "smart" rifles were devastatingly accurate. Men and women fell, writhing, screaming; or lay silently where they'd fallen, looking as limp and inconsequential as discarded clothing. One-armed Dr. Levassier and the young Lebanese woman who was his medic scurried to the wounded, crouching as they went to stay below the lethal hailstorm that came through the windows.

An enemy commando stuck his head too far above the protective barrier to take aim—and Torrence dropped his crosshairs on the blurred oval of the man's head, squeezed off a burst—the head vanished; the body staggered back and fell. Torrence fired at someone else but knew he hit the barrier. He wasn't likely to hit many more of the enemy. Torrence shouted over the noise at Steinfeld. "They're chewing us up! We're just wasting ammo!"

Steinfeld shook his head, yelling, "If we stop, they'll charge us!"

"No, not for a while! It'll give us a chance to—" He broke off, exasperated with trying to explain under these conditions; he saw another guerrilla shot in the face—his teeth flying out through the back of his head. Heart hammering, Torrence felt like he was exploding himself. *Bibisch. Claire.*

Steinfeld changed his mind. "Hold your fire!"

It took a full minute for the word to pass down the train. The guerrillas stopped firing. The Second Alliance barrage continued—and then stopped, the enemy waiting to see if the resistance fighters were about to surrender.

The train car was cloudy with gunsmoke, turned violet in the red emergency lights; it stank of cordite and blood and the burning smell of metal sparking metal. Bodies strewed the aisle; men and women begged for help and raised a dissonant chorus of moans.

Others crouched just below the windows, their faces white with fear and anger, quivering with suppressed emotion, knuckles white on their guns.

All of them were looking to Steinfeld and Torrence.

And Torrence wondered what to do next; and wondered if Bibisch were still alive. She might be lying in that next car, hugging herself. Gut-shot.

The bullhorn was booming out some sort of demand, garbled and echoey, mostly lost in the battering noise of the chopper gunship hovering over the train.

What next, what next, *what next*?

Torrence wanted to scream it.

Instead, he turned to Steinfeld. "I'm going to see what's happening with Bones and Bibisch—maybe they've got something set up."

Steinfeld nodded and went to the window. He crouched out of the line of fire, tried to stall the enemy, shouting, "We cannot surrender our entire force! But we will negotiate something!"

The bullhorn replied with a demand for unconditional surrender. Steinfeld shouted back, suggesting they were considering it—another time-wasting tactic.

• • •

Torrence worked his way past sodden bodies and the shaking, squirming wounded. Past sobbing men and grim-faced women. He sprinted between cars.

He found Bones and Bibisch hunched by the rear door of the car; Bones was aiming the transmitter antenna of the radio programmer out the doorway at a slant, holding its metal box in his hands. His face was lined with concentration, eyes squeezed shut, headset jacked into the transmitter box; using the transmitter to get to the Plateau—he couldn't augment directly into it from their present position. Bibisch hunkered beside him, her submachine gun still smoking. Tears streaking her face.

She saw Torrence, scrambled to him on her haunches; came into his arms. "We all of us die now."

"Did you link up? Did Bones get there?"

"He linked, sent two transmissions, but I don't know if it's—" She broke off, tilting her head to listen.

He heard it then. The hum and rumble.

Looked out the window and saw it—the autotank they'd stolen from the refugee camp; the autonomous weapon they'd hidden in the abandoned factory. It was responding to Bones' chip-implanted control and Bibisch's recording, rumbling up the gravel utility road that ran between the train tracks and the flower fields.

The Fascists cheered, thinking that they had robotic reinforcements.

Maybe they did, Torrence thought with a chill. Maybe this wasn't the one he thought it was. Maybe—

The autotank opened fire at close to point-blank range . . .

It opened fire on the SA, from behind them, blasting with cannon and machine guns.

The autotank fired the cannon again and again, like a semiautomatic rifle; *thud thud thud thud thud thud,* blowing soldiers and broken Eagle-Feather deflectors into the air, strobe-lighting the countryside with muzzle flashes. Steinfeld bellowed an order and the guerrillas resumed fire, catching the panicked SA in a cross fire. Torrence popped up like a jack-in-the-box, firing with the AMD-65, using up his clip, instantly ducking down and attaching a rifle-propelled rocket-grenade. Popping up, firing the grenade at a high angle so that, on its way back down, it detonated in the midst of the SA. Bullets sucked air around him. Crouching, he attached another grenade, hands trembling but efficient. He fired. Attached another. The train shook as the enemy gave up trying to keep it intact, fired rockets into the third car. The whole train shuddered, rocked as the car was torn from its coupling. Tilting off the track, falling half onto its east side, smashing into the concrete wall. The west-side windows tilted up so the Second Alliance helicopter gunship could fire into them, 16mm rounds ripping the inside of the third car. Men screamed . . .

And then the Bell-Howell armored car swung away from the front of the train, jouncing and clanking over the tracks, its cannon swiveling smoothly, computer microprocessors aiming it precisely—at the autotank. A flash as it fired; a thud as the round impacted dead center in the autotank—stopping it, totaling its engine and wheel system. Leaving the turret and command center intact. The autotank fired back, four times in succession.

Exploding, the Bell-Howell blossomed like a heavy-metal flower, flame its stamens. A man on fire, a figure made of flame with a human core of shadow, streaked from the burning wreck with a high-pitched wail that was all one long note. The French SS fired an armor-piercing round and the autotank heaved itself into scrap iron and an oily twist of smoke.

Shivering stalks of flame from the burning wrecks and burning sections of train cast a jittery light, made the battlefield quiver, made the bodies lying on the blasted turf seem as animated as the living soldiers: the dead doing a hideous horizontal dance among the cloying, blackening flowers.

Something gleamed on the horizon, a glittering oval. The transport VTOL Badoit had sent. They'd planned to meet it at the outskirts of the airport; Steinfeld had called it here by radio.

Hope lifted its head—and then ducked back into its hole.

The Second Alliance chopper was headed straight for Badoit's VTOL, on its way to shoot their only hope of escape out of the sky.

Bibisch wailed in frustration, picked up the Stinger, and ran to the door.

Torrence, at the window, shouting at her, not even sure what was coming out of his mouth. Some way of saying: *Don't!*

Then she was outside, kneeling among the flowers, aiming the preloaded Stinger into the night sky.

Torrence gaped at her watching through a shattered window, seemed to see her in some kind of compositional frame then: *French Woman With Missile Launcher Amid Flame, Flowers, and Moonlight.*

Torrence wanted to run to Bibisch, but he was afraid to take his eyes from her, insanely sure that if he looked away for a moment she'd be dead. So he stood there, firing furiously past her at the confused SA soldiers, trying to give her cover.

She braced to fire the Stinger . . .

And she fell, as SA rounds found her. They shot her through the side, the hip, and a forearm.

Torrence yelped like a kicked dog. Should he run to her? What could he do for her, now?

And then she was up, gushing blood but getting to her knees. She raised the weapon, fired the Stinger. The rocket, before launching, flared a pool of mystic light around her. It arced into the sky . . .

As she spun around, struck by another burst of enemy gunfire, smashed flat onto her back. Blood splashed, mixing with a sweet confetti of yellow flower petals.

Torrence found himself running toward the door, shouting wordlessly—shrilly and uncontrollably, because he couldn't do anything else.

Then the Stinger struck home. The heat-seeking missile ignited the Second Alliance chopper, made it a ball of blue and yellow fire in the night sky, rivaling the moon.

Ran out the door, jumped down off the train. Metallic *smack* sounds as bullets hit the train near his head. Shouting, sirening his way to her, he kicked the Stinger launchtube aside. Bullets searing past him so close he could smell the friction of their passage in the air.

Glimpsed, in moonlight and fire, the slick blue and red of her insides showing through a hole in her belly.

Flashing red lights.

As he picked her up in his arms, ran back to the train. It seemed to take forever. The other resistance fighters giving him cover. He made it to the chrome steps. Going to make it inside.

Something smacked him hard in the back of his head. He was falling . . .

Failing forward, toward the chrome steps of the train. Never hitting the steps: Falling right through them.

• • •

"I don't know," someone said in French. "Maybe trauma, cerebral hemorrhage, maybe only a bad graze. I have no equipment. Don't know." Levassier's voice.

Daniel Torrence was surprised he could understand this Frenchman. He'd picked up a lot of French after all. He congratulated himself, feeling childishly proud. His mom would be pleased. Wait till he told Kitty, his sister Kitty, that he could understand French.

She'd be impressed.

He wasn't sure if his eyes were open or not. After a moment, he decided they were. He was beginning to make out the ceiling of a train. What train was it?

I open my eyes in the morning, and for a minute or two I'm just here . . . and then I remember . . . you know . . . that I'm dying . . .

The train. Bibisch. "Is she okay?" His tongue felt thick.

He could see Levassier now, with Steinfeld, bending over him. Steinfeld, from this angle, looked like he was mostly beard.

Torrence slowly began to get feeling in his arms and legs. He became aware that the world was vibrating, shaking—each movement rippling pain through his skull.

The train was moving.

"Bibisch . . . "

"She's badly hurt," Steinfeld said. "But still alive."

"Do not move," Levassier said in English, tightening the bandage around Torrence's head.

"The train . . . "

"Bones contacted their computer, found a way to get the train's power back on," Steinfeld said. "Not for long, probably. But we've moved away from them. We disabled their trucks. They're closing in on us, of course, but we're going to—"

The train ground to a halt. Torrence heard Bones's voice. "That wasn't me. They overrode me."

Steinfeld moved out of Torrence's line of vision. "It's okay—there's the transport from Badoit."

"How many did we lose?" Torrence asked. Shit-motherfucker, but it hurt to talk.

Steinfeld said, "Too many. I should have sent only two or three with Hand, slip them out of the city that way. But I was afraid they'd get caught, and I thought if we escorted them, we could fight our way through . . . his information, his reporting to the world—it could be the difference between winning or losing. It may be our only hope. But it was a stupid decision. A decision out of fatigue. I should have sent you with them, alone, underground perhaps. But I thought the train . . . Stupid . . . "

"How . . . many . . . ?"

"Hand is alive, and Barrabas and the American—"

"How many?"

"We lost all but seven, with four surviving wounded. Eleven left. The others are all dead."

"They shot me in the . . . head?"

"Your head was turned when you were hit," Levassier said. "I think it is just a graze. But you have concussion. Maybe."

Torrence heard the thunder and shriek of Vertical Take-off and Landing engines—a big one. The transport. It might be able to get them out of the country. Or it might be shot down.

No. Hand had to get through. Tell the world.

Get up. Protect Hand. Bibisch.

Torrence turned slowly on his side, groaning, levering to get up. Levassier tried to restrain him. "Wait for the stretcher, imbecile!"

Torrence shook loose from Levassier. Nausea gushed up in him. He turned over and vomited.

And then fell forward in it.

• 11 •

FirStep, the Space Colony, Admin Conference Room.

"How are things going in Admin?" Stoner asked distractedly as they waited for Russ to get there.

Stoner wasn't really interested, Claire thought. There was something else . . .

"Lester's faction is a serious pain in the butt," Claire said. "They want to declare the Colony its own sovereign socialist state. Confiscate all UNIC funds for people living at the Colony. They talk about striking—but they're a minority of the technickis. I doubt a strike'll happen."

"Lester's charismatic," Stoner said. Still sounding as if he were thinking about something else entirely. "That can make a minority into a majority. Maybe you should . . . " He broke off, embarrassed. "Sorry. CIA reflexes. Old habits die hard. Never mind."

What had he been about to suggest? she wondered. Assassination?

"Lester's not angry enough to pull it off," she said, chuckling. "We're not mistreating the technickis enough."

Stoner nodded, not giving a hot damn himself. Claire glanced at the broad, high-resolution screen on the left-hand wall, just now coded to *window*—it was a shot of space from the astronomical camera at the "north" end of the colony. It showed a fiercely bright field of stars, one of them a little bigger and more colorful. *Venus.* There was a fringe of glow on one side of the colony, from the sun just out of shot, and on the other a sort of violet and scarlet aurora, like a smeared crab nebula, that was the result of solar wind reacting with the anti-ionization shield of ice-fog they manufactured from the ice asteroid. It was a nonbreathable but protective atmosphere, of sorts, for the outer skin of the Colony on the sunward side. "Pretty view today. Looks almost like a real window, this new screen. Good resolution."

"Uh-huh." Stoner was drumming his fingers.

Russ came in then, looking just a little smug. All right, Claire thought, so he made her come twice the night before—did he have to be so pleased with himself? He sat next to her at the S-shaped table. Squeezed her hand under the table. She suppressed an urge to roll her eyes. He was a bit of a romantic.

He'd already proposed to her twice. Marriage? Ridiculous.

But Claire squeezed his hand back.

She wondered at herself. Since her life had changed so radically—forced out of FirStep, guerilla fighting on Earth, all that she'd seen, she'd reacted by falling into her sexuality, as if it were a refuge. Dan Torrence, Lila— Lila!—Karakos, Russ . . . She'd thrown herself at Russ, almost literally. Not like her, all that sexual wildness.

Stress has turned me into a slut, she thought ruefully. Time to tone it down . . .

"I've been doing some surveillance on Witcher," Stoner said. Adding: "With Steinfeld's permission."

"*Steinfeld's* permission?" She looked at him in a way that made him shrink back in his seat a little. "Witcher is registered personnel on the Colony. How about *my* permission? How about Russ's?"

Russ cleared his throat apologetically. "I've been working with him on this."

She removed her hand from his. "Who the hell do you people think you are?"

Russ winced. "I'm still head of Security, Claire. I never had to approve every move I made with Admin before."

"But this is bugging someone's quarters."

"Not exactly," Stoner broke in. "We're listening in on his unauthorized communications with Earth."

"Still . . . " She sighed. "You had a good reason?"

Both men nodded hastily. Like naughty boys.

"And what did you find out?"

"Witcher made some contacts with certain people in the SA, through intermediaries," Stoner said. "Making purchases from them. I don't think they know who the buyer really is. The Second Alliance has some kind of viral genetic-engineering program going on in secret. A secret most of the officials in SPOES and the Unity Party and the rest don't know about. Apparently they're trying to develop a racially selective virus. I don't know how successful they've been. They developed one that's *not* racially selective—but does have one quality they were after. It dies out after it spreads in a roughly predictable epidemiological pattern. It's called S1-L. Apparently, Witcher has purchased samples of S1-L. Seems he's planning to use it some way."

She blinked. "On the Colony?"

"I don't think so. He seems to be deploying it for specific areas of Earth . . . We think he's planning to use it on Earth while he's on the Colony. While he's safe here, you see."

She shook her head in amazement. "I don't believe it. That's—beyond megalomaniacal. It's crazy. He seems perfectly sane. A little neurotic maybe, but—Well, what the hell is he doing it *for?* Who exactly does he want to kill? The SA?"

"No, uh-uh," said Russ. "Not specifically. The instructions he gave for distributing the things . . . I'd say he wants to kill a large part of the world. In general."

"What do you mean, 'a large part'?" Russ asked. "What exactly does that mean?"

"What it says. A majority."

Russ said, "Holy shit."

Claire stammered for a moment and then managed: "Well—alert people on Earth. Arrest him!"

"We need you to sign a warrant," Russ said, taking a printout and a pen from his pocket.

She looked it over. And signed.

Stoner chewed a thumbnail. "But as for alerting people—our information is too nonspecific. It's more or less hearsay. We're going to inform people, but . . . how seriously they'll take us"—he shrugged gloomily—"I just don't know."

• • •

THE BADOIT COMPLEX, EGYPT.

"I was shot in the leg?" Torrence said sleepily. "I thought I was just shot in the head."

"No. Leg, too. Zuh head wound," Levassier said, "zis is superficial."

"I don't remember that. Being shot in the leg. I didn't feel it."

"Zuh back of zuh left leg," Levassier said. "Thigh."

"Move the leg, Torrence," Steinfeld said a trace mischievously.

Torrence tried. The pain expanded from the wound like a hot ripple in cold water, spreading through his body. "Ouch! Shit! Now I feel it. But at the time . . . nothing. "

"It happens zat way sometimes," Levassier said. "You still have head pain?"

"No. Long as I don't move, I'm almost too comfortable." The bed in the private clinic room was small but soft, tilted up a little. There was a TV, and a bathroom within hobbling distance. The room was the perfect temperature. His Arab nurse, he saw now, as she took his blood pressure, wore a veil and a long black gown, so he didn't know if she was pretty, but otherwise it was ideal.

He didn't like it that way. He understood Roseland a little better now. The shame of survival.

"Hand got through all right?" he asked.

"Yes. His assistant was killed. The technicki. A stray round. But Hand got through. With all the digi-vid, everything."

"That's something any—shit!" A white bolt of pain sizzled through Torrence's head—and then vanished. He felt a little strange. Unreal. "I didn't get any brain damage?"

"I do not sink so," Levassier said, looking into Torrence's eyes with a small, cylindrical optical instrument. "There was some danger of it, some concussion, but head wound, *c'est seulement un*—what word. A graze. A little trauma—we control it with some nimodipine. You feel . . . normal?"

"Mostly. A little out of it, maybe." He'd only just woken, was still a little fuzzy—the trip to Malta and then to Egypt was all a fog. He was forgetting something. Someone. A sense of someone important, crying near him, whimpering with pain . . .

Bibisch.

He grabbed Steinfeld's wrist. Tightly. "Where is she?"

The weariness in Steinfeld's eyes spoke before he did. "She's gone, Danny. Died this morning in surgery. They tried everything. Badoit had the best people flown in, waiting for her. But she had six wounds . . . "

Torrence's eyes burned, but the tears didn't come. Choking on the words, he said, "I don't fucking think it's worth it, Steinfeld. Chances are, we're going to lose. We're outnumbered. And a virus—what the hell do we do about that? It was all wasted. She's wasted." Feeling a great relief and at the same time a growing emptiness as he said it. "She was wasted. Rickenharp, wasted. Yukio, wasted. Danco, wasted. All the others. How many on that train? Forty? Fifty? We're fucked anyway—we should just try to find some little corner of the world and live there . . . Until the virus hits . . . "

"We *do* matter—we liberate concentration camps. We give people hope. It matters. And the race-selective virus—they are far from being ready to deploy it, so far as we can tell. There's still time. I understand how you feel, Danny. We all feel that way sometimes. But we've saved lives. We've saved other lives by destroying their computer files. We've delayed them seriously. And Bibisch saved Hand and the other witnesses. They're important—especially Hand. He could make the difference. We'd never have got him through if she hadn't taken out that gunship when she did. It would have shot the transport out of the sky—the SA reinforcements would have come. We'd all be dead and all Hand's witnessing would be lost, if not for her. She was the only one who reacted fast enough. She wasn't *wasted*, Dan. Her sacrifice mattered."

Torrence leaned back and closed his eyes. And tried to believe it.

Steinfeld went on. "Listen—she asked for something just before she went into surgery. It's kind of . . . perhaps a little grotesque. But it seemed important to her. She said if she didn't make it . . . "

Torrence opened his eyes, saw Steinfeld looking confused and embarrassed. "Well?"

"She wants you to have one of her ears."

"What?"

"With her love."

"Her ear?"

"Something about Van Gogh. And you missing an ear. She said you looked like an alley cat after a bad fight all the time, with that ear shot off. What I mean is—she wanted to have one of her ears transplanted onto you, to replace the one you lost. The visible ear. They'll mold it with surgery to make it symmetrical with your other one, use grafting and tissue-bonding agents to get it to, ah, take once it's implanted and . . . You see, it would actually be quite helpful. We're tired of looking at you. Frankly"—he smiled grimly—"we're sick of your face."

•••

New York City.

"Apparently, I got out of Paris in the nick of time," Smoke said. "They had some trouble there after I left. Just a day after."

"You are okay?" Alouette's image compressed and expanded like an accordion, yawed left and right, and then stabilized. Mexico had notoriously bad fone transmission.

"Yes, I'm all right. No one even shot at me. But some of the others . . . " He broke off, wondering how much to tell her. She was still just a kid. She'd stayed in the hospital with him after he'd been wounded in D.C.; she knew about the danger to him, and to the resistance. But maybe it was best he didn't tell her about the massacre at the train. "It's worked out all right," he finished lamely.

Smoke was in the relatively modest suite Badoit kept at the New York Fuji-Hilton, leaning back in an easy chair, looking out through the glass wall at the sunset breaking though the Manhattan skyline. In this smoggy sunset light, the city looked like a cluster of red-hot smokestacks. He was tired, jet-lagged, but was fighting sleep. He had too much to do. He hadn't even unpacked yet. He tapped a console to order espresso from a serving table beside the chair. A plastic cup emerged from a chute; a jet shpritzed hot black espresso.

"Are *you* okay, Alouette?"

"Yes. I miss you. Someone here, he wants to see you." She clucked her tongue, chirped in Merinese at someone off-camera. The crow hopped onto her arm, tilting its head with one of those birdlike movements that was like bad cartoon animation: not enough frames per second.

"Well, hello, Richard," Smoke said.

The crow shook itself and made a raucous noise in its throat. Smoke grinned. He remembered when the bird had come to him in Amsterdam on that ruined balcony. They'd both survived a great deal since then. The crow was a link to a Jack Smoke who seemed like a dream now—a homeless, half-mad babbler to birds.

"Are you going to come and see me?" Alouette said. Sounding as if she might cry.

Smoke said, "Soon! Um—as soon as I can. I'm about to start a media blitz, try and get Grid-Entry for . . . " He hesitated, unsure as to how secure this line was. Especially since this was Badoit's suite. Badoit had his share of enemies. He didn't want to even say Hand's name. "A campaign to explain to people what's really going on over there."

She nodded. "You have a guard?"

"Yes. A bodyguard." He sipped espresso. Not bad for out of a cred-vend machine. "He's doing push-ups in the next room."

It was a lie. He should have a bodyguard, and didn't. Bodyguards made him feel conspicuous, and that feeling was scarier to him than the risk of going without a bodyguard. And he didn't think the enemy knew he was here.

"Okay. You come and see me soon?"

"Yes. Are you studying hard?"

"I'm learning so much. You want me to show you some chip readouts? Ask me a math question. I can tell you what day of the week it'll be, any day of any Year—like April twelfth, the year 3503."

"Never mind." Thinking that the chips made people into a variation of autistic savants. "I believe you. I heard you did some trans-Atlantic work with our Jerome-X."

"They didn't have anybody in London that processed genetic cores as good as me."

"Do you know what it was you were processing?"

"No. Something about germs."

"Uh-huh." Good. He didn't want her to know what that was about if she didn't have to. She had enough to be afraid of. He sipped more espresso. The sun went down, the sunset drawing in on itself like a hermit crab into a shell; the adumbration of night made itself known over the city: lights became more brilliant, shone out of the city's deeper places like the reflective pupils of Rousseau jungle animals. More and more lights shone, more clearly electric now; each one marking a person, or people.

He wondered how close the SA was to using the racially selective virus. He wondered how many of those lights would be switched off when they used it.

It might be a dark city soon.

"On satellite news they said you had an acid rainstorm there," she said. Looking more excited than worried.

"Yes. It delayed the plane. A particularly acidic storm. That sort can be deadly for the homeless over a period of hours, I hear. The rains aren't so bad this year, though, as the last five years. The stuff's finally beginning to work its way out of the biosphere, I suppose. Global warming complicates things so it's hard to say for sure . . . "

"They waited too long to make the laws."

"Yes. For those kinds of laws, they always do. Have you got someone to play with there?"

"Julio plays with me. He showed me how to catch a scorpion in the desert."

"What! Isn't anybody *watching* the kids in that facility? Is Bettina there?"

"She's not back from London yet. Tomorrow."

"Tell her to call me. And don't go playing with scorpions in the desert, Alouette."

In any sense, he thought, *don't play with scorpions in the desert.*

• • •

PARIS.

Roseland wanted to hit Pasolini. He wanted to scream at her. She was so fucking sure of herself. And God, she loved being in charge.

They were in what had been a security monitoring room for the old Metro subway system. The portable, caged electric lights were hanging on the hook in the doorframe by their orange industrial extension cords, parasitically drawing on cables NR techs had exposed in the cracked concrete ceiling of the old station. Roseland and Pasolini and two other NR were sitting cross-legged on the floor across from the little computer screen they'd patched into the city's one working channel. Watching the Unity Party news on "unconfirmed reports of the capture of the terrorist Hard-Eyes." The Fascists, gloating about their omniscience. No one escaped the long arm of the Special Police. And so forth.

Fuck you, Roseland thought. *I got away. Torrence will too.*

"Pasolini—Torrence is important to us. He's like a linchpin. Ask Lespere if you don't believe me. I don't think you're considering this in an unbiased way. We've got to get him out."

"And lose how many people? It's foolish. He got himself caught—he walked into it like an imbecile."

"He was trying to liberate some prisoners—"

"He should never have come back to Paris so soon. It was stupid! He had a bandage on his head in that picture. I think he must have had some brain damage. Stupid. No, I will not risk everything to try to get a single man out of SA prison. Do you know how many political prisoners they have? They are all important to me. Just as important as Torrence. They have *children* in prison—"

"Torrence is valuable to the Resistance."

"Not that much."

"You're prejudiced against him. You were rivals. Think past your own biases, Pasolini."

"I said *no*. Steinfeld made the chain of command quite clear. If you don't like it—" She waved her stubby Russian cigarette imperiously. "—find another cause."

"This is more my cause than yours—"

"Oh, your precious Jewish heritage. The martyrs of the world."

"Don't give me any of your anti-Semitic shit, Pasolini, or I swear to God I'll put a . . . " He broke off, staring at the TV. "Oh, shit."

They saw Dan Torrence on TV. He was marched out across a prison compound. A doll-size Torrence on a little, snowy TV screen in the corner of a concrete floor—an image of someone they knew intimately, seeming like a stranger, like some video-abstracted figure from TV news. Treated like just another faceless terrorist caught out in the floodlights.

And marched into the featureless brown building. The camera, handheld and wobbling, following them into the gas chamber. Something more ignominious about gassing an enemy of the state—less heroic than putting him in front of a firing squad. The Second Alliance had chosen the means of execution thoughtfully.

"And what have they learned from him, with their extractors?" Pasolini was saying.

The commentator speaking in a low, serious voice, and in French, but Roseland knew the sort of thing being said. *The criminal shows no emotion as he is taken to his death; he has had every opportunity to express remorse, and has shunned those opportunities . . . There is, perhaps, even a sneer on his face as he is led into the chamber . . . But now we see the truth behind the mask as his cowardice shows, and he begins to panic . . .*

Roseland thinking: God. Dan looked awful. Sunken, sick. What have they done to him? Broken him with torture. Must have been dead for days, psychologically.

Roseland stood up, walked to the screen, and kicked it in.

Whop, the screen imploding. Glass tinkling to the floor. Sparks and a burning smell.

"*Idiota!*" Pasolini shouted.

Roseland turned and started for the door—then he stopped, staring at the monitors on the old Metro security console. The resistance techs had rigged the cameras to work again—and they showed armed men coming down the corridor, too far from the camera to see clearly.

"Intruders," Roseland said, grabbing his Royal Army surplus Enfield. He ran out onto the disused Metro platform, scuffing through the plaster dust that had fallen during the shellings, shouting at the guerrillas playing cards near the stairs. "Company coming!"

Pasolini was beside him, shouting orders. Roseland was rounding a corner, running up the ramp the intruders were coming down. Somewhere in the back of his head, Roseland as thinking, *Do it now. Take some of these assholes out, push 'em.* Not quite thinking, consciously, the rest of it:

Make them kill you.

Because seeing Torrence marched into the gas chamber had been one death too many. It was time to join his friends . . .

He was halfway up the ramp when the intruders rounded a corner. He raised his rifle.

And recognized Steinfeld. "Shit!" He stopped, staring. Steinfeld and four other guerrillas, including a Japanese guy. "I almost blew you assholes away! Why didn't you signal down?"

"We did," Steinfeld said. "No one acknowledged. Where's your communications man?"

"Uh—watching the execution on TV, I guess. We were distracted. Torrence . . . "

"I know." Steinfeld came closer, the others at his heels. Put a big hand on Roseland's shoulder. "It was terrible."

"*Steinfeld,*" the Japanese guy said, sounding exasperated.

Tall for a Japanese, probably a half-breed. Bandage on one ear. Something familiar about his voice.

The guy smiled. A familiar smile.

Roseland stared at him.

Blurting, "You sons of bitches."

Steinfeld laughed.

"You fuckheads."

The guerrillas chortled.

"You shit-eating *putzim!*"

Daniel Torrence embraced him.

Roseland didn't try to stop the tears. He laughed as they rolled down his cheeks. "You motherfucking assholes!"

He stood back, and looked at Torrence. "Who are you supposed to be?"

Torrence grinned. "John Ibishi. Son of a Japanese businessman and an American masseuse. Microcomputer consultant to several French companies."

Steinfeld put in, "The kind of foreigner the French Fascists leave alone—for the moment—because they need them for the economy."

Roseland admired the surgical craftsmanship displayed in Torrence's new face; the epicanthic folds on Torrence's eyes, the higher cheekbones, the faint tint to the skin. "Badoit hired the best."

"You guessed it."

Roseland looked at the other guerrillas. Started to ask where Bibisch was, and didn't. He could see it in the sag of Torrence's shoulders, hear it in the strain that went in his banter. Bibisch was dead.

But Torrence was alive. And free from the reprisals.

"Who the hell did they execute?"

"One of their own people," Torrence said. "A processing-center guard we captured. About my size, close to my looks. We wiped his brain with an extractor, planted a bunch of stuff that seemed to be garbled-up Torrence memories in him. Nothing useful to them. Just tantalizing stuff. Levassier gave him a nasty bash on the head—making it look like he was garbled from brain damage. From a gunshot wound. And whacked off an ear. Planted him where he'd be captured . . . " He shrugged. "Was an American, too. Some real asshole. Never knew what hit him."

"Must've been confused as all hell." Roseland tilted his head to one side, rubbed his chin, and looked Torrence over thoughtfully. "You know something, Dan—"

"Don't say it."

"Now that I look you over—"

"I'm warning you."

"You really—look—"

"Don't say it!"

"—much better as a Japanese."

"I told you not to say it."

"If only they'd made you Jewish."

•••

PARIS, A BOAT ON THE SEINE.

Watson sat in one of the rows of canvas chairs on the afterdeck of the big patrol boat, between Giessen and Rolff. Just behind the boy Jebediah.

You deal with one problem, Watson thought, and five more crop up to take its place. The Hydra of chaos. The sword of order, the Second Alliance's new order, must keep chopping at the proliferating heads of the Hydra of chaos—cutting short the vector of disorder they called subversion. That was just part of the job—a perpetual tidying-up.

Giessen wasn't making it any easier.

It was time to see if Giessen could be transferred out. "You're needed in America, Giessen," Watson said. "That's where Hand is hiding out, where this Barrabas traitor is, where the gadfly Jack Smoke is—if you'll excuse the pun, it's where he's blowing smoke up the asses of the American public. We need you there."

Giessen shook his head. "America is unfriendly to our people these days."

They were in the back of one of the new UPSS patrol boats, moving upstream on the Seine. It was a warm evening. There were silver and black clouds wreathing the horned moon, and streetlights glowing softly from the bridges; the natural and man-made light melting together in the silk fan of the boat's wake. The living smell of the river melded with the boat's methanol vapors.

Watson could have enjoyed it, as a tourist, under different circumstances. But he had to deal with Giessen and the Unity Party officials, and the blasted kid Jebediah.

"A little wine, Colonel Watson?" Bisse, the party's general vice secretary, was acting the steward. He was a stooped, vulpine man with bad teeth and a cheap government-issue suit—which he wore piously to show his dedication to the U.P. austerity program.

"No, thank you," Watson said.

Bisse's corroded smile didn't waver; he took his tray of plastic bubbly to Rolff, who accepted politely.

There were guards to either side of them, of course, in armor, standing at the rail, wearing night-seeing goggles; they were watching the stone walls along the banks of the river, and scanning the bridges. The U.P. had invited them along on this ceremonial boat ride at the last moment. Chances were small the Resistance had found out about the cruise. But it was a bit of a risk here. Put a man on that bridge coming up, say, crouching with a sniperscope behind the big ornately laurel-wreathed N for Napoleon . . .

Watson and most of the others were wearing bullet-proof vests. He would like to have worn a helmet too, but he needed to project a certain confident bravado today. And of course a helmet was no use in the event of a hit from a missile launcher. The bastards were just as likely to use a hand-held launcher as a rifle or a machine gun . . .

Giessen interrupted his thoughts. "This man Torrence was not my only assignment here, Herr Watson. I was under orders from Rick Crandall to do a general review of the security arrangements . . . "

"Were you indeed? This is the first I've heard of it." This was interesting. Why hadn't it occurred to him before? He could work up an animation of Crandall "ordering" Giessen to get out of his hair. "Crandall" could have Giessen arrested. But no—Giessen was useful. Would be quite useful—in some other arena. Mustn't allow himself to waste resources. He'd simply have Crandall order him out of the country.

Watson smiled in relief, knowing he'd soon be rid of Giessen. Who looked at him with suspicious puzzlement, wondering why Watson was so much at ease of a sudden.

Watson stretched, pleased with himself. Sometimes you didn't see the forest for the trees. Elegant simplicity. That was similar to the RSV. The Racially Selective Virus was elegant simplicity—would be, anyway, once it was deployed. So much simpler than the old Nazi Final Solution. And, should things go awry, so much more difficult to trace.

He wondered if he should move up the date for the viral dissemination. And he wondered whether people like Bisse, who likely had some Jewish blood in them, would blow a gasket if they knew about the virus. Oh, yes.

Watson noticed the boy Jebediah watching him. Was it his imagination, or was the little martinet glaring at him?

Watson shrugged. He turned to Giessen, feeling at ease enough to bait him now. "You've been crowing about capturing this Torrence, who essentially just blundered into our hands—but really, my dear fellow, it was you who took matters into his own hands to retrieve Steinfeld and Hand and this Barrabas creature—and then lost them."

"Barrabas—A man notably well named," said Jebediah with the casual pretentiousness only a boy could come out with. "His first name ought to be Judas. But maybe that name ought to be reserved for someone else."

What the devil did he mean by *that*? Watson decided to ignore him, going on, "And it was you, Herr Giessen, who lost them. By now they're probably in the States."

"I am not a specialist in military strategy," Giessen said stiffly. "That is Rolff's work. I located them—and pinpointed the place to stop them. I could not do everything. We had logistical problems getting enough troops there."

"I think that what we're hearing from you now, Giessen, is what the Americans call 'passing the buck,'" Watson said.

"Giessen's right," Rolff said. "It was my failure. I did not anticipate that the autotank was controlled by the NR. I can only say that one cannot anticipate everything."

"Well, you will have no military stresses on you when you work in the States, Giessen," Watson went on relentlessly.

"I could not possibly work in the United States, the way things are there now," Giessen said, prissily adjusting the set of his antique tweed jacket. He showed his irritation in the excessive briskness of the movement. "America is awash with liberalism now."

"Yes," Jebediah said, nodding, trying to be part of the adults' discussion. "Secular humanism."

Giessen said, "They've done away with the AntiViolence Laws—no more public executions, no more public beatings. Scrutinizing every court case with maddening slowness. In such an atmosphere one cannot work fruitfully with the police. One is on one's own."

"Liberalism? America?" Watson laughed. "Only on the surface. A little media oil to quiet the turbulent waters of the Grid, my dear fellow. So long as Mrs. Anna Bester is still president, so long as her administration is still in place, America will be functionally a conservative nation. And that means we will have sympathizers in high places. There are many of us still in the CIA, the NSA—you will have help, Giessen. I rely on you to find Hand and this Smoke before they poison the waters of the media—"

"I am taking orders from Rick Crandall," Giessen said. "He is my employer. We shall see what he says."

Giessen stood and walked forward, to join the U.P. officials in the pilot's cabin.

Yes, Watson thought with some satisfaction. *We will see what Rick Crandall says . . .*

• • •

They sat on the edge of the subway platform, Steinfeld and Torrence and Roseland, feet dangling over as if they sat on the bank of a dry underground river, waiting for a ghostly UPSS boat that would come only in fancy.

"And he's on the boat with Watson now?" Torrence asked.

Steinfeld nodded. Looking into the shadowy riverbed of the subway tracks, as if seeing the boat there. Seeing the boy Jebediah on it.

"How did you get the story to him?" Roseland asked.

"Through Cooper. When we found out that Cooper was Witcher's Second Alliance contact, we were able to use the same intermediary to inform Cooper. And Cooper saw the potential; he's scared of Watson and Rolff. We knew Cooper was in touch with Jebediah's father. Father told son, trying to decide what to do about it. The boy, being a boy, will probably confront Watson—some sort of interesting schism should develop."

"How did you get onto this thing in the first place?" Barrabas asked.

"Why do I feel as if I'm on one of those talk-show things," Steinfeld said, tugging his beard. "Well, now. We found out by accident that was not entirely accident. We had our video-propaganda man scanning all the SA output. Our man Kessler. He's very good. When we got the vid of Crandall talking about his new version of the Bible, Kessler noticed a few telltale signs. He realized that Crandall is now animated. Which might mean that the real Crandall is too paranoid to go to wherever it is he does his video recording—but we think it means he's dead. There've been changes out at Cloudy Peak Farm. No sign of him out there. None of his favorite foods ordered in . . . Lots of secretiveness . . . We think Watson may have, well, taken over by puppeting the image of Crandall. The one we see on the net is most definitely a phony."

"A computer animation? Maybe he was all along," Roseland said.

"No," Steinfeld said. "He was quite flesh and blood, I assure you. At one time."

"Now he's ascended to video heaven," Roseland said. He grinned. "TV-evangelist heaven."

Torrence looked at him. "Having fun? You don't snow me. What the fuck were you doing running up there by yourself when we came in? If you thought we were SA."

"Uh . . . I don't know."

"Bullshit. You were taking them on alone. Confronting what you thought was the SA. What was that all about?"

Roseland shrugged. Looked at them with raised eyebrows. "Uh . . . heroism?"

Steinfeld snorted. "The opposite. Cowardice. You wanted to be killed, man. And I understand how you feel." He put a big, clumsy hand on Roseland's shoulder. "But . . . if you desert us that way, you are a coward. You paid attention when they trained you. You are a good shot. You are motivated. We are undermanned. We need you, Roseland."

Roseland swallowed, hard. The lump didn't go away.

Across from him was an old subway billboard advertising a cocaine fizz. "COU-COU! La Boisson De Vos Jeune Petiller!" A swatch of light from behind them fell onto an old, dusty billboard photo of a young woman's sparkling eyes seeming to fizz the same color as the drink in her hand. She was a satire of being alive, he thought.

Seeing, in his mind's eye, her pretty blond head exploding the way Gabrielle's had. Gabrielle falling . . .

What was that old Rickenharp song lyric?

Something like: *Just bein' alive is the Original Sin . . . And steppin' outdoors is givin' in . . .*

But Steinfeld needed him. Torrence needed him. They needed him alive.

"Yeah," Roseland said. "Okay."

He looked down at the subway tracks, into the river of shadows.

• • •

The boat was heading downstream, back to the gendarme marina. The other guests had gone forward, were standing at the rail of the prow, praising the sleekness and speed and stability of the boat. But they held on to the rail for dear life, fighting queasiness as it went through choppy water set up by another boat.

Watson had decided he wanted a drink after all. He went down the stairs to the afterdeck, made himself a Scotch and water at the temporary bar set up there. He was alone on the deck but for the solitary silhouette of an SA bull, standing guard at the rail, staring out over the wake, his back to Watson.

And then suddenly the boy Jebediah was there. Coming from the bathroom below, Watson supposed.

Jebediah was staring up at Watson accusingly. "You didn't think God would let you get away with it, did you?" the boy asked smarmily.

"I beg your pardon?"

"I've been trying to talk to Rick Crandall for two months. He always took my calls before. He was always willing to see my father. Now he won't see anyone, won't take calls. And those videos of him. They're fake. I'll tell you what we think, my father and I. We think he's dead. We think you *killed* him."

Watson was unable to resist looking around to see if anyone was within earshot. The noise of the boat would prevent the guard from hearing. The others were well forward.

"It's true, isn't it," the boy said, with his childish self-righteousness. "I can see it in your face."

Watson took a deep breath. To think that once he had rather admired this pestilential little bugger. Well. This was a sticky wicket, as his father had been fond of saying. He sipped his Scotch, and then said, "Don't be absurd. I can arrange a meeting with you and Rick, if you like."

"You can?" The boy's eyes widened.

"Quite." Thinking: Can't even stall this thing. He mustn't so much as breathe a word of this to anyone. "And anyone else you've told. We'll bring them along, have Rick reassure them."

"It's just me and my dad. He didn't want me to tell anyone until he'd decided what to . . . " The boy's voice trailed off as he realized he'd said more than he should have.

Watson looked at his watch. They'd be at the marina in ten minutes. There wasn't much time. "Wait here. That guard is carrying the, ah, communications codebook for me. He always contacts Crandall for me, you see, it's a security, ah, method."

The boy nodded. One good thing, despite his precocity, he was still a boy. He'd swallow any technical-sounding spy gibberish you fed him.

Watson went to the guard at the taffrail. What was the man's name?

Stuart. Jock Stuart. Big, muscular, balding fellow with bristling red eyebrows. He'd been hinting about a transfer to England.

"Jock," Watson said. "Open your helmet."

Stu moved the curved mirror of the helmet aside, looked at Watson. "Jock—I can fiddle you a posting in England, anywhere you like, but there's something messy you've got to do for me. Not only will you get the posting you want—you'll get a promotion. And even a nice bit of cash. This little thing you've got to do, you've got to do very discreetly.

It's a sort of purge, in a small way. Something only you and I will know about . . . "

Jock nodded. "Very good, sir. How can I be of service?"

A minute later, Watson returned to the boy, waiting at the bottom of the stairs. "Hold on here a moment, Jock will explain the top-secret procedure for seeing Rick. Maximum security these days, you see."

The boy did a poor job of hiding his skepticism. "But why the video animation . . . "

"It was a security procedure. Rick will explain. Actually—best you come forward with me a minute. See if we have time to arrange this now."

The boy frowned, not quite believing Watson, but following him up the ladder. They went to the small crowd at the forward rail. Wind and fine spray on their faces. The others greeted them. Clearly saw Watson arriving with the boy. Watson looked around as if gauging the boat's whereabouts, then nodded to the boy, pointed his chin aft.

Puzzled, the boy shrugged and returned to the aft deck. Alone.

Right, Watson thought, *you wanted to see Rick, boy, you're going to see him.*

No one but Watson, who was listening for it, heard the faint sound of a cry, and then a splash coming from the rear of the boat. The others were a little tipsy, and busy drinking.

All but Giessen, who was watching Watson closely.

• 12 •

LONDON.

The loading dock at the lab was a drafty place. It was a chilly, damp evening, an unseasonal mockery of summer, and Cooper wanted badly to be indoors. He didn't take to cold well. He fantasized again about moving to some place warm. Gibraltar, say. Only, in a warm clime the hot sun was dangerous for an albino. There was always something wrong with any place he chose to live.

Where was the sodding bastard who was bringing his supply?

Cooper hugged himself, glaring at the bugs, bugs dusty white as an albino, banging themselves against the single two-hundred-watt bulb overhead. The insta-platform was barren; the alleyway was empty but for a few bits of gravel. There was nothing to look at. One could only wait, growing more impatient with each passing second.

He wished he could have brought his coat, but they'd have noticed that in the lab.

For the fifth time in five minutes, he thought of getting past the checkpoint at the other end of the alley by sneaking out with his supplier, hide in the back of his truck. But he was frightened to try it. Frightened of the SA, frightened of what the supplier might do later. Might blackmail him, hold him hostage or something. Some sort of criminal drug dealer, after all. Capable of anything, he supposed.

Soon the Security chief would check up on him and notice he was not in the building.

Cooper tried to think of his projects—of his triumphs on two fronts.

Experiments in crowd control through activation of socio-biological triggers; development of the primary Racially Selective Virus. And then there were the "puppies."

He was a bloody Renaissance man, a Da Vinci, is what he was, with these interdisciplinary triumphs, and no one appreciated it! Of course, he was only a partner on the Viral Program and the development of the subhuman work force, not too terribly hands-on. But he'd helped conceive it, helped guide it, and he was head of department. They were his projects too.

But not only was he underappreciated, he was in effect incarcerated. Had been under house arrest in the lab living quarters for weeks. It was enough to drive a man dotty.

They might kill him, because of the Barrabas thing, if he became less than vital to their plans . . .

And suppose they found out that he'd been selling some of the earlier viral gen-codes through the supplier? God only knew who was buying them on the other end. Some wog terrorist, he supposed. Probably use them on another faction, kill more of their own people, do everyone a spot of good.

It was not as if he'd sold the calibrations for the Racially Selective Virus. No, indeed. That was sacred, don't you know. He'd sold them a failure, really. A virus that was short-lived but non-racially selective. A throwaway.

But would Rolff appreciate that? No. Would they be furious with him, perhaps punish him dreadfully, if they found out he'd sold the S1-L? Yes. Dreadfully, don't you know.

He began to pace, whining faintly to himself to relieve the tension, the chill. The frustration.

He needed to get *off*. It was that simple. He needed to get out of himself. To have the orgasm of the nervous system that would get him free for a while. Open the spillway, let the pressure drop.

But where was the supplier?

The whir of the electric fence opening, down the alley. Headlight beams pooling on tarmac. The lights swinging toward him. Relief and exhilaration.

The supplier left the panel truck's headlights on, its electric motor humming. He got out of the car . . .

Who the bloody hell?

Not the usual chap. Not the little cockney fellow this time. Damn damn damn. Someone delivering lab supplies, he supposed—and *only* lab supplies.

Someone big as a house. Big, bulky, dark silhouette behind the headlight glare. "Dr. Cooper, I presume." A husky woman's voice, with an American accent. Southern States, he thought.

She came into the light. An enormous black woman. Good God! Why had the guards let her through?

But of course they were used to seeing Negroes in service jobs. She was supposed to be delivering chemicals for the lab. Same truck as usual.

"Yes . . . ?" he said tentatively.

"I got yo' supplies. You know? Sarky couldn't make it. Sent me over. I work wid him. Know what I mean? De whole deal."

She was carrying Sarky's little black belt pouch in her hand. Sarky usually wore it, but this woman would have a bit of a struggle getting it around a leg, let alone her middle.

She climbed the insta-steps with some effort, grunting and cursing under her breath. "Oughta make you come down to me," she muttered. But she came up, and simply handed him the belt with his drugs on it. "It's all dere. Some lab supplies in de truck too, natcherly, make it look good."

He stared at her. An American? A black? A woman? He took a nervous step back from her. "What's happened to Sarky?"

"Got inna tussle, couldn't make it. I'm doin' de deal for him, is all. It's the righteous shit, man, jus' de same zalways."

His heart was banging in his chest. This felt wrong. But he wanted to get off ever so badly. And this woman couldn't be a revolutionary agent, or a police agent. She was too odd to fit the profile. The New Resistance used the inferior races for their cannon fodder, he was quite sure, but never, he assumed, in so sensitive a position as an undercover agent of some kind. They didn't have the brains to pull it off.

Fingers shaking, he zippered the canvas pouch open, found the little bottle and the balancer-charging unit. Without the one-shot unit, the bottle was useless—he couldn't get another charge for his balancer without leaving here. And Security was supposed to monitor his balancer, officially, while he was under house arrest. And they wouldn't let him get really high.

Addictive that way, they said. Made you prone to unsound decisions, they said.

Sod 'em. He gave her the cred number for this week, for the floating account he'd set up for this sort of thing, and she turned and waddled away, making an inordinate amount of noise. She began to unload a few cardboard boxes from the back of the truck, for the sake of appearances.

"Just leave them on the dock," he said, hurrying to the door. "I'll get them later."

He went eagerly into the building, directly to the men's restroom and locked himself in. With fingers that worked all on their own, so exactingly and quickly they were almost a blur, he charged the balancer on his thigh.

Oh, yes. There it was. Yes. His friend was back. Yes, yes, there it was, that's it, that was . . .

Was something else. Something different.

There was something else in with the euphoric. Something . . . What was it? Some minor impurity. It would pass.

But it made him restless. Normally he got off in the bathroom, stayed there for the rush. But it seemed so cramped now, cramped like his life under this bloody house arrest. Trapped in the lab like one of his own lab mice. Suddenly he was claustrophobic. Needed badly to get *out*.

Cooper found himself stalking down the hall, his pants not even done up properly. Not caring, feeling a tidal push behind him, a growing swell of inchoate rage.

How dare they treat him like this. A Da Vinci, a Newton, a Mendel. A genius. Treat him like a half-breed, like some pathetic wog who'd cocked things up.

He'd straighten them out. Knew just the thing.

He had the presence of mind to put on the protective helmet before he smashed the vial containing the universal-kill virus in the coffee room, where the others were on their break. Had the pleasure of watching the virus take effect immediately—that immediacy was his own addition to the molecular design—watching them writhe on the floor, screaming.

Spitting blood. Dying.

But then realized he hadn't done up the protective helmet properly, either.

Oh, bugger.

* * *

PARIS, THE OLD METRO STATION.

"I shot this in the tunnels," Roseland said.

He held up what looked like a smashed electronic clock. Aluminum and silicon and glass and a lot of micromotor parts: a machine the size of a small bird, lying in the palm of his hand.

"It's a bird's eye," Steinfeld said. "Where did you spot it?"

Torrence walked up then, into the monitoring office, looking around. "Anyone seen Pasolini? She's late for her watch. Not like her. "

Steinfeld was distracted by the bird's eye. "Pasolini? No. Look at this, Dan. Roseland shot it like a quail."

"That was the shot I heard? I thought it was another of those fucking pipes exploding. Yeah, that's a bird's eye. Shit. Maybe we should just get the hell out of here now. Did it see you first?"

Roseland shook his head. "It was a quarter mile down the tunnel, on the other side of the barricade. I was on watch, thought I heard something, so I looked through the barricade and saw it looking around. Shot it from behind. They'll figure it just ran into a wall or something. They must lose a lot of them, they break down all the time."

"That barricade's well camouflaged," Steinfeld said, nodding. "Looks like shelling debris."

"But they're getting close," Roseland said.

"A miss by an inch's as good as a mile," Torrence said. "Where's Pasolini?"

"I really don't know," Steinfeld said. "We'll probably have to move again soon anyway. Things are in place, events in motion. Latest is, our good Dr. Cooper's dead."

"Is he?" Torrence smiled. Something you didn't often see.

"Bettina got onto his supplier. Decided she'd be the one to give him the stuff, figured he'd never believe someone like her was an agent. Used an OD of the Army's aggression drug. He killed a bunch of 'em with his own virus. The S1-L. Non-racially selective. We were counting on them to shoot him, but it didn't happen that way. Accidently exposed himself to the virus."

"Dead is dead," Torrence observed.

"Not only Cooper, but half a dozen other SA researchers. Plus three SA Security men."

"Should put a crimp in their racist-virus project."

"One hopes."

"Maybe Smoke'll come through in time," Torrence said.

Absently, Torrence put a hand up to touch his new ear. Unless you looked close, it was symmetrical with the other. The skin color was a little different, but only a little. Torrence caressed it once, with the tip of his index finger.

Roseland watched in morbid fascination. Shuddered. *Weird keepsake to have.*

Steinfeld glanced at the calendar on his watch. "I only wish we knew how much RSV they have in storage. In the meantime, at least, they're going to have to put a new scientific team together, to work out the vectoring."

"It's just a delay," Roseland said lugubriously. "It's coming."

"Where's Pasolini?" Torrence asked again.

The other two turned to look at him. And then looked around.

Where was she?

• • •

FIRSTEP, THE SPACE COLONY.

There were three women in Witcher's little Colony apartment, and they were all beautiful, and all in various states of undress.

It was a little crowded, certainly, a little claustrophobic for his taste. He didn't like being pushed in so close to them. Not this much. But then, if you have to be stuck in a small apartment with three people, Marion, Jeanne, and Aria were the sweetest kind of discomfort.

Administrative assistants, that's what he'd called them when he'd filled out the forms to bring them to FirStep. They'd arrived a long, lonely week after he'd settled in here.

He felt so much safer now.

Speaking of filling out forms, Aria filled out hers marvelously, he thought, in that off-white negligee. It had been a good choice. Deliberately one size too small for her. She was oiling her Walther, the gun-cleaning kit open beside her. The strong smell of its solvents annoyed him in the close quarters, but it was important, today, that the gun be ready.

It had been, he reflected, more difficult getting permission to bring the girls in than it was smuggling the guns in. The colony people had strange priorities. Well, he supposed, perhaps it made sense. Guns don't use up air or food or water.

Jeanne was in the shower. He considered going in, scrubbing her with the brush. No, she was moody this morning, best leave her alone.

And Marion. Sitting cross-legged in a corner, in her tight black neoprene skirt, neoprene bikini top with brutal uplift. Watching a minimono show on video. "Whatabuncha assholes, these minimono dwips," she said. Clicking her black nails against the barrel of her 9mm H & K. But she didn't turn the console off. "You know what I heard, I heard the minimonos wanta come here, think the Colony's their intended homeland. Like the Rastas were with Ethiopia. They think they're destined to live on the Space Colony, like, but they can't get permission to come here because this Claire bitch, like, thinks they're half crazy or something. Whud she say . . . 'psychologically inappropriate.' Fuck, that ain't half. I mean, Gridfriend, gimme a break, they're fucking out of their weasely little minds." Marion pretending to play a guitar solo on her submachine gun; like the gun was an air guitar. "Pisses me off," she said, "they won't let me smoke here. Couldn't I sneak one, Dad?"

Witcher said, "Uh-uh. They have smoke detectors."

"But we're locked in here anyway. Under siege, like."

"I was referring to even the possibility of your smoking it in the hall. You know I don't tolerate smoking in the house with me."

"In the bathroom? Please, Dad? When Jeanne gets out?"

"No. Take another pill if you need nicotine. Get a patch."

"Not satisfying that way."

She was pouting now. He liked seeing her pout. It was sexy.

He imagined taking her, then. Her and her pout. Actually, really fucking her. He almost got a hard-on thinking about it. The excitement was like a vibrating piano wire in him.

"I'm thinking about this plan, this locking ourselves in here," Aria said. "I don't like it. I want to go to the pool, and go jogging."

"It's just for a few hours, till things cool off," Witcher told her. "They want to arrest me. It's that simple. In a few hours things will be different. It will be a *fait accompli*, and they'll see the error of their ways, and we'll negotiate with them."

"There's just the three of us, against all their people. And that Claire woman doesn't approve of us. How you keep us. She was here, she saw us. She acted very superior. I don't know if she's going to negotiate much."

"Oh, she will."

He wondered if he should tell them about the strategy. The purging. No. Unknowable, how they might react. They would have relatives on Earth.

"Don't worry about it."

Jeanne came out of the bathroom, nude except for the towel on her hair, bringing a scent of soap and scrubbed skin with her.

Witcher added, "Why don't you go take a shower, Aria? You'll feel better."

She sighed. On the Colony, he made them all shower two or three times a day. Not so he could watch, but because he liked them clean in this crowding. Completely clean. She went to the bathroom, muttering in Scandinavian.

"And douche while you're in there!" he called after her.

Thinking that he might have them play with one another, while he was waiting to see if the Colony would break down his door.

• • •

PARIS, THE HÔTEL DE VILLE.

Watson felt a little better, seeing his new suite of rooms. It wasn't a proper suite at the moment, of course, since most of the furniture had been moved against the walls to allow for the cardboard boxes the movers had left in the middle of the sitting room. They hadn't even bothered to put the boxes marked "bedroom" in the bedroom, blast them. Frog bastards.

But God, what a beautiful room. He had developed a taste for ornate French decor lately. This one was 1890s, Belle Époque he supposed, ornate almost to a fault and yet lovingly composed, lovingly preserved. Perhaps he ought to purchase some paintings for that wall, though, it looked a little—

"Colonel Watson?"

Giessen. Always breaking in on him. "Yes?"

The natty little German was standing in the doorway. With him were two SA guards.

"It should be obvious, Giessen, that I'm quite busy. Is it important?" He was sorry he hadn't yet made up the video-animated "message" from Crandall informing Giessen of his new posting. Shouldn't have put it off till the evening. But he'd been eager to get into his more spacious flat.

"It is, *ja,* quite important," Giessen said. Adding, "Herr Watson." Knowing it irritated Watson. "We found the boy's body in the river this morning. Bruises on his neck. From a man's hand. Apparently he'd been strangled, although not quite successfully, before being dropped in the Seine."

"Indeed." Stuart! That bloody idiot. Supposed to make it took as if the boy fell in by accident. Another cock-up.

"So I decided to have another talk with the guard who was the last one to see the boy. A Sergeant Stuart. I became convinced Stuart was lying—so we had him extracted."

"What! No one is to use an extractor without my authorization!"

"Or Rolff's." Giessen smiled.

Rolff! The bastard had betrayed him. Or possibly Giessen had intimidated him into it. The bloody fool should have realized that if Watson went down, Rolff, his co-conspirator, went down with him.

"And the extractor told us some very interesting things," Giessen said, insufferably smug. A very faint smile on his liverish lips. "That you ordered the boy killed. That you asked Stuart to do it. And the boy tried to tell Stuart something, to talk him out of it. He didn't get out much. Enough. Something about Crandall being dead. Video animation. That would explain why Crandall always seemed to take up your case when things were not going your way . . . "

Watson felt the warmth and comfort of the room recede from him, like an elevator failing down a shaft. "Disinformation," he sputtered. "NR disinformation. Planted in Stuart, in the boy . . . "

"No. We've had the Crandall video decrypted. They're animations. Is he dead?"

"Certainly not. He—he wanted animations. Security reasons. Can't reveal."

"Oh, yes? Very improbable. I've spoken to the Inner Circle. You are to be detained pending an investigation. Please come along."

Watson pointed at the guards, spoke in his most authoritative tone. "This man is attempting a coup. Drag him out of here and lock him up."

They didn't respond. They walked across the room, stepping around the boxes, but working their way implacably to him. Giessen had chosen men loyal to him.

The mirror-visored helmets reflected his face as they came toward him. He saw himself, doubly reflected. Shaking, angry.

Saw his own image get closer and bigger. And saw the expression on his face change as they took him by the wrists.

Change from anger to fear.

• • •

FirStep: the Space Colony.

Russ Parker blurted the whole thing as he rushed through the hatch of Claire's office, barely clearing the low doorframe with his head as he came in. "He's frozen the doors! He brought one of those autohacker programs with him, booted it into the door control. They're locked but good. Permanently. Shutting off the power wouldn't help."

Stoner, sitting on the only other chair in the little office, was staring at the monitor that showed Witcher's apartment door. Two Colony Security guards were there, working at it with tools. "How long will it take them to get through?"

Claire, sitting at her desk nursing a cup of cold coffee, said, "Two hours. It's pretty well reinforced. Could take even longer, in fact. We can't blast through—he's too near the outer hull. Too much risk we'd rupture the Colony. Anyway, he's got bodyguards in there. Those women—with their guns. They could hold off our people indefinitely from in there."

The fone on Claire's desk chimed. Witcher smiled out of the little monitor. "Hello, all," he said. "And how are we today? One big happy family?"

Claire switched on the fone's cam so Witcher could see her. "We've got the full story now, Witcher," she said, trying to control the tone of her voice. Best not to provoke this paranoid. "We know about the S1-L and the timetable. What we don't know is why. You want to tell me about it?"

"Is this some sort of delaying tactic till they can break through the door? They've got a long way to go. You can tell them to stop, though. First of all—I'm well protected here." He gestured, and the big busty blonde stepped into the shot, brandishing an autopistol.

God, Claire thought, what an arrested adolescent this old man is. Keeping walking-talking soft-core porn foldouts around him. Barbie-on-Her-Honeymoon dolls with GI Joe accessories. Too much James Bond in his youth. Why hadn't she realized before how sick he was? Psychopaths are clever. That's why.

"Second," Witcher went on, "don't try it, because if you do, I'll transmit the signal ahead of time, if anyone interferes with me here. I prefer to time things my way, to get all my people under cover, but if I have to . . . " He shrugged. "And don't think about interfering with my transmitter. I have a monitor on it for spacecraft. If any of your EVA pods come near it, I'll know. I'll transmit." He clapped his hands together once. "You've got thirty seconds to tell them to stop." He kept smiling, pleasant as a kiddy-show host.

Claire hesitated, then said, "Hold on." She cut to another line, called the guards, gave the order and quickly came back to Witcher.

"It sounds as if they've stopped," he said.

"They have. So now it's not a delaying tactic, you can tell us what the fuck you think you're doing."

He looked at her with a little surprise. "Hanging out with those streetfighters affected your speech mannerisms. Well, yes, I'll tell you. I was planning to tell you, a little later, anyway. I was going to warn the resistance people to take refuge just before it all went down. Minutes before."

"Killing how many others?" she asked hoarsely.

"With luck, ninety percent of the population of the world, Claire. Across racial boundaries. Across the spectrum. The S1-L virus is not racially selective. And I'm no racist. I will, in fact, be *killing* most of the racists. I'm having the canisters placed that way. This will eliminate the Second Alliance. And that's just the beginning. We'll have a chance to make the world a just place to live, for the first time."

"Yeah," Russ muttered, "you're real morally uplifting."

Claire gestured at Russ for silence. She bent closer to the fone-cam. "Go on." Thinking that if she understood his logic, maybe she could talk him out of it.

Witcher sipped a mineral water reflectively, and then said, "Why do you suppose racism arises? Why conflicts of any kind, really. It's all instinct. Sociobiological necessity. Xenophobia coming out of territoriality responses. Ultimately, from a territory that's overburdened by population, strain on its resources. Smoke believes much the same thing."

"Up to a point, maybe."

"But, you are implying, he would never advocate mass extermination for population control. Ah, now. True. It's an ugly thing for me to do. It will create, in fact, major health problems on Earth due to all those decomposing bodies. For a while. But I'll be up here, and most of the survivors will manage to protect themselves. The virus will die out. The bodies will be dealt with. The population of the Earth will be a tiny fraction of what it was—and suddenly, for the first time, *Utopia will be possible, Claire.*" Real fervor was coming into his voice now. "We've had the technology for Utopia for years—but population stresses made that technology more a disadvantage than an asset. Wipe out most of the population, and suddenly everything becomes manageable. We can let most of the planet revert to its healthy, natural state. We can afford to end pollution. We can organize a world government at last—in this situation, it would be inevitable. Think of it! One world! My company'll be ready. My trained security people. We'll take control. Slowly we'll bring the population back up—but only a bit, to manageable levels. Most of the people in the world, Claire, are suffering—they are better off dead. We have to think of those who will come: they'll live in a world without racism—I'll outlaw even the faintest tinge of racism! A world without organized religion! I'll outlaw that, too! A world without crime, because there'll be abundance. A world without pollution. Without urban sprawl, or suburban blight. All those damnable housing projects. *Gone,* all of it. Look at that side of it. I'll restructure things for *real* social justice. No more slums. An end to exploiting the Third World."

"Christ," Stoner said. "A liberal's version of fascism."

"It's *order,* is what it is, order and peace. No armies when I'm done," Witcher went on smoothly. "No more fighting. No wars! Not one more war!"

"Not one more *word,*" Russ interrupted. "I can't handle one more word of this crap. This is some kind of special blasphemy against God. It's as bad as the Second Alliance and as bad as Hitler."

Claire nodded. Numb with disbelief. "You've been planning this all along, Percy?"

"No. I expected the NR would be a vehicle to overthrow the competition. Rid me of the other ones who want to unify the planet—enslaving it is their way of unifying it. I thought I'd see my chance at some point. And then one of my people made contact with Dr. Cooper, and after our London computer break-in cued me on their viral experimentation . . . Well, the

S1-L has a short life. The other bioagents are too unpredictable, too long-lived. And of course, I didn't want the racially selective one."

Claire thought: *All* males get crazy when they get powerful enough. "You've got agents who're going to release this stuff on your signal—all over the planet?"

"Not precisely," Witcher said, glancing away.

"What it is, most of them are in two central locations, where the labs are," Stoner said. "They're supposed to pick up the stuff, spread out from there. Most of 'em don't know what they're going to release."

Stoner was at another fone, watching the chronometer digitalizing the seconds and minutes in the corner of the screen. A text message flashed onto the screen then. Something he'd been waiting for, Claire thought, judging from his expression.

"That's it. It's all over." Stoner turned to the other fone. "It's already over with, 'Dr. Strangelove.' We traced your operation, busted your labs. I hipped some old acquaintances in the NSA to it. You can transmit all you want. We've got your people. And your viruses."

Claire sagged with relief.

Stoner went on, "It was too fucking ludicrous to work."

"You people . . . " Witcher shook his head, tears in his eyes. Gaping. "You have no perspective. Well, I'm cutting the NR off. Not one penny more, not one page of intelligence more."

"We don't need you, it turns out," Claire said. "We've found . . . another backer."

"Have you." His voice shrill. Breaking as he went on, "Have you now. The New Resistance was practically my creation. It should be under my guidance. And if it's not, it'll go completely wrong. It seems it already has! Fine. We'll see how much credibility the NR has after tonight. Stoner, you didn't get all the agents there were to get. There was one who *was already deployed*. Already has the canister at ready. She'll be at the receiver in about two hours. I'm going to signal her. I'm going to tell her: *Use it!*"

"Who is it, Witcher?" Russ asked. "Where are they?"

"Oh, she's ostensibly an NR agent," Witcher said. "I have an arrangement with her. To release the virus in a certain population center. She doesn't know the whole of my strategy." He wiped his eyes with a sleeve. Gave a cavalier smile. Had his aplomb back. "I'll make a start and I'll destroy you people. And then I'll start over."

"Where's the virus?" Russ asked.

Witcher chuckled.

That kiddy-show-host smile came back.

And then he switched off the fone.

• 13 •

Mexico.

Smoke was there. Jerome was there. Bettina was there. Kessler was there. Richard the crow was there.

Kessler was a medium-tall, round-faced man with short black hair, streaked blue-white to signify his work as a video tech. Big brown eyes, rather girlish mouth. Looked soft, Smoke thought, but he was sharp and tough as nails. He wore, like Smoke and Barrabas, feather-light white peon pajamas, and sandals. Jerome wore jeans, no shirt, mirror sunglasses.

The crow was on Smoke's shoulder, Jerome was sitting across the terrace table from Smoke, Kessler on one side of Jerome, Bettina on the other. All of them on the sun-baked, stone-flagged terrace outside the NR's chip-training installation. It was only eleven in the morning, but the day was bright and already hot; the big table umbrella didn't make enough shade. The tall glasses of iced tea they were drinking weren't cooling enough. Especially for Bettina, who wore a ghastly little orange-print housedress and thongs. She got up and moved gelatinously to the other terrace table, dragged it over, making it squeal across the stone, so its umbrella blocked the sun at her back.

She heaved herself back into the creaking wrought-iron chair and, wiping sweat from her face with a dish towel, said, "Where Patrick and Jo Ann at?"

"Here they are," Smoke said, nodding toward the glass sliding doors that let onto the terrace.

Carrying ice teas, Barrabas and Jo Ann came blinking out into the sunlight; pulled chairs up from the other table and hunched beside Smoke in the shade.

"It's hot out here," Jo Ann said, "but it's worse indoors." She looked out at the desert stretching away brown and purple to her right. "Smells good. Smells like sage. What's that noise?"

"Cicada, or something like it," Smoke said.

"You nature boys done with de vague entomology, let's get on wid dis shit," Bettina said. "I wanna get in de wading pool. Alouette's filling it up for me 'n' her."

"Won't be room for her in it," Jerome said.

She took a swipe at him; he was prepared, and ducked it.

"I get yo' skinny white ass later," she said. She turned to Smoke. "Let's talk and get it over wid."

"Things are serious now," Smoke said. "Find some patience, Bettina."

"Things always serious. Serious for years now."

"It's come to a head," said Smoke. He sipped his tea, his ice clinking, looking at the horizon. A distant jet doodled a curly contrail on the blue-white sky. He went on, "It's all timing, you see. And the timing has to be decided *now.*"

Jerome said, "I think you oughta just go ahead, let Hand spill the beans, let Barrabas witness for us, hit 'em with a frontal attack. Now. Their computers are fucked up, their bosses are arresting each other, fighting for top control. We ain't sure what the timetable with the RSV is. Why don't you just go for it?"

"Because of certain military factors. And because of the Leng Entelechy."

Jerome groaned. "We're not really going to try that, are we? You'll have us wearing crystals for good vibes next."

Bettina ducked her head in a way peculiar to her that signified bafflement. "The Leng *what*-uh-hicky?"

"Don't play dumb just because you're not in a mood to work today, Bettina," Smoke snapped. Thinking: *The heat's making us all irritable.* "The word is 'entelechy.' It means fulfillment of potential—a system coming to a fulfillment that something in it is . . . is reaching for."

"A term from vitalism, isn't it?" Kessler asked.

"Yes. But in this case we're interested in the entelechy of the collective psychic field."

"The collective psychic field?" Kessler smiled, chuckling urbanely. "You mean the one which probably doesn't exist?"

Jo Ann said, "This Leng guy—is he the Shrimp Man?"

"I doubt he'd appreciate that nickname, but yes. Dioxin birth defects, born without arms and legs. Body shaped sort of like a shrimp. Gets around in a very nice exoskeletal prosthesis. One of the best microbiologists around. Combined Earth science with microbiology and physics. Nobel prize in 2016."

"Nobel prize doesn't mean he couldn't have a crank idea," Kessler said.

"You work hard on being cynical, Mr. Kessler?" Jo Ann said.

"I just think that 'supernatural' phenomena is psychological, not psychic," Kessler said. "It's a question of conditioning input, shared psycho-programming symbols, myth-symbol projection, that sort of thing."

"I don't think this *is* a supernatural phenomenon," Smoke said. He reached up and scratched under the crow's beak. It bit his finger, but only playfully. Then cocked its head as something rustled in the sere grass and stony ground beside the patio. Smoke went on, "Leng doesn't regard it as supernatural. He regards it as a weak bioelectric field uniting all life on Earth. He got interested in it as a young man when he read about a study done in the 1980s. The study found that under certain circumstances, if you taught a trick to a group of rats . . . "

"Come on, man," Bettina interrupted, swabbing her forehead and jowls, "I don' have time for scientific studies about no damn *rats*. Get to de fucking point."

Smoke went on as if he hadn't heard her. "—then other rats who *weren't around* suddenly knew the trick too . . . as if it had simply been in the air. The effect was more pronounced when there was a greater conductivity in the air. And among people we have the phenomenon of an 'idea being in the air'—sometimes it's because of parallel stimulus, social reasons, but other times it happens with disparate cultures at opposite ends of the Earth who had no contact at all. Simultaneously. What it all boils down to—"

"Yeah, boil it down before I boil down," Bettina snapped.

"—is a body of evidence that indicates there's a collective unconscious mind of some sort linking people."

"Well, fuck," she said, "who don't know *that*?"

Jerome nodded. "I've felt it at gigs."

Smoke nodded. "Rickenharp used to talk about that. The field is weak and it's subject to a variety of stresses, but it's there. Leng found a way to sense it and measure it and predict its cycle of intensity. Its impulses travel around the world in waves. Like a big psychic tsunami. Subtle, but affecting the brain of every human on the planet—on some level." He saw Bettina's impatience about to erupt, and he added hastily, "We can use this stuff ourself, perhaps, yes, Bettina. I'm coming to it. It might be possible to introduce electromagnetically encoded information into the Group Mind Wave at certain times—and use it to communicate an insight to everyone on the planet. Just a little psychic nudge, you see. Through the Plateau. Leng has the technique—there's a specific frequency . . . "

Kessler turned Smoke a pained and puzzled look. "You're going to delay our move just to wait for the optimum time for this . . . this entelechy? What about the virus? You're going to risk the life of every person of color on the planet just to test your theory?"

Smoke shook his head. "No. We're waiting for Torrence and Steinfeld to line up their strikes. They're working things out with Badoit, getting some gear together for the EMP action."

"The what?" Jerome said.

"Electromagnetic pulse. They want to completely pull the plug on Second Alliance finances so they can't finance counter-propaganda, can't pay their people, whole SPOES falls apart."

"Electromagnetic pulse. I was afraid that's what you meant," Jerome grimaced. "Don't be doing that shit around *me*. Or around anyone else with a chip implant." He tapped his head. "Fuck 'em up."

"The military operations are supposed to get us some hard evidence about the virus, to back up Jo Ann here," Smoke said.

Kessler was shaking his head. "No. You're gambling they won't use the thing before you get this all set up. You *can't* gamble that way. We should announce the thing now, start raising people's consciousness about it, do our best with what we have. Now."

"De man's right!" Bettina burst out. "You ain't gambling wid you own motherfucking race, Smoke! It's wid mine! And a whole lot of de rest of de world!"

"We don't think we're gambling. We know a bit about the Racially Selective Virus. We know it's isolated now in one lab and one storage facility. Both in London. It's not the sort of thing they can simply release in any city and let it do its work. Temperature conditions have to be optimal. Plus they have to have multiple simultaneous releases—the virus dies out fast. They designed it that way so it would be less likely to mutate. And they're worried that it might not be as selective as they think—one gene wrong in your DNA and it could kill you. They're not all certain about their own ancestors. How much Jewish blood is enough to make the pathogen kill you? They've got those technical problems. I heard they thought they had that under control, but they're still testing. It's going to take them a while to set this up—"

"That's what your intelligence tells you. Your Badoit, your NR espionage," Kessler said. Shaking his head. "That's basically hearsay. You're just gambling that it's true. I say don't gamble."

"I think he's right too, Smoke," Jerome said.

Barrabas spoke for the first time. "The thing's got to be stopped. People should be told with all speed. Maybe there's some sort of preventive antiviral measures . . . "

"If it comes to that. We're watching them. We have a man on the inside. We'll know if they start to move."

"You *hope* you'll know," Kessler said. "You hope you know about where they're storing the stuff. You'd better be right. He stood up and walked away from the table, into the building.

Bettina drank the rest of her tea and most of Jerome's, then began crunching up the ice in her teeth. All the time eyeing Smoke balefully.

"Man's right," she said. Crunch, crunch. "You gambling."

"It would be gambling to do things precipitously," Smoke said. "Gambling that it'd work best that way. We don't think it would."

In the silence that followed, something rustled in the dry grass again.

"You know what, Smoke," Jerome said finally, "when you were talking about the entelechy, you sounded like a religious convert, man. It's something you'd like to believe in. Maybe some connection to God. Makes you feet less lonely. That's cool. But maybe it's slanting the way you're planning things."

"It isn't just me," Smoke said. Feeling odd. Wondering if Jerome was right. "It's Torrence and Steinfeld and Badoit. Witcher approved it. Steinfeld and Badoit . . . " He paused, allowing himself to look a little hurt. " . . . are threatened by the virus, too. Their races."

"Look, man," Bettina said, "I don't mean to say you don' give a fuck about black people, but let's face it—"

"My race is threatened by this thing," Smoke said. "The human race. Homo sapiens. That's my race, Bettina."

They looked at him; he looked out at the desert.

A rustling. Then a dusty-gray tarantula, bristly and kinklegged, crawled up onto the edge of the flagstones about thirty feet away. Jo Ann saw it and cringed in her seat. "Oh, God, I hate those things. I can't stand them, I really can't. I hate spiders, and those are the worst. Patrick—"

Barrabas said hastily, "They give me the willies, too, love. Can't stand spiders, not me."

"Why's it comin' out inna daytime?" Bettina wondered. "They nocturnal."

"It's supposed to be an omen," Jerome said, "when animals act unnaturally."

Jo Ann looked at Smoke. "Could you . . . ?"

Smoke was thinking about something else. About gambles. About death.

Jo Ann had gone white. She said, "Oh, God, it's coming this way. Somebody. I can't move. I'm really arachnaphobic. Please."

Bettina said, "Jerome, git that damn thing so this woman'll shut up."

"*Me?*"

Bettina made a snorting sound of disgust and stood up, the suddenness of it knocking her chair over with a clang. She stalked over to the tarantula—and stomped it, once, hard, with the bottom of her thong. Squish.

Jo Ann looked away, covering her mouth, as Bettina took off her thong, scraped spider mush off it onto the edge of a flagstone, and flicked the mess into the grass. Then she went to the spigot in the side of the building to wash the thong. There were still pieces of tarantula legs sticking out from the bottom of it.

The crow fluttered up into the air, flew over to the edge of the flagstones . . .

• • •

FIRSTEP, THE COLONY.

Russ had never done EVA work. He didn't think he was going to like it. He was right.

Russ Parker was walking ponderously through a vacuum, across a steel plain. His magnetic boots grabbed the hull with a clink that rang inside his suit. Every step was an effort; he was only a quarter mile along and already getting winded. He looked for Lester, panicked for a moment when he didn't see him. Then realized the crappy peripheral vision on this old helmet had lost Lester in its blind spot.

He turned his head, saw him a stride or two behind, plugging on strong. It made him feel better to see Lester there. He was a good man, and knew what he was doing out here. He had a fair amount of EVA time.

Coming out of hull airlock 70 had been a thrill, despite his fears about Witcher. They were on the cold side, facing away from the sun, and there was no solar glare. The stars out there . . .

You saw the stars in the shuttle, and from inside the Colony. But the parallax here, the horizonless openness of it, made him feel that the Colony— millions of tons of crystallized alloy—was a single spore of pollen, and he was less than a dust mite clinging to it. The stars out here had a certain regal brittleness to their shine, sharp-edged as the tone of a synthesizer's high-C. The Earth was a Christmas-tree bulb. The moon a night-light.

After that . . .

His pressure suit was ballooned-out in the pressureless void, the arms becoming stiff, almost rigid. It was one of the cheap, old-fashioned kind the Colony got surplus from the Korean moonbase. Would have been nice to have one of the more flexible gas-permeable suits. This one smelled like the inside of a tramp's shoe, for one thing. The lining fibers were coming loose, prickling him, the rest of the interior feeling faintly vitreous from years of bodies in it. And there was no telling when it might decide it couldn't maintain airtight integrity any longer. In which case, he'd be dead in seconds.

Russ kept plodding, clinking, on toward the distant abstract tree of Witcher's antenna. His limbs fighting the restraint of the clumsy pressure suit, his own breathing rasping loud in the helmet. Rattles and tickings came from the clamps for the backpack control box against his chest, the electric cable angling across his rib cage, the communication and ventilation umbilical bumping his hip; the small cutting torch clacking against the zipper of his utility pocket. A crackle came in the headset: Lester's voice, once, "We can stop if you need to, Russ. It's . . . " Something more, fuzzed out by static.

"I ain't that goddamn old yet."

"This shit takes getting used to. I'm tired already, and I'm pretty used to it. You sure we can't take the maneuverers? The guy's probably bluffing about being able to detect anything flying over the hull."

"I don't want to take the chance he's not bluffing."

"I'm gonna make my oxymix a little richer, Russ. You might wanna try it. It helps when you get tired."

"You think I don't know you're patronizing me, Lester? I ain't that goddamn old yet, I'm telling you." But he reached down and turned the knob on the backpack control, enriched his oxygen flow.

It made him feel a little light-headed; not particularly stronger.

Sweat itched between skin and suit lining. He had to hit the defogger switch on his helmet about every thirty seconds now.

Maybe there was a better way to do this. Maybe Lester was right and the guy had been bluffing. But they were committed now. And if he hadn't made the right decision, fuck it, the decision couldn't be unmade.

The chrome tree—though stark and clearly defined against a pocket of starless black—never seemed to get any closer.

Maybe they'd figured the air wrong. People didn't normally *walk* very far across the outer hull. They used maneuverers or a repair module, usually. The amount of air they'd taken had been a function of guesswork. Maybe they'd run out before they got there. Or before they got back.

Just keep going.

His breath was rasping louder and louder in his ears. Sweat stung his eyes, blurred his vision. His heart pounded. His lungs heaved. This was no time for masculine pride. This was something like crossing a bad stretch of the Sahara on foot. Exhaustion out here could mean death.

He spoke into his headset, "Lester—wait a sec."

Crackle. "Sure."

They stopped. Empyrean jewelry wheeled around them. The occluded sun lit the stunted horizon.

Russ's breathing quieted. The ache in his muscles subsided a little.

"Okay." They plodded onward.

He wished he could talk to Claire. Damn, what a babe. Tough as nails, but when she wanted to be, pliant as a willow. Be nice to get a report from her, but she was afraid Witcher might have a way to monitor a long-range EVA transmission.

Hell. He had to pee.

The urine transfer collector was cinched onto his dick. It was supposed to work. But if it didn't work right, he'd have piss floating around in his suit . . .

Maybe it was nerves, but he couldn't wait. He pissed. It took an effort of will—bucking a lifetime of inhibition against pissing his pants. That's what it felt like: infantile self-wetting. Except the collector got most of it.

Only a few drops of golden urine floated past his eyes, wobbling with surface tension.

Distances were playful out here, and suddenly the antenna was there, glazed by starlight so it looked like an ice-bound, leafless tree in the dead of winter. Bigger than he'd thought it was, forty feet high. Must have been a major conspiracy and a lot of payoffs to get it out here, planted right under his nose. But then, there was a lot of EVA work that went on, and the hull wasn't security-monitored much.

He glanced at his chronograph. About twenty minutes left to deadline. Pretty soon now they'd be breaking through the door of Witcher's apartment. This had to be done *fast*.

He and Lester set to work, one on either side, burning through the ten-inch metal trunk of the "tree."

The cutting torch, spitting its own oxygen in defiance of the vacuum, eating slowly but steadily through the gray alloy.

Time eating steadily away at their margin of error . . .

● ● ●

"I just don't like it, is all," Marion was saying. "It's fucked, that's all. It sucks."

"You're so articulate, dear. How very charming that is."

"You're pissing me off, Dad."

She'd never spoken to him like that before.

Witcher swallowed the hurt and leaned back against the wall, drawing his feet up onto the bed, knees against his chest. "It's getting rather close in here."

A renewed *whi-ii-ine* came from the door, a noise that set his teeth on edge: the moronic techies, boring into his privacy.

"I don't think we should think about all this now," Witcher went on. "We're all rather claustrophobic and under pressure. Marion, why don't you sit down, hmm?"

She was pacing past Jeanne and Aria, who were sitting on the edge of the bed, at Witcher's feet. Guns in their hands. Their heads turned to watch her pace, as if they were at a slow-motion tennis match.

"I don't want to sit down, I'm thinking, I'm deciding, I can't do it sitting down. I just wish there was more room to walk in here, you can't go but three steps without fucking having to turn around." She reached into her pocket and, to his amazement, took out a cigarette, triggered the end with a thumb so it flared alight.

"What are you doing?" he asked in his most emotionless voice. A voice he rarely used with them.

"I'm smoking a fucking cigarette."

"I don't allow it and the Colony doesn't allow it."

"I don't care what Mama don't allow, I'm gonna smoke my cigarette anyhow."

"What?"

"Forget it." She stopped pacing with startling abruptness, and turned to squint past a curl of smoke at him. "Dad—you were really gonna let that shit go, the virus, or was that, like, a bluff. Or maybe a fantasy . . . "

He glared at her. If he pretended it weren't true, she'd have won a challenge to his authority. He'd have backed down. And his authority must be absolute, because these girls were armed.

He hedged. "Marion, you're a very lovely girl, and very talented, but it's a big, complex world—too big and too complex, that's it's chief problem—and . . . and it's just not something you're going to understand."

"Is that right."

Aria stood up, took the cigarette from Marion's hand, flicked it through the bathroom door into the toilet bowl.

Witcher felt some relief. Aria was still with him, then.

But she kissed Marion on the cheek and said, "It's just too close to smoke in here, pretty doll. Take a pill and you can have a smoke when we get into the Open." She sounded too conciliatory . . .

Aria turned to Witcher. "Answer her question. Is it true or not? About the virus?"

"You wouldn't understand."

"I take that to mean it is true."

Stall them, Witcher thought, glancing at his watch. In a few minutes, Pasolini would be in the Paris sat-receiving station he'd set up. And he could signal her. He wished he'd set up some sort of repeating loop signal.

"The world stinks with suffering," Witcher said. "I want to free it from suffering, lead the survivors into Utopia. Into the first real possibility of freedom. *But freedom needs room.*"

Not turning around, Jeanne said, "I don't think freedom needs mass murder . . . *Merde.* No. I just didn't know you'd go that far . . . "

There was a red light blinking on his transmitter console. He was grateful for the interruption. He swung his feet off the bed, moved to the console. Stared. "There's someone tampering with the antenna." He hit the transmit button. Another red light. The antenna was too damaged to transmit.

"They'll go to hell," he said, "if there is one."

He tapped the keyboard for antenna adjustment . . .

• • •

It was standing up on not much more than a finger's width of metal now, holding upright in a way that would have been defiance of gravity—if there had been much gravity . . .

The torches were whittling at that metal finger from either side.

And then a vibration tickled up through his boots, and the antenna torqued suddenly.

Clop. *Crunch.* Pain in Russ's chest. His feet kicking nothingness.

Seeing the impossibly right-angled tree receding from him; the stark shadows sucking into it. Lester suddenly looked like a midget—and then a doll. Receding.

"Russ!" Crackle. "Russ! Fuck! Don't thrash around like that, you'll use up oxygen! We'll come and—" Crackle.

The fucker had detected them; had swung the antenna with its angle-adjuster, knocked Russ off his feet. Into space. With enough force to best the small gravitational pull of the Colony . . . *(Please, God. I know I've fucked up in my life.)*

Lester was getting smaller and smaller. The sun was rising like the blazing furnace of Death as he angled out into space. Into the restless nothing.

His heart was like an amateur drummer playing an inconsistent drumroll. *(Look, God, I'll try to be a better person. I'll marry Claire. I'll get closer to Jesus. Please.)*

Seeing the edges of the Colony, the whole place shrinking to fit into his field of vision.

He said it aloud, a hoarse whisper. "Please . . . "

• • •

Claire's office. Claire and Stoner. The smell of fear.

Claire said, "Witcher didn't transmit. The antenna has to be down by now. I'm gonna call Russ."

"Maybe you should wait," Stoner said. "We can't be sure—"

"I can't wait." She patched into the EV radio. "Russ? I mean, uh, Admin One to EVA Two and Three."

Static like spittle spraying. "*Claire?*" Lester's voice.

"Is the antenna down?"

"*Yeah, but—Claire, get an RM out now, track Russ. Witcher knocked him into freefall. He's floating free . . . *"

Claire's eyes blurred. She hit a switch, a siren hooted throughout the Colony. She hit a button and spoke to Airlock Supervisor Six:

"EVA 2 is adrift, repeat, adrift, you should be able to get a fix from his transmitter . . . "

"We're not getting anything. Where is he?"

"Russ?" She waited. "Russ? Are you reading me. Russ, it's Claire . . . " She changed bands. "Oh, shit. Lester? They're not picking up a signal from him, and he isn't answering me."

"The damn antenna hit him in the control box. Busted it—" Crackle. *"I can't even see him anymore. Man, I feel helpless. Get somebody out here!"*

She spoke to Airlock Six. "Fix on EVA One, spiral outward from there and do a search. Get everything you've got out there. Is there a shuttle in the vicinity?"

"No."

"Do your best."

A buzz from another fone. "Claire? We're through the lock in the door . . . "

What did she do now? If she didn't supervise the taking of Witcher's quarters, people would probably get killed in the confusion. If she didn't supervise the search for Russ, they might lose him. Someone had to be there to push them into doing everything fast.

"Stoner—can you handle the Witcher thing?"

"I can try. It's not my expertise. You're the one with the combat experience."

"Shit!" They'd do all right on their own, looking for Russ.

She yelled at the fone. "Leave Witcher alone till I get there!"

She ducked through the door, ran down the corridor.

She wanted to be outside, herself, in an RM, looking for Russ. She wanted to scream.

Now she knew why her father had gone off the deep end.

• • •

One minute of air left. Spinning around some axis he'd never known he had before. There was the Colony. A bar of light. Now it was gone. There it was. Now it was gone.

Thirty seconds of air left.

No one coming. His transmitter was broken.

You want to choke to death in the suit, Russ?

He said, "Okay, Lord Jesus, if that's the way you want it. Take me, please, warts and all. I'm sorry for anything I did that I shouldn't have done. I love you. I love Claire."

He opened his visor.

• • •

"They're gonna rush the door," Marion said. A little sweat ran from her palm, running down the gun-grip.

She stood rigidly in front of the door. Aria and Jeanne beside her. Three guns, three women, focused on the door.

"Maybe we block it off some way," Jeanne said.

"Nothing here to move big enough for that," Marion said. "Bed's built into the floor."

"When they come through," Witcher said, deciding it right then, "shoot to wound one, kill the others. Then we'll pull the wounded one in for a hostage. They'll have to make arrangements with me."

Marion said, in a voice that, somehow, he knew was meant for the other women, "Don't do *anything*."

The door was kicked, *clang*, and swung inward.

Marion moved at the same time in a blur, to one side of the door, using the gun like an aikido staff, the speed of a scorpion's stinger, hitting the Colony Security heavy in the side of the head. The guy went right down, out cold. She kicked the next one in the gut. He folded up, fell back.

She pushed the unconscious one out. A hostage set free after only one second of captivity.

She kicked the door shut.

Witcher was standing ramrod straight, back against the wall. Staring at Marion in hurt disbelief. "I told you to shoot!"

"Not taking your orders anymore, Dad."

"You low-class little bitch. You whining little punk cunt." He turned, reached under his pillow, drew out his little explosive-bullet pistol.

Regrettable, the mess it was going to make.

"Don't even think it, Dad. We're gonna give ourselves up to 'em, all of us. This shit is all over. So put that down."

He swung the weapon toward her.

Her Spigon submachine gun spat like an angry cat.

Witcher was slammed back against the wall, his face bleary with amazement.

He slid down the floor, the gun dropping from twitching fingers. He stared a question at her.

"What'd you think?" Marion said. "We're stupid little chicks that shit when you say shit? We're people, man, and we're not stupid and we're not robots and we didn't take this job to murder a bunch of children we never even heard the names of. You know?"

But he couldn't hear her.

A thunk, and running feet, then the door swung in again, more cautiously this time. Claire and a heavily armed man in a cowboy shirt looked in at them from behind a transparent portashield down the hall.

Marion took her gun to the door, put it on the corridor deck, slid it well out of reach. Aria and Jeanne did the same.

Claire stepped out from behind the plastic wall. She looked drained, scared, lonely. Marion raised her hands. "You going to put us in some kind of brig, or kill us, or what?"

Claire sighed, stepping into the room, looking at Witcher's body. Seeing the gun in his hand.

"We didn't know what he was doing until just a little time ago," Aria said.

Claire nodded. "If that's true, no one'll bust you. In fact . . . " She turned and headed out the door, off on some other mission. Saying almost as an afterthought, "If you want a job, you can stay here. We can use some more intelligent women."

• 14 •

PARIS.

She knew that something had gone wrong when the signal didn't come through. This Witcher was anal, fanatically punctilious. If his timetable was out of kilter, something had interfered with him.

Shit on his timetable, Pasolini decided. *I don't need it. I have my own agenda.*

She turned away from the sat-link and walked out of the old tenement, carrying the pouch containing the glass canister. And carrying the ID and the bogus Nazi manifesto that would make her seem to be a Second Alliance agent.

She headed for the train station, for the one working train to Germany. To Berlin. To NATO command center, Berlin.

It was a warm night outside. The stars were pretty. She thought about a beach on Sardinia, and a little blue fishing boat, and a poem she'd once buried in the sand. Now the poem would come true.

There was a glass canister in the pouch, and in the canister was death, and in death was freedom, and the end of all loneliness.

• • •

FREEZONE, OFF THE COAST OF MOROCCO.

Torrence hated being in West Freezone.

Part of it was the way this section of the floating artificial island reminded him of the USA. These truncated skyscrapers, only thirty or forty stories but the same kind of combination of tinted-glass monoliths and revisionist early-twentieth-century-style architecture, humorous and faintly deco embellished—with their excruciatingly well-planned little malls around the foundations.

It was a hot day, too, and the African coastal sun blazed from the ten thousand reflective planes. He was glad of his mirror shades, but they weren't enough. Need a mirror suit, he thought.

What he was wearing, though, was the cheap blue printout jumpsuit of a delivery boy, and a hat, covering the bandage on his head. The hat said "West Freezone Messengers" on it. He was carrying a book-size package and a teleclip. The package in his hands, addressed to Freezone Savings and Investments, was standard FedEx cardboard envelope, supposed to be records coming from the East Freezone branch of the Bank of Brazil, one of the biggest banking multinationals. A standard delivery coming though a messenger service they used regularly. It should work. In case it didn't, he had a pistol in a side pocket that fired sedative darts, and he hoped they were as quick-acting as Badoit claimed.

He rode up in an elevator. The Muzak was playing a treacly version of the Living Dead's hit single, "My Death is Your Death Because It's the Whole Fucking World's Death." An entirely nihilistic and anarchist-rooted song, subsumed, in equal entirety, in glutinous co-optation. We'll be hearing Jerome-X on Muzak soon, he thought. Jerome won't care as long as he gets the residuals.

He reached up and stroked his new ear. It had taken very nicely. His body wasn't going to reject it. No.

You bitch, you just had to be a hero.

Then he was on the fifteenth floor, walking down the hall to the receptionist. Seeing that long hall as if through an old suspense movie's long-shot movie camera. Hitchcockian, getting closer and closer to the secretary, as she looks up; the walk down the hall seeming to take forever. Maybe the limp from his wounded leg would make them wonder about him.

What am I nervous for? What's this bimbo going to notice about a tallish half-Oriental delivery boy? She sees every mongrel kind of delivery boy every day. They don't use the same one all the time. Nothing to worry about.

There was a guy standing behind her with a little plastic card clipped to his real-cloth gray jacket, looking at Torrence with the flat but interrogatory gaze of professional security. SA trained, probably.

This bank was owned by a Bolivian firm. Probably founded on last century's cocaine money. Bolivian Nazi war criminal connections.

Maybe. So if the SA had those kind of connections with these people, then maybe the wipe wouldn't stop the bank from giving them their money and all this shit was for nothing.

Or maybe it was a legitimate bank. In which case—

Don't think about that stuff. You're a delivery boy. Smile vacantly. Chew gum. Look like you're in a hurry to go on your break.

"Gotta delivery for Yost," he said, glancing the address. "Henry Yost. Vice manager of something-or-other-I-can't-read."

"You kind of old for this work," the Security guy said. No particular accusation to it, maybe just thinking aloud.

"Yeah, by now I should have a job standing around noticing crap like that," Torrence said.

"Oh, I see. You're just stupid. Okay."

Torrence gave him a *fuck you* look and put the package on the girl's desk. She had the light-pen ready, absentmindedly scribbled her signature on the glass of his teleclip. "Here you go, then," the secretary said. English girl. How come having an English girl receptionist was so damn de rigueur. It had been fashionable ever since he could remember. Some kind of unconscious class thing, he supposed.

Her signature vanished into the records. It was the only thing in the teleclip records, but they didn't know that.

What if this security dude wants to look through the clip's records, or wants to call the company, see if I'm on the level? Torrence thought. Why'd Steinfeld pick me for this? Fuck. I'm no actor. It should have been Roseland. More the show-offy type.

But the security guy was watching a woman executive walk by; watching her bare legs, the way her ass snugged into the West African business exec's bathing suit. Bathing suits in the office. It's a Freezone thing, he thought.

"There you go," the secretary said.

"Thanks." Torrence tried not to hurry to the elevator.

He was in, the doors shutting, when he heard the alarm go off. *Goddamn it to hell, goddamn it to hell, Steinfeld told me the fucking thing was supposed to be insulated against detectors.*

And then he felt the ripple. And the elevator stopped. The light went out. He was in pitch darkness, stuck between floors.

Oh, great.

The EMP had done its thing sooner than it was supposed to, which was good, maybe, because that meant that its work was probably done. The Electromagnetic Pulse generated by the gear in the package had wiped out their records, completely destroyed their computers. Fried their chips. They were limited to hard-copy records, and that would take time. The bulk of the SA's assets—if Musa had done his own delivery-boy acting in Geneva—would be frozen, maybe indefinitely gone.

Very cool, only now the fucking pulse had wiped out the elevator's controls and he was trapped in it and building security would be looking for him. They'd have it all sealed off downstairs.

No, wait. Fones would be out too. It'd take them time to get down the stairs by foot.

Thinking all this, he was ripping at the ceiling panel with the teleclip, finding no exit that way. Try the door.

Torrence had a ballistic knife strapped to his right ankle, a hardened plastic blade, for getting past metal detectors. Tough as steel. He tossed the teleclip aside, felt for the knife, feeling sweat gather on the tip of his nose, his cheekbones. He found the knife, carefully disengaged the launch spring, then used the blade to pry at the door. Got it open an inch, got his fingers in there—pushed the doors apart without a little effort. Blank wall—between floors. There was maybe just enough space to shinny through, between this side of the elevator and the wall, down between two shaft buttresses. A washed-out blue light came from a skylight somewhere above. He thought he heard shouting somewhere below him. He put the knife back on its launcher, sheathed it, and began to wriggle downward, between the floor of the elevator and the wall, kicking his feet over to the metal rungs of a maintenance ladder off to the side. He missed the ladder; the leg wound was burning, throbbing.

And his chest was stuck. He wasn't going to get through. He was fucking *stuck*. And they'd get the power back on and the elevator was going to squash him against the wall, crush his head against the cold concrete.

He swung a foot over, again—caught a rung with his toe. The ladder was about three and a half feet to the side. He hooked his foot on the rung and pulled himself downward, forcing his chest past the bottleneck. It hurt. Thought he felt his breastbone crack—

Falling through. Flailing at the rungs.

Ouch. Caught them but felt like his arms were wrenched from the sockets. He got his footing, took the pressure off his arms. His arms were still in their sockets. But maybe he had two more inches of reach he hadn't had before. Roseland would make some lame joke, if he were here, about becoming a basketball player.

He climbed down the ladder, into deepening darkness.

A hundred feet below him, a square of light opened. Someone stuck their head from the square, looking up. He didn't see the guy's gun, but there must have been one, because a bullet whined and ricocheted, and the crack of the shot echoed up the shaft.

Torrence, holding on with one hand, drew his weapon and returned fire with the other.

Sedative gun was all he had. Shit. Like that would work fast enough.

But the guy was falling. The sedative *did* work fast.

What was the point of using a sedative to save their lives if they fell down elevator shafts?

He hoped the guy was Second Alliance and not just some Security guard. Either way, he was dead now.

Torrence kept going, fast as he could, his leg wound aching. Once he slipped, started to fall, caught himself, kept going.

Then he reached the open elevator door—tried to swing through.

Someone in the hall fired a shot at him and he lurched back, around the edge of the door, back onto the ladder—and dropped his gun, *goddamn fuck it,* in the process. He held on with one sweaty hand and grabbed the ballistic knife with the other as the guy in the hallway moved into a shooting angle, off to the side of the door, aiming carefully at Torrence's head through the elevator doorway—Torrence fired the knife without taking time to aim. The spring hummed, the knife-blade whistled softly, the guy went down with the knife in his belly, screaming, his gun shooting holes in the ceiling tiles.

Torrence thought, *Man, I hope they're SA—not just family men hired on for this . . .*

Suppressing the twinge of guilt as he swung through the door, he kicked the guy's gun aside, ran down the hall to the stairway . . .

Should have taken the gun, he thought. *I'm defenseless now.*

He clattered down the stairs to the lobby—and then he was in the lobby. The lobby guard stood across from him with his back turned, cursing at the fone, trying to get it to work. Torrence ran quietly past on the balls of his feet, out the door—it was frozen halfway open—and into the crowd.

• • •

PARIS. THE OLD METRO STATION.

"Smoke's not going to wait any longer?" Roseland asked.

Steinfeld shook his head. They were in the storage room they used for computer work, Steinfeld sitting at the console, Roseland looking over his shoulder as the decrypting program unscrambled the latest message. "He got worried. I guess Jerome-X talked him into going ahead. Not waiting for the whole Leng Entelechy thing. They're going to do that later, but—I always thought it was pretty doubtful. Witcher liked it, he had a mystical streak, so that's part of the reason he went along with Smoke on that—" He broke off, staring. "What the hell?"

An image of a man appeared in the corner of the screen, in a box, as the copy scrolled by—a digital image of Bones. "Steinfeld," Bones said, voice coming from the computer's speakergrid, "I didn't want to use the fone—Um—I don't know if you've gotten to that part on the copy but it boils down to this: Two hundred thousand people died in Berlin today. Witcher's Sl-L pathogen. Not racially selective."

"Oh, God," Roseland breathed.

"I saw a picture of the agent who released the stuff. The agent was dead too, of course. It's Pasolini. I guess she did it wrong, only got one of the canisters open. She had some ID and some racist pamphlet shit in her pocket, so the NATO authorities—she released this in the Berlin NATO offices—so they, you know, think she's a Second Alliance agent. Fake name and everything. I mean, she did it to *hit* the SA, to set them up but—Christ, Steinfeld, two hundred thousand people are dead! I want to know, man. Did you authorize this?"

Roseland looked at Steinfeld. There was no use his answering now—Bones couldn't hear him, this was a computer-animated recording of Bones, not a fone transmission. But Roseland wondered what the answer would be . . .

"I mean, this could hurt the enemy. Will hurt them. But didn't you—or Pasolini, if she was acting alone—think that this might force their hand? They might decide to release the Racially Selective Virus ahead of time. Anyone think of that? Tell you the truth, hodey, I'm scared for my own ass now . . . That RS pathogen's got my DNA written on it . . . "

He gave the reply code, and his image rezzed out.

Roseland looked at Steinfeld. "*Did* you tell her to do it?"

Steinfeld, after a scary second of hesitation, said, "No. I didn't tell her to do it. I had no idea she was going to do it."

He just sat there, staring into the blank screen. Shoulders slumped.

Two hundred thousand dead.

Killed by an NR operative.

• • •

Mexico.

They were in the cool cinder-block rec room. Kessler and Bettina sat at the card table, Jerome on the ratty, legless sofa, Alouette on the floor. Kessler and Bettina were playing chess. Bettina was winning. She moved her rook, shifting her weight at the same time. Her folding metal chair groaned under her as she shifted; Kessler groaned at the same moment, seeing the chess move.

Jerome was drinking a San Miguel and watching console TV. Alouette was singing to herself, sitting Indian style on the floor, and drawing with colored pens in a sketchbook, complex geometrical designs executed with inhuman exactitude; she was using her chip for the straight-edged geometry, her right-brain for the design. The crow was perched on a high bookshelf, on a copy of Crandall's bogus Bible, sleeping, its head tucked under a wing.

The satellite broadcast of Nicholas Roeg's *Performance* ended. Jerome said, "What a fucking great flick. They don't make 'em with that kind of detailed mastery this century, no way no mo'."

And then a news special came on. With Smoke. With Barrabas and Jo Ann.

"Bettina—Kessler—!"

They were already looking up, riveted to the big screen.

Smoke was being interviewed on InterNet TV, the Biggest Grid station in the world. The interviewer was a smooth, composed black Creole in an understated Japanese Action Suit.

And with him were Barrabas and Jo Ann.

"Thank you, Gridfriend,"

"It's about time," Kessler said.

"Shhhhh!" Alouette told them.

Smoke was saying: "—the new Holocaust has been ongoing for months. The video that Norman Hand has just shown you is available for examination, to determine computer enhancement or animation—"

"Some of it could simply have been staged," the interviewer pointed out.

Hand, sitting beside the interviewer, snorted. He didn't have much of his TV journalist's persona left. He seemed simply tired and scared and angry. "*Staged?*" he said, a little shrilly. "We staged a Jægernaut crushing a building? Crushing those people? What are you saying, we made miniatures and matted in the people? Look at it closer. Watch it again."

Barrabas was squirming on his seat, eager to say something. Finally he put in, "You can check the video of the subhumans. That's all quite authentic as well."

"And quite sickening," the interviewer said.

"You think that's sickening?" The camera moved in close on Barrabas, the director sensing emerging emotional drama. "That's nothing. What's sickening is how they make you part of it. I mean—how they could do it to anyone?" He swallowed. "To me! They—you have buttons you don't even know you have. And they push 'em and you find yourself hating anyone they want you to hate! I mean . . . I mean, some of it, right, was in me already. My parents and . . . But they . . . it's like they inflated it, made me . . . " There were tears in his eyes. "Took advantage of me." Jo Ann took his hand. It was obvious he was fumbling along, trying to find his way out of the maze of guilt, trying to see himself as a victim. "The scary thing is—how easily they can do it to people . . . " He slumped back in his seat, embarrassed.

Smoke said gently, "Patrick is right—we're all of us too vulnerable to this kind of manipulation. Media-cultivated racism. It makes any kind of atrocity thinkable—because they think it for you first, in the media. By dehumanizing other races, nationalities. And by laying down a foundation of rationales to build on . . . "

"Now you have your own media reply," the interviewer said. "The video of the Jægernaut destroying the apartment building does seem very . . . authentic."

"We also have corroborating documentation," Smoke said. "And when NATO does some investigating they will find they have hundreds of thousands of witnesses."

"And we have this . . . " He nodded to a technician. The screen's image changed to show victims of the Berlin mass murder. Smoke said, "The canister had been set off near the ghettos—but not directly in it. Between NATO headquarters and the ghettos." The unsteadily panning eye of the camera showed hundreds of people, many of them black and Arab, dead on a street, sprawled and splayed and in some places heaped, fallen in the midst of their workday. A small portion of the two hundred thousand dead. "This is actually NATO video," Smoke added. "We obtained a copy . . . Here's a shot of the pathogen canister on the street. You can see there's a minidisk taped to it . . . " The vid ended, the screen showed Smoke again. "On the disk is a recorded manifesto from a right-wing terrorist. She was probably—and this conclusion is in NATO's report too—probably associated with the Second Alliance. A follower of Rick Crandall's, in fact, who'd worked at a lab run by the Second Alliance International Security Corporation lab—the two hundred thousand dead in Berlin is the end result of one of the Second Alliance's viral warfare experiments gone wrong. At the very least, the SA's leadership, even if they didn't plan this, are guilty of the negligent homicide of two hundred thousand people . . . "

"There were white people as well as people of color, dead, in that film . . . "

"All whites who are not allies are enemies, from the SA fanatic's viewpoint," Smoke said. "But when they deploy the Racially Selective Virus—if we let them—they believe they'll be killing only people of color. Perhaps it'll work . . . "

"This Racially Selective Virus—that whole business is a bit hard to believe," the interviewer said. "It's something you're going to have trouble backing up."

"No, I don't think that'll be a problem," Smoke said. "Not after—" He looked at his watch. "After, say—another ten minutes."

• • •

LONDON.

Early evening on a dark, rain-wet South London street. The streetlights had been smashed out in a food riot the previous winter. The street was consigned to blank warehouses and abandoned buildings. And three identical vans, parked in a row, lights out.

Torrence sat in the driver's seat of the front van, huddled into a brown leather flight jacket that was a size too big for him. He'd lost weight. He rarely ate.

His assault rifle was behind him, leaning up against the metal wall. On his lap was a canvas bag of noise grenades. Roseland and Steinfeld and two other guerillas were in the back of the van.

Torrence was both tired and wired. He hadn't slept since before the action in Freezone. He'd met Musa and Roseland and Steinfeld at the airport. The airport had been unprotected, at least by Second Alliance people—because they'd lost two-thirds of their auxiliary staff after the bank-records action. No money to pay them. Only the ideological hard core were left.

Now Torrence and thirty others were poised a block away from the SAISC's second London storage facility. It was night and it was drizzly, and imminence crackled in the air. Or maybe it was only in Torrence's head.

A dark limosine turned the corner up ahead, cutting its headlights as it came. The limo pulled up, a car length away, facing the van. Two men got out, one a big white guy in a long brown mac, carrying a riot shotgun, looking sharply up and down the street. The other, in a long coat and shiny black shoes, was a tall black man with hair shaved close to his head, a suit and tie under the great coat. He walked confidently up to the van.

"That's Bill Marshall," Steinfeld said from the back. "Open the door for him."

Torrence reached across and opened the passenger-side door. The tall black man climbed in, stooping, bringing the smell of wet streets with him. The bodyguard waited outside the door, standing in the drizzle, the auto shotgun resting in the crook of an arm. Marshall closed the door and said, in tones as modulated as his expression, "Good evening, gentlemen. A light rain, tonight, but it's not at all cold. Rather a relief from last night, don't you think?" With precise, delicate motions of his hands, he tugged off thin ocher calfskin gloves. It wasn't cold enough for gloves, but the well-dressed man wore gloves these days in London. "I mean," Marshall went on, "it was dreadfully humid last night,"

Eton and Oxford, probably, Torrence guessed. The guy was MI-6, according to Steinfeld, which was run by Lord Chalmsley: a closet liberal and New Resistance sympathizer. Chalmsley was the only major figure in British intelligence who wasn't either a rampant conservative or a Second Alliance puppet. The fascists, Steinfeld had said, were walking a narrow tightrope, however, in British politics. They were losing more supporters every day, in light of the recent revelations; were already political poison to many. And there had always been those who'd regarded the SA and SPOES as a threat to British sovereignty.

Marshall was as black a man as Torrence had ever seen. He had an immaculate tie and diamond cuff links. Marshall had been sent to school in England after his parents had seized a diamond mine from its white owners in Zimbabwe.

Marshall looked at Torrence expectantly.

Torrence decided the guy was waiting for him to respond to the small talk. He said, "Yeah. It's, like, humid."

Marshall smiled. "An American. And one resonant with charming authenticity." He put the tips of his fingers together, making a little cage with his hands and pressed his thumbnails against his lower lip. His diamond-crusted Rolex counted off the minutes and seconds. "The situation is somewhat precarious," he began.

"Do we have the green light or not?" Steinfeld asked.

Marshall turned sideways in his chair so he could see Steinfeld. Or anyway, Steinfeld's silhouette. Somehow even in the cramped space of the van's front passenger seat Marshall managed to strike a modelesque pose.

"You have the green light if you turn up something that can be verified without question. If this is a red herring, the green light never existed. We'll lie copiously and persistently, and the Ministry will believe us over you."

"Clear enough," Steinfeld said.

Torrence was thinking: *Yeah, clear as mud.* "You got people ready to take the stuff, make the ID and everything?"

"Yes. Quite nearby."

"Why don't you just get a warrant or some kind of surprise building inspection or something? Check it out yourself. Say it was the wrong address if it turns out bunk."

"Political subtleties make it difficult. If we came up wrong, the SA's supporters would put two and two together . . . A New Resistance sympathizer—yours truly—would be identified in MI6. And there's no time to go through the courts."

Steinfeld said, "Torrence, let's go."

Torrence nodded, took a headset from his jacket pocket, and put it on. He pressed the stud. "Let's go, Blue Flag."

He heard the reply in his headset as he reached back for his rifle and soundproof helmet.

Marshall was already on his way back to the limo. By the time that Torrence and the other guerrillas were moving down the street, Marshall's limo was already gone from sight.

• • •

Torrence and Roseland went ahead of the main group. They kept in the lee of the seemingly broken-down, robot-driven semitruck which an NR operative had remote-stalled slantwise on the street an hour before. Orange lights blinked on the semi. The Second Alliance guards had long since looked it over and decided it was harmless. It was. Except it was crucial cover for the two guerrillas, enabling them to get within thirty feet of the side door without being seen.

There were enemy sentries on the roof, so there was no coming in on a helicopter. But this side door was remote enough from the others, they might not see what happened there if the truck did the rest of its bit.

The truck cab's emergency lights strobed wobbly golden streaks on the rainy street. Torrence ran hunched over up to the semi's cab; rifle tightly strapped across his back, noise grenades in one hand and ballistic knife in the other. Roseland close behind him. Torrence spoke into his headset, and the guerrilla on the roof of the building to his left responded, throwing a switch on a remote-control unit. The truck suddenly started itself up. The cameras on its robot snout swiveled as if it were coming back to consciousness and wondering just where it was.

Torrence was cheek by jowl with the truck cab when it began to roll toward the SA storage building. He ran along beside it in a crouch, the truck hiding him from the building as it drove past. Then he hung back when he was parallel to the corner of the building, let it go on, honking and revving, rolling past the SA guards—holding their attention, he hoped, distracting them as he sprinted to the side door. But the guard there saw him coming, raised a gun, and opened his mouth to shout.

The shout came out in a bubbling moan as the ballistic knife parted the man's windpipe. The cry was lost in the roar of the truck vanishing down the street. Torrence finished the guard, then he and Roseland plunged through the unlocked door, Torrence hissing orders into his headset, blinking in the sudden light of the bright interior. He sealed the soundproof helmet, was now locked into silence, except for headset crackle—and he flung the first of the noise grenades at a group of guards at the end of the hall. They went down, thrashing, clutching at their heads. The noise grenades were designed to put them out for a while with a vicious sonic pulse. Couldn't risk major explosions in here, where the virus was kept.

"Those things really work," Roseland said over his headset. "I want some for next time I got to visit my relatives at Passover. Stun my Uncle Irving . . . "

Torrence kept going, in eerie silence. Not hearing the gunfire as outdoor SA sentries spotted the follow-up guerrilla strikeforce outside.

They were intended to spot them; intended to think they were the point men.

Torrence ran down the corridor. Again he had a sense of seeing things as if through a camera, a length of the corridor panning past him. He wondered what that kind of distancing from the world meant psychologically. He unslung his rifle . . .

He caught peripheral flashes, Roseland firing behind him at someone at the other end of the hall. There: the door to the central storage room. Torrence burst through, tossing noise grenades. Like toys, with no explosion—but four men went down. There: the walk-in vault. And it was open. Torrence and Roseland opened their helmets as they jogged toward the vault . . . And then there were two more Second Alliance guards coming in through a side door a few yards away. Bullets sizzled the air. Torrence ran at the enemy, worried about bullets hitting viral canisters, but firing his weapon. The guards were armored, but the bullets made them stagger, cracked one of the helmets, and then Torrence was upon them, slapping the suction disks onto them. The guards screaming as the disks drilled and detonated in them. They fell, writhing, blood pooling around them; thrashed a bit and then lay quiet . . .

Roseland was already inside the walk-in safe, carrying out a crate of viral canisters.

There was gunfire outside, but it was becoming sporadic. And the guys in here who were stunned weren't getting up. They were coming out of it—but they just lay there, staring up at Torrence's rifle. Torrence stood guard over them, letting Roseland get the goods.

Roseland walked past him, carrying the crate, and said to the guys huddled on the floor: "Better lay still. My friend here's from the Half-British Half-Japanese Liberation Front for the Free Distribution of Sushi and Chips to All Underprivileged Gaijin, and he means business."

Torrence sighed. After Roseland was gone from the room, he allowed himself to laugh.

The gunfire from outside ceased completely, and in another two minutes Torrence heard Steinfeld's voice in the hall. And then Marshall's.

● ● ●

NEW YORK CITY.
Jerome and Bettina held hands. That was one connection between them. The other one was on the Plateau.

They were remote-jacked into the consoles in Badoit's suite in the New York Fuji-Hilton Hotel; most of the year, the suite was empty. Badoit kept it just in case he should need it.

The gear had been moved in this afternoon, all of it selected and tweaked to Leng's specifications. It was ten p.m. Outside, there were sirens and traffic and the yellow guttering on the horizon of a fire in one of the rooftop shantytowns.

But here, the shades were drawn, the suite's sound-block fields dialed to silence. And the two of them sat in a dark room, closed eyes sealing them into deeper darkness, consciousness turned inward, fixed on the particular continuum of sheer data and signification that was the Plateau. They roamed a cybernetic steppe where there was no night or day, and eyeless wolves stalked and sniffed, sensing everything. For Jerome and Bettina, there was only the Plateau and the communion.

At first it was a communion with one another, through the chips. Like jamming on instruments together, only it was the riffing of an immaculate symmetry of numbers, of frequency coordinates and geometrical imagery; of key words and phrases and rippling concatenations of triggered mental associations. Then a new stage, the joining: they were working as one unit, moving into the System, finding their way together into the computer linkage that informed the Grid.

There they met the others.

From all over the planet: the wolves of the Plateau, tolerating, now, intruders on their turf; certain computer criminals with an urge to tinker with global politics. And the anarchist underground, the Libertarian information networks, the revolutionaries with other orientations: Communist, Socialist, anarcho-syndicalist; the Liberal Democratic Capitalist party; the apolitical who simply hated the Fascists; Catholic nuns and other Christians acting out of Christ-inspired conscience; the Buddhists; the Mossad; reps from the intelligence service of the People's Democratic Republic of China; chip-aug'd agents working with Marshall at MI-6; agents from Sweden, from the NSR, from India, from Egypt; Badoit's own chip-aug'd agents; agents from the People's Republic of South Africa; from Cuba; from Iceland; from Mexico, Brazil, Nicaragua, the People's Democratic State of Chile; from Canada's intelligence service; from the Democratic State of Unified Korea; from Australia, from New Zealand; from Arabia, from the Palestinian state; from Libya, Chad, and Algeria. And one from Luxembourg.

Many were normally enemies. Now they were united in fear, hatred, or repugnance for the Second Alliance.

Each of them was cerebrally implanted, chip-augmented, skilled on the Plateau. All were linked to the Grid through the international televid system. Each performed two functions at once.

Top function: transmitting the media capsule that Smoke had put together.

The ground had been prepared by Smoke's media conferences, the furor over Hand's testimony; by the images of the subhumans, of the Jægernaut, of the Processing Centers. And there was a sudden interest by the Internet newspaper, the *Washington Post*, kindled by Hand's connections there.

Worldwide curiosity was whetted. Now came the blitz, entirely illegal but grounded in an inarguable moral foundation: the warning about the Racially Selective Virus.

The blitz, the capsule:

Poignant selections from Hand's video. Hand's testimony. Barrabas's vid. Barrabas's testimony. Jo Ann's testimony. Her extractor data (editing out some of the key specs for the racially selective pathogen). A spokesman for Lord Chalmsley and British intelligence confirming that the captured viral samples were large amounts of lethal racially selective pathogen—an announcement sponsored by the British Labor Party, the opposition. Over the objections of the prime minister's staff. Quotes from Jerome's computer-break-in documentation further linking the SA to the pathogen. The relationship between the SA and the virus that killed two hundred thousand people in Berlin overnight: something the world was still reeling from. Then there was the strong implication that the SA had been testing a variation of the Racially Selective Virus that went wrong. There was digi-vid from the Processing Centers, testimony from Processing Center survivors, testimony from escaped SA political prisoners. The information that Crandall was dead, his version of the Gospel as fallacious as his appearance on television: an animation put together by SA's Inner Circle; evidence that Larousse's appearances were computer and holographically enhanced. The true relationship between the SA and SPOES. The Second Alliance's hidden agenda for Europe . . .

And then they saw the video of the dead in Berlin—Army trucks carting their stacked bodies . . . A wide camera angle on the square outside the Brandenburg Gate . . . An unconstructed jigsaw puzzle of corpses; a field of the dead. The street curb to curb a river of vomit and blood, an archipelago of the dead in the monstrous flow of it; the dead in cafés and shops . . . The dead in their cars, in frozen traffic, still sitting at their steering wheels . . . In one section of Berlin, around the NATO headquarters and near the ghettos, it was a city of the Dead. A necropolis.

Statements crackled from angry NATO authorities. NATO officials who'd previously collaborated with the Second Alliance were now carefully distancing from them. The political tide was turning.

The pirate blitz was slickly put together, edited for minimum dryness and maximum impact. Three versions had been worked up by Hand—all of it narrated by Hand—in A, B, and C formats: versions dubbed into seven languages.

And all of it went into the Grid whether the Grid wanted it or not, carrying, somehow, the immediacy and urgent authority of a Civil Defense alert. The aug-chip conspiracy worked together, overwhelming the cybernetic defenses of the media network. It broke in all over the world, effecting political revelation through media piracy, simultaneously and continuously, over and over, saturating the world with truth. Even the billboard-size propaganda TV screens in Paris and in other SA-held territories were co-opted, taken over, pirated: appropriated. *Liberated*. In most cases, the viewers saw the whole thing twice before the Second Alliance gave up trying to block it cybernetically and simply switched off the power.

Via satellite. Via ground-based transmitter. Via cable. Via wifi. Via microwave and even radio. The truth as guerrilla action.

And each media capsule ended with a challenge to the Second Alliance: *Meet us at the United Nations to repudiate us. Bring your evidence that what we say isn't true. Meet us in Geneva. Meet us in the International Court. Anywhere! Our facts against yours. Let the world decide who's telling the truth. We challenge you!*

No, that's not the absolute end of the capsule; there was one thing more. Video of the Jægernaut that smashed the Arc de Triomphe; of Rickenharp and Yukio, rocking and fighting, as the inexorable juggernaut of oppression crushed them into the rubble . . .

At the climax of the video, coming up gradually from a soft background whisper to consummate as a thunderous, echoing chord: Rickenharp's music, his Song Called Youth, his electric guitar playing the score for this movie, this documentary that was also a military assault. Rickenharp's composition as martial marching music. The beat of an insistence on justice; the squeal, the rock 'n' roll peal, of a demand for freedom; the medium as the message.

All of that went into the Grid, the worldwide media network.

And all that was just the top function of the aug chips working on the Plateau. Pumped out by a kind of electronic, on-line telepathy; by fakirs of the chip, deep in silicon contemplation; electromagnetic communion: the framework of an electronic global mind.

There was—or so Smoke and Leng believed—another kind of global mind, one accessed during the secondary function of the aug-chip communion.

Impulses sent out at the peak of the collective mind's cycle of intensity—or in accordance, anyway, with Leng's calculations—carried electromagnetically encoded information that would be instantaneously received by human bioelectric fields, drawn into the unconscious mind of every human brain on the planet. *An idea, a living meme, launched on the great, ethereal psychic tsunami that invisibly paces the globe at predictable intervals . . .*

"Man, this is probably bullshit," Jerome-X said. "But if it isn't, could be it's something worse. Some kind of brainwashing." Smoke told him that only the truth can be introduced into the entelechy wave. Anything else breaks down from misalignment with the wave's internal structure, made up of consensual observation. The wave is accreted from agreed-on perceptions, and those perceptions have gradually evolved from super-stition to consensual truths. There are exceptions, Smoke said, but for the most part the Collective Mind harbors truth. This Truth is usually submerged. But coupled with the information coming through the Grid, at the right moment, it would surface, emerge as an idea. An insight; a repudiation of racism; a recognition of oppression; a vision of all human-ity's kinship with the oppressed; a realization that the time had come to confirm that kinship.

It was like the 1989 student-led rebellion in China, coming in alignment with Gorbachev's *perestroika* and *glasnost*, and the triumph of *Solidarity* in Poland. Or later, the Arab Spring: Partly a function of global telecommunications, social media; partly emerging from a shared idea riding the wave through the collective mind . . .

Jerome had thought about it—and decided to take part. It was an intuitive decision. It felt right.

And now he let his chip transmit the program Smoke had provided, impulses that his brain would transmit to the global psychic field, adding its microscopic ripple to the Big Ripple.

Maybe it was bullshit. Maybe it was wishful thinking. Maybe Smoke was still a little crazy, hungry for meaning in a world of random violence.

Maybe it was just more psychological comfort, the way a prayer was.

Like a prayer, it was worth a shot.

• • •

PARIS.

They came from the surrounding countryside; they poured in from the south of France, from Spain; they'd come from North Africa, some of them, just across the Mediterranean. They came out of their hiding places in the city. They came from certain Processing Centers deserted by panicked and unpaid SA guards, where the cameras and automated guns had been neutralized by the New Resistance hackers. They came across the Channel from England. They were led by Badoit's troops, and by the NR, but most of them were civilians, armed with whatever was handy or nothing at all.

They were Jews and Arabs and Iranians and Indians and Blacks and Orientals. They were people of color, people of varied religion. They were Judaic and Muslim and Hindu and Buddhist and Sikh and Sufi. And there were thousands of sympathetic Christians.

In all, about half a million people came, that morning.

It was a sunny morning in the Place de Hôtel de Ville. The sky was a cloudless expanse of blue like the New Resistance flag. The great, ornate building the Second Alliance had taken as its headquarters was inscrutably unresponsive to the chanting, surging crowd outside. The chant Roseland had initiated: *JAMAIS PLUS!* NEVER AGAIN! *JAMAIS PLUS!* NEVER AGAIN! *JAMAIS PLUS!* NEVER AGAIN! As they waved their blue flags, most of them homemade. Fists pumped the air, charged with consensus.

• • •

Inside the Hôtel de Ville, Watson sat in the janitor's room that constituted his jail cell, watching the event on the watery image of an ancient portable television.

He could hear them, chanting and shouting, outside; could see them on the console, could hear the excited voice of the commentator who sensed he was witnessing a turning point in history. There had been a few skirmishes that morning—resistance fighters clashing with the Soldats Superieurs, and the Paris skinheads. But most of the Unity Party's "fighting elite" had deserted, were in hiding, or running, trying to buy new identities. They'd panicked after NATO investigation teams closed down the remaining Processing Centers that morning. There were about five hundred refugee Second Alliance in the building. The hard-core five hundred inside against the five hundred thousand outside. There were autotanks lined up in front of the Hotel, of course—completely impotent. The New Resistance had taken over their guidance systems, overridden them with their remote-control hackers. This Badoit had provided the money that in turn provided the technology. Surgical strikes from the Mossad and Badoit's forces had rendered the Jægernauts inoperable, if not entirely destroyed.

Watson changed channels, came to another report from London, showing another kind of rabble loose in the streets. Watson laughed bitterly, seeing the subhumans; the "Puppies" wandering about. Resistance provocateurs had incited a riot outside Second Alliance research facilities—looters had broken in and smashed into the cages—recoiling in horror at what they'd seen. They'd left the gates open. The subhumans, the late Dr.

Cooper's pets, shuffled and crawled and toddled out of the lab, into the street . . . were wandering, starkers nude, down the street.

The commentator babbling it all: the SAs genetic research experiments, gotten loose; attempt to create a race of subhuman lumpen-workers; the commentator's impromptu editorializing called the experiment illegal and ethically deplorable . . .

The Puppies. Pausing now and then to defecate and lick a filthy wall, or to paw through a heap of trash. Looking repugnantly stunted, physically warped, like animated wads of much-chewed pink bubble gum badly sculpted into something almost human. Making noises like donkeys and monkeys and . . . hairless bipedal stunted subhumans . . .

God, what a sight.

And down in the corner of the screen a prompter flashed: "3D AVAILABLE." Lovely. If you had a holoset, you could watch the twisted little wankers defecate in 3D.

Watson began to laugh. He laughed for a long time. There were tears in his eyes, and his sides were aching, when he heard the click of the lock at the door and looked up to see Giessen there, with Rolff.

So Rolff had worked out a deal with him.

Both men, Watson noticed, wore ordinary printout street clothing. Giessen had abandoned his curious antiquated costume.

Watson stopped laughing, but only for a moment. The look on Giessen's face made him laugh again. The little prig was scared.

"Rolff, he's hysterical," Giessen said in German.

Rolff, gun in hand, expressionless, advanced on Watson, and pistol-whipped him twice, hard, splitting his lip and knocking the laughter from him.

"Rolff," Watson said, tasting blood, blood mixing with the words, "you are a traitorous coward."

Rolff stared at him impassively then took him by the elbow and pulled him to his feet. The other hand pressing the gun against Watson's side. "Come along."

"You think you're going to trade me to them? To the mobs outside?" Watson asked, his voice going shrill. "Do you really think they're going to mistake you for their kind?"

Giessen murmur, "It all depends on what is said, and who it is said to, it seems to me. Bring him into the hall, Rolff."

"They're not going to let you leave," Watson said as they dragged him out. "And if they do, then what? We're bloody war criminals now."

"The dead can't hold us to trial," Giessen said. "There's still the final phase of Total Eclipse."

"Is there, indeed?" Watson laughed as they shoved him into the hall. "Total Eclipse is Bugger All. The RSV is done, Giessen. The only cultures of the virus we had have been taken from storage by the Resistance, before we could deploy them. *There is no more of the virus, Giessen.* They got it all. You understand?"

Giessen stared at him. "You idiot. Keeping it all in one place!"

"It was only for a day," Watson said, shrugging. "But they knew which day. Their hackers were into our logistics schedules . . . " He shrugged once more, hugely, imitating a Frenchman, and then burst out laughing again. "The dead can't hold us to trial? You'd be surprised at how the dead can speak, Giessen! And I'll speak too! Let's put all our cards on the table and see who's cheating, eh?"

"One thing won't go wrong," Giessen said. "You won't speak." He nodded to two burly SA guards in armor and mirror helmets. They helped Rolff hold Watson down as Giessen drew a scalpel from a coat pocket, pried Watson's mouth open with a gun barrel, and cut off his tongue.

• • •

Larousse had gone on TV, of course, to try to calm things down, pour the oil of rhetoric on the troubled waters, but not one of his transmissions got through without NR jamming. The NR pirates were everywhere now, it seemed.

The Inner Circle were waiting pensively in the Hôtel De Ville, for the helicopter that was supposed to take them out of there . . . until they got word that the Mossad had shot it down. And that two Israeli gunships were circling the building.

The Inner Circle had come to Paris to discuss the crisis. None of them had been expecting this spontaneous—or perhaps not so spontaneous—eruption of the masses. It was Larousse who stepped out onto the front steps of the Hôtel de Ville, raising the bullhorn to his lips to speak to the sea of faces. Trying to tell them that the giggling, bloody-mouthed man the guards held beside him was the perpetrator of the great infamy, the terror carried out under the nose of the French government, concealed from Larousse, who had not been "in on the loop," who'd not known what was going on in the processing centers or the Second Alliance labs . . . this man, this monster, this Colonel Watson was their villain . . .

Watson just stood there, giggling in his throat, blood bubbling from his mouth. *Speaking blood,* he thought. *I'm speaking to them, speaking with deep sincerity, speaking the truth: Speaking with blood.*

Larousse got only a third the way through his speech—which was lost under the noise of the crowd—before the gunshots rang out, and he fell, and the crowd surged forward, and the guards were trampled and crushed . . .

The rioters had Watson, then, had him down and underfoot; they kicked in his ribs, his skull, crushing ideas and being into meaningless pulp; wiping out information the old-fashioned way.

He was brain-dead, but life still pumped through him in a desultory, automatic way, until he was killed, almost as an afterthought, by an old Afghan woman wielding a pair of scissors,

She used the scissors working in the garment district every day. With the same methodical precision she brought to her craft, she used the scissors to snip Watson's jugular.

• • •

Steinfeld was there, of course, at the edge of the crowd, sincerely trying to keep some order. Lespere—emerged from his deep cover—was with him, both men with Mossad-issue Uzis in hand. They were hoping to take the Inner Circle alive, make them stand trial, get the whole truth incontrovertibly out in the open. Shouting at their men to contain the crowd. But the New Resistance troops were pushed aside, were overwhelmed, unwilling to open fire on civilians. And the Muslim contingent was particularly inflamed, the Muslim world enraged by Crandall and Watson's spurious Bible, the Bogus Jesus' slandering of Mohammed. In the face of this outrage, military strategy became irrelevant.

"*Attente!*" Lespere shouted. "Wait!"

But hunger fed hunger: a hunger for revenge; outrage became true rage. The frustration of war, privation, and persecution erupted in one. The doors were smashed in, the crowd surged across the lobby, bullets and bricks smashed the painted moldings and knocked the ancient portraits down, shattered the receptionist's computer console, exploded windows—and struck down startled guards. Most of the guards were armored, but it was no use against ten people prying at them, like psychotic starfish prising seashells, tearing the armor open, getting at the soft and vulnerable men inside; at men who wondered how they'd come here, to this, as they were clubbed to death . . .

The SA switched off the elevators, but soon the crowd boiled up the stairs onto the upper floors, smashing through the Comm Rooms, and through the rooms containing the controls for Larousse's faux image. An assault, as W.S. Burroughs had longed for, on the reality-control room.

Here they found Giessen and Rolff.

Giessen they pulled from under a secretary's desk. He spat insults at them until the first gunshot smashed into his gut, and then he folded up, all his brittle punctilio shattered by the bullet, and he cried out like a lost child, and took a long time crying and whimpering . . . Steinfeld and Lespere tried to get through to him, hoping to save him for trial, but the crowd shoved them back and bore Giessen up, toted him to the window . . .

He had been recognized. *The Thirst*. A man—a person whose interrogations Giessen had supervised . . . a torture victim . . . this man recognized him—and was the first to shout, "Throw him out the window!" Giessen went flying head first, trailing a streamer of blood, out the window and into the crowd chanting in the square.

In the hallway, trying to get to the roof, were several hundred Second Alliance, some in armor, some in fine suits. The rioters found them harder to get to. But partisans with guns were brought to the front of the mob and opened fire, killing methodically. Some of the fascists returned fire, rallied by Rolff, who came howling Aryan blood oaths down the hallway, firing a carbine, shrieking about *Juden Swine* . . .

Steinfeld and Lespere sighed as one, and—also as one—opened fire themselves. Steinfeld's Uzi ripping into Rolff's mouth, flinging his racist epithets back into his skull on a fist of bullets. A reply that couldn't be argued with.

• • •

The ancient building was looted. Everyone found in it was killed including some who were relatively innocent. The place was sacked and burned to the ground.

Most of the top Second Alliance administrators died in the first twenty minutes, and died with great suffering.

Steinfeld was sorry he couldn't bring them to trial somewhere. But as to their suffering—he didn't give a hang about that at all.

• • •

The thing was won, so there was no reason, Torrence thought, for what Steinfeld did on the rooftop helicopter pad.

The Inner Circle SA were there—those four who'd survived thus far, including old Jæger himself—surrounded by the fanatic elite of the Soldats Superieurs and half a dozen Second Alliance bulls in full armor. They were entirely at the mercy of the uprising. They could be captured, or, if they refused surrender, their escape choppers could be blown up with grenade launchers. There was really no reason for Steinfeld to lead a charge into them. None at all.

But that's what Steinfeld did. He ran at them, rather clumsily, since he usually left this sort of thing to Torrence. He charged them with an assault rifle in his hands, firing, the gun spitting the only kind of rhetoric that mattered today.

Torrence shouted, "Steinfeld, what the hell are you—?" Hobbling up behind him, trying to give him supporting fire, but moving slowly on his wounded leg.

Jæger went down, and another fascist too—and then the bulls opened fire on Steinfeld and Torrence. Steinfeld staggered as a dozen rounds tore into him. He spun and fell, still firing. Torrence blowing away the guy who'd shot Steinfeld.

Torrence got it then. Feeling a punch in the chest, another in the right hip. Going down.

Steinfeld, what the hell did you do that for? It was pointless. We had them. We had them. There was no reason . . .

• • •

"There was a reason," Roseland said.

Roseland was sitting beside Torrence's hospital bed in an overburdened government hospital run by the new French Republic. Four other beds were crammed into the room. Torrence didn't respond aloud, because of the tube going down his throat, into his right lung—the lung the bullet had gone through—but he looked at Roseland in a way that meant, *What the fuck are you talking about?*

"He kept a personal journal, written in Hebrew," Roseland said. Roseland looked as ill as Torrence, though he hadn't been wounded. He looked as if he was having trouble sitting up straight. Hadn't slept in a few days, Torrence guessed. "I found the journal in his stuff when I was getting it together to send to the Mossad. I couldn't help it. I read it. Most of it wasn't anything the enemy could've used for intelligence if they'd found it—all that part was real elliptical and general. It was mostly personal thoughts, ideas, feelings. And he talked about Pasolini at the end. Turns out he had been having Pasolini followed.

"Steinfeld knew she was in touch with some of Witcher's operatives. He found out about the virus—had one of Witcher's contacts picked up and extracted. He wrestled with himself about it. He knew she was the only one left with the non-racially-selective virus. Thinking that if she went ahead and did it, released it in Berlin with the fake manifesto recording, it would hurt the enemy bad, and in the long run that'd save lives. Then he decided he was being as bad as they were—that there was no excuse for allowing tens of thousands of civilians to die as part of some damn political strategy. He came to this, see, he really did. But by the time he'd made up his mind, it was too late. She was on her way to Berlin. He tried to find her, tried to stop her . . . " He shook his head. "I saw his face when we got the news about Berlin. I never saw such open emotion in the guy before . . . "

Torrence nodded, very slightly. But he thought: *Steinfeld could have stopped it. He let hate for the SA get in the way of saving two hundred thousand lives.*

Steinfeld knew that, of course. Which is why the charge on the rooftop.

He had joined those he had failed. The guilty dead had joined the innocent dead.

• • •

THE ISLAND OF MERINO.

"What are we going to do today?" Alouette said, kicking spray into the air with her bare feet. She ran from the lapping fringe of ocean, chased it back to the surf, ran from it again.

"Anything you want," Smoke said.

"How about tomorrow?"

"Anything you want."

"You're going to stay in Merino?"

"This is my home now. That's why we came back here. It's my home, with you. I have a grant, and I'm going to stay here and write a book just to have something to do, but mostly I'm going to go swimming with you, and tell you to do your homework, and tell you: no, you can't watch satellite TV."

"Can too watch TV."

"Cannot either."

"Can too. Sometimes a little."

"Maybe sometimes a little."

She danced happily around him. He smiled sadly, looked at the sunwashed beach, the palms along the beachside road, the high shaggy trees nodding in the easy breeze. Here and there were stumps of palms left by the shelling—but most of the trees had made it. And so had most of the islanders.

"Alouette," he said, "did the crow really die at that moment?"

"When we sent out the message into that entelechy thing? That Leng field thing?"

"Yes. Did you make that up?"

"No. That's when he died. He flew down onto my shoulder and then fell in my lap. I didn't really notice it much, I was in chip communion, see, but afterward it made me cry when I found him. But part of me notices things around me, those times. That's when he died. When we sent that message."

"Huh. Be damned."

"Daddy Jack?"

"What?"

"Mr. Kessler says that entelechy thing is 'hooey.' He says it does not work. Do you think it worked? It seemed like it worked. Everybody saw what was happening and they did something."

"But maybe that was just the media, the timing. I don't know if it worked. With those things, it's hard to tell if they're real or not. And if they are real—whoever made them, whoever put the world together, must want it this way. I mean, they must want it, so we can't be sure if it's real or not: The things people call spiritual . . . "

"Can we get some ice cream?"

"You're too fat for ice cream."

She wasn't even remotely fat, but she pretended outrage. "I am not! My metabolism rate likes ice cream!"

"Your metabolism rate. Oh. Well, in that case. Yes. Let's get some ice cream."

"And can we get another bird?"

"Another crow?"

"No. A cockatoo. A yellow cockatoo. I know a man who is selling one."

"Yeah. Ice cream and a cockatoo. Why not."

He took her hand, and they walked back to the hotel.

•••

FirStep: The Colony. Four months later.

Claire was pruning roses.

She was working on a patch of red roses at the new technicki housing project. It was her way of taking a day off. The sunlight was coming strongly despite the filters, and the air was sweet with rose scent, and the protestation of her muscles felt good. Maybe afterward she'd go for a swim.

"Can I help?"

She looked up at the stranger and smiled politely. An Oriental, maybe Japanese. But tall for a Japanese. He was probably half American, judging by his size and accent. Rather thin and tired. Vaguely familiar. She'd probably seen him around the Colony somewhere.

"You can help if you like," she said. "I don't have any extra clippers, though. Do you know about gardening?"

"Not a damn thing."

His voice . . .

He smiled. And that smile was familiar. She found herself staring at one of his ears. It was slightly off-color. There was a faint scar around the base of it.

"My sister," he was saying, "used to try to get me to help her in Mom's garden when we were kids. I'd tell her, 'Kitty—I'll garden when I haven't got anything else to do. Which'll probably be never.'" He shrugged. "I guess it's never now."

"Your sister's name is Kitty?"

"Yes."

"Danny?"

"Yes."

"*Danny?*"

"Uh-huh. I—"

He didn't get the rest out. She nearly knocked him over when she threw her arms around him. "Danny . . . "

• • •

A while later, maybe an hour and maybe three—neither of them could have told you how long they had been talking—they were strolling through the little woods, next to the old monument to space techs who'd died building the Colony. She looked up at it, and real pain flared in her eyes. "Dan—when I was . . . while we were separated, I had a relationship with someone."

"Did you? So did I." He touched his new ear.

"He died, though. In space."

"Yours died? So did mine."

They were quiet for a while, just walking, strolling slowly through an artificial twilight, till Torrence said, "Listen—I didn't come alone. There's a friend of mine, guy named Roseland. Abe Roseland. He . . . he's kind of suicidal. He was one of the best NR men. After it was over he was going to join the Israeli army—and there's a good chance Israel's going to have a war with this new fundamentalist loon that's running Libya, if Badoit can't make the peace. Abe's just looking for a way to get killed. He's just like Steinfeld, except he's got a different kind of guilt. Or maybe not so different. I practically had to shanghai him, but I talked him into coming up here. He needs . . . sanctuary. A place to start over. So do I. Abe, though, won't come out of his room. I thought maybe if you offered him a job here in Security, he'd—"

"Consider it done. I'll send our new chief of Security over to talk to him. She'll recruit him. In fact, he sounds like her type. She might recruit him for more than a job."

"She who?"

"Her name's Marion. Listen—you recovered from those wounds?"

"Mostly. I'm working on it. I'm supposed to do aerobics to build up my lungs."

"I know just the thing. You ever been in freefall?"

"Freefall? Weightless?" He grimaced. "On the ship over here, briefly. Made me sick."

"That's because you weren't adapting right. Got to get the blood moving, see. Get a feel for it."

He looked at her. There was something mischievous . . . "Yeah?"

"Yeah. There're parts of the Colony that are low-grav, so low they're almost freefall. Some real nice rooms there. Private rooms." She stopped and looked into his eyes.

He was still Hard-Eyes. He was Daniel Torrence behind the Oriental mask. Her lover was in there still.

"Okay," he said. "Where's the freefall room?"

She took his hand. "Come on," she said. "I'll show you."

THE END

OF THE

A SONG CALLED YOUTH

TRILOGY

John Shirley is the author of more than thirty novels. He is considered seminal to the cyberpunk movement in science fiction and has been called the "postmodern Poe" of horror. His numerous short stories have been compiled into eight collections including *Black Butterflies: A Flock on the Darkside*, winner of the Bram Stoker Award, the International Horror Guild Award, and named as one of the best one hundred books of the year by *Publishers Weekly*. He has written scripts for television and film, and is best known as co-writer of *The Crow*. As a musician, Shirley has fronted several bands over the years and written lyrics for Blue Öyster Cult and others.

The father of three sons, he lives in the San Francisco Bay area with his wife, Michelina.

To learn more about John Shirley and his work, please visit his website at john-shirley.com.